O F
LOVE
AND
LIFE

O F
L O V E
A N D
L I F E

Three novels selected and condensed
by Reader's Digest

The Reader's Digest Association Limited, London

The Reader's Digest Association Limited
11 Westferry Circus, Canary Wharf, London E14 4HE

www.readersdigest.co.uk

ISBN 0-276-42998-2

For information as to ownership of copyright in the material of
this book, and acknowledgments, see last page.

CONTENTS

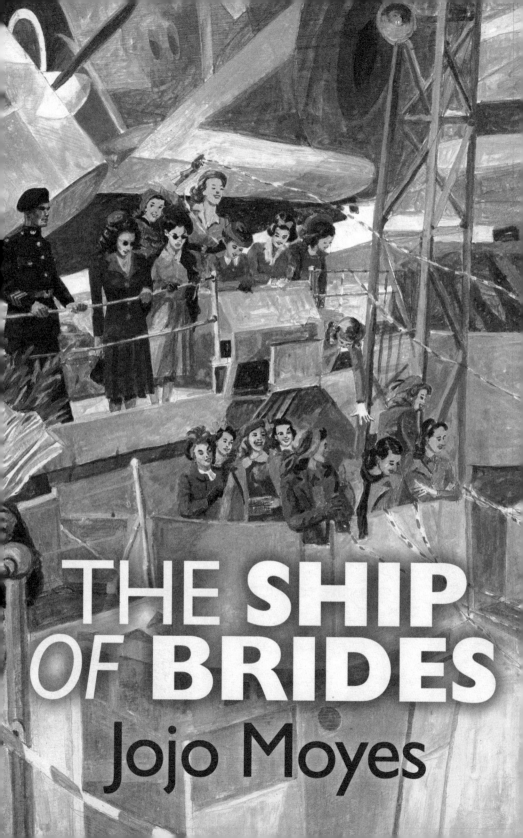

THE SHIP
OF BRIDES

Jojo Moyes

It is 1946, and four Australian war
brides, their hearts full of hope and
excitement, are setting sail on HMS
Victoria for England. Margaret is leaving
a remote farm and five brothers; spoilt
Avice has high hopes of English society;
flighty Jean, only sixteen years old, is
looking for stability, and Frances
is desperate to put the past behind her.

PROLOGUE

THE FIRST TIME I saw her again, I felt as if I'd been hit.

I have heard that said a thousand times, but I had never until then understood its true meaning: there was a delay, in which my memory took time to connect with what my eyes were seeing, and then a physical shock that went straight through me, as if I had taken some great blow. I can say truthfully that it left me winded.

I hadn't expected ever to see her again. Not in a place like that. I had long since buried her in some mental bottom drawer. Not just her physically, but everything she had meant to me. Everything she had forced me to go through. In myriad ways she had been both the best and the worst thing that had ever happened to me.

But it wasn't just the shock of her physical presence. There was grief too. I suppose in my memory she existed only as she had then, all those years ago. Seeing her as she was now, surrounded by all those people, looking somehow so aged, so diminished . . . I grieved for what had once been so beautiful, magnificent, even, reduced to . . .

I don't know. Perhaps that's not quite fair. None of us lasts for ever, do we? If I'm honest, seeing her like that was an unwelcome reminder of my own mortality. Of what I had been. Of what we all must become.

Whatever it was, there, in a place I had never been before, in a place I had no reason to be, I had found her again. Or perhaps she had found me . . . I suppose I hadn't believed in fate until that point. But it's hard not to, when you think how far we had both come.

Hard not to when you think that there was no way, across miles, continents, vast oceans, we were meant to see each other again.

9

INDIA, 2002

THE OLD WOMAN lifted her head away from the car window, rubbing the back of her neck where the air-conditioning had cast the chill deep into her bones, and tried to straighten up. She had woken to the sound of bickering. Yapping, irregular, explosive, like the sound a small dog makes. In those first few blurred moments of wakefulness she was not sure where, or even who, she was.

'I'm not saying I didn't like the palaces or the temples. I'm just saying I've spent two weeks here and I don't feel I got close to the real India.'

'What do you think I am? Virtual Sanjay?' From the front seat of the car, his voice was gently mocking. 'I am Indian. Ram here is Indian. Just because I spend half my life in England does not make me less Indian.'

'Oh, come on, Jay, you're hardly typical of most of the people who live here.'

The young man shook his head dismissively. 'You want to be a poverty tourist. You want to be able to go home and tell your friends about the terrible things you've seen. How they have no idea of the suffering. And all we have given you is Coca-Cola and air-conditioning.'

There was laughter. The old woman squinted at her watch. It was almost half past eleven: she had been asleep almost an hour.

Her granddaughter, beside her, was leaning forward between the two front seats. 'Look, I just want to see something that tells me how people really live. All the tour guides want to show you are princely abodes or shopping malls.'

'So you want slums.'

From the driver's seat Mr Vaghela's voice: 'I can take you to my home, Miss Jennifer. Now this is slum conditions. Look closely at Mr Ram B. Vaghela here and you will also find the poor, the downtrodden and the dispossessed.' He shrugged. 'You know, it is a wonder to me how I have survived this many years.'

'We, too, wonder almost daily,' Sanjay said.

The old woman pushed herself fully upright, catching sight of herself in the rearview mirror. Her hair had flattened on one side of her head, and her collar had left a deep red indent in her pale skin.

Jennifer glanced behind her. 'You all right, Gran?'

'Fine, dear. I'm terribly sorry, I must have nodded off.'

'Nothing to apologise for,' said Mr Vaghela. 'We mature citizens should be allowed to rest when we need to.'

'Are you saying you want me to drive, Ram?' Sanjay asked.

'No, no, Mr Sanjay, sir. I would be reluctant to interrupt your scintillating discourse.'

The old man's eyes met hers in the rearview mirror. Still fogged from sleep, the old woman forced herself to smile. They had, she calculated, been on the road for nearly three hours. Their trip to Gujarat, a last-minute incursion into the touring holiday, had started as an adventure ('My friend from college—Sanjay—his parents have offered to put us up for a couple of nights, Gran! They've got the most amazing place, like a palace. It's only a few hours away'), and ended in near-disaster when the failure of their plane to meet its scheduled slot left them only a day in which to return to Bombay to catch their flight home.

Already exhausted by the trip, she had despaired. She had found India a trial, and the thought of being stranded in Gujarat, even in the palatial confines of the Singhs' home, filled her with horror. But then Mrs Singh had volunteered the use of their car and driver.

'I can drive them,' Sanjay had protested. But his mother had murmured something about an insurance claim and a driving ban, and her son had agreed instead to accompany Mr Vaghela, to make sure they were not bothered when they stopped. She was grateful for such old-fashioned courtesy. She did not feel capable of negotiating her way alone through these alien landscapes, and found herself anxious with her risk-taking granddaughter, for whom nothing seemed to hold any fear.

'Are you OK back there, madam?'

'I'm fine, thank you, Sanjay.'

'Still a fair way to go, I'm afraid. It's not an easy trip.'

'It's very kind of you to take us.'

'Jay! Look at that!'

She saw they had come off the fast road now and were travelling through a shanty town, studded with warehouses full of steel girders and timber. The road, flanked by a long wall created from sheets of metal haphazardly patchworked together, had become increasingly pockmarked and rutted so that the black Lexus could travel at no more than fifteen miles an hour. It crept onwards, swerving periodically to avoid the potholes or the odd cow.

The prompt for Jennifer's exclamation had not been a cow but a mountain of white ceramic sinks.

'From the ships,' said Mr Vaghela, apropos apparently of nothing.

'Do you think we could stop soon?' she asked. She was now desperate for a drink and a chance to stretch her legs.

'Not here.' Sanjay frowned, gazing around him.

'Let me see the map,' Jennifer said. 'There might be somewhere off the beaten track. Somewhere a bit more . . . exciting.'

'I tell you what,' said Sanjay, 'we'll get a couple of bottles of cola and stop out of town somewhere to stretch our legs.' He waved at the driver to stop. 'Stop there, Ram, at that shop. The one next to the temple. I'll get some cold drinks.'

'We'll get some cold drinks,' said Jennifer. The car pulled up. 'You all right in the car, Gran?' She didn't wait for an answer. The two of them sprang out of the doors and went, laughing, into the sunbaked shop. A short way along the road a group of men squatted on their haunches, drinking from tin mugs. Outside, the heat shimmered off the earth.

'You know this place?' Mr Vaghela turned in his seat.

She shook her head.

'Alang. Biggest shipbreaker's yard in the world.'

'Oh.' Her mouth was dry and she swallowed awkwardly.

'Four hundred shipyards here. And men who can strip a tanker down to nuts and bolts in a matter of months.'

'Really?'

'Some of the biggest ships in the world have ended up here. You would not believe the things that the owners leave on cruise ships—dinner services, Irish linen, whole orchestras of musical instruments.' He sighed. 'Sometimes it makes you feel quite sad, yaar.'

The old woman tried to show a semblance of interest, conscious that exhaustion and thirst were poisoning her normally equable mood.

'They say on the road to Bhavnagar one can buy anything—chairs, telephones, musical instruments. My brother-in-law works for one of the big shipbreakers in Bhavnagar, yaar. He has furnished his entire house with ship's goods. It looks like a palace.' He picked at his teeth.

'Mr Vaghela?'

'Yes, madam?'

'Is that a teahouse?'

Diverted from his monologue, Mr Vaghela followed her pointing finger to a shopfront, where several chairs and tables stood haphazardly on the dusty roadside. 'It is.'

'Then would you be so kind as to take me there and order me a cup of tea?' she asked. 'I really do not think I can spend another moment waiting for my granddaughter.'

'I would be delighted, madam.' He climbed out of the car and held open the door for her.

The young people came out as she was drinking her cup of what Mr Vaghela called 'service tea'. The cups were scratched, but they looked clean, and the man who had looked after them had made a prodigious show of serving their tea. She had sat under the canopy and gazed out at what she now knew, from her slightly elevated vantage point, lay behind the steel wall: the endless, shimmering blue sea.

'I said I didn't think we should stop here,' said Sanjay, eyeing first the group of men nearby, then the car, with barely hidden irritation.

'I had to get out,' she said firmly, 'and Mr Vaghela was kind enough to accommodate me.' She sipped her tea. She felt a little better now: the heat was tempered by the faintest of sea breezes. In the distance she could hear the whine of a cutting instrument.

'Wow! Look at all those ships!'

Jennifer was gesticulating at the beach, where her grandmother could just make out the hulls of huge vessels, beached like whales upon the sand. She half closed her eyes. 'Is that the shipbreaking yard you mentioned?' she said to Mr Vaghela.

'Four hundred of them, madam, along ten kilometres of beach.'

At the water's edge, a group of men squatted on their haunches, dressed in faded robes of blue, grey and white, watching as a ship's deckhouse swung out from a still-white hull anchored several hundred feet from the shore and crashed heavily into the sea.

'Looks like an elephant's graveyard,' said Jennifer. Her hand was lifted to shield her eyes against the sun. Her grandmother gazed at her bare shoulders and wondered if she should suggest the girl cover up. 'This is the kind of thing I was talking about, Jay. Let's go and have a look.'

'There's a guard on the gate,' said Sanjay. 'You would be required to seek permission from the port office.'

But Jennifer had jumped up and was halfway across the road.

'I'd better go with her,' said Sanjay, a hint of resignation in his voice.

'Young people,' said Mr Vaghela. 'There is no telling them.'

A huge truck trundled past, the back filled with twisted pieces of metal to which six or seven men clung precariously. After it had passed, she could see Jennifer in conversation with the man on the gate. She watched as the girl ran her hand through her blonde hair and then reached into her bag and handed the man a bottle of cola. As Sanjay caught up with her, the gate opened and they were gone.

Twenty minutes later she was struggling to suppress her irritation that her granddaughter had behaved in such a selfish, reckless manner. Yet she knew that her response was due partly to fear that something would happen to the girl while she was in her charge.

'She won't wear a watch, you know.'

'I think we should go and bring them back,' said Mr Vaghela.

She let him pull back her chair and took his arm gratefully. She stayed close to him until they halted at the gate, where Mr Vaghela said something to the security guard. His tone was belligerent, as if the man had committed some crime in allowing the young people to go through. The guard said something apparently conciliatory in reply, then shepherded them in. Men swarmed over the rusting hulks like ants. They held welding torches, hammers, spanners, the beating chimes of their destruction echoing disconsolately in the open space.

'Please be careful where you walk,' said Mr Vaghela, gesturing towards the discoloured sand, grey with years of rust and oil.

'I shall hold on to you, Mr Vaghela, if you don't mind.'

'I think this would be recommended,' he said.

A small group of people had gathered on the sand, some clutching binoculars, others resting against bicycles, all looking out to sea. She took a firm hold of Mr Vaghela's arm and paused for a second, adjusting to the heat. Then they moved slowly down to the shore, to where men with walkie-talkies and dusty robes talked excitedly to each other.

Jennifer was nowhere to be seen.

'Another ship is coming in,' said Mr Vaghela, pointing.

They watched what might have been an old tanker, towed by several tugs, becoming gradually distinct as it drew towards the shore. A Japanese four-wheel drive roared past, screeching to a halt a few hundred yards ahead. And it was then that they became aware of voices raised in anger and, as they turned past a pile of gas cylinders, of a small crowd further along, standing in the shadow of a huge metallic hull.

The man in the centre of the commotion had jumped from his car and was gesturing at the ship, his indignant speech accompanied by sprays of spittle. Sanjay stood before him in a circle of men, his hands palms down in a conciliatory gesture. The object of the man's ire, Jennifer, was standing with her arms folded defensively across her chest.

'Madam, we should probably head this way,' said Mr Vaghela.

She nodded. She had begun to feel anxious.

'You can tell him,' Jennifer was saying, as they approached, 'that there's no law against looking at his bloody ship.'

Sanjay turned to her. 'That's the problem, Jen. There *is* a law against looking when you're trespassing on someone else's property.'

Around Sanjay, the men stood watching with unconcealed interest, nudging each other at Jennifer's jeans and vest-top. As the old woman came closer, several moved back, and she caught the smell of sweat.

'He thinks Jennifer is from some environmental group, that she's here to gather evidence against him,' Sanjay told her.

'It's obvious I'm only looking,' said Jennifer. 'I haven't even got a camera on me,' she enunciated at the man, who scowled at her.

'Jen, you're really not helping,' Sanjay remonstrated.

The old woman tried to assess how much of a threat the man might be. His gestures had become increasingly abrupt and dramatic, his expression florid with rage. She looked at Mr Vaghela, almost as if he were the only adult present.

Perhaps mindful of this, he detached himself from her, moved towards the shipbreaker and thrust out his hand, so that the man was forced to take it. 'Sir, I am Mr Ram B. Vaghela,' he announced. He began to talk rapidly, in Urdu, his voice wheedling and conciliatory one minute, determined and assertive the next. Occasionally he waved towards the old lady and she fanned herself, conscious that her presence would probably aid their cause.

In an attempt at nonchalance, she began to walk towards the bow of the ship, keen to be away from her irresponsible granddaughter and the blank-eyed men. It was hard to see much from so far underneath, but she could just make out a couple of gun turrets. She studied them, frowning at their familiarity, at the peeling pale grey paintwork, a soft colour you saw nowhere but on British naval ships.

She lifted her hand to shield her eyes from the fierce sun until she could see what remained of the name on the side.

And then, as the last of the letters became distinct, the arguing voices receded, and even in the oppressive heat of an Indian afternoon, the old woman beneath the bow of the ship felt herself possessed of an icy cold.

The shipbreaker, Mr Bhattacharya, was unconvinced. Mr Vaghela wiped his forehead with a handkerchief. He could tell that the man was offended by Miss Jennifer's barely decent mode of dress, and he suspected that while Mr Bhattacharya knew the young people were innocent of his charges, he had worked himself into such a rage that he was determined to continue the argument.

'I don't like the way he is talking to me.' Miss Jennifer was kicking sand angrily, her expression sulky.

Mr Sanjay moved towards the girl. 'But you don't even know what he's saying, Jen. Go back to the car and take your gran with you.'

'Don't tell me what to do, Jay. I—' Miss Jennifer stopped abruptly.

Mr Vaghela followed the eyes of the crowd to the shaded area under the hull of the next ship, where the old lady was sitting slumped forward, her head supported in her hands.

'Gran?' The girl sprinted over to her. 'Are you all right?'

'Yes. Yes, dear.' The words seemed to come out automatically, Mr Vaghela thought. Forgetting Mr Bhattacharya, he and Mr Sanjay walked over and squatted in front of the old lady.

'You look rather pale, *Mammaji*, if I may say so.'

The shipbreaker was beside them. He muttered to Mr Vaghela. 'He wants to know if you'd like a drink,' he told her. 'He says he has some iced water in his office.'

She lifted a hand feebly. 'That's very kind, but I'll just sit for a minute.'

'Gran? What's the matter?' Jennifer had knelt down, her eyes wide with anxiety. The posturing arrogance had evaporated in the heat.

'Please ask them to go away, Jen,' the old woman whispered. 'Really. I'll be fine if everyone just leaves me alone.'

'Is it me? I'm really sorry, Gran. I should have been more thoughtful. Look, we'll get you back to the car.'

Mr Vaghela was gratified to hear the apology. She should not have caused the old lady to walk such a distance in this heat.

'It's not you, Jennifer. It's the ship,' she whispered.

Uncomprehending, the young people stared at each other.

'It's just a ship, Gran,' said Jennifer.

'No,' she said, and Mr Vaghela noted that her face was as bleached as the metal behind it. 'That's where you're quite wrong.'

PART ONE

AUSTRALIA, 1946

Four weeks to embarkation

LETTY McHUGH straightened her blouse, picked up the letters she had collected on her weekly visit to the post office and peered out at the blurred landscape through the windscreen of the pick-up truck. The rain probably wouldn't let up no matter how long she waited. She pulled a piece of tarpaulin over her head and shoulders, leapt out of the truck and ran for the house.

'Margaret? Maggie?'

The screen door slammed behind her, muffling the insistent timpani of the deluge outside, but only her own voice and the sound of her shoes on the floorboards echoed back at her. Letty put her handbag and the letters on the scrubbed wooden table and went to the stove, where a stew was simmering. She lifted the lid and sniffed. Then, guiltily, she reached into the cupboard and added a pinch of salt, some cumin and cornflour, stirred, and replaced the lid.

She went to the little liver-spotted mirror by the medicine cupboard and tried to smooth her hair, which had already begun to frizz in the moisture-filled air, then turned back to the kitchen.

Her solitude allowed her to see it with a dispassionate eye. She surveyed the cracked linoleum, ingrained with years of agricultural dirt that wouldn't lift, no matter how many times it was mopped. She took in the faded paintwork, the calendar that marked only this or that agricultural show, the arrival of vets, buyers or grain salesmen, the dogs' baskets with their filthy old blankets lined up round the range, and the packet of Bluo for the men's shirts, spilling its grains onto the bleached work surface. The only sign of any female influence was a copy of *Glamor* magazine, its straplines advertising a new story by Daphne du Maurier, and a heavily thumbed article entitled 'Would You Marry A Foreigner?'

She glanced at the clock: the men would be in shortly for lunch. She walked to the coathooks by the back door and pulled off an old stockman's jacket. The rain was now so heavy that in places around the yard it ran in rivers; the drains gurgled in protest and the chickens huddled in ruffled groups. Letty cursed herself for not having brought her gumboots but ran from the back door of the house to the barn. There she made out what looked like a brown oilskin-proofed lump on a horse, circling the paddock, no face visible under the wide-brimmed hat.

'Margaret!' Letty stood under the eaves of the barn and shouted, waving halfheartedly.

The horse was plainly fed up: its tail clamped to its soaking hindquarters, occasionally cowkicking in frustration while its rider patiently turned it to begin each painstaking manoeuvre again.

'Maggie! Maggie, will you get over here!'

The brim of the hat lifted and a hand was raised in greeting. The horse was steered round and walked towards the gate, its head low. 'Been there long, Letty?' she called.

'Are you insane, girl? What on earth do you think you're doing?' She could see her niece's broad grin under the brim of the hat.

'Just a bit of schooling. Dad's too big to ride her and the boys are useless with her, so there's only me. Moody old girl, isn't she?'

Letty shook her head, exasperated, and motioned for Margaret to dismount. 'For goodness' sake, child. Do you want a hand getting off?'

'Hah! No, I'm fine. Is it lunchtime yet? I put some stew on earlier, but I don't know what time they'll be in. They're moving the calves down to Yarrawa Creek and they can be all day down there.'

'They'll not be all day in this weather,' Letty responded, as Margaret clambered down from the horse and landed heavily on her feet. 'You're soaked. Look at you! I can't believe you'd even consider riding out in this weather. What your dear mother would have said . . .'

There was a brief pause.

'I know . . .' Margaret wrinkled her nose as she reached up to undo the girth.

Letty wondered if she had said too much. She hesitated, then bit back the awkward apology that had sprung to her lips. 'I didn't mean—'

'Forget it. You're right, Letty,' said the girl, as she swung the saddle easily under her arm.

The men returned shortly before one o'clock, arriving in a thunderous cluster of wet overshoes and dripping hats, shedding their coats at the door. Margaret had set the table and was dishing up steaming bowls of beef stew.

Murray Donleavy, a towering, angular man whose freckles and pale eyes signalled his Irish origins, sat down at the head of the table and began to work his way through a hunk of bread that his sister-in-law had sliced for him. 'How are you, Letty? Did you get up to town yesterday?'

'I did, Murray.'

'Any post for us?'

'I'll bring it out after you've eaten.' Otherwise, the letters would be splashed with gravy and fingered with greasemarks. Her sister, Noreen, had never seemed to mind.

Margaret had had her lunch already, and was sitting on the easy chair by the larder, her socked feet on a footstool. Letty watched as the men settled to eat. Not many families, these days, could boast five sons round a table with three of them having been in the services. No, this table lacked someone else entirely. She sighed, pushing Noreen from her thoughts, as she did countless times every day.

'You make this?' Murray lifted his head from his newspaper and jerked a thumb at his bowl, which was nearly empty.

'Maggie did,' said Letty.

'Nice. Better than the last one.'

'I don't know why,' said Margaret, her hand held out in front of her the better to examine a splinter. 'I didn't do anything any different.'

'There's a new picture starting at the Odeon,' Letty said, changing the subject. That got their attention. She knew the men pretended not to be interested in the snippets of gossip she brought to the farm twice a week, gossip being the stuff of women, but every now and then the mask of indifference slipped. She rested against the sink, arms crossed. 'Well?'

'It's a war film. Greer Garson and Tyrone Power.'

'I hope it's got lots of fighter planes. American ones.' Daniel, the youngest, glanced at his brothers, apparently searching for agreement, but their heads were down as they shovelled food into their mouths.

'How are you going to get to Woodside, short-arse? Your bike's broke, if you remember.' Liam shoved him.

'He's not cycling all that way by himself, whatever,' said Murray.

'One of youse can take me in the truck. Ah, go on.'

'Oh, Dad, Betty says to tell you their good mare is in foal finally, if you're still interested,' Colm told him.

Murray exchanged a glance with his eldest son. 'Might swing by there later in the week, Colm. Be good to have a decent horse.'

'Which reminds me.' Letty took a deep breath. 'I found Margaret riding that young filly of yours. I don't think she should. It's not safe.'

Murray didn't look up from his stew. 'She's a grown woman, Letty. We'll have little or no say over her life soon enough.'

'You've no need to fuss, Letty. I know what I'm doing,' Margaret said.

'She's a mean-looking horse.' Letty began to wash up, feeling vaguely undermined. 'I'm just saying I don't think Noreen would have liked it.'

The mention of her sister's name brought a brief, melancholy silence.

Murray pushed his empty bowl to the centre of the table. 'It's good of you to concern yourself about us, Letty. Don't think we're not grateful.'

If the boys noted the look that passed between the two 'olds', as they were known, or that their aunt Letty's was followed by the faintest pinking of her cheeks, they said nothing. Just as they had said nothing when, several months previously, she had started to wear her good skirt to visit them. Or that, in her mid-forties, she was suddenly setting her hair.

Margaret, meanwhile, had risen from her chair and was flicking through the letters on the sideboard. 'Bloody hell!' she exclaimed. 'Look! Look, Dad, it's for me! From the navy!'

Her father motioned for her to bring it over. He turned the envelope in his broad hands, noting the official stamp. 'Want me to open it?'

'He's not dead, is he?' Daniel yelped as Colm's hand caught him a sharp blow to the back of the head.

'You don't think he's dead, do you?' Margaret reached out to steady herself, her normally high colour draining away.

'Course he's not dead,' her father said. 'They send you a wire for that.'

She looked at him, then down at the letter, which she now held. Her brothers were on their feet, standing tightly around her. Letty, watching from the sink, felt superfluous, as if she were an outsider.

Margaret ripped open the envelope and began to read the letter. Then she gave a little moan, and Letty whirled round to see her sit down heavily on a chair that one of her brothers had pushed out for her.

'You all right, girl?' Her father's face was creased with anxiety.

'I'm going, Dad,' she croaked. 'To England. They've got me aboard a ship. Oh my God, Dad.'

'Mags is going to England!' Colm now held the letter and was reading it. 'She's really going! They've actually managed to squeeze her on!'

'Less of your cheek,' said Margaret, but her heart wasn't in it.

'"Due to the change in status of another war bride, we can offer you a passage on the—"'

'Change in status? What do you suppose happened to that poor soul, then?' Niall scoffed.

'It's possible the husband might have been married already. It happens, you know,' Letty said.

'Letty!' Murray protested.

'Well, it's true, Murray. You only have to read the papers. I've heard of girls who've gone all the way to America to be told they're not wanted. Some with . . .' She tailed off.

'Joe's not like that,' said Murray. 'We all know he's not like that.'

'Besides,' said Colm cheerfully, 'when he married Mags I told him if he ever let her down I'd hunt him down and kill him.'

'You did that too?' said Niall, surprised.

'With you lot looking after me it's a wonder he stuck around at all,' Margaret said, ignoring her aunt.

A hush descended as the import of the letter settled on the occupants of the room. Margaret took her father's hand and held it tightly.

'Does anyone want tea?' said Letty. A lump had risen in her throat: she had been picturing the kitchen without Margaret in it. There were several subdued murmurs of assent.

'Is that it?' said Daniel. 'I mean, do you go to England and that's it?'

'That's it,' said Margaret, quietly.

'But what about us?' said Daniel, his voice breaking, as if he had not yet taken seriously his sister's marriage or its possible ramifications. 'We can't lose Mum *and* Mags. I mean, what are we supposed to do?'

Across the table, Murray had been sitting in silence. Now he smiled reassuringly at his daughter. 'We, son, are going to be glad, because Margaret is going to be with a good man. A man who's fought for his country and ours. A man who deserves to be with our Margaret just as much as she deserves him.'

'Oh, Dad.' Margaret dabbed at her eyes.

'And more importantly,' here his voice rose, as if to stave off interruption, 'we should be glad as anything because Joe's grandfather was an Irishman. And that means'—he laid a roughened hand gently on his daughter's expanded belly—'this little fellow here is going to set foot, God willing, in God's own country.'

'Oh, Murray,' whispered Letty, her hand pressed to her mouth.

Margaret hauled another clean wet undershirt from the bucket and handed it to her aunt, who fed the hem into the mangle and began to turn the handle.

'Why don't you sit down, Maggie?' Letty said, eyeing her legs. 'You know you should rest. Most women have their feet up by now.'

'Ah, there's ages yet,' Margaret said.

'Less than twelve weeks, by my reckoning.' Letty was conscious of her inability to talk of childbirth with any authority. She continued wringing in silence, the rain drumming noisily on the tin roof of the outhouse. The mangle squeaked, a geriatric creature forced unwillingly into effort.

'Daniel's taken it worse than I thought,' Margaret said eventually. 'He's really angry. I didn't expect him to be angry.'

Letty paused. 'He feels let down, I suppose. What with losing his mum and you . . .'

Margaret thought of her brother's outburst, of the words 'selfish' and 'hateful' hurled at her in temper. 'When Joe and I got married, you know, I didn't think about leaving Dad and the boys. Who's going to look after them all? There's not one of them can put together a meal. And they'd leave the sheets on their beds until they walked themselves to the linen basket.'

As she spoke, Margaret began almost to believe in this picture of herself as a domestic linchpin, which position she had held with quiet resentment for the past two years. 'It's a huge worry, Letty. I really think they won't be able to cope without a woman around the place.'

There was a lengthy silence.

'I suppose they could get someone in, like a housekeeper,' said Letty eventually, her voice deceptively light.

'Dad wouldn't want to pay for that. You know how he goes on about saving money. And, besides, I don't think any of them would like a stranger in the kitchen.'

The two women were silent for a few minutes, Margaret spoke again. 'Actually, I'm wondering whether I should leave at all.'

'I suppose,' Letty ventured, 'that I could help out. If you're that worried about them all'—her voice was measured—'I might be able to come most days.'

'Oh, Letty, would you?' Margaret had ensured that her voice held just the right amount of surprise, just the right level of gratitude.

'I wouldn't want to be treading on anyone's toes. I wouldn't want you or the boys thinking . . . that I was trying to take your mother's place. But, it's not like I've got a job or anything, now they've shut the munitions factory. And family should come first.'

'It certainly should.'

If Margaret noticed the faint blush of pleasure creeping across her aunt's face she said nothing. If the price of her own guiltless freedom was for her mother's place to be usurped, she would be careful only to see the benefits.

Letty's angular face was lit now by a smile. 'If it will help you, dear, I'll take good care of them all,' she said. 'Yes, I'll make sure they're all all right.' Anticipation had apparently made her garrulous. 'You won't need to worry about a thing.' Suddenly galvanised, she wrung out the last shirt by hand and dumped it in the washing basket. 'Right. Now. Why don't I go and make us both a cup of tea? You write your letter to the navy, telling them you'll accept, and then we'll know you're all set.'

Margaret made her smile seem readier than it felt. Her aunt was now hauling the basket across the room with the same proprietorial familiarity as her mother once had. She shut her eyes and breathed deeply as Letty's voice echoed across the laundry room.

'I might fix up a few of your father's shirts, while I'm at it. I couldn't help noticing, dear, that they're looking a bit tired . . .' Letty's face was suddenly anxious, her forty-five-year-old features as open as those of a young bride.

'Maggie?'

'Mm?'

'Do you think your father will mind? I mean, about me?'

Afterwards, on the many nights when she thought back, Margaret wasn't sure what had made her say it. She wasn't a mean person. She didn't want either Letty or her father to be lonely, after all.

'I think he'll be delighted,' she said. 'He's very fond of you, Letty, as are the boys.' She looked down and coughed. 'He's often said he looks on you like . . . a kind of sister. Someone who can talk to him about Mum, who remembers what she was like . . . And, of course, if you're washing their shirts for them you'll have their undying gratitude.' For some reason it was impossible to look up but she was aware of the acute stillness of Letty's skirts, of her thin, strong legs, as she stood a few feet away. Her hands, habitually active, hung motionless against her apron.

'Yes,' Letty said at last. 'Of course.' There was a slight choke in her voice. 'Well. As I said. I'll—I'll go and make us that tea.'

Three weeks to embarkation

Ian darling,

You'll never guess what—I'm on! I know you won't believe it, as I hardly can myself, but it's true. Daddy had a word with one of his old friends at the Red Cross, who has some friends high up in the RN, and the next thing I had orders saying I've got a place on the next boat out. Now I'm here, holed up at the Wentworth Hotel in Sydney, waiting to nip on board.

Darling, I can't wait to see you. I've missed you so terribly. Mummy says that when we've got our new home sorted she and Daddy will be over ASAP. She has asked me to ask you for your mother's address so she can send on the rest of my things once I'm in England. I'm sure they'll be better about everything once they've met your parents.

So, anyway, darling, here I am practising my signature, and remembering to answer to 'Mrs', and still getting used to the sight of a wedding band on my finger. It was so disappointing us not having a proper honeymoon, but I really don't mind where it happens, as long as I'll be with you. I'll end now, as I'm spending the afternoon at the American Wives' Club at Woolloomooloo, finding out what I'll need for the trip. Take care my love, and write as soon as you have a moment.

Your Avice

In the four years since its inception the American Wives' Club had met every two weeks at the elegant white stucco house on the edge of the Royal Botanic Gardens, initially to help girls who had travelled from Perth or Canberra to while away the endless weeks before they were allowed a passage to meet their American husbands. A number of middle-aged ladies taught them how to make American patchwork quilts, sing 'The Star Spangled Banner', and offered a little matronly support to those who were pregnant or nursing.

Latterly the club had ceased to be American in character: the previous year's US War Brides Act had hastened the departure of its 12,000 newly claimed Australian wives, so the quilts had been replaced by bridge afternoons and advice on how to cope with British food and rationing.

Many of the young brides who now attended were lodged with families. They were in a strange hinterland, their lives in Australia not yet over and those elsewhere not begun.

Apart from Avice, there were twelve other young women at today's gathering; few had spent more than a week at a time with their husbands, and more than half had not seen them for the best part of a year. The shipment home of troops was a priority; the 'wallflower wives', as they had become known, were not. In other times, Avice would not have spent five minutes with this peculiar mixture of girls—some of whom seemed to have landed straight off some outback station with red dust on their shoes—or, indeed, have wasted so many hours enduring interminable lectures. But she had been in Sydney for almost ten days now and the Wives' Club was her only point of social contact.

Avice was the newest member. Listening to their tales of the families with whom the other young women were billeted, she had silently thanked her parents for the opulence of her hotel accommodation.

'When's the next boat due in?'

'Around three weeks, according to my orders,' said a dark-eyed girl sitting beside Avice. Avice thought she might have said her name was Jean. 'She'd better be as nice as the *Queen Mary*.' The liner had been held up as the holy grail of transport. 'She even had a hair salon with heated dryers. I'm desperate to get my hair done properly before I see Stan.'

'She was a wonderful woman, Queen Mary,' said Mrs Proffit, from the end of the table. 'Such a lady,' she said, benignly, as she checked the stitching of a green hat on a brown woollen monkey. Today they were Gift-making for the Bombed-out Children of London.

'You've got your orders?' A freckled girl on the other side of the table was frowning at Jean.

'Last week.'

'But you're low priority. You said you didn't even put in your papers until a month ago.'

There was silence. Around the table, several girls exchanged glances, then fixed their eyes on their embroidery. Mrs Proffit looked up; she had apparently picked up on the subtle cooling in the atmosphere. 'Anyone need more thread?' she asked, peering over her spectacles.

'Yes, well, sometimes you just get lucky,' said Jean, and excused herself from the table.

'How come she gets on?' said the freckled girl, turning to the women on each side of her. 'I've been waiting nearly fifteen months and she's getting on the next boat out. How can that be right?' Avice made a mental note not to mention her own orders.

'She's carrying, isn't she?' muttered another girl.

'What?'

'Jean. She's in the family way. You know what? The Americans won't let you over once you're past four months.'

'Who's doing the penguin?' said Mrs Proffit. 'You'll need to keep that black thread for whoever's doing the penguin.'

'Hang on,' said a redhead threading a needle. 'Her Stan left in November. She said he was on the same ship as my Ernie.'

'So she can't be in the family way.'

'Or she is . . . and . . .'

Eyes widened and met, accompanied by the odd smirk.

'Are you up for a little roo, Sarah dear?' Mrs Proffit beamed at the girls and pulled some pieces of fawn felt out of her cloth bag.

Several minutes later Jean returned to her chair, and folded her arms rather combatively.

'I met Ian, my husband, at a tea dance,' said Avice, in an attempt to break the silence. 'He was the second man I offered a cup of tea to.'

'Was that all you offered him?'

That was Jean. She might have known. 'From what I've heard I don't suppose everyone's idea of hospitality is quite the same as yours,' she retorted. She remembered how she had blushed as she poured.

Petty Officer Ian Stewart Radley. At twenty-six, a whole five years older than her, which Avice considered just right, he was tall and straight-backed with eyes the colour of the sea, a gentlemanly British accent and broad, soft hands that had made her tremble the first time they ever brushed hers. He had asked her to dance—even though no one else was on the floor—and with him being a serviceman, and look-ing death in the face, she had thought it mean-spirited to refuse.

Less than four months later they were married, a tasteful ceremony in the Collins Street register office. Her father had been suspicious, had made her mother quiz her as to whether there was any reason for such a hasty marriage other than Ian's imminent departure. Ian had told her father, rather honourably, she thought, that he was happy to wait, that he would do nothing to upset them, but she had been determined to become Mrs Radley.

'But we know nothing about him, dear,' her mother had said, wring-ing her hands.

'What do you need to know? Doesn't protecting our country, putting his own life at risk twelve thousand miles from his home to save us from the Japs, make him worthy of my hand?'

'No need to be melodramatic, sweetheart,' her father had said.

They had given in, of course. They always did. Her sister Deanna had been furious.

'My Johnnie was billeted with my aunt Vi,' said another girl. 'I thought he was gorgeous. I sneaked into his room the second night he was there and that was that.'

'Best to get in early,' said another, to raucous laughter. 'Stake your claim.'

'Especially if Jean's around.'

Even Jean found that funny.

Mrs Proffit sighed and laid down her craftwork. Really! It was only to be expected, as embarkation drew closer—but really!

'So, when are you out?'

Jean's host family were two streets away from the Wentworth Hotel and, despite the air of mutual dislike between them, the girls had ended up walking back together, dawdling. They were both reluctant to sit alone in their rooms for yet another evening.

'Avice? When are your orders for?'

Avice wondered whether to answer truthfully. She was pretty sure that Jean—immature and coarse as she was—was not the kind of girl she would normally want to associate with, especially if what had been said about her condition was true. But neither was Avice a girl used to self-restraint, and the effort involved in keeping quiet for an entire afternoon about her own plans had been a strain. 'Same as you. Three weeks. What's she called? The *Victoria*?'

'It's a bugger, isn't it?' Jean lit a cigarette, cupping her hands against the sea breeze. 'They get the *Queen Mary* and we get the old tin can.'

'I'm sorry, I don't understand what you mean.'

Jean laughed humourlessly. 'Didn't you hear Mrs Proffit? She's married to the commander and our *Victoria* is a bloody aircraft carrier.'

Avice stared at the girl for a minute, then smiled. It was the kind of smile she reserved at home for the staff when they did something particularly stupid. 'I think you must be mistaken, Jean. Ladies don't travel on aircraft carriers. There'd be nowhere to put us all.'

'You really don't know anything, do you?'

Avice fought back irritation at being addressed in this manner by someone who had to be at least five years younger than herself.

'They've run out of decent transport. They're going to stick us on anything to get us over there.'

'An aircraft carrier?' Avice felt a little wobbly. She reached for a nearby wall and sat down. 'But where will we sleep?'

Jean seated herself comfortably beside her. 'Dunno. On the deck with the planes?'

Avice's eyes widened.

'Strewth, Avice, you're even more gullible than I thought.' Jean cackled, stubbed out her cigarette, stood up and began to walk on. 'They'll find some way to fit us on. Got to be better than sticking around here, anyway.'

'Oh, I don't think so.' Avice stood up. 'I can't possibly travel on something like that. My parents thought I'd be travelling on a liner. You know, one of the ones that had been requisitioned for transport.'

'You take what you're given in times like these, girl. You know that.'

Not me, said Avice silently. She was now running towards the hotel. If she rang now she might catch her father before he left for his club.

'Avice darling, is that you? Wilfred! It's Avice!' She could picture her mother sitting on her telephone seat, the Persian rug on the parquet floor, the ever-present vase of flowers on the table beside her. 'How are you, sweetheart?'

'Fine, Mummy. But I need to speak to Daddy.'

'You don't sound all right. Are you really fine?'

'Yes.' Avice struggled to keep her impatience out of her voice.

Her father came on the line. 'Is that my littlest princess?'

'Oh, Daddy, thank goodness. There's a problem with the ship.'

'I don't understand, Princess.'

'It's an aircraft carrier.'

'*What?*'

'It's an aircraft carrier. They're expecting us to sail to England on an aircraft carrier.'

There was a brief silence. 'They want her to travel on an aircraft carrier,' her father told her mother.

'What? A warship?'

Avice could almost hear her reeling in horror. Deanna had started laughing in the background. She would: she hadn't forgiven Avice for marrying first.

'You're going to have to talk to whoever it was who got me on,' Avice said urgently. 'Tell him I need to travel on something else.'

'What's the matter? Are you the only girl on board, Princess?'

'Me? Oh, no, there's six hundred or so wives travelling.' She frowned.

27

'It's just that it will be awful. They'll have us sleeping on bedrolls and there won't be any facilities. Can you sort it out?'

Her father sighed heavily. 'Well, it's not as easy as that, Princess. I had to pull quite a few strings to get you on board. And I'm not sure how many more transports there are going to be.'

'Well, fly me over. I'll go with Qantas.'

'It's not as easy as that, Avice.'

'I can't go on that awful ship!'

She stamped her foot and the receptionist glanced at her. She lowered her voice to a whisper: 'I know what you're doing, Daddy. Don't think I don't know why you're refusing to help me.'

Her mother broke in on the line, her voice firm. 'Avice, you're right. I think the ship thing is a very bad idea.'

'You do?' Avice felt a flicker of hope. Her mother understood the importance of travelling comfortably.

'Yes. I think you should come home. Get on a train first thing tomorrow morning.'

'Home?'

'The whole thing has too many ifs and buts. This ship business sounds awful; you haven't heard from Ian in goodness knows how long—'

'He's at sea, Mummy.'

'—and I just think all the signs are against you. You know nothing about this man's family. Nothing. You have no idea if there's even going to be anyone to meet you at the other end. That's if this warship even gets there. Come home, darling, and we'll sort it all out from here. Plenty of girls change their minds.'

'Plenty of girls get dumped too,' called Deanna.

'I'm married, Mummy.'

'Well, we could have it annulled or something.'

Avice was incredulous. 'Annulled? Ugh! You're both such hypocrites! I know what you're doing. You got me on the rottenest old ship you could find just so I wouldn't want to travel.'

The receptionist had given up any pretence of not listening and was agog, leaning over her counter.

Her father broke back in: 'You there? Avice? Look, I'll wire you some money. Leave it a while, if you want. Sit tight at the Wentworth. We'll talk about this.'

'No, Daddy,' she said. 'Tell Mummy and Deanna I'll be on the ship to meet my husband, even if it does mean swimming in diesel fuel and stinking troops, because *I love him*. I won't ring again, but I'll wire Mummy at the other end. When Ian—my husband—has met me.'

HALMAHERAS ISLANDS ~ SOUTH PACIFIC, 1946

One week to embarkation

THERE WAS A FULL MOON over Morotai. With a melancholy lucidity, it illuminated the still night, the heat so stifling that even the gentle sea breezes were deadened. The leaves of the palm trees hung limp. The only sound was a periodic muffled thud as a coconut hit the ground. There was no one left to take down the ripe ones, and they fell unchecked, a hazard to the unwary.

For the past five years that end of the island had been clamorous with the traffic of the Allied Forces, the air filled with the roar of aircraft engines, but now there was silence, broken only by bursts of distant laughter and, just audible in the still night, the clink of glasses. In the tented confines of the nurses' mess, a few hundred yards from what had been the American base, Matron Audrey Marshall of the Australian General Hospital, finished her day's entry in the Unit War Diary.

The ward was one of the few still open: forty-five of the fifty-two were now closed, their patients restored to families in England, Australia, or even India, nurses discharged. The *Ariadne* would be the last hospital ship, carrying with it a raggle-taggle of a dozen POWs and one nursing sister. From now on it would be just the odd car accident and civilian illnesses until she, too, received her orders to return home.

'Nurse Frederick says I should tell you Sergeant Wilkes is foxtrotting Nurse Cooper around the operating theatre . . . She's fallen over twice already.' Staff Nurse Gore stuck her head round the sheeted doorway. She was flushed with excitement. With the hospital so close to abandonment, the girls were skittish and silly, their former reserve and authority evaporating in the moisture-filled air. She didn't have the heart to reprimand them, not after what they'd seen these last weeks. She couldn't forget their shocked faces when the first POWs arrived from Borneo.

'Go and tell the silly girl to bring him back in. He's only been on his feet forty-eight hours.'

'Will do, Matron.' The girl started to leave, then stopped briefly. 'Are you coming? The boys are asking where you are.'

'I'll be along shortly, Nurse,' she said, shutting her book.

'Yes, Matron.' With a giggle she departed.

The majority of beds in the long tent known as Ward G had been moved back so that half of the room now formed an unofficial, sand-based dance floor and those men still confined to their beds could see it. On the desk in the corner the gramophone huskily issued the songs that had not been scratched to nothing through years of sand and overuse. A couple stopped when Audrey Marshall entered, but she nodded at them in a way that suggested they should carry on.

She moved along the row of beds, checking the temperatures of those with suspected dengue fever and peering under dressings.

'Share a nip with us, Matron?'

The captain lifted the bottle, an invitation. She eyed him for a moment. He shouldn't be drinking with the medication he was taking. 'Don't mind if I do, Captain Baillie,' she said. 'One for the boys who aren't going home.'

'Wish the Americans were still here,' said Staff Nurse Fisher, mopping her brow. 'I don't half miss those buckets of crushed ice.' A few British patients were all that remained.

There was a swell of agreement.

'I just want to get to sea,' said Private Lerwick, from the corner. 'I keep dreaming of the breezes.'

Normally heat like this would have left them all listless, the patients dozing on their beds, the nurses moving slowly between them, wiping damp faces with cool cloths. But the imminent departure of the POWs had injected something into the atmosphere. Perhaps it was the sudden realisation that tightly knit groups, which had supported each other through the horror of the last years, were about to be disbanded and might not meet again.

Audrey Marshall, watching the people before her, felt her throat constrict. Suddenly she understood the girls' need to party, the men's determination to drink, dance and plough their way with forced merriment through these last hours together. 'Tell you what,' she said, gesturing towards what had been the dressings station, but which was now an impromptu bar offering whisky and beer. 'Make mine a large whisky.'

The singing started not long afterwards: 'Shenandoah'. The reedy, drink-lubricated voices drifted through the canvas into the night sky. It was halfway through the chorus that the girl entered. Audrey didn't see her at first, but as she raised her own voice in song, she became aware of the girl's pale, freckled face framed in the doorway, her thin shoulders erect in her uniform. She was holding a small suitcase and a kitbag. Not much to show for six years in the Australian General Hospital. She stared into the crowded tent as if she were about to change her mind.

Then she caught Audrey Marshall looking at her, and walked over.

'Packed already, Sister?'

The girl hesitated before she spoke. 'I'll be boarding the hospital ship tonight, Matron, if it's all right by you. They could do with a bit of help with the very sick men.'

'They didn't ask me,' said Audrey, trying not to sound aggrieved.

The girl looked at the floor. 'I—I offered. I hope you don't mind. I thought that you probably didn't need me any more.'

'You don't want to stay and have a last few drinks with us?' Even as she said it Audrey wasn't sure why she'd asked. In the four years they had worked together Sister Mackenzie had never been one for parties.

'You're very kind, but no, thank you.' She was already looking at the doorway, as if calculating how soon she could leave.

Audrey was about to press the point, unwilling to let this be the way her years of service should end. But as she tried to find the right words, she became aware that most of the girls had stopped dancing. 'I'd like to say—' she began, but one of the men interrupted.

'Don't you go anywhere, Sister. You made me a promise, remember?' Private Lerwick was trying to get out of bed. He had put his feet on the ground and was steadying himself with one hand on the iron bedstead.

Audrey caught the knowing smirk between Nurse Fisher and the two girls beside her. She glanced at Sister Mackenzie, and realised that she had seen it too. Sister Mackenzie's hands had tightened on her two bags. She said quietly, 'I can't stay, Private. I have to board the hospital ship.'

'Ah, will you not take a drink with us, Sister? A last drink?' asked Sergeant O'Brien.

'Sister Mackenzie has work to do, Sergeant,' the matron said firmly.

'Ah, come on. At least shake my hand.'

The girl took a step forward, then went to shake the hands of those men who proffered them. The music had started up again, deflecting attention from her, but even as Sister Mackenzie moved from bed to bed, Audrey Marshall noted the cold, assessing eyes of the other nurses.

'Sister! Sister, come here.' Private Lerwick was beckoning. 'You wouldn't break a promise to a wounded man, would you, Sister?' Private Lerwick's expression was comically hangdog.

The men on each side of him joined in chorus: 'Come on, Sister, you promised.'

Unable to bear the girl's dilemma any longer, Audrey Marshall intervened: 'Private, I'll thank you to get back into your bed.' She walked briskly across to where he sat. 'Promise or no promise, you're not ready to be out of it.'

31

She was lifting his leg back onto the mattress when a voice said, 'It's all right, Matron.' She turned to see the girl standing behind her, face bright. Only the fluttering of her pale hands betrayed her discomfort. 'I did promise.'

She was tall, so she had to stoop as, arm under his shoulders in a long-practised manoeuvre, she hauled him to his feet.

'Go on, Scottie,' said the man behind her. 'Just don't step on her toes.'

'I couldn't dance before,' he joked, as they moved slowly onto the sandy area that had passed as the dance floor. 'Two pounds of shrapnel in my knees isn't going to help none.'

They began to dance, and those men still nearby broke into spontaneous applause. Audrey Marshall found she was clapping too, moved by the sight of the frail man standing tall and proud, beaming to have achieved his modest ambition: to stand on a dance floor again with a woman in his arms. She watched the young nurse, braving her own discomfort for him, arms tensed to support him if he lost his balance. A kind girl. A good nurse.

That was the saddest part of it.

The music stopped. Private Lerwick sank gratefully into his bed, still grinning despite his obvious exhaustion. Audrey felt her heart sink, knowing that the act of kindness would count against the young nurse.

Private Lerwick was still hanging onto the nurse's hand. 'We know what you've all done, coming here in your time off . . . You've all been like—like our sisters.' He broke down and, after a brief hesitation, Sister Mackenzie bent over him, murmuring to him not to upset himself. 'That's what I'll think of when I think of you, Sister. Nothing else. I just wish poor Chalkie . . .'

Audrey placed herself swiftly between them. 'I'm sure we're all very grateful to Sister Mackenzie, aren't we? And I'm sure we'd like to wish her all the best for the future.'

A few nurses clapped politely. A couple of the men exchanged a smirk.

'Thank you,' the girl said quietly. 'Thank you. I'm glad to have known you . . . all . . .' She bit her lip and glanced towards the door of the tent, apparently desperate to be away.

'I'll see you out, Sister,' Audrey said.

The two women walked slowly towards where the hospital ship sat in the glinting water at the end of the peninsula, illuminated by the moon.

They reached the checkpoint and stopped. Sister Mackenzie stared at the ship and Audrey Marshall wondered what was going through the girl's head, suspecting she knew the answer. 'You're doing the right thing, Frances,' she said, eventually. 'I'd do the same, if I were you.'

The girl looked at her, back straight, eyes level. She had always been guarded, Audrey thought, but in the past weeks her expression seemed as if it had been cast in marble. 'Fresh start, eh?' she said, holding out her hand.

'Fresh start.' Sister Mackenzie shook it firmly. Her hand was cool, despite the heat. Her expression was unreadable. 'Thank you.'

PART TWO

SYDNEY, JULY 1946

Embarkation

AFTERWARDS, SHE REALISED she wasn't sure what she had expected; perhaps some orderly queue of women, suitcases in hand, making their way past the captain. With a shake of his hand and some discreet, perhaps tearful goodbyes, they would walk up the gangplank onto their big white ship.

What she had not imagined was this: the traffic jams all the way to Sydney Harbour, cars bumper-to-bumper under the grey city skies; the crowds of people thronging the entrance to the docks, the jostling of a million elbows and stumbling feet, all trying to force their way to the quayside. Innumerable young women, clutching parents, bawling grief-stricken or giddy with excitement as they attempted to haul baggage and food parcels through the thick crowd towards the huge grey vessel.

'Bloody hell! We'll never make it at this rate.' Murray Donleavy sat behind the wheel of the pick-up truck, his freckled face set.

'Be fine, Dad.' Margaret laid a hand on his arm. 'If it gets any worse I can always get out and walk.'

'She can bat them out the way with her bloody stomach.' Daniel, behind her, had been increasingly rude about her 'lump', as he called it.

'I'll bat you out of the way, if you don't mind your language.' Margaret leaned forward to stroke the terrier that sat in the footwell between her feet. Maud Gonne, now half-blind, her nose speckled with flecks of grey, had been Margaret's tenth birthday gift from her mother.

She pulled her hand basket onto her knee, then checked for the fourteenth time that her papers were in order.

Her father glanced over. 'Looks like you've got bugger all in that basket. I thought Letty put a few sandwiches in for you.'

33

'I must have taken them out when I was fussing with it at home. Sorry—too much on my mind this morning.'

'Let's hope they feed you on board.'

'Course they'll feed us, Dad. Especially me.'

'They'll need another ship just to carry the food she needs.'

'Daniel!'

'Dad, it's OK.' Her brother's fierce features were half hidden behind his overgrown fringe. He seemed to find it increasingly difficult to look at her, now that they were near to saying goodbye.

'Got your papers?' They had reached the gates of Woolloomooloo wharf. The officer leaned through the window of the truck and Margaret pulled her well-thumbed documents out of her basket and handed them to him.

His finger traced the line of names until, apparently satisfied, he waved them on. 'All brides, *Victoria*. Number six berth. You might be lucky and find a space over on the left. Follow the signs to the quayside, then head left by the blue pillar.'

'Cheers, mate.'

Murray shoved his hat further down on his head and negotiated his way towards the quayside. He didn't like crowds at the best of times. Despite Woodside's relative proximity to the city, Margaret thought he had probably been to Sydney no more than a handful of times since she was born. She didn't much like crowds herself, but today she felt curiously detached, as if she were an observer, unable to take in the magnitude of what she was about to do.

'How we doing for time?' Murray said, as they sat, engine idling, waiting for another crocodile of people to pass, dragging bulging suitcases.

'Dad, we're fine, I've told you. I could get out and walk from here. It's only a couple of hundred yards and I'm hardly an invalid.'

'I promised I'd see you onto your ship, Maggie. You just sit tight.' His jaw had tightened and she wondered absently to whom he had made the promise.

'Look, Dad!' Daniel was rapping on the back window, gesticulating wildly to where an official-looking car was just leaving a parking space.

'Right.' Her father's chin jutted, and he revved the engine, causing the people in front of him to skip out of the way. Within seconds he had wedged the truck into the little space, thwarting several other cars that had edged towards it. 'There!' He turned off the ignition and turned to his daughter. 'There,' he said again, not quite as firmly.

She reached across and took his hand. 'I knew you'd get me here,' she said.

The ship was huge. It took up the entire length of the dockside, blocking out the sea and the sky so that only its flat grey surfaces met the crowds who now swarmed up to the barriers, trying frantically to communicate with those already on the water. On its side, gun turrets bulged like balconies and on the flight deck, just visible from this far back, aircraft were poised in three formations, their wings folded above them. Hundreds of girls were aboard already, lining the flight deck or sitting astride gun barrels, waving from walkways, their coats and head-scarves tied tight against the brisk sea breeze.

To one side a brass band was playing: she could just identify snatches of 'The Maori's Farewell'. As they stood, a girl was being helped down the gangplank, crying, brightly coloured paper streamers stuck to her coat. 'Changed her mind,' she heard one of the officers say. 'Someone take her to the cargo sheds with the others.'

Margaret allowed herself to feel the slightest trepidation.

'Nervous?' said her father. He had seen the girl too.

'Nope,' she said. 'I just want to see Joe again.'

Her answer seemed to satisfy him. 'Your mum would be proud.'

'Mum would say I should be wearing something smarter.'

'That too.' He nudged her and she nudged him back, then reached up to adjust her hat.

'Any more brides?' A Red Cross woman with a clipboard elbowed her way past. 'Brides, you need to board now. Have your papers ready.'

Her father had taken her trunk to Customs. Now she peered round him to where her youngest brother was standing, eyes averted from her and the ship. She stared at his thin shoulders, overwhelmed by the urge to hug him, to tell him how much she loved him. But he had recoiled from contact with her since she had confirmed she was leaving.

'Shake my hand, Daniel?'

There was a long pause, then Daniel's hand snaked out and took hers in a brief, firm clasp.

'I'll write to you,' she said. 'You'd better bloody reply.'

He said nothing.

Her father stepped forward and hugged her.

'Tell that man of yours he's to look after you,' he said, his voice strangled as he spoke into her hair. Then he pulled away from her and took several swift glances around him, as if his mind was already elsewhere. He swallowed. 'Well, we'd better let you get on board. Want me to carry your bag?'

'I'll be fine.' She slung the big bag over her shoulder, jamming her hand basket under her free arm, then made towards the ship.

Her father's hand shot out. 'Hang on, girl! You've got to go through Customs first.'

She peered through the jostling crowds to where he was pointing: a huge corrugated-iron shed across the quayside.

Two girls were talking to the officers at the doorway. One was gesturing at her bag and laughing.

Her father peered at her. 'You all right, girl? You've gone awful pale.'

'I can't, Dad,' she whispered. 'I don't feel good.'

Her father took her arm. 'Do you need to sit down?'

'No . . . It's the crowds. I'm feeling a bit faint. Tell them they've got to get me aboard.' She closed her eyes. She heard her father bark at Daniel, and him sprinting off.

Several minutes later, two naval officers were standing beside her.

'This isn't like her,' her father was saying, his voice concerned. 'She's a strong lass. Never seen her come over faint before.'

'We've had a few already,' said one of the officers. 'It's all this commotion. We'll get her aboard. Give us your bag, madam.'

She let go of her bag.

'You got a doctor aboard?' Her father hovered nearby, his face drawn.

'Yes, sir. Please don't worry.' She felt him pause beside her. 'Sorry, sir. You can't come any further.'

The other officers reached for her basket. 'Want me to take this for you?'

'No,' she snapped, pulling it to her. 'No, thank you,' she added, and tried to smile. 'It's got all my papers in it. Be terrible if I lost it.'

He grinned at her. 'You're probably right, madam. Today's not the day to lose anything.'

They had each supported her under an elbow and were now propelling her towards the ship. 'Bye then, Maggie,' her father called.

'Dad.' Suddenly it seemed too hurried. She wasn't sure if she was ready after all. She tried to blow a kiss with her free hand in an attempt to convey something of what she felt.

'Dan? Daniel? Where is he?' Her father had spun round to locate the boy. He waved his hand for her to wait, to hang on, but the crowd was pushing against the barrier and he was already being swallowed into it.

'We should really get you aboard, Madam,' said the officer beside her.

'I can't see him, love,' Murray called. 'I don't know where he is.'

'Tell him it's OK, Dad. I understand.'

'You take care,' her father yelled. 'You hear me? You take care of yourself.' Then his voice, his face and the top of his battered hat were lost in the melee.

The executive officer, or XO as he was known to the men, had tried three times to get his attention, bobbing up and down like a child. Dobson. Always a little more informal than the occasion deserved. Captain Highfield, already in a foul mood, was determined to ignore him. He turned away, rang down to the Engine Control Room.

The damp was making his leg ache. He rested it briefly by placing his weight on the other in a lopsided stance unusual to him. He was a stocky man, whose ramrod-straight posture had become ingrained over years of service—and led to countless irreverent imitations below decks.

'Hawkins, let me know about the port outer engine. Is it still locked?'

'I've got two men down there at the moment, sir. We're hoping to free it up in the next twenty minutes or so.'

Captain Highfield exhaled. 'Do your best, man. Otherwise we're going to need another two tugs to get us clear.'

'Bridge, wheelhouse, Coxswain at the wheel.'

'Very good, Coxswain. Stand by to steer one-two-zero.' Captain Highfield stood up from the voice-pipe.

From the bridge, the whole harbour was visible: the huge, teeming crowds that stretched as far as the dry docks, the bunting strung below, and, one by one, the women who made their way slowly up the gangplank. Highfield had groaned inwardly at every one.

'I came to talk to you about the mess report, sir.' Dobson hesitated. 'We're still missing a few.'

Captain Highfield glanced at his watch. 'At this hour? How many?'

Dobson consulted his list. 'At this moment, sir, almost half a dozen.'

'Bloody hell.' Captain Highfield slammed his hand down on the dial. 'What on earth were the men doing last night?'

'Sounds like there was something of a shindig at one of the drinking clubs, sir.'

Highfield stared out of the bridge. 'Bloody shambles,' he said. Those around him knew that the ferocity in his voice did not relate entirely to the missing men. 'Six hundred flapping girls can make their way aboard on time, but not England's finest.'

'There's something else. Four of the brides are in with the Red Cross.'

'What? They've only been on board five minutes.'

'Didn't listen when we said they'd need to duck through the hatches. Too excited, I suppose.' He smacked his forehead, mimicking the most common injury on board ship. 'One's a stitches job.'

'Can't the surgeon see to it?'

'Ah. He's—erm—one of those missing.'

There was a lengthy silence.

'Twenty minutes,' Highfield said eventually. 'Just till we get the port outer engine working again. After that you can tell the mess men to start offloading their belongings. I won't have this ship held up.'

Avice leaned on the rail, one hand keeping her new hat in place. Astride a gun turret, Jean was making a spectacle of herself. The dark-haired girl had her arms slung over two ratings, as if she were drunk and leaning on them for support. Perhaps she *was* drunk: with that kind of girl little would have surprised Avice.

She looked down at the pleats on her new suit, satisfied by how superior her outfit was compared with those of the girls around her. Avice had been worried about what to wear, unsure of the etiquette for such an occasion. Now, with a clear view of at least a hundred other girls, hardly any of whom seemed to have dressed for the occasion, she wondered why she had fretted. She straightened her shoulders and forced herself to think about what she was heading to. In six weeks, she would discover what her new life held. She would get to know Ian's parents, take tea at the Rectory, meet the ladies of the quaint English village where they lived, and perhaps the odd duke or duchess. She would begin to make their home . . .

She was brought back to the present by the realisation that the deck was vibrating gently under her feet. Looking over the edge she saw, with a start, that the gangplank had been hauled up. A short distance away a winch was hoisting up several sailors who had apparently missed their opportunity to get aboard by normal means. They were laughing and cheering, covered with lipstick kisses. Possibly even drunk.

Disgraceful, thought Avice, smiling despite herself as they were dumped unceremoniously on the flight deck above. Around them, small tugs bossed and bullied the vast ship, negotiating its slow release from the harbour. The crowd, a sea of Australian flags and the odd Union Jack, frothed and bubbled as people pushed towards the edge of the quay.

She found herself gazing around the port, then at the hills beyond. Is this it? she thought suddenly, her breath catching in her throat. My last view of Australia? Then, with a lurch, the streamers snapped, their cobwebby strands releasing the ship from the dockside.

There was a collective gasp. The engines began to power, and over the din the band on the quayside struck up with 'Waltzing Matilda'. The thin ribbon of blue water widened beneath them, then became an expanse. The ship, as if oblivious to the madness around it, glided, surprisingly quickly, away from the harbour.

Murray Donleavy placed his arm round his sobbing son and sat silently as the crowds melted away. It was getting chilly and the boy was shivering. He took off his jacket and threw it round Daniel's shoulders, then hauled the boy against him for warmth.

Every now and then Daniel raised his head as if he wanted to speak, but was unable to find words and sank back into silent weeping, his face thrust into his hands as if the tears were a cause of shame.

'Nothing to be sorry for, boy,' Murray murmured. 'It's been a tough day.'

Theirs was one of the few vehicles remaining, sitting in a sea of muddied streamers. Murray walked round to the driver's side of the pick-up, then halted when he noticed that his son was standing still and staring at him. 'You all right now?'

'Do you think she'll hate me, Dad?'

Murray moved round and hugged his boy again. 'Don't be so soft.' He ruffled his hair. 'She'll be banging on about you visiting her soon.'

'In England?'

'Don't see why not. You keep saving up that rabbit money and you'll be able to fly there before you know it. Things are changing fast.'

Daniel smiled then, and his father's heart ached to see him meet another loss so bravely. They sat in the cab for a few moments, watching people trail out through the dockyard gates. He sighed, suddenly conscious of the length of the drive home.

'Dad, she's left her sandwiches.' Beside him, Daniel held aloft the greaseproofed package that Letty had put together that morning.

Murray frowned. Oh, well, he thought. That's women when they're carrying. All over the place. Noreen had been the same.

'Can I have them, Dad? I'm starving.'

Murray stuck his key into the ignition. 'Don't see why not. They're no use to her now. Tell you what, save one for me.' He started the truck, and reversed out slowly onto the dockside. Suddenly he hit the brake, sending Daniel shooting forwards. 'Hang on,' he said, his face electrified with the memory of an empty basket and his daughter's inexplicable hurry to get on board. 'Where's the bloody dog?'

One Day In

HMS *Victoria* comprised nine floors below the flight deck and four decks above it up to the vertiginous heights of the bridge and island. Even without the brides' specially created berths it would have housed in its gigantic belly some 200 different rooms, stores and compartments, equalling the size, perhaps, of several department stores. The hangars alone, where most of the brides were housed, fed and entertained, were nearly 500 feet long and situated on the same floors as the canteens, bathrooms, the captain's sleeping area and at least fourteen sizable store-rooms. They were linked by narrow passageways, which, if one confused the decks, were as likely to lead to an aircraft repair shop or engineers' mess as a brides' bathroom—a situation that had already caused several red faces.

It was a floating world of unintelligible rules and regulations, of ordered and as yet unrevealed routines, a labyrinthine rabbit warren of low-ceilinged rooms, corridors and lockers, the vast majority of which led to places where the women were not meant to be. It was vast yet cramped, and noisy. With the sheer numbers of people moving around, and a general unfamiliarity with the placing of the different flights of stairs and gangways, it frequently took the best part of half an hour simply to traverse one deck.

And still Avice could not lose Jean.

From the moment she discovered they had been allocated the same cabin (more than 600 brides and they had lumped her with Jean!) the girl had decided to take on a new role: that of Avice's Best Friend. Having conveniently forgotten the mutual antipathy that had characterised their meetings at the American Wives' Club, she had spent the greater part of the last twenty-four hours trailing Avice, who knew she should be nicer to Jean, especially since she had discovered she was only sixteen—but, really! The girl was awfully trying.

And Avice wasn't convinced that she was entirely truthful either. There had been an exchange when Jean had chattered on at breakfast about her plans to get a job in a department store where her husband's aunt held a managerial post. 'How can you work? I thought you were expecting,' Avice had said coldly.

'Lost it,' said Jean blithely. Then, after a pause, 'Do you think they'll let me have a second helping of bacon?'

Jean, Avice noted as she walked briskly up the last flight of stairs, hardly ever mentioned her husband, Stanley. She herself would have mentioned Ian more often, but on the few occasions when she had, Jean had tried to elicit from her some smutty confidence ('Did you let him do it to you before your wedding night?' And, even worse: 'Did it give you a fright the first time you saw it?'). They were all due upstairs on the flight deck at eleven for the captain's address. It should be simple enough to lose her among more than 600 other women, shouldn't it?

'Do you fancy going to one of these lectures?' Jean shouted, chewing gum as they made their way past the projection room. 'There's one on the strains of marrying a foreigner next week.'

Avice pretended not to hear her.

'I fancy the one on common difficulties in the first year,' Jean went on. 'Except our first year has been dead easy so far. He wasn't even there.'

'The ship's company of HMS *Victoria* will do their best to make your passage to the United Kingdom an enjoyable one . . . At the same time you must remember you are not in a liner, but are privileged to be a passenger in one of His Majesty's ships. Life on board must be governed by service rules and customs.'

Margaret stood on the flight deck, which was three deep in rows of brides. The sea, sparkling blue, was benign and calm, and the deck— the size of a two-acre field—hardly moved. Margaret cast surreptitious glances along its shining length, sniffing the salted air, feeling the breeze-blown sea mist on her skin, enjoying her first sense of space and freedom since they had slipped anchor the previous day.

'Every person aboard one of His Majesty's ships is subject to the Naval Discipline Act, which means no spirits, wine or beer, and that gambling in any form is forbidden. There is to be no smoking near the aircraft at any time. You are allowed nearly everywhere on the ship except the men's living spaces, but work must not be interrupted.'

At this some of the girls glanced around and one of the ratings winked. A giggle rippled through the female ranks. Margaret shifted her weight to her other foot and sighed.

'If there is a general complaint about some matter, the duty women's service officer should be informed, and she will bring the matter to the notice of one of the lieutenant-commanders. Meanwhile, the following spaces are out of bounds to women: ratings' living spaces and messes, officers' cabins and messes, below the level of the hangar deck, one deck above the flight deck, gun positions and galleries, and inside boats.

'A more comprehensive guide, in booklet form, will be distributed to each of you later today. I'd like you all to read it and ensure you follow its regulations. I cannot emphasise strongly enough how grave the consequences will be for those who choose to disobey them.'

A silence descended on the deck, as he allowed the weight of his words to resonate.

'Eight women's service officers are on board to advise, help and assist you. Each WSO has a group of cabins under her special care and will always be available to help you.' He fixed the women in front of him with a stern gaze. 'The ship's company is not allowed in the women's quarters and living spaces, except as required for duty. The WSOs will do rounds during the night.'

'And naughty girls will have to walk the plank.' There was a surreptitious but clear outbreak of giggling, a pressure valve loosening.

'Lord knows what he takes us for,' said the girl beside Margaret, fiddling with a brooch.

The captain appeared to be at the end of his interminable speech. He stared at his papers, then fixed them all with a look that might have been cold or simply weary resignation.

'Friendly soul,' said Margaret, under her breath.

'I feel like I'm back at school,' murmured Jean, in front of her.

Highfield looked at the women in front of him, nudging, whispering, fidgeting, not even capable of standing still for long enough to hear him list the rules and regulations that would govern their lives for the next six weeks. Even in this last twenty-four hours, he had watched every new outrage, every new example of why this had been a catastrophic idea, and wanted to telegraph McManus to say, 'See? Didn't I tell you this would happen?'

Admittedly there was no dramatic difference in the men's behaviour, but he knew it was only a matter of time. He could feel a subtle sense of disquiet in the air, as when dogs scent an approaching storm.

Or perhaps it was simply that nothing had felt settled since Hart's death. The company had lost the cheerful sense of purpose that had characterised its last nine months in the Pacific. Several times since they had slipped anchor, he had caught them muttering among themselves and wondered to what extent they blamed him. He concluded his speech and forced the thoughts, as he often did, from his mind. The women looked wrong. The colours were too bright; the hair was too long; scarves dangled all over the place. His ship had been an ordered thing of greys and whites, of monochrome. The mere introduction of colour was unbalancing, as if someone had unleashed a flock of exotic birds around him and left them, flapping and unpredictable, to create havoc.

It's not that I don't like women, he thought, as he did several times an hour. It's just that everything has its place. People have their place. He folded the booklet under his arm and strode into the lobby.

Dear Joe,

Well, here I am on the Victoria *with the other brides. Our four-berth cabin is one of many in what was apparently a giant liftwell, and I am sharing with three girls, who seem to be all right. One girl, Jean, is only sixteen. Another has been working for the Australian General Hospital out in the Pacific, and says almost nothing, and the third girl is a bit of a society type. I can't say any of us has much in common.*

The men are all pretty friendly, but we're not meant to talk to them much. Some girls go silly whenever they walk past one. Honestly, you'd think they'd never seen a man before, let alone married one. The captain has read us the Riot Act already, and everyone keeps going on about water and how we're not meant to use any.

I think of you often, and it is a comfort to me to think that we are probably, even at this minute, sailing on the same ocean.

Your Maggie

These were the other things that she hadn't told Joe: that she had lain awake for most of the first night, listening to the clanking of chains and feeling the vibrations of the great ship moving under her, like some groaning prehistoric beast. That the ship was a bewildering mass of ranks and roles, from marines to stokers to airmen. That the canteen was big enough to seat 300 girls at once and that she had eaten better food at last night's supper than she had for the last two years. That almost the first naval custom they had been taught—with great emphasis on its importance—was the 'submariner's dhobi': a shower of several seconds to soak oneself, a soaping with the water turned off, then a brief rinse under running water. It was vital, the Red Cross officer had impressed upon them, that they conserve water so that the pumps could desalinate at a rate fast enough to replace it. From what she had heard in the shower rooms, she was pretty well the only bride to have followed those instructions.

Behind her, hidden by her size and a carefully folded blanket, Maud Gonne lay sleeping. After the captain's address, Margaret had raced back and subdued the little dog's yelps with stolen biscuits, then smuggled her along to the bathroom to make sure she didn't disgrace herself. She had only just got back to the bunk when Frances came in, and she had thrust herself onto her bed, willing the dog to stay quiet. She had thought she would be allocated a single cabin—most of the pregnant brides had been. It hadn't occurred to her that she might have to share. She shifted on her bunk, trying to get comfortable.

'You want my pillow?' On the opposite bunk, Frances had emerged from her novel. She was gesturing towards Margaret's stomach.

'No. Thanks.'

'Go on—you can't be comfortable.'

It had been the longest sentence she had uttered since introducing herself. Margaret hesitated, then accepted the pillow with thanks and wedged it under her thigh. It was true: the bunks offered all the width and comfort of an ironing board.

'When's it due?'

'Not for a couple of months or so.' Margaret sniffed, pushed tentatively at her mattress. 'It could have been worse, I suppose. They might have given us hammocks.'

The other girl's smile faltered, as if, having opened the conversation, she was now unsure what else to say. She returned to her book.

Maud Gonne shifted and whined in sleep, her paws scrabbling against Margaret's back. The noise was disguised by the thrum of the engines and the chatter of girls passing outside the half-open door. But she would have to do something. Maud Gonne couldn't stay in here for the whole six weeks. Even if she only left to go to the bathroom there were bound to be occasions when the other girls were here. How would she keep her quiet then?

The cabin door was open and Avice stepped in, remembering to duck, and raised a smile for the two girls lying on the bottom bunks. Made of a naval-issue bedroll lying on a raised platform of webbing, the bunks were less than five feet apart.

A small quantity of their belongings were stacked against the temporary sheet-metal wall that divided their cabin from the next. Their bags and cases, with the majority of their clothes and belongings, were stored in the quarterdeck lockers, which smelt of aircraft fuel and to which they had to beg access from a sour WSO, who had already told Avice that life on board was not a fashion parade.

Avice was desperately disappointed in her travelling companions. Almost everywhere she had been this morning she had seen girls in smarter clothes, the kind that spoke to Avice of a social standing not dissimilar to her own. She might have found consolation in their company for the awfulness of the ship. Instead she had been landed with a pregnant farm girl and a surly nurse. And, of course, there was Jean.

'Hey there, shipmates.' Jean scrambled onto the bunk above Margaret, her thin limbs like a monkey's, and lit a cigarette. 'Avice and me have been checking out the action. There's a cinema up near the bow, on the lower gallery. Anyone fancy coming to the pictures later?'

'No. Thanks, anyway,' said Frances.

'Actually, I think I'll stay here and write some letters.' Avice had made her way on to her top bunk, holding her skirt down over her thighs with one hand. It took some effort. 'I'm feeling a little weary.'

'How 'bout you, Maggie?' Jean leaned over the side of her bunk.

Her head heaving suddenty into view made Margaret jump and contort into a peculiar shape. 'No,' she said. 'Thank you. I—I should rest.'

'Yeah. You do that,' said Jean, hauling herself back into her bunk. 'The last thing we want is you dropping it in here.'

Avice was searching for her hairbrush. 'I'm sorry to bother you all, but has anyone seen my brush? It's silver. It has my initials—AR.'

'Not up here,' said Jean. 'Have you looked on the floor?'

Avice knelt down, cursing the inadequate light from the one unshaded overhead bulb. If they'd had a window, she would have been able to see better. In fact, everything would have been more pleasant with a sea view. She was just stretching her arm under Frances's bunk when she felt a cold wet touch high on the inside of her thigh. She shrieked and jumped up.

'What, in heaven's name—' She pulled her skirt tight round her legs, twisting round in an effort to see behind her. 'Who did that? Was it someone's idea of a joke?'

'What's the matter?' asked Jean, wide-eyed.

'Someone goosed me.' She gazed round suspiciously, as if perhaps some madman had stowed away when no one was looking.

No one spoke.

Frances was watching her silently, her face impassive.

'I'm not imagining it,' Avice told her crossly.

It was then that all eyes fell on Margaret, who was leaning over the edge of her bunk, muttering. She looked up with a guilty expression, then stood up, went to the door, closed it and sighed. 'Oh, hell. I need to tell you all something. I'd thought I'd get a cabin to myself because of being pregnant.' She shook her head and lowered herself onto her hands and knees and uttered a soft crooning sound. Seconds later, her broad hand emerged from under her bunk. In it she held a small dog. 'Girls,' she said, 'meet Maud Gonne.'

Four sets of eyes stared at the dog, who stared back with disinterest.

'I knew it! I knew you were up to something!' crowed Jean.

'Oh, for goodness' sake.' Avice grimaced.

Frances studied the dog. 'You're not allowed pets on board,' she said. 'I know that.'

'I'm sorry, but you can't hope to keep it quiet,' Avice said. 'And it'll make the dorm smell.'

Margaret sat down, ducking to avoid banging her head on the top bunk. The dog settled on her lap. 'She's very clean—and I've worked it all out. She doesn't smell. I'll make sure I keep her "business" well out of your way. But please, please, don't dob me in. She's . . . old . . . My mum gave her to me. And'—she blinked furiously—'look, she's all I've got left of my mum. I couldn't leave her.'

There was silence as the women exchanged looks. Margaret stared at the floor, flushed with emotion. It was too soon for this level of confidence. She knew it, and so did they.

The nurse looked at her shoes. 'If you want to try to keep her in here, I don't mind.'

'Nor me,' said Jean. 'Long as she doesn't chew up my shoes.'

Avice knew she couldn't be the only one to complain: it would make her seem heartless. 'What about the Royal Marines they're posting outside our doors from tomorrow night? You won't be able to get her out.'

'A marine? For what?'

'He's coming at nine thirty. I suppose it's to stop the men below coming up and ravishing us,' said Jean. 'Think about it—a thousand desperate men lying just a few feet below us.'

'Oh, for goodness' sake!' Avice's hand flew to her throat.

'Well, I'll have to get her out before the marine comes.'

'Gangway's too busy,' said Jean.

'Perhaps we should just tell someone,' said Avice. 'I'm sure they'd understand. And perhaps they'll have . . . facilities for this kind of thing.'

'No,' said Margaret, her face darkening. 'You heard the captain this morning. I can't take the risk.'

'We'll keep it quiet,' said Jean, stroking the little dog's head. Avice thought that Jean would have been up for anything that smacked of subverting authority. 'Won't we, girls? It'll be a gas.'

'Avice?' said Margaret. It was as if, Avice thought afterwards, she had already been earmarked as a killjoy.

'I won't say a word,' she said, her voice strained. 'Just keep her well away from me.'

Two days in

Frances dressed in pale khaki slacks and a short-sleeved shirt—the closest she could come to her old uniform—and slipped out. She nodded a greeting to the girls she passed, and made her way down the gangway.

She had had to knock twice before she got a response.

'Come in.'

She stepped into the infirmary, whose walls were lined with bottles and jars, secured on narrow shelves behind glass doors.

'Come right in. You're making the place look untidy.' The man behind the desk had short red hair and was dressed in civilian clothes. His eyes were creased from years of what might have been squinting but, judging from his actions now, was probably smiling.

Frances flushed briefly, realised he had been joking, then took a few steps towards him. 'Are you the surgeon? Mr Farraday?'

'No.' He gazed at her, apparently weighing up whether to enlighten her. 'Vincent Duxbury. Civilian passenger. Mr Farraday—er—failed to make the trip. Captain Highfield asked me to step in. How can I help you?'

'I'm a nurse.' She held out a hand. 'Frances Mackenzie. Sister Frances Mackenzie. I thought I might offer my services here.'

Vincent Duxbury shook her hand, and motioned to her to sit down. 'A nurse, eh? I thought we might have a few on board. Seen much duty?'

'Five years in the Pacific,' she said. 'Last posting was the Australian General Hospital, Morotai.'

'My cousin was out in Japan, back in 'forty-three. Your husband?'

'My? Oh.' She looked briefly wrong-footed. 'Alfred Mackenzie. Royal Welsh Fusiliers.'

'Royal Welsh Fusiliers . . .' He said it slowly, as if it had significance, then leaned back in his chair, fiddling with the top of a brown glass bottle. Suddenly it dawned on her that the smell of alcohol was not necessarily medicinal.

She took a deep breath. 'I've had special experience in burns, treatment of dysentery, and revival of impaired digestive systems. That was the POWs,' she added. 'We had significant experience of those.'

'Uh-huh.'

'I don't have much specialist feminine or obstetric knowledge, but I would appreciate the chance to gain a little more experience . . . I'm a good learner,' she added, when he didn't speak.

'Do you sing?' he said eventually.

'I'm sorry?'

'Sing, Mrs Mackenzie. You know, show tunes, hymns, opera.' He began to hum something she didn't know.

'I'm afraid not,' she said.

'Pity.' He wrinkled his nose, then slapped his hand on the desk. 'I thought we might get some of the girls together and put on a show.'

The brown bottle, she saw, was empty and now the scent of what it had contained burst softly onto the air with his every utterance.

She took a deep breath. 'I'm sure that would be a . . . a useful idea, Doctor. But I really wondered whether we could just discuss—'

'Do you know *Showboat*?'

'No,' she said. 'I'm afraid I don't.'

47

'Pity. "Old Man River" . . .' He closed his eyes and started to sing.

She sat, her hands clasped in her lap, unsure whether or not to interrupt. 'Doctor? Do you have any idea of when you might like me to start?'

'"He just keeps rollin' . . ."' He opened an eye.

'I can start today, if you'd like. If you'd find it . . . useful.'

He had stopped singing and smiled broadly.

'You know what I'm going to say to you, Frances? May I call you Frances?' He was pointing at her now with his bottle. 'I'm going to tell you to go away.'

'I'm sorry?'

He laughed. 'That got you, didn't it? No, Frances Mackenzie. You deserve a little break. I'm going to prescribe a six-week holiday.'

'But I want to work,' she said.

'No buts, Mrs Mackenzie. The war's over. In a few short weeks you're going to be engaged in the hardest job of your career. You'll be raising children before you know it and, believe me, those sick soldiers will look like a holiday then. I'm going to insist you enjoy your last days of freedom. Get your hair done. Watch some movies. Make yourself look pretty for that old man of yours. So go. Go on—now.'

It took her several seconds to grasp that she had been dismissed.

She could hear him singing the entire length of the gangway.

That evening the marine arrived at a minute before 9.30. A slim man with dark, slicked hair, he positioned himself at the entrance to their dormitory, and stood with his back to the door. He was responsible for watching over the two cabins on each side of theirs, and the five above.

'Trust us to have one actually outside our door,' muttered Margaret, looking down at her sleeping dog.

The brides had been lying on their bunks reading or writing. Able to see a sliver of his body through the half-open door, they glanced at each other, then waited in case he uttered some greeting or instruction, but he just stood there.

At 9.45, Jean stepped outside with her cigarettes, and offered him one. When he refused, she lit one for herself and began to ask him questions. Where was the cinema? Did the men get the same food as the brides? He answered monosyllabically. 'So, where do you sleep?' she asked coquettishly.

The marine looked straight ahead.

'I'm only curious . . .' She peered into his face. 'Oh, come on, I've had toy soldiers that talked more than you.'

'Ma'am.'

'Actually,' she said, stubbing out her cigarette, 'I wanted to ask you something . . . but it's a bit embarrassing.'

The marine looked wary. As well he might, thought Avice.

Jean traced a pattern on the floor with her toe of her shoe. 'Please don't tell anyone, but I keep getting lost,' she said. 'It's made me a bit of a joke with the other girls. I even missed dinner because I couldn't find the canteen.'

The marine had relaxed a little. He was intent, listening.

'It's because I'm sixteen, you see. I didn't do too good at school. Reading and stuff. And I can't'—she let her voice drop to a whisper—'I can't understand the map of the ship. You couldn't explain it to me, could you?'

The marine hesitated, then nodded. 'There's one pinned up on that notice board. Want me to talk you through it?'

'Oh, would you?' said Jean, a heartbreaking smile on her face.

'Golly, Moses, she's brilliant,' said Margaret, who was listening from behind the door. When Margaret and Avice looked out the pair were standing in front of the map, fifteen or so feet along the gangway. Margaret, carrying an oversized washbag, gave them a merry wave as she hurried along in her dressing gown. The marine saluted her, then turned back to Jean.

'It's not ideal,' said Margaret afterwards, sitting down heavily on her bunk as the dog plodded round the dormitory, sniffing at the floor. 'I mean, she's used to fields.'

Avice stifled the urge to remark that she should have thought of that beforehand, when the door opened.

'Great,' said Margaret, as Jean came in, closing the door behind her. 'You were great, Jean. That bit about not being able to read was a masterstroke. You must really be able to think on your feet.'

Jean gave her an odd look. 'No thinking about it, mate.' She directed her next words at the floor. 'Can't read a word. 'Cept my name.'

There was an awkward silence. Avice tried to gauge if this was another of Jean's jokes, but she wasn't laughing.

It was on the second night that homesickness struck. Margaret lay awake in the darkened cabin, listening to the odd creak and sniff as her travelling companions shifted on their bunks.

She had never shared a room in her life; it had been one of the few advantages of growing up female in the Donleavy household. Now the little dormitory, without the door open, without light or a breath of air, felt stifling, and she was gripped by a childlike desire to turn round and run for the familiar safety of the only house in which she had ever spent a night. She swung her legs over the side of the bunk and sat there for a minute. She thought of Joe, his expression warm and faintly mocking. 'Get a grip, old girl,' he was saying, and she closed her eyes, trying to remind herself of why she was making this journey.

'Margaret?' Jean's voice cut into the darkness. 'You going somewhere?'

'No,' said Margaret, sliding her feet back under the covers. 'No, just having trouble getting to sleep.'

'Me too.'

Her voice had sounded uncharacteristically small. Margaret felt a swell of pity for her. 'Want to come down here for a bit?' she whispered.

She could just make out Jean's slender limbs climbing rapidly down the ladder, and then the girl slid in at the other end of her bunk. Jean fidgeted for a while, and Margaret felt Maud Gonne lift her head.

'What's your husband's name?' Jean asked eventually.

'Joe.'

'Mine's Stan.'

'You said.'

'Stan Castleforth. He's nineteen on Tuesday. From Nottingham,' said Jean. 'He said it's where Robin Hood came from. So I reckon it's probably in a forest. I think about Stan loads. He's dead handsome. I met him outside the cinema and he and his mate offered to pay for me to go in. *Ziegfield Follies*. In Technicolor.' She exhaled. 'He told me he hadn't kissed a girl since Portsmouth and I couldn't really say no in the circumstances. I got married in parachute silk. My aunt Mavis got it for me from a GI she knew. My mum's not really up for all that stuff.' She paused. 'In fact, I get on better with my aunt Mavis. Always have done. My mum reckons I'm a waste of skin.'

Margaret shifted onto her side, thinking of her own mother. She found her mouth had dried.

'Did you have to do it differently . . . to have a baby, I mean.'

'Jean!'

'What?' Jean's voice rose in indignation. 'Someone's got to tell me.'

Margaret sat up, careful not to bang her head on the bunk above. 'You mean no one's ever told you . . . about the birds and the bees?'

Jean snorted. 'I know where he's got to put it, if that's what you're talking about. But I don't know how doing that leads to babies.'

Margaret was shocked into silence, but a voice came from above: 'If you're going to be so coarse as to discuss these matters in company, you could at least do it quietly. Some of us are trying to sleep.'

'I bet Avice knows,' giggled Jean.

50

'I thought you said you'd lost a baby,' said Avice, pointedly.

'Oh, Jean. I'm so sorry.' Margaret's hand went to her mouth.

There was a silence.

'Actually,' Jean said, 'I wasn't exactly carrying as such. I was . . . well, a bit late with my you-know-what. And my friend Polly said that meant you were carrying. So I said I was because I knew it would help me get on board. When they did my medical check I said I'd lost it and I started crying because by then I'd almost convinced myself that I was and the nurse felt sorry for me and said no one needed to know one way or the other, and that the most important thing was getting me over to my Stan. It's probably why they've stuck me in with you, Maggie.' Her voice took on a defensive edge: 'But if any of you tell on me, I'll just say I lost it.'

Margaret laid her hands on her stomach. 'Nobody's going to tell on you, Jean,' she said.

There was a deafening silence from Avice's bunk.

'Frances?' said Jean. 'You won't tell on me, will you?'

'No,' said Frances, from the bunk opposite. 'I won't.'

Jean got out of bed and climbed nimbly back up to her bunk, where she could be heard rustling herself into comfort. 'So, come on, then,' she said eventually. 'What is it that makes you get a baby?'

On the flight deck, a 1,000-pound bomb from a Stuka aircraft looks curiously like a beer barrel. It rolls casually from the underbelly of the sinister little plane and, surrounded by its brothers, it seems to pause momentarily in the sky, then float down towards the ship, guided, as if by an invisible force, towards the deck.

This is one of the things Captain Highfield thinks as he stares up at his impending death. This, and the fact that, when the wall of flame rises up from the armoured deck, engulfing the island, the ship's command centre, he has forgotten something he had to do. And in his blind paralysis even he is dimly aware of how ridiculous it is to be casting around for some unremembered task while he faces immolation.

Then, in the raging heart of the fire, as the bombs rain around him, he looks up to see a plane, where now there is no plane. It, too, is engulfed, flames licking at the cockpit, the tilted wings blackened, but not enough to obscure, within, Hart's face, which is untouched, his eyes questioning as he faces the captain.

I'm sorry, Highfield weeps, unsure if, through the roar of the fire, the younger man can hear him. I'm sorry.

When he wakes, his pillow damp and the skies still dark above the quiet ocean, he is still speaking these words into the silence.

Two weeks previously

According to her log, HMS *Victoria* had seen action in the north Atlantic, the Pacific and, most recently, at Morotai, where she helped force back the Japanese and bore the scars to show it. She, and many like her, had stopped repeatedly over the past few years at the dock-yards at Woolloomooloo to have her mine-damaged hull repaired, bullet and torpedo holes plugged, the brutal scars of her time at sea put straight before she was sent out again.

Captain George Highfield was not much given to fanciful thinking, but as he walked along the dry dock, staring up through the sea mist at the hulls of the *Victoria* and her neighbours, he often allowed himself to think about the vessels as his fellows. Hard not to see them as having some kind of personality when they had allied themselves to you, given you their all, braved high seas and fierce fire. In forty years' service, he'd had his favourites: those that had felt undeniably his. He had bitten back private tears of grief when he left them, less privately when they had been sunk. He supposed this was how previous generations of fighting men must have felt about their horses.

'Poor old girl,' he muttered, glancing at the hole ripped in the aircraft carrier's side. She looked so much like *Indomitable*, his old ship.

The surgeon had said he should use a stick. Highfield suspected that the man had told others he shouldn't be allowed back to sea at all. 'These things take longer to heal at your age,' he had observed, of the livid scar tissue and ridged skin of the burns on his leg. 'I'm not convinced you should be up and about on that just yet, Captain.'

Highfield had discharged himself from the hospital that morning. 'I have a ship to take home,' he had said, closing the conversation.

Like everyone else, the surgeon had said nothing. Sometimes it seemed to Highfield that no one knew what to say to him now. He hardly blamed them. In their shoes he would have felt the same.

'Ah, Highfield. They told me you were out here.'

'Sir.' He stopped and saluted. The admiral approached through the light rain, waving away the umbrella-bearing officer beside him.

'Leg all better?'

'Absolutely fine, sir. Good as new.'

He watched the admiral glance down at it. McManus was a good sort, who always knew somehow what was going on and missed nothing.

Highfield fought the urge to shift the weight off his leg again. He was conscious suddenly that McManus probably knew all about that too.

'Thought I'd take a look at the *Victoria*,' he said. 'Haven't seen her since I went aboard during the Adriatic convoys.'

'You may find her a little changed,' said McManus. 'She's taken a bit of a bashing.'

'I suppose you could say the same for most of us.' It was the closest Highfield would come to a joke, and McManus acknowledged it in his quiet smile.

The two men walked slowly along the dock.

'Terrible business, what happened. We all felt for you, Highfield.'

Highfield kept his face to the front.

'Yes,' McManus continued. 'Hart would have gone all the way to the top. Bloody shame when you were all so close to getting home.'

'I contacted his mother, sir, while I was in hospital.'

'Yes. Good man. Best coming from you.' The admiral stopped and faced him. 'You mustn't blame yourself, you know. We've all suffered such losses, and we've all lain awake at nights wondering if we could have prevented them.' His assessing gaze passed over Highfield's face. 'Don't dwell on it, Highfield. These things happen.' McManus tailed off, as if he were deep in thought, and Highfield stayed silent, listening to the sound of his feet on the now slick dockside.

They had almost reached the gangplank. Even from here he could see the engineers on board, replacing the metal that had been buckled by impact, hear the banging and drilling that told him welders were busy inside. *Victoria* would win no beauty contests but, as his eyes rested upon her, Highfield felt the misery of the past weeks melt away.

They paused at the foot of the gangplank, squinting up into the rain.

'So, what next when you get back, Highfield?'

Highfield hesitated. 'Well, I'll be retired, sir.'

'I know that, man. I meant what are you going to do with yourself? Got any hobbies? No Mrs Highfield that you've been hiding all these years?'

'No, sir.'

'Oh.'

Highfield thought he detected pity in the word. He wanted to say that he had never felt the lack of a female presence in his life, but on the occasions when he had said this, men had looked at him curiously.

The admiral turned back towards *Victoria*. 'Well, golf's my thing. I plan to be on the links morning till evening. Think my wife'll like it that way too.' He laughed. 'She doesn't relish the prospect of me under her feet. She's got used to doing her own thing, over the years. Not something you'll have to worry about, eh? You can play all the golf you like.'

'I'm not a golfing man, sir. Think I'm happier on the water.' He nearly

53

said what he thought: that he wasn't sure what he was going to do. And that he felt discomfited at not knowing. Several times in the past he had fought the urge to beg the admiral to let him stay on.

'Going up then, Highfield?'

'Thought I might inspect the work.' Now that he was going on board again, Highfield felt the sense of surety and order returning. The admiral said nothing, but went briskly up the gangplank.

The pegging-in board had been turned towards the wall. The captain paused at the doorway, turned it round and slid his name tag across to confirm his presence aboard; a reassuring gesture. Then they stepped over the sill of the doorway, ducking simultaneously as they entered the cavernous hangar.

Not all of the lights were illuminated, and it took Highfield a couple of minutes to adjust to the gloom. He looked in front of him at the huge liftwell that transported the planes to the deck. Several men were at work, one on a scaffold platform, apparently securing metal struts at regular intervals all the way up to the flight deck. He stared at the scene, trying to work out a possible explanation. He failed.

'Hey! You!' A young welder on the platform lifted his safety helmet. The captain moved to the edge of the liftwell. 'What on earth do you think you're doing to the liftwells? Have you gone mad? Do you know what liftwells do? They allow the bloody planes to go up and down. Who told you to put bunk supports in the liftwells?'

'This is what I came to talk to you about.' The admiral placed his hand on Highfield's arm. 'He's doing it under my orders, Highfield.'

'I'm sorry, sir?'

'The *Victoria*. There have been new orders from London.'

Highfield's face fell. 'More POWs?'

'No.' The admiral let out a long breath, his eyes steady on the captain's face. 'They're for women. You'll still be taking your men home, but you've got extra cargo. Six hundred-odd Australian war brides bound for their men in Blighty. The liftwells will be used for the extra berths.'

The welder resumed his work, his torch sending sparks skittering off the metal frame.

Captain Highfield turned to the admiral. 'But they travel on troop ships, sir. Liners, where they can cater for them. You can't have girls and suchlike on an aircraft carrier. It's madness.'

'I can't say I was entirely happy about it either. But needs must, old chap. All the liners have already been commandeered.' He patted Highfield's shoulder. 'It's only six weeks. Be gone before you know it.'

But it's my last voyage. My last time with my men. With my own ship.

Highfield felt a great wail build inside him, a fury at the humiliation of it. 'Sir—'

'Look, George, the telephone lines to London have been burning up on this one. It's caused bad feeling with the Aussie men, having so many of their women marry out. All sides feel the best thing is to get the women away as soon as possible and let the whole thing settle down.'

'But what about my men?'

'Well, they'll be on different decks. The liftwells—with the cabins— will be closed off. There's a few—the, er, ones in the family way—in single cabins. Your men's work will continue as normal. And we're putting in all sorts of safeguards to stop any improper mixing.'

Captain Highfield turned to his superior. The urgency of his position had stripped his face of its habitual impassiveness: his whole self was desperate to convey how wrong this was and how impossible. 'Look, sir, some of my men have been without . . . without female company for months. This is like sticking a match in a box of fireworks. It's impossible, sir. It stands to destabilise the whole atmosphere on the ship.'

'These are married women, Highfield.' The admiral's voice was sharp. 'They're going home to be with their husbands. That's the whole point.'

'Well, with respect, sir, that shows just how much you understand about human nature.'

His words hung in the air, shocking both men. Highfield took a quivering breath. 'Permission to be dismissed. Sir.' He hardly waited for the nod. For the first time in his career, Captain Highfield turned on his heel and walked in anger from his superior.

Five days in

With a change of mood as abrupt and capricious as those of the brides on board, the sea conditions altered dramatically outside the stretch of water known as Sydney Heads. The cheerful blue sea darkened, muddied and swelled into threatening peaks. The winds, born as whispered breezes, grew to stiff gusts, then amplified to gale force. Beneath them, the ship bucked and rolled her way through the waves.

It was at this point that the passengers, who had spent the previous days meandering round the decks like a restless swarm, retired, at first one by one, then in greater numbers, to their bunks.

Avice and Jean (it would be Jean, wouldn't it?) were lying on theirs, locked into their private worlds of nauseous misery. Avice was asleep.

'You not coming for some tea, then?' said Margaret, standing in the doorway. The dog was asleep on her bed, apparently unaffected by the rough weather.

Jean was turned to the wall. Her reply was unintelligible.

'Come on, then, Frances,' said Margaret. 'I guess it's just you and me.'

Margaret Donleavy had met Joseph O'Brien eighteen months previously when her brother Colm had brought him home from the pub, along with six or seven other mates who became regular fixtures in the Donleavy household in the months leading up to the end of the war. It was her brothers' way of keeping the house busy after their mother had gone, she said. For several months they had brought the pub to the farm, sometimes fourteen or fifteen American and Irish men hanging off the back of the pick-up truck.

'Joe was the only one who didn't ask me out or make a nuisance of himself,' she told Frances, as they sat in the near-empty canteen. 'The others either treated me like some kind of barmaid, or tried to give me a squeeze when my brothers weren't looking. I had to whack one with a shovel when he came on a bit fresh.' She grabbed her metal tray as it slid across the table. 'After that they stopped bringing men home.'

Except Joe, who had come every day, had teased Daniel into good humour, had offered her father advice gleaned from his father's own smallholding in Devon.

They had walked out for the first time three months to the day before the US Air Force dropped the atom bomb on Hiroshima, and had wed several weeks afterwards, Margaret in her mother's wedding dress, on the last occasion Joe could get leave. She had known they'd be all right together. Joe, she said, was like her brothers.

'Was he pleased about the baby?'

'When I told him I was expecting, he asked me whether it was due at lambing season.' She snorted.

'Not the romantic kind.' Frances smiled.

'Joe wouldn't know romance if it smacked him in the face,' Margaret said. 'I don't mind, though. I'm not really one for all that sappy stuff.' She grinned, took another mouthful. 'I wasn't even going to get married. To me marriage was just more cooking and wet socks.' She glanced down at herself, and the grin disappeared. 'I still ask myself every now and then how I've managed to end up like this.'

'I'm sorry about your mum,' said Frances. 'How did she die? Oh, I'm sorry,' she said hurriedly, as Margaret's pale skin coloured. 'I don't mean to be . . . indelicate. It's the nursing.'

'No . . . no . . .' said Margaret.

They clutched the table, which was clamped to the floor, arms shooting out to stop salt, pepper or beakers sliding off.

'It came out of nowhere,' she said eventually, as the wave subsided. 'One minute she was there, the next minute she was . . . gone.'

'I'd say that was rather a good way to go,' said Frances. Her eyes, when she looked at Margaret, were clear and steady, a vivid blue. 'She wouldn't have known a thing.' She paused, then added, 'Really. There are far worse things that could have happened to her.'

Margaret might have dwelt on this statement longer had it not been for the sound of giggling in the corner. The two women turned in their chairs to see that a group of women had been joined by several men in engineers' overalls. Margaret recognised one—she had exchanged a greeting with him as he had scrubbed the decks the previous day.

Frances turned her head away and stared out of the window at the water heaving and churning around them. She was reserved, thought Margaret, the kind who always seemed to have a second conversation taking place in her head even as she spoke.

'Hello, ladies.'

It was the engineer. Margaret jumped, then glanced behind him at the skittish girls he had just left, some of whom were peering over their shoulders at him. 'G'day,' she said neutrally.

'I've just been speaking to my friends over there, and I thought I'd let you ladies know that there's a little party in the stokers' mess tonight.'

'Nice thought,' said Margaret, sipping her tea. 'But we've got a bloke posted outside our door.'

'Not tonight you haven't, ladies,' he said. 'Big shortage of morality monitors because of the weather.' He winked at Frances. He had probably been born winking. 'It'll just be a bit of a laugh. We'll play cards and maybe introduce you to a few English customs.'

Margaret raised her eyes to the ceiling. 'Not for us, thanks.'

'Cards, missus, cards.' His expression was of shock and offence. 'I don't know what you had in mind. You a married woman and all . . .'

Despite herself Margaret laughed. 'I don't mind a game of cards,' she said. 'What do you play?'

'Gin rummy. Newmarket. Perhaps the odd game of poker.'

'Only card game there is,' she said, 'but I only play for stakes.'

'My kind of girl,' he said.

'I'll probably thrash you,' she said. 'I've learned from the best.'

'I'll take my chances,' he said. 'I'm not fussy who I take money off.'

'Ah. But will there be room for me?' she said, pushing herself back in her chair, so that the full expanse of her belly was revealed.

His hesitation lasted a fraction of a second. 'We'll make room for you,' he said. 'Any decent poker player's welcome in the stokers' mess.' He thrust out a hand. 'Dennis Tims.'

She took it. 'Margaret—Maggie—O'Brien.'

He nodded at Frances, who had failed to proffer her own hand. 'We're four decks below. Make your way down the stairs by the officers' bathrooms, then follow the sound of a good time.'

The prospect of a few hours in male company made Margaret feel distinctly chipper. She let out a huge sigh: Dennis's arrival had shown her what a strain she had found her all-female existence. 'He seemed all right,' she said cheerfully, heaving herself out from behind the table.

'Yes,' said Frances. Already she had picked up her tray and was taking it towards the washing-up trolley.

'You coming with me? Frances?'

Margaret had to jog to keep up as the tall, slim girl strode down the passageway. Frances had kept her face turned away from Dennis for almost the entire time he was talking, she thought. It was several minutes more before she realised that during the entire two hours they had spent together Frances had told her not a thing about herself.

Dear George,

I hope this letter finds you well, and that your leg is much recovered. I was not sure that you received my last letter as I have not had a reply. The garden is looking simply lovely here in Tiverton, and my new borders are filling out nicely. Patrick is working hard, as always, and has taken on a new chap to help him with some of the bigger accounts.

I am rather anxious to hear from you, George, as I have asked you several times now whether you want to take up the rental of the cottage on the edge of the Hamworth estate. I have spoken to Lord Hamworth personally and he has said he is happy to consider you, with your glowing service record, but he does need to know soon, dear. There is a retired teacher next door, Mrs Barnes, a nice sort, from Cheltenham.

Another retired serviceman and his wife have just moved in locally, although I think he might be RAF, so you would have someone to exchange your 'war stories' with. He is a quiet sort and seems to have something wrong with his eye. I assume it is a war injury, but Marjorie Latham swears he is winking at her.

I must go now, George. But I thought I should let you know that our sister is a little better. She says to tell you she is grateful for all you did.

I pray, as always, that your voyage is a safe one.

Your loving sister, Iris

Captain Highfield sat in his rooms for his meal, one steadying hand on his wineglass as he read the letter he had put off opening since Sydney. When he reached the end, he put the piece of paper down, then pushed away the congealing gammon steak and boiled potatoes.

He had been rather glad of the change in the weather: the women were easier to manage in the confines of their berths and cabins and the sickbay had not been unduly troubled. That said, the doctor was much on his mind at the moment.

At first he had wanted to ascribe it to the damp, the rheumatic twinge caused by the sudden drop in pressure. But the ache in his leg had become steadily more insistent. He knew he should go and get it seen to, but he knew also that if they found what he suspected they would have a reason to deprive him of this last voyage. They'd have him flown home. And even a ship full of women was preferable to no ship at all.

There was a knock on his door and Dobson entered, bearing a thick sheaf of papers. 'Sorry to disturb you, sir, but I've brought you the revised sick list. I thought you'd want to know that we're down five of the eight WSOs.'

'All sick?'

'Four sick, sir. One confined to bed. She fell down the stairs by the transmitter room and sprained her ankle.'

'What on earth was she doing outside the transmitter room?'

'Lost, sir.' Dobson shifted his balance expertly as the floor rose beneath him and spray obliterated the view from the window. 'Seems an awful lot of the girls can't read a map.'

Highfield exhaled. 'So what will we do about going rounds tonight?'

'I thought we could get a few of the marines to do it, sir. Clive and Nicol are pretty responsible fellows. To be honest, I can't see there'll be too much trouble with the ladies. At least half are too busy moaning on their bunks to get up to any mischief.'

Highfield hoped absently that the foul weather would last the entire six weeks. 'Fine. Get the men to do it. How's the water level?'

'Not too bad, sir. We're just about keeping on top of things, although I have to say the systems on this old girl are pretty tired. Still, it's helped that so many of the women are in bed.' He grinned. 'Less hair-washing, that sort of thing.'

'Yes, well, I've been thinking about that. Make sure we introduce another lecture on the dhobi. Make it compulsory.'

Dobson left, something a little irritating in his swagger. He fancied himself for captain, Rennick, Highfield's steward, had told him. He had been glad to see other men who had served beneath him promoted, but there was something about Dobson's manner that stuck in his craw.

'That man's an ass,' Rennick said, arriving to take the captain's plate. 'The men have no respect for him. He'll do you no good on this voyage.' He had been with Highfield almost ten years and his opinions were expressed with the confidence of their long acquaintance.

'You know what, Rennick? Right now, ass or not, Dobson is the only executive officer I've got and the least of my worries.'

The steward shrugged, his lined Scottish face fixing the captain with an expression that suggested they both knew more than they chose to say. As Rennick left the room, Highfield's eyes fell to the letter in front of him. He picked up his wineglass and abruptly swept the piece of paper off the mahogany table and into the bin below.

Dennis Tims had been wrong about the marine. When Margaret and Frances arrived back at their cabin, he was standing outside, his hand raised as if to knock. 'Hey!' yelped Margaret, trying to run down the passageway. 'Hey!'

He lowered his hand long enough for Margaret to slide between him and the door.

'Can I help?' she said, panting, one hand under her belly.

'I've brought you some crackers. Captain's orders, ma'am. We're doing it for everyone who's sick.'

'They're asleep,' said Margaret. 'Best not to disturb them, wouldn't you say, Frances?'

Frances glanced at the man, and then away. 'Yes.'

'Frances here's a nurse,' added Margaret. 'She knows what's best.'

There was a short silence.

'Crackers tend to help.' The marine was holding the box stiffly in both hands. 'Shall I leave them with you, then?'

'Yeah. Thanks.' Margaret took the box.

The marine was staring at Frances. When he realised Margaret was watching him, he looked away quickly. 'I won't be here tonight,' he said. 'There's a few gone sick so I'll be helping with the rounds. I've got permission to look in on you later if you'd prefer.' He had a clipped way of talking, as if uncomfortable with casual conversation.

'No,' said Margaret. 'We'll be fine.' She smiled broadly. 'Thanks for offering, though.'

'Right.' He lifted a hand in a half-salute.

''Bye, then. And thanks for the crackers.' Margaret was praying that Maud Gonne, alerted by her voice, wouldn't bark.

When they opened the door Jean woke, raising a pale face from under her blanket. She refused the crackers and sat up slowly, revealing the upper half of a flannelette nightgown garlanded with little pink rosebuds. She looked, Margaret thought, shockingly young.

'Do you think we should take anything?' Maud Gonne had leapt onto Margaret's lap and was trying to lick her face.

'Take anything where?'

'The stokers' mess. A drink or something.'

'I'm not going,' Frances said.

'You must! I can't go by myself.'

Jean squinted. Her eyes were shadowed. 'Go where?' she murmured.

'Bit of a do downstairs,' said Margaret. 'I'm promised a game of poker. I'm going to head down there once I've given Maudie a quick run. Come on, Frances, you can't sit here all night. You'll be miserable.'

'It's really not my thing,' said Frances. But she sounded halfhearted.

'Then I'll teach you.'

'You're not leaving me here,' said Jean, and she swung her legs over the edge of the bunk. 'I'm not missing out if there's a party.'

If Margaret had thought the brides' cabins cramped, little had prepared her for the sheer numbers of men who could be crowded into a single mess area. Thirty-two men were billeted in the stokers' mess, and even with only half of that number present, the women found themselves in a proximity to the opposite sex that in normal circumstances would have left them awaiting imminent betrothal.

Frances spent the first half an hour pressed up against the only spare six inches of wall. Jean was giggling and blushing, and kept saying, 'Saucy!' in a scolding voice. Margaret was perhaps the least perturbed: her condition and her ease in the company of large numbers of men enabled them to treat her like an honorary sister. Within an hour, she had won several hands of cards.

'You ladies want a drink?' Dennis Tims was leaning over them with a bottle of amber liquid and a couple of tumblers. They had quickly established that he did not operate by the normal rules of the ship. Alcohol, smokes, a sub till payday—all of these flowed either to or from him like water. Frances, who had been persuaded to sit down beside Margaret, shook her head. She was apparently immune to the men's admiring looks, and had spent so much time staring at her shoes that Margaret felt guilty for having insisted she come. Jean, meanwhile, had drunk two tumblers already and was getting sillier by the second.

'Steady now, Jean,' Margaret whispered. 'Remember how sick you were earlier.'

'Davy here says it will settle my stomach,' said Jean, prodding the man beside her.

'You don't want to believe anything this lot tell you,' said Margaret, raising her eyebrows. 'Settle your stomach, indeed.'

Around them, those men not playing cards at the wooden tables lay in their hammocks, writing letters, sleeping, smoking, reading or just watching—simply enjoying the presence of women. Despite the close confines, the men were hospitable, friendly and only mildly flirtatious.

'Frances? You sure you won't play a hand?' Margaret had won again. Dennis had whistled and thrown down his cards.

'No. Thank you.'

Several times now Maggie had mentioned that Frances was a nurse, and several times Frances had rebuffed any attempt to get her to talk about her time in service.

'Your mate all right?' Dennis murmured to her.

'I think she's shy.' Margaret had no other explanation.

They played two, three, several more hands. The room grew smokier and without natural light it was impossible to tell whether time had stalled or sped on into the early hours. It became a matter of good or bad hands and of Jean's giggling.

At a quarter to twelve, Frances, the only one of them who was still stiff and formal, looked pointedly at her watch and then at Jean, who, helpless with giggles, was lying on a hammock, looking at a young rating's comic book.

Margaret stood up heavily. 'It's been great, guys,' she said, 'but I suppose we should go. Thanks ever so much for the hospitality.'

'Our pleasure,' said Dennis. 'Want one of us to check the passageway's clear?' Then his voice hardened. 'Oi, Plummer, have a little respect.'

All eyes turned towards Dennis's line of sight. The owner of Jean's comic book had rested a hand casually on the back of her thigh.

For a second or two, nobody spoke. Then Frances stepped forward. 'Yes, come on, Jean. Get up. We must get back.'

'Spoilsports.' Jean half slid, half fell off the hammock, blew a kiss to the rating, and allowed her arm to be linked by Frances's rigid one. "Bye, lads. Thanks for a lovely time.' Her hair had fallen across her face, half concealing a beatific smile. 'Got to shake a leg in the morning.'

Margaret nodded to the men round the table, then made her way to the door, suddenly awkward, as if only just aware of the potential pitfalls of their position.

Dennis seemed to grasp this. 'Sorry about that,' he said. 'It's just the drink. No harm meant.'

'None taken,' said Margaret, raising a neutral smile.

He held out a hand. 'Come again.' He stooped forward and murmured, 'I get sick of the sight of this lot.'

She knew what he was trying to say, and was grateful. 'I'm sure we'll be back,' she said, as Frances dragged Jean out of the door.

Seven days in

The master-at-arms stood in front of one of the younger boys who was being supported under each arm by two mates. He shot out a broad, pudgy finger, and chucked the offender under the chin, frowning as he caught a whiff of his breath. He turned to the boys. 'He your mate?'

'Sir.'

'How'd he get like this? Scotch mist, is it? As opposed to just Scotch?'

'Dunno, sir.'

'Dunno, sir,' the man repeated, fixing them with a well-practised glare. 'I bet you don't.'

Henry Nicol, Marine, stepped back against the wall. The young dabber beside him was wringing his cap in bruised hands.

'Soames, eh?'

The younger man nodded unhappily at the master-at-arms. 'Sir.'

'What's he in for, Nicol?'

'Quarrels and disturbances, sir. And drunkenness.'

The older man shook his head. 'You speaking for him, are you, Nicol?'

'Yes, sir.'

'Make sure you get some sleep afterwards. You're on watch again tonight. You look bloody awful.' He nodded at the younger man. 'Soames, it's a bad business. Use your loaf next time, not your fists.'

Soames slumped back against the wall. 'I'm going to get it, aren't I?' he groaned.

In normal circumstances Nicol might have been reassuring, upbeat. But with one hand still resting against the letter in his trouser pocket, he had neither the energy nor the desire to make someone else feel better. He had put off opening it for days, guessing, dreading the nature of its contents. Now, seven days after they had left Sydney, he knew.

'You'll be all right,' he said.

Dear Henry,

I'm disappointed but not surprised I haven't heard back from you. I want to say again how sorry I am. I never set out to hurt you. But we have had hardly a word from you in so long, and I am very fond of

Anton. He is a good man, a kind man, who pays me a lot of heed . . .

This is not meant to be a criticism of you. I know we were awfully young when we married, and perhaps if the war had not come when it did . . . Still, our world today is full of such if-onlys . . .

He had read the first paragraph and thought that, ironically, life was easier when his letters were still censored.

It was almost twenty minutes before they were up. They paused outside the captain's office, then Nicol followed the younger man in and they saluted. Captain Highfield was seated behind the desk.

An officer standing beside the captain read out the charge: the boy had been scrapping with another dabber in the seamen's mess. He had also been drinking in excess of the daily ration.

'How do we plead?' said Captain Highfield.

'Guilty, sir,' said Soames.

Yes, I am guilty. And weak. But, to be truthful, for the last four years I might as well have been a widow for the word I have had from you. I spent three of those years lying awake week after week praying for your safety. When you did come back you were like a stranger.

The captain eyed the young man, then addressed the marine. 'What can you tell me about this young man's character, Nicol?'

Nicol cleared his throat. 'He's been with us a little over a year, sir. He's been steady, hard-working, quiet.' He paused. 'A good sort.'

'So, Soames, given this glowing character reference, what turned you into a brawling idiot?'

'Sir.' He blushed. 'It's my girl, sir. She . . . she was to see me off in Sydney. But she's been . . . well, it's one of the others in C Deck, sir.'

When Anton started paying me some attention, Henry, it's not even that he stepped into your shoes. There were no shoes for him to step into. The children are very fond of him. You will always be their father, and they know that, but they will love America and have all sorts of chances there that they would never have had in a sleepy old village in Norfolk.

'. . . and he started taunting me . . . and then the others, well, they said as how I couldn't keep hold of a woman, and you know what it's like in the mess, sir, well, I'd had a bellyful of it and I suppose I saw red.'

'You suppose you saw red.'

'Yes, sir.' He coughed into his hand. 'I'm very sorry, sir.'

'You're very sorry,' said the captain. 'So, Nicol, you say he's been a good sort up to this point?'

'Yes, sir.'

The captain put down his pen and clasped his hands. His voice was icy. 'You know I don't like fighting on my ship. I especially don't like fighting when there's alcohol involved. Even more, I dislike discovering that there may be social events taking place on my ship without my knowledge that involve alcohol.'

'Sir.'

'I don't like surprises, Soames.'

But here, dear, I have to tell you something hard. If there is an urgency to my letter it is because I am carrying Anton's child, and all we are waiting for is your permission to divorce, so that we can marry and bring this baby up together.

'You're a disgrace.'

'Yes, sir.'

Nicol cleared his throat.

The captain stared at the boy from under his brows. 'I'm conscious of your previous good character, Soames, and you should consider yourself lucky you have someone of better character to speak for you.'

'Sir.'

'I'm going to let you off with a fine. But I want you to be clear on one thing—little escapes me on this ship. Very little. And if you think I am not aware of the little get-togethers that are springing up, then you are very much mistaken.'

'I didn't mean any harm, sir.'

I did not intend things to turn out this way. Please do not make this child grow up a bastard, Henry, I implore you. I know I have hurt you, but please do not inflict whatever you feel for me on the little one.

Please write me or wire me when you can. I am happy to leave you the house and everything. I just want your permission to go.

Yours, Fay

'You meant no harm,' Highfield muttered, and began to write. 'Nobody ever does.' There was a brief silence in the room. 'Two pounds. And don't let me see you in here again.'

'Sir.'

The two men saluted, and left the office.

The summary trials ended shortly after eleven. Captain Highfield laid down his pen and motioned to Dobson, who had entered some minutes previously, and the marine captain that they should sit down. A steward was sent for tea.

'It's not good, is it?' he said, leaning back in his chair. 'We're hardly a week in and look at it.'

The marine captain said nothing. The marines were a disciplined lot and never drank on board; they tended to appear only as character witnesses, or occasionally when the natural friction between marines and seamen boiled over into blows.

'It's bringing tension into the ship. And alcohol. When did we last have so many drunkenness offences at sea?'

The two men shook their heads. 'We'll organise a locker search, captain. See if we can flush it out,' said Dobson.

Out of the window, behind them, the skies had cleared to a bright, vivid blue, the sea becalmed. It was the kind of sight that couldn't help but fill the heart with optimism. But Highfield took no joy from it: his leg had throbbed dully all morning, a permanent, intermittent reminder of his failure. If Bertram, the ship's regular surgeon, had been aboard, he could have asked him to take a look at it. But Bertram had failed to show at Sydney, was now the subject of a court-martial, and that damn fool Duxbury was in his place.

Dobson leaned forward, his elbows resting on his knees. 'The women's officers tell me they're pretty sure there's movement at night. The one on B Deck had to break up a situation only last night.'

'Fighting?'

The two seated men glanced at each other, then at the captain.

'No, sir. Er . . . physical contact between a bride and a rating. He had hold of her round the—round the back of the bilge pump.'

'I knew this would happen,' Highfield said. The thought that, even as he sat here, such things were going on aboard his own ship . . . But then he saw that the other two men seemed markedly less disturbed by it than he felt. In fact, Dobson looked as if he was trying to contain mirth.

The marine captain, a more diplomatic sort, leaned forward. 'I think, sir, that much of the problem this past week may have been to do with the conditions over the Bight,' he said. 'The fact that so many of the monitors were absent increased the levels of . . . erm . . . interaction. Give it a few days more and I suspect things will settle down.'

Highfield studied Nicol. 'You think we should let things be?'

'Yes, I do, sir.'

'I agree, sir,' said Dobson. 'Best not to rattle things up too much.'

Highfield ignored him. As he closed the ledger, he turned to Nicol. 'Very well,' he said. 'We'll go softly for now. But I want to know everything. If there is the slightest hint of misbehaviour, I want us to be down on it like a ton of bricks.'

Dear Deanna,

I hope you, Mother and Father are all well. I'm not sure when I will be able to post this, but I thought I would write and let you know a little of our exciting voyage, and how surprising are the conditions we travel in, given my reservations.

I have made three delightful new friends: Margaret, whose father owns a large estate not far from Sydney; Frances, who is terribly elegant and has been doing admirable things in nursing; and Jean. They are all so much more interesting than our old crowd.

My accommodation is situated in the largest part of the boat, a short distance from the part known as the bridge and the captain's 'sea cabin'. We are told there may well be some cocktail parties once we get to Gibraltar as it is possible that several governors are coming aboard.

Every day they lay on new entertainments to keep us girls busy; needlework, dancing, all the latest films. I am off to watch National Velvet this afternoon. I don't believe it has reached Melbourne yet but, believe me, you must go when it does. Apparently, Elizabeth Taylor is perfectly wonderful. The sailors are charming and are always bringing one little things to eat. And, Deanna, you would die for the food.

There is a fully fitted hair salon at the far end of the ship. After I finish writing I think I might take a look. I shall, of course, let you know all about London. I am hoping to hear from Ian before we meet, as to the plans for our little holiday there.

As I said, I hope my letter finds you all well, and please do pass on my happy news to the old crowd. I'll write again when I'm not so busy!

Your loving sister

Avice

Avice was sitting in the small canteen on the flight deck, staring out of the salt-spattered window at the seagulls swooping alongside the ship and the bright skies beyond. For the half-hour it had taken her to write her letter, she had almost begun to believe in the version of the voyage she had created. So much so, in fact, that she had felt rather deflated when she signed off to find herself back in this rusting hangar, surrounded not by cocktail parties and adorable new friends but by the scarred noses of the aeroplanes on the deck.

'Cup of tea, Avice?' Margaret was leaning over her. 'I'm going to get some. You never know, it might settle your stomach.'

'No. Thank you.' Avice swallowed, then allowed herself to imagine the taste. An immediate wave of nausea confirmed her refusal.

'You've got to have something.'

'I'll have a glass of water. Perhaps a dry cracker, if they've got some.'

'Sure thing, Ave.'

Ave. If Avice had been feeling less awful, she would have corrected her: there was nothing worse than an abbreviated name. But Margaret had already waddled off towards the counter, leaving her with Frances, an even more uncomfortable proposition.

Margaret had told her that Frances had been turned down when she offered to work in the infirmary. The less generous-spirited part of Avice wondered what the navy had felt was not fitting about the girl; the other thought how much easier life would have been without her hanging around all day, with her awkward conversation and serious face.

'Have you anything planned for this afternoon?'

Frances had been studying a copy of *Daily Ship News*. She looked up sharply with the guarded expression that made Avice want to yell, 'It isn't a trick question, you know.' Her pale red hair was pulled into a tight chignon. She'd be pretty if she brightened herself up.

'No,' said Frances. Then, when the ensuing silence threatened to overwhelm them both. 'Have you finished your letter?'

Avice's hand closed over her writing-pad, as if its contents might somehow become visible. 'Yes.' It had come out sharper than she'd intended. She made a conscious effort to relax. 'It's to my sister. And I've written one to Ian, too.'

'Oh.'

Avice sighed. 'I don't know when we'll be able to post them, though. I'd love to know when I'll get one from Ian.' She examined her finger-nails. 'I've been told they might bring aboard post at Ceylon.'

She had dreamed of a fat little cushion of Ian's letters, waiting in some sweltering tropical post office. She would tie them with red ribbon and read them in private, luxuriously, one at a time, like someone enjoying a box of chocolates. 'It's rather strange,' she said, almost to herself, 'going all this way and not speaking for so long.' Her finger traced Ian's name on the envelope. 'Sometimes it all feels a bit unreal. Like I can't believe I married this man, and now I'm on this boat in the middle of nowhere.'

Five weeks and four days since his last letter. The first she had received as a married woman.

'I try to imagine what he's thinking now, because the worst thing about waiting so long for letters is that things he might have told me about then will have passed. The one thing we all count on, I suppose, is that their feelings for us haven't changed. I suppose that's our test of faith.'

Her voice had dropped, become contemplative. She realised that for several minutes she had forgotten to feel sick. 'Don't you think?'

At that question, something odd happened to Frances's expression: it closed over, became neutral, mask-like. 'I suppose so,' she said.

Avice felt as though her gesture towards intimacy had been deliberately rebuffed. She was almost tempted to say something to that effect, but at that moment Margaret waddled back to the table bearing a tea tray. Propped in her mug was a vanilla ice-cream.

'Listen to this, girls. Old Jean will love it. There's going to be a crossing-the-line ceremony. It's a sailors' tradition, apparently, about crossing the equator, and there's going to be all sorts of fun on the flight deck. The guy at the tea urn just told me.'

Frances's rudeness was forgotten. 'Will we have to get dressed up?' Avice's hand had risen to her hair.

'Dunno. They're going to post something on the notice board later.'

'Ugh. I'm not joining in. Not with my stomach.'

Margaret had bitten the top off her cone. A small blob of ice cream was stuck to the tip of her nose. 'Frances?'

'I don't know.'

'Ah, come on,' said Margaret. The chair creaked in protest as she sat down. 'Let your hair down, woman. Cut loose a little.'

Frances gave her a tentative smile, showing small white teeth. She might even, Avice saw, with a start, be beautiful. 'Perhaps,' she said.

Frances had known she would resent the man outside. On the first night he had stood there, on the other side of their door, she had been unable to sleep, conscious of the stranger's proximity. His presence highlighted the fact that they were cargo, a consignment to be ferried safely from one side of the world to the other, in many cases from fathers to husbands, one set of men to another. She resented him for making her feel like a possession, someone's property to be safeguarded.

The others seemed to indulge in little such philosophical consideration. In fact, they didn't notice him; for them, like so much on board, he was part of the nightly furniture, someone to call good evening to, to smuggle the dog past, or even themselves. Tonight Margaret and Jean were off to meet Dennis for another poker session.

'You sure you won't come with us, Frances?' They had been to several parties now. Jean had stayed sober during at least one.

Frances shook her head.

'You don't need to behave like a nun.' Margaret finished doing up her shoe. 'I'm sure your old man won't mind you enjoying a bit of company. You'll go nuts if you spend every evening in here, you know.'

'I'll take my chances.' Frances smiled.

'Avice?'

'No, thank you. I'll rest this evening.' Avice's nausea had worsened again, and she lay, pale and limp, on her bunk.

They had not expected the marine to be standing outside. He had not been there the previous evening, and none of them had heard the footsteps that usually signalled his arrival. Jean, then Margaret, stopped dead in the doorway. 'Oh . . . we're just going for some fresh air,' said Margaret, speedily closing the door behind her.

'We'll be back by eleven,' said Jean.

Frances, who had stood up to retrieve her dressing gown from a hanger, paused on the other side of the door, hearing the surprise and slight strain in the women's voice.

'I'd avoid the Black Squad, if that's how you like your fresh air,' he said now, so quietly that no one could be sure of what they'd heard.

Frances leaned closer to the door, her dressing gown raised in the air.

'The stokers' mess. Bit of a crackdown tonight,' he explained.

'Oh. Right,' said Margaret. 'Well. Thanks.'

She heard their shoes clattering down the passageway, then the marine coughing quietly. Out of sight they would explode with shock and laughter, clutching each other briefly before, with a furtive glance behind them, they made for the stokers' mess.

Avice wasn't asleep. It would have been easier, Frances thought, if she had been. She lay back on her bunk and tried to read, but found she had scanned the same paragraph several times without taking anything in. The dog whimpered quietly in sleep, just visible under Margaret's cardigan. She glanced down to check that its water bowl was full.

Outside, the marine muttered to someone as they passed. Time stretched out, became elastic.

Frances sighed. Quietly, so that Avice would not hear. Margaret was right. If she spent another evening in here, she'd go insane.

He turned when she opened the door. 'Stretching my legs,' she said.

'Strictly speaking, ma'am, you shouldn't be leaving your cabin at this time.'

She didn't protest, or plead, just stood, waiting, and he nodded her on. 'Stokers' mess?'

'No,' she said, smiling at her feet. 'No. Not my cup of tea.'

She walked briskly along the passageway, conscious of his eyes on her back, fearful that he might call out to her that it was too close to the curfew. But he said nothing.

Out of his range, she went up the stairs near the cinema projection room, past rows of tin trunks secured to the wall with webbing straps, and the redundant stores for life jackets, weaponry and ammunition. She strode up the temporary steps towards the captain's sea cabins two at a time, ducking to avoid hitting her head on the metal struts. Reaching the hatch, she glanced back to check no one was watching, then opened it and stepped out onto the flight deck. There she stopped abruptly, almost reeling from the sudden expanse of inky black sea and sky.

She stood there for some time, breathing in the cool, fresh air, enjoying the gentle movement of the ship. Up here, the vibration of the engines was a low purr, the ship benign and obedient, carrying her safely forward, like some mythical beast, across the vast ocean.

Frances peered across the deserted deck, out of bounds after dark. Some moonlit, some in shadow, the silhouettes of the aircraft stood around her, noses up, as if they were scenting the air. She walked slowly among the shining metal, then, finally, sat down under a streamlined belly. She folded her hands round her knees and stared out at the million stars, and at the unknowable point where the inky sea met the infinite black sky. And for possibly the first time since they had embarked, Frances Mackenzie closed her eyes and allowed herself to breathe out.

She had been sitting there for almost twenty minutes when she saw the captain. She watched him close the door carefully so that it did not slam. Then, with the same furtive air as, presumably, she had displayed, he stepped forward and began to limp towards the starboard side of the ship and a point just out of sight of the bridge. He stopped by one of the planes, his uniform spotlit by the moonlight, and reached out as if to support himself on a wing strut. Then, he bent and rubbed his leg. Afterwards, he stood there some minutes, his weight on one leg, shoulders slumped, staring out to sea. Then he straightened his shoulders and walked back to the hatch, his limp no longer perceptible.

Afterwards, she could not articulate what it was about this brief time that she had found comforting, but as she came back down the stairs she found herself somehow less conscious of the glances of those who passed, with a little of her confidence restored to her.

She would not normally have asked a man for a cigarette. She would not usually have allowed herself to be drawn into conversation. She would certainly not have begun one. But she felt so much better and there was something so melancholy about his face.

He was leaning against the wall beside their door, cigarette cupped between thumb and forefinger, eyes fixed on a point on the floor in front of him. His hair had flopped forward and his shoulders were hunched, as if he was lost in thought. As he caught sight of her he pinched out the cigarette and dropped it into his pocket.

'Please don't bother,' she said. 'Not on my account.'

He shrugged. 'Not meant to, really, on duty.'

And for some reason, instead of disappearing into the cabin, she had stood there, and asked whether she might have one too. 'I don't feel like going in yet,' she explained. Then, self-conscious, she had stood beside him, already regretting her decision.

He pulled a cigarette from the pack, handed it to her and lit it, his hand briefly touching hers as it cupped the flame. Frances tried not to flinch, then wondered how quickly she could smoke it. Plainly, he had not wanted company. 'Thanks,' she said. 'I'll just have a few puffs.'

'Take your time.'

They stood, one on each side of the door frame, looking at their feet, until the silence became uncomfortable.

She looked sideways at his sleeve. 'What rank are you?'

'Corporal.'

She took a deep drag of her cigarette. She was already nearly a third of the way down it. 'I thought three stripes meant sergeant.'

'Not if they're upside-down.'

'I don't understand.'

'They're for long service. Good conduct.' His eyes flickered over them, as if he had rarely considered them. 'Stopping fights, that kind of thing. It's a way of rewarding someone who doesn't want promotion.'

'Why didn't you want promotion?'

'Don't know.' His eyes, while not unfriendly, told of his discomfort with casual conversation. His gaze briefly met hers and slid away. 'Perhaps I never wanted the responsibility.'

It was then that she spotted the photograph. He must have been looking at it before she came back. A black and white picture, a little smaller than a man's wallet, tucked into his right hand between finger and thumb. 'Yours?' she said, nodding towards his hand.

He lifted it, and looked at it as if for the first time. 'Yes.'

'Boy and girl?'

'Two boys. My youngest needed a haircut.' He handed it to her. She took it, held it under the light and studied the beaming faces, unsure what she was meant to say. 'They look nice.'

'Picture's eighteen months old. They'll have grown some. You?'

'Oh. No . . .' She handed back the photograph. 'You miss them?'

'Every day.' Then his voice hardened. 'They probably don't even remember what I look like.'

She did not know what to say: whatever she was intruding on would not be eased by a few minutes of small talk. She felt suddenly that engaging him in conversation had been misjudged. His job was to stand outside their door. He had no choice if she chose to talk to him.

'I'll leave you,' she said, quietly. 'Thank you for the cigarette.' She trod it out, then bent down to pick up the butt. What should she do with it? As she hesitated by the door he turned. 'Here,' he said, holding out a hand.

She shook her head, but he held his hand closer, insistent. She placed the little butt on it, and blushed. 'Sorry,' she whispered.

'No problem.'

'Good night, then.'

She opened the door, was sliding silently round it into the darkness when she heard his voice. It was quiet enough to reassure her that her judgment of him had been right, but light enough to show he had not taken offence. Light enough to suggest some kind of offering.

'So, whose is the dog?' it asked.

Sixteen days

The first 'Not Wanted Don't Come' arrived on the morning of the sixteenth day the brides had been on board. The telegram arrived just after 8 a.m. in the radio room. Its content was noted by the radio operator. He carried it swiftly to the captain, who was eating toast and porridge in his rooms. He read it, then summoned the chaplain, who summoned the relevant women's officer, and all three spent some time pontificating on what was known of the character of the bride concerned, and how well—or otherwise—she was likely to take the news.

The subject of the telegram, a Mrs Millicent Newcombe (née Sumpter) was called in to the captain's office at 10.30 a.m. She arrived white-faced, convinced that her husband, a pilot, had been shot down and was missing, presumed dead. So great had been her distress that none of the three was quick to tell her the truth. Eventually, Captain Highfield put matters straight. Then he had handed her the telegram.

Afterwards, he told his steward, she had asked, several times, whether they thought it was a joke, and when she heard that all such telegrams were investigated and verified as a matter of course, she had sat down, squinting at the words in front of her.

Captain Highfield had wired the girl's parents, then contacted London, who had advised that they should put her off at Ceylon where a representative of the Australian government would take charge of the arrangements to bring her home. They would not let her go until they were sure that her parents or other family members were able to meet her at the other end. These procedures were laid out in the paperwork recently sent from London and had been put in place for the earlier return of GI brides.

'I'm very sorry,' she said, once the arrangements had been made, 'to put you all to so much trouble. I'm very sorry.'

'It's really no trouble, Mrs . . . erm . . . Millicent.'

The women's officer had placed an arm round the girl's shoulders; it was hard to tell whether the gesture was protective or merely indicative of her determination to steer her out from the captain's office.

For several moments after she had left the room was silent.

'I'll get on to the Red Cross in Ceylon, sir,' said the chaplain, eventually. 'Make sure there's someone who can give her a bit of support.'

'That would be a good idea,' said Highfield. He scribbled something meaningless on the notepad in front of him. 'I suppose we should contact the pilot's supervising officer as well, just to make sure there are no extenuating circumstances. You take charge of that, Dobson, will you?'

'Yes, sir,' said Dobson. He had entered just as Millicent was leaving, and had since started whistling a jaunty tune that Highfield found intensely annoying. 'She'll be all right, sir,' Dobson said. 'She'll probably have found another young dope by the time she leaves Ceylon. Pretty girl like that.' He grinned. 'I don't think these Aussie girls are too fussy, as long as they find someone to get them off the old sheep farm.'

Highfield was speechless.

'Besides, it's one less bride on board, eh, Captain?' Dobson laughed, apparently pleased with his own humour. 'With a bit of luck we could have jettisoned the lot by the time we reach Plymouth.'

Rennick, who had been standing in the corner, briefly met his captain's eye, then quietly left the room.

Until that point the world as the brides had known it had steadily receded by nautical miles, and the *Victoria* had become a world of its own, existing discretely from the continuing life on land. The routines of the ship had become the routines of the women, and those faces who daily moved around them, scrubbing, painting or welding, their community. With food provided, and their lives dictated by the rules, there were few decisions to make. Marooned on their floating island, they became passive, surrendered themselves to these new rhythms, surrounded by nothing except the slowly changing climate, the increasingly dramatic sunsets, the endless ocean.

In this stilled atmosphere, news of the Not Wanted Don't Come filtered through the ship as rapidly and pervasively as a virus. A new low note of anxiety underlaid the conversation in the canteen; a spate of headaches and palpitations presented themselves to the sickbay. At least one bride confided in the chaplain that she thought she might have changed her mind, as if by saying the words, and hearing his reassurance, she could ward off the possibility of her husband doing the same.

That one piece of paper, and its four bald words, had brought home to them rudely the reality of their situation. It reminded them that many had married in haste, and that no matter what they felt, what sacrifices they had made, they were now waiting, like sitting ducks, for their husbands to repent at leisure.

Despite this, or perhaps because of it, the arrival that afternoon of King Neptune and his cohorts prompted an atmosphere on board that could at best be described as fevered and at worst as manic.

After lunch Margaret had dragged the others up onto the flight deck. Avice had declared she would rather rest on her bunk, that she was feeling too delicate to enjoy herself. Frances had said, in her cool little voice, that she didn't think it was her kind of thing. Margaret, who had not failed to notice the chill in the air between the two, had determined it would do them all good to go. Jean, at least, had needed no persuading.

When they had emerged outside, the flight deck was a seething mass of people, their chatter lifting above the sound of the engines as they seated themselves around a newly constructed canvas tank. It was several seconds before Margaret noticed the chair suspended above it from the mobile crane.

'Good God! They're not going to stick us in that, are they?' she said.

'Need a dockyard crane for you,' said Jean, as she pushed, through the crowd, oblivious to sharp looks and muttering. 'Come on, plenty of room over here. Mind your backs! Pregnant lady coming through.'

Now that most were seated, Margaret could see that the crowd was mixed. It was the first time since they had slipped anchor that so many men and women had been gathered together without formal separation. The officers, though, stood apart in their whites.

She lowered herself into the space Jean had cleared for her, trying to prop herself up on the hard surface. Minutes later she found herself ducking as a large crate was passed over the women's heads by one of the ratings to an engineer, who she recognised from Dennis's mess. 'There you go, missus,' he said, placing it beside her. 'Sit yourself on that.'

At that moment 'Neptune' arrived, in a wig made of unbraided rope, his face painted a violent green. He was surrounded by a number of equally outlandishly dressed companions, who were introduced as (a rather hairy) Queen Amphitrite, the Royal Doctor, Dentist and Barber, and the oversized Royal Baby, modesty protected by a towelling napkin and slathered in a layer of the grease more commonly associated with a well-tuned engine. Behind them, accompanied by a trumpet-player, came a band of bare-chested men, cheered loudly by the assembled troops and women, who were apparently to act as enforcers. They were introduced without explanation as 'Bears'.

'Look. There's all sorts of ranks here,' Avice said happily, neck craned to make out who was in the crowd. 'Look at all the stripes! I thought it was just going to be a load of horrid old engineers.' It was clear to Margaret, Frances and Jean that Avice was feeling better.

'And horrid old engineers' wives?' said Margaret, drily, but Avice didn't appear to hear.

'Hear ye, hear ye,' said Neptune, lifting his trident so that it glinted in the sun. Slowly the noise subsided to a barely suppressed communal giggle, the odd whisper rippling through the crowd like a breeze. Satisfied that he had the women's attention, he lifted a scroll of paper.

> 'You ladies now by Britain claim'd
> Will find our company is shamed.
> And offences grave and numerous here
> Old Neptune's court has come to hear.
> Rating, captain, all the same,
> Before our sea king's judgment famed
> And all will find their sins are met
> With punishment both foul and wet. . .'

'It's hardly Wordsworth, is it?' sniffed Avice.
'Who?' said Jean.

> '. . . Now our ratings, our tadpoles, pollywogs
> Will have to fight like cats and dogs
> To save themselves from Neptune's pack
> And earn the right to be "Shellback".
> Captain, chaplain, or humble docker,
> They've sent too many to Davy Jones's locker.
> So we will decide, O ladies fair,
> Just who gets a spell in our dunking chair.'

Eventually, after much catcalling and something that might have qualified as a scuffle, the first 'tadpole' was called up. As the women howled their approval, the young rating was first charged with 'failing to acknowledge the territory of Neptune', then, as the enforcers held him down, the Royal Dentist filled his mouth with what looked like soap-suds, leaving him gagging and choking. He was subsequently lifted into the chair and, at the lowering of Neptune's trident, summarily ducked.

'It's not very dignified, is it?' said Avice.

At this point, the Bears moved into the crowd, eyeing the women with theatrical intent. The brides, in turn, shrieked obligingly and clutched each other, vowing loudly and without any intent whatsover, to protect each other. They were melodramatic enough for Margaret to roll her eyes. Beside her, Frances, wearing a large, floppy sunhat, didn't flinch. But, then, she seemed so little moved by the presence of men that Margaret wondered how she had ever come to be married at all.

One of the Bears stopped in front of them. Green-faced, with a string of shells round his neck, he bent low and peered at the women. 'What sinners and miscreants do we have here, then?' he said. 'Which of you is deserving of punishment?' He paused in front of Frances, who sat very still, her hands folded tightly in her lap. Realising he would get no sport from her, he prowled off after other game.

The sun grew fiercer and Margaret envied Frances her hat. She shifted on her crate, one hand raised to her hairline as she watched the enter-tainment. 'You've been on ships before. Is it always like this?' she said to Frances, who was now wearing sunglasses.

Frances forced a smile. 'I couldn't tell you,' she murmured. 'I've always been working.' Then she was distracted by something off to her right.

'Who are you nodding at?'

'That's our marine,' Frances said.

'It is?' Margaret squinted at the dark-haired man standing a short dis-tance away from them. She hadn't ever really looked at his face, had been too busy hurrying past him, hunched over her concealed dog. 'He looks bloody awful. Shouldn't he be asleep if he's on watch all night?'

Frances didn't answer. The marine had spotted them and her eyes were now on her feet.

'He's nodding at you,' said Margaret, waving cheerfully. 'There! You not going to wave back?'

But Frances didn't appear to have heard.

'Look!' interrupted Jean, grabbing Margaret's elbow. 'Bloody hell! They've got one of the officers!'

'And he's no ordinary officer,' said Avice. 'He's the executive officer. He's terribly high up, you know. Oh, my goodness!'

Swearing and spluttering, the XO had been carried from beside the captain to the ducking stool and strapped in. There, set upon by Bears, his shirt was removed and, as the brides shrieked their approval, he was smothered in grease and his face plastered with what might have been oatmeal. Several times he twisted in the seat, as if to appeal to someone, but syrup was rubbed into his hair and feathers scattered on top. With every humiliation the noise level grew higher.

Margaret was distracted by a tap on her shoulder. Frances seemed to be gesturing that she was leaving. She looked pale, Margaret thought, then turned back to the XO's misery.

'Look at him,' yelled Avice, marvelling. 'He looks absolutely furious.'

'Mad as a cut snake,' said Jean. 'I didn't think they'd do it to someone that high up.'

At the urging of the now delirious crowd, the Royal Barber applied foam to the officer's hair, then took a pair of oversized scissors and hacked at it. Then his mouth was cranked open by gleeful men and he was fed what Neptune announced as 'seafarer's medicine'. As he retched and spluttered, he was ducked, emerging twice to express his outrage.

'I really can't believe they're meant to do that,' said Avice fizzing with excitement. 'I'm sure someone so high up isn't meant to be included.' Then she took on the stillness of a gun dog scenting sport. 'Oh, my goodness! That's Irene Carter!'

Neptune's court—and her companions—forgotten, she stood up and pushed her way through the jeering crowd. 'Irene! Irene! It's Avice!'

'Do you think the captain will report them for it?' Jean said, wide-eyed, as the spluttering victim was unstrapped from the ducking chair.

'I've no idea,' said Margaret. She scanned the deck for Frances and spotted the captain. It was hard to tell from that distance, and with so many people moving around, but she could have sworn he was laughing.

Frances was talking about life on board a hospital ship. As her quiet, precise voice detailed some of the injuries she had treated when positioned off the Solomon Islands, Margaret thought of home. The temperature had not cooled as much as it had on previous evenings, and a balminess in the air reminded her of sitting out on the front porch in summer, bare feet warm against the rough boards.

She tried to imagine what her brothers would be doing that night. She thought of Letty. Of the brief, blushing youthfulness of her; that strange almost-prettiness that beset her features when she had dared briefly to believe in a future with Murray Donleavy. She pushed away the memory, feeling darkly ashamed.

Suddenly she became aware of what Frances was telling her. She stopped. Got Frances to repeat herself. 'Are you sure? He knows?'

Frances's hands were thrust deep into her pockets. 'That's what he said. He asked whose she was.'

'So what did you say?'

'I didn't say anything.'

'What do you mean, you didn't say anything?'

'I didn't say anything. I shut the door.'

They fell back against the pipe-lined wall as two officers walked past. Margaret waited until they were far down the gangway before she spoke again. 'He told you he knew about the dog and you didn't ask him whether he was going to tell on us?'

'Well, he hasn't told on us yet, has he?'

'But we don't know what he's going to do.' Frances's jaw, Margaret realised, was peculiarly set.

'I just . . . I didn't want to get into a discussion about it.'

'Why not?' Margaret asked incredulously.

'I didn't want him to get any ideas . . .'

'Ideas? About what?'

Frances managed to look furious and defensive at once. 'I didn't want him to think he could use the dog as a bargaining ploy. I thought he might want something . . . in return.'

Margaret shook her head in incomprehension. 'Jeez, Frances. You've got a strange view of how people go about things.'

They had arrived at their cabin. Margaret was trying to think whether there had been some hidden meaning in the way the marine had waved to them but she was distracted by the sight of a girl running up the passageway. She skidded to a halt when she reached them, and scanned their door. 'You live here? 3G?' she panted.

'Yeah.' Margaret shrugged. 'So?'

'You know a girl called Jean?' she asked, still breathless. And when they nodded: 'You might want to get downstairs. She's got herself into a bit of trouble.'

'Where?' said Margaret.

'Seamen's mess. E Deck. Go left by the second flight of stairs. It's the blue door near the fire extinguisher. You'll have to hurry.'

'I'll go,' said Frances to Margaret. 'I'll be faster. You catch me up.' She slipped off her shoes, then sprinted down the passageway, her long thin legs flying up behind her as she went.

There were all manner of hardships one could endure, Avice thought, if one happened to be in the right company. Since she had found Irene Carter that afternoon, and had been invited to join her and her friends

79

for tea, then a lecture and finally supper, she had forgotten not only the time but how much she detested the old ship.

Irene Carter's father owned Melbourne's most prominent tennis club. She was married to a sublieutenant just returned from the Adriatic; the son of (here Avice paused for breath) someone high up in the Foreign Office. Irene Carter was most definitely the right sort. And she had determined to surround herself only with other girls of the right sort.

'Of course, you know what happened to Lolicia Tarrant, don't you?' Irene was saying, her arm lightly linked through Avice's as they tripped down the steps into the main hangar.

'No.'

'Well, you know she was engaged to that pilot? The one with the . . . unfortunate moustache? No? Well . . . he wasn't five weeks in Malaya when she took up with an American soldier.'

'So what happened?' Avice was wide-eyed.

'Well, her fiancé came back and was not best pleased to find Lolly promenading around with this GI, as you can imagine. Let's just say it was more than the Brisbane line he'd been holding.'

'Oh,' said Avice.

'And nor was Lolly's father best pleased when he found out. The GI had let all his friends know, in graphic detail, what he'd been up to with Lolly. And his commanding officer apparently got the wrong end of the stick and sent Lolly's father a letter, suggesting he keep better watch on his daughter. Her fiancé wants nothing to do with her, of course.'

'Oh my goodness! Is she all right?'

'I don't know,' said Irene.

'I thought you and she were friends,' said Avice.

'Now?' Irene pulled a face and she shook her head. There was a long silence. 'So,' she continued, 'are you going to enter for Queen of the *Victoria*? They're having a Miss Lovely Legs contest next week.'

They were halfway along the hangar deck when they came across Margaret. She was leaning against a notice board, one hand above her head, palm down, as if to support herself.

'Are you all right?' said Avice, paralysed with the fear that the farm girl was about to give birth. She would have to get involved. Goodness only knew what Irene would think.

'Stitch,' said Margaret, through gritted teeth.

Avice felt almost faint with relief.

'Would you like some help getting back to your cabin?' asked Irene, courteously.

'No.' Margaret looked at Avice, then at her friend. Her nose, Avice noticed, had reddened with the sun. 'I've got to go downstairs. Jean's got herself involved in a little . . . episode.'

'She shares our cabin,' Avice explained.

Irene looked into Margaret's flushed face. 'Well, you can't possibly go and get your friend like that,' she said. 'Not down all those stairs. We'll come with you.'

Avice began to remonstrate: 'No, I don't think we should. I mean—'

But Irene had already slid her arm from Avice's and was reaching for Margaret. 'Better? Come on, take my arm. We'll have a little adventure.'

Come on, girls, she had said. Let's go and rescue a damsel in distress. And Avice heard Jean's bawdy laugh in her ears and watched Irene—her only lifeline to a proper social life during this voyage—prepare to float away from her on a mist of disapproval.

But Jean, when they found her, was not laughing. She wasn't even standing. They saw her legs before they saw her, emerging awkwardly from behind a stack of canisters, her shoes, half on her feet, pointing towards each other. As they came closer their voices stilled as they took in the tableau. They could see enough of her top half to gather that she was drunk. Drunk enough not to care that her blouse was unbuttoned.

Frances stood over her, her usually pale, grave face flushed and animated, her hair somehow uncoiling from its usually severe pinning. A man, possibly a seaman, equally drunk, his flies undone, was reeling away from her, clutching his shoulder. As the new arrivals stared in mute, shocked horror, Jean stirred, muttered something, her hair in dark, sweaty fronds over her face. Amid the shocked silence, Margaret knelt down and tried to pull Jean's skirt over those pale thighs.

'You bastard,' Frances screamed at the man. They could see she was holding a large spanner in her hand. He moved and her arm came down, the spanner connecting with his shoulder in an audible crack. As he ducked away, the blows rained down on him with the relentless, manic force of a jackhammer. As one hit the side of his head, a fine arc of blood spattered.

Before they had a chance to digest this scene, to let its ramifications sink in, Dennis Tims was running towards them, his taut bulk bringing renewed threat, followed by another man. 'What the hell's going on?' he shouted. 'Mikey said— Oh Jesus,' he said, taking in Frances, the bleeding man's trousers, Jean on the floor, now supported by Margaret. 'Oh, Thompson, you bloody—' He grabbed at Frances, who tried to shake him off, her face contorted.

'All right, girl,' he said. 'All right now.' As his mate pulled the man away from Frances, Tims closed his forearms around her collarbone and pulled her back, until the spanner was waving futilely in the air.

Tims's mate released the man who, too shocked or perhaps too inebriated to react, fell like a stone.

Irene shrieked.

Tims let go of Frances and shoved the man onto his side. He was checking the head wound, muttering something under his breath.

Margaret, behind the men, had begun to haul Jean away.

Frances was shaking convulsively.

'We should call someone,' said Avice to Irene.

'I don't . . . I . . .'

It was then that they caught sight of the women's officer running towards them, her feet echoing on the floor. 'What is going on here?'

Tims straightened up and looked at Margaret, his eyes wide and strained. He shook his head, as if to say something, to apologise perhaps. And then the woman was there, her eyes darting between them, a regulatory air emanating from her like a bad perfume.

'What is going on here?' she said again.

'Bit of an accident,' said Tims, wiping bloodied hands on his trousers. He did not look at the woman. 'We've just been sorting it out.'

The officer looked from his hands to Avice, to Margaret. 'What are you girls doing down here?'

She waited for an answer. No one spoke. Beside her, Avice realised, Irene's hand was pressed to her chest, clutching a handkerchief, in the manner of a consumptive heroine.

When she turned back Tims and his mate had disappeared. The injured man sat lopsidedly on the floor, his knees drawn up to his chest.

'You do know there are grave penalties for being in the men's area?'

There was a heavy silence. The officer bent down, took in the state of the man, the fact that the other had vanished. Then she saw Jean. 'Oh, my goodness. Please don't tell me this is what I think it is.'

'It's not,' said Margaret.

The woman's eyes moved to her. 'Oh, my goodness,' she said again. 'The captain will have to be informed.'

'Why? It wasn't us.' Avice had yelled to be heard over the engines. 'We only came to get Jean.'

'Avice!' Frances stood between the woman and Jean's prostrate form. 'Leave it to us. We'll get her back to her room.'

'I can't do that. I've been told to report any parties, any drinking, any misdemeanours. I'll need all your names.'

'But it wasn't us!' said Avice, with a glance at Irene. 'It's only Jean who's disgraced herself!'

'Jean?'

'Jean Castleforth,' said Avice, desperately. 'We really are nothing to do with it. We just came down because we heard she was in trouble.'

'Jean Castleforth,' said the woman. 'And your name?'

'I said we'll take her to her room,' interrupted Frances. 'I'm a nurse. I'll look after her.'

'You're not suggesting I ignore this? Look at her!' The woman wrinkled her nostrils against the smell of alcohol on Jean's breath.

'She's sixteen years old,' Frances said. 'They've obviously got her drunk and . . . abused her. You think she should lose her reputation, possibly her husband, because of this? You can't ruin the girl's life because of one drunken moment!'

It was impossible to say why Frances, flushed and electric, was standing over the officer, her arm raised, but Margaret was already pulling her back. 'Frances,' she was murmuring, 'calm down. You're not helping her. You hear me? You've got to back off.'

Frances blinked several times, then let out a deep, shuddering breath. 'She's just a kid.'

But the officer had turned and was walking briskly, with purpose, down the passageway.

Eighteen days

Henry Nicol did not like the hour between five and six in the morning. Once he had enjoyed the early watch, when the seas had been new and magical to him, when, unused to living in such close quarters with other men, he had relished the quietest time aboard ship.

Later, when he had been home on leave and the children were babies, one or both would inevitably wake at this time, and he would hear his wife slide heavily out of bed, half seeing, if he chose to open an eye, her hand reaching for her dressing gown. He would turn over, pinned to his pillow by the familiar mix of guilt and impatience, aware even in half-sleep, of his own failure to feel what he should for the woman padding across the linoleum: gratitude, desire, even love.

For some time now 0500 hours had become not the herald of a new dawn but a bald figure of timing for conversion: in America, it would be five o'clock the previous evening. Now there would be no more thinking of the children in the present tense, imagining, as he sometimes did, They'll be having breakfast. They'll be brushing their teeth. Now they might be outside, playing with a ball.

Some other man's hands throwing the ball.

On the other side of the steel door a woman murmured in sleep, her voice rising as if in a question. Then silence.

Nicol stared at his watch, adjusted the previous day as they entered another time zone. My hours are speeding towards nothing, he thought. No home, no sons, no heroic return. Nicol leaned back, trying to dislodge the huge weight that had settled upon him, willing the last hour to pass faster. Willing the dawn to come.

Tims, a broad, taut figure, stood beside Nicol on the hangar deck. He was subdued. When he spoke, his words were careful and considered. There might be a bit of bad blood between the seamen and the stokers, he said. There had been an incident with a woman a couple of nights ago. Things, he said, had got a little out of hand.

Such a bald admission was out of character. At first Nicol wondered if he was asking him obliquely to make an arrest. But before he had a chance to ask why, Tims spoke again: 'It's your lot who were involved.'

Your lot. Nicol felt a flush of incomprehension that the reserved bride who had chatted with him that evening might have been the cause of some kind of drunken fracas. That was women for you, he thought bitterly. Unable to stay faithful, sober, even for a six-week voyage.

Then Tims, a bloodsoaked bandage visible round his knuckles, explained further. It had not been the tall girl, Frances, but the silly young girl. The one who was always giggling. Jean.

'I need you to do us a favour, Marine. I can't go along there, obviously.' Here Tims jerked a thumb towards the cabins. 'Just make sure Maggie's all right, will you? The one who's expecting. She's a nice girl, and she was a bit shocked. I don't like to think of her being troubled. And if anyone says anything, the girls were in their bunks all night. Right?'

It was not the norm for a marine to be addressed in such a way by a stoker. But Nicol suspected this unusual confidence was prompted by genuine concern, and he let it go. 'No problem,' he said.

Now he thought back, there had been a change in atmosphere that evening. From the other side of the door he had heard urgent whispering, and at one point, there had been the sound of crying, an argument.

'I tell you,' Tims was saying. 'Thompson's lucky I didn't get to that spanner first.'

'Spanner?' He glanced behind him.

'One of the girls had it. The tall one. By all accounts it was her who got the bastard off. Gave him a crack on the shoulder, then tried to stove his head in for good measure.' Tims laughed humourlessly. 'Anyway, tell

Mags I'm sorry. If I'd got to her little mate first . . . well, it wouldn't have happened.'

'Where's Thompson now?' said Nicol. 'Shouldn't we be taking him in?'

'Think about it, Nicol. If we haul him in for what he's done, the girl gets done too, right? The WSO who came down didn't have a clue, only got Jean's name. But little Jean's not going to tell the truth about what went on. Not if she wants to get to Blighty and her old man without a fuss. Besides, I am sure you don't want a fuss made about your girls getting into trouble. Can't look good, can it? Them all being down in the engine rooms that close to the start of your watch . . .' He kept his voice soft, at odds with the implied threat of his words. 'I'm just letting you know, out of courtesy, that me and the boys will deal with Thompson, even if we have to wait till we're ashore.'

'It'll get out,' said Nicol. 'You know it will.'

Tims glanced behind him. When he turned back, his eyes held something that made Nicol feel vague pity for the offender. 'Not if everyone keeps their gobs shut it won't.'

Margaret leaned over the rail as far as her belly would allow, and hauled up the wicker basket. Below her, in the glinting waters, lithe brown boys dived over the sides of their small craft for coins that the sailors threw from the deck. Alongside them slim canoes wobbled under the movements of thin, tanned men holding armfuls of trinkets. The port of Colombo, Ceylon, shimmered in the heat, punctuated by the occasional tall building and set behind with dense forest.

There had been several reported cases of smallpox and it had been announced earlier that it was not considered wise for the women to go ashore. Here, anchored in the clear blue waters several hundred feet from shore, was as close as they were going to get to Ceylon.

Margaret, who had spent days anticipating the feel of solid earth under her feet, had been furious. 'They're still going to allow the men ashore so it's OK for us to catch the bloody smallpox off our own.' She had almost wept with the unfairness of it.

'I suppose it's because the men are inoculated,' said Frances. Margaret chose not to hear her.

Perhaps in consolation, one of the storemen had lent them a cable to which he had attached a basket. They were to lower it and pull it up when it was full, so they could examine the goods at their leisure.

'This batch looks good, girls. Get your purses ready.'

Margaret, puffing with exertion, brought the basket carefully over the rail, then placed it on the floor of the gun turret where they were seated.

She rummaged through, holding up beads, strings of shell and coral that rippled through her fingers. 'Look, Jean. This would go well with your blue dress. See how the mother-of-pearl catches the light.'

'Nice,' said Jean. She lit another cigarette, her shoulders hunched around her ears as if she were cold, despite the heat.

'We should get something for poor Avice. Might make her feel better.' She heard her voice, determinedly cheerful, and in the answering silence the suggestion that Frances might not want Avice to feel better.

There had been an argument between the two after they had returned to the cabin the previous night. Frances, her normal reserve dissolved, had screamed at Avice that she was selfish, a traitor. Avice, flushed with guilt, had retorted that she couldn't see why she should jeopardise her future because Jean had the morals of an alleycat. They would have found out her name in the end.

The voices of the traders floated up to them: 'Mrs Melbourne! Mrs Sydney!' They gestured prices with their fingers. In the midst of their boats, a small boy's head broke through the surface of the water. He was grinning as he held aloft something metallic. Then he looked closely at it and hurled it at the ship. It pinged off the side like a bullet.

'What's that all about?' said Margaret, peering down.

'The sailors throw them old nuts and dowels. They let them dive thinking they're coins,' said Frances. 'Their idea of fun.' She stopped. They had new views on sailors' ideas of fun.

But Jean didn't appear to have heard. She had been examining a little pearl necklace and now stuffed it into her pocket.

'Want me to get that for you?' said Margaret. 'I don't mind if you forgot your purse.'

Jean's eyes were still pink-rimmed. 'Nah,' she said. 'I'm not paying. More fool them for sending it up.'

There was a brief silence. Then, wordlessly, Margaret got up, removed a few coins from her purse and lowered them, with the remaining trinkets, to the boat below. Then, perhaps to comfort herself as much as the younger girl, she said to Jean, 'Did I ever tell you how Joe proposed?'

She sat down, nudged her. 'This'll make you laugh. He'd already decided he wanted to ask me. He'd got Dad's permission. And he'd bought a ring. Anyway, he decides Wednesday's the day—it's his last but one day before the end of his shore leave, and he turns up, nervous, his boots shining like mirrors and his hair slicked. He's got it all planned in his head. He's going to go down on one knee and make the one romantic gesture of his life.'

'Wasted on you,' said Frances.

'Well, he knows that now.' Margaret grinned. 'So, anyway, he gets to ours, and he knocks on the door, and just as he's stepping in, Dad runs in, yelling that the cows have got out. He grabs Joe and says, "Come on, lad. Look alive," and hauls him out to the back.'

Margaret leaned back. 'Well,' she said, 'it was chaos. There's around forty of them out and they've brought down one of the fences, and there's two tearing up what's left of Mum's garden, so Dad's beating them with a stick, tears falling down his face, trying to prop up Mum's flowers. There's Colm racing down the track in the truck, horn blaring, trying to head off the ones stampeding towards the road. Liam's on one of the horses, acting like John Wayne. And then there's me and Joe trying to corner the rest of them in the shed.'

She looked around the faces opposite her. 'Ever seen a frightened cow, girls?' She lowered her voice. 'They shit like you've never seen. Poor old Joe is covered with it, top to toe, everything.'

'How disgusting,' said Jean, raising a small smile.

'And then, to add insult to injury, our biggest girl decides to make a break for it, and she goes straight over him. Bam.' She mimed falling backward to the ground.

Even Margaret, supposedly immune to the farmyard smell, had held her nose when she helped him get up, tried to wipe him down. She had thought he was swearing, but eventually realised he was saying, 'The ring, the ring.' The two of them had spent almost half an hour on their hands and knees in the cowshed, trying to find Joe's token of everlasting devotion in the slurry.

'And you—you still wear it?'

'Cow dung included. To me that's part of the romance.' Then, as Jean's hand went to her mouth, 'Oh, Jean! Of course I washed it before I put it on. I had to do the same for Joe. My first evening as his fiancée was spent washing and ironing his uniform.'

'Stan asked me while we were at a dance,' said Jean. 'I reckon I was the youngest there—I was still fifteen. But it was lovely. I was wearing a blue shantung silk two-piece, it belonged to my friend Polly, and he said I was the most beautiful girl in the room. When they struck up with "You Made Me Love You" he turned to his mate and said, "This is the girl I'm going to marry. You hear that?" And then he said it louder. And I made out I was dead embarrassed but, to be honest, I really liked it.'

'I'm sure you did,' said Frances, smiling.

'He was the first person to tell me he loved me.' Her eyes glittered with tears. 'No one ever told me that. Not my mum. Never even met my dad.' She pushed her hair off her face. 'Stan's the best man I ever met.'

They had sat, in near silence, for almost half an hour more. As the heat grew fiercer, and the sun moved across, taking their vantage point out of the shade, Margaret thought about moving. But no entertainments had been planned for the day, owing to the former expectation that they would be ashore, and the thought of them bickering with each other in the little dormitory was unbearable.

She was squinting listlessly at a small propeller craft humming towards them, the naval cap of its skipper, the clumsy grey shapes on board, watching them become increasingly distinct at it drew closer, when 'Girls!' she yelled. 'It's the post! We've got post!'

An hour later, they sat in the canteen as a Red Cross officer collected all mail to be sent and distributed small bundles of letters from a trestle table at the end. The announcement of each name was greeted with squeals from the recipient and her friends. Around them the windows were propped open to allow the sea breezes to penetrate the room.

Jean had been among the first called to the table: her impressive seven letters from Stan had restored some of her vitality. She had handed them to Frances, who read them aloud in her low, sonorous voice, while Jean puffed nervously at a cigarette. 'Did you hear that?' she kept interrupting. 'My name tattooed on his right arm. In two colours!'

Margaret and Frances had exchanged a glance. 'And,' Frances continued, 'he's won four pounds in a boxing match. He says the other fellow's idea of boxing involved trying to block Stan's punches with his nose.'

'Hear that?' Jean nudged Margaret. 'Trying to block punches with his nose!' If her laughter was a little too high to suggest genuine mirth, no one said anything. It was enough that she was laughing at all.

Later Frances would confide that she had left out several paragraphs: those that warned Jean to 'behave herself', and the story of a sweetheart deserted by one of his friends once he heard she had been 'playing fast and loose'.

'Margaret O'Brien?'

Margaret was out of her chair with a speed that belied her cumbersome frame. Breathless, she launched herself at the sheaf of letters proffered towards her, and returned, glowing and triumphant, her failure to get ashore forgotten. She wondered whether she could go to the cabin and read them in private without causing offence. But just as she was about to ask, she heard a chair scrape back, and looked up from the envelopes to see Avice seat herself carefully in front of them.

There was a brief pause. Margaret, a little taken aback that Avice had chosen to seat herself among them after the previous evening's quarrel, wondered if she might be about to apologise.

'I've got news,' Avice said.

'So have I,' said Jean. 'Look. Seven letters. Seven!'

'No,' said Avice. She had a contained smile on her face, as if she harboured some great secret. 'I have real news,' she said, her chin jutting out. 'I'm expecting.'

There was a stunned silence.

'Expecting what?' said Jean.

'A baby, of course. I've been to the doctor.'

'Are you sure?' said Frances. 'Dr Duxbury doesn't strike me as . . . the most reliable . . .'

'Oh, so nurses know more than doctors now, do they?'

'No, I'm just—'

'Dr Duxbury has taken a blood test, but in the meantime he asked me lots of questions and did an examination. He's pretty certain.'

'I guess it makes sense,' said Margaret, 'now I think about it.'

Avice couldn't retain her composure. Her face lit up, cheeks pink with excitement. 'A baby! Can you imagine? I knew I couldn't be seasick. I've been yachting loads of times and that didn't make me ill. Margaret, you must tell me everything I need to buy. I shall have to get Mummy to send over all sorts of things.'

Margaret stood up and reached over the table to hug her. 'Avice,' she said, 'it's great news. Congratulations.'

'Strewth,' said Jean, wide-eyed. 'So all that seasickness was really you expecting?' She looked genuinely pleased. Frances hasn't told her of Avice's betrayal, Margaret thought, and felt suddenly sad for her.

'He thinks I'm already nine or ten weeks along. I was rather shocked when he told me. But I'm so excited. Ian's going to be thrilled.'

Margaret marvelled at Avice's ability to wipe out the events of the previous evening.

'Stan got a tattoo of my name,' Jean told her, but Avice didn't hear.

'I think I shall put in a special request to the captain to wire my family and tell them the news. I don't think I can bear to wait until we reach England.' Her name, called in clipped tones, echoed through the canteen. 'Letters!' she said, standing. 'Letters! In all the excitement I hadn't even thought—oh, you two have got yours.' She looked at Frances, as if suddenly remembering, and said nothing.

'Congratulations,' said Frances. She didn't look at Avice.

Frances's name was called an hour later; it was almost the last, and cut across the nearly empty canteen. Margaret had thought several times about leaving them all so that she could drink in Joe's words in private, but there was such bad blood between the other girls now, and Jean was still so fragile, that she felt obliged to wait.

Avice had received two letters from her family, and two very old ones from Ian, sent only days after he had left Sydney. 'Look at the date on them,' she had said crossly. 'Ian's are nearly six weeks old. Honestly, you'd think the least the navy could do is make sure we get our letters on time. It's really not on. I should have had lots more by now.'

'I think you were just unlucky, Avice,' said Margaret, absently. She had reread Joe's first letter several times now. He had numbered them thoughtfully so that she could read them in the correct order. She sneaked a look at Jean, who was gazing intently at Stan's letters. 'Want me to teach you?' she asked. 'While we're on board? Bet we could have you reading by the time we disembark.'

'Really?'

'Nothing to it,' said Margaret. 'An hour or two a day and you'll be a regular bookworm.'

'Stan doesn't know . . . about the reading. I always got my mate Nancy to write letters for me, see? But then I remembered when I came aboard that if anyone else writes them it'll be in different handwriting.'

'All the more reason to get you started,' said Margaret. 'You'll be able to write your own. And I bet you Stan won't know any different. Here, give us an envelope. I'll write out your ABCs.'

Frances had arrived back at the table. Avice glanced up from her letters at Frances's hand. 'Only one?' she said loudly. Frances was unperturbed. 'It's from one of my old patients,' she said, with shy pleasure. 'He's home and walking again.'

'How lovely,' said Margaret, patting her arm.

Having failed to elicit a reply from you to any of my correspondence, I am writing out of courtesy to let you know that I have applied for a divorce, on grounds of three years' desertion. While you and I know this might not be quite correct, I am hoping you will not contest. Anton is paying for the children's and my passage to America, so that we can join him there. We leave Southampton on the 25th. I would have liked us to do this in a civilised manner, for the children's sake as much as anything, but you are obviously determined to show me the same lack of concern as you have displayed the whole time you have been gone.

Where is your humanity? Perhaps there is nothing left of you underneath your rules and regulations. I know things must have been hard for you. I know you have seen and coped with no end of horrors. But we, here, are living. We would have been your lifeline if you had let us.

I feel no guilt in choosing life, a better life, for me and my children . . .

'What's the matter, Nicol? You look a bit pale. Got a Not Wanted Don't Come?' Jones-the-Welsh was lying on his hammock, flicking through a dozen or so letters.

Nicol stared, unseeing, at his. Crumpled it into his pocket. 'No,' he said, then coughed to stop his voice cracking. 'Just news from home.'

A few of the men around him exchanged glances.

'No one ill?' said Jones.

'No,' said Nicol. His tone halted further enquiries.

'Well, you look terrible. Working middle watch does that to you, doesn't it, lads? You know what you need, man?' Here he punched Nicol's arm. 'You're off tonight, right? Come ashore with us.'

'Ah . . . I think I'll just get some sleep.'

'Sorry, man, can't have it. Get a couple of hours' kip now. Then you're coming out with us. And we're going to get absolutely pissed.'

They had eaten together—less, Margaret suspected, out of any great desire on Avice's part to share her meals with them, but because Irene and her friends had made it clear, by their whispers and cold stares, that she was no longer welcome in their set.

Avice had smoothed her hair and sat down opposite Margaret. 'You know,' she said lightly, 'I've just remembered what I couldn't stand about that Irene Carter. She's terribly rude. I can't imagine what I ever saw in her.'

'It's nice for us all to eat together for a change,' Margaret said equably, ignoring Frances's silence.

'Nice not to have Avice puking anyway,' said Jean.

'Did they make a mistake with your post, Frances,' said Avice, 'or did you really get just one letter?'

'Do you know what, Avice?' said Margaret, loudly, pushing away her plate. 'We had a chat earlier about how our husbands proposed to us. I bet you'd love to tell us how Ian proposed to you, wouldn't you?'

Margaret caught Frances's look. It might have been of gratitude or something else entirely.

'Have I not told you? Really? Oh, it was the best day of my life. Well, next to our wedding, of course. That's always a girl's best day, isn't it? And in our case we couldn't have the kind of wedding I might normally have expected—with my family's position in society and all . . . No, it had to be a bit more intimate. But, oh, Ian's proposal. Oh, yes . . .' She closed her eyes. 'I knew he was the one as soon as I saw him. He's the most romantic man alive. I didn't think I'd marry into the services. I wasn't one of those uniform-hunters, always fluttering her eyelashes at anything in whites. But I saw him at one of the tea dances and that was it. I knew I had to be Mrs Radley.'

'So what did he do?' said Jean, lighting a cigarette.

'Well, we knew we loved each other—he told me he was obsessed with me at one point—can you imagine?—but he was worried about whether I could cope with being a services wife. I mean, what with all the separations and insecurity . . . He told me he didn't know if it was fair to put me through that. But I told him, "I may look like a delicate flower"—that's what my father used to call me, his little jasmine blossom—"but I'm actually quite strong and I'm very determined." And I think even Ian recognised that in the end.'

'So, what happened?' said Margaret, sucking her teaspoon.

'Well, we were both in agony. Daddy wanted us to wait. And Ian didn't want to upset him, so he said he would. But I couldn't bear the thought of us leaving each other simply "engaged".'

'Worried he'd bugger off with someone else?' said Jean.

'So he got permission from his commander and we just ran off and got married in front of a justice of the peace. It was terribly romantic.'

'What a lovely story, Avice,' said Margaret.

'What about your bloke, Frances?' Jean rested her chin on her hands, her head tilted to one side. 'How did he propose?'

Frances began gathering plates. 'Oh, it's not very interesting.'

'I'm sure we'd be fascinated,' said Avice.

Frances gave her a hard look, but after a moment's hesitation, told them in quiet, unemotional tones. She had met him in Malaya while she had been nursing. Private Engineer Alfred 'Chalkie' Mackenzie, twenty-eight years old. From a town called Cheltenham. He had shrapnel wounds, which had become infected because of the tropical humidity. She had nursed him and, over the weeks, he had grown fond of her.

'So, when did he ask you?' said Jean. Above her, the neon lights came on abruptly, illuminating the women's faces. Outside it was almost dark.

'Well . . . he asked me lots of times, actually. There wasn't really one occasion. I think it was about sixteen before I agreed.'

'Sixteen times!' said Avice. It was as if she couldn't believe Frances could provoke such persistence.

'What made you say yes?' said Margaret. 'In the end, I mean.'

'What made him keep asking?' muttered Avice.

But Frances stood up and glanced at her watch. 'Goodness, Maggie! Look at the time. That dog of yours will be desperate for her walk.'

'Oh, darn. You're right. Better get back downstairs,' said Margaret. With a nod to the others, she and Frances half ran towards the cabin.

At some point in the evening he had lost his watch, and no longer had any idea what time it was. Men catcalled or fought incompetently in the street outside the bar. Girls disappeared upstairs, came down again and chattered or squabbled with their colleagues. Outside, the neon bar sign cast the blue light of a cold grey dawn across the entrance.

Across the room, half lying on a banquette, Jones-the-Welsh was placing cigarettes in a girl's mouth and laughing as she coughed them out again. 'Don't inhale so much,' he was saying, as she hit him playfully with a slim hand. He caught Nicol watching him. 'Ah . . . no . . . Don't tell me you like Annie here too?' he called.

Nicol tried to formulate some reply, but it turned to powder in his mouth.

'To wives and sweethearts,' Jones-the-Welsh announced, his drink aloft. 'May they never meet.'

Nicol raised his glass to his mate and took a slug.

A girl in a green dress was tugging his sleeve. She closed her hand round his with the proprietorial confidence of a child and led him up the stairs. He had to let go of her to negotiate them, clutching the banister as the wooden steps rose and fell beneath his feet like a deck in a storm.

The door of the room was paper light in his hand; the fragility of the dividing walls apparent in the noises he could hear from the next room.

'Nice time, uh?' The girl followed his gaze and giggled.

He felt suddenly weary, and seated himself heavily on the side of the bed, watching as she undid her dress. The knobs of her spine were distinct under her pale skin.

The thin coverlet was immaculately laundered. Beside it, on a rickety table, stood a bottle with several blossoms. These two domestic details made his eyes fill with tears. 'I'm sorry,' he said. 'I don't think—'

She turned, and he caught something raw in her expression. 'Yes, yes,' she said, her smile rapidly in place again. 'I make you happy man.'

'I'm sorry,' he said.

She clasped his hand then. 'You wait little while,' she pleaded.

He realised then that something weary and resigned in her eyes made her seem older than she was. Now that he looked, her nails were bitten as his sister's once were. Nicol closed his eyes, feeling ashamed to have been complicit in such corruption. This is what war does, he said silently.

He felt her weight upon him then, light hands stroking his face.

'Please you wait little while,' whispered the voice in his ear. He could smell her perfume, something heavy and cloying, at odds with her youth, the insubstantial nature of her frame.

She had reached round his neck, was pulling him down.

'There's nothing left in me,' he said. 'I'm empty.'

Then, as she lay against him, her dark eyes searching his for some sign of his intention, he lay back on the pillow. He took her hand. 'You tell me something,' he said. He could feel her breath on his neck, careful, expectant, and realised he was drifting towards sleep. 'What time is it in America?'

Twenty-one days

It had never happened before. She had never meant it to happen at all. But Frances was forced to concede that she was falling in love.

Every evening she would tell herself that she should stay away, that it would do her no good, that by her actions she was putting her passage in danger. And in spite of that, every evening, with the minimum explanation to her cabin mates, she found herself disappearing through the metal door. With a furtive glance towards each end of the gangway, she would tread swiftly past the other cabins, lightly up the stairs and along the upper length of the hangar deck until she reached the heavy steel hatch that opened out onto the flight deck.

It was the ship she loved: the size of it, like a leviathan, propelled by an epic strength through the roughest seas. She loved the scars, the streaks of rust that, despite years of painting and repainting, were visible on her skin. She loved the infinite space visible all around her, the sense of possibility that the ship bestowed on her.

If it wasn't too cold at night, she would sit on the flight deck for hours, glancing up occasionally to make sure she couldn't be seen by whoever was on watch at the bridge. Now, in the increasing heat, it offered sweet relief; she would locate her favoured spot under the aircraft and enjoy in solitude the soft breezes and the sound of the waves rushing beneath. She liked the way you could see the sky's mood changing miles away, hear a distant storm. And there were the sunsets, the primeval oranges and blues that bled into the edge of the earth until you could no longer see where the sky ended and the sea began.

At night, alone, she could just sit and be; a tiny, meaningless nothing amid the sky, the sea and the stars.

'So, how's your ship of brides?'

The warship *Alexandra* was the first British vessel the *Victoria* had passed within radio distance since they had left Sydney. But Highfield had taken Captain Edward Baxter's call with less enthusiasm than he might have done in other circumstances, having something of an inkling as to how the exchange would run.

'I think the question all the chaps want an answer to is how's your water consumption?'

'Fine,' said Highfield, thinking back to that morning's report. They had had some trouble with one of the desalination units, but the chief engineer had told him they were now running as normal.

Baxter was talking too loudly, as if conscious that he was listened to by other people at his end. 'It's just that we hear on the grapevine you've set up a hair salon, and we were wondering how you looked after a shampoo and set . . .' He guffawed heartily, and Highfield thought he heard an echoing laugh behind him.

He was alone in the meteorological office, high above the shimmering deck, and his leg had throbbed steadily all day. He had felt a vague sense of betrayal when it started; for days it had given him hardly any trouble.

'I spoke to Dobson before they put me through to you. He says those Aussie girls are giving you all a run for your money. Can't say I envy you, old man. Load of women littering up the place with their washing, wandering around in their next-to-nothings, distracting the men.'

There had been a noticeable lightening in the way senior naval personnel talked to each other since the end of the war. Highfield, not for the first time, found himself hankering after the old ways. 'My men are conducting themselves properly.'

'It's not the men's behaviour I'm thinking of, George. I've heard about these colonial girls. Not quite the same reserve as their British sisters. . .'

'These girls are fine. Everything's under control.' He thought uncomfortably of the incident the women's service officer had reported the previous week. Baxter and his like would know soon enough.

'Yes, well . . . we've all had a bit of a chuckle at the thought of you and the hair salon. Still . . . it's nice to know there's a use for the old girl after she retires. You could set up the world's first mobile beauty parlour.'

Highfield's attention snapped away from his leg. 'Retires?'

'You know, when she's decommissioned.'

'The *Victoria's* being decommissioned?'

There was a brief silence. 'I thought you knew, old man. She's done. When the engineers were all over her in Woolloomooloo they decided it wasn't worth patching her up again. She's finished when you get back to Blighty. They're going to concentrate on a new class of carrier now that the war's over. Not that it's going to affect you, eh?'

Highfield sat down. Around him, the various dials and maps of the meteorological office stared back mutely, oblivious of their imminent redundancy. So, he told the ship silently, you and me both.

'But jesting aside, how are you, old boy? Heard you took a knock with *Indomitable*. You had a few people worried.'

'I'm fine.'

'Of course, of course. Shame, though. Young Hart served with me a couple of years ago. Stood out from the crowd.'

'Yes. Yes, he did.'

'Met his wife once, when we were out in Singapore. I seem to recall she had just had twins. Which rather brings me to my reason for calling. London wired me this morning. They tell me you might have a few brides on board who are married to my men. We're going to be along-side for a day or two and London thought it would be a nice gesture if we allowed them radio contact. What do you think?'

'I don't know . . .'

'Well, don't decide just yet. As I understand it, there's only a handful of them. But it would mean a lot to my boys.'

Below him, on deck, two young women strolled towards the deck canteen, the setting sun bouncing off their set, shining hair. They ducked together under the wing of one of the aircraft. Behind them, the other fighter planes stretched across the deck, their smooth surfaces radiating heat. As redundant as the rest of the ship.

'Highfield?'

'Get your man to speak to my number one,' Highfield said, eyes still fixed on the deck below. 'We'll send over a passenger list and you can let me know who your boys want to speak to. We'll organise something.'

He put down his headphones. Then he turned to the radio operator. 'Get me the commander-in-chief of the British Pacific Fleet.'

The cabin had been empty that evening; Avice was at a fabric-flower-making session, which apparently counted towards the Queen of the *Victoria* contest. Having decided Irene Carter was now her sworn enemy, she was intent on beating her to the title.

Jean, having whined about the oppressive heat, had tired of her read-ing lesson and was watching a film with two brides from the dormitory above theirs.

Frances, having enjoyed an hour's solitude, was feeling restless in the airless confines of the dormitory. She went to the bathroom and splashed her face several times with cold water. She returned to the dor-mitory, but was about to go up to the flight deck when Margaret burst in, flushed and breathless. 'Ohmygoodness,' she was saying, one plump hand at her throat. 'Ohmygoodness.'

'Are you all right?' Frances leapt towards her.

Margaret mopped a faint sheen from her face. A heat rash had spread from her chest to her neck. She sat down heavily on her bunk.

'Margaret?'

'I've been summoned to the radio room. You'll never guess—I'm to speak to Joe!'

'*What?*'

Margaret's eyes were wide. 'Tonight! Can you believe it? The *Alexandra* is just a short distance away, apparently, and we can pick her up on radio.' She grabbed the dog from her bed and kissed her vigorously. 'Oh, Maudie, can you believe it? I'm going to speak to Joe! Tonight!' Then she glanced at her reflection in the mirror Avice had propped beside the door and groaned. 'Oh, no! Look at the state of me. My hair always goes mad in the humidity.'

'I don't think he'll be able to see you over the radio,' Frances ventured.

'But I still want to look nice for him.' Margaret pursed her lips. 'Will you come with me?' She bit her lip. 'It's months since I spoke to him.'

Frances took her hand. 'I'd be delighted,' she said.

'Joe?'

The radio operator, earphones clamped to his head, adjusted the microphone in front of her. 'Put your face close to there,' he said, placing his hand gently on Margaret's back to encourage her in. 'That's it. Now try again.'

'Joe?'

In the radio room tucked beneath the bridge, the handful of chosen brides, some accompanied by friends, nudged each other. The room was small, and they stood stiffly, arms pressed to their sides.

'Mags?' The voice was distant, crackly. But, from Margaret's expression, definitely his.

There was a collective sharp intake of breath. Margaret had been first up and it was as if until the brides heard this evidence it had been impossible to believe in the proximity of their men.

Margaret put out a hand to the microphone.

'Joe, it's me. How are you?'

'I'm grand, love. Are you keeping well? Are they looking after you?'

Margaret closed her hand round the microphone. 'I'm fine. Me and Joe Junior both. It—it's good to hear you,' she faltered, conscious that just as she was surrounded by strangers it was likely he was too.

'Are they feeding you well?' came the voice, and the occupants of the radio room laughed. Margaret's eyes flicked towards the captain, who stood back, smiling benignly. 'They're looking after us fine.'

'Good. You . . . watch out in this heat. Drink lots of water.'

'Oh, I am.'

'I've got to go, sweetheart, give the next fellow a turn. You take care. I'll see you in Plymouth. Not long now.'

Margaret moved in to the microphone, as if she could somehow get closer to him. 'Not long at all,' she said. 'Bye, Joe.'

As she turned from the microphone, she sagged and Frances stepped forward to hold her, alarmed by the tears coursing down Margaret's cheeks. It had been a pretty mean exchange, she thought. She should have been allowed a few more minutes and some privacy.

But when Frances looked at her now, Margaret's smile illuminated the darkness. 'Oh, Frances, that was wonderful,' she whispered.

Nicol moved along the half-lit gangway towards the lobby, trying to make himself inconspicuous as he passed the captain's rooms. Finally, with a quick glance to left and right, he opened the hatch door beside the lieutenant-commander's office and emerged onto the unlit deck.

He had been told where to find her. He had knocked on the door rather awkwardly (it felt like an intrusion, even speaking into this feminine lair) to tell them what had been decided. Perhaps he had told them early because he wanted them to have the best spot. They had laughed, incredulous. Made him say it twice before they would believe it. Then, with Avice and Jean galvanised into action, Margaret, still glowing from her radio contact, had whispered confirmation to him of what he already suspected.

The sky was mostly covered with cloud, revealing only a handful of stars, so it was several minutes before he saw her. He could just make out her angular shape under the furthest plane, her arms wrapped round her knees. As he drew closer and she turned to him, he felt a rush of relief. As if her presence there could reassure him of something.

Nicol saw now that she had been crying, and his pleasure in seeing her was clouded by awkwardness. 'I'm sorry if I disturbed you. Your friend told me I might find you here.'

She made as if to stand. 'Is everything all right?'

She looked so alarmed that he realised his sudden unannounced presence might have suggested a feared telegram. 'Nothing wrong. Please.' He motioned for her to remain seated. 'I just wanted to tell you . . . to warn you . . . that you won't be alone for long.'

She looked almost appalled. 'What?' she said. 'What do you mean?'

'Captain's orders. It's too hot in the liftwells—your cabins, I mean.

He's ordered that you brides should sleep out here tonight.'

Her shoulders relaxed a little. 'Sleep out here? On deck?'

He found himself smiling. 'We can't have you all boiling down there, so Captain Highfield has decided all brides are to bring their bedrolls up here. You can sleep in your swimwear. You'll be a lot more comfortable.'

She looked away from him then, out at the dark ocean. 'I suppose this means I'll have to stay away from here now,' she said wistfully.

He could not take his eyes off her profile. Her skin, in the moonlight, was opalescent. When he spoke, his voice cracked and he coughed to disguise it, to pull himself together. 'Not on my account,' he said. 'You wouldn't be the first to need a few minutes alone with the sea.'

Alone with the sea? Where had that come from? He didn't talk like that. She probably thought him a fanciful fool.

That night, Frances thought afterwards, had been the high point of the voyage. Not just for her but for most of them. It was something about them all being together on the open deck, about the sweet release of the open sea and the sky after the days of encroaching heat, that lifted their spirits and made them all, briefly, equal.

Avice had spent several hours making friends with the girls around them, capitalising on her new status as pregnant wife. Margaret, after fretting a little while about Maud Gonne and being reassured by Frances, who had sneaked down on a pretext and found her sleeping comfortably, had flaked out on Frances's pillow.

Frances was pleased to see it: she had felt pangs of sympathy for Margaret, swollen and uncomfortable in the heat, twisting and turning on her bunk in a vain attempt to get comfortable.

Initially Frances had felt a little self-conscious in her bathing suit, but confronted with the exposed limbs and midriffs of several hundred women of all shapes and sizes (some in the minuscule new bikinis), she soon realised that such self-absorption was ridiculous. Once the marines had got over the shock of what they were guarding they had lost interest too; several were now playing cards on crates by the bridge, while others chatted among themselves, apparently oblivious to the near-naked sleeping bodies behind them.

She must have slept for a few hours after midnight. Most of the girls around her had slept soundly, but she couldn't help herself: being among so many people made her uncomfortable. Eventually, she had sat up and decided, gracefully, to give in to wakefulness. She wrapped her cotton sheet loosely round her shoulders, and trod carefully to the edge of the group. Eventually she found a spot away from everyone, and sat, thinking of nothing, staring into the distance.

'You all right?' It was said quietly, so that only she could hear.

The marine was standing a few feet away from her, his face carefully turned to the front.

'I'm fine,' she murmured. She kept her face towards the sea, as if they were in mutual pretence that they were not in conversation.

He stood there for some time. Frances was acutely conscious of the stillness of his legs beside her, braced a little as if in preparation for some unseen swell.

'You like it up here, don't you?' he asked eventually.

'Very much. I've found the sea makes me feel . . . well, happy.'

'You didn't look very happy earlier.'

She wondered that she could talk to him like this. 'I suppose I didn't feel comforted . . . the way I usually do.'

'Ah.' She felt, rather than saw his nod. 'Well, she rarely does what you expect her to.'

They were silent for a while, Frances unbalanced because they were no longer divided by a steel door.

'Your whole face changes when you're up here.'

She glanced up at him quickly, but he kept his eyes on the ocean. 'I know how it feels,' he said. 'It's why I like to stay at sea.'

What about your children? she wanted to ask, but couldn't frame it so that it didn't sound like an accusation. She wondered why he seemed so sad when he had so much to return to.

He turned and their eyes locked. 'Do you want me to leave you alone?' he said quietly.

'No,' she said. The word was out before she had had time to think about it. And then both silenced, by awkwardness or surprise, he stayed beside her, her personal sentry, as they stared out over the dark waters.

The first slivers of light, fierce and electric, appeared thousands of miles distant on the horizon shortly before five. He told her of how the sunrises could change, depending on which part of the equator they were travelling through, sometimes slow and languorous, a gentle flooding of the sky with creamy blue light, at others a brief, almost aggressive sparking, short-circuiting the sky into dawn.

'Have you served on this ship for long?'

It took him a minute to focus on what she was saying.

'No,' he said. 'Most of us were on *Indomitable*. But she was sunk at the end of the war. Those of us who got out ended up on the *Victoria*.'

Such a few tidy words, well rehearsed now. They did little to convey the chaos and horror of the final hours of that ship, the bombs, the screams and the holds that turned into geysers of fire.

She turned her face towards him. 'Did you lose many?'

'A good few. Captain lost his nephew.'

'Everyone has lost someone,' she said, almost to herself.

He asked her about the prisoners of war, and listened to her litany of patients she had cared for and lost. He didn't ask her how she had coped with all the injuries. Those who had lived through it rarely did, she noticed.

'Quite a thing to choose to do,' he said.

'We all have to find some way,' she said, 'of atoning.'

You? he wanted to say incredulously. You didn't start this war. You were not responsible for the damage, the torn limbs, the suffering. You are one of the good things. You, of all people, of all these women lying here, have nothing to atone for.

Perhaps it was the strangeness of the hour, or the simple fact that for what seemed like years he had not exchanged a single word that was not smothered with uniformed bluff and bravery, but he wanted to crack open like the dawn in front of her, to reveal himself, faults and all, and be absolved by her warmth and understanding. He wanted to scream at her husband—no doubt some wisecracking engineer, who, even as they spoke, might be straightening his trousers as he crept out of some Far-Eastern brothel—'Do you know what you've got?'

He thought briefly, insanely, that he might try to put at least some of this into words. And then Captain Highfield appeared on the bridge. Following his gaze, she turned and watched as the captain consulted two officers.

Nicol drew back reluctantly from Frances. 'I'd better go and find out what's going on,' he said.

Minutes later he returned. 'The planes are going over the side,' he said. 'Captain's decided we need more room. He's just got permission from London to put them overboard.' He shook his head, disbelieving.

'But he's right,' she said eventually. 'It's over. Let the sea take them.'

And as dawn finally broke, touching the near-naked bodies with its cold blue light, a few of the girls woke, pulling their sheets round them, watching mutely with sleep-filled eyes as silently, one by one, the aircraft were wheeled to the edge by pairs of engineers. There they teetered, spending the shortest moment in midair before they disappeared on their concluding flight, the splash of each impact surprisingly muted as they drifted down, down, down towards a final, gentle landing on some unseen seabed at the bottom of the Indian Ocean.

Twenty-two days

Dear Mum,

This is a hard letter to write. I guess I've put off writing it for as long as I could. But you probably know without me having to explain what it is I want to tell you that I have done, and how I've carried it round ever since. I'm not sure who I thought I was protecting—you or myself . . .

'Avice,' said Margaret, 'do you have any blotting paper?'

'Here,' said Avice, stretching downwards. 'You can have that sheet. I've got plenty.' She adjusted her skirt as she settled on her bunk again.

. . . so that's why I'm going to write to Letty, Mum, and tell her the truth. That Dad, while he'll never love anyone like he loved you, deserves to have a bit of company. He deserves to be looked after. I've finally realised I don't have to protect some perfect image I have of the two of you. I don't have to feel angry with her for being in love with him all these years. I can just feel sad for her that she wasted them on someone she knew she couldn't have. Didn't even try to have.

I know you'll agree with this, Mum. I think Letty, after all her years alone, deserves to be loved.

'I'm going upstairs to sit on the deck for a bit. Are you all right if I leave you with Maudie?'

Avice glanced up, pen in hand, and looked at Margaret. She looked, Avice thought, a little red round the eyes. 'Sure,' she said.

'It's not so bad up there now the heat has died down a bit.'

Avice nodded and, as the door closed behind Margaret, she resumed writing on the tissue-thin navy-issue writing-paper.

Perhaps you might find it silly, but do you know what, Ian? I have felt strangely nervous about telling you. I know you're not desperately keen on surprises, but this is a truly special sort of surprise, isn't it? Of course it would have been nice for us to have a little time to ourselves, but once the baby is born we can sort out a nurse for it, and you and I can go on being just how we were in Australia—except with a darling little baby to love too. I know some men rather miss the attention of their wives once the little ones come along but, darling, I want to assure you that no baby would ever come between you and I. You are first in my heart, and always will be. The important thing is for us to be together. That's what you always said to me. I hold that thought close to my heart.

Your Avice

Avice lay back on her bunk, listening to the distant thrum of the ship's engines. She placed her sealed letter on her chest, holding it to her with both hands, and thought back.

The check-out time would normally have been 11 a.m., but it being wartime, and needs being what they were, she had known that even at 2.15 in the afternoon they were unlikely to be disturbed by the maid. The Melbourne Flower Garden Hotel, like many local establishments, did a brisk trade these days in what were known as 'extended check-outs'.

Avice calculated that if they left in the next hour they could nip into the zoo before going home, so that then she wouldn't have to lie about where they'd been. Her mother was bound to ask her something pointed about Sumatran tigers or some such.

Ian had been dozing, one heavy arm pinning her to the bed. Now he opened an eye. 'What are you thinking?'

She let her head turn slowly until their faces were only inches apart. 'I was thinking we were not supposed to do this until after the wedding.'

'Don't say that, gorgeous girl. I couldn't have waited that long.'

'Would it have been so hard?'

'Sweetheart, you know I've only got a forty-eight-hour pass. Wasn't this more fun than fussing about plans for flowers and bridesmaids?'

Avice thought secretly that she would probably have liked fussing over flowers and bridesmaids, but she didn't want to spoil the mood so she smiled enigmatically.

'God, I love you.'

She could feel his words on her skin, as if he were giving her tiny particles of himself even in his breath. She closed her eyes, savouring them: 'I love you too, darling.'

'You're not sorry?' he said.

'To be marrying you?' Her eyes widened.

'To have done . . . you know. I didn't hurt you or anything?'

He had, a little, if she was honest. But not in any way that had made her want to stop. She blushed now, shocked at the things she had found herself doing, at how easily she had surrendered to him.

'You don't think any less of me . . .' she murmured '. . . for having let you . . .' She swallowed. 'I mean, I'm not sure I was meant to enjoy it quite as much as I did . . .'

'Oh, my darling girl, no! God, no, it was wonderful that you liked it. In fact, that's one of the things I love about you, Avice,' Ian pulled her close and spoke into her hair. 'You're a sensual creature. A free spirit.'

A free spirit. She had found herself believing this new version of herself, as Ian described it. Some time earlier, when she had found herself naked and self-conscious before him, he had said she was a goddess, the most alluring creature he had ever seen, and she had found herself determinedly becoming alluring and goddess-like when she really wanted to reach for a dressing gown.

This must mean he's right for me, she told herself. He has it in him to make me better than I am.

Outside, the traffic was picking up. Somewhere below the open window a car door slammed.

'So,' she said, disentangling their legs and sliding round so that she was leaning over him. 'You really, really love me, do you?'

He smiled at her and she thought she'd never seen a more handsome man in her entire life. 'Do you really have to ask?'

'And I never do anything to upset you, or irritate you?'

'Couldn't,' he said, reaching over to the bedside table for a cigarette.

'And you want to be with me for ever?'

'More than. For infinity.'

She took a deep breath. 'Then I'm going to tell you something, and you're not to be angry with me.'

He pulled a cigarette from his packet with neat white teeth, and paused, using the arm looped round her neck to cup the flame of the match as he lit it. 'Mm?' he said. A soft plume of blue smoke rose into the still air beside her head.

'We're getting married.'

He looked at her for a moment. His eyes creased upwards. 'Of course we're getting married, my little duck.'

'Tomorrow.'

'*What?*'

'I've fixed it up. With a justice of the peace. We're getting married tomorrow. At the Collins Street register office. Mum and Dad and Deanna are going to be there and the Hendersons have agreed to be our witnesses.' Then, when he didn't say anything, 'I couldn't bear the thought of you going off again and us only being engaged. And I thought seeing as you do love me and I love you and we only want to be together there wasn't any point in waiting. And you did say you'd got permission from your commander.'

Ian sat up abruptly, so that she fell against the pillow, and leaned forward, his back to her. She pushed herself upright against the headboard, the sheet gathered round her chest.

'Now, darling,' she said, playfully, 'you're not to be cross.'

He didn't move.

Eventually, when she could bear it no longer, she put out a hand to him. His skin, where it met hers, sang to her of the previous hours. 'Are you really cross with me?'

He was silent. He put out his cigarette, then turned back to her, running a hand through his hair. 'I don't like you organising things over my head . . . especially not something as—as important as this.'

Now she dropped the sheet, leaned forward and put her arms round his neck. 'I'm sorry, darling,' she whispered, nuzzling his ear. 'I thought you'd be pleased.'

'It's a man's place to arrange these things. You make me feel . . . I don't know, Avice. Who wears the trousers here?' His face was clouded.

'You!' she said, and the last of the sheet dropped away as she slid a slim leg over him.

'This isn't some joke, is it? It's all set up? Guests and everything?'

She lifted her lips from his neck. 'Only the Hendersons. Apart from family, I mean. It's not like I organised some huge do.'

He covered his face with a hand. 'I can't believe you did this.'

'You do still want me, don't you, darling?' It had never occurred to her that Ian might change his mind.

'You know I do . . . It's just—'

'You want to make sure you're head of the household. But you know I think you're simply masterful. And if we had had more time I would have left it as long as anything. Oh, Ian, it's only because I wanted to be Mrs Radley so badly.' She pressed her nose to his and widened her blue eyes. 'Oh, Ian, darling, I do love you so much.'

He had said nothing initially, just submitted to her kisses, her murmured entreaties, the gentle exploration of her hands. Then, slowly, she felt him thaw. 'It's only because I love you, darling,' she whispered, and as he gave himself up to her, a little part of her reflected with satisfaction that, difficult as these things could sometimes be, through intelligence, charm and a bit of luck, Avice Pritchard usually had her way.

He had been a little odd at the wedding. She knew her mother thought so. He had been distracted, selectively deaf. Given that there were only eight of them, and that he was an officer, she had thought his nervousness a little excessive.

'Don't be silly,' her father had said. 'All grooms are supposed to look like condemned men.' Her mother had hit him playfully.

Deanna had sulked, and Avice had complained about it to her mother, who had told her not to fuss. 'It's very hard for her, you being the first to get married,' she had whispered.

Avice's parents had paid for everyone's dinner and a night for the two of them at the Melbourne Grand. Her mother had wept at the table and told her in a stage whisper, as she and Ian left to go upstairs, that it really wasn't all that bad and it might help if she had a drink or two first. Avice had smiled—a smile that reassured her mother and irritated her sister, to whom it said, I'm going to do It: I shall be a woman before you.

'Ian? Do you still love me, now that I'm just boring Mrs Radley?'

They had reached their room. He closed the door behind her, took another swig of his brandy and loosened his collar. 'Of course I do,' he said. He seemed more like himself. He pulled her to him, and slid a warm hand chaotically up her thigh. 'I love you to bits, darling girl.'

'Forgiven me?'

His attention was already elsewhere. 'Of course.' He dropped his lips to her neck, and bit her gently. 'I told you. I just don't like surprises.'

'I reckon there's a storm brewing.' Jones-the-Welsh checked the barometer at the side of the mess door, and lit another cigarette, then generated a shudder. 'I can feel it inside me. A real wild woman of a storm, lads. The kind that stands your hair on end, whips you round the chops and shreds your trousers afore you can say, "Ah, come on now, love. I was just calling you her name for a joke."'

There was a rumble of laughter from various hammocks. Nicol, lying in his, heard the sound as a dull harbinger of darkening skies. Jones was right. He felt tense, jittery. He told himself it was the storm.

In his mind Nicol saw, again, the imprint of that pale face, illuminated by moonlight. There had been no invitation in her glance, no coquettishness. But there was something in her gaze that told him of an understanding between them. She knew him. That was what he felt.

'Oh, for God's sake,' he said, swinging out of the hammock. He had not meant to speak, and as his feet hit the floor he felt self-conscious.

'What's the matter, Nicol, my love?' Jones-the-Welsh put down his letter. 'Someone done up your corset too tight?'

'Headache,' he said now, rubbing his forehead. 'The pressure.'

He had told himself he was incapable of emotion. So shocked by the horrors of war, by the loss of so many around him that, like so many men, he had closed off. Now, forced to examine his behaviour honestly, he thought perhaps he had never loved his wife. He had had to marry her after she had revealed the consequence of what they had done. You married, you had your children and you grew old. Your wife grew sour with lack of attention; you grew bitter and introverted for your lost dreams. He found it hard to admit that war had freed him from that.

'You know, Nic, the stokers are talking of having a party tonight. It seems a waste for all that female talent to miss out on the experience of a bit of naval hospitality. I thought I might look in later.'

Nicol reached for a boot and began to polish it. 'You can't do it, Jones. They're all married, for God's sake.'

'Ah, come on, Nicol. Those who don't want a bit of Welsh rarebit must be proper in love with their old men. So that's lovely. Don't come over all married and judgmental on us. Just because you're happy living by the rule book doesn't mean the rest of us can't enjoy ourselves.'

'I think you should leave them alone,' he said, closing his ears to the communal 'woohoo!' that met his words. There was a creeping lack of respect for the women that made him uncomfortable.

'And I think you should buck up a bit. Lidders here is coming, aren't you, boy? And Brent and Farthing. Come with us—then you can see we're behaving ourselves.'

'I'm on duty.'

'Of course you are. Pressed up to that dormitory door listening to those girls pant with longing.' He cackled and jumped into his own hammock. 'Oh, come on, Nicol. Marines are allowed a bit of fun too. Look . . . think of what we're doing, right, as some kind of service. The entertainment of the Empire's wives. For the benefit of the nation.'

The men were boxing on the flight deck. Someone had set up a ring where the aircraft had sat and in it Dennis Tims was battering one of the seamen. His naked upper body a taut block of sinewy muscle, he moved without grace or rhythm around the ring, until the young seaman succumbed and was hauled unconscious through the ropes.

Frances stood with her back to them. There was something in the power of his swing, in the brutal set of his jaw as he ploughed into the pale flesh presented to him that made her feel cold, even in this heat.

'Hope they don't get too hot and bothered,' Jean said now, folding herself neatly into the spot beside Margaret. She had spent the last hour wandering back and forth between the ringside and their deck chairs. 'Have you heard? The water's run out.'

Margaret looked at her. 'What?'

'Not drinking water, but the pump isn't working properly and there's no washing—not hair, clothes or anything—until they've mended it. Can you imagine? In this weather!' She fanned herself with her hand. 'I tell you there's a bloody riot in the bathrooms.'

Over the past week or so, Jean had recovered her good humour and her ceaseless chatter had taken on a new momentum. 'You know Avice is taking Irene on for Queen of the *Victoria*? They've got the Miss Lovely Legs competition this afternoon. Avice persuaded an officer to let her go down to the cases and get her best pair of pumps. Four-inch heels in dark green satin to match her bathing suit.'

Jean got up and straightened her skirt. 'I'm going to see if anyone wants to have a wager with me.' She skipped over to the other onlookers.

Margaret and Frances sat in silence. In the distance, a tanker moved across the horizon, and they followed its steady progress until it was no longer visible.

'What's that?' Frances asked, looking at the letter in Margaret's hand.

Margaret looked down and saw that the name of the addressee was showing.

'Were you going to throw it into the water?'

Margaret gazed out at the turquoise waves. 'No. I was going to post it,' she said.

Frances looked back at the envelope, checked that she'd read the name correctly. Then she turned to Margaret, perplexed.

'I lied,' said Margaret. 'I let you think she was dead but she's not. She left us. She's been gone nearly two and a half years.'

'Your mother?'

'Yup.' She waved the letter. 'I don't know why I brought it up here.'

Then Margaret began to talk, at first quietly, and then as if she no longer cared who heard.

It had been a shock. That much was an understatement. They had come home one day to find dinner bubbling on the stove, the shirts neatly pressed over the range, the floors mopped and polished and a note. She couldn't take it any more, she had written. She had waited until Margaret's brothers were home from the war, and Daniel had hit fourteen and become a man, and now she considered her job done. She loved them all, but she had to claw back a little bit of life for herself. She hoped they would understand, but she expected they wouldn't.

She had got Fred Bridgeman to pick her up and drop her at the station, and she had gone, taking with her only a suitcase of clothes, forty-two dollars in savings, and two photographs of the children.

'Mr Leader at the ticket office said she'd got the train to Sydney. From there she could have gone anywhere. We figured she'd come back when she was ready. But she never did. Daniel took it hardest.'

Frances took Margaret's hand.

'Did you ever hear from her?'

'She wrote a few times, and Dad wrote begging her to come back, but when she didn't, he stopped. He couldn't cope with the idea of her not loving him any more. Once they accepted she wasn't coming back, the boys wouldn't write at all. So . . . he just . . . they . . . behaved as if she had died. It was easier than admitting the truth.' She paused. 'She's only written once this year. Maybe I'm a reminder of guilt she doesn't want to feel. Sometimes I think the kindest thing I could do would be to let her go.' She turned the envelope in her free hand.

'I'm sure she wouldn't want to cause you pain,' said Frances, quietly.

'But she is. All the time.' Margaret threw the envelope onto the deck.

Frances fought the urge to pin it down with something. She didn't want a stray breeze to take it overboard.

'But she said she loved you—'

'You don't get it. I'm her daughter, right?'

'Yes . . . but—'

'So what am I meant to feel, if motherhood is so bad that my mum had to run away?' She rubbed swollen fingers across her eyes. 'What if, Frances, what if when this baby gets here . . . I feel exactly the same?'

The weather had broken at almost four thirty, just as the boxing finished. As the first large drops of rain landed heavily, the women swiftly disappeared below decks.

Margaret retreated to the cabin to check on Maud, and now Frances sat with Jean in the deck canteen, watching the rain trickling through the salt on the windows. Margaret had seemed a little better once she'd spoken out, but Frances had felt helpless. She had wanted to tell her a little about her own family, but felt that to do so would require further explanation, which she wasn't prepared to give, even to Margaret. The other woman's friendship had become valuable to her, which made her vulnerable. Also, it brought with it a sense of foreboding. She toyed with the metal spoon in her empty cup, hearing the ship groan.

Where is he now? she thought. Is he sleeping? Dreaming of his children? His wife? Just as Margaret's friendship had introduced new emotions into her life, so thoughts of the marine's family now brought out something in her that filled her with shame. She was jealous. She had thought of him as a friend, a kindred spirit, but it had changed into something she couldn't identify.

She thought of her husband, Chalkie. What she had felt on first meeting him had been quite different. She put down the spoon. I won't do this, she told herself. There is no point in hankering for things you can't have. She made herself think back to the beginning of the voyage, to a time when the mere fact of the journey was enough. She had been satisfied then, hadn't she?

Frances and Jean were about to leave, standing beside each other at the canteen doorway, waiting for the rain to ease off a little, when the rating arrived. He pushed through the door, dripping wet after having made the short journey across the deck, bringing with him a gust of the rain-soaked cool air.

'I'm looking for a Jean Castleforth,' he said.

'That's me.' Jean grabbed the man's arm. 'Why?'

The rating's expression was unreadable. 'You've been called to the captain's office, madam.' Then, as Jean stood still, her expression rigid, he said to Frances, as if Jean were no longer there, 'She's one of the young ones, right? I've been told it's best if someone comes with her.'

Those words halted any further questions. He led them briskly across the hangar deck, past the torpedo store and up some stairs to a door. The rating rapped on it sharply. When he heard, 'Enter,' he opened it, stood back, one arm out, and they walked in. Jean had slid her hand into Frances's and was gripping it tightly.

Three people were silhouetted against one of the windows, and two faced them. Frances saw with alarm that the chaplain was there, then recognised the women's officer who had come across them that night in the engine area. The temperature seemed to drop and she shivered.

Jean's eyes darted round the grim faces in front of her and she was shaking convulsively. 'Something has happened to him, hasn't it?' she said. 'Oh God, is he all right? Tell me, is he all right?'

The captain had been gazing out to sea. Now he turned and exchanged a brief look with the chaplain, before stepping forward and handing Jean a telegram.

'I'm very sorry, my dear,' he said.

Jean looked at the telegram, then up at the captain. 'M . . . H . . . Is that an H?' She traced the letters with her finger. 'A? You read it for me,' she said, and thrust it at Frances.

Frances took the telegram in her left hand, keeping hold of Jean's hand in the other. She took in the content for a second, then the words dropped from her mouth like stones. '"Have heard about behaviour on board. No future for us."' She swallowed. '"Not Wanted Don't Come."'

Jean stared at the telegram, then at Frances. 'I don't understand.'

'News travels between ships,' said the WSO, quietly. 'Someone must have told one of the other carriers when we docked at Ceylon.'

'But no one knew. Apart from you . . .'

'When we spoke to your husband's superiors to verify the telegram, they said he was rather disturbed by news of your pregnancy.' She paused, then added rather cruelly, 'I understand that, according to your given dates, it would be impossible for him to be the father.'

Jean had gone white. 'But I'm not pregnant—that was—'

'I think, in the circumstances, he probably feels that is irrelevant.'

'But I haven't had a chance to explain to him. I need to speak to him.'

Frances stepped in. 'It wasn't her fault. It was a misunderstanding.'

'I'm sorry,' the captain said to Jean. 'We have spoken to the Red Cross and arrangements will be put in place for your passage back to Australia.'

With the ferocity of a whirlwind, Jean launched herself at the women's officer, fists in tight balls. 'You bitch! You fucking old bitch!' Before Frances dived in she had landed several flailing punches on the woman's head. 'I never did nothing!' she shouted, tears streaming down her cheeks, as Frances and the chaplain held her back, faces flushed with effort. 'I never did nothing! You've got to tell Stan!'

The air had been sucked from the room. Even the captain looked shocked. He stepped back.

'Sir,' said Frances, breathing hard, holding the shaking girl in her arms. 'With respect, you have done her a great disservice.' Her head whirled with the unfairness of it. 'She was a victim in this.'

'You're a nurse, not a lawyer,' hissed the women's officer. 'I saw.'

It was too late. As Frances led Jean out of the captain's office, she could hear, over the noise of Jean's sobbing, the women's officer: 'I can't say it surprises me,' she was saying. 'Those Aussie girls are all the same.'

Twenty-three days

Jean was taken off the ship during a brief, unscheduled stop at Cochin. No one else was allowed to disembark, but several brides watched as she climbed into the little boat, and, refusing to look at them, was motored towards the shore, an officer of the Red Cross beside her, her bag and case balanced at the other end. She didn't wave.

Frances and Margaret could just, if they shielded their eyes from the sun, make out the boat as it came to a halt by the jetty. There were two figures waiting under what looked like an umbrella, one of whom took Jean's luggage, while the other helped her onto dry land. It was impossible, at this distance, to see any more than that.

'It wasn't my fault,' said Avice, when the silence became oppressive. 'You don't need to look at me like that.'

Margaret wiped her eyes and made her way heavily inside. 'It's just bloody sad,' she said.

Frances said nothing.

In the days that followed Captain Highfield found that he could not get Jean Castleforth's face out of his mind. It had been uncomfortably like dealing with a POW: the putting ashore, the handing over into safe custody. Several times he had asked himself whether he had done the right thing. The brides had been so adamant, and the nurse's tones of quiet outrage haunted him. *You have done her a great disservice.* But what else could he have done? The WSO had been certain of what she'd seen.

Besides, he had other concerns. The ship, as if she had heard of her own planned fate, had suffered a series of breakdowns. The rudder had jammed, necessitating an emergency switch to steam steering, for the third time in the past ten days. The water shortage continued, with the engineers unable to work out why the desalination pumps kept breaking down. He was supposed to pick up a further fourteen civilian passengers at Aden, including the Governor of Gibraltar and his wife who had been visiting the port, for passage back to their residence, and was not sure how he was going to cater for them all. And he was finding it increasingly hard to disguise his limp. Dobson had asked him pointedly if he was 'quite all right' the previous day and he had been forced to put his full weight on it even though it throbbed so hard he had had to bite the inside of his cheek to contain himself. Three more weeks, he told himself. Three more weeks, if I can hang on that long.

And that, in the end, was why he decided to hold the dance. A good captain did everything to ensure the happiness and well-being of his passengers. He, of all people, understood the need for a diversion.

The Royal Marines Band sat on their makeshift pedestal outside the deck canteen, a little way distant of the ship's island, and struck up with 'I've Got You Under My Skin'. The *Victoria's* engines were shut down for repairs and she floated serene and immobile in the placid waters. On the deck, several hundred brides in the finest dresses they had access to, were whirling around, some with the men and others, giggling, with each other. Around the island, tables and chairs had been brought up from the dining area. Above them, in the Indian sky, the stars glittered like ballroom lights.

It could have been—if one bent one's imagination a little and ignored the presence of the guns—any one of the grand ballrooms of Europe. The captain had felt an unlikely joy in the spectacle, considering it no less than the old girl deserved in her final voyage. A bit of a do.

Highfield thought the men, in their good tropical kit, were looking more cheerful than they had done for days, while the brides—mutinous after the closure of the hair salon—had also perked up considerably, thanks to the introduction of emergency salt-water showers.

Some sat in now well-established huddles or chatted in groups, the men temporarily unconcerned by the lack of defining rank structure.

'How long does the *Victoria* take to refuel, Captain Highfield?'

Beside him sat one of the passengers, a Wren to whom Dobson had introduced him earlier. She was small, dark and intensely serious, and had quizzed him so lengthily about the specifications of his ship that he had been tempted to ask her if she was spying for the Japanese.

'Do you know, I don't think I could tell you offhand,' he said now.

'A little longer than your boys do,' muttered Dr Duxbury, and laughed.

In thanks for their fortitude over the water situation, Captain Highfield had promised everyone extra 'sippers' of rum. He suspected, however, that Duxbury had somehow obtained more than his share. What the hell? he thought. The man would be gone soon. His leg was painful enough tonight for him to consider taking extra sippers himself.

'Did you serve alongside many of the US carriers?' the little Wren asked. 'We came up alongside the USS *Indiana* in the Persian Gulf.'

Dr Duxbury didn't appear to have heard. 'You have a look of Judy Garland about you. Did you ever see her in *Me and My Girl*?'

'I'm afraid not.'

Here we go, thought Captain Highfield. He had already endured several dinners with his proxy medic, at least half of which had culminated in the man singing his terrible ditties. He took a last look at the merriment in front of him; the band had struck up a reel and the girls were whooping and spinning. Then he looked at Dobson and the marine captain, who were talking to a flight captain over by the lifeboats. They could take over from here. He had never been a great one for parties.

'Excuse me,' he said, pushing himself upright painfully, 'I've got to attend to a little matter.' And with that he went back inside.

'Jean would have loved this,' said Margaret. Seated in a comfortable chair that had been brought up from the officers' lounge, a light shawl round her shoulders, she was beaming.

'Poor Jean,' said Frances. 'I wonder what she's doing.'

Avice, a short distance away, was dancing with one of the white-clad officers. Her hair gleamed honey under the arc-lights, while her neat waist and elaborate gathered skirt betrayed nothing of her condition.

'I don't think your woman there is worrying too much, do you?' Margaret nodded.

Avice was still celebrating having won that afternoon's cleverest-use-of-craft-materials competition with her decorated evening bag. Not, she told the girls afterwards, that she would have had it within six feet of her on a night out. The important thing had been beating Irene Carter. She was now two points ahead of her for the Queen of the *Victoria* title.

'I don't think she worries about anything—' Frances stopped herself.

'Let's not think about it tonight, eh? Nothing we can do now.'

'No,' said Frances.

She had never been interested in clothes and had fallen with relief into her nurse's uniform. She smoothed her skirt: the dress she had once considered smart looked dowdy. On a whim, she had released her hair from its tight knot at the back of her head, letting it hang loose on her shoulders, but now she felt unsophisticated and wished for the reassurance of her hairpins. She wondered if she could voice her fears to Margaret, but the sight of her friend's perspiring face stopped the question on her lips. 'Can I get you a drink?' she said instead.

'You beauty! Thought you'd never ask,' Margaret said companionably.

'I'll get you some soda.'

'Bless you! Though you don't have to stay with me. Go and enjoy yourself.'

Frances wrinkled her nose. 'I'm happier at the edge of things.'

It wasn't strictly true. She had felt a creeping longing to be one of those girls whirling around on the dance floor.

She collected two glasses of soda and returned to Margaret, who was watching the dancers.

'I never was one for dancing,' said Margaret, 'yet looking at that lot right now I'd give anything to be up there.'

Frances nodded towards Margaret's belly. 'Not long,' she said. 'Then you can foxtrot halfway across England.'

She had told herself it didn't matter, not seeing him. That, looking like she did, she might even prefer it. He was probably lost in that dark crowd, dancing with some pretty girl in a brightly coloured dress. She wouldn't have known how to make small talk, would have felt too self-conscious in her dull pale blue dress beside everyone else's gowns.

'Hello there,' he said, seating himself beside her. 'I wondered where I might find you.'

She could barely speak. His dark eyes looked steadily out at her from a face softened by the night. His hand lay on the table in front of her and she fought an irrational urge to touch it.

'I wondered if you'd like to dance,' he said.

She stared at that hand, faced with the prospect of it resting on her waist, of his body close to hers, and felt a swell of panic. 'No,' she said abruptly. 'Actually, I—I was just leaving.'

There was a brief silence.

'It is late,' he conceded. 'I was hoping to get up here earlier, but we had a bit of an incident downstairs in the kitchens.'

'Thank you, anyway,' she said. 'I hope you enjoy the rest of your evening.' There was a lump in her throat. She gathered up her things and he stood to let her pass.

'Don't go,' said Margaret. 'For God's sake, woman, you've kept me company all bloody night and now the least you can do is have a turn round the dance floor. Let me see what I'm missing.'

'Margaret, I'm sorry, but I—'

'Sorry but what? Ah, go on, Frances.'

She looked back at him, then at the crowded deck, the endless whirl of white and colour, unsure whether she was fearful of entering the throng or of being so close to him.

'Get on with it, woman.'

He was still beside her. 'A quick one?' he said, holding out his arm.

Not trusting herself to speak, she took it.

She wouldn't think tonight about the impossibility of it all. About the fact that she was feeling something she had long told herself it was unsafe to feel. About the fact that there would inevitably be a painful consequence. She just closed her eyes, lay back on her bunk, and allowed herself to sink into those moments she had stored deep inside: the four dances in which he had held her, one hand clasping hers, the other resting on her waist; of how, during the last, even as he kept himself inches from her, she could feel his breath against her bare neck.

Of how he had looked at her when he let go. Had there been reluctance in the way his hand had separated slowly from hers? Was there not a strange emphasis on the way he'd lowered his head to hers and said, so quietly, 'Thank you'?

What she felt for him shocked her. The chaotic, overpowering emotions she had experienced this evening made her wonder if she was in the grip of some seaborne virus. She bit down on her hand, forced herself to breathe deeply, tried to restore the inner calm that had provided solace in the last six years.

It was just a dance. 'A dance,' she whispered to herself, pulling the sheet over her head. 'Why can't you be grateful for that?'

She heard footsteps, then men's voices. Someone was talking to the marine outside the door, a young substitute with red hair and sleepy eyes. She lay, only half listening, wondering if it was time for the watch to change. Then she sat up.

It was him. She sat very still for a minute longer, checking that she was not mistaken, then slid out of her bunk, her heart hammering in her chest. She thought of Jean and grew cold. Perhaps she had been so blinded by her own attraction to him that she had not seen what was before her. She placed her ear to the door.

'What do you think?' he was saying.

'It's been a good hour,' the other marine replied, 'but I don't suppose you've got a choice.'

'I don't like it,' he said. 'I don't like doing it at all.'

She stepped back from the door, and as she did, the handle turned and it opened quietly. His face slid round it and he had caught her there, shocked and pale in the illuminated sliver of the passage lights.

She grappled for her wrap, and flung it on, tying it tightly around her.

'I'm sorry to disturb you.' His voice was low and urgent. 'But there's been an accident. I was wondering—Look, we need your help.'

The dance had ended in several unofficial gatherings in various parts of the ship. In the sweaty confines of the rear port-side engine room, a stoker had been waltzing a bride along one of the walkways that flanked the main engine. It seemed that the couple had fallen into the engine pit. The man was unconscious; the bride had a nasty cut on her face.

'We can't call the ship's doctor for obvious reasons. But we need to get them out of there before the watch changes.' He hesitated. 'I thought . . . I thought you might help.'

She wrapped her arms round herself. 'I'm sorry,' she whispered. 'I can't go down there. You'll have to get someone else.'

'I'll be there. You don't need to worry, I promise. They know you're a nurse. There's no one else who can help,' he said, and glanced at his watch. 'We've only got about twenty minutes. Please, Frances.'

He had not used her name before. She hadn't been aware he knew it.

Margaret's voice cut through the darkness. 'I'll come with you.'

She was in an agony of indecision, thrown by his nearness.

'Just have a look at them. If it's really bad we'll wake the doctor.'

'I'll get my kit,' she said. She reached under her bunk for the tin box. Opposite, Margaret got up heavily and put on her dressing gown. She gave Frances's arm a discreet squeeze.

'Where are you going?' said Avice, and pulled the light cord.

'We're going to help a couple of people who have been hurt down-stairs,' said Margaret. 'Come with us, if you want.'

Avice looked at them, as if weighing up whether to go, then slid off her bunk and into her peach silk robe. She walked past the marine, who held the door back, a finger to his lips, and followed them as they went silently down the passageway towards the stairs.

Behind them, the red-headed marine shuffled back into place, guarding a cabin that was now empty but for a sleeping dog.

Margaret reached the engine room after everyone else. When she opened the hatch, the heat was such that she had to stand still for a moment to acclimatise. Then she stepped onto the walkway inside and looked down. Some fifteen feet below them, in a huge pit in the floor, a young seaman was half lying on the ground, supported on one side by a weeping bride and on the other by a friend. In the centre a huge engine—a labyrinthine organ of pipes and valves—pumped and ground a regular, deafening beat from its huge metal parts, its valves hissing steam.

Ahead, Frances was clambering down a metal ladder that led to the pit. Finally, she pushed her way through the crowd and fell to her knees beside the seaman. There was no caution in her demeanour now: she was galvanised. Beside her, the marine, loosening his good bootneck collar, was following her instructions, searching out items in her medical kit. He shouted orders to the remaining seamen, two of whom darted back up the ladder, apparently glad to be out of the way.

Avice was standing on the walkway with her back to the wall. The uneasy look on her face told Margaret that she had already decided this was not a place she wanted to be. But then she looked back at Frances as she bent over the unconscious man, and knew she couldn't leave. She watched as the marine handed Frances what looked like a sewing kit.

It was as she turned away that a man in the corner drew her attention. Margaret realised that in several minutes he had not taken his eyes from Frances. The peculiar nature of his gaze made her wonder if perhaps Frances's robe was too revealing. He looked, she thought, not quite salacious, but oddly knowing. She moved closer to Avice.

'When did they say the watch was changing?' asked Avice, nervously.

'In fourteen minutes,' said Margaret. She wondered whether she should go down and remind them of the time, but it seemed pointless: their movements were filled with urgency.

'I think we should leave,' Avice said.

'She won't be long,' said Margaret. But secretly she agreed.

Nicol looked down at his watch. 'We've got eight minutes, Frances, before we have to get them both out of here.'

Beside him, on the floor, Frances had finished cleaning the cut on the bride's face. The girl had stopped weeping and was in a state of white-faced shock. Frances's hair, wet with sweat, hung lank round her face.

'Pass me the morphine, please,' she said. He got the little brown bottle out of her box. She took it, removed the top from the bottle and filled a syringe. 'Soon feel better,' she said to the injured girl, and as Nicol shifted to give her room, she placed the needle next to her skin. 'I'll have to stitch it,' she said, 'but I promise I'll make them as tiny as I can. Most of them will be covered by your hair anyway.'

The girl nodded mutely.

Some men were carrying the young seaman out, passing him between them up the ladder, shouting to each other to watch his leg, his head.

'Your friend here isn't going to say anything, right?' Jones-the-Welsh, who had been watching for some time, asked Nicol. 'I mean, can we trust her?'

Nicol nodded. It had taken her several attempts to thread the needle; he saw that her fingers were trembling.

He was struggling to find ways in which he might thank her, express his admiration. He had never seen a woman so confident in duty.

'Time?' said Frances.

'Four minutes,' he said.

She shook her head as if faced with a private impossibility. Time inched forwards, the hands of his watch moving relentlessly from one digit to the next.

Nicol found himself standing, glancing at the hatch, convinced even over the deafening sound of the engine that he could hear footsteps.

And then she turned to him, face flushed from the heat. 'We're done,' she said, with a brief smile.

'A little over a minute and a half,' said Nicol. 'Come on, we've got to get out of here. Leave it,' he called to some ratings who had been trying to fix the guard rail, 'there's no time. Just help me get her up.'

Margaret and Avice were standing by the hatch on the walkway above them, and Frances motioned to them as if to say they could leave now.

He stood and offered his hand so that she could stand. She hesitated, then took it, smoothing her hair from her face. He tried not to let his eyes drop to her robe, which now clearly outlined the contours of her breasts. Sweat glistened on her skin.

'Hang on,' said Jones-the-Welsh from beside him. 'Don't I know you?'

At first she seemed to assume that he was addressing the injured girl. Then she registered that he was talking to her and something hardened in her expression.

'You were never at Morotai,' said Nicol.

'Morotai? Nah.' Jones was shaking his head. 'It wasn't there. But I never forget a face. I know you from somewhere.'

'I don't think so,' Frances said quietly. She gathered up her medical kit, pulled her robe tightly round her and picked her way past the engine towards the ladder.

'I know it'll come to me.' Jones shook his head. 'Oh, no . . .'

Nicol tore his gaze from Frances to Jones-the-Welsh. The man was staring at her, a wicked smile on his face.

'What?' said Nicol.

'No . . . can't be . . . never . . .' Jones glanced behind him. 'Hey, Duckworth, are you thinking what I'm thinking? Queensland? It isn't, is it?' Frances had climbed up the ladder and was now walking towards Margaret and Avice, head down.

'Saw it straight away,' came the broad Cockney accent. 'The old Rest Easy. You wouldn't credit it, would you?'

'A nurse!' said Jones-the-Welsh, and burst out laughing. 'A nurse!'

'What the hell are you talking about, Jones?'

'Well, your little nurse there, Nicol,' Jones said, 'used to be a brasser. Duckworth knows—we came across her at a club in Queensland, must be four, five years ago now.'

'Don't be ridiculous, man.' Nicol looked up at Frances, who was nearly at the hatch. 'She's married.'

'What? To her bludger? Manager's prize girl, she was! And now look! Can you credit it! She's turned into Florence Nightingale!' His burst of incredulous laughter followed Frances along the passageway.

AUSTRALIA, 1939

FRANCES HAD CHECKED the biscuit tin four times before Mr Radcliffe came. She had also checked the back of the cutlery drawer, in the pot behind the screen door and under the mattress in what had once, many years previously, been her parents' room. She had asked her mother several times where the money was, and in her mother's snoring, alcohol-fumed reply the answer was obvious.

But not to Mr Radcliffe. 'So, where is it?' he had said, smiling. The same way that a shark smiles when it opens its mouth to bite.

'I'm real sorry. I don't know what she's done with it.' Her ankle was hooked behind the door to restrict his view inside, but Mr Radcliffe leaned to one side and gazed through the screen to where her mother lolled in the armchair.

'No,' he said. 'Of course.'

'She's not very well,' she said, pulling at her skirt awkwardly. 'Perhaps when she wakes up she'll be able to tell me.'

Behind him, she could see two neighbours walking along the street. They murmured something, their eyes trained on her.

'What? Like your mum did last week? And the week before that?'

She said nothing, locked in an uneasy waiting game.

'You've not been around here for a while.' It wasn't quite a question.

'I've been staying with my aunt May.'

'Oh, yes. She passed on, didn't she? Cancer, wasn't it?'

Frances could answer now without her eyes filling. 'Yes,' she said.

'I'm sorry for your loss. You probably know your mother didn't do too good while you were gone. She dropped behind on her payments. Not just with me. You'll get no tick at Greens now, or Mayhews.' He glanced past her through the door again. 'Your mother was a pretty woman when she worked for me. That's what the drink does to you.'

He turned to the gleaming motor car that stood in the road. Two boys were peering at themselves in the wing mirror. He turned back. 'How old are you, Frances?' he said.

'Fifteen.'

He studied her, as if assessing her. Then he sighed, as if he were about to do something against his better judgment. 'Look, I tell you what, I'll let you work at the hotel. You can wash dishes. Do a bit of cleaning. Don't let me down, mind, or you and she will be out on your ears.' He had been back at his car, shooing away the boys before she'd had a chance to thank him.

She had known Mr Radcliffe for most of her life. Most people in Aynsville did: he was the owner of the only hotel, and landlord of several clapboard properties. She could still remember the days when her mother had disappeared in the evening to work at the hotel bar and Aunt May had looked after her.

Frances's own experience of the hotel was rather better. For the first year, anyway. Every day, shortly after nine, she would report for work in the back kitchen, alongside Hun Li, a near-silent Chinese man, who scowled and raised a huge knife at her if she didn't wash and slice the vegetables to his satisfaction. She would clean the kitchens, slapping at the floors with a mop, help prepare food until four, then move on to washing up. Her hands chapped and split with the scalding water; her back and neck ached from stooping at the sink, and she learned to keep her eyes lowered from the girls who sat around bad-temperedly in the bar during the afternoons, with little to do but drink.

Mr Radcliffe kept the rent and paid her just enough to cover food and household expenses. She managed to buy herself a new pair of shoes, and her mother a cream blouse with pale blue embroidery. The kind of blouse she could imagine a different sort of mother wearing.

But then, freed of the responsibility of earning, her mother had begun to drink more heavily. She would come to the hotel bar and lean over the counter in her low-cut dresses and, inevitably, late into the evening, she would harangue the men around her and the girls who worked there. Finally she would clatter into the kitchens to attack her daughter verbally for her failures—for allowing herself to be born and for ruining her mother's life—until Hun Li grabbed her in his huge arms and threw her out. In the face of their poverty, Frances could never work out how her mother acquired the money to get as drunk as she did.

Then, one night, her mother disappeared with the evening's takings.

Frances had been taking a five-minute break when Mr Radcliffe had stormed into the kitchen.

'Where is she, the thieving whore?'

Frances froze, wide-eyed. She knew, with a familiar sinking feeling in her stomach, who he was talking about.

'She's gone! And so has my bloody cash! Where is she?'

'I—I don't know,' Frances had stammered.

Mr Radcliffe, normally so urbane and gentlemanly, had become an enraged, puce-faced creature, his fists balled as if in an effort to contain himself. He had stared at her for what seemed like an eternity, apparently weighing up the possibility that she was telling the truth. Then he had gone, the door slamming behind him.

They had found her mother two days later, unconscious, at the back of the butcher's. There was no money, just a few empty bottles. Her shoes were missing. One evening that same week, Mr Radcliffe went round 'to have a word with her' then came back to the hotel to tell Frances that he and her mother had decided it might be best if she left town for a while. He had personally helped her out. 'Just till she straightens herself out a bit.'

Frances had been too shocked to react. When she arrived home that evening, took in the heavy silence of the house, the bills sitting on the table, the note that failed to explain where her mother was going, she had laid her head on her arms and stayed like that until, exhausted, she slept.

It had been almost three months later that Mr Radcliffe had called her in. Her mother's shadow had diminished; people in town had stopped murmuring to each other as she passed—some even said hello. Hun Li had been conciliatory—had made sure that there were scraps of beef and mutton in her dinner, that she had regular breaks. The girls in the bar had asked if she was doing all right, had tweaked her plaits in a sisterly manner. When one had popped her head round the kitchen door and asked her to nip up to Mr Radcliffe's office, she had flinched, afraid that she was about to be accused of theft too. Like mother like daughter—that was what they said in the town. But when she knocked and entered, Mr Radcliffe's face was not angry.

'Sit down,' he said. The way he looked at her seemed almost sympathetic. She sat. 'I'm going to have to ask you to leave your house.'

Before she could open her mouth to protest, he continued, 'The war's going to change things in Queensland. We've got troops headed up here and the town's going to get busy. I'm told there are people coming in who can pay me a much better rent on it. Anyway, Frances, it doesn't make sense for a young girl like you to be rattling around in it alone.'

'I've kept up with my rent,' said Frances. 'I haven't let you down once.'

'I'm well aware of that, sweetheart, and I'm not the kind of man to turf you out on the street. You'll move in here. You can have one of the rooms at the top. And I'll take a reduced rent for it. How's that sound?'

His confidence that she would be pleased with this arrangement was so overwhelming that she found it hard to say what she felt: that the house on Ridley Street was her home. That since her mother's departure she had started to enjoy her independence. And that she did not want to be indebted to him in the way this arrangement suggested.

'I'd really rather stay in the house, Mr Radcliffe. I—I'll work extra shifts to make up the rent.'

Mr Radcliffe sighed. 'I'd love to help you there, Frances, really I would. But when your mum took off with my takings she left a hole in my finances. A great—big—hole that I'm going to have to fill.'

He stood up, and walked over to her. His hand on her shoulder felt immensely heavy.

'But that's what I like about you, Frances. You're a grafter, not like your old mum. So, you'll move in here. A girl like you shouldn't spend the prime of her life worrying about the rent. You should be out, dressed up a bit, having fun. Besides, it's not good for a young girl to be seen to be living on her own . . .' He squeezed her shoulder. 'No. You move your stuff in Saturday week and I'll take care of everything else. I'll send someone over to give you a hand.'

Afterwards, she realised that perhaps the girls had known something she couldn't. That their sympathy, their friendliness, stemmed not from the fact that they lived under one roof, all girls together, as she had assumed, but from what they understood about her position.

And that when Miriam, a short Jewish woman with hair that stretched to her waist, announced she would spend an afternoon helping her to smarten herself up a bit, it had perhaps been the result not of girlish friendliness, but of someone else's instruction.

Either way, Frances had found herself too intimidated by the unfamiliar attention to protest. At the end of the day, when Miriam had set her hair, pulled tight the waistband of the deep blue dress she had altered to fit her and presented her to Mr Radcliffe, boasting about the transformation, Frances had assumed she should be grateful.

'Well, look at you,' Mr Radcliffe said, puffing at his cigarette. 'Who'd have thought, eh, Miriam?'

'Doesn't scrub up too bad, does she?'

Frances felt her cheeks burn under their scrutiny and the make-up.

'Good enough to eat. In fact, I think our little Frances has been wasted on old Hun Li, don't you?'

'I'm fine,' said Frances. 'Really. I'm very happy working with Mr Hun.'

'Sure you are, sweetheart, and very fine work you do too. But looking at how pretty you've got, I think you're more use to me out front. So, from now on you'll serve drinks.'

She should be grateful. She should be grateful that Mr Radcliffe had given her the attic room at a cheaper price. She should be grateful that he paid her so much attention, that he had ordered those two good dresses for her, that he took her out to dinner once a week and protected her from the attentions of the troops flooding into town. She should be grateful that someone found her as pretty as he did.

She should have paid attention to Hun Li when he took her aside one night and hissed at her in pidgin English that she should leave. Now. She wasn't a stupid girl, no matter what the others were saying.

So that first night when, instead of waving her off to bed, Mr Radcliffe invited her to come to his rooms after dinner, it was hard to say no. When she had pleaded tiredness, he had pulled such a sad face and said she couldn't possibly leave him alone after he had entertained her all evening, could she? He had seemed so proud of the specially imported wine that it had been vital that she drink some too. Especially that second glass. And when he had insisted she sit on the sofa beside him, it would have been rude to refuse.

'You know, you're actually a very beautiful girl, Frances,' he had said. There had been something almost hypnotic about the way he kept murmuring it into her ear. About his broad hand, which, without her noticing, had been stroking her back, as if she were a baby. About the way her dress had slipped from her bare skin. Later, when she had thought back, she knew she had hardly tried to stop him because she hadn't realised, until it was too late, what she should have been stopping. And it hadn't been so bad, had it? Because Mr Radcliffe cared about her. Like no one else cared. Mr Radcliffe would look after her.

She might not be sure what it was she actually felt about him. But she knew she should be grateful.

Frances stayed at the Rest Easy Hotel for three more months. For two of those months she and Mr Radcliffe (he never invited her to use his first name) settled into a twice-weekly routine of his nocturnal 'visits'.

She realised pretty quickly that she did not love him, no matter what he said to her. She knew now why he employed so many female staff. She saw, with not a little curiosity, that none of them envied her position as his girlfriend, even though he favoured her—in wages, dresses and attention—best of all.

But on the day when he suggested she 'entertain' his friend for a little while, she had understood everything. 'I'm sorry,' she said, smile wavering as she looked at the two men, 'I don't think I heard you right.'

He laid his hand on her shoulder. 'Neville here has a proper soft spot for you, sweetheart. Do me a favour. Just make him feel better.'

'I don't understand,' she said.

His fingers tightened on her. 'I think you do, sweetheart.0'

She refused, flushed to the roots of her hair at what he had suggested. 'Get off me!' she whispered. 'I can't believe you're asking me to do such a thing!' She half ran towards the stairs, desperate to escape to the safety of her own room, conscious of the eyes of the other girls upon her, the catcalling of the now ever-present troops. But by the time she reached the door to her room he was behind her.

'What do you think you're doing?' he yelled at her, whipping her round to face him. 'How dare you embarrass me like that! After all I've done for you. Neville's a good friend of mine, and his son's off to war and he's blue as anything and I'm just trying to take his mind off it all.'

She tried to interrupt but he stopped her.

'I thought you were better than that, Frances.' Here his voice dropped, became conciliatory. 'One of the things I always liked about you was that you were a caring sort of a girl.'

'But I—' She didn't know how to answer him. She began to cry.

'Look, sweetheart, Neville's a nice man, isn't he?'

A small, grey-haired moustachioed man. He had grinned at her all night. She had thought he found her conversation entertaining.

'It would mean such a lot to him. Come on, sweetheart, it's half an hour of your life. And it's not like you don't enjoy it, is it?' He lifted her hands from her face. Forced her to open her eyes.

She didn't know how to reply. She had never been sober enough to remember. He seemed to take her silence as acquiescence and led her into her room.

'You straighten yourself up a bit,' he said. 'No one wants to see a face full of tears. I'll have a couple of drinks sent up to you and then I'll send Neville up.' He hadn't looked at her as he'd left the room.

After that she lost count of the number of times she did it. She knew only that each time she had been progressively more drunk. She spent as much time as she could hiding in the bathroom, scrubbing her skin.

Finally, on the last occasion, as the bar grew noisier, Hun Li had caught her after she had ducked into the cellar. Faced with two off-duty servicemen who had gleaned the impression from Mr Radcliffe that they might get the chance to spend some time with her, Frances now stood in the corner swigging from a half-empty bottle of rum.

'Frances!'

She had whipped round. Drunk, it had taken her time to focus, and she recognised him only by his blue shirt and broad arms. 'Don't say nothing,' she slurred. 'I'll put the money in the till.'

He had stepped closer to her, under the bare light bulb, and she wondered whether he wanted to paw at her too. 'You must go from here. This place no good.'

'What?'

He stood awkwardly in front of her. 'I got this for you.' And then she saw that his fist was full of money. 'That man last week. The one with the flash suit. He got a gambling place. I stole this from his car.' He thrust his fist at her. 'You take it. There's a train leaves tomorrow.'

She didn't move, and he shook his fist insistently. 'This is no good for you, Frances. You're a good girl.'

A good girl. She stared at this man, whom she had thought hardly capable of speech, let alone such kindness. She took the money and put it into her pocket.

'What about you?' she said. 'You don't need this for yourself?'

His face was unreadable. 'I never needed it like you,' he said.

Twenty-five days

'Poor old girl. It wasn't a fate you deserved, however you look at it.' He laid his hand gently on her, sensing, he fancied, the years of struggle echoing through the cool metal. 'Too good for them. Far too good.'

He straightened up, then glanced behind him, conscious that he was talking aloud to his ship and keen to ensure that Dobson had not witnessed it.

There had not been a square inch of *Indomitable* that Highfield hadn't known, no part of her history with which he wasn't familiar. He had seen her decks submerged in high seas in the Adriatic, he had steered her through the Arctic in the winter of '41, he had held her steady as she fought off the suicide bombers of the Sakishima Gunto airfields. He had swept her through the Atlantic, listening for the ominous echo that told of enemy submarines, and he had seen her at her last. Watched her deck canting as she slid down, taking with her his beloved nephew. When her bow had sunk and the waves closed over her, there had been no sign left that she had existed at all.

The *Victoria's* layout was identical to that of her twin; there had been something almost eerie about it when he had first stepped aboard. For a while he had been resentful. Now he felt a perverse obligation to her.

They had contacted him that morning. The *Victoria* would be examined in dry dock at Plymouth before being modified and sold off to some merchant shipping company or broken up. 'Nothing wrong with the old girl,' he had wired back. 'Suggest most strongly the former course.'

He had not told the men. He suspected most would not notice what ship they were on, as long as the messes were of a decent size, the money regular and the food edible. With the war over, many would leave the navy for good. He, and the old ship, would be no more than a dim memory when war stories were exchanged over dinner.

'What you do, ladies, is mix one level tablespoon of the powdered egg with two tablespoons of water. Allow it to stand for a few minutes, then work out any lumps with a wooden spoon . . .'

Margaret sat with her notebook on her lap, her pen in her hand. She had given up writing several recipes ago, distracted by the murmur of conversation around her.

'A prostitute? I don't believe it. Surely the navy wouldn't let one travel with all the men.'

'Well, they didn't know, did they? They can't have.'

'But who on earth would have married her?'

'And what if he doesn't know?'

It had been the same story all over the ship. Those who had had any dealings with Frances Mackenzie were fascinated that this supposedly demure young woman had such a chequered past. Others found the story of her former career compelling, and felt obliged to embellish it.

'I heard she was on the train. You know, the one they used to send up to the troops. It was full of . . . those sorts.'

'Do you think they had to check her for diseases? I mean, we might have been sharing a bathroom with her.'

Margaret had fought the urge to interrupt, to inform these stupid, gossiping women that they didn't know what they were talking about. But it was difficult when she herself had no idea of the truth.

It wasn't as if Frances was saying anything. She had barely spoken, keeping her conversation to an absolute practical minimum. She had avoided the canteen. Margaret wasn't sure that she was eating anything.

Avice had asked, rather ostentatiously, to be moved to another cabin, and when the only other bunk on offer had proven not to her liking, she had announced that she wanted as little to do with Frances as possible.

Margaret had told her not to be so ridiculous, and not to listen to a load of bloody gossip. There would be no truth in it. But it was difficult to be as vehement as she would have liked when Frances was doing so little to defend herself. She stared at the recipes in front of her, then stuffed her notebook into her basket, got up and left the room.

Dear Deanna,

I can't tell you what fun I'm having on board—quite a surprise, all things considered. I somehow find myself in the running for Queen of the Victoria, *a prize they award to the bride who has proven herself a cut above in all matters feminine. I have so far won points in craft, dressmaking, musical ability and—you'll never guess—Miss Lovely Legs! I wore my green swimsuit with the matching satin heels. I do hope you didn't mind me taking them. You seemed to wear them so seldom.*

How are you? Mummy's letter said you were no longer in correspondence with that nice young man from Waverley. I find it very hard to think anyone would so cruelly drop a girl like that. Unless he had found someone else, I suppose. Men can be such an enigma, can't they? I thank goodness every day that Ian is such a devoted soul.

I will post this when we next dock.

Your loving sister, Avice

Avice finished her letter and headed out onto the foredeck for a swim.

It was the first time the brides had been allowed to bathe and all around her hundreds of women were submerged in the clear waters, squealing as they floated around lifeboats, while the marines and officers not manning the boats leaned over the ship's side watching them.

She examined herself with some pride, noting the still-flat stomach but an attractive hint of fullness to her bosom. There was no sign of the baby yet. She wouldn't be one of these flabby whales, like Margaret. She would make sure she stayed trim and attractive until the end.

Now that she no longer felt nauseous, she was sure that pregnancy would positively agree with her: aided by the constant sunshine, her skin glowed, her blonde hair had new highlights. Avice shed her sundress and straightened up a little, just to make sure that she could be seen to her best advantage before she lay decoratively on the deck to sunbathe. Apart from that unfortunate business with Frances (and what a turn-up that had been for the books!), and what with her steady notching up of points for Queen of the *Victoria*, she thought she had probably made the voyage into rather a success.

A short distance away, on the forecastle, Nicol was propped against the wall. Normally he would not have smoked on deck, especially not on duty, but over the past days he had smoked with a grim determination.

'Going in later?' One of the seamen appeared at his elbow. The men would be piped to bathe when the last of the women were out.

'No.' Nicol stubbed out his cigarette.

'I'm surprised old Highfield let 'em in. Would have thought the sight of all that female flesh'd be too much for him.' Below them, in the glassy waters, two women writhed and squealed their way onto one of the lifeboats. The man gazed at them in appreciation. 'Cold fish, that Highfield. You got to wonder about a man always wants to be by himself.'

Nicol said nothing and lit another cigarette.

She was not there. He hadn't thought she would be.

He had lain awake for the rest of that dreadful night, Jones's words haunting him almost as much as his own sense of betrayal. Slowly, as the night gave way to day, his own disbelief had evaporated. Standing in the bowels of the ship, he had wanted her to deny it indignantly; wanted to hear her outrage at the slur. None had been forthcoming. Now he wanted her to explain herself.

When he returned to the mess she had still been the talk of the men. Wide-eyed little thing she had been, Jones-the-Welsh said, leaning out of his hammock for a cigarette. A ton of make-up on her. Almost like the others had done it for a joke.

Nicol had paused in the hatch, wondering whether he should turn round. He wasn't sure what made him stay.

Jones himself had apparently been presented with her but declined. 'Thin as a whippet,' he said, 'with no tits to speak of.' And because she was drunk, he said, curling his lip.

The manager had sent her upstairs with one of his mates and she'd fallen up the steps, her legs all over the place. They had all laughed. Actually, he said, more seriously, 'I thought she was under age, you know what I'm saying? Didn't fancy having my collar felt.'

Duckworth, an apparent connoisseur of such things, had agreed.

'Bloody hell, though. You'd never know now, would you? Looks like butter wouldn't melt.'

No, Duckworth had observed, but for them recognising her, no one would have known.

Nicol had begun to pull down his hammock. He had thought he might try for some sleep before his next watch.

'Now, now, Nicol,' came Jones's voice from behind him. 'Hope you're not thinking about slipping in there for a quickie later. Need to save your money for that missus of yours.' He had guffawed. 'Besides, she's a bit better-looking now. She'd probably charge you a fortune.'

He had thought he might hit him. Instead he had pasted a wry smile on his face, feeling even as he did that he was engaged in some sort of betrayal, and disappeared into the wash cubicle.

Night had fallen. The *Victoria* pushed forward in the black waters, oblivious to the time or season, to the moods and vagaries of her inhabitants, her vast engines powering obediently beneath her. Frances lay in her bunk, listening for the now familiar sounds, the slowing of breath that told the same story of the two other women in her cabin. The sounds of solitude, the sounds that told her she was free once again to breathe. And outside, just audible to the trained ear, the sound of two feet shifting on the corridor floor.

He arrived at 4 a.m. She heard him murmuring something to the other marine as they changed guard, the muffled echo of the other man's steps as he went. She listened to the man outside until, finally, when she could bear it no longer, she rose from her bunk. Unseen by the two sleeping women on each side of her, she tiptoed towards the steel door, her footsteps sure and silent in the dark. Just before she reached it, she stood still, eyes closed as if she were in pain.

Then she stepped forward and carefully laid her face against it. Slowly she rested her entire length, her thighs, her stomach, her chest against it, palms pressed flat on each side of her head, feeling the cool metal through her thin nightgown.

If she turned her head, kept her ear pressed against the door, she could almost hear him breathing.

She stood there, in the dark, for some time. A tear rolled down her face and plopped on to her bare foot. It was followed by another.

Outside, apart from the low rumble of the engines, there was silence.

Twenty-six days

A major port, especially one that had formed an important staging-post for most of the war years, can safely be assumed to have seen most things pass through its gates. But the sight of some 600 women waiting to go ashore at Bombay brought the traffic at Alexandra Lock to a standstill. The women, lining the decks in their summer dresses, waved at the onlookers with hats and handbags. Small tugboats, hovering beneath the great bow like satellites, noisily dragged the *Victoria* round, pulling her into position. And all along the quay eyes lifted to the great aircraft carrier that no longer carried aircraft. Men and women stood in brightly coloured robes and saris, troops, dockyard workers, traders, all paused to watch the Ship of Brides manoeuvre her way in.

'You must stick together and stay in the main thoroughfares.' The WSO was struggling to be heard over the clamour of those desperate to disembark. 'And you must return by twenty-two hundred hours at the latest. Captain Highfield has made it clear he will not tolerate lateness. The duty officer will be taking names as each woman returns aboard. Make sure yours is among them.'

The heat was fierce and Margaret clung to the side of the ship, wishing, as the crowd pressed and writhed around her, that she could find somewhere to sit down. Avice, beside her, kept standing on tiptoe, shouting back what she could see, one hand shielding her eyes against the bright sunlight.

There was a queue for the gharries, the little horse-drawn carriages that would take the women to the Red Gate at the entrance to the dock. Those who had already made it down the gangplank were clustered around them, pointing out the distant views of the city.

Through the gate, Margaret could see wide, tree-lined avenues, flanked by large hotels, houses and shops, the pavements and roads thick with movement.

'There's a dinner-dance at Green's Hotel.' Avice was checking notes in her pocket book. 'Some of the girls are heading there later. I said we might meet them for tea. But I'm desperate to go shopping.'

'I just want a bloody seat,' Margaret muttered. 'I don't care about sightseeing or shopping. I just want dry land and a bloody seat.'

It was then that Margaret became aware of a shushing. She wondered what had caused it. Following the others' gaze, she turned to see Frances walking down the gangplank behind them. She wore her wide-brimmed sunhat and glasses, but her red-gold hair and long limbs confirmed her identity.

She hesitated at the bottom, conscious perhaps of the quiet. Then, seeing Margaret's hand held aloft, she made her way through the women to where Margaret and Avice stood.

'It'd drive you nuts to stay aboard too long, eh?' Margaret looked at Avice. 'Especially in heat like this.'

Frances stood very still, her eyes fixed on Margaret. 'It is pretty close,' she said.

'Well, I vote we find some bar or hotel where we can—'

'She's not walking around with us.'

'Avice!'

'People will talk. And for all we know her former customers are walking the streets. They might think we're one of those . . .'

'Don't be so ridiculous. Frances is perfectly welcome to walk with us.'

'You, perhaps,' said Avice. 'I'll find someone else to walk with.'

'Frances,' Margaret said, 'I'd be glad of your company. You can help me find somewhere nice to sit down.'

'Just watch out she doesn't find somewhere to lie down.'

Frances's head shot round and her fingers tightened on her handbag. 'Actually, I've changed my mind. I—I'll see you later.' Before Margaret had a chance to say any more she had disappeared back through the crowd.

The women closed ranks, murmuring in righteous indignation. Margaret watched the distant gangplank, just able to make out the tall, thin figure walking slowly up it. She knew she should go to Frances: by even participating in this outing she would condone Frances's treatment. But she was desperate to feel land under her feet. And it was so difficult to know what to say.

Frances was a few steps away from the little dormitory when she saw him. She had told herself that her previous outings around the ship had been to give herself some fresh air; to make herself leave the sweaty confines of the cabin. Now, as she recognised the man walking towards her, she knew she had not been honest with herself.

She glanced down at her pale blue blouse and khaki trousers, unconsciously checking herself as she had once done while on duty, feeling her skin prickle with a mixture of anxiety and anticipation. She was unsure of what she could possibly say to him.

They stopped. Looked at each other for just the briefest moment.

'Going ashore?' He indicated the harbour.

She could see nothing on his face, no clue. 'No . . . I—I decided to stay here.'

'Enjoy the peace and quiet.'

'Something like that.'

Perhaps he hadn't wanted to talk to her but was too gentlemanly to hurt her feelings.

'You should make the most of it,' he said. 'It's . . . hard to find a bit of space to yourself on board. I mean real space . . .'

Perhaps he might understand more than he was saying, she thought.

'Yes,' she said. 'Yes, it is.'

'Hey, Marine.'

The rating walked towards them, his cap pulled at a jaunty angle over one eye. 'They want you in the control room before your watch. Briefing for the governor's visit.' As he came closer she could see he had recognised her. The look the younger man gave her made her wince. 'Excuse me,' she said, cheeks reddening.

Moments later she wrenched open the door to the dormitory and let it shut heavily behind her. She leaned against it, her jaw clenched so tightly that it ached. Until now she had never thought about life's fairness, at least not in relation to herself. But now, with all the other emotions swirling around inside her in some infernal cocktail, she felt the pendulum swing from bleak despair to blind fury at the way her life had turned out. Had she not suffered enough?

Maud Gonne, perhaps understanding that Margaret had gone ashore, scratched restlessly at the door. Frances stooped, picked her up and sat down with her on her lap, but the dog took no comfort from this. In fact she paid Frances no attention, the milky, unseeing eyes, the quivering body desperate for only one person. Frances held the dog close to her, pitying her plight. 'I know,' she whispered, laying her cheek against the soft head. 'Believe me, I know.'

Accustomed to the intense heat of Bombay, and oblivious to the huge fans that whirred overhead, the waiters in the cocktail bar of Green's Hotel were visibly perspiring. The sweat glistened on their burnished faces and seeped into the collars of their immaculate white uniforms.

But their discomfort was less to do with the heat—it was a relatively mild evening—than with the endless demands of the hundred or so brides who had chosen that bar to end their day's shore leave.

'If I have to wait one more minute for my drink I swear I'll have words with that man,' said Avice, wafting the fan she had bought that afternoon and eyeing the unfortunate waiter as he ducked through the crowd, tray held aloft. 'I'm wilting,' she said, to his departing back.

'He's doing his best,' said Margaret. She had been careful to sip her drink slowly, having guessed from the packed bar that service was likely to be slow. She was feeling restored: she had been able to elevate her feet for half an hour, and now let her head rest on the back of the chair, enjoying the light breeze created by the overhead fan.

Heedless of the heat, Avice had dragged her everywhere that afternoon. They had walked round all the European shops, spent at least an hour in the Army and Navy Stores and another bartering with the men and small boys who besieged them with apparently unmissable bargains.

Margaret had been shocked at the sight of Indians bedding down in the street. At their thin limbs next to her own milk-fed plumpness, at their physical disabilities and barely dressed children.

Her drink appeared, and she made a point of tipping the waiter. Then, as he departed, she stared out at the *Victoria*, floating serenely in the harbour, and wondered guiltily if Frances was asleep. All its lights were on, giving it a festive appearance, but without either aircraft or people the flight deck looked like a vast, unpopulated plain.

'Ah! A seat! Mind if we join you?' Margaret looked round to see Irene Carter, flanked by one of her friends, pulling out the chair opposite. She gave a wide, lipsticked smile that did not stretch to her eyes. Despite the heat she looked cool and brought with her a vague scent of lilies.

'Irene,' said Avice, her own smile something of a snarl. 'How lovely.'

'We're exhausted,' said Irene, throwing her bags under the table and lifting a hand to summon a waiter. He arrived at her side immediately. 'All those natives following you around. I had to get one of the officers to tell them to leave me alone.'

'We've hardly noticed. We've been so busy shopping, haven't we, Margaret?' Avice gestured at her own bags.

'Really? I heard you'd bought something for the Queen of the *Victoria* final.' Margaret fancied there was a steely glint in Irene's eye.

'To be honest, I haven't given a thought to what I'll wear. It's only a bit of fun after all, isn't it?'

Margaret snorted quietly into her drink. Avice had spent the best part of an hour parading in front of a mirror in a variety of outfits. 'I wish I knew what Irene Carter was wearing,' she had muttered. 'I'm going to make sure I knock her into a cocked hat.' She had spent more money on three dresses than Margaret's father would spend on cattle feed in a year.

'Couldn't agree more,' said Irene. 'You know what, Avice? I shall tell all those girls who've been whispering that you're taking it too seriously that they're quite wrong. There.' She paused. 'And that I've heard that direct from the horse's mouth.' She lifted her drink as if in a toast.

Margaret had to bite her lip hard to stop herself laughing.

The four women, forced together through lack of spare tables rather than camaraderie, ordered a fish curry; Margaret found it delicious but regretted it when indigestion struck. The other brides, however, pronounced it inedible.

'I hope it hasn't done any harm to the baby,' said Avice, laying a hand on her non-existent bump.

'I heard your news. Congratulations,' said Irene. 'Does your husband know?' She laughed, a tinkling sound.

'I believe we're getting post tomorrow,' said Avice, whose own graceful smile had gone a little rigid. 'I imagine he'll have told everyone by now. We're having a party when we get to London,' she said. 'We felt we rather missed out, with the war, so we're going to have a do. Probably at the Savoy. And now, of course, it will be a double celebration.'

The Savoy was a good one, Margaret thought. Irene had looked briefly furious.

'In fact, Irene, perhaps you'd like to come. Mummy and Daddy will be flying from Australia—the new Qantas service?—and I'm sure they'd love to see you.' Avice leaned forward conspiratorially. 'Always makes you feel better to have at least one date in the social diary, doesn't it?'

Ka-*pow*! thought Margaret, who was enjoying herself now.

'I shall be delighted to come to your little gathering, if I can,' said Irene. 'But I do think it's lovely that you'll have something to take your mind off things.'

Avice raised an eyebrow.

'Oh, this horrid business with you having befriended a prostitute. I mean, who on earth could have known? And so soon after your other little friend was caught fraternising with those grubby engineers.'

'I hardly—' Avice began.

Irene's voice was concerned: 'It must have been so worrying for you, not knowing if you were going to be tarred with the same brush . . . you know, with what everyone's been saying about your dormitory and what goes on there. We've all so admired your stoicism. No, your little social do is a very good idea.'

The afternoon had stretched into evening, and with the fading of the light her thoughts had grown darker. Unable to face the confines of the cabin any longer, she had toyed with the idea of leaving the ship. But Bombay seemed to require a certain robustness of spirit that she did not own. She had stepped out and headed for the boat deck.

Now she stood, while the harbour lights glinted steadily on the inky water, interrupted occasionally by the noisy passage of tugs and barges. Across the bay, voices called to each other and from somewhere further distant Indian music drifted, one long, mournful filigree note.

'You want to watch out. You're not meant to be here.'

She jumped. 'Oh,' she said. 'It's you.'

'It's me,' he said, stubbing out his cigarette. 'Maggie not with you?'

'She's ashore.'

He was wearing his engineer's overalls; it was too dark to see the oil on them but she could smell it under the scent of the smoke. She hated the smell of oil: she had treated too many burned men who had been saturated with it.

I shall start nursing again in England, she told herself. Audrey Marshall had sent her off with a personal letter of recommendation. With her service record there would be no shortage of opportunities.

'Ever been to India before?'

She was annoyed at the interruption of her thoughts. 'No.'

'Seen a lot of countries, have you?'

'No more than anyone else who's seen service, I imagine.'

He lit himself another cigarette and blew the smoke meditatively into the sky. 'But I bet you could answer me a question,' he said.

She looked at him.

'Is there a difference?'

She frowned. 'I'm sorry?'

'In the men.' He smiled, revealing white teeth in the darkness. 'I mean, is there a nationality you prefer?'

From his expression she knew she had heard what she suspected. 'Excuse me,' she said. She moved past him, her cheeks burning, but as she reached for the handle of the hatch, he stepped in front of her.

'No need to have an attack of modesty on my account,' he said. 'We all know what you are. No need to skirt round it.' He spoke in a sing-song voice so that it was a second before she had gauged the menace in what he was saying.

'Please would you let me pass?'

'You know, I had you all wrong.' Dennis Tims shook his head. 'We called you Miss Frigidaire in the mess. Miss Frigidaire. We couldn't

135

believe you'd even married. How wrong we were, eh?'

Her heart was racing as she tried to assess whether she would be able to push past him for the door. One of his hands rested lightly on the handle. She could feel the confidence behind his strength, the sureness of a man who always, physically, got his own way.

'So prim and proper, with your blouses buttoned up to your neck. And really you're just some whore who no doubt persuaded some fool sailor to stick a ring on your finger. How'd you do it, eh? Tell him he was the only one who meant anything?' He put out a hand towards her breast and she batted it away.

'Let me pass,' she said.

'What's the matter, Miss Priss? Not like anyone's around to know.' He gripped her arms then, pushed her towards the guard rail. She stumbled as his weight met her like a solid wall. 'I've seen girls like you in a million ports. Shouldn't allow your sort on board,' he muttered wetly into her ear.

'Get off me!'

'Oh, come on! You can't expect me to believe you're not making a bit on the side while you're here—'

'Step away, Tims.'

The voice came from her right. Tims's head lifted, and she glanced across his shoulder. He was standing there, his eyes burning black in the dim light.

'Step away, Tims.' His tone was icy.

Tims turned and checked the other man's identity. 'A little dispute over payment,' he said, backing away from her and ostentatiously checking his trousers. 'You know what these girls are like.'

She closed her eyes, not wanting to see the marine's face. She was shaking violently.

'Get inside.' The marine spoke slowly.

Tims seemed remarkably cool. 'Like I said, Marine, just a disagreement about price. She wants to charge twice the going rate.'

'Get inside,' said Nicol. 'If I see you so much as look in Mrs Mackenzie's direction for the remainder of the voyage, I'll have you.'

'You?'

'It might not be on board. It might not even be on this voyage. But I'll have you.'

'You don't want to make an enemy of me, Marine.' Tims was at the hatch. 'Don't suppose you want the captain to know he's carrying a brasser. Or who her friends are.' His eyes glittered in the darkness.

'You aren't listening to me.'

There was a moment of exquisite stillness. Then, with a final, hard look at the two of them, Tims backed through the hatch.

'Are you all right?' he said, quietly.

She smoothed her hair off her face and swallowed hard. 'I'm fine.'

'I'm sorry,' he said. 'You shouldn't have to . . .' His voice tailed off, as if he were unsure of what he wanted to say.

She was unable to determine if she was brave enough to look at him. Finally, 'Thank you,' she whispered, and fled.

When he returned there was only one other marine in the mess: the young bugler, Emmett, was fast asleep, arms stretched behind his head. The little room smelt stale. Nicol removed his uniform, washed, and then, his towel round his neck and the water already evaporating from his skin, pulled his writing-paper from his locker and took a seat.

He was not a letter-writer. Many years ago, when he had tried, he had found that the sentiments on the page rarely mirrored what he felt inside. Now, however, the words came easily. He was letting her go. 'There is a passenger on board,' he wrote, 'a woman with a bad past. Seeing what she has suffered has made me realise that everyone deserves a second chance, especially if someone out there is willing to give them one, in spite of what they carry with them.'

Here he lit a cigarette, his gaze fixed ahead on nothing. He stayed like that for some time, oblivious to the men who were now climbing into their hammocks around him.

Finally, he put the nib of his pen back onto the paper. He would take it ashore tomorrow and wire it. No matter the cost. 'I suppose what I am trying to say is that I'm sorry. And that I'm glad you've found someone to love you, despite everything. I hope he will be good to you, Fay.'

He reread it twice before he saw that he had written Frances's name.

Thirty-three days

The Governor of Gibraltar was known throughout the navy and the British civil service as an unusually intelligent man. His diplomatic career had seen him rewarded for his hawklike tactical and observational skills, but even he had stared at the forward liftwell for several moments before he could acknowledge what he was seeing.

Captain Highfield, in the process of taking him up onto the flight deck ready for the welcoming performance by the Royal Marines Band, cursed himself for not checking the route beforehand. A liftwell was a liftwell. He had never thought they'd be bold enough to string their underwear along it. White, flesh-coloured, grey with overuse or cobweb-delicate and edged with French lace; the brassières and foundation garments waved merrily all the way up the cavernous space, mimicking the pennant that had welcomed the great man aboard.

Dobson. The man would have known about this, yet had chosen not to warn him. Captain Highfield cursed his leg for confining him to his office that morning and allowing the younger man the opportunity. He might have known Dobson would find a way to undermine him.

'I would say, Your Excellency, that this is something of an unconventional crossing. It is by no means an indication of the level of our respect.' He tried to inject a note of humour into his voice, but it fell flat.

The governor's wife, handbag held in front of her, nudged her husband surreptitiously. She inclined her head. 'Nothing we haven't seen before, Captain,' she said graciously, her mouth twitching. 'The war has exposed us all to far more frightening scenes than this one.'

'Quite,' said the governor. 'Quite.' The tenor of his voice suggested that this was unlikely.

'In fact, it's admirable that you're going to such lengths to keep your passengers comfortable.' She laid a hand on his sleeve, a glimmer of understanding in her face. 'Shall we move on?'

Things improved on the flight deck. Having embarked the governor and fourteen other passengers at Aden, the *Victoria* had begun to make her way slowly north along the Suez Canal. The brides were gay under parasols and sunhats, the band keeping up gamely despite the discomfort of the heat.

The men having resumed their duties, the governor and his wife had agreed to judge the tap-dancing competition, the latest in the series of the Queen of the *Victoria* contests devised to keep the women occupied. Shielded by a large umbrella from the worst of the sun, armed with iced gin and tonic and faced with a line of giggling girls, even the governor had warmed. His wife, who had taken the time to chat to each contestant, eventually awarded the prize to a pretty blonde girl, a popular choice given the hearty congratulations of the other brides. She had confided to Highfield afterwards that she thought the Australians were 'rather a nice lot. Terribly brave to leave their loved ones and come all this way.' Infected with a little of the merriment of the afternoon, he had found it hard to disagree.

And then it had all gone wrong again.

The *Victoria* was moving sedately past a military camp on the starboard side and the brides, spotting large numbers of Caucasian men, had flocked to the edge of the flight deck. Their dresses fluttering in the breeze, they waved gaily at the bronzed young men, who had stopped work to watch them pass, calling down greetings.

Highfield stared at the bare-chested men below, now jammed up against the wire perimeter fence, making sure his suspicions were correct. Then it was with a heavy heart that he reached for the Tannoy. 'I am gratified that you have given our guests, the governor and his wife, such a rousing welcome,' he said, watching the governor's back stiffen in his tropical whites as he too took in the scene below. 'There will be extra refreshments in the forward hangar for those who would like tea. In the meantime, you might be interested to know that the young men you are waving to are German prisoners.'

Irene Carter had approached her after the contest to tell her she was glad Avice had won—'Best to make the most of those legs before the old varicose veins set in, eh?'—and to show off her latest delivery of post. She had received seven letters, no less than four from her husband.

'You must read us yours,' she said, sunglasses masking her eyes. 'My mother says she's been inviting yours round for tea since they discovered we were shipmates. Did you get many?'

'Oh, heaps,' said Avice, brandishing hers in the air. There had been only one from Ian. She had tucked it under her mother's so that Irene couldn't tell. 'Good luck with the next contest, anyway,' she said. 'It's fancy dress, I believe, so I'm sure you'll do much better. You're getting so tanned you could wear a scarf round your waist and go as a native.' And clutching her 'certificate', Avice walked away.

Frances wasn't in the dormitory. Margaret was attending a lecture on places to visit in England. Avice kicked off her shoes and lay down, preparing to read Ian's latest communication in an atmosphere of rare privacy. She scooted through the letters from her father and sister . . . then came to Ian's envelope.

She glanced at her wristwatch: there was ten minutes before the first lunch shift. She had just time to read it. She peeled it open and gave a little sigh of pleasure.

A quarter of an hour later, she was still staring at it.

Frances and Margaret were seated in the deck canteen when the rating found them. They had been eating ices. Frances was now accustomed to the relative hush that descended whenever she dared show herself in public. Margaret had chattered away with grim determination.

'Mrs Frances Mackenzie?' the rating had asked.

She nodded. She had been half expecting him for days.

'Captain would like to see you in his offices, ma'am. I'm to bring you.'

The canteen had gone quiet.

Margaret blanched. 'Do you think it's the dog?' she whispered.

'No,' said Frances, dully. 'I'm pretty sure it's not that.'

Avice lay on the bed. From somewhere nearby there was a strange sound, a low, guttural moan, and it was with distant surprise that she realised it was emanating from her own throat.

She stared at the hand holding the letter, then at the wedding ring on her slim finger. The room receded around her. Suddenly, she threw herself off her bunk, fell onto her knees, and vomited violently into the bowl that had never been removed after her early days of sickness. Finally, spent, she pushed herself back against the bunk, her hair plastered in sweaty tendrils round her face, limbs awkward and ungainly on the hard floor, her dress, her make-up unheeded. She wondered if the whole thing had been a dream. Perhaps the letter didn't exist.

But there it was on her pillow.

Outside, she could hear the clicking heels of a group of women who were chattering as they passed. She lay down on the ribbed metal floor, eyes on the other letter open beside her. Her mother had written:

I've told everyone that the celebration will be at the Savoy. Daddy got a very advantageous rate because of one of his contacts in the hotel business. And, Avice darling—you'll never guess—the Darley-Hendersons are going to make it part of their round-the-world trip. If that wasn't exciting enough the governor and his wife have said they're coming too. That will ensure we get your picture into Tatler. Darling, I might have had my doubts about this wedding, but we'll put on a do that will have not just Melbourne but half of England talking for months!

Your loving Mother

PS We've not heard yet from Ian's parents, which is a pity. Could you ask him to send us their address so we can contact them ourselves?

It had been a long, rather wearing afternoon, and it was something of an effort to stand when the young woman entered the room, so Captain Highfield stayed behind his desk to allow himself the chance to lean on it. She stood in the doorway when the rating announced her and stayed there after he had left, clutching a small bag. He had seen her at close quarters twice now and she was physically striking. Only her demeanour stopped her being a compelling figure. She had seemingly developed the trick of receding into the background; now that he had briefed himself through her notes, he understood why.

Captain Highfield gestured to her to sit down. Perhaps to save her blushes, he had chosen to hold this meeting without the aid of either the chaplain or WSO. He stared at the floor for some moments, trying to work out how to address the issue. Disciplinary matters with his men were straightforward: one followed procedure, gave them a bawling-out if necessary. But women were different, he thought, exasperated. They brought all their problems on board along with their tons of baggage.

Come on, man, he told himself. Get it over and done with. 'It has come to my attention that several days ago you were involved in something of an incident downstairs. In the course of looking into the matter, I've heard things that . . . have left me a little concerned.'

It was Rennick who had told him, the previous evening.

'It's about your . . . your life before you came aboard. I'm afraid for the welfare of my men and for the good conduct of everyone on board, I have to know whether these . . . these rumours are true.'

She said nothing.

'Can I assume from your silence that they are not . . . untrue?'

When she failed to answer him a second time, he felt ill-at-ease. This, allied with his physical discomfort, caused him to become impatient. He stood and moved round the desk.

'I'm not trying to deliberately persecute you, Miss—'

'Mrs,' she said. 'Mrs Mackenzie.'

'But rules are rules, and as it stands I cannot allow women of . . . your sort to travel on a ship full of men.'

'My sort?'

'You know what I'm saying. I've looked into your—your circumstances, and I can't allow your presence to destabilise my ship.'

She stared at her shoes, then raised her head. 'Captain Highfield, are you putting me off the ship?' Her voice was calm.

He was half relieved that she had said it. 'I'm sorry,' he said. 'I feel I have no choice.'

She appeared to be considering something. Her demeanour suggested that there was nothing surprising in what he had said to her.

'You are free to say something,' he said, when the silence became oppressive. 'In your defence, I mean.'

There was a lengthy pause. Then she placed her hands in her lap. 'In my defence . . . I am a nurse. A nursing sister, to be more precise. I have been a nurse for four and a half years. In that time I've treated several thousand men, some of whose lives I saved.'

'It's a very good thing—that you managed to—'

'Become a worthwhile human being?' Her tone was sharp. She smoothed her dress over her knees and took a deep breath, as if she were having some trouble containing herself. 'What I was going to say, Captain Highfield, before you interrupted me, is that I nursed men, who had been terrorised and physically brutalised, some of whom were my enemies, many of whom were only half alive. And not one,' she paused for breath. 'Not one of them treated me with the lack of consideration you have just shown.'

He had not expected her to be so composed. So articulate.

He had not expected to find himself the accused.

He glanced down at the papers that detailed the procedures for putting off brides. 'Put her off at Port Said,' the Australian Red Cross supervisor had said. 'She might have to wait a bit for a boat back. Then again, a lot of them disappear in Egypt.' Her 'them' had contained an unmistakable note of contempt.

God, it was a mess. A bloody mess. He wished he'd never embarked on the conversation. But she had entered the system now.

Perhaps recognising something in his expression, she got to her feet. Her hair, scraped back from her forehead, emphasised the high, almost Slavic bones of her face, the shadows under her eyes.

'Look, Mrs Mackenzie, I—' He was struggling for something to say, something that might appropriately convey the right mixture of authority and regret.

She was halfway towards the door, when she said, 'Do you want me to look at your leg?'

His final words stalled on his lips. He blinked.

'I've seen you limping. When you thought you were alone. You might as well know that I used to sit out on the flight deck at night.'

Highfield was now completely wrong-footed. He found he had moved his leg behind him.

They stood across the office from each other. Neither moved.

'I've not . . . I've not mentioned it to anyone,' he found himself saying.

'I'm fairly good at keeping secrets,' she said, her eyes on his face.

He sat down heavily on his chair and drew up his trouser leg. He hadn't liked to look too closely at it for some days.

She stepped forward and examined it. 'It's clearly infected. Is your temperature raised?'

'I've felt better,' he conceded.

She studied it. 'I think you may have an infection that has spread into the bone. This should be drained, and you need penicillin.'

'Do you have some?'

'No, but Dr Duxbury should.'

'I don't want Duxbury told,' he said.

'Then I've given you my professional opinion, Captain, and I respect your right to ignore it.'

She got up and wiped her hands on her trousers. He asked her to wait, then moved past her and opened the door. He summoned the rating from the corridor.

The boy stepped in, his gaze flickering between the captain and the woman before him. 'Take Mrs Mackenzie here to the dispensary,' Highfield said. 'She is to fetch some items.'

When she took the key from him, she made sure her fingers did not touch his.

The needle went into his leg. Despite the pain of the procedure, Highfield felt the anxiety that had plagued him start to dissipate.

'You need another dose of penicillin in about six hours. Then one a day. A double dose to start with to push your system into fighting the infection. And when you get to England you must go straight to your doctor. It's possible he'll want you in hospital.' She returned to the wound. 'But you're lucky. I don't think it's gangrenous.'

She said this in a quiet, unemotional tone, declining to look at his face for most of it. Finally, she placed the dressing on his leg and sat back on her heels so that he could pull down his trouser leg.

He sighed with relief at the prospect of a pain-free night. She was gathering together the medical equipment she had brought from the dispensary. 'You should keep some of this here,' she said, eyes still on the floor. 'You'll need to change that dressing tomorrow.' She scribbled some instructions on a piece of paper. 'Keep your leg elevated whenever you're alone. And try to keep it dry. You can take the painkilling tablets two at a time.' She put the dressing and tape on his desk.

'I'm going to say there has been a misunderstanding.' Her head lifted at his voice. 'A case of mistaken identity. If you could spare some time during the voyage to administer those injections I would be grateful.'

She stared at him, raised herself to her feet. She looked, perhaps for the first time that day, startled. She swallowed hard. 'I didn't do it for that,' she said.

He nodded. 'I know.'

He stood up, testing his weight on the injured leg. Then he held out his hand. 'Thank you,' he said, 'Mrs . . . Sister Mackenzie.'

Given the astonishing composure she had shown so far, when she took it and looked up, he was surprised to see tears in her eyes.

Thirty-five days

The marine officer's attendant had motioned to him twice now to help clear the wardroom. It took Jones's urgent 'C'mon, man, shake a leg,' to rouse Nicol from his reverie.

Around him the officers had finished their meal and were retiring to smoke pipes and read letters or old newspapers. There had been a long-running joke throughout lunch about the state of the *Victoria's* engines, and an open book on whether they were going to last until Plymouth.

During lunch he had been imagining her put off, and him following. He had allowed himself the daydream that her husband might send her a Not Wanted Don't Come, then cursed himself for wishing that shame upon her. But he couldn't help it. When he closed his eyes, he saw the brief, bright smile she had bestowed on him when they had danced.

Who had she married? Had she told him of her past? Worse, had the man been part of it? There seemed no way to ask her without implying that he, like the rest of them, was entitled to some sort of opinion on her life. She had created a future for herself, found some stability. He had no right to say or do anything that might interfere with it.

Last night he had stared up at the constellations that had once intrigued him, now cursing the conjunction of planets that had caused their paths to veer past each other at a point that might have redeemed them both. I could have made her happy, he thought. How could the unknown husband say the same? Or perhaps some selfish part of him just wanted to diminish his own sense of guilt by being her saviour.

It was this uncomfortable revelation that forced him to his conclusion, which prompted him to swap his shifts with Emmett and kept him, for the next few days, well away from her.

It was no longer her past that troubled him. It was that she had escaped it.

A burst of laughter brought him back to the present. He stared up at the picture of the King, in pride of place on the wall, then stood next to Jones, preparing to file out of the wardroom. He had received a wire four days after he had sent his own. It had said simply, 'Thank you!' The exclamation mark, with all it conveyed, had made him wince.

Unexpectedly, the dog began to howl when Margaret opened the door. She placed her hands frantically round Maud Gonne's muzzle and stumbled for the bed, hissing, 'Shush! Shush, Maudie! Shush now!' The dog had barked twice, and Margaret had come as close as she ever had to smacking her. 'Come on, now, settle down,' she murmured, and the dog turned tight circles on her bunk.

Only then did she realise Avice was lying motionless on her bunk, facing the wall, her knees drawn up to her stomach. It was, she calculated, the fourth day that Avice had lain like this. Seasickness, she had said, to enquiries. But the water hadn't been choppy.

Margaret stepped forward and bent over the prostrate figure. She had wondered whether to talk to Frances: perhaps Avice was suffering from some medical complaint. But given the bad blood between the two women, she didn't feel it fair on either of them.

Besides, Frances was rarely here now. She had been helping out in the infirmary, Dr Duxbury having gleefully accepted the responsibility of organising the final of the Queen of the *Victoria* contest. At other times she went out for several hours every day, and offered no explanation as to where she was going. Margaret supposed she should be glad to see her so much happier, but she missed her company.

'Avice?' she whispered now. 'Are you awake?'

She did not reply until a second prompt. 'Yes.'

Margaret stood awkwardly in the centre of the little dormitory, trying to work out what to do for the best. 'Can I . . . can I get you a cup of tea?'

'No.'

Margaret lay down on her bed and read for almost an hour, not feeling able to leave either Avice or the dog. She had begun a letter to her father, then discovered she had nothing to say about life on board that she had not already told him. She had written to Daniel instead: a series of questions about the mare, an urgent demand that he should skin as many darn rabbits as he could so that he could get over to England to see her. Daniel had written once, a letter she had received at Bombay. It comprised just a few lines and told her little, other than the state of the cows, the weather, and the plot of a movie he had seen in town, but her heart had eased. She had been forgiven, those few lines had told her.

There was a sharp rap on the door, and she leapt on her dog, cutting short her bark. 'Hold on,' she said, her broad hand clamped gently but firmly round Maud Gonne's muzzle. 'Just coming.'

'Is Mrs A. Radley there?'

Margaret faced Avice's bunk. Avice, blinking, sat. Her clothes were crumpled, her face pale and blank. She slid slowly to the floor, lifting a hand to her hair. 'Avice Radley,' she said, opening the door a little way.

A young rating stood before her. 'You've had a wire. Come through the radio room this afternoon.'

Margaret dropped the dog behind her and stepped forward to take

Avice's arm. 'Oh my God,' she said involuntarily.

The rating registered the two wide-eyed faces. Then he thrust the piece of paper into Avice's hand. 'It's good news, missus. Your folks are going to be in Plymouth to meet you off the ship.'

Avice had sobbed for almost twenty minutes, which had initially seemed excessive and had now become alarming. Margaret, her previous reticence forgotten, had climbed onto Avice's bunk and now sat beside her, trying not to think about the way it creaked ominously under her weight. 'It's OK, Avice,' she kept saying. 'He's all right. Ian's all right. That bloody wire just gave you a bit of a fright.'

The captain wasn't best pleased, the rating had said gleefully. Said he'd be using the radio room for taking down shopping lists next. But he'd allowed the message through.

Margaret tutted. 'They shouldn't have sent someone down here like that. They must have known it would scare you half to death. Specially someone in our condition, eh?' She tried to get the girl to smile.

Avice failed to answer her. But eventually the sobbing subsided and Margaret stepped down. She lay on her own bunk and began to chat about Avice's preparations for the Queen of the *Victoria* final, anything to shake her out of her depression. 'You've got to wear those green satin shoes again,' she rattled on gamely. 'You don't know how many girls would give their eye teeth for them, Avice. That girl from 11F said she'd seen some just like them in *Australian Women's Weekly*.'

Avice's eyes were raw and red-rimmed. You don't understand, she thought, as she stared at the blank wall, not registering the endless stream of words that floated up from below. Just for a moment, I thought that there was going to be a way out of this for me. Just for a moment, I thought they had come to tell me he was dead.

'Sister Mackenzie . . . can I offer you a drink? I often have a little tot at this time of day.'

'Thank you, but I don't drink.' She began to place the medical instruments back in the carrying case.

'Sensible girl. Do please sit down for a while.'

She knew he felt better. It was in his demeanour; something in him was no longer quite so grimly contained. Now his smile came readily. When he stood straight, it was with pride rather than the desperation to prove he still could. She closed the case and sat down, watching as he manoeuvred himself round his desk. The captain's private room could have sat happily in any well-to-do house, with its carpet, paintings and comfortable upholstered chairs. She thought of the sparse conditions of the men below; their hammocks, lockers and bleached tabletops. 'How did you do it?' she asked, as he poured his drink.

'What?'

'Your leg. You never said.'

He was standing with his back to her and for a moment it went still enough for her to understand that her question had not been as inconsequential as she had intended. 'You don't have to tell me,' she said. 'I'm sorry. I didn't mean to pry.'

It was as if he had not heard her. He stoppered the decanter, then sat down again. He took a long slug of the amber liquid, and then he spoke. The *Victoria*, he said, was not his ship. 'I served on her sister, *Indomitable*. From 'thirty-nine. Then shortly before VJ Day we came under attack. I knew from the start we were done.

'My nephew was a pilot. Robert Hart. Twenty-six years old. My younger sister Molly's boy. We were close. He was a good chap.'

They were interrupted by a knock on the door. Highfield rose and walked heavily across the floor. He opened the door, glanced at the papers that were handed to him and nodded at the young telegraphist. 'Very good,' he muttered.

Frances, still lost in the captain's previous words, barely noticed.

The captain sat down again, dropping the papers beside him on the desk. There was a long silence.

'Was he . . . shot down?' she said.

'No,' he said, after another slug of his drink. 'No. One of the bombs dropped into number two hold and blew out several decks, from the officers' berths to the centre engine room. I lost sixteen men in that first explosion.'

Frances could imagine the scene on board, her nose scenting the smoke and oil, the screams of trapped and burning men in her ears. 'Including your nephew?'

'No . . . no, that's the problem. I was too late getting them out, you see. I'd been blown off my feet and I was a bit dazed. I didn't realise how close the explosion had been to the ammunition stores. Fifteen minutes after the first explosion, they caught and blew out half the innards of the ship.' He shook his head. 'I thought the heavens themselves had cracked open. I should have had more men down there, checking the hatches were closed, stopping the fire. I lost fifty-eight, all told. My nephew was trapped in one of the planes. I couldn't get to him.'

Frances sat very still. 'I'm sorry,' she said.

'They made me get off,' he said, his words coming thick and fast now as if they had waited too long. 'She was going down, and I had my men—those who could still stand—in the boats. It was so hot. Those of us still aboard were spraying ourselves with the hoses, just to try to stay on the ship. And while we were trying to reach our injured men, while bits of the ship were cracking open and burning, the bloody Japanese kept circling.' He took a gulp of his drink. 'I was still trying to find him when they ordered me off.' He dropped his head. 'Two destroyers came alongside to help us. Finally saw off the Japanese. And all my men sat there and watched as I let the ship go down, knowing that there were probably men alive down there, injured men.'

He paused. 'None of them said a word to me. They just stared.'

Frances closed her eyes. She had heard similar stories, knew the scars they caused. There was nothing she could say to comfort him.

'Not much of a way to end a career, is it?'

She heard the break in his voice. 'Captain,' she said, 'the only people who still have all the answers are those who have never been faced with the questions.'

Captain Highfield stared at his feet, then at her, digesting the truth of what she had said. He had a long slug of his drink, his eyes not leaving hers as he finished it. 'Sister Mackenzie,' he said, as he put his glass on the table, 'tell me about your husband.'

Nicol had stood outside the cinema projection room for three-quarters of an hour. His attention was focused on the other end of the corridor.

'I can't believe this,' Jones-the-Welsh had said, as he dried himself in the mess. 'I heard she was being put off. The next thing captain's saying it's all a bloody misunderstanding. It was not, I can tell you. Don't understand it.' He rubbed briskly under his arms.

'I know why,' said another marine. 'She's in there having a drink with the skipper.'

'What?'

'The weather-guesser took him in the long-range reports, and there she is, curled up with him on the settee having a drink.'

'The sly old dog,' Jones said.

'She's not silly, eh?'

'It's one rule for us and another for them, that's for sure,' said Duckworth, bitterly.

'You must be mistaken.' Nicol had spoken before he realised what he was saying. 'She wouldn't be in the captain's rooms.' He lowered his voice. 'I mean, there's no reason for her to be there.'

'Taylor knows what he saw. I can tell you something else. It's not the first time, either. He reckons it's the third time this week he's seen her in there.'

'Third time, eh? C'mon, Nicol. You know the reason as well as I do.' Jones's braying voice had exploded into laughter. 'How'd you like that, boys? Our skipper's finally discovered the joys of the flesh!'

At last he heard voices. As he stood back against the pipes, the captain's lobby door opened. The air was punched silently from his lungs as he saw the slim figure step out and turn to face the captain. He didn't have to look long to confirm who it was: her image, every last detail, was now as deeply imprinted on his soul as if it had been etched there.

'Thank you,' Highfield was saying. 'I don't really know what else to say. I'm not usually given to . . .'

She shook her head, as if whatever she had bestowed upon him was nothing. Then she smoothed her hair. He found himself stepping back into the shadows. *I'm not given to . . .* to what? Nicol's breath lodged in his chest and his mind went blank.

They muttered something he couldn't catch, and then her voice rose again. 'Oh, Captain,' she called, 'I forgot to say . . . Sixteen.'

Nicol could just make out Highfield staring at her, his expression quizzical.

She began to make her way towards the main hangar. 'Sixteen penicillin left in the big bottle. Seven in the smaller one. And ten sealed dressings in the white bag. At least, there should be.'

Two days to Plymouth

In the absence of horses and a track, it should perhaps have been of little surprise that such fierce betting lay on the immaculately coiffed heads of the Queen of the *Victoria* contestants. It was possible that knowing she was five to two on might have put a swagger into Irene Carter's already undulating step, but for days now it had been common knowledge that the real favourite was Avice Radley.

'Foster says there's some fair-sized punts on her,' yelled Plummer, the junior stoker.

'There's some fair-sized somethings,' roared the departing watch.

Within hours they would have entered the cool, choppy waters of the Bay of Biscay, but more than a hundred feet below the flight deck, down in the engine pit, the temperature was still at a shirt-drenching hundred or so degrees. Tims, naked to the waist, swung the polished wheels that sent the steam into the engine's turbines while Plummer, who had been oiling the main engine, felt round the bearings for overheating.

Between them, the bridge telegraph dial relayed the orders from above to put the engines over to 'full speed' in an effort to get through the rough as soon as possible, and around them the tired old ship creaked and groaned in protest. Steam persisted in escaping through valves in little belches of effort; the rags that tried to quell them were damp and sodden with scalding water.

Plummer finished tightening a bolt, secured his spanner in its wall-mounting, then turned to Tims. 'You not had a few bob on one of them girls, then? There's a lot of money riding on it.'

'Load of rubbish,' said Tims, dismissively. He wiped his shining forehead with a rag, then reached down for a wrench. 'Don't know what you're getting so excited about,' he growled. 'You're on duty all night.'

'Two pounds I've got on that Radley girl,' Plummer said. 'Two pounds! I got my bet on when she was still three to one against so if she wins I'm bloody quids in. If not, I'm in the drink. I promised my old ma I'd pay for us all to go to Scarborough. But I reckon I can't lose.'

Tims, apparently oblivious, was staring at his watch.

Plummer rambled on: 'All the officers get to see it, you know. How's that fair, eh? Two more nights on board, and all the officers get to see the girls in their swimsuits and we're stuck down here in bloody centre engine. You know the marines are switching shifts at nine so even they'll catch some of it. One rule for one lot, another rule for us.'

Plummer checked a dial, swore, then glanced at Tims, who was staring at the wall.

'You all right, Tims? Something got on your wick, has it?'

'Cover me for half an hour,' Tims said, turning towards the exit hatch. 'Something I need to do.'

Had he been able to see the opening stages of the Queen of the *Victoria* contest, young Plummer might have felt less confident about his trip to Scarborough.

Perched on the makeshift stage alongside her fellow contestants, Avice Radley looked pale and preoccupied, despite the glowing scarlet of the silk dress she wore and the glossy wheat sheen of her blonde hair. As the other girls giggled and clutched each other, trying to keep their balance in high heels as the ship dipped under them, she stood alone and aside, smile fading, eyes shadowed. And when you compared her to the glowing Irene Carter, resplendent in pale peach and blue and apparently heedless of the heaving waters, it was hard to disagree.

Dr Duxbury, the host for the evening's proceedings, had tried to get

Avice to elaborate on her plans for her new life, but she had seemed not to notice him. He tailed off to polite, scattered applause.

'Ladies,' said Highfield, standing quickly. He waited as the audience gradually fell silent. 'As you know, this is our last night's entertainment on the *Victoria*. Tomorrow night we will dock at Plymouth, and in the morning I will discuss the arrangements on the flight deck, but for now I just wanted to say a few words. I can't—I can't pretend this has been the easiest cargo I have ever had to transport,' he said. 'But I can tell you that it has been the most . . . educational.

'Now I won't bore you with a lengthy speech about the difficulties of the course you have chosen. But I will say that you, like all of us, will probably find the next twelve months the most challenging—and hopefully rewarding—of your lives. So what I wanted to tell you is this: you are not alone.'

He looked around at the hushed, expectant faces. Under the harsh lights of the hangar deck the gilt buttons of his uniform shone.

'Those of us who have always served are going to have to find new ways of living. Those of us who have found ourselves profoundly changed by the experience of war will have to find new ways of dealing with those around us. Those who have suffered are going to have to find ways of forgiving. We are returning to a country that is likely to be unfamiliar to us. We, too, may find ourselves strangers in that land. So, yes, brides, you face a great challenge. But it has been both a pleasure and a privilege to be part of your journey and we are proud to claim you as our own. And I hope that when you look back, in happiness, to the early years of your time in Britain, you think of this as not simply the journey to your new life but the start of it.'

Few would have noticed that during some of this speech he seemed to be speaking to one woman in particular, that when he said, 'You are not alone,' his gaze might have rested on her a little longer than on anyone else. But it was irrelevant. There was a brief silence, and then gradually applause and cheering ignited the entire room.

Captain Highfield took his seat, having nodded gratefully at the blur of faces. It had not come solely from the women below him, he observed, trying not to smile as much as he wanted to. It had also come from the men. 'What did you think?' he murmured to the woman beside him, his chest still puffed with pride.

'Very nice, Captain. Your words were . . . beautifully chosen.'

Highfield felt the ship lift under him as it broke another wave.

'Glass of cordial, Sister Mackenzie? You sure you wouldn't like anything stronger?' He waited until it had ridden out, then lifted his glass.

It would only be for twenty minutes. The engine was running much better, or at least as well as she was ever going to. And Davy Plummer was buggered if he was going to sit down there by himself in the engine room. Besides, he was leaving the navy once they got back to Blighty. What were they going to make him do if they found him off duty for once? Make him swim home?

He checked the temperature gauges, ran a cloth over the more problematic pipes, stubbed out his cigarette underfoot and, with a swift glance behind him, ran two at a time up the steps onto the gangway and towards the exit hatch.

The votes were in and Avice Radley had lost. The judging panel all agreed that they had wanted to give the prize to Mrs Radley but felt that, given her extremely lacklustre performance on the final night, her marked disinclination to smile and her perplexing answer to the question, 'What do you most want to do when you finally get to England?' ('I don't know') and her immediate disappearance after it, there was only one choice for overall winner.

Irene Carter wore her hand-sewn sash with cooing, tearful delight. It had been, she announced, the finest trip she had ever undertaken. She felt, frankly, as if she had made at least 600 new friends. And she hoped they would all find the happiness in England she was sure they deserved. It was when she started thanking her former neighbours in Sydney by name that Captain Highfield intervened and announced that if the officers and men would like to clear the tables to the sides of the room, the Royal Marines Band would provide music for a little dancing.

Davy Plummer, standing near the back of the bandstand, glanced in disgust at the handwritten betting slip Foster had given him, screwed it up and thrust it into the pocket of his overall. Bloody women. He was about to return to the engine room when he saw two brides standing in the corner. They whispered something behind their hands.

'Never seen a working man before?' he said, holding out the sides of his overalls.

'We were wondering if you were going to dance,' said the smaller, blonder girl, 'but whether you could do it without getting us all oily.'

'Ladies, you have no idea what a stoker can do with his hands.' Davy Plummer stepped forward, his betting slip forgotten.

Frances ran lightly along the corridor that led from the hangar to the dormitories, occasionally touching the wall to keep her balance.

Then she stopped.

He was standing outside the dormitory, removing a cigarette from a packet. She had not seen him since he had arrived on the gun turret as she struggled with Tims, and had had to fight the suspicion that he had avoided her since then. She had several times considered asking the younger marine, Emmett, why he had taken over the night watch.

Even as her feet took her towards him she felt her own reticence return. She paused at the door, unsure whether to step inside.

'Want one?' he said, holding the packet towards her.

She took a cigarette and he held the flame towards her so that she didn't have to bend towards him as it lit. She could not take her eyes off his hands.

'I saw you at the captain's table,' he said eventually. His voice sounded strange. 'Quite unusual for him to invite one of the women to join him.'

The temperature of her blood dropped a couple of degrees. 'Is there something you want to say?'

He looked blank.

She forgot her previous awkwardness. 'Surely what you're asking is why I, of all people, was seated at the captain's table?'

He set his jaw. 'I was . . . curious. I came to see you the other afternoon. And then I saw you . . . outside the captain's—'

'Ah. Now I see. You weren't asking, just implying.'

'I didn't mean—'

'So you've come to question me over the standard of my conduct?'

'No, I—'

'What will you do, Marine? Report the captain? Or just the whore?'

The word silenced them both.

'Why are you talking like this?' he asked quietly.

'Because I'm tired, Marine. I'm tired of having every single one of my actions judged by ignorant people who then find me wanting.'

'I didn't judge you.'

'The hell you didn't.' She was suddenly furious. 'You're as bad as the rest of them. I thought you were different. I thought you understood something about me, understood what I was made of. God knows why!'

'Frances—'

'What?'

'I'm sorry about what I said. I just saw you . . . and . . . I'm sorry. Really. Things have happened that have made me . . .' He tailed off, then continued. 'Look, I came to see you because I wanted you to know something. I did things in the war . . . that I'm not proud of. I haven't always behaved in a way that people—people who don't know the full circumstances—might consider to be admirable. There's none of us—not even your husband probably—who can say they did.'

She put out a hand to the wall, feeling the floor rise and fall under her feet. 'I think you'd better go,' she said quietly. She could not look at him, but she could feel his eyes on her. 'Good night, Marine,' she said.

In the centre engine room, somewhere below the hangar deck, the high-pressure feed pump that transferred fuel to the boiler, succumbed to what might have been age, and split.

It is impossible to see the hot spots in a ship's engine, the places where small areas of metal, weakened by fractures or the strain on its joints, reach terrible internal temperatures. If they cannot be detected by the many gauges around the engine room, or by the treacherous act of feeling for them through rags, one discovers them by chance—conclusively when fuel leaks onto them.

Unseen and unheard by the humans who relied upon it, the *Victoria's* centre engine hammered energetically, unseen, too red, too hot. The fuel hung briefly in the air in tiny, unseen droplets. Then the exhaust duct, inches from the cracked fuel pipe, glinted, like malice in a devilish eye, ignited and, with a sudden whumph! took its chance.

Fool. Bloody fool. Nicol slowed outside the oilskin store. One more night until she left for good, one more in which he could have said a thousand things to her, shown her a little understanding. If nothing else, she would have known then. As bad as the rest of them, she had told him. The worst of what he had always suspected of himself.

'Blast it,' he said, and slammed his fist into the wall.

'Something bothering you, Marine?' Tims was blocking the passageway. 'Run out of people to discipline?'

Nicol glanced at his bleeding knuckles. 'Get on with your work, Tims.' Bile rose in him.

'Get on with your work? Who d'you think you are? Commander?'

Nicol glanced behind him at the empty corridor. No one was visible. Those not on duty were all in the hangar area, enjoying the dance.

'Your ladyfriend not giving it up, like you thought?'

Nicol took a deep breath. 'You might think you're a big man on this ship, Tims, but in a couple of days' time you'll just be another unemployed matelot like the rest of them. A nothing.' He tried to keep his voice calm, but he could still hear in it the vibration of barely suppressed rage.

Tims crossed his forearms across his chest. 'Perhaps you're not her type.' He lifted his chin, as if a thought had occurred to him. 'Oh, sorry,

I forgot. Everyone's her type, provided they've got two bob . . .'

The first punch Tims seemed to expect and ducked away. The second was blocked by the stoker's own blinding upper cut. It caught Nicol unawares, sending him crashing backward into the wall.

'Think your little whore will still find you pretty now, Marine?' The words came at him like another blow, cutting through the sound of the engines, the blood in his ears. 'Perhaps she just didn't think you were man enough for her, with your prissy uniforms.'

He felt the stoker's breath on his skin, could smell the oil on him. 'Did she tell you how she liked to feel my hands on them titties, liked to—'

With a roar, Nicol threw himself at Tims and brought them both crashing down. He pummelled blindly at the flesh before him, not even sure what his fists were connecting with. He felt the man wrench his body underneath him, saw the great fist come round as it caught him again. But he could not stop now, even if he felt himself in danger. He hardly felt the blows that rained down upon him. A blood mist had descended, and all the anger of the past six weeks, of the past six years, forced their way out of him through his fists. In their welter of blood and blows neither man registered the siren, despite the proximity of the Tannoy above their heads.

'Fire! Fire! Fire!' came the piped instruction. 'Standing Sea Emergency Party, close up at Section Base Two. All marines to the boat deck.'

The Queen of the *Victoria* contestants were being led from the stage, their polished smiles vanished from their faces, Irene Carter clutching her winner's sash round her like a life jacket. Margaret glimpsed them briefly as, wedged in the sea of bodies, she found herself moving towards the door.

A voice shouted from somewhere ahead, 'Quickly, ladies, please. Those with surnames N to Z gather at Muster Station B, all others to Muster Station A. Just keep moving now.'

Margaret had made her way to the edge of the crowd when the women's service officer caught her arm.

'This way, madam.' She held out her arms, pointing in front of her, a physical barrier to the starboard exit.

'I have to pop downstairs.' Margaret cursed under her breath as someone elbowed her in the back. 'I have to fetch something.'

The woman looked at her as if she was a fool. 'There is a fire on board,' she said. 'There is no going downstairs. Captain's orders.'

Margaret's voice rose, a mixture of anxiety and frustration. 'You don't understand! I have to make sure—I have to look after my—my—'

The WSO's temper flared right back. She blew her whistle, trying to steer someone to the right, then pulled it from her pursed lips and hissed, 'Can you imagine the chaos if we let everyone start digging around for photograph albums or pieces of jewellery? It's a fire. Now, please move on or I'll have to get someone to move you.'

Two marines were already locking the exit hatch. Margaret gazed around her, trying to locate another way down, and then, her chest tight, moved forward in the crush.

'Avice.' Frances stood in the doorway of the silent dormitory, staring at the motionless form on the bunk. 'Avice? Can you hear me?'

There was no response. For a minute, Frances had thought this was because Avice now declined to speak to her. She would not normally have persisted, but something made her ask again.

'Just go away,' came the reply. It sounded reduced, at odds with the aggression of the words.

Then the siren had started. Outside, in the gangway, a fire alarm rang, shrill and insistent, followed by the sound of rapid footfalls outside.

'Attack party close up at fire in centre engine. Location centre engine. All passengers to the muster stations.'

Frances glanced behind her, all else forgotten. 'Avice, that's the alarm. That means there's a fire on board. We've got to go.'

'No. I'm not going.' Avice lifted her head. 'You're OK,' she said, her voice hard. 'You've got your husband, in spite of everything. Once you get off this ship you're free, you're respectable. I've got nothing but disgrace and humiliation ahead of me.'

The alarm had been joined by a distant Tannoy. 'Fire! Fire! Fire!' Frances was having trouble keeping her thoughts straight.

'Avice, I—'

'Look!' Avice was holding out a letter. It was as if she were deaf to the anxious voices, feet running outside. 'Look at it!'

Fear meant that Frances could not make sense of the words on the paper in front of her. Every nerve was screaming at her to move towards the door, to safety. With Avice's eyes on her, she ran her gaze distractedly over the letter, picking out 'sorry' and grasped that she might be in the presence of some personal catastrophe. 'You can sort it out later,' she said, gesturing towards the door. 'Come on, Avice, let's get to the muster station. Think of the baby.'

'Baby? The baby?' Avice stared at Frances as if she were an imbecile. 'Oh, just go,' she said. She buried her face in her pillow, leaving Frances to stand dumbly by the door.

It took Nicol several seconds to realise that the arms hauling at him were not Tims's. He had been flailing around, fists flying, head moving dully back and forth with each impact, but he was dimly conscious that the last time they had landed on flesh the wail of protest had not been the stoker's. He reeled back, eyes stinging as he tried to focus. Tims lay several feet away, two seamen bent over him.

'What the hell are you doing, Nicol?' Emmett was pulling at his jacket. 'You've got to get upstairs, to the muster stations. Got to get the brides into the boats. Jesus Christ, man! Look at the state of you.'

It was then that he became aware of the alarm, and was surprised he had not noticed it before.

'It's centre engine, Tims,' the young stoker was shouting. 'Shit, we're in trouble.'

The fight was forgotten.

'What happened?' Tims was on his feet now, leaning over the young stoker. A long cut ran down his cheek. Nicol, struggling to his feet, wondered whether he had bestowed it.

'I don't know.'

'What have you done?' Tims's huge, bloodied hand shot out and gripped the boy's shoulder.

'I—I don't know. I took five minutes to go and see the girls. Then I went back down and the whole bloody passage was filled with smoke.'

'Did you shut it off? Did you close the hatch?'

'I don't know—there was too much smoke. I couldn't even get past the bomb room.'

'Shit!' Tims looked at Nicol. 'I'll head down there.'

'Anyone else in centre engine?'

Tims shook his head, wincing. 'No. It was just the damn fool boy.' The first wisp of smoke found its way into the men's nostrils, prompting a short, loaded silence.

'It's the captain,' said Tims. 'He's jinxed. He'll do for us all.'

The stoker firefighter coughed and wiped soot from his eyes, then straightened and faced his captain. 'Beaten back, sir. We've closed all the hatches we can, but it's spread to the starboard engine room. Drenching system hasn't worked.' He coughed black phlegm onto the floor, then looked up again, eyes white in his sooty face. 'I don't think it's reached the main feed tank, because it would have blown out the machine control room.'

'Foamite?' said the captain.

'Too late for that, sir. It's no longer just a fuel fire.'

Around him the team of marines and stokers, the naval firefighters, stood waiting for the orders that would send them in. Highfield mentally traced the possible route of the fire through *Indomitable's* sister ship. 'Do we know which way it's headed?'

'We can only hope it spreads to starboard. That way we might lose the starboard engine, sir, but it will hit the air space. But I can't guarantee it's spreading in that direction, sir.'

'You think it might be heading towards the machine-control room?'

The man nodded.

'If it blows out the machine-control room, it will reach the warhead and bomb rooms.'

'Sir.'

That plane. That face. Highfield forced himself to push away the image. 'Get the women off the ship. Lower the lifeboats.'

Dobson glanced out of the bridge at the rough seas. 'Sir, I—'

'I'm not taking any chances. Take a bloody order, man. Green, grab your men and equipment. Dobson, I need at least ten men. We're going to empty the bomb rooms as far as possible, then flood the bloody thing. Tennant, I want you and a couple of others to see if you can get to the passage below the mast pump room. Get the hatches open on the lub oil store and flood it. Flood as many of the compartments around both engine rooms as you can.'

'But it's above water level, sir.'

'Look at the waves, man. We'll make the seas work for us.'

On the boat deck, Nicol was trying to persuade a weeping girl, her arms wrapped round her life jacket, to climb into the lifeboat. 'I can't,' she shrieked, pointing at the churning black seas below. 'Look at it!'

Around them, the marines struggled to keep order and calm. The weeping girl was not the only one unwilling to climb into the boats, which, after the solidity of the *Victoria*, bobbed like corks in the foaming waters below.

'You've got to get in,' he yelled, his tone becoming firmer.

With a sob of reluctance, the girl allowed herself to be handed into the boat and the queue shuffled forward a few inches. Behind him the crowd of several hundred women waited, having been marshalled out of the hangar deck towards the lifeboats, most still in their evening dresses. The wind whistled around them, goosepimpling the girls' arms; they clutched themselves and shivered.

The next female hand was in his. It was Margaret, her moon face pale. 'I can't leave Maudie,' she said.

It took him several seconds to understand what she was saying. 'Frances is down there,' he said. 'She'll bring her.'

'But how do you know?'

'Margaret, you have to get into the boat.' He could see the anxious faces of those swaying in the suspended lifeboat. 'C'mon, now.'

Her grip was surprisingly strong. 'You've got to tell her to get Maudie.'

Nicol peered back through the smoke and chaos below the bridge. His own fears were not for the dog.

'You get into that one, Nicol.' His marine captain appeared behind him, pointing to the cutter alongside. 'Make sure they've all got their jackets on.'

'Sir, I'd rather wait on deck, if that's—'

'Nicol, in the boat. That's an order.' The marine captain nodded him towards the little vessel, as Margaret's lifeboat disappeared down the side of the ship, then did a double take. 'What the bloody hell has happened to your face?'

Several minutes later, Nicol's boat hit the waters with a flat wet thud that made several girls shriek. Fumbling with safety straps and the problem of getting a life jacket round a particularly hysterical bride, Nicol scanned the boats already on the water until he spotted Emmett. The young marine was gesturing at his single oar. 'There's no bloody ropes,' he was shouting, 'and half the oars are missing.'

'They were halfway through replacing them,' said another voice.

Nicol searched for and found his own oars—he was lucky. They were safe. They could float all night for all it mattered. Around them, the sea churned dark grey, the waves not high enough to induce real fear, but sizable enough to keep the women's hold firm on the sides of the little boats. He stared at the creaking ship; the faint but distinct plume of smoke that had emerged from the space below the women's cabins.

Get out, he told her silently. Get to somewhere I can see you.

'I'm not going.'

Frances could smell smoke now. It made all the hairs on the back of her neck stand on end. She could hear the sound of the lifeboats hitting the water, the shouts of those leaving the ship, and was filled by the blind fear that they would not get out.

'There's nothing for me now,' said Avice, and her voice rasped like sandpaper. 'You hear me? Everything's ruined. I'm ruined.'

'I'm sure it can be sorted out—'

'Sorted out? What do I do? Unmarry myself? Row myself back to Australia? My life is over. I may as well stay here.'

'Avice, this is not the time—'

A man's face appeared round their door. 'You shouldn't still be in here,' he said. 'Leave your things and go. Now!' he said, and vanished.

Frances stared in horror at the door, just long enough to see the back legs of the little dog disappear through it. She toyed with the idea of going after her, but a glance at Avice's wild expression told her where her priorities lay.

There was a crash on the deck above them and a man's voice at the end of the hangar deck yelling, 'Secure hatches! Secure hatches now!'

'Oh, for God's sake.' Frances's grip was strong. She grabbed an arm and a handful of Avice's dress and pulled her out of the cabin. The corridor was full of smoke. 'Gun turret,' she yelled, pointing, and they stumbled, half blinded, their lungs scorched and protesting, towards it.

They fumbled with the hatch door and fell outside, gasping and retching. Frances made her way to the edge and leaned over, so relishing the clearer air that it took her a minute to register the scene below: a web of boats spanning beneath them. She glanced up at the empty gantries and saw that all the boats were in the water.

Someone saw them and shouted. Arms gesticulated from below. 'Get out!' someone was shouting. 'Get out now!'

Frances stared at the water. She was a strong swimmer: she could dive down, emerge among the lifeboats. She owed Avice nothing. 'We can't head up to the flight deck. There's too much smoke in the corridor,' she said. 'We're going to have to jump.'

'I can't,' said Avice.

'It's not that far. Look—I'll hold on to you.'

'I can't swim.'

Frances heard the crack of something giving outside, the hint of an inferno she did not want to face. She grabbed Avice and tried desperately to drag her towards the edge.

'Get off me!' Avice screamed. 'Don't touch me!' She was wild, scratching and pounding at Frances's arms, her shoulders. Smoke was seeping under the hatch. Her heart filled with fear, Frances grabbed a handful of Avice's silk dress and dragged her on to the gun turret. Her foot slipped, the rubber sole of her shoe sliding off metal, and, entangled, they were falling, arms and legs flailing, towards the inky black below.

The captain had the wrench in his hands, and was struggling to get the bomb off its clamp on the wall. 'Get out!' he shouted at the men carrying the penultimate bomb from the magazine. 'Get the hose! Flood the compartment! Flood it now!' He had removed his mask to be better heard.

'Captain!' yelled Green, through his mask. 'Got to get out now.'

'She's not going up. Got to be safe.'

'You don't have time to get them all off, sir. We can flood it now.'

Afterwards, Green thought Highfield might not have heard him. He did not want to leave his skipper there, but he knew there was only so much a man could do before the need to keep the other men safe overrode his concern.

'Start the flooding,' Highfield was shouting. 'Just go.'

He turned, and as he did so, he heard something fall. He threw his smoke helmet blindly towards the captain, hoping it would reach him, that somehow he would see it through the smoke. His heart heavy with foreboding, he was out, pushing his men before him.

Frances broke through the surface, her hair plastered over her face. She could hear voices, feel hands pulling at her. At first the sea had not wanted to relinquish her: she felt its icy grasp on her clothes. And then she was flopping, gasping, on the floor of the little boat like a landed fish, retching as voices tried to reassure her, and a blanket was wrapped round her shoulders.

Avice, she mouthed. And then as the salt sting in her eyes eased, she saw her being hauled like a catch over the other end of the cutter, her beauty-pageant dress slick with oil.

Is she all right? she wanted to ask. But an arm slid round her, pulled her in tightly so that she felt the closeness of this solid body, the intensity of its protection, and suddenly she had no words. Frances, a voice said, close by her ear, and it was dark with relief.

Captain Highfield was laid out on the flight deck by the two stokers who had carried him there. The men stood round him, hands thrust in pockets, some wiping sweat or soot from their faces. In the distance, under the dark skies, there were shouts of confirmation as different parts of the ship were deemed to have stopped burning.

It's out, Captain, they told him. It's under control. We did it. They half whispered these words as if unsure whether he could still hear them. Then there was silence for a whole minute, as the men stared at his slumped figure, still in his good dress uniform, wet and smoke-stained, eyes still fixed on some distant drama.

The men looked at him, and then, surreptitiously, at each other. One man wondered aloud whether to summon the ship's doctor. Then Highfield raised himself on his elbow, his eyes bloodshot. He coughed once, twice more, and moved his neck as if in pain. 'Well, what are you waiting for?' he asked, voice gravelly, eyes full of fury. 'Check every last bloody compartment. Then get the bloody women out of the bloody boats and back on bloody board.'

It was several hours before the temperature had cooled enough to check it, but it was pretty clear once the working party got down there that the centre engine room was beyond repair; the heat had melted pipework and welded rivets to the floor. The walls and hatches had buckled, and above it half of the seamen's messes were gone.

'Think you can limp into harbour?'

Highfield sat in the bridge, watching the grey skies clear to reveal patches of pure blue, as if in apology for the evening before. 'We're less than a day away. We've got one working engine. I don't see why not.'

'Sounds like the old girl suffered a bit.' McManus's voice was low. 'And a little bird tells me you were a little too stuck in for comfort.'

Highfield dismissed thoughts of armament clamps and his raw throat. 'Fine, sir. Nothing to worry about.'

'Good man. I'll take a look at your report. Glad you were able to bring it all under control—without frightening the ladies too much, I mean.' The admiral's laugh echoed tinnily down the wire.

Highfield stepped out of the bridge and stood on the flight deck. At the aft end, a row of men were making their way along it, scrubbing off traces of the smoke that had filtered upwards, their buckets of grey, foaming water slopping as they went. Several marines had been busy constructing barriers around the areas that were not safe to walk on. When they sailed into Plymouth, Highfield's ship would be under control.

He had not lost a single person.

No one was close enough to hear the shaking breath that Highfield slowly let out as he turned to go back into the bridge.

At least a hundred women had queued patiently by the main hatch since breakfast, waiting to be allowed back to their cabins. There had been hushed conversations about the state of their belongings, fears for cherished arrival outfits now perhaps wrecked by water and smoke.

Margaret, heavily pregnant as she was, tore through the hatch the minute it was opened, and was in her cabin by the time the other brides had made it to the bottom of the stairwell. 'Maudie! Maudie!'

The door had been open. She knelt down and peered under the two bottom bunks. 'Maudie!' she cried.

She checked under every blanket, lifting bedrolls and tearing the sheets from the bunks in her desperation. Nothing. Then she heard the scream. She stood very still for a moment, before throwing herself out of the door and down the passageway to the bathrooms.

Afterwards she thought she had probably known even before she got there. It was the only other place Maudie knew on the ship, the only other place she must have thought she might find Margaret. She stood in the doorway, staring at the girls gathered by the sinks. She followed their eyes to the little dog on the damp floor.

Margaret stepped forward and fell to her knees. A great sob escaped her. The dog's limbs were stiff, the body cold. 'Oh, no. Oh, no.' She gathered the little dog's body into her arms. 'Oh, Maudie, I'm so sorry. I'm so, so sorry.'

She stayed there for some minutes, trying to will the body into life, knowing that it was hopeless. Eventually, she peeled off her cardigan and folded the dog into it. Then she got to her feet.

'Would you . . . would you like me to fetch someone?' A woman laid a hand on her arm.

Margaret didn't seem to hear, but walked back along the passageway, clasping her swaddled burden.

The WSO placed a hand under her arm as Frances lifted herself onto the bed, surprised by how tired that small act made her feel. The woman pulled a blanket over her, then made to adjust a second one round her shoulders. The marine removed his own supporting arm, and let go of her hand with a hint of reluctance. She caught his eye and her exhaustion briefly disappeared.

'I'm fine,' she said, to the WSO. 'Thank you, but really I am. I'd be just as good in my own bunk.'

'Dr Duxbury says anyone who's been in the water needs to spend a few hours under observation. You'll probably be out by teatime.' The WSO moved to Avice's bed, tucking in her blankets in a brisk, maternal gesture. They were in a small room opposite the infirmary, some kind of detergent store, Frances guessed, from the boxes around them and the pervasive smell of bleach. She shivered.

'Sorry about the room,' the WSO was saying. 'We need the infirmary for the men who inhaled smoke, and we couldn't have you mixing. This was the only place we could put you two.'

The marine, inches from her bed, was staring at her. Frances felt the warmth of his eyes and savoured it. She could still feel the imprint of his arm round her as he had half walked, half carried her back on board, his head so close to hers that, if she had inclined her neck a little further, she could have felt his skin against hers.

'Now, Mrs Radley, are you all right?'

'Fine,' Avice said, into her pillow.

'Good. I've got to pop next door and get the men comfortable, but I'll be back as soon as I can. I've brought you both some dry clothes for you to change into, when you're feeling up to it. I'll put them just here.' She placed the carefully folded pile on a cabinet. 'Now, I'm sure you ladies could do with a cup of tea. Marine, would you do the honours?'

'I'd be delighted.'

She felt the brief squeeze of his hand, and she forgot about this room, about Avice, the fire. She was on a lifeboat, her eyes locked onto this man's, saying everything she had ever wanted to say, everything she had never believed she would want to say, without uttering a word.

'I'll take a look at those cuts later,' she murmured to him, and fought the urge to touch his face. She imagined how his skin would feel under her fingertips, the tenderness with which she would care for him.

He glanced back at her as he walked towards the door. Smiled when he saw she was still watching him.

'I don't suppose you particularly want to be stuck with me, do you?' As he closed the door, Avice's voice cut into the silence.

Reluctantly, Frances brought her thoughts to the woman in front of her. 'I don't mind who I'm with,' she replied coolly.

It was as if their hours in the lifeboat had never happened, as if Avice was now determined to restore the distance between them.

'I've got a stomach ache. This bodice is too tight. Will you help me out of my dress?'

Avice slid slowly out of her bed, her hair separated into pale, salted fronds. Frances helped her out of the ruined party dress and into a peach silk dressing gown left by the WSO. It was only as she helped Avice back onto the bed that she saw the mark spreading slowly across the back of the dressing gown. 'I have to tell you something, Avice,' she said, as the girl lay down. 'You're bleeding.'

In the little room, piled high with boxes, they examined the dressing gown in silence. Avice stared at the ruby stain. She saw in Frances's face what it meant. There was no visible change in her demeanour. She accepted the clean towel that Frances fetched without comment.

'I'm so sorry,' said Frances, a pebble of discomfort lodged inside her. 'It may have been the shock of the water.' She had been prepared for Avice to scream at her, but she said nothing, just acceded to Frances's quiet requests to lie still.

Finally she spoke. 'Just as well, really,' she said. 'Poor little bastard.'

There was a brief, shocked silence. Frances's eyes widened.

Avice shook her head. Then suddenly, lurching up and forward like somebody choking, she began to wail. Frances clambered quietly onto Avice's bed and sat beside her, stunned. Unable to bear the terrible sound any longer, she put her arms round the girl and held her.

It was some time before the sobbing subsided. Frances fetched more painkillers from the dispensary and a sedative. When she returned, Avice was lying back against the wall, a pillow propped behind her. She wiped her eyes, then gestured to Frances to pass her the ruined dress. Then she pulled a piece of tattered, damp paper from a side pocket in the skirt. 'Here, you can read this properly now,' she said.

Avice thrust it towards her and Frances took the sodden letter and read the bits that had not run in the waters of the Atlantic.

I should have told you this a long time ago. But I love you, darling, and I couldn't bear the thought of your sad face when I told you, or the slightest possibility of losing you . . . Please don't misunderstand me— I'm not asking you not to come. You need to know that the relationship between me and my wife is far more like brother and sister than any- thing. You, my darling, mean far more to me than she ever could . . .

I want you to know I meant every word I said in Australia. But you must understand—the children are so young, and I am not the type to take my responsibilities lightly. Perhaps when they are a little older we can think again?

So, I know I'm asking a lot of you, but just think about this in your days left on board. I've got a fair bit put away, and I could set you up in a lovely little place in London. And I can be with you a couple of nights a week, which, when you think of it, is more than most wives see their men in the navy . . .

Avice, you always said that us being together was all that mattered. Prove to me, darling, that this was the truth . . .

As Frances handed the letter back to Avice, she didn't know whether she should look the girl full in the face. She did not want her to think she was gloating. 'What will you do?' she said carefully.

'Go home, I suppose. I couldn't while there was . . . but now it can be like none of it happened. My parents didn't want me to come anyway.' Her voice was thin and cold. She dropped the letter onto the bed. The way she looked at Frances now was unembarrassed. 'How do you carry on living,' she asked, 'with all that hanging over you? All that disgrace?'

Frances understood that, for once, the words were not as harsh as they sounded. There was genuine curiosity in Avice's eyes. Frances chose her words carefully as she handed her another towel. 'I suppose I've discovered . . . we all carry something. Some burden of shame.'

Avice shifted on the bed as she took the towel. 'And yours has been lifted. Because you found someone prepared to take you on. Despite your . . . your history.'

'I'm not ashamed of who I am, Avice.' She sat down on the bed. 'I've done one thing in my life that I'm ashamed of. And that wasn't it.'

The Australian Army Nursing Service had set up a recruiting depot in Wayville, near the camp hospital. She had been a trainee nurse for some time at the Sydney Showground Hospital, had worked for a good family in Brisbane to finance her training, and now, single, medically fit, without dependants and with a glowing reference, the newly formed Australian General Hospital was keen to take her.

Joining the AGH, she said, had been like coming home. The nurses were stoic, capable, cheerful, compassionate and, above all, professional. They came from all over Australia, had no interest in her history and appreciated her effort and dedication. The necessities of their job meant they lived from day to day, in the present.

Over several years they had served together in Northfield, Port Moresby and, lastly, in Morotai, where she had met Chalkie. During that time she had learned that what had happened to her was not the worst thing that could happen to a person, not when you considered the cruelties inflicted in the name of war. Men had fallen for her. It was almost par for the course in the hospital—a few kind words, a smile, and they bestowed on you all sorts of qualities you might or might not have. She had assumed Chalkie was one of those. He asked her to marry him at least once a day and, as with the others, she had paid him little attention. She would never marry.

Until the day the gunner arrived.

Here she swallowed. 'He came from the same unit that had been stationed by the hotel where I had lived all those years ago. And I knew that I had to leave Australia, that it would be the only way I could ever get away from . . .' She paused. 'So I decided to say yes to Chalkie.' She allowed herself a small smile. 'I never knew a man as gentle. The night I told him I would marry him, he cried with happiness.'

Avice's eyes closed with pain, and Frances waited until the cramp had passed. Then she continued. 'He had this CO, Captain Baillie, who knew Chalkie had no family. He knew, too, that I had nothing much to gain from the marriage, so he gave his permission where, I suppose, plenty wouldn't. I did care for Chalkie.'

'And you knew you would get your passage out.'

'Yes.' A half-smile played across her lips. 'Ironic, really, isn't it? A girl with my history marrying the only man who never laid a finger on me.'

'But at least you kept your reputation intact.'

'No. That didn't happen.' Frances fingered her skirt. 'A few days before Chalkie and I were married I was sitting outside the mess camp, when that gunner came up and'—she choked—'tried to put his hand up my skirt. I screamed, and hit his face quite hard. Some of the other nurses ran out and he told them it was all I was good for. That he had known me in Aynsville. That was the decider, see? I had told them where I had come from. They knew it had to be true.'

'Did anyone tell Chalkie?'

'No. They all knew how he felt about me, and he was frail . . .'

'But the nurses did what I did in judging you?'

'Most of them, yes. The matron took a different view. She just told me I should make the most of what Chalkie had given me. That not many people get a second chance in life.'

Avice lay down and stared at the ceiling. 'I think she was right. No one has to know. No one has to know . . . anything.'

Frances raised an eyebrow, unconvinced. 'Even after all this?'

Avice shrugged. 'England's a big place. Chalkie will look after you now.'

As Frances failed to reply, Avice asked, 'No one told him in the end, did they? Not after all that?'

'No,' Frances said. 'No one told him.'

On the other side of the door, where he had been listening, still holding two stone-cold tin mugs of tea, the marine closed his eyes.

MOROTAI, HALMAHERAS ISLANDS, 1946

'I KNOW IT'S IRREGULAR,' said Matron Audrey Marshall, 'but you saw them. You saw what it's done to her.'

'I find it all rather hard to believe.'

'She was a child, Charles. Fifteen, from what she told me.'

'He's very fond of her, I'll grant you.'

'So what harm would it do? The man's got no money, has he? You said he had no family.' Her voice dropped. 'You know as well as I do how ill he is. It would bring him some happiness and give her a lifeline. She can't stay in nursing in Australia now everyone knows. She'd be entitled to go to England. She'll make a superb nurse over there. Think what she's done for your men, Charles. Think of O'Halloran and those wretched sores. She's a good nurse. A good girl.'

'I know.' Charles Baillie sighed deeply. 'And it's hard to refuse you anything, Audrey.'

She smiled with the satisfaction of someone who knows the battle is won. 'I'll do what I have to do,' she said.

The chaplain was a pragmatic man. Weary of the pain and suffering he had seen, he had been easily persuaded to help. The young nurse was a perfect illustration of the redemptive powers of marriage, he told himself. He felt pretty sure his God would understand.

Congratulating themselves on their solution, and with perhaps the faintest curiosity as to how their plan would be received by its subjects, the three sat in the matron's office long enough to celebrate their good sense with a drink. They toasted Sister Luke, her future husband, the end of the war and Churchill for good measure. Shortly after ten o'clock they walked out into the tented ward and through the sandy pathway between the beds, careful not to wake those men already sleeping. Then pushed back the curtain to enter the next ward.

Sister Luke glanced up as she heard them enter. She looked at them with wide, unreadable eyes. She was leaning over Alfred 'Chalkie' Mackenzie's bed, three-quarters of which was still covered by a mosquito net. She was pulling a white sheet over his face.

Avice was sleeping when the marine returned with two new, still-hot cups of tea. He placed the two mugs on the table between the beds.

Frances had been standing over Avice and jumped, evidently having not expected to see him. He thought she looked exhausted. A few hours ago he might have given in to the urge to touch her. Now, having heard her words, he knew he should not. He moved back towards the door.

'I'm sorry I took so long.'

'Dr Duxbury's given me the all-clear. I'm going to go back to the dormitory. Avice will probably spend tonight in here. I will come back later to make sure she's OK. Do you know how Maggie is?'

'Not too good. The dog . . .'

'Oh.' Her face fell.

'I'm sure she'd be glad of your company.' He ached to wipe the dark smudge from her cheek.

She stepped forward, glanced back at the sleeping Avice. 'I thought about what you said,' she told him, her voice low, 'that the war has made us all do things we're not proud of. Until you said that, I had always thought I was the only one . . .' She tailed off, and her eyes flashed up at him. 'But I wanted to thank you for that. You've . . . I'll always be so grateful that we met.' The last words were rushed, as if she had had to force them out while she still had the courage to say them.

He felt suddenly small, wretched. 'Yes. Well,' he said, when he could form words, 'it's always nice to have made a friend.' He felt mean even opening his mouth as he added, 'Ma'am.'

There was a little pause.

'Ma'am?' she repeated. The shy smile had disappeared.

I have no choice, he wanted to shout at her. It is for you I'm doing this. 'I'm sorry,' he said. 'I've got to go now. But . . . you'll like England.'

'Thank you. I've heard a lot about it from the lectures.'

The rebuke in her words felt like a blow. 'Look . . . I hope you'll always think of me'—his hands were rigid at his sides—'as your friend.' That word had never sounded so unwelcome.

She blinked a little too swiftly, and in shame he looked away.

'That's very kind, but I don't think so, Marine,' she said. Her voice was sharp with hurt. 'After all, I don't even know your name.'

Margaret stood towards the aft end of the flight deck by the lashings, a headscarf trying and failing to stop her hair whipping too hard round her face. Her back was to the bridge and her head was dipped over the bundle in her arms.

The wind and her headscarf meant that she didn't hear Frances arrive beside her. When she saw her she could not be sure how long she'd been there. 'Burial at sea,' she said. 'Just trying to pluck up the courage to actually do it, you know?'

'I'm so sorry, Maggie.' Frances's eyes were bleak. The hand she reached out to Margaret was tentative.

Some time later, Margaret stepped forward, hesitated for a moment, then stooped and dropped the little bundle into the sea. She held the rail with white-knuckled fingers, even now shocked at how far above the waves she stood, fighting the urge to stop the ship, to retrieve what she had lost. The sea seemed suddenly too huge, a cold betrayal rather than a peaceful end. Her arms felt unbearably empty.

'Have we been mad, Frances?' she said, at last.

'I'm not sure what—'

'We've left everything, all the people we love, our homes, our security.

And for what? Because there's no guarantee, right? There's nothing says these men and their families are going to want us, right? What the hell do I know about England? What do I really know about Joe or his family? About babies? I couldn't even look after my own bloody dog . . .' Her head dipped. 'You know . . . I have to tell you . . . I think I've made a terrible mistake. I got carried away with the idea of something, maybe escaping from cooking and cleaning for Dad and the boys. And now I'm here, all I want is my family. I want my family back, Frances. I want my mum.' She was crying bitterly. 'I want my dog.'

Eyes blinded by tears, she felt Frances put her thin, strong arms round her. 'No, Maggie, no. It's going to be fine. You have a man who loves you. Really loves you.'

Margaret wanted to be convinced. 'How can you say that?'

'Joe is one in a million, Maggie. And you have a wonderful life ahead of you because it will be impossible for his family not to love you. And you're going to have a beautiful baby and you will love him or her more than you ever imagined. Oh, if you only knew how much I . . .'

Frances's face contorted with an unstoppable torrent of tears. She tried to apologise, to pull herself together, waved her hand in mute apology, but she could not stop.

Margaret, shocked into togetherness, held her. 'Hey now,' she said weakly. 'Hey now, Frances, c'mon . . . c'mon, this isn't like you . . . You're right. We'll be OK,' she murmured, stroking Frances's hair. 'We might end up living near each other, right?'

'I'm not what you think. I can't begin to tell you—'

'Ah, c'mon, it's time to leave all that behind.' Margaret wiped her own eyes. 'Look, as far as I'm concerned, you're a great girl. I know what I need to know, and a little bit that I didn't. And you know what? I still think you're a great girl. And you'd better bloody keep in touch with me.'

'You're . . . very . . . kind.'

'Hey! You two! Come away from there!'

They turned to see an officer standing by the island, waving them in. Margaret turned back to Frances. 'Ah, c'mon, girl. Don't get sappy on me now. Not you of all people.'

'Oh, Maggie . . . I'm so . . .'

'No,' she said. 'This is our new start, Frances. New everything. Like you said, it will be all right. We'll make it all right.'

As they came through the hatch into the dormitory area after dinner, a small part of her hoped the marine would be standing there, his feet locked in their habitual position, his eyes sliding to hers in silent complicity. But the corridor was empty, as was the one above it, for there were to be no marines on duty tonight. Perhaps it was for the best.

She left Margaret asleep in the dormitory some time after 9.30 and made her way to the women's lavatories down the corridor. On her way back she turned off to check on Avice in the infirmary.

She walked along the silent passageway, her soft shoes making almost no noise as she passed the closed doors. In other cabins tonight the air was thick with the scent of face cream liberally applied, the walls bright with carefully laundered dresses, sleep disturbed by the prickle of rollers, hairpins and excited dreams. Not in our little cabin, Frances thought. Margaret had attempted to pin her hair and then, swearing, given up.

Frances heard the singing before she reached the infirmary and deduced that Dr Duxbury had the men singing show tunes. From the loose quality of the harmonies, she thought perhaps the infirmary might be a little lighter on sterile alcohol than it had been. In another time, she might have reported him, but there were just a few hours left on board. Who was she to judge whether the men should sing or not?

The song collapsed in a melancholy trail. Frances let herself into the little room opposite, eyeing in the dim light the girl who lay pale and motionless on the bed. The worst, for Avice, was over. She was asleep now, the blanket pulled high round her neck.

Frances walked over to the little chair beside the bed and sat down. Here she stayed, listening to the sounds of the singing, which had begun again, and the noise of the remaining engine, weaker and less dynamic than it had been. She imagined the curses of the stokers who sweated away in their efforts to bully the unwilling ship into harbour. She thought of the navigator, the radio operator, the duty watch, all the others still awake across this vast ship, contemplating their return to their families. She thought of Captain Highfield, in his palatial quarters above them, knowing that tonight might be the last he spent at sea. We all have to find new ways of living, he had told them.

She thought she might have drifted off to sleep when she heard the sound. A cough so discreet, so far on the periphery of her consciousness that she was never quite sure afterwards why it had woken her.

She sat upright and listened. Another cough. The kind that denotes the desire to draw attention. She slid out of the chair and made her way across the floor to the door.

'Frances,' a voice said, so quietly that only she could have heard it.

She wondered briefly if she was still asleep. Next door Dr Duxbury was singing 'Danny Boy'.

'You shouldn't be here,' she murmured. She did not open the door. They were under instructions: there was to be no mixing this evening.

'I wanted to make sure you were all right. What I said . . .'

'Please don't worry.' She didn't want to have this conversation again.

'I wanted to tell you . . . I'm glad. I'm glad to have met you. And I wish . . . I wish . . .' There was a long silence.

Barely knowing what she was doing, Frances laid her cheek against the door, waiting in silence until she heard what she was waiting for. Then she stepped back and opened the door. She stared up at him, knowing that this was the last time she would see this man, trying to make herself accept he was not hers to want.

'Well.' Her wavering, brilliant smile would have broken his heart. 'Thank you. Thank you for looking after me. Us, I mean.'

Frances held out a slim hand to him. After a moment he took it, and they shook solemnly, their eyes not leaving each other's face.

'Time to get to bed, boys. Got to be fresh for the morning!' Vincent Duxbury's voice increased in volume as the infirmary door began to open, throwing out a rectangular flood of light. 'Home, boys! You're going home tomorrow!'

She tugged the marine into the little room and closed the door silently behind them. They stood inches apart, listening as the men fell out of the infirmary into the passageway.

She was so close he could feel her breath upon him. Her body was rigid, listening, her hand still unwittingly in his. If it hadn't been that she had chosen that moment to look up at him he might never have done it. But she had raised her face, lips parted, and put her hand to the cut above his brow, tracing it with her fingertips. Instead of stepping away from her, as he had intended, he raised his hand to hers, enclosing it within his own.

The voices outside increased in volume and someone fell over. From a distance there was a muffled 'You there!', the brisk steps of someone in authority. Nicol hardly heard them. He heard instead her faint exhalation, felt the answering tremble in her fingertips. His skin burning, he brought her hand down and pressed it to his mouth. She hesitated, and then pulled back her hand and lifted her mouth to his, her hands gripping his now as if she would make them stay on her for ever.

It was sweet, so sweet as to be indecent. Nicol wanted to absorb her into him, to fill her, enclose her, take her in to his very being. I knew this! some part of him rejoiced. I know her! His eyes opened and locked with hers, and it was she who pulled back, one hand raised to her lips, her eyes still on his. 'I'm sorry,' she whispered. 'I'm so, so sorry.' She glanced briefly at Avice, still asleep on the bed, and lifted a hand to his cheek, as if imprinting the sight and feel of him on some hidden part of her. Then she was gone, and the storeroom door closed gently between them.

The ceremony was carried out at nearly half past eleven on the Tuesday night. In different circumstances, it would have been a beautiful night for a wedding: the moon hung low and magnified in a tropical sky, bathing the camp in a strange blue light.

Aside from the bride and groom, there were just three people in attendance: the chaplain, Audrey Marshall and Captain Baillie. The bride, her voice barely audible, sat by the groom for the entire service. The chaplain crossed himself several times after the ceremony, and prayed that he had done the right thing. The bride placed her pale face in her hands and sat still for some time, until her face emerged again, gasping slightly, like a swimmer breaking through water.

'Are we done?' said the matron, who seemed the most composed.

The chaplain nodded, his brow still furrowed, eyes cast down.

'Sister?' The girl opened her eyes.

'Right,' said Audrey Marshall, looking at her watch and reaching for her notes. 'Time of death, eleven forty-four.'

Eight hours to Plymouth

Highfield stared at his uniform, carefully pressed by his steward, ready for its last outing when the *Victoria* docked the following day. What does that uniform say about me? he thought, running his hand down the sleeve. Does it tell of a man who only knew who he was when he was at war? Or of a man who realises now that the thing he thought he was escaping from, intimacy, humanity, was what he had lacked all along?

He turned to his half-packed trunk. He knew where his steward would have placed it, did not have to slide his hands too far under the carefully packed clothes before he found the photograph that had spent the last six months face down in his drawer. It was a silver-framed photograph of a young man, his arm round a smiling woman who tried, with one hand, to stop the wind blowing her hair across her face.

It would make a man of the lad, he had told his sister. The navy turned boys into men. He would take care of him. He stared at the image of the young man grinning back at him. Then he moved the chart a little and placed the photograph upright on the table. It would be the last thing he would take from this ship.

They were a matter of hours from Plymouth. By the time the women woke, the ship would be preparing to disgorge them into their new lives. Tomorrow, from the earliest pipes, the ship would be a vortex of activity: endless lists crossed and checked, women and men queuing for their trunks, the procedural and ceremonial duties involved in the bringing of a great ship into harbour. He had seen it before, the excitement, the nervous anticipation of the men waiting to disembark. Except this time the war was over. This time they knew their leave was safe, their return permanent. They would pour off the ship, straight into those tearful embraces, eyes shut tight in gratitude, the pawing excitement of their children.

And then, on board, there were those like himself. Those who made their way inconspicuously through the crowds of jostling, reunited families, perhaps to be met miles away by the muted pleasure of relatives who tolerated them through familial pity or duty.

Highfield stared again at the uniform he would wear for the last time tomorrow. Then he sat down at his desk and began to write.

Dear Iris,

I have some news for you. I am not coming to Tiverton. Please send Lord Hamworth my apologies and tell him I will be happy to make up any financial disadvantage my decision might cause on his part.

I have decided, upon reflection, that a life on land is not for me . . .

Nicol could think of nowhere else to go. Even at a quarter to one at night the mess was a seething mass of noisy men, high on anticipation and extra sippers, pulling their photographs from their lockers and packing them into overstuffed kitbags, exchanging stories about where they would be, what they wanted to do first. He needed to be alone, to digest what had happened to him.

The captain was standing on the foredeck, in front of the bridge. He was in his shirtsleeves, head bare to the wind. Nicol, emerging onto the deck, halted in the doorway and prepared to retreat, but Highfield had spotted him and Nicol realised he would have to acknowledge him.

'Finished your watch?'

Nicol stepped forward so that he was standing beside the captain. 'Yes, sir. We're not posted outside the brides' area tonight.'

'You were outside Sister Mackenzie's lot, weren't you?'

Nicol looked up sharply. But the captain's look was benign, lost in thought. 'That's the one, sir.'

The captain's hands were thrust deep into his pockets. 'They all all right, are they? I heard two of them were in the sickbay.'

'All fine, sir.'

'Good. Good.' The captain gave him a sideways look. 'You married, Nicol?'

Nicol stared at the point where the black sea met the sky and a patch of stars were revealed as the clouds parted. 'No, sir,' he said. 'Not any more.' He noted the captain's enquiring look.

'Don't become too enamoured of your freedom, Nicol. A lack of responsibility, of ties . . . can be a two-edged sword.'

'I'm starting to understand that, sir.'

They stood there for some time in companionable silence. Nicol's thoughts churned like the seas, his skin prickling when he thought of the woman below. What should I have done? he asked himself, over and over. What should I do?

Highfield stepped a little closer to him. He pulled a cigar box from his pocket and offered one to Nicol. 'Here. Celebration,' he said. 'My last night as a captain. My last night after forty-three years in the navy.'

Nicol took the cigar and allowed the older man to light it, his hand braced against the sea breeze. 'You'll miss it. Out here.'

'No, I won't.'

Perplexed, Nicol turned to him.

'I'm going to go straight back out,' Highfield said. 'See if I can crew merchant ships. I'm told there's plenty of demand. These girls have made me think, Nicol. If they can do it . . .' He shrugged.

'You don't feel . . . like you've earned your time on land, sir?'

The captain exhaled. 'I'm not sure, Nicol, that I'd know how to be on land. Not for any length of time.' He drew on his cigar. 'Did you know she served in the Pacific?'

'*Victoria*?'

'Your charge. Sister Mackenzie. Brave woman. Brave the lot of them, really. Think about it. This time tomorrow they'll know which way their future lies . . .'

With that man, the man Nicol wanted to hate. But the way she had described him—how could he hate the gentle, affectionate soldier?

'Poor girl. She's the second one on board, you know.'

'Second what, sir?'

'Widow. Had a telegram yesterday for one of the girls on B Deck. Husband's plane went down on a training flight.'

'Mrs Mackenzie's husband was killed?' Nicol froze. He felt a stab of guilt, as if he had willed this to happen.

'Mackenzie? No, no, he . . . he died some time ago. Back in the Pacific. Odd decision, really, to leave Australia with nothing to come to.

Still, that's the war for you.' He sniffed the air, as if he could detect the proximity of land.

Widowed?

'Look at that. Hardly worth going to sleep now. Here, Nicol, come and have a drink with me.'

Widowed? The word held a glorious resonance. He wanted to shout, 'She's a widow!' Why hadn't she told him? Why hadn't she told anyone?

'Nicol? What do you fancy? Glass of Scotch?'

'Sir?' He glanced towards the hatch, desperate suddenly to get back to her cabin, to tell her what he knew. Why didn't I tell her the truth? he thought. She might have confided in me. He understood suddenly that she had probably believed her status as a married woman offered her the only protection she had ever had.

'Your devotion to duty is admirable, man, but just this once I'm ordering you. Let your hair down a little.'

Nicol felt himself lean towards the hatch. 'Sir, I really—'

'Come on, Marine, indulge me.'

By the time he leaves the captain's rooms it is too late to wake her. He does not mind now: he knows he has time. His stomach full of whisky, and his mind still ringing with that word, he has all the time in the world. He squints against the too-bright blue of the skies as he heads across the flight deck, slows along the hangar deck, and then, stops, savouring the dawn silence, the sound of the gulls crying from Plymouth Sound, the sound of home.

PLYMOUTH, AUGUST 1946

As some of the WSOs had predicted, it was chaos. Brides ran up and down corridors, shrieking over mislaid belongings or missing friends. There had been an endless stream of piped instructions to the men, all in preparation for disembarkation, while the air was filled with the sound of seamen calling to each other.

The WSOs were already congregating at the gangplank, ready for their final duties: to confirm that each bride had been checked off, was in possession of her cases, that she would be passed into safe hands.

'Brides second sitting, last call for the canteen.' The Tannoy hissed and clicked off.

Insulated from all the activity, and without Avice and Frances, the dormitory was silent. Margaret glanced down at her outfit; she could only squeeze into one of her dresses now, and it was straining at the seams. This was the first morning she had not been able to eat even a piece of dry toast. She felt sick with nerves.

Suddenly, she was conscious of a shuffling against her door. Puzzled, she opened it and stepped back as the marine fell into the cabin, a heavy tumble of limbs.

'Hello,' said Margaret, as he tried to push himself upright. It was obvious to her that the man was barely awake. She sniffed, noting with some surprise the faint whiff of alcohol that emanated from him.

Suddenly he seemed to register where he was. 'I need to speak to Frances.' He scrambled to his feet.

'She's not here.'

He looked startled. 'What?'

'She came back last night and then she went again.' Then she understood something that had been nagging at her for weeks. 'I guess I thought she might be with you.'

Avice stood in the infirmary bathroom, applying a final coat of lipstick. Her eyelashes, under two layers of block mascara, widened her marble-blue eyes. Her skin, which had been ghostly pale, was now apparently glowing with health. That was the marvellous thing about cosmetics. No one would know what awful things were going on inside one, given some pressed powder, rouge and a good lipstick.

He would not be there to meet her. She knew this as surely as she believed that now, finally, she knew him. He would wait until he had heard from her, until he knew which way the land lay. If she said yes, he would fall on her with protestations of eternal love. If she told him she didn't want him, she suspected he would grieve for a few days, then probably consider himself to have had a lucky escape.

The WSO stuck her head round the door. 'You all right, Mrs Radley?' She smiled brightly. 'There, now. Don't you look a hundred per cent better than yesterday?'

'Thank you. I'll be ready in two minutes,' Avice said.

After the WSO had gone, she placed her lipstick back in its case and stood for a moment, turned a few degrees to each side, checking her reflection. I look, she thought . . . wiser.

Highfield stood on the roof of the bridge, flanked by Dobson, the first lieutenant and the radio operator, and gave orders down the intercom to the coxswain as the aircraft carrier negotiated her way by degrees into the narrower water, and the English coastline grew into solid reality around them. Below him the sailors stood in perfect lines round the outside edge of the flight deck, while officers and senior ranks manned the island area. Coming alongside was traditionally one of the finest moments of a captain's journey: it was impossible not to be filled with pride, standing on a great warship with one's men below, the noise of the welcoming crowd already in their ears.

The light was peculiarly bright, the kind of light that heralds a fine, clear day. Plymouth Sound was beautiful, an appropriate send-off for the old ship, and a good welcome, he thought, for the brides. The sea, flecked with white horses, glinted around the ship. After Bombay and Suez, after the endless muddied blue of the ocean, everything looked an impossible green.

The docks had begun to fill almost at first light. First a few anxious-looking men, their collars turned up against the cold, then larger groups, families, standing in huddles on the dockside, occasionally pointing and waving at the approaching ship.

The captain stood, his hands on the rail in front of him. They were coming home. Whatever that meant.

Nicol had checked the dormitory, the infirmary, the deck canteen and the brides' bathroom, prompting a shrieking near-riot in the process. Now he ran swiftly along the hangar deck towards the main brides' canteen, oblivious of the curious glances of the last women returning from breakfast. Twice he had passed other marines as they headed for the flight deck; seeing him at speed, they had assumed him to be on some urgent official duty. Only afterwards, as they registered the crumpled state of his uniform, his unshaven face, might they have remarked that Nicol was looking a bit rough.

He skidded to a halt at the main doorway, and scanned the room. There were only thirty or so brides still seated: so close to disembarkation, most were finishing their packing, waiting on the boat deck or in turrets, skirts billowing in the stiff sea breeze. He paused for a moment, waiting for this girl to turn, or that one to look up, making sure neither of them was her. Then he cursed his befuddled head.

There were people milling about everywhere. In half an hour, how was he meant to find one person in this rabbit warren of rooms and compartments, among sixteen hundred others?

'Trevor, Mrs Annette.' The WSO stood at the top of the gangway and waited for Mrs Trevor to fight her way to the front of the group. There was a brief hush before a blonde woman appeared, hat askew as a result of struggling through the others. 'Your belongings have been cleared by Customs. Your trunks will be on the dockside, and you will need proof of identity when you collect them. You may disembark.' The WSO moved her clipboard to her left hand. 'Good luck,' she said, and held out a hand.

Mrs Trevor, her eyes on the bottom of the gangplank, distractedly shook it, and then made her way down, wobbling in her high heels.

The noise was deafening. On board the women's voices rose in a swell of anticipation, their heads bobbing as they fought to catch a glimpse of a loved one in the crowd. Around the bottom of the gangplank, several marines now stood firm, holding back the crowds.

Margaret stood in the queue, her heart thumping, hoping it wouldn't be too long before she could sit down. It had all seemed so abrupt, so rushed. She had had no chance to say goodbye to anyone, not even her cabin-mates, both of whom had vanished into thin air. Was this it? she thought. My last links with home, just vanishing on the breeze?

As the first bride reached the bottom of the gangplank, a cheer went up and the air was lit with a battery of flashbulbs. The band struck up 'Waltzing Matilda'.

'Wilson, Mrs Carrie.' The names reeled off, faster now. 'Your belongings have been cleared by Customs . . .'

What have I done? Margaret thought, staring out at this strange new country. She had never felt more alone in her life.

And suddenly there it was. Spoken twice before she heard it: 'O'Brien, Mrs Margaret . . . Mrs O'Brien?'

'Come on, girl,' said a neighbour, shoving her to the front. 'Shake a leg. It's time to get off.'

The captain had just begun to show the Lord Mayor round the bridge when an officer appeared at the door. 'Bride to see you, sir.'

'Show her in.'

She stood in the doorway, flushing as she saw the company he was in. 'I'm sorry,' she said, faltering. 'I didn't mean to interrupt.'

'XO, look after the Mayor for a moment, would you?' Ignoring Dobson's glare, Highfield walked over to the doorway. She was dressed in a pale blue short-sleeved blouse and khaki trousers, her hair pinned at the back of her head. She looked exhausted and unutterably sad.

'I just wanted to say goodbye and check that there was nothing else you wanted me to do. I mean, that everything is OK.'

'All fine,' he said, glancing down at his leg. 'I think we can say you're dismissed now, Sister Mackenzie.'

She gazed down at the dockside below them, teeming with people.

'Will you be all right?' he asked.

'I'll be fine, Captain.'

'I don't doubt it.' He realised he wanted to say more to this quiet, enigmatic woman. He had friends in high places: he wanted to ensure that she would find a good job. That her skills would not be wasted. There was no guarantee, after all, that any of these women would be appreciated. But in front of his men, he could say nothing.

She stepped forward and they shook hands. 'Thank you for everything,' he said quietly.

'Just glad to have been able to help, sir.'

'If there is ever any way in which I might help you, I'd be delighted if you would allow me . . .'

She smiled at him, the sadness briefly lifting from her eyes, and then, with a shake of her head, which told him he could not be the answer, she was gone.

Margaret stood in front of her husband, stunned into muteness. The sheer handsomeness of him in his civilian clothes. The redness of his hair. The way he was staring at her belly. She pushed back a strand of hair and wished that she had made the effort to set it. She tried to speak, then found she did not know what to say.

Joe looked at her for what seemed an eternity. Then he stepped forward with a huge grin. 'Bloody hell, woman, you look like a whale.' He threw his arms round her, saying her name over and over, hugging her so tightly that the baby kicked in protest, which made him jump back in surprise.

'Would you credit that, Mother? A kick like a mule, she said, and she wasn't wrong. How about that?' He rested his hand on her belly, then took hers. He gazed into her face. 'Ah, Maggie, it's good to see you.'

He enclosed her in his arms again, then reluctantly released her, and Margaret found herself clinging to his hand, as if it were a lifeline in this new country. It was then that she saw the woman standing with him, a couple of steps back, as if she did not want to interfere. As Margaret attempted to straighten her too-tight dress, all fingers and thumbs, the woman stepped forward, a smile breaking over her face. 'Margaret, dear. I'm so glad to meet you. Look at you—you must be exhausted.'

There was the briefest pause and then Mrs O'Brien folded her into her chest. 'How brave you are,' she said into her hair. 'All this way . . . away from your family . . . Well, don't you worry. We'll look after you now. You hear me? We're all going to get along grand.'

She felt those hands patting her back, smelt the faint, maternal smell of lavender, rosewater and baking. Margaret did not know who was more surprised, she or Joe, when she burst into tears.

Avice saw them before they saw her. She stood beneath the gun turret, her hat pinned tightly to her head so that it wouldn't blow away, and watched the little group below. Her mother was wearing a hat with a huge turquoise feather in it. It looked curiously ostentatious among all the tweeds, dull browns and greys. Her father, his own hat wedged low on his brow as he preferred it, kept glancing around him. She knew who he was looking for. In the melee of naval uniforms, he would be wondering how on earth they would ever find him.

'Radley. Mrs Avice Radley.'

Avice took a deep breath, brushed the front of her jacket and made her way slowly to the bottom of the gangplank, her back as straight as that of a model, her chin held high.

'There she is! There she is!' She heard her mother's squawk of excitement. 'Avice, darling! Look! Look! We're here!'

In front of her, where the gangplank met the dockside, a bride was ambushed at the bottom of the steps and swept into the arms of a soldier. Unable to get past them, Avice had to stand there, trapped on the gangplank, trying to look away as the couple were reacquainted.

'Avice!' Her mother was bobbing up and down on the other side of them like a brightly coloured cork. 'There she is, Wilf! Look at our girl!'

Finally, the soldier realised he was holding up the other brides, uttered a halfhearted apology, then swept his girl off to the side.

Her mother ran the last few steps to meet her, her face tearful with happiness. 'Oh, darling, it's so good to see you!'

Her father moved forward and held her. 'Your mother hasn't stopped fretting since you left. Couldn't bear the thought of you two on bad terms on opposite sides of the world. How's that for devotion, eh, Princess?'

There was such love and pride on both their faces. Avice realised, with horror, that if they carried on her face would crumple.

Deanna stepped forward. She was wearing a new cerise suit. 'Which one was the prostitute? Mummy nearly came out in hives when she got Mrs Carter's letter.'

'Where's Ian?' Her mother was peering into the faces of the men in

181

naval uniform. 'Do you think he's brought his family?'

'You'd better not have lost my shoes,' said Deanna, under her breath. 'I want them out of your case before you disappear.'

'He won't be here,' Avice said.

'He's never been sent off already. I thought the men were going to be allowed to meet you!' Her mother's gloved hand pressed to her face. 'Well, thank goodness we came, Wilf. Don't you think?'

'Is his family coming to meet you? We've heard nothing from them.' Her father took her arm. 'I've brought them a wireless. Top of the range.'

Avice stopped, set her face as straight as she could. 'He's not coming, Dad. He's never coming. There's been . . . there's been a change of plan.'

There was a short silence. Her father turned to her. 'What do you mean? You're not telling me I've just spent four hundred dollars on flights when there's no bloody celebration going to take place? Have you any idea how much this trip has—'

'Wilf!' Her mother turned back to her daughter. 'Avice, darling—'

'I'm not going to talk about it here, on a dockside full of people.'

Her parents exchanged a glance, then her mother adjusted her hat, took Avice's arm and tucked it into the crook of her own. Perhaps understanding something in her daughter's expression, she chose not to look her full in the face. When she spoke, there was a faint but definite break in her voice.

'Well, dear, when you're ready we'll have a little chat at the hotel.' She began to walk. 'It's a very nice hotel, you know. Beautiful-sized rooms and views all the way to Cornwall . . .'

Frances walked slowly down the gangplank, her suitcase in her right hand, the other trailing lightly down the handrail. She was, she thought, invisible in this crowd of cheering, embracing people. As she drew closer to the dockside, she kept walking. A new start, she told herself. I have made a new start.

'Frances!' She turned to see Margaret, her dress riding up over her knees as she waved wildly. Joe stood beside her, an arm round her shoulders. An older woman held her other arm. She had a kind face, not unlike Margaret's own, which was now beaming and tear-stained.

Frances went towards her. Her steps felt surprisingly unsteady on dry land and she struggled to walk without lurching. The two women dropped their bags and embraced.

'You weren't going to go without my address, were you?'

Frances shook her head, sneaking a glance at the two proud people who had claimed her friend as their own.

Margaret took a pen from her husband and accepted a scrap of paper from her mother-in-law. She put pen to paper, paused and laughed. 'What is it?' she said.

He laughed too, then scribbled something on the paper, which Margaret placed in Frances's hand. 'As soon as you get settled, you write to me with your address, you hear? My good friend Frances,' she explained to the two of them. 'She helped look after me. She's a nurse.'

'Pleased to meet you, Frances,' said Joe, thrusting out a huge hand. 'You come and see us. Whenever.'

Frances tried to return some of his warmth in her own grasp. The older woman nodded and smiled, then glanced at her watch. 'Joseph, train,' she mouthed.

'You take care now,' Margaret said, squeezing her arm.

'I'll look forward to hearing how it all goes,' said Frances.

'It'll be fine,' Margaret said, with confidence.

Frances watched the three of them as they made their way to the dockyard gates, still chatting, arms linked, until people closed round them and she couldn't see any more.

She took a deep breath, trying to dislodge the huge lump in her throat, and glanced back at the ship. There were men moving around, women still waving. She could see nothing, no one. I'm not ready, she thought. I don't want to go. She stood, a thin woman jostled by the crowds, tears streaming down her face.

Nicol pushed his way to the front of the queue and several of the waiting women protested loudly. 'Frances Mackenzie,' he shouted at the WSO. 'Where is she?'

The woman bristled. 'Do you mind? My job is to sign these ladies off the ship.'

He grabbed the clipboard.

'She's gone,' she said, snatching it back. 'She's already disembarked. Now, if you'll excuse me.'

Nicol ran to the side of the ship and leaned over the rail, trying to see her in the crowd, trying to make out the distinctive, strong, slim frame, the pale hair. Below him thousands of people were still on the side, jostling, weaving past each other, disappearing and reappearing.

His heart lodged somewhere high in his throat, and, in despair, he began to shout, 'Frances, Frances,' already grasping the scale of his loss, his defeat.

His voice, roughened with emotion, hovered for a moment over the crowds, caught, and then sailed away on the wind, back out to sea.

Captain Highfield was almost the last man to leave the ship. He had undergone his ceremonial goodbye, flanked by his men, but at the gangplank, he stood, looking out, as if reluctant to disembark. When they realised he was in no hurry to move, a number of senior officers had filed past, wishing him well in his future life.

And then he was alone, standing at the top of the gangplank.

Those few who were watching from the dockside, the few who were minded to pay him any attention, remarked afterwards that it was strange to see a captain all by himself on such an occasion. And that, strange as it might sound, they had rarely seen a grown man look more lost.

It was the last time I ever saw her. There were so many people, screaming and yelling and pushing to get to each other, and it was impossible to see. And I looked up, and someone was pulling at my arm and then a couple ran towards each other and just locked onto each other right in front of me and kissed and kissed, and I don't think they could even hear me when I asked them to get out of the way.

And I think it was then that I realised it was a lost cause. It was all lost. Because I could have stood there for a day and a night and hung on for ever but sometimes you just have to put one foot in front of the other and move on. So that was what I did.

And that was the last I saw of her.

PART THREE
2003

THE STEWARDESS walked down the aisle, checking that all seat belts were fastened for landing. She did not notice the old woman who dabbed her eyes a few more times than might have been necessary. Beside her, her granddaughter fastened her belt. She placed the in-flight magazine in the pocket on the back of the seat in front of her.

'That's the saddest story I've ever heard.'

The old woman shook her head. 'Not that sad, darling. Not compared to some.'

'I guess it explains why you had such a reaction to that ship. My God, what are the chances of that happening, after all those years?'

She shrugged, a delicate gesture. 'Pretty small, I suppose. Although perhaps I shouldn't have been surprised. Lots of ships that leave the navy are recycled, as it were.'

She had recovered her old composure. She had even managed to scold Jennifer several times, for mislaying her passport, for drinking beer before lunchtime. Jennifer had been reassured. Because by the time they had got onto the flight her grandmother had said almost nothing in sixteen hours. She had been reduced somehow, more frail, despite the restorative comforts of the luxurious hotel and the first-class lounge in which the airline staff had allowed them to wait. Jennifer, holding her hand, had felt the guilt bear down on her with even more determination. You shouldn't have brought her to India, it said.

And then, shortly after take-off, she had begun to talk.

The old lady had pushed herself upright and then spoke as if they had spent the last hours not in terrible silence but deep in conversation.

'I hadn't thought of it as anything but a travel arrangement, you see?' she said suddenly. 'A means of getting from A to B, a hop across the seas.'

Jennifer had shifted uncomfortably, unsure how to respond. Or whether a response was even required.

Her grandmother's voice had dropped and she had turned to the window. 'And there I was, feeling things I never expected to feel. And so exposed to all those people, knowing it was only a matter of time . . .' She gazed out at the rippled carpet of white clouds sitting in space.

'A matter of time?'

'Till they found out.'

'About what?'

Her grandmother's eyes landed on Jennifer and widened, as if she was surprised to find her there. She frowned a little. Her voice, when it came, was polite, unemotional. A coffee-morning voice. 'Would you be kind enough to get me a drink of water, Jennifer dear? I'm rather thirsty.'

The girl waited a moment, then got up, found an obliging stewardess from whom she took a bottle of mineral water. She poured it into a glass and her grandmother drank it in efficient gulps.

'What did they find out?'

Nothing.

'You can tell me, Gran,' she whispered, leaning forward. 'What it was that upset you back there? Let it out. There's nothing you could say that would shock me.'

The old woman smiled. Then she stared at her granddaughter with an intensity the young woman found almost unnerving.

'You with your modern attitudes, Jenny. Your little arrangement with

185

Sanjay and your "letting it all out" . . . I wonder just how modern your views really are.'

She didn't know what to say to that. There was something almost aggressive in her grandmother's tone. They had sat, watched the in-flight film and slept.

And then, finally, as she woke, her grandmother had told her the story of the marine.

He was waiting, as they had known he would be, by the arrivals barrier. Even in that crowd of people they would have recognised him any-where: the erect bearing, the immaculately pressed suit. Despite his age and failing eyesight, he saw them before they saw him and his hand was already signalling to them.

Jennifer stood back as her grandmother picked up speed, and then, dropping her cases on the floor, embraced him. They held on to each other for some time, her grandfather's arms wrapped tightly round his wife, as if fearful that she would absent herself again.

'I've missed you,' he murmured into her grey hair. 'Oh, my darling, I've missed you,' so that Jennifer, kicking at the toes of her shoes, looked around at the other families, wondering if anyone had noticed. She felt somehow as if she was intruding. There was something pretty unsettling about passion in a pair of eighty-year-olds.

'Next time, you come with me,' her grandmother said.

'You know I don't like to go far,' he said. 'I'm quite happy at home.'

'Then I'll stay with you,' she said.

In the car, their bags stowed behind them, her grandmother some-how rejuvenated, Jennifer had begun to tell her grandfather the story of the ship. She had just got to the part where they had discovered the broken vessel's name when he turned off the ignition and she saw that he was staring at her with unexpected intensity.

'The same ship?' he said. 'It was really the *Victoria*?'

The old lady nodded.

'I thought I'd never see her again,' she said. 'It was . . . It gave me quite a turn, I can tell you.'

Her grandfather's eyes didn't leave his wife's face. 'Oh, Frances,' he said. 'When I think of how close we came . . .'

'Hang on,' Jennifer said. 'Are you saying you were the marine?'

The two old people exchanged a glance.

'You?' She turned to her grandmother. 'Grandpa? You never said! You never said Grandpa was the marine.'

Frances Nicol smiled. 'You never asked.'

He had run, he told Jennifer, as he drove out of the sprawling mass of Heathrow, the equivalent of a mile and a half by the time he had searched the ship and worked out she had already gone. All the time he had been shouting her name. Frances! Frances! Frances! And then he had done the same on land, pushing his way through the throng of people on the dockside.

Then, as he had despaired, chest heaving, hands thrust onto his knees, the crowds at the jetty had thinned, and by chance he had seen her. A tall, thin figure, standing with her suitcase, her back to the sea, staring at her adopted homeland.

'What happened to the others?'

Frances smoothed her skirt. 'Margaret and Joe went back to Australia after his mother died. They had four children. She still writes to me at Christmas.'

'What about Avice?' She laid a heavy emphasis on the A, as if still amused by the anachronistic nature of her name.

'I don't really know. She wrote once to say she'd gone back to Australia and to thank me for everything I'd done. Rather a formal letter, but I suppose that wasn't a surprise.'

Jennifer sat back in the upholstered seat. She pulled her phone from her back pocket to see if Jay had texted her again, but her inbox was empty. She would text him when she got home. 'You know, I don't understand why you two didn't just get it together on the ship, if you liked each other so much,' she said, putting her phone away. She was vaguely irritated by the way they looked at each other then, as if what they had shared had been something she would not understand.

Her voice became more assertive. 'It just strikes me that people of your generation often made things far more difficult for yourselves than they needed to be.'

They said nothing. Then, from the back seat, she watched her grandfather's hand slide over to take her grandmother's and give it a squeeze. 'I suppose that's possible,' he said.

When he had told her the truth about his marriage, about what it meant for the two of them, she had been silent. She had sat down on the grass, her expression stilled, as if she were only just able to absorb what he was telling her.

'Frances?' He seated himself beside her on the grass. 'Remember what you said to me, the night the planes went over the side? It's over, Frances. It's time to move on.'

She had turned to him slowly, her expression almost fearful, as if she could not trust herself to believe what he was saying.

'This is the beauty in it, Frances. We're allowed this. No, we're entitled to it.' Underlying the determination, there was a faint note of panic in his voice. 'We're entitled, you hear me? Both of us.'

She had stared fiercely at her feet, and then a faint sound escaped her, and he saw she was smiling and crying at the same time, her hand reaching clumsily across the ground for his.

They had stayed there for some unknown period of time, their hands entwined, pressed into the grass. Chattering families passed them on their way home, eyeing them knowingly but without curiosity, a marine and his sweetheart, reunited after a lifetime spent apart.

'You are Nicol,' she had told him, as she traced the still bruised lines of his face with her fingers. 'The captain told me. Nicol. Your name is Nicol.' The way she said it was joyful. It made it sound like treasure.

'No,' he said, with certainty, and as he spoke his voice sounded strange, unfamiliar even to himself, for it had been years since anyone had said this word. 'I am Henry.'

JOJO MOYES

'Grandparents just don't seem to realise how interesting their lives are to the younger generation,' Jojo said reflectively as we lunched together close by Liverpool Street station. She had dashed up to London by train in between her new baby son's feeds. 'It was only when I became a teenager, and started asking my grandparents questions, that I began to discover what a fascinating life they'd led.' Although Jojo and her parents lived in London, and her grandparents had a home in Devon, Jojo says they were a very close family. 'My grandfather was a naval commander, but he was also very creative. He used to make up fantastic stories. I wish I'd written them down.'

In fact, from the age of seven, Jojo was busy writing her own stories. It was years later, when she was working as a journalist on the *Independent*, and had written three unpublished novels, that the story of her grandparents' wartime courtship gave her the idea for *Sheltering Rain*, her first best seller. She wrote two further novels before a conversation with her grandmother, Betty McKee (pictured here with Jojo) inspired *The Ship of Brides*.

'I knew she'd grown up in Australia and had married my grandfather— then a young lieutenant in the Royal Navy—during the war, but I didn't know how she'd got from Sydney to England. She told me that, at the age of twenty-two, she had been one of 650 war brides who had sailed to Plymouth on an aircraft carrier to meet up with their husbands.' Jojo was so intrigued

that she searched for more information about their extraordinary and coura-
geous journey, and what she discovered fired her imagination.

'I started without knowing anything about Australia, or the navy,' she
laughed. 'It was a huge technical challenge. I badgered the navy to let me
spend time on board an aircraft carrier and enlisted the help of a lieutenant
who answered questions like "How would a stoker react to a naval commander" and "What would happen if there was a fire on board?" I visited the
Imperial War Museum and discovered that an aircraft carrier is just like a
floating city. I took home a detailed diagram of a carrier and kept it pinned
up on the wall. It was the only way to keep track of where everyone was and
how they moved around the ship. And then there was lots of background
reading about the war . . . Anyway, my grandmother has read the book and
I'm thankful to say she likes it!'

Betty McKee supplied Jojo with some specific memories of the voyage 'like
the scene where all the brides slept on the top deck in their swimsuits', but
the characters are imaginary. 'At the outset, I had no idea whether my main
characters were going to get together or not. For example, I hadn't anticipated that there would be this weird chemistry between Frances and the captain
of HMS *Victoria*—they decided that for themselves. When I wrote the scene
where they are both in his cabin, I just couldn't stop, and I found myself writing and crying at the same time! If you really inhabit your characters, then
their actions and reactions work in the book.'

Anne Jenkins

The Undomestic Goddess

Sophie Kinsella

My name is Samantha Sweeting.

I am twenty-nine years old and about to

be made a partner at Carter Spink, one

of the biggest law firms in London.

OK, there are a few drawbacks—

I spend all my waking hours

at work, have no home life and have

never had time to learn

to cook or sew on a button.

But then, who needs to be

a domestic goddess?

One

WOULD YOU CONSIDER **yourself stressed?**

No. I'm not stressed.

I'm . . . busy. Plenty of people are busy. It's the way the world is. I have a high-powered job, my career is important to me and I enjoy it.

OK. So sometimes I do feel a bit tense. Kind of pressured. But I'm a lawyer in the City, for God's sake. What do you expect?

On average, how many hours do you spend in the office every day?

~~14~~

~~12~~

~~8~~

It depends.

Do you exercise regularly?

~~I regularly go swimming~~

~~I occasionally go swim~~

I am intending to begin a regular regime of swimming. When I have time.

Do you drink 8 glasses of water a day?

~~Yes~~

~~Someti~~

No.

I put down my pen and clear my throat. Across the room, Maya looks up from where she's rearranging all her little pots of wax and nail varnish. Maya is my beauty therapist for the day.

'Everything all right with the questionnaire?' she says in her soft voice.

'Are all these questions absolutely necessary?' I say politely.

193

'We like to have as much information as possible to assess your beauty and health needs,' she says in soothing yet implacable tones.

I glance at my watch. Nine forty-five. I don't have time for this. But it's my birthday treat and I promised Aunt Patsy.

To be more accurate, it's *last* year's birthday treat. In the card that came with the 'Ultimate De-stress Experience' voucher she wrote *Make Some Time For Yourself, Samantha!!!*

Which I did fully intend to do. But we had a couple of busy patches at work and somehow a year went by without my finding a spare moment. I'm a lawyer with Carter Spink, and just at the moment things are pretty hectic. It's a blip. It'll get better. I just have to get through the next couple of weeks.

Anyway, then Aunt Patsy sent me *this* year's birthday card—and I suddenly realised the voucher was about to expire. So here I am, on my twenty-ninth birthday. Sitting on a couch in a white towelling robe and surreal paper knickers. With a half-day window. Max.

Do you smoke?

No.

Do you drink alcohol?

Yes.

Do you eat regular home-cooked meals?

I look up, a bit defensive. What does that have to do with anything? What makes home-cooked meals superior?

I eat a nutritious, varied diet, I write at last.

Which is absolutely true. Everyone knows the Chinese live longer than we do—so what could be more healthy than to eat their food?

'I'm done,' I announce, and hand the pages back to Maya, who starts reading through my answers. Her finger is travelling down the paper at a snail's pace. Like we've got all the time in the world. Which she may well have. But I have to be back in the office by one.

'I've read your answers carefully.' Maya gives me a thoughtful look. 'And you're obviously quite a stressed-out woman.'

What? Where does she get that from? I specifically put on the form, I am *not* stressed out.

'No, I'm not.' I give her a relaxed, see-how-unstressed-I-am smile.

Maya looks unconvinced. 'Your job is obviously very pressured.'

'I thrive under pressure,' I explain. Which is true. I've known that about myself ever since . . .

Well, ever since my mother told me, when I was about eight. *You thrive under pressure, Samantha.* Our whole family thrives under pressure. It's like our family motto or something.

194

I love my job. I love the satisfaction of spotting the loophole in a contract. I love the adrenaline rush of closing a deal. I love the thrill of negotiation, and arguing, and making the best point in the room.

I suppose, occasionally, I do feel as though someone's piling heavy weights on me and I have to keep holding them up, no matter how exhausted I am. But then everyone probably feels like that. It's normal.

'Well.' Maya gets up. She presses a button set in the wall and gentle panpipes music fills the air. 'All I can say is, you've come to the right place, Samantha. Our aim here is to de-stress, revitalise and detoxify.'

'Lovely,' I say, only half listening. I've just remembered, I never got back to David Elldridge about that Ukrainian oil contract.

'The aim of the Green Tree Centre is to provide a haven of tranquillity, away from all your day-to-day worries.' Maya presses another button in the wall and the light dims to a muted glow. 'Before we start,' she says softly, 'do you have any questions?'

'Actually, I do.' I lean forward. 'Could I send a quick email?'

'Samantha, Samantha . . .' Maya shakes her head. 'You're here to relax. Not to send emails. It's an obsession! An addiction!'

That's ridiculous. I'm not *obsessed*. I check my emails about once every . . . thirty seconds, maybe. A lot can change in thirty seconds.

'This is why we ask that you leave all electronic equipment in the safe. No mobile phones are permitted. No little computers.' Maya spreads her arms. 'This is a retreat. An escape from the world.'

'Right.' I nod meekly.

Now is probably not the time to reveal that I have a BlackBerry hidden in my paper knickers. I did see the rule about no electronic equipment. And I did surrender my Dictaphone. But three hours without a BlackBerry? I mean, what if there was an emergency?

'So, let's begin.' Maya smiles. 'Lie down on the couch, under a towel.'

She turns away discreetly and, a little awkwardly, I arrange myself on the couch, trying to avoid squashing my precious BlackBerry.

'I'm going to begin with a relaxing foot rub,' says Maya, and I feel her smoothing some kind of lotion over my feet. 'Try to clear your mind.'

I stare dutifully up at the ceiling. Clear my mind.

What am I going to do about Elldridge? He'll be waiting for a response. What if he tells the other partners I was lax? What if it affects my chances of partnership? I feel a clench of alarm. Now is not the time to be leaving anything to chance.

'Try to let go of all your thoughts . . .' Maya is chanting.

Maybe I could send him a very quick email. Surreptitiously I reach down and feel the hard corner of my BlackBerry. Gradually I inch it out of my paper knickers. Maya is still massaging my feet, totally oblivious.

'Your body is growing heavy . . . your mind should be emptying . . .'

I edge the BlackBerry up onto my chest until I can just see the screen underneath the towel. Trying to keep my movements to a minimum, I furtively start typing an email with one hand.

'Imagine you're walking along a beach . . .' Maya is saying soothingly.

'Uh huh . . .' I murmur.

David, I'm typing. *Re ZFN Oil contract. I read through amendments. Feel our response should be*

'What are you doing?' says Maya, suddenly alert.

'Nothing!' I say, hastily shoving the BlackBerry back under the towel. 'Just . . . er . . . relaxing.'

Maya comes round the couch and looks at the bump in the towel where I'm clutching the BlackBerry.

'Are you hiding something?' she says in disbelief.

'No!'

From under the towel the BlackBerry emits a little bleep. Damn.

Maya's eyes narrow. 'Samantha,' she says in slow, ominous tones. 'Do you have a piece of electronic equipment under there?'

I have the feeling that if I don't confess she'll rip my towel off anyway.

'I was just sending an email,' I say at last and sheepishly produce the BlackBerry.

'You workaholics!' She grabs it out of my hand in exasperation. 'Emails can *wait*. It can all *wait*. You just don't know how to relax!'

'I'm not a workaholic!' I retort indignantly. 'I'm a lawyer! I can't just switch off! Especially not right now. I'm . . . well, I'm up for partnership at the moment. They make the decision tomorrow. If it happens, I'll be the youngest partner in the whole history of the firm. Do you know how big a deal that is? Do you have any idea—'

I stop with a squeak of surprise, as from inside my paper knickers there comes a judder. My mobile phone. I shoved it in there along with the BlackBerry and turned it on to 'vibrate' so it wouldn't make a noise.

Suspicion snaps through Maya's eyes. 'You smuggled in a *mobile phone as well*?'

'Look,' I say, trying to sound apologetic, 'I know you've got your rules and everything, which I do respect, but the thing is, I *need* my mobile.' I reach under the towel for the phone.

'*Leave it!*' Maya's cry takes me by surprise. 'Samantha, if you've listened to a single word I've said, you'll switch the phone off right now.'

The phone vibrates again in my hand. I look at the caller ID and feel a twist in my stomach. 'It's the office.'

'They can leave a message. They can wait. This is your own time.'

God, she really doesn't get it, does she? I almost want to laugh.

'I'm an associate at Carter Spink,' I explain. 'I don't *have* my own time.' I flip the phone open and an angry male voice bites down the line.

'Samantha, where the hell are you?'

It's Ketterman. The head of our corporate department. He must have a Christian name, but no one ever calls him anything except Ketterman.

'The Fallons deal is back on. Get back here now. Meeting at ten thirty.'

'I'll be there as soon as I can.' I snap the phone shut and give Maya a rueful glance. 'Sorry.'

As I arrive at the office, Ketterman is standing by my desk, looking at the mess of papers and files strewn everywhere with distaste.

'Meeting in ten minutes,' he says, looking at his watch. 'I want the draft financing documentation ready.'

'Absolutely,' I reply, trying to stay calm. But just his presence is giving me the jitters.

Ketterman is unnerving at the best of times. He emanates scary, brainy power like other men emanate aftershave. But today is a million times worse, because Ketterman is on the decision panel. Tomorrow he and thirteen other partners decide on who will become a new partner.

Tomorrow I discover whether I've made it or whether my life has been one big useless failure. No pressure, or anything.

'The draft documentation is right here . . .' I reach into a pile of folders and pull out what feels like a box file with an efficient flourish.

It's an old box of Krispy Kreme doughnuts.

Hastily I shove it in the bin. 'It's definitely here somewhere . . .' I scrabble frantically and locate the correct file. Thank God. 'Here!'

'I don't know how you can work in this shambles.' Ketterman's voice is sarcastic. 'You know, the old rule was that desks were completely cleared every night by six. Perhaps we should reintroduce it.'

'Maybe!' I try to smile.

'Samantha!' A genial voice interrupts us and I look round in relief to see Arnold Saville approaching along the corridor.

Arnold is my favourite of the senior partners. He's got woolly grey hair which always seems a bit wild for a lawyer, and a flamboyant taste in ties. Today he's wearing a bright-red paisley affair, with a matching handkerchief in his top pocket. He greets me with a broad smile.

I'm sure Arnold's the one who's rooting for me to be made partner. Just as I'm equally sure Ketterman will be opposing it.

'Letter of appreciation about you, Samantha.' Arnold holds out a sheet of paper. 'From the chairman of Gleiman Brothers, no less.'

I take the headed sheet in surprise and glance down the handwritten note. '. . . *great esteem . . . her services always professional . . .*'

'I gather you saved him a few million pounds he wasn't expecting,' Arnold twinkles. 'He's delighted.'

'Oh, yes.' I colour slightly. 'Well, it was nothing. I just noticed an anomaly in the way they were structuring their finances.'

I glance at Ketterman, just to see if by any remote chance he might look impressed. But he's still wearing his impatient frown.

'I also want you to deal with this.' Ketterman plonks a file on my desk. 'I need a due diligence review in forty-eight hours.'

My heart sinks as I look at the folder. It'll take me hours to do this. Ketterman's always giving me extra bits of mundane work he can't be bothered to do himself. In fact, all the partners do it. Even Arnold. Half the time they don't even tell me, just dump the file on my desk with some illegible memo and expect me to get on with it.

'Any problems?' His eyes are narrowing.

'Of course not,' I say in a brisk, can-do, potential-partner voice. 'See you at the meeting.'

As he stalks off I glance at my watch. Ten twenty-two. I have precisely eight minutes to make sure the draft documentation for the Fallons deal is all in order. I open the file and scan the pages swiftly, checking for errors. I've learned to read a lot faster since I've been at Carter Spink.

In fact, I do everything faster. I walk faster, talk faster, eat faster . . . have sex faster . . . Not that I've had much of that lately. But a couple of years ago I dated a senior partner from Berry Forbes. He was called Jacob and worked on huge international deals, and he had even less time than me. By the end, we'd honed our routine to about six minutes.

Anyway, then Jacob was made a huge offer and moved to Boston, so that was the end of it. I didn't mind very much. I didn't really fancy him.

'Samantha?' A voice interrupts my thoughts. It's my secretary, Maggie. She only started a few weeks ago and I don't know her very well yet. 'You had a message while you were out. From Joanne?'

'Joanne from Clifford Chance?' I look up, my attention grabbed.

'Not that Joanne,' says Maggie. 'Joanne your new cleaner. She wants to know where you keep your vacuum cleaner bags.'

'Why does the vacuum cleaner need to go in a bag?' I say, puzzled. 'Is she taking it somewhere?'

Maggie peers at me as though she's not sure if I'm joking.

'The bags that go *inside* your vacuum cleaner,' she says carefully. 'To collect the dust? Do you have any of those?'

'Oh!' I say, quickly. 'Oh, *those* bags. Er . . .'

'Maybe it's a Dyson,' suggests Maggie. 'They don't take bags. Is it a cylinder or an upright?' She looks at me expectantly.

I have no idea what she's talking about.

'I'll sort it,' I say in a businesslike manner, and start gathering my papers together. 'Thanks, Maggie.'

'She had another question.' Maggie consults her paper. 'How do you switch on your oven?'

For a moment I continue gathering my papers, as though I haven't quite heard. Obviously I know how to switch on my own oven.

'Well. You turn the er . . . knob,' I say at last, trying to sound nonchalant. 'It's pretty clear, really . . .'

'She said it has some weird timer lock.' Maggie frowns thoughtfully. 'Is it gas or electric?'

OK, I think I might terminate this conversation right now.

'Maggie, I really need to make a call,' I say regretfully.

'So what shall I tell your cleaner?' Maggie persists. 'She's waiting for me to call back.'

'Tell her to . . . leave it for today. I'll sort it out.'

As Maggie leaves my office I reach for a pen and memo pad.

> 1. *How switch on oven?*
> 2. *Vacuum cleaner bags—buy*

I put the pen down and massage my forehead. I really don't have time for this. I mean, vacuum bags. I don't even know what they look like, for God's sake, let alone where to buy them—

A sudden brainwave hits me. I'll order a new vacuum cleaner. That'll come with a bag already installed, surely.

'Samantha.'

'What? What is it?' I give a startled jump and open my eyes. Guy Ashby is standing at my door.

Guy is my best friend in the firm. He's six foot three with olive skin and dark eyes, and normally he looks every inch the smooth, polished lawyer. But this morning his dark hair is rumpled and there are shadows under his eyes.

'Relax.' Guy smiles. 'Only me. Coming to the meeting?'

'Oh. Er . . . yes I am.' I pick up my papers, then add carelessly, 'Are you OK, Guy? You look a bit rough.'

He broke up with his girlfriend. They had bitter rows all night and she's walked off for good . . . No, she's emigrated to New Zealand . . .

'All-nighter,' he says, wincing. 'Ketterman's inhuman.'

'Bummer.' I grin in sympathy, then push back my chair. 'Let's go.'

I've known Guy for a year, ever since he joined the corporate department as a partner. He's intelligent, and funny, and works the same way I do, and we just somehow . . . click.

And yes. It's possible that some kind of romance would have happened between us if things had been different. But there was a stupid misunderstanding, and. . . anyway. It didn't. The details aren't important. It's not something I dwell on. We're friends—and that's fine by me.

OK, this is exactly what happened.

Apparently Guy noticed me pretty much the first day at the firm, just like I noticed him. And he was interested. He asked if I was single. Which I was. This is the crucial part: I was single. I'd just split up with Jacob. It would have been perfect. But Nigel MacDermot, who is a stupid, stupid, *thoughtless* behind-the-times moron, told Guy I was attached to a senior partner at Berry Forbes. *Even though I was single.*

There was a slightly embarrassing few weeks where I smiled a lot at Guy—and he looked awkward and started avoiding me.

I didn't understand what was going on, so I backed off. Then I heard on the grapevine he'd started going out with a girl called Charlotte who he'd met at some weekend party.

I mean, it's fine. Really. That's the way it goes. Some things happen—and some things don't. This one obviously just wasn't meant to be.

'So,' says Guy as we walk along the corridor to the meeting room. 'Partner.' He cocks an eyebrow.

'Don't say that!' I hiss in horror. He'll totally jinx it.

'Come on. You know you've made it.'

'I don't know anything.'

'Samantha, you're the brightest lawyer in your year. And you work the hardest. Haven't you practised in the mirror for the firm's website?' Guy adopts a pose with his finger poised thoughtfully at his chin. 'Ms Samantha Sweeting, Partner.'

'I haven't even thought about it,' I say, rolling my eyes with disdain.

This is a slight lie. I've already planned how to do my hair for the photo. And which black suit to wear. And this time I'm going to smile. In the photo on my Carter Spink web page, I look way too serious.

'I heard your presentation blew their socks off,' says Guy seriously.

My disdain vanishes in a second. 'Really?' I say, trying not to sound too eager. 'You heard that?'

'And you put William Griffiths right on a point of law in front of everybody?' Guy folds his arms and regards me humorously. 'Do you ever make a mistake, Samantha Sweeting?'

'Oh, I make plenty of mistakes,' I say lightly. 'Believe me.'

Like not grabbing you and telling you I was single, the first day we met.

'A mistake isn't a mistake,' Guy pauses, 'unless it can't be put right.'

'Ready?' Ketterman's whiplash voice behind us makes us both jump and I turn to see a whole phalanx of soberly suited men, together with a pair of even more soberly suited women.

'Absolutely.' Guy nods at Ketterman, then turns back and winks at me.

Nine hours later we're all still in the meeting.

The huge mahogany table is strewn with photocopied draft contracts, financial reports, notepads covered in scribbles, polystyrene coffee cups and Post-its. Two of the lawyers from the opposition have got up from the table and are murmuring intently in the break-out room. Every meeting room has one of these: a little side area where you go for private conversations, or when you feel like breaking something.

The intensity of the afternoon has passed. It's like an ebb in the tide. Faces are flushed around the table, tempers are still high, but no one's shouting any more. The clients have gone. They reached agreement at about four o'clock, shook hands and sailed off in their shiny limos.

Now it's up to us, the lawyers, to work out what they said and what they actually meant (and if you think these are the same thing, you might as well give up law now), and put it all into a draft contract in time for the meeting tomorrow.

When they'll probably begin shouting some more.

The fluorescent lights are flickering in my eyes and I feel drained. It's seven nineteen, and in eleven minutes I'm supposed to be halfway across town, sitting down to dinner with my mother and brother Daniel.

I'll have to cancel. My own birthday dinner.

Even as I think the thought, I can hear the outraged voice of my oldest school friend Freya ringing in my mind.

They can't make you stay at work on your birthday!

What she doesn't understand is, the deadline comes first, end of story. Prior engagements don't count, birthdays don't count. Holidays are cancelled every week. Across the table from me is Clive Sutherland from the corporate department. His wife had twins this morning and he was back at the table by lunchtime.

'All right, people,' Ketterman's voice commands immediate attention. 'We have to adjourn.'

What? My head pops up.

Other heads have popped up too; I can detect the hope around the table. We're like school kids sensing a disturbance during the maths test, not daring to move in case we land a double detention.

'Until we have the documentation from Fallons, we can't proceed. I'll see you all tomorrow, here at nine a.m.' He sweeps out, and as the door closes, I exhale. I was holding my breath, I realise.

Clive Sutherland has already bolted for the door. People are already on their mobile phones all over the room, discussing dinner, films, uncancelling arrangements. There's a joyful lift to the proceedings. I have a sudden urge to yell 'Yippee!'

But that wouldn't be partner-like.

As my taxi edges through the traffic on Cheapside, I quickly rifle in my bag for my new make-up bag. I nipped into Selfridges in my lunch-hour the other day, when I realised I was still using the eyeliner and mascara I bought for my graduation six years ago. I didn't have time for a demonstration, but I asked the girl at the counter if she could just quickly sell me everything she thought I should have.

I didn't really listen as she explained each item, because I was on the phone to Elldridge about the Ukrainian contract. But the one thing I do remember is her insistence I should use something called bronzer powder. She said it might stop me looking so dreadfully—

Then she stopped herself. 'Pale,' she said at last.

I take out the compact and huge blusher brush, and start sweeping the powder on to my cheeks and forehead. Then, as I peer at my reflection in the mirror, I stifle a laugh. My face stares back at me, freakishly golden and shiny. I look ridiculous.

I mean, who am I kidding? A City lawyer who hasn't been on holiday for two years doesn't have a tan. Or even a glow.

I look at myself for a few more seconds, then take out a cleansing wipe and scrub the bronzer off until my face is white again, with shades of grey. Back to normal. The make-up girl kept mentioning the dark shadows under my eyes, too.

Thing is, if I *didn't* have shadows under my eyes, I'd probably get fired.

I'm wearing a black suit, as I always do. My mother gave me five black suits for my twenty-first birthday, and I've never broken the habit.

I free my hair from its elastic band, quickly comb it out, then twist it back into place. My hair has never exactly been my pride and joy. It's mouse colour, medium length, with a medium wave. At least, it was last time I looked. Most of the time it lives screwed up into a knot.

'Nice evening planned?' says the taxi driver.

'It's my birthday, actually.'

'Happy birthday!' He twinkles at me. 'You'll be partying, then.'

'Er . . . kind of.'

My family and wild parties don't exactly go together. But even so, it'll be really great for us to see each other. It doesn't happen very often.

It's not that we don't want to see each other. It's just we all have very busy careers. There's my mother, who's a barrister. She's quite well known, in fact. And then there's my brother Daniel, who is thirty-six and head of investment at Whittons. He was named last year as one of the top deal-makers in the City.

There's also my dad who lives in South Africa with his third wife. I haven't seen much of him since I was three. But that's OK. My mother's got enough energy for two parents.

We come to a halt outside the restaurant and I pay the taxi driver.

'Have a great evening, love!' he says. 'And happy birthday!'

'Thanks!'

As I hurry into Maxim's, I'm looking all around for Mum or Daniel, but I can't spot either of them.

'Hi!' I say to the maître d'. 'I'm meeting Ms Tennyson.'

That's Mum. She disapproves of a woman taking the name of her husband. She also disapproves of women staying at home, cooking, cleaning, or learning to type, and thinks all women should earn more than their husbands because they're naturally brighter.

The maître d' leads me to an empty table in the corner and I slide on to the suede banquette.

As I scan the menu I feel suddenly ravenous. I haven't had a proper meal for a week, and it all looks so yummy. Glazed *foie gras*. Lamb with spiced hummous. And on the specials board is chocolate-mint soufflé with two homemade sorbets.

'Miss Sweeting?' I look up to see the maître d' approaching, holding a mobile phone. 'I have a message. Your mother has been held up at her chambers.'

'Oh.' I try to hide my disappointment. But I can hardly complain. I've done the same thing to her enough times.

'I have her here on the telephone. Her secretary will put her through . . . Hello?' he says into the phone. 'I have Ms Tennyson's daughter.'

'Samantha?' comes a crisp, precise voice in my ear. 'Darling, I can't come tonight, I'm afraid.'

'You can't come at *all*?' My smile falters.

'Far too much to do. I'm in court tomorrow . . . No, get me the other file,' she adds to someone in her office. 'These things happen,' she resumes. 'But have a nice evening with Daniel. Oh, and happy birthday. I've wired three hundred pounds to your bank account.'

'Oh, right,' I say after a pause. 'Thanks.'

'Have you heard about the partnership yet?'

'Not yet.' I can hear her tapping her pen on the phone.

'How many hours have you put in this month?'

'Um . . . probably about two hundred . . .'

'Is that enough? Samantha, you don't want to be passed over.'

'Two hundred is quite a lot,' I explain. 'Compared to the others—'

'You have to be *better* than the others!' Her voice cuts across mine as though she's in a court room. 'You can't afford for your performance to slip below excellent. This is a *crucial time*—Not *that* file!' she adds impatiently to whoever it is. 'Hold the line, Samantha—'

'Samantha?'

I look up in confusion from the phone to see a girl in a powder-blue suit approaching the table. She's holding a gift basket adorned with a bow, and has a wide smile.

'I'm Lorraine, Daniel's PA,' she says. 'He couldn't make it tonight, I'm afraid. But I've got a little something for you—plus he's here on the phone to say hello.'

She holds out a lit-up mobile phone. In total confusion, I take it and press it to my other ear.

'Hi, Samantha,' comes Daniel's businesslike drawl. 'Look, sweets, we're on a mega deal. I can't be there.'

I feel a plunge of total dismay. *Neither* of them is coming?

'I'm really sorry, babe,' Daniel's saying. 'One of those things. But have a great time with Mum, won't you?'

I swallow several times. I can't admit she blew me out too. I can't admit that I'm sitting here all on my own.

'OK!' Somehow I muster a breezy tone. 'We will!'

'I've transferred some money to your account. Buy something nice. And I've sent some chocolates along with Lorraine,' he adds proudly. 'Picked them out myself.'

I look at the gift basket Lorraine is proffering. It isn't chocolates, it's soap.

'That's really lovely, Daniel,' I manage. 'Thanks very much.'

'*Happy Birthday to You . . .*'

There's sudden chorusing behind me. I swivel round to see a waiter carrying over a cocktail glass. A sparkler is fizzing out of it and 'Happy Birthday Samantha' is written in caramel on the steel tray, next to a miniature souvenir menu signed by the chef. Three waiters are following behind, all singing in harmony.

After a moment, Lorraine awkwardly joins in. '*Happy Birthday to You . . .*'

The waiter puts the tray down in front of me, but my hands are full of phones.

'I'll take that for you,' says Lorraine, relieving me of Daniel's phone.

'Samantha?' Mum is saying in my ear. 'Are you still there?'

'I'm just . . . they're singing Happy Birthday . . .'

I put the phone on the table. After a moment's thought, Lorraine puts the other phone carefully down on the other side of me.

This is my family birthday party. Two mobile phones.

I can see people looking over at the singing, their smiles falling a little as they see I'm sitting on my own. I can see the pity in the faces of the waiters. My cheeks are burning with embarrassment.

'So anyway . . .' Lorraine retrieves Daniel's mobile phone and pops it into her bag. 'Happy birthday—and have a lovely evening!'

As she tip-taps her way out of the restaurant, I pick up the other phone to say goodbye—but Mum's already rung off. The singing waiters have melted away. It's just me and a basket of soap.

It doesn't matter. The truth is, we were never all going to make a dinner. It was a fantasy idea. We shouldn't even have tried. We're all busy, we all have careers, that's just the way my family is.

As I stand outside the restaurant, a taxi pulls up right in front of me and I quickly stick my hand out. The rear door opens and a tatty beaded flip-flop emerges, followed by a pair of cut-off jeans, an embroidered kaftan, familiar tousled blonde hair . . .

'Stay here,' she's instructing the taxi driver. 'I'll be five minutes.'

'*Freya?*' I say in disbelief. She wheels round and her eyes widen.

'Samantha! What are you doing on the pavement?'

'What are *you* doing here? I thought you were going to India.'

'I'm on my way! I'm meeting Lord at the airport in about . . .' She looks at her watch. 'Ten minutes.'

She pulls a guilty face, and I can't help laughing. I've known Freya since we were both seven years old and starting boarding school together. On the first night she told me her family were circus performers and she knew how to ride an elephant and walk the tightrope. For a whole term I believed her, until her parents arrived to pick her up and turned out to be a pair of accountants from Staines.

'I'm here to gatecrash your birthday dinner.' Freya's eyes swivel to the restaurant in suspicion. 'But I thought I was late. What happened?'

'Well . . .' I hesitate. 'The thing was . . . Mum and Daniel . . .'

'Left early?' As she peers at me Freya's expression changes to one of horror. 'Didn't turn *up?*'

'It doesn't matter,' I say, with a rueful shrug. 'Really. I've got a pile of work to get through anyway.'

'*Work?*' She stares at me. 'Now? Are you serious? Doesn't it ever *stop?*'

'We're busy at the moment,' I say defensively. 'It's just a blip.'

'There's always a blip! There's always a crisis! Every year you tell me it'll get better soon. But it never does!' Her eyes are burning with concern. 'Samantha, what happened to your life?'

I stare back at her for a few moments, not sure how to reply. To be honest, I can't remember what my life used to be like.

'I want to be a partner of Carter Spink,' I say at last. 'That's what I want. You have to make sacrifices.'

'And what happens when you make partner?' she persists.

I shrug evasively. The truth is I haven't thought beyond making partner. It's like a dream. Like a shiny ball in the sky.

'You're twenty-nine years old!' Freya gestures with a bony, silver-ringed hand. 'You should be seeing the world!' She grabs my arm. 'Samantha, come to India. Now!'

'Do what?' I give a startled laugh. 'I can't come to *India!*'

'Take a month off. Come to the airport, we'll get you a ticket . . .'

'Freya, you're crazy, but I love you.'

Slowly, Freya's grip on my arm loosens. 'Same,' she says. 'You're crazy, but I love you.'

Her mobile starts ringing, but she ignores it. Instead, she's rummaging in her bag. At last she produces a tiny, intricately worked silver perfume bottle, haphazardly wrapped in a piece of purple shot silk.

'Here.' She thrusts it at me.

'Freya,' I turn it over in my fingers, 'it's amazing.'

'I thought you'd like it.' She pulls her mobile out of her pocket. 'Hi!' she says impatiently into it. 'Look, Lord, I'll be there, OK?'

Freya's husband's full name is Lord Andrew Edgerly. Freya's nickname for him started as a joke and just kind of stuck. They met five years ago on a kibbutz and got married in Las Vegas. Technically, this makes her Lady Edgerly—but nobody can quite get their heads round this idea.

'Thanks for coming. Thanks for this.' I hug her. 'Have a fabulous time in India.'

'We will.' Freya is climbing back into her taxi. 'And if you want to come out, just let me know. Invent a family emergency . . . anything. Give them my number. I'll cover for you. Whatever your story is.'

'Go,' I say, laughing, and give her a little push. 'Go to India.'

The door slams, and she sticks her head out of the window.

'Sam . . . good luck for tomorrow.' She seizes my hand, suddenly serious. 'If it's really what you want, then I hope you get it.'

'It's what I want more than anything else.'

'You'll get it. I know it.' She waves goodbye. 'And don't go back to the office! Promise!' she shouts as her taxi roars off into the traffic.

'OK! I promise!' I yell back. I wait until she's disappeared, then stick my hand out for a taxi. 'Carter Spink, please,' I say as it pulls up.

I was crossing my fingers. Of course I'm going back to the office.

I arrive home at eleven o'clock, exhausted and brain dead, having got through only about half of Ketterman's file. Bloody Ketterman, I'm thinking, as I push open the main front door of the 1930s mansion block where I live. Bloody Ketterman. Bloody . . . bloody . . .

'Good evening, Samantha.'

I nearly jump a mile. It's Ketterman. Right there, standing in front of the lifts, holding a bulging briefcase. For an instant I'm transfixed in horror. What's he doing here?

'Someone told me you lived here.' His eyes glint through his spectacles. 'I've bought number 32 as a pied-à-terre. We'll be neighbours during the week.'

No. Please tell me this is not happening. He *lives* here?

'Er . . . welcome to the building!' I say, trying as hard as I can to sound like I mean it. The lift doors open and we both get in.

Number 32. That means he's only two floors above me.

As we rise up in silence I feel more and more uncomfortable. Should I make small talk? Some light, neighbourly chitchat?

'I made some headway on that file you gave me,' I say at last.

'Good,' he says shortly, and nods.

So much for the small talk. I should just cut to the big stuff.

Am I going to become a partner tomorrow?

'Well . . . good night,' I say awkwardly as I leave the lift.

'Good night, Samantha.'

The lift doors close and I emit a silent scream. I cannot live in the same building as Ketterman. I'm going to have to move.

I'm about to put my key in the lock when the door to the opposite flat opens a crack. 'Samantha?'

My heart sinks. As if I haven't had enough this evening. It's Mrs Farley, my neighbour. She has silver hair and an insatiable interest in my life. But she is very kind and takes in parcels for me, so I basically let her poke and pry at will.

'Another delivery arrived for you, dear,' she says. 'Dry-cleaning this time. I'll just fetch it for you.'

'Thanks,' I say gratefully, swinging my door open. A small pile of junk leaflets is sitting on the doormat and I sweep them aside, onto the bigger pile building up at the side of my hallway.

'You're late home again.' Mrs Farley is at my side, holding a pile of polythene-covered shirts. 'You girls are so busy!' She clicks her tongue.

'Thanks very much.' I make to take my dry-cleaning, but Mrs Farley pushes past me into the flat, exclaiming, 'I'll carry it in for you!'

'Er . . . excuse the . . . er . . . mess,' I say as she squeezes past a pile of pictures propped against the wall. 'I keep meaning to put those up . . . and get rid of the boxes . . .'

I steer her hastily into the kitchen, then wish I hadn't. On the kitchen counter is a stack of old tins and packets, together with a note from my new cleaner, all in capitals:

DEAR SAMANTHA

1. ALL YOUR FOOD IS PAST ITS SELL-BY-DATES, SHOULD I THROW AWAY?
2. DO YOU HAVE ANY CLEANING MATERIALS?
3. ARE YOU COLLECTING CHINESE FOOD CARTONS FOR ANY REASON? DID NOT THROW THEM AWAY, JUST IN CASE.
YOUR CLEANER JOANNE

I can see Mrs Farley reading the note. I can practically *hear* the clucking going on in her head.

'So . . . thanks.' I hastily take the dry-cleaning from her and dump it on the hob, then usher her out to the front door, aware of her swivelling, inquisitive eyes. 'It's really kind of you.'

'It's no trouble.' She gives me a beady look. 'Not wishing to interfere, dear, but you know, you could wash your cotton blouses very well at home, and save on all that money.'

I look at her blankly. If I did that I'd have to iron them.

'And I *did* just happen to notice that one of them came back missing a button,' she adds. 'The pink and white stripe.'

'Oh, right,' I say. 'Well . . . I'll send it back. They won't charge.'

'You can pop a button on yourself, dear!' says Mrs Farley, sounding shocked. 'It won't take you two minutes. You can sew a simple button on, surely!' she exclaims.

'No,' I say, a bit rankled at her expression. 'But it's no problem. I'll send it back to the dry-cleaners.'

'In my day,' says Mrs Farley, shaking her head, 'all well-educated girls were taught how to sew on a button, darn a sock and turn a collar.'

None of this means anything to me. *Turn a collar?* It's gibberish.

'Well, in my day we weren't,' I reply politely. 'We were taught to study for our exams and get a career worth having.'

Mrs Farley looks me up and down for a few moments.

'It's a shame,' she says at last, gives me a sympathetic pat on the arm, and heads across the hallway to her flat.

I'm trying to keep calm, but the tensions of the day are rising inside me. I've had a non-existent birthday, I feel bone-tired and hungry . . . and now this old woman's telling me to sew on a *button?*

'How is it a shame?' I demand, stepping out of my doorway. 'How? OK, maybe I can't sew on a button. But I can restructure a finance agreement and save my client thirty million pounds. That's what I can do.'

Mrs Farley regards me from her doorway. If anything she looks more pitying than before. 'It's a shame,' she repeats, as though she didn't hear me. 'Good night.' She closes the door and I emit a squeal of exasperation.

Two

THIS IS IT. All the work, all the late nights . . . it's all been for this day.

Partner. Or not partner.

As I arrive at the office, I'm determined I'm not going to acknowledge this is any kind of special day. I'll just keep my head down and get on with my work.

But as I travel up in the lift, three people murmur 'Good luck'.

I head hurriedly into my office and close the door, trying to ignore the fact that through the glass partition I can see people talking in the corridor and glancing at me.

It's fine. I'll just start on some work, like any other day. I open Ketterman's file, find my place and start reading through a document on a five-year-old share transfer.

Somehow I get through the morning. I finish up on Ketterman's file and make a start on my report. I'm halfway through the third paragraph when Guy appears at my office door.

'You did it, Samantha,' he murmurs. 'You're a partner. You'll hear officially in an hour.'

A white dazzling heat shoots across my chest. I made it. *I made it.*

'You didn't hear it from me, OK?' Guy's face creases briefly in a smile. 'Well done.'

'Thanks . . .' I manage.

'I'll see you later. Congratulate you properly.' He turns and strides away, and I'm left staring unseeingly at my computer.

I made partner. Oh my God. *Oh my God.* Oh my GOD!

I take out a hand mirror and glance at my own exhilarated reflection. My cheeks are bright pink. I'm feeling a terrible urge to leap to my feet and cry out 'YES!' How do I survive an hour? How can I just sit here calmly? I can't possibly concentrate on Ketterman's report.

I stand up and walk over to my filing cabinet, purely for something to do. I open a couple of drawers at random, and close them again. Then, as I swivel round, I notice my desk, crammed with papers and files.

Ketterman's right. It is a disgrace. It doesn't look like a partner's desk. I'll tidy it up. This is the perfect way to spend an hour.

I had forgotten how much I loathe and detest tidying.

All sorts of things are turning up as I sift through the mess on my desk. Company letters . . . contracts that need to be filed . . . memos . . . a Pilates pamphlet . . . last year's Christmas card from Arnold, which depicts him in a woolly reindeer costume . . . And . . . oh God, half a Snickers bar I obviously didn't finish eating at one time or another. I dump it in the bin and turn with a sigh to another pile of papers.

Partner! shoots through my mind. *PARTNER!*

Stop it, I instruct myself sternly. Concentrate on the task in hand. As I pull out an old copy of *The Lawyer* and wonder why on earth I was keeping it, some paper-clipped documents fall to the floor. I reach for them, and run my gaze down the front page, already reaching for the next thing. It's a memo, from Arnold.

Re: Third Union Bank.
Please find attached debenture for Glazerbrooks Ltd. Please attend to registration at Companies House.

I peer at it without great interest. Third Union Bank are Arnold's client, and I've only dealt with them once. The deal is a loan for £50 million to Glazerbrooks, and all I have to do is register it within twenty-one days at Companies House. It's just another of the mundane jobs that partners are always dumping on my desk. Well, not any more, I think with a surge of determination. In fact, I think I'll delegate this to someone else, right now. I glance automatically at the date.

Then I look again. It's dated May 26.

Five weeks ago? That can't be right.

Puzzled, I flip quickly through the papers, looking to see if there's been a typo. There *must* be a typo—but the date is consistent. May 26.

I sit, frozen, staring at the document. Has this thing been on my desk for *five weeks*?

But . . . it can't. I mean . . . that would mean I'd missed the deadline.

I swallow hard. I have to be reading this wrong. I can't have made such a basic mistake. I cannot possibly have failed to register a charge before the deadline. I *always* register charges before the deadline.

My happy glow has gone. There's a kind of iciness about my spine. I'm trying desperately to remember if Arnold said anything about the deal to me. I can't even remember him mentioning it. But, then, why would he? It's one simple loan agreement. The kind of thing we do in our sleep. He would have assumed I'd carried out his instructions.

What am I going to do? A wall of panic hits me as I take in the consequences. Third Union Bank has lent Glazerbrooks £50 million. Without the charge being registered, this loan—this multi-million-pound loan—is unsecured. If Glazerbrooks went bust tomorrow, Third Union Bank would go to the back of the queue of creditors. And probably end up with nothing.

I bury my head in my hands. I'm trying to keep calm, but inside is a great well of terror. I have to face it. *I have made a mistake.*

What am I going to do?

Then suddenly Guy's words from yesterday ring in my ears, and I feel a flood of relief. *A mistake isn't a mistake unless it can't be put right.*

Yes. The point is, I can put this right. I can still register a charge.

It will be excruciating. I'll have to tell the bank what I've done—and Glazerbrooks—and Arnold—and Ketterman. I'll have to have new documentation drawn up. And, worst of all, live with everyone knowing I've made the kind of stupid, thoughtless error a trainee would make.

It might mean an end to my partnership, runs through my mind, but there's no other option. I have to put the situation right.

Quickly I log on to the Companies House website and enter a search for Glazerbrooks. As long as no other charge has been registered in the meantime, it will all come to the same thing . . .

I stare at the page in disbelief. No. It can't be.

A charge of £50 million was entered last week by BLLC Holdings. Our client has been bumped down the creditors' queue.

My mind is helter-skeltering. This isn't good. I have to do something before any more charges are made. I have to . . . call the bank.

I search through the attached contact sheet and find the name and number of the guy at Third Union. Charles Conway.

With trembling hands I dial the number. I feel as though I'm psyching myself up to dive into a noxious swamp full of leeches.

'Charles Conway.'

'Hi!' I say, trying to keep my voice steady. 'It's Samantha Sweeting from Carter Spink. I don't think we've met.'

'Hi, Samantha.' He sounds friendly enough. 'How can I help?'

'I was phoning on a . . . a technical matter. It's about . . .' I can hardly bear to say it. 'Glazerbrooks.'

'Oh, you've heard about that,' says Charles Conway.

The room seems to shrink. I grip the receiver more tightly. 'Heard . . . what?' My voice is higher than I'd like. 'I haven't heard anything.'

'Oh! I assumed that's why you were calling. They called in the receivers today. That last-ditch attempt to save themselves didn't work . . .'

He's still talking but I can't hear him. I feel light-headed. Black spots are dancing in front of my eyes.

Glazerbrooks is going bust.

I won't be able to register the charge.

I've lost Third Union Bank £50 million.

Charles Conway's voice suddenly hits my consciousness. 'It's a good thing you phoned.' I can hear him tapping at a keyboard, totally unconcerned. 'You might want to double-check that loan security.'

For a few moments I can't speak.

'Yes,' I say at last, my voice hoarse. I put down the receiver, shaking all over. I think I might throw up.

Barely knowing what I'm doing, I push back my chair. I have to get out. Away.

I walk through reception on autopilot. Out onto the sunny crowded lunchtime street, one foot in front of the other, just another office worker walking along.

Except I'm different. I've just lost my client £50 million.

I don't understand how it happened. My mind keeps turning it over. I never even saw the document. It must have been put on my desk, then covered up with something. A pile of contracts, a cup of coffee.

One error. One mistake. The only mistake I've ever made. I want to wake up and find this is all a bad dream, it happened in a movie, it happened to someone else.

But it was me. It is me. My career is over.

The last person at Carter Spink who made a mistake like this was Ted

Stephens in 1983, who lost a client £10 million. He was fired on the spot.

My breaths are getting shorter; my head is dizzy; I feel like I'm being smothered. Suddenly I jump in terror as my mobile phone vibrates in my pocket. I pull it out and look at the caller ID. It's Guy.

I can't talk to him. I can't talk to anybody. Not right now.

A moment later, the phone tells me a message has been left. I lift the phone to my ear and press '1' to listen.

'Samantha!' Guy sounds jovial. 'Where are you? We're all waiting with the champagne to make the big partnership announcement!'

Partnership. I almost want to burst into tears. But . . . I can't. It's too big for that. I thrust my phone in my pocket. I begin to walk faster and faster, weaving through the pedestrians. I have no idea where I'm going. But I just can't stop.

At last, when my legs are starting to ache, I slow down and come to a halt. My mouth is dry; I need water. I look up, trying to get my bearings. Somehow I seem to have reached Paddington Station, of all places.

Numbly, I turn my steps towards the entrance and walk inside. The place is noisy and crowded with travellers. The fluorescent lights and air conditioning and the blaring announcements make me flinch. As I'm making my way to a kiosk selling bottled water, my mobile vibrates. I pull it out and look at the display. I have fifteen missed calls and another message from Guy. He left it about twenty minutes ago.

I hesitate, my heart beating with nerves, then press '1' to listen to it.

'Samantha, what *happened*?' He doesn't sound jovial any more, he sounds totally stressed. I feel prickles of dread all over my body.

'We know,' he's saying. 'OK? We know about Third Union Bank. Charles Conway called up. Then Ketterman found the paperwork on your desk. You have to come back to the office. Now. Call me back.'

They know. They all know.

As I'm standing there, something catches the corner of my eye. A familiar face is just visible through the crowd. I turn my head and squint at the man, trying to place him—then feel a fresh jolt of horror.

It's Greg Parker, one of the senior partners. He's striding along, holding his mobile phone. His brows are knitted together and he looks concerned. 'So where *is* she?' His voice travels across the concourse.

Panic hits me like a lightning bolt. I have to get out of his line of vision. I have to hide. I edge behind a vast woman in a beige mac and try to cower down so I'm hidden. But she keeps wandering about, and I keep having to shuffle along with her.

'Did you want something? Are you a beggar?' She suddenly turns and gives me a suspicious look.

'No!' I say in shock. 'I'm . . . er . . .' I can't say 'I'm hiding behind you.'

'Well, leave me alone!' She scowls and stalks off towards Costa Coffee. My heart is hammering in my chest. I'm totally exposed in the middle of the concourse. Greg Parker has stopped striding now. He's standing about fifty yards away, still talking on his mobile phone.

If I move, he'll see me. If I stay still . . . he'll see me.

Suddenly the electronic Departures display board renews itself with fresh information. A group of people who have been gazing up at it all pick up their bags and newspapers and head towards Platform Nine.

Without thinking twice I join the throng. I'm hidden in their midst as we sweep through the open barriers. I get on the train along with everyone else, walking swiftly down the carriage as far as I can.

The train pulls out of the station and I sink into a seat, opposite a family all wearing London Zoo T-shirts. They smile at me—and somehow I manage to smile back. I feel totally, utterly unreal.

'Refreshments?' A wizened man pushing a trolley appears in the carriage and beams at me. 'Hot and cold sandwiches, teas and coffees, soft drinks, alcoholic beverages?'

'The last, please.' I try not to sound desperate. 'A double. Of anything.'

No one comes to check my ticket. No one bothers me. The train seems to be some sort of express. Suburbs turn into fields, and the train is still rattling along. I've drunk three small bottles of gin, mixed with orange juice. My heart rate has subsided, but I have a throbbing headache. I feel weirdly distanced from everything.

I have made the biggest mistake of my career. I have quite possibly lost my job. I will never be a partner.

'Ladies and gentlemen . . .' The conductor is crackling over the loudspeaker. 'Unfortunately . . . rail works . . . alternative transport . . .'

I can't follow what he's saying. I don't even know where I'm headed. The train is pulling into a station. Lower Ebury. Everybody is gathering up their stuff and getting off.

Like an automaton I get up too. I follow the London Zoo family off the train and out of the station, and look around. I'm standing outside a tiny, twee country station, with a pub called The Bell over the road. The road bends round in both directions and I can glimpse fields in the distance. There's a coach standing on the side of the road, and all of the passengers from the train are piling onto it.

London Zoo mother is gesturing at me. 'You need to come this way,' she says helpfully. 'If you want the bus to Gloucester?'

The thought of getting on a coach makes me want to heave. I don't want the bus to anywhere. I just want a painkiller. My head feels like my skull is about to split open.

'Er . . . no, thanks. I'm fine here.' I smile as convincingly as I can and start walking down the road, away from the coach.

Inside my pocket, my phone suddenly vibrates. I pull it out. It's Guy. Again. This must be the thirtieth time he's rung. And every time he's left a message telling me to call him back; asking if I've got his emails.

I haven't got any of his emails. I was so freaked out, I left my BlackBerry on my desk. My phone is all I have. It vibrates again and I stare at it for a few moments. Then, my stomach clenched with nerves, I lift it to my ear and press Talk.

'Hi.' My voice is scratchy.

'Samantha?' His voice blasts down the line. 'Where *are* you?'

'I don't know. I had to get away. I . . . I went into shock . . .'

'Samantha, I don't know if you got my messages. But . . .' He hesitates. 'Everyone knows.'

'I know.' I lean against an old crumbling wall and squeeze my eyes shut, trying to block out the pain. 'I know.'

'How the hell did you make a simple error like that?'

'I don't know,' I say numbly. 'I just didn't see it. It was a mistake—'

'You never make mistakes!'

'Well, I do now!' I feel tears rising and fiercely blink them down. 'What's . . . what's happened?'

'It's not good.' He exhales. 'Ketterman's been having some damage-limitation talks with Glazerbrooks' lawyers and talking to the bank . . . and the insurers, of course.'

The insurers. The firm's professional indemnity insurance. I'm suddenly gripped by an almost exhilarating hope. If the insurers pay up without making a fuss, maybe things won't be as bad as I thought.

But even as I feel my spirits lift I know I'm like some desperate traveller seeing the mirage through the haze. Insurers never cough up the whole amount. Sometimes they don't cough up anything.

'What did the insurers say?' I gulp. 'Will they . . .'

'They haven't said anything yet.'

'Right.' I wipe my sweaty face, screwing myself up to ask the next question. 'And what about . . . me?'

Guy is silent.

As his meaning hits me I feel myself swaying as though I'm going to faint. There's my answer.

'It's over, isn't it?' I'm trying to sound calm but my voice is wobbling out of control. 'My career's over.'

'I . . . I don't know that. Listen, Samantha, you're freaked out. It's natural. But you can't hide. You have to come back.'

'I can't.' My voice rises in distress. 'I can't face everyone. I need some time . . .'

'Saman—' I flip my phone shut.

I feel faint. My head is bursting. I have to get some water. But the pub doesn't look open and I can't see any shops.

I totter along the road until I reach a pair of tall, carved pillars decorated with lions. Here's a house. I'll ring the bell and ask for a painkiller and a glass of water. And ask if there's a hotel near by.

I push open the wrought-iron gates and crunch over the gravel towards the heavy, oak front door. It's a rather grand house, made out of honey-coloured stone, with steep gables and tall chimneys and two Porsches on the drive. I raise a hand and tug the bell pull.

There's silence. I stand there for a while, but the whole house seems dead. I'm about to give up and trudge back down the drive, when all of a sudden the door swings open.

There before me is a woman with blonde, lacquered hair to her shoulders and long, dangly earrings. She has a cigarette in one hand and a cocktail in the other.

'Hello.' She drags on her cigarette and looks at me a bit suspiciously. 'Are you from the agency?'

I have no idea what this woman's talking about. My head's hurting so much, I can barely look at her, let alone take in what she's saying.

'Are you all right?' She peers at me. 'You look terrible!'

'I've got a rather bad headache,' I manage. 'Could I possibly have a glass of water?'

'Of course! Come in!' She waves her cigarette in my face and beckons me into a huge, impressive hall with a vaulted ceiling. 'You'll want to see the house, anyway. *Eddie?*' Her voice rises to a shriek. 'Eddie, another one's here! I'm Trish Geiger,' she adds to me. 'You may call me Mrs Geiger. This way . . .'

She leads me into a luxurious maple kitchen and tries a few drawers, apparently at random, before crying 'Aha!' and pulling out a plastic box. She opens it to reveal about fifty assorted bottles and packets of tablets.

'I've got aspirin . . . paracetamol . . . ibuprofen . . . *very* mild valium . . .' She hands me three green tablets and, after a few attempts, locates a cupboard full of glasses. 'Here we are. They'll zap any headache.' She runs me some iced water from the fridge. 'Drink that up.'

'Thanks,' I say, swallowing the tablets down with a wince. 'I'm so grateful. My head's just so painful. I can barely think straight.'

'Your English is very good.' She gives me a close, appraising look.

'Oh,' I say, thrown. 'Right. Well, I'm English. That's . . . you know, probably why.'

'You're *English*?' Trish Geiger seems galvanised by this news. 'Well! Come with me. Those'll kick in, in a minute.' She sweeps me out of the kitchen and back through the hall. 'This is the drawing room,' she says, gesturing around the large, grand room, dropping ash on the carpet. 'As you'll see, there's quite a lot of hoovering . . . dusting . . . silver to be kept clean . . .' She looks at me expectantly.

'Right.' I nod. I have no idea why this woman is telling me about her housework.

'We'll go in here.' She's leading me through another huge, grand room into an airy glassed conservatory furnished with opulent teak sun-loungers, frondy plants and a well-stocked drinks tray.

'Eddie! Come in here!' She bangs on the glass and I look up to see a man in golfing slacks walking over the well-manicured lawn. He's tanned and affluent-looking, probably in his late forties.

Trish is probably in her late forties, too, I think, glimpsing her crow's-feet as she turns away from the window. Although something tells me she's going for thirty-nine and not a day older.

'Lovely garden,' I say.

'Oh.' Her eyes sweep over it without much interest. 'Yes, our gardener is very good. Now, sit down!' She makes a flapping motion with her hands and, feeling a little awkward, I sit down on a lounger. Trish sinks into a basket chair opposite and drains her cocktail.

'How's your head?' she demands and carries on before I'm able to reply. 'Better? Ah, here's Eddie!'

The door opens and Mr Geiger comes into the conservatory. He doesn't look quite as impressive close up as he did striding over the lawn. His eyes are a little bloodshot and he has the beginnings of a beer belly.

'Eddie Geiger,' he says, holding out his hand. 'Master of the house.'

'Eddie, this is . . .' Trish looks at me in surprise. 'What's your name?'

'Samantha,' I explain. 'I'm so sorry to bother you, but I had the most terrible headache . . .'

'I gave Samantha some of those prescription painkillers,' puts in Trish.

'Good choice.' Eddie unscrews a Scotch bottle and pours himself a drink.

I manage a half-smile. 'You've been very kind, letting me trespass on your evening.'

'Her English is good, isn't it?' Eddie raises his eyebrows at Trish.

'She's English!' says Trish triumphantly, as though she's pulled a rabbit out of a hat. 'Understands everything I say!'

I am really not getting something here. Do I *look* foreign?

'Shall we do the tour of the house?' Eddie turns to Trish.

My heart plummets. People who give tours of their houses should be abolished. The thought of trailing round, trying to find different things to say about each room, is unbearable. I just want to sit here and wait for the pills to kick in.

'Really, it's not necessary,' I begin. 'I'm sure it's beautiful—'

'Of course it's necessary!' Trish stubs out her cigarette. 'Come on.'

As I get up my head swims and I have to clutch onto a yucca plant to steady myself. This all feels like a bit of a dream.

OK, this woman cannot have a life. All she seems interested in is housework. As we trail round one splendid room after another she keeps pointing out things that need special dusting and showing me where the Hoover is kept. Now she's telling me about the washing machine.

'It seems . . . very . . . efficient,' I say, as she seems to be waiting for a compliment.

'We do like fresh linen *every* week. Well ironed, of course.' She gives me a sharp look.

'Of course.' I nod, trying to hide my bewilderment.

'Now upstairs!' She sweeps out of the kitchen.

Oh God. There's more?

'You come from London, Samantha?' says Eddie Geiger as we head up the stairs.

'That's right.'

'And you have a full-time job there?'

He's only asking to be polite—but for a few moments I can't bring myself to answer. Do I have a job?

'I did,' I say at last. 'To be honest . . . I don't know what my situation is at the moment.'

'What sort of hours did you work?' Trish wheels round.

'All hours.' I shrug. 'I'm used to working all day and into the night. Through the night, sometimes.'

The Geigers look absolutely stunned at this revelation. People just have no idea what the life of a lawyer is like.

'You used to work *through the night?*' Trish seems stupefied. 'On your own?'

'Me and the other staff. Whoever was needed.'

'So you come from . . . a big set-up?'

'One of the biggest in London.' I nod.

Trish and Eddie are darting glances at each other. They really are the weirdest people.

'Well, we're *far* more relaxed, you'll be glad to hear!' Trish gives a little laugh. 'This is the master bedroom . . . the second bedroom . . .'

As we walk down the corridor she opens and closes doors and shows me four-poster beds and handmade drapes, until my head swims even more. I don't know what was in those pills, but I'm feeling weirder by the minute. We descend a flight of stairs and I grab the wall to keep myself steady, but it seems to run away in a tangle of wallpaper flowers.

'Are you all right?' Eddie catches me as I'm about to topple to the floor.

'I think those painkillers were a bit strong,' I mumble.

'They *are* a bit vicious.' Trish gives me a considering look. 'You haven't drunk any *alcohol* today, have you?'

'Er . . . well, yes . . .'

She pulls a face. 'Well, it's all right as long as you don't start *hallucinating*. Then we'd have to call a doctor. And . . . here we are!' she continues, and opens the last door with a flourish. 'The staff accommodation.'

All the rooms in this house are huge. This one is about the size of my flat, with pale walls and stone mullioned windows overlooking the garden. It has the plainest bed I've seen yet in this house, vast and square and made up with crisp white bed linen.

'Lovely,' I say politely. 'It's a gorgeous room.'

'Good!' Eddie smacks his hands together. 'Well, Samantha, I'd say you've got the job!'

I look back at him through my daze. Job? What job?

'Eddie!' snaps Trish. 'You can't just offer her the job! We haven't finished the interview!'

Interview? Did I miss something?

'We haven't even given her a full job description!' Trish is still laying into Eddie. 'We haven't been through any of the details!'

'Well, go through the details, then!' retorts Eddie. Trish shoots him a look of fury and clears her throat.

'So, Samantha,' she says in formal tones, 'your role as full-time housekeeper will comprise all cleaning, laundry and cooking. You will wear a uniform and maintain a respectful . . .'

My role as—these people think I'm applying to be their *housekeeper*?

For a moment, I'm too dumbfounded to speak.

'. . . full board and lodging and four weeks holiday a year. Do you have any questions about the post?'

This is the moment where I have to explain there's been a big mistake. That I'm not a housekeeper, I'm a lawyer.

But nothing comes out of my mouth.

I could stay here one night, flashes through my brain. *Just one night. I could sort out the misunderstanding tomorrow.*

'Um . . . would it be possible to start tonight?' I hear myself saying.

'I don't see why not—' begins Eddie.

'Let's not jump ahead of ourselves,' Trish interrupts. 'We have had *quite* a few promising applicants for this post, Samantha. Several quite dazzling. One girl even had a diploma in French cordon bleu cookery!'

She drags on her cigarette, giving me a pointed look. And something inside me stiffens, like an automatic reflex. I can't help it. Is she implying that I might not *get* this job?

I regard Trish silently for a few moments. Somewhere, down inside my befuddled state of shock, I can feel a tiny flicker of the old Samantha returning. I can feel my ingrained ambition lifting its head and sniffing the air, rolling back its sleeves and spitting on its hands. I can beat some French-cordon-bleu-cookery girl.

I have never failed an interview in my life. I'm not about to start now.

'So.' Trish looks at her list. 'You're cordon bleu trained?'

'I trained under Michel de la Roux de la Blanc.' I pause gravely. 'His name obviously speaks for itself.'

'Absolutely!' says Trish, glancing uncertainly at Eddie.

We're sitting in the conservatory again. Trish is firing questions at me that sound like they come from a 'How To Hire Your Housekeeper' pamphlet. And I'm answering every single one with total confidence.

Deep down in my brain I can hear a little voice calling out, 'What are you doing? Samantha, what the hell are you *doing*?'

But I'm not listening. Somehow I've managed to block out real life, the mistake, my ruined career, the whole nightmare of a day . . . everything else in the world except this interview.

'Could you give us a sample menu?' Trish lights another cigarette. 'For a dinner party, say?'

Food . . . Impressive food . . . Suddenly I remember Maxim's, the night before. The souvenir birthday menu.

'I'll just consult my notes.' I unzip my bag and surreptitiously scan the Maxim's menu. 'For a formal dinner, I would serve . . . er . . . seared foie gras with an apricot glaze. . . lamb with spiced hummous . . . followed by chocolate-mint soufflé with two homemade sorbets.'

Take *that*, cordon bleu girl.

'Well!' Trish looks astounded. 'I must say, that's very impressive.'

'Marvellous!' Eddie looks like he's salivating.

Trish shoots him an annoyed look. 'I'm assuming you have a reference, Samantha?'

A reference?

'My referee is Lady Freya Edgerly,' I say, in sudden inspiration.

'*Lady* Edgerly?' Trish's eyebrows rise.

'I have been associated with Lord and Lady Edgerly for many years.' I nod. 'I know Lady Edgerly will vouch for me.'

Trish and Eddie are both staring at me, agog. Maybe I should add some housekeeperly detail.

'A lovely family,' I embellish. 'Quite a job it was, keeping the manor house clean. And . . . polishing Lady Edgerly's tiaras.'

Shit. I've gone a step too far with the tiaras.

But to my amazement, not a note of suspicion crosses either face.

'You cooked for them?' enquires Eddie. 'Breakfasts and so forth?'

'Naturally. Lord Edgerly was very fond of my Eggs Benedict.'

I can see Trish pulling what she clearly imagines are cryptic faces at Eddie, who is surreptitiously nodding back. They might as well have 'Let's Have Her!' tattooed on their foreheads. They look like all their Christmases have come at once.

Three

I WAKE THE NEXT MORNING to an unfamiliar, smooth white ceiling above me. I stare at it for a few moments in bewilderment, then lift my head a little. The sheets make a strange rumpling sound as I move. What's going on? My sheets don't sound anything like that.

But of course. They're the Geigers' sheets.

I sink comfortably back into my pillows—until another thought strikes me. Who are the Geigers?

I screw up my face, trying to remember. Snatches of yesterday are vivid in my mind, amidst a dense fog. I'm not sure what's real and what's a dream. I came on the train . . . yes . . . I had a headache . . . Paddington Station . . . walking out of the office . . .

Oh God. Oh please, no.

With a sickening whoosh the whole nightmare is back in my brain. The memo. Third Union Bank. Fifty million pounds. Asking Guy if I had a job left . . . His silence.

I lie very still for a while, letting it all sink in again. My career is wrecked. I have no chance of partnership. I probably have no job. Everything is over as I knew it. I squeeze my eyes tight shut, trying to escape the thoughts starting to float into my mind. Sickening, if-only thoughts. If I'd seen the memo earlier . . . If I had a tidier desk . . . If Arnold hadn't given that piece of work to me . . .

But there's no point. Ignoring my throbbing head, I walk to the window. What happened, happened. And now I find myself in a strange room in the middle of the countryside. With my career in ruins. Plus there's something nagging at me. A final piece of the jigsaw still missing in my dazed brain. It'll come to me in a minute.

I turn round and focus on a blue dress hanging on the wardrobe door. Some kind of uniform, with piping. Why would there be a—

It's coming back to me like some kind of terrible, drunken dream.

Did I take a job as a housekeeper?

For an instant I cannot move. What have I *done*?

My heart starts to thump as I take in my situation properly for the first time. I am staying in a strange couple's house under completely false pretences. I've slept in their bed. I'm wearing one of Trish's old T-shirts. They even gave me a toothbrush, after I invented a 'suitcase stolen on the train' story. The last thing I remember before crashing out is hearing Trish gloating on the phone. 'She's English!' she was saying. 'Yes, speaks English perfectly! *Super* girl. Cordon bleu trained!'

I'll have to tell them it was all lies.

There's a rapping at my bedroom door and I jump in fright.

'Samantha? May I come in?'

'Oh! Um . . . yes!'

The door opens and Trish appears, wearing pale pink exercise clothes with a diamanté logo.

'I've made you a cup of tea,' she says, handing me the mug. 'Mr Geiger and I would like you to feel very welcome in our house.'

'Oh!' I swallow nervously. 'Thanks.'

Mrs Geiger, there's something I need to tell you. I'm not a housekeeper.

Somehow the words don't make it out of my mouth.

Trish's eyes have narrowed as though she's already regretting her kind gesture. 'Don't think you'll be getting this every day, of course! But since you weren't feeling well last night . . .' She taps her watch. 'Now you'd better get dressed. We'll expect you down in ten minutes. We only have a light breakfast as a rule. Toast, coffee and whatnot. Then we can discuss the other meals of the day.'

'Er . . . OK,' I say feebly.

She closes the door and I put the tea down. What am I going to do?

OK. Calm down. Prioritise. I need to call the office. Find out exactly how bad the situation is. With a spasm of apprehension I reach inside my bag for my mobile phone.

The display is blank. The battery must have run out.

I stare at it in frustration. I must have been so spaced out yesterday I forgot to charge it. I pull out my charger, plug it into the wall and attach the phone. At once it starts charging up.

I wait for the signal to appear . . . but it doesn't. There's no signal.

I feel a thrust of panic. How am I going to call the office? How am I going to do *anything*? I cannot exist without my mobile phone.

Suddenly I remember passing a telephone on the landing. It was on a table in a little window bay. Maybe I could use that. I open my bedroom door and look up and down the corridor. No one's about. Cautiously I creep into the bay and lift the receiver. The dial tone rings calmly in my ear. I take a deep breath—then dial the direct line for Arnold.

'Arnold Saville's office,' comes the cheerful voice of Lara, his secretary.

'Lara,' I say nervously, 'it's Samantha. Samantha Sweeting.'

'*Samantha?*' Lara sounds so gobsmacked, I wince. 'Oh my God! Where *are* you? Everyone's been—' She draws herself up.

'I . . . I'm out of London right now. May I talk to Arnold?'

'Of course. He's right here.' She disappears briefly into chirpy Vivaldi, before the line clears again.

'Samantha.' Arnold's friendly, assured voice booms down the line. 'My dear girl. You've got yourself in a pickle, haven't you?'

Only Arnold could describe the loss of a client's £50 million as a 'pickle'. In spite of everything, a tiny half-smile comes to my lips.

'I know,' I say, trying to match his understated tones. 'It's not great.'

'I'm obliged to point out that your hasty departure yesterday did not help matters.'

'I know. I'm so sorry. I just panicked.'

'Understandable. However, you left a bit of a mess behind.'

Underneath Arnold's jolly veneer I can detect unfamiliar levels of stress. Arnold never gets stressed. Things must be really bad.

'So—what's the latest situation?' I'm trying to sound composed. 'Is there anything the receivers can do?'

'I think it unlikely. They say their hands are tied.'

'Right.' It's like a hammer blow to the stomach. So that's it. The £50 million is gone for good. 'And the insurers?'

'That is the next step, of course. The money will be recovered eventually, I'm sure. But not without complications. As you will appreciate.'

For a few moments neither of us speaks. There's no good news, I realise with a dull ache of comprehension. There's no silver lining.

'Arnold,' I say, my voice quivering, 'I have no idea how I could have made such a . . . a *stupid* mistake. I don't understand how it happened. I don't even remember seeing the memo on my desk—'

'Where are you now?' Arnold breaks in.

'I'm . . .' I look helplessly out of the window. 'To be honest, I don't even know exactly where I am. But I can come in. I'll come back now.' My words come tumbling out. 'I'll get on the first train.'

'I don't think that's a good idea.' There's a new edge to Arnold's voice.

'Have I . . . have I been fired?'

'It hasn't been addressed yet.' He sounds testy. 'There have been slightly more pressing matters to consider, Samantha.'

'Of course. I'm sorry.' My throat is thickening. 'I've been with Carter Spink all my working life. All I ever wanted was . . .'

I can't even say it.

'Samantha, I know you're a very talented lawyer.' Arnold sighs. 'I'll do everything I can. There's to be a meeting this morning to discuss your fate.'

'But you don't think I should come in?' I bite my lip.

'It might do more harm than good at the moment. Stay where you are. Leave the rest to me.' Arnold hesitates, his voice a little gruff. 'I'll do my best, Samantha. I promise.'

'I'll be waiting,' I say quickly. 'Thank you so much.' But he's gone. Slowly I put down the phone. I have never felt so powerless in my life. I have a sudden vision of them all sitting round a table: Arnold, Ketterman, maybe even Guy, deciding whether to give me a break.

'*Super* girl.'

I jump at the sound of Trish's approaching voice.

'Well, of course I'll check her references, but, Gillian, I am a *very* good judge of character. I'm not easily fooled—'

Trish rounds the corner, holding a mobile to her ear, and I quickly move away from the telephone.

'Samantha!' she says in surprise. 'What are you doing? Still not dressed? Buck up!' She heads off again and I scuttle back to my room. I close the door and stare at myself in the mirror.

I suddenly feel a bit bad.

In fact, I feel really bad. How are the Geigers going to react when I tell them I'm a total fraud? That I'm not a trained cordon bleu housekeeper at all, I just wanted a place to stay for the night?

I have a sudden image of them bundling me furiously out of the house. Feeling totally used. Maybe they'll even call the police. Have me arrested. Oh God. This could get really nasty.

But, I mean, it's not like I have any other option. It's not like I could actually . . . Could I?

I pick up the blue uniform and finger it, my mind whirling round and round. They've been pretty kind, putting me up. It's not like I'm doing anything else right now. It's not like I have anywhere else to go. Maybe it'll even take my mind off things, doing a little light housework.

Abruptly I come to a decision.

I'll busk it for a morning. It can't be that hard. I'll make their toast and dust the ornaments. I'll think of it as my little thank-you to them. Then as soon as I hear from Arnold I'll find a convincing excuse to leave. And the Geigers will never know I wasn't a proper housekeeper.

It'll be fine.

As I walk down the stairs, the Geigers are both standing at the bottom, looking up at me. I have never felt more self-conscious in my life.

I'm a housekeeper. I have to behave like a housekeeper.

'Welcome, Samantha!' says Eddie as I arrive down in the hall. 'Sleep all right?'

'Very well, thank you, Mr Geiger,' I reply demurely.

'That's good!' Eddie rocks back and forth on the soles of his feet. He seems just a little awkward. In fact, they both seem awkward.

'You'll be wanting to get to know your new kitchen!' says Trish brightly.

'Of course!' I say with a confident smile. 'I'm looking forward to it!'

It's only a kitchen. It's only one morning. I can do this.

Trish leads the way into the vast, maple kitchen, and this time I look around more carefully, trying to take in the details. There's a huge, hob-type thing set into the granite counter to my left. A bank of ovens built into the wall. Everywhere I look I can see shiny chrome gadgets plugged into sockets. Racks of saucepans and implements of all descriptions are hanging overhead in a jumble of stainless steel.

I have not one single clue what anything is.

'You'll want to get it the way you like it, of course,' says Trish.

'Absolutely,' I say in a businesslike way. 'Obviously I have my own . . . um . . . systems. That shouldn't be there, for example.' I point randomly at some gadget. 'I'll have to move it.'

'Really?' Trish looks fascinated. 'Why's that?'

There's a momentary beat of silence. Even Eddie looks interested.

'Kitchen . . . ergonomic . . . theory,' I improvise. 'So, you'd like toast for breakfast?' I add quickly.

'Toast for both of us,' says Trish. 'And coffee with skimmed milk.'

'Coming up.' I smile, feeling slight relief. I can make toast. Once I've worked out which of these things is the toaster.

'So, I'll just bring that through in a moment,' I add, trying to chivvy them out. 'Would you like to eat in the dining room?'

There's a small crash from the hall.

'That'll be the newspaper,' says Trish. 'Yes, you may serve breakfast in the dining room.' She hurries out, but Eddie loiters in the kitchen.

'You know, I've changed my mind.' He gives me a jovial smile. 'Forget the toast, Samantha. I'll have your famous Eggs Benedict. You whetted my appetite last night!'

Last night? What did I say last—

Oh no. Eggs Benedict. My famous signature dish as beloved by Lord Edgerly. What was I *thinking*?

I don't even know what Eggs Benedict *are*.

'Are you sure that's what you want?' I manage in a constricted voice.

'I wouldn't miss your speciality!' Eddie rubs his stomach appreciatively. 'It's my favourite breakfast.'

OK. Keep calm. It must be simple enough. Eggs and . . . something.

Eddie leans against the granite counter with an expectant look. I have a nasty suspicion he's waiting for me to start cooking. Hesitantly I get down a gleaming pan from the rack, just as Trish bustles in with the newspaper. She eyes me with bright curiosity.

'How will you be using the asparagus steamer, Samantha?'

Shit.

'I just wanted to . . . examine it. Yes.' I nod briskly, as though the pan has confirmed my suspicions, then hang it back on the rack again.

I'm feeling hotter and hotter. I have no idea even how to begin. Do I crack the eggs? Boil them? Throw them against the wall?

'Here are the eggs.' Eddie plonks a huge box on the counter and lifts the lid. 'Should be enough there, I'd imagine!'

I stare at the rows of brown eggs, feeling a little light-headed. What do I think I'm doing? I can't make Eggs Benedict. I can't make these people breakfast. I'm going to have to come clean.

I turn round and take a deep breath. 'Mr Geiger . . . Mrs Geiger . . .'

'*Eggs?*' Trish's voice cuts across mine. 'Eddie, you can't have eggs! Remember what the doctor said!' She looks at me, eyes narrowed. 'What did he ask you for, Samantha? Boiled eggs?'

'Er . . . Mr Geiger ordered Eggs Benedict. But the thing is—'

'You're not eating Eggs Benedict!' Trish practically shrieks at Eddie. 'It's full of cholesterol!'

'I'll eat what I like!' Eddie protests.

'The doctor gave him an eating plan.' Trish is dragging furiously on her cigarette. 'He's already had a bowl of cornflakes this morning!'

'I was hungry!' says Eddie, defensive. 'You had a chocolate muffin!'

Trish gasps as though he's hit her. Small red dots appear on her cheeks. For a few moments she seems unable to speak.

'We will have a cup of coffee each, Samantha,' she announces at last in dignified tones. 'You may serve it in the lounge. Use the pink china. Come along, Eddie.' And she sweeps out before I can say anything else.

Ten minutes later I've arranged a tray with a pink coffeepot, pink cups, creamer, sugar, and a sprig of pink flowers I snipped from a hanging basket outside the kitchen. I'm rather proud of it, if I say so myself.

I approach the sitting-room door, put the tray down on the table in the hall and knock cautiously.

'Come in!' Trish calls.

As I enter, she's sitting in a chair by the window, holding a magazine at a rather artificial angle. Eddie is on the other side of the room, examining a wooden carving.

'Thank you, Samantha.' Trish inclines her head graciously as I pour out the coffee. 'That will be all for the moment.'

I feel as though I've stumbled into a Merchant Ivory costume drama, except the costumes are pink yoga wear and golfing sweaters.

'Er . . . very good, madam,' I say, playing my part. Then, without meaning to, I bob a curtsy.

Both Geigers just gape at me in astonishment.

'Samantha, did you just . . . curtsy?' says Trish at last.

I stare back, frozen. What was I thinking? Housekeepers don't bloody curtsy. This isn't Gosford Park. They're still goggling at me. I have to say something. 'The Edgerlys liked me to curtsy. It's a habit I got into. I'm sorry, madam, I won't do it again.'

Trish's head is leaning further and further over, her eyes all screwed up. She's squinting at me as though she's trying to make me out.

She must realise I'm a fake, she must.

'I like it,' she pronounces at last, and nods her head in satisfaction. 'Yes, I like it. You can curtsy here, too.'

What? I can do what? This is the twenty-first century. And I am being asked to curtsy to a woman called Trish? I take a breath to protest—then close it again. It doesn't matter. It's not real. I can curtsy for a morning.

I can see *The Times* lying on the table. It's open at the business pages and a headline reads GLAZERBROOKS CALLS IN RECEIVERS.

My eyes run down the text but I can't see any mention of Carter Spink. The PR department must have managed to keep a lid on the story.

'Mr Geiger and I will be going out in a minute,' Trish says. 'Kindly prepare a light sandwich lunch for one o'clock, and get on with the downstairs cleaning. We'll talk about dinner later. I might tell you, we were both very impressed by your seared *foie gras* menu.'

'Oh . . . um . . . good!'

It's fine. I'll be gone by dinner time.

By 11.30 I'm a nervous wreck. My mobile's charged up and I've finally found a signal in the kitchen, but it hasn't rung. And there are no messages. I've checked it every minute.

I gave up on the 'light sandwich lunch' almost straight away. I sawed away at two loaves of bread—and ended up with ten huge, wonky slices, each one more misshapen than the last.

All I can say is, thank God for *Yellow Pages* and caterers. And American Express. It's only going to cost me £45.50 to provide Trish and Eddie with a 'gourmet sandwich lunch' from Cotswold Caterers. To be honest, I would have paid twice that.

Now I'm just sitting on a chair, my hand clasped tightly over my mobile in my pocket, desperately willing it to ring. At the same time I'm utterly terrified that it will.

All of a sudden I can't bear the tension any more. I need something to relieve it. *Anything.* I wrench open the door of the Geigers' enormous fridge and pull out a bottle of white wine. I pour myself a glass and take an enormous, desperate gulp. I'm about to take another when I feel a tingling on the nape of my neck. As if . . . I'm being watched.

I swivel round. There's a man at the kitchen door. He's tall and broad, and deeply tanned, with intense blue eyes. His wavy hair is golden brown with bleached-blond tips. He's wearing old jeans and a torn T-shirt and the muddiest boots I've ever seen.

His eyes run doubtfully over the ten wonky, crumbly bread slices on the side, then on to my glass of wine.

'Hi,' he says at last. 'Are you the new cordon bleu cook?'

'Er . . . yes! Absolutely.' I smooth my uniform down. 'I'm the new housekeeper, Samantha. Hello.'

'I'm Nathaniel.' He holds out his hand and after a pause I take it. His skin is so hard and rough, it's like shaking a piece of tree bark. 'I do the garden for the Geigers. You'll be wanting to talk to me about vegetables.'

Why would I want to talk to him about vegetables?

'I can supply pretty much anything,' he continues. 'Seasonal, of course. Just tell me what you want.'

'Oh, *vegetables*,' I say, suddenly realising what he means. 'For cooking. Er . . . yes. I'll be wanting some of those. Definitely.'

'They told me you trained with some Michelin-starred chef?' He gives a small frown. 'I don't know what kind of fancy stuff you use, but I'll do my best.' He produces a small, mud-stained notebook and a pencil. 'Which brassicas do you like to use?'

Brassicas? What are brassicas? They must be some kind of vegetable. I search my mind frantically but all I can see is an image of brassieres, waving on a washing line.

'I'd have to consult my menus,' I say at last with a businesslike nod.

'But just generally.' He looks up. 'Which do you use most? So I know what to plant.'

'I use . . . all sorts, really.' I give him an airy smile. 'You know how it is with brassicas. Sometimes you're in the mood for one . . . sometimes another!' I'm really not sure how convincing that sounded. Nathaniel looks baffled.

He puts down his notebook and surveys me for a moment. His attention shifts to my wineglass again. I'm not sure I like his expression.

'I was just about to put this wine in a sauce,' I say hastily. With a nonchalant air, I take a saucepan down from the rack, put it on the hob and pour the wine in. I shake in some salt, then pick up a wooden spoon and stir it.

'Where did you say you trained?' he says.

'At . . . cordon bleu school.' My cheeks are growing rather hot. I shake more salt into the wine and stir it briskly.

'You haven't turned the hob on,' Nathaniel observes.

'It's a cold sauce,' I reply, without lifting my head. I keep stirring for a minute, then put down my wooden spoon. 'So. I'll just leave that to . . . marinate now.'

At last I look up. Nathaniel is leaning against the doorframe, calmly watching me. There's an expression in his blue eyes that makes my throat tighten.

He knows. He knows I'm a fake. *Please don't tell the Geigers*, I silently transmit to him. *Please. I'll be gone soon.*

'Samantha?' Trish's head pops round the door and I start nervously. 'Oh, you've met Nathaniel! Did he tell you about his vegetable garden?'

'Er . . . yes.' I can't look at him. 'He did.'

'*Marvellous!*' She drags on a cigarette. 'Well, Mr Geiger and I are back now, and we'd like our sandwiches in twenty minutes.'

I feel a jolt of shock. Twenty minutes? But it's only ten past twelve. The caterers aren't coming till one o'clock.

'Would you like a drink first?' I suggest desperately.

'No, thanks!' she says. 'Just the sandwiches. We're both rather famished, actually, so if you could hurry up with them . . .'

'Right.' I swallow. 'No problem!'

I automatically bob a curtsy as Trish disappears and hear a kind of snorting sound from Nathaniel.

'You curtsy,' he says.

'Yes, I curtsy,' I say defiantly. 'Anything wrong with that?'

Nathaniel's eyes rest again on the misshapen bread slices lying on the breadboard. 'Is that lunch?' he says.

'No, that's not lunch!' I snap, flustered. 'And please could you get out of my kitchen? I need a clear space to work in.'

'See you around then. Good luck with the sauce.' He nods his head towards the pan of wine.

As he closes the kitchen door behind him I whip out my phone and speed-dial the caterers. But they've left their machine on.

'Hi,' I say breathlessly after the bleep. 'I ordered some sandwiches earlier? Well, I need them *now*. As soon as you can. Thanks.'

Even as I put the phone down I realise it's pointless. The caterers are never going to turn up in time. The Geigers are waiting.

Determination rises in me. OK. I can make a few sandwiches.

Quickly I pick up the two least wonky of my bread slices. I pick up the bread knife and start cutting off the crusts until they're about an inch square but presentable. There's a butter dish on the side and I gouge some out with a knife. As I spread it on the first slice the bread tears into two pieces.

I'll patch them together. No one'll notice.

I fling open a cupboard door and frantically root through pots of mustard . . . mint sauce . . . strawberry jam. Jam sandwiches it is. An English classic. I hastily smother one piece of bread with jam, spread some more butter on the other, and sandwich the two together. Then I stand back and look at it.

It's a total disaster. Jam is oozing out of the cracks. I've never seen a more revolting sandwich in my life.

Slowly I put the knife down in defeat. So this is it. Time for my resignation. As I stare at the jammy mess I feel strangely disappointed in myself. I would have thought I could last a morning.

A knocking sound breaks me out of my reverie. I whip round to see a girl in a blue velvet hairband peering through the kitchen window.

'Hi!' she calls. 'Did you order sandwiches for twenty?'

It all happens so fast. One minute I'm standing there looking at my botch of jam and crumbs. The next, two girls in green aprons are trooping into the kitchen with plates of professionally made sandwiches.

Clean-cut, white and brown sandwiches, stacked in neat pyramids, garnished with sprigs of herbs and slices of lemon. They even have little handwritten paper flags describing the fillings. *Tuna, mint and cucumber. Smoked salmon, cream cheese and caviar. Thai chicken with wild rocket.*

'I'm *so* sorry about the numbers mix-up,' the girl in the hairband says as I sign for them. 'It honestly looked like a twenty. And we don't often get an order for sandwiches for just two people . . .'

'It's fine!' I say, edging her towards the door. 'Really. Whatever. Just put it on my card.'

The door finally closes and I look around the kitchen, totally dazed. I've never *seen* so many sandwiches.

'Samantha?' I can hear Trish approaching. 'It's five past one, and I did ask *most* clearly for . . .'

Her voice trails off into silence as she reaches the kitchen door, and her whole face sags in astonishment. I turn and follow her gaze as she surveys the endless plates of sandwiches.

'My goodness!' At last Trish finds her voice. 'This is . . . impressive!'

'I wasn't sure what fillings you'd prefer,' I say. 'Obviously next time I won't make quite so many . . .'

'Well!' Trish appears totally at a loss.

'I'll put a selection on a plate for you,' I suggest. 'And bring it out to the conservatory.'

'*Marvellous.* Nathaniel!' Trish raps on the kitchen window. 'Come in and have a sandwich!'

I stop dead. No. Not him again.

'We don't want to waste them, after all.' She arches her eyebrows. 'If I did have a criticism, Samantha, it would be that you were a *little* profligate. Not that we're *poor*,' she adds suddenly. 'It isn't *that*.'

'Er . . . no, madam.'

'Mrs Geiger?' Nathaniel has appeared in the kitchen doorway again.

'Have one of Samantha's delicious sandwiches!' exclaims Trish, gesturing around the kitchen. 'Just look! Isn't she clever?'

There's total silence as Nathaniel surveys the endless mounds of sandwiches. I can't bring myself to meet his eye.

'That didn't take you long,' he says, a slight question in his voice.

'I'm pretty quick when I want to be.' I give him a bland smile.

'Samantha's wonderful!' says Trish, biting greedily into a sandwich and practically swooning. 'This Thai chicken is divine!'

Surreptitiously I pick up one from the pile and bite into it.

Bloody hell, that's good. Though I say it myself.

By half past two the kitchen is empty. Trish and Eddie devoured over half the sandwiches, and have now gone out. Nathaniel is back in the garden. I'm pacing up and down, looking at the clock every thirty seconds. Arnold will call soon. It's been hours.

Suddenly I feel my mobile vibrate and my whole chest seems to explode in painful fright. I grab the phone out of my uniform pocket with a suddenly trembling hand.

The caller ID tells me it's Ketterman.

As I stare at his name I feel real fear in a way I never have before.

'Hello.'

'Samantha. John Ketterman here.'

'Right.' My voice is scratchy with nerves. 'Hello.'

'Samantha, I'm ringing to tell you that your contract with Carter Spink has been terminated.'

I feel all the blood drain from my face.

'A letter is on its way to you giving the reasons.' His tone is distant and formal. 'Gross negligence compounded by your subsequent unprofessional behaviour. Your P45 will be sent to you. Your pass has been disabled. I don't expect to see you at the Carter Spink offices again.'

'Please don't . . .' My voice comes blurting out in desperation. 'Please give me another chance. I made one mistake. One.'

'Lawyers at Carter Spink don't make mistakes, Samantha. You've disgraced the reputation of the firm and yourself.' Ketterman's voice sharpens as though he, too, might be finding this difficult. 'You have lost fifty million pounds of a client's money through your own negligence. And subsequently absconded with no explanation. Samantha, you cannot have expected any other outcome, surely?'

There's a long silence. My forehead is pressed hard against the heel of my hand. I try to focus on breathing. 'No,' I whisper at last.

It's over. My entire career. Everything I've worked for since I was twelve years old. All gone. Everything ruined. In twenty-four hours.

At last I realise Ketterman has disappeared from the line. I get to my feet and stagger over to the shiny fridge. I look greenish-grey in its reflection. My eyes are huge, burning holes.

I've been fired. The phrase echoes round my mind. *I've been fired.*

Suddenly I hear the sound of a key in the front door. My eyes snap into focus and I move away from the fridge.

I can't be found like this. I can't face any probing; any sympathy. Otherwise I'm afraid I might just collapse into sobs and never stop. Distractedly I reach for a cloth and start sweeping it over the table.

'There you are!' Trish comes tripping into the kitchen on her high-heeled clogs, holding three bursting shopping bags. 'Samantha!' She stops at the sight of me. 'Are you all right? Is your headache back?'

'I'm . . . fine.' My voice shakes a little. 'Thanks.'

'You look *dreadful*! Goodness me! Have some more pills!'

'Really . . .'

'Go on! I'll have some too, why not?' she adds gaily. 'Now, sit down, and I'll make *you* a cup of tea!'

She plonks the bags down and switches on the kettle, then rootles around for the green painkillers.

'These are the ones you like, aren't they?'

'Um, I'd rather just have an aspirin,' I say quickly. 'If that's OK.'

'Are you quite sure?' She runs me a glass of water and gives me a couple of aspirin. 'Now, you just sit there. Relax. Don't even *think* of doing anything else! Until it's time to make the supper,' she adds.

'You're very kind,' I manage.

As I say the words I have the dim realisation that I mean them. Trish's kindness may be a bit warped, but it's real.

My mind is beating like a butterfly's wings. What am I going to do?

Go home.

But the thought of returning to that flat, with Ketterman living two floors above, makes me sick. I can't face him. I can't do it.

Phone Guy. He'll have me to stay. They have that huge house in Islington with all those spare rooms. Then I'll . . . sell my flat. Find a job.

What job?

'Here we are.' Trish puts a cup of tea down and scrutinises me for a few moments. 'This will cheer you up,' she says, patting the shopping bags with suppressed glee. 'After your *stunning* performance at lunch . . . I've been shopping. And I've got a surprise for you!'

'A surprise?' I look up, bewildered, as Trish starts producing packets from the bag.

'Foie gras . . . chick peas . . . shoulder of lamb . . .' She hefts a joint of meat on to the table and looks at me expectantly. Then she clicks her tongue at my bewildered expression. 'It's *ingredients*! Your dinner-party menu! We'll eat at eight, if that's OK?'

It'll be all right.

If I say it often enough to myself, it must be true.

I need to call Guy. I flip open my phone and dial Guy's number.

'Samantha.' He sounds guarded. 'Hi. Have you—'

'It's OK,' I squeeze my eyes shut. 'I've spoken to Ketterman. I know.'

'Oh, Samantha.' He exhales hard. 'I'm so sorry . . . All sorts of stories are going round.'

'Stories?' My heart is thudding. 'What . . . what stories?'

'There's a rumour you've skipped the country.' He sounds reluctant. 'Apparently people are saying you're . . . unreliable. That you've made errors before.'

I can't take all this in. I cannot stand his pity. If he says anything else I might burst into tears. 'It's fine,' I say, cutting him off. 'Really. Let's not talk about it. Let's just . . . look forward. I have to get my life on track.'

'Jesus, you're focused!' There's a note of admiration in his voice. 'You don't let anything faze you, do you?'

'I just have to . . . get on with things.' Somehow I keep my voice even and steady. 'I need to get back to London. But I can't go home. Ketterman bought a flat in my building. He *lives* there.'

'Yes, I heard about that.' I can hear the wince in Guy's voice.

'I just can't face him, Guy. So . . . I was wondering. Could I come and stay with you for a few days?'

There's silence. I wasn't expecting silence. 'Samantha, I'd love to help,' says Guy at last. 'But I'm not sure it's possible . . . we're having some work done to the bedrooms . . . it's just not a good time . . .'

He sounds halting, as if he wants to get off the line. And suddenly it hits me. He doesn't want to be near me. It's as though my disgrace is contagious; as though his career might get blighted, too.

I know I should stay quiet, keep my dignity, but I just can't contain myself. 'You don't want to be associated with me, do you?' I burst out.

'Samantha!' His voice is defensive. 'Don't be ridiculous.'

'I'm still the same *person*. I thought you were my friend, Guy.'

'I am your friend! But you can't expect me to . . . Look, call me in a couple of days, maybe we can meet up for a drink . . .'

I try to control my voice. 'I'm sorry to have bothered you.'

I switch off my phone, light-headed with disbelief, wondering what to do next. When the phone suddenly vibrates in my hand, I nearly jump out of my skin. *Tennyson*, my display reads.

Mum. I feel a clutch of apprehension inside. I guess she's heard. I guess I could go and stay with her, it occurs to me. How weird. I didn't even think of that before. I open up the phone and take a deep breath.

'Hi, Mum.'

'Samantha.' Her voice pierces my ear with no preamble. 'How long were you going to leave it exactly before you told me about your debacle? I have to find out about my own daughter's disgrace from an *Internet joke*.' She utters the words with revulsion.

'An Internet joke?' I echo faintly. 'What do you mean?'

'You didn't know? Apparently in certain legal circles the new term for fifty million pounds is "a Samantha". I was not amused.'

'Mum, I'm so sorry—'

'Where are you?' She cuts across my faltering words.

'I'm . . . at someone's house. Out of London.'

'And what are your plans?'

'I don't know.' I rub my face. 'I need to . . . find a job.'

'Yes, and be thankful that I have acted for you. I've called in all my favours. It wasn't an easy job. But the senior partner at Fortescues will see you tomorrow at ten.'

'You've organised me a job interview?'

'Assuming all goes well, you will enter at senior associate level.' Her voice is crisp. 'You're being given this chance as a personal favour to me. As you can imagine, there are . . . reservations. So, if you want to progress, Samantha, you are going to have to perform. You're going to have to give more than you did at Carter Spink. No slacking. No complacency. You will have to prove yourself *doubly*. Do you understand?'

'Yes,' I say automatically. I shut my eyes, my thoughts whirling. I have a job interview. A fresh start. It's the solution to my nightmare. Why don't I feel more relieved? More happy?

More hours. More work. More late nights. It's almost as if I can feel the concrete blocks being loaded onto me again. Heavier and heavier.

'I mean, no,' I hear myself saying. 'No. I don't want that. I don't want it. I can't . . . it's too much . . .'

The words come out of my mouth all by themselves. I wasn't planning them; I've never even thought them before. But now they're out in the air they somehow feel . . . true.

'I'm *sorry*?' Mum's voice is sharp.

'I was thinking . . . I could take a break, maybe.'

'A break would finish your legal career.' Her voice snaps dismissively.

'I could do something else.'

'You wouldn't last more than two minutes in anything else!' She sounds affronted. 'Samantha, you're a *lawyer*.'

'There are other things than being a lawyer!' I cry, rattled.

'Samantha, if you're having some kind of breakdown—'

'I'm not!' My voice rises in distress. 'Just because I question my life, it doesn't mean I'm having a breakdown! I never *asked* you to find me another job. I need a bit of time to . . . to think.'

'You will be at that job interview, Samantha.' Mum's voice is like a whip. 'You will be there tomorrow at ten o'clock.'

'I won't!'

I switch off my phone, and almost savagely throw it down on to the table. My face is burning. Tears are pressing hotly at the back of my eyes. The phone starts vibrating angrily on the table but I ignore it. I'm not going to answer it. I'm not going to talk to anyone. I'm going to have a drink. And then I'm going to cook this bloody dinner.

I slosh some white wine into a glass and take several gulps. Then I address myself to the pile of raw ingredients waiting on the table.

I can cook. I can cook this stuff. Even if everything else in my life is in ruins, I can do this. I have a brain, I can work it out.

Without delay I rip the plastic covering off the lamb. This can go in the oven. In some kind of dish. Simple. And the chick peas can go in there too. Then I'll mash them and that will make the hummous.

I open a cupboard, select a baking tray and scatter the chick peas onto it. I grab a bottle of oil from the counter and drizzle it over the top. Already I'm feeling like a cook.

I shove the tray into the oven and turn it on full blast. Then I plonk the lamb in an oval dish and shove that in too.

So far so good. Now all I need to do is leaf through all Trish's recipe books and find instructions for seared *foie gras* with an apricot glaze.

By seven o'clock I'm still cooking.

At least I think that's what I'm doing. Both ovens are roaring with heat. Pots are bubbling on the hob. The electric whisk is whirring busily. I've burnt my right hand twice, taking things out of the oven.

I've been going for three hours. And I haven't yet made anything that could actually be eaten. So far I've discarded a collapsed chocolate soufflé, two pans of burnt onions, and a saucepan of congealed apricots that made me feel sick just to look at them.

The Geigers, meanwhile, have no idea. They're drinking sherry in the drawing room. They think everything is going splendidly.

A kind of frenzied hysteria has come over me. I know I cannot do this. But somehow I can't give up either. I keep thinking a miracle will happen. I'll pull it all together. I'll manage it somehow—

Oh God, the gravy's bubbling over.

I grab a spoon and start stirring it. It looks like revolting lumpy brown water. Frantically I start searching in the cupboards for something to chuck in. Flour. Cornflour. Something like that. This'll do. I grab a small pot and shake in vigorous amounts of the white powder, then wipe the sweat off my brow. OK. What now?

Suddenly I remember the egg whites, still whisking up in the food mixer. I grab the recipe book, running my finger down the page. I changed the dessert course to pavlova after I chanced upon the line in a recipe book: 'Meringues are so easy to make.'

So far so good. What next? 'Form the stiff meringue mixture into a large circle on your baking parchment.'

I peer at my bowl. *Stiff* meringue mixture? Mine's liquid.

It has to be right, I tell myself feverishly. It has to be. I followed the instructions. Maybe it's thicker than it looks. Maybe once I start pouring it out, it'll stiffen up by some weird culinary law of physics.

Slowly I start to pour it on to the tray. It doesn't stiffen up. It spreads in a white oozing lake and starts dripping off the tray onto the floor.

A big splodge lands on my foot and I give a frustrated cry. I feel near tears. Why didn't it work? A pent-up rage is rising up inside me: rage at myself, at my crappy egg whites, at cookery books, at cooks, at food . . . And most of all at whoever wrote that meringues were 'so easy to make'.

'They're not!' I hear myself yelling. 'They're bloody not!' I hurl the book across the kitchen, where it smashes against the kitchen door.

'What the hell—' a male voice exclaims in surprise.

The next minute the door flies open and Nathaniel is standing there, his hair glinting in the evening sun. A rucksack is hefted over his shoulder; he looks like he's on his way home. 'Is everything OK?'

'It's fine,' I say, rattled. 'Everything's fine. Thank you. Thank you so much.' I make a dismissive motion with my hand, but he doesn't move.

'I heard you were cooking a gourmet dinner tonight,' he says slowly, looking around at the mess.

'Yes. That's right. I'm just in the . . . most complex stage of the . . .' I glance down at the hob, and give an involuntary scream. 'The gravy!'

Brown bubbles are expanding out of my gravy saucepan, all over the cooker and down the sides onto the floor.

'Get it off the heat, for God's sake!' exclaims Nathaniel. He snatches up the pan and moves it. 'What on earth is in that?'

'Nothing!' I say. 'Just the usual ingredients . . .'

Nathaniel has noticed the little pot on the counter. He grabs it and stares at it incredulously. '*Baking soda?* You put baking soda in gravy? Is that what they taught you at—' He breaks off and sniffs the air. 'Hang on. Is something burning?'

I watch helplessly as he opens the bottom oven, grabs an oven glove with a practised air and hauls out a baking tray covered in what look like tiny black bullets. My chick peas. I forgot all about them.

'What are *these*?' he says incredulously. 'Rabbit droppings?'

'They're chick peas,' I retort. 'I drizzled them in olive oil and put them in the oven so they could . . . melt.'

Nathaniel stares at me. '*Melt*?'

'Soften,' I amend hurriedly.

Nathaniel puts down the tray and turns round, his face working with disbelief. 'You know bugger all about cooking! This is all a bluff! You're not a housekeeper. I don't know what the hell you're up to—'

'I'm not up to anything!' I reply, in shock.

'The Geigers are good people.' He faces me square on. 'I won't have them exploited.'

Suddenly, he looks really aggressive. Oh God. What does he think? That I'm some kind of confidence trickster?

I rub my sweaty face. 'I'm not trying to rip anyone off. OK, I can't cook. But I ended up here because of . . . a misunderstanding.'

'A misunderstanding?' He gives a suspicious frown.

'Yes,' I say, a little more sharply than I meant to. I sink down onto a chair. 'I was running away from . . . something. I needed a place to stay for the night. The Geigers assumed I was a housekeeper. And then in the morning I felt bad. I thought I'd do the job for a morning. But I'm not planning to stay. And I won't take any money from them, if that's what you're thinking.'

There's silence. At last I look up. Nathaniel is leaning against the counter, his huge arms folded. His wary frown has eased a little.

'What were you running from?' he says. 'A bad relationship?'

I think back over all my years at Carter Spink. All the hours I gave them; everything I sacrificed. Finished in a three-minute phone call.

'Yes,' I say slowly. 'A bad relationship.'

'How long were you in it?'

'Seven years.' To my horror I can feel tears seeping out of the corners of my eyes. 'I'm sorry,' I gulp. 'It's been quite a stressful day.'

Nathaniel tears off a square of kitchen towel from the wall-mounted roll behind him and hands it to me. 'If it was a bad relationship, you're well out of it,' he says calmly. 'No point staying. No point looking back.'

'You're right.' I wipe my eyes. 'Yes. I just have to decide what to do with my life. I can't stay here.'

'The Geigers are good employers,' says Nathaniel with a tiny shrug. 'You could do worse.'

'Yeah.' I raise a half-smile. 'Unfortunately I can't cook.'

'I could speak to my mum. She can cook. She could teach you.'

I look at him in astonishment, almost laughing. 'You think I should *stay*? I thought I was supposed to be a confidence trickster.' I shake my head. 'I have to go.'

'Shame. It would have been nice to have someone around who speaks English. And makes such great sandwiches,' he adds, totally deadpan.

I can't help smiling back. 'Caterers.'

'Ah. I wondered.'

A faint rapping at the door makes us both look up.

'Samantha?' Trish's voice outside is hushed and urgent. 'Don't worry, I won't come in. I don't want to disturb anything! You're probably at a very *crucial* stage.'

'Kind of . . .' I catch Nathaniel's eye and a sudden wave of hysteria rises through me.

'I just wanted to ask,' Trish continues, 'if you will be serving any kind of *sorbet* between the courses?'

I look at Nathaniel. His shoulders are shaking with silent laughter. I can't stop a tiny snort escaping. I clamp my hand desperately over my mouth, trying to get control of myself.

'Samantha?'

'Er . . . no,' I manage at last. 'There won't be any sorbet.'

Nathaniel has picked up one of my pans of burnt onions. He mimes taking a spoonful and eating it. *Yummy*, he mouths. Tears are streaming from my eyes. I'm almost asphyxiating, trying to keep quiet.

'Well! See you later!'

Trish tip-taps away and I collapse into helpless laughter. I've never laughed so hard in my life. My ribs hurt; I almost feel like I'll be sick.

At last I somehow calm down, wipe my eyes and blow my runny nose. Nathaniel's stopped laughing too, and is looking around the bombshelled kitchen.

'Seriously,' he says, 'what are you going to do about this? They're expecting a fancy dinner.'

'I know.' I feel a fresh wave of hysteria and fight it down. 'OK.' I exhale with a little shudder and push back my damp hair. 'I'm going to rescue the situation.'

'You're going to rescue the situation.' He looks disbelieving.

'In fact I think this might solve everyone's problems.' I get to my feet and start busily sweeping packets into the bin. 'First I need to clear up the kitchen a bit . . .'

'I'll help.' Nathaniel stands up. 'This I have to see.'

Companionably, we empty pans and pots and packets into the bin. I open the oven and pull out the lamb in a cloud of smoke, then scrub all the smeared surfaces while Nathaniel mops up the meringue.

'How long have you worked here?' I ask him.

'Three years. Before that, I was working at Marchant House. It's a stately home, near Oxford. Before that, university.'

'University?' I say, my ears pricking up. 'I didn't know—'

I halt. I was about to say 'I didn't know gardeners went to university.'

'I did natural sciences.' Nathaniel gives me a look that makes me think he knew exactly what I was thinking.

I open my mouth to ask him where and when he was at university— then on second thoughts, close it and switch on the waste-disposal unit. I don't want to start getting into details, going down the 'Do we know anyone in common?' road. Right now, I could do without remembering the particulars of my life.

At last the kitchen looks a bit more normal. I take a deep breath.

'OK. Show time.'

'Good luck.' Nathaniel raises his eyebrows.

I open the kitchen door to see Trish and Eddie loitering in the hall.

'Ah, Samantha! Everything ready?' Trish's face is all lit up with anticipation, and I feel a huge twinge of guilt for what I'm about to do.

'Mr and Mrs Geiger.' I take a deep breath and put on my best breaking-bad-news-to-a-client face. 'I am devastated.' I look from one face to the other, then close my eyes and shake my head.

'Devastated?' echoes Trish nervously.

'I have done my best.' I open my eyes. 'But the dinner I created was not up to my own professional standards. I could not allow it out of the kitchen. I will of course reimburse all your costs—and offer my resignation. I will leave in the morning.'

There. Done. And no casualties.

'*Leave?*' Trish stares at me in consternation, her blue eyes practically bulging out of their sockets. 'You can't leave! You're the best housekeeper we've ever had! We'll give you a pay rise! Name your price!'

This conversation is really not going the way I planned.

'Well . . . we never actually discussed pay . . .'

'*Eddie!*' Trish rounds on him savagely. 'This is *your* fault! Samantha's leaving because you're not paying her enough!'

'I didn't say that—' I begin helplessly.

She digs Eddie in the ribs with her elbow. 'Say something!'

'Ah . . . Samantha.' Eddie clears his throat awkwardly. 'We'd be very happy if you would consider staying with us. We've been delighted with your performance and whatever your salary expectations are . . . we'll match them.' Trish digs him in the ribs again. 'Exceed them.'

They're both gazing at me with a kind of eager hope.

I glance at Nathaniel, who cocks his head as though to say 'Why not?'

The strangest feeling is coming over me. Three people. All telling me they want me within the space of ten minutes. I could stay. It's as simple as that. *I can't cook,* a little voice reminds me. *I can't clean. I'm not a house-keeper.* But I could learn. I could learn it all.

The silence is growing in tension. Even Nathaniel is watching me closely from the door.

'Well . . . OK.' I feel a smile coming to my lips. 'OK. If you want me to . . . I'll stay.'

Four

THE ONLY THING IS, now I actually have to be a housekeeper.

Having set my alarm early, the next morning I arrive downstairs in the kitchen before seven, in my uniform. The garden is misty and there are no sounds, except a couple of magpies chacking at each other on the lawn. I feel as though I'm the only person awake in the world.

Breakfast is a bit of a nightmare. It takes me three failed attempts before I realise how you're supposed to cut a grapefruit in half. You'd think they'd draw guidelines round them, or have perforations, or something. Meanwhile the milk for the coffee boils over—and when I plunge down the cafetière, the coffee explodes everywhere. Luckily Trish and Eddie are so busy arguing about where to go on their next holiday, they don't seem to notice what's going on in the kitchen.

On the plus side, I really think I'm getting the hang of the toaster.

When they've finished, I stack the dirty dishes in the dishwasher and am desperately trying to remember how I made it work yesterday, when Trish comes into the kitchen.

'Is everything all right?' she asks. 'Have you got your routine sorted, Samantha?'

'Absolutely.' I grope for a competent-sounding phrase. 'I'm pretty much . . . on top of everything.'

'Good!' she exclaims. 'I knew it! You don't need mollycoddling! You know your way around a house!'

'I should say so!'

Trish beams back. 'I expect you'll be tackling the laundry today.'

The laundry. I hadn't even thought about the laundry.

'Only I'd like you to change the sheets when you make the beds,' she adds.

Make the beds? That hadn't occurred to me either.

I feel a twinge of slight panic. Not only am I not remotely 'on top of everything', I don't have a clue what 'everything' is.

'Obviously I have my own . . . er . . . established routine,' I say, trying to sound casual. 'But it might be an idea if you give me a list of duties.'

'Oh.' Trish looks a little irritated. 'Well, if you think you need it. Now, Samantha, Mr Geiger would like to see you in his study. To discuss your pay and conditions. Don't keep him waiting!'

'Er . . . very good, madam.' I curtsy, then head out into the hall. I approach the door of Eddie's study and knock twice.

'Come in!' comes a jovial voice. As I walk into the room, Eddie is sitting behind his desk: a huge affair of mahogany and tooled leather with an expensive-looking laptop.

'Ah, Samantha.' Eddie gestures to an upright wooden chair and I sit down. 'Here we are! The document you've been waiting for!'

With a self-important air he hands me a folder marked HOUSEKEEPER'S CONTRACT. I open it up to find a title sheet on cream vellum paper printed to look like an old scroll. Printed in an ornate, medieval-style font are the words

CONTRACT OF AGREEMENT
Between Samantha Sweeting and Mr and Mrs Edward Geiger, this 2nd day of July in the year of our Lord two thousand and four.

'Wow,' I say in surprise. 'Did a . . . lawyer draw this up?'

I cannot imagine any lawyer I know drawing up a contract in Disney-medieval lettering. Let alone putting it all in a fake scroll.

'I didn't need a lawyer.' Eddie chuckles knowingly. 'I'm not playing at that game. Charge you an arm and a leg, those guys will, just for a bit of fancy Latin. Take it from me, Samantha, these things are simple enough to draw up if you've half a brain.' He gives me a wink.

'I'm sure you're right,' I say at last. I turn over the title sheet and run my eyes down the printed clauses.

Oh my God. What *is* this gibberish? I have to bite my lip as I take in phrases here and there.

. . . Insofar, notwithstanding the provision of culinary services, in a manner which shall be deemed, prima facie, to include yet not exclude light snacks and beverages . . .

My lips are clamped together. I must not laugh.

Pursuant to the aforetaining, ipso facto, all parties will retain the afore-mentioned rights beyond reasonable doubt.

The whole thing is a total nonsensical mishmash. Bits of legal jargon soldered together in meaningless, would-be-impressive phrases. I scan the rest of the page, desperately keeping a straight face, trying to think of a suitable response.

'Now, I know it looks frightening!' says Eddie, misinterpreting my silence. 'But don't be intimidated by all these long words. It's quite simple, really! Did you have a chance to look at the pay?'

My eye flicks to the figure quoted in bold under 'Weekly Salary'. It's slightly less than I charged per hour as a lawyer.

'It seems extremely generous,' I say after a pause.

'Is there anything you don't understand?' He beams jovially. 'Just say!'

Where do I start?

'Um . . . this bit.' I point to *Clause 7: Hours*. 'Does this mean I have the whole weekend off? Every weekend?'

'Of course.' Eddie seems surprised. 'We wouldn't expect you to give up your weekends! Unless it's a special occasion, in which case we'll pay you extra . . . you'll see in Clause 9 . . .'

I'm not listening. Every weekend free. I can't get my head round this. I don't think I've had a totally free weekend since I was twelve.

'That's great.' I look up, unable to stop myself smiling.

'I'll leave you alone to study the agreement before you sign.'

As Eddie disappears from the room, I look down at the contract again, rolling my eyes. I pick up a pencil and automatically start correct-ing the text, rephrasing, scoring out and adding queries in the margin.

Then, abruptly I stop myself. *What the hell am I doing?*

I grab a rubber and hastily erase all my amendments. I reach for a Biro and turn to the bottom of the page, where a cartoon owl in lawyer's garb is pointing to a dotted line.

Name: Samantha Sweeting.
Occupation:

I hesitate for a moment, then put *Domestic Help*.

As I write the words I have a fleeting blink of incredulity. I'm really doing this. I'm really taking this job, miles away from my former life in every sense. And no one knows what I'm doing. I have a sudden flash of the expression on my mother's face, if she knew where I was right now . . . if she could see me in my uniform . . . I'm almost tempted to call her up and tell her.

But I'm not going to. I have laundry to do.

It takes me two trips to bring down all the washing to the laundry room. I dump the overflowing baskets on the tiled floor and look at the high-tech washing machine. This should be simple enough.

I'm not exactly experienced in this area. At home I send everything except underwear to the dry-cleaners. But that doesn't mean I *can't* do it. Experimentally I open the door of the machine and at once an electronic display starts flashing at me. WASH? WASH?

Immediately I feel flustered. *Obviously* I want you to wash, I feel like snapping back. Just give me a chance to get the bloody clothes in.

I take a deep breath. Stay calm. One thing at a time. First step: fill the machine. I pick up a bundle of clothes—then stop myself.

No. First step: sort the clothes. Feeling pleased with myself for having thought of this, I start sorting out the dirty clothes into piles on the floor, consulting the labels as I go.

Whites 40.

Whites 90.

Wash inside out.

Wash colours separately.

Wash with care.

By the end of the first basket I'm totally bewildered. I've made about twenty different piles on the floor, most consisting of only one item. This is ridiculous. I can't put on twenty washes. It'll take all week.

OK . . . let's just be rational. People do washing every day, all over the world. It cannot be that hard. I'll just have to mix and match a bit.

I pick up a bundle of clothes from the floor and shove it into the drum. Then I open a nearby cupboard and grab a packet covered in pictures of white T-shirts, shake some powder into the little tray at the top. I close the door firmly. Now what?

WASH? the machine is still flashing at me. WASH?

'Er . . . yes!' I say. 'Wash them.' I jab randomly at a button.

ENTER PROGRAM? it flashes back.

Program? My eyes dart about for clues and I spot a manual tucked behind a spray bottle. I grab it and start leafing through.

The half-load option for small washes is only available for pre-wash programs A3–E2 and super rinse programs G2–L7 not including H4.

What? Come on. I have a degree from Cambridge. I know Latin, for God's sake. I can work this out. I flip to another page.

Programs E5 and F1 exclude spin cycle UNLESS button 'S' is depressed for five seconds before commencing.

I can't cope. My exam on international corporate litigation was a million times easier than this. OK, let's forget the manual. Let's just use common sense. I briskly press at the key pad in my best competent-housekeeper manner.

PROGRAM K3? the machine flashes at me. PROGRAM K3?

'No,' I say aloud, jabbing at the machine. 'I want something else.'

YOU HAVE CHOSEN PROGRAM K3 it flashes back.

'But I don't want program K3!' I say, flustered.

K3 COMMENCING, flashes the display. HEAVY DUTY UPHOLSTERY PROGRAM.

Heavy duty? *Upholstery?*

'Stop it,' I say under my breath, and start banging all the buttons. 'Stop!' I kick the machine in desperation. '*Stop!*'

'Everything all right?' comes Trish's voice from the kitchen and I leap away from the machine, smoothing my hair down.

'Er . . . fine! Fine!' I plaster on a professional smile as she appears at the door. 'Just . . . getting some washing on.'

'Well done.' She holds out a stripy shirt to me. 'Now, Mr Geiger needs a button sewn on this shirt, if you would be so kind . . .'

'Absolutely!' I take it from her with an inward gulp.

'And here's your list of duties!' She hands me a sheet of paper. 'It's by no means complete, but it should get you *started* . . .'

As I run my eyes down the endless list, I feel a bit faint.

Make beds . . . sweep and clean front steps . . . arrange flowers . . . polish all mirrors . . . store cupboards tidy . . . laundry . . . clean bathrooms daily . . .

'Now there's nothing here that should present you with a problem, is there?' adds Trish.

'Er . . . no!' My voice is a little strangled. 'No, it should all be fine!'

'But make a stab at the ironing *first*,' she continues firmly. 'There is quite a lot, I'm afraid.' For some reason, Trish is looking upwards. With foreboding, I follow her gaze. There, above us, is a mountain of crumpled shirts hanging on a wooden drying rack. At least thirty.

As I stare up at them, I feel wobbly. I can't iron a shirt. I've never used an iron in my life. What am I going to do?

'I expect you'll whip through these in no time!' she adds gaily. 'The ironing board's just there,' she adds with a nod.

'Um, thanks!' I manage.

The important thing is to look convincing. I'll get the ironing board out, wait till she leaves . . . then come up with a new plan.

I reach for the ironing board, trying to look matter-of-fact, as if I do this all the time. I tug briskly at one of the metal legs, but it won't move.

Trish takes the board from me, and in two movements has put it up. 'I expect you're used to a different model,' she adds as she clicks it shut. 'They all have their own little tricks.'

'Absolutely!' I say, seizing on this excuse in relief. 'Of course! I'm far more used to working with a . . . a . . . a Nimbus 2000.'

Trish peers at me in surprise. 'Isn't that the broomstick out of Harry Potter?'

Fuck. I knew I'd heard it somewhere.

'Yes . . . it is,' I say, my face flaming. 'And also a well-known ironing board. In fact, I think the broomstick was named *after* the ironing board.'

'Really?' Trish looks fascinated. 'I never knew that!' To my horror she leans expectantly against the door and lights a cigarette. 'Don't mind me!' she adds, her voice muffled. 'Just carry on!'

Carry on?

'There's the iron,' she adds with a gesture. 'Behind you.'

'Er . . . great! Thanks!' I take the iron and plug it in, as slowly as possible, my heart banging in fright. I'm going to have to start ironing. I reach for one of the shirts overhead, and spread it out awkwardly on the ironing board, playing for time.

Unable to believe what I'm doing, I pick up the iron. It's far heavier than I imagined and emits a terrifying cloud of steam. Very gingerly, I start lowering it towards the cotton fabric. I have no idea which bit of the shirt I'm aiming for. I think my eyes might be shut.

Suddenly there's a trilling from the kitchen. The phone. Thank God.

'Sorry, Samantha,' says Trish, frowning. 'I should get this . . .'

'That's fine!' My voice is shrill. 'No worries! I'll just get on . . .'

As soon as Trish is out of the room I put the iron down with a crash and bury my head in my hands. I must have been mad. This isn't going to work. I'm not made to be a housekeeper. The iron puffs steam in my face and I give a little scream of fright. I switch it off and collapse against the wall. It's only nine twenty and I'm already a total wreck.

And I thought being a lawyer was stressful.

Later, when time Trish comes into the kitchen I'm a little more composed. I can do this. It's not quantum physics. It's *housework*.

'Samantha, I'm afraid we're going to *desert* you for the day,' says Trish, looking concerned. 'Mr Geiger is off to golf and I'm going to see a *very* dear friend's new Mercedes. Will you be all right on your own?'

'I'll be fine!' I say, trying not to sound too joyful. 'Don't worry about me. Really. I'll just get on with things . . .'

'Is the ironing done?' She glances at the laundry room, impressed.

Done? What does she think I am, Wonder Woman?

'Actually, I thought I'd leave the ironing for now and tackle the rest of the house,' I say. 'That's my normal routine.'

'Absolutely.' She nods vigorously. 'Whatever suits you. Now, I won't be here to answer any questions, I'm afraid, but Nathaniel will!' She beckons out of the door.

'Oh,' I say as he walks in, wearing ripped jeans, his hair dishevelled. 'Er . . . hi, again.'

This is a bit weird. Seeing him this morning, after the drama of last night. As he meets my eye there's the twitch of a smile at his mouth.

'Hi,' he says. 'How's it going?'

'Great!' I say lightly. 'Really well.'

'Nathaniel knows *all* there is to know about this house.' Trish picks up her handbag. 'So if you can't find anything he's your man.'

'I'll bear that in mind,' I say. 'Thanks.'

'Toodle-oo!' calls Trish from the hall, and the front door bangs shut.

'Right!' I say. 'Well . . . I'll get on.'

I wait for Nathaniel to leave, but he leans against the table and looks at me quizzically. 'Do you have any idea how to clean a house?'

I'm starting to feel quite insulted here. Do I *look* like someone who can't clean a house?

'Of course I know how to clean a house.' I roll my eyes.

'Only I told my mum about you last night and she's willing to teach you cooking. And I said you'd probably need cleaning advice too—'

'I do not need cleaning advice!' I retort. 'I've cleaned houses loads of times. In fact, I need to get started.'

'Don't mind me.' Nathaniel shrugs.

I'll show him. In a businesslike manner I pick a can out of the cleaning cupboard and spray it on to the counter. There. Who says I don't know what I'm doing?

The spray has solidified into crystalline little grey droplets. I briskly rub them with a cloth—but they won't come off. Shit.

I look more closely at the can. 'DO NOT USE ON GRANITE'. *Shit.*

I hastily put the cloth down to hide the droplets. 'You're in my way.' I grab a feather duster from the blue tub and start brushing crumbs off the kitchen table. 'Excuse me . . .'

'I'll leave you then,' says Nathaniel, his mouth twitching again. He looks at the feather duster. 'Don't you want to be using a dustpan and brush for that?'

'I have my methods,' I say, lifting my chin. 'Thank you.'

'OK.' He grins. 'See you.'

I'm not going to let him faze me. I'm perfectly capable of cleaning this house. I just need . . . a plan. Yes. A time sheet, like at work.

As soon as Nathaniel's gone I grab a pen and piece of paper and start scribbling a list for the day.

> 9.30–9.36 Make beds
> 9.36–9.42 Take laundry out of machine and put in dryer
> 9.42–10.00 Clean bathrooms

I get to the end and read it over with a fresh surge of optimism. This is more like it. At this rate I should be done easily by lunchtime.

9.36 Fuck. I cannot make this bed. Why won't this sheet lie flat?
9.54 This is sheer torture. My arms have never ached so much in my entire life. The blankets weigh a ton, and the sheets won't go straight and I have no idea how to do the wretched corners. How do chambermaids do it? How?
10.30 At last. A whole hour of hard work and I have made precisely one bed. But never mind. Laundry next.
10.36 No. Please, no.

I can hardly bear to look. It's a total disaster. Everything in the washing machine has gone pink. Every single thing.

With trembling fingers I pick out a damp cashmere cardigan. It was cream when I put it in. It's now a sickly shade of candy floss. I knew K3 was bad news. I knew it—

Keep calm. There must be a solution. My eye starts flicking frantically over cans of products stacked on the shelves. Stain Away . . . Vanish. There has to be a remedy . . . I just need to think . . .

10.42 OK, I have the answer.
11.00 I've just spent £852 replacing all the clothes in the machine. Harrods personal-shopping department was very helpful, and will send them Express Delivery tomorrow.
11.06 The ironing. What am I going to do about that?
11.12 Right. I've looked in the local paper and I have a solution to that, too. A girl from the village will collect it, iron it all overnight at three pounds a shirt, and sew on Eddie's button.

So far this job has cost me nearly £1,000 pounds.

11.42 I've got the Hoover on, I'm cruising along nicely—

Shit. What was that? What just went up the Hoover? Why is it making that grinding noise? Have I broken it?

11.48 How much does a Hoover cost?

12.24 My legs are in total agony. I've been kneeling on hard tiles, cleaning the bath, for what seems like hours. All I want is a rest. But I have to keep moving. I can't stop for a moment. I am *so* behind . . .

12.30 What is wrong with this bleach bottle? Which way is the nozzle pointing, anyway? Why won't anything come out? OK, I'm going to squeeze it really, really hard—

12.32 Fuck. What has it done to my HAIR?

By three o'clock I am utterly knackered. I'm only halfway down my list and I can't see myself ever making it to the end. I don't know how people clean houses. It's the hardest job I've ever done, ever.

Right now I'm standing on a chair, cleaning the mirror in the drawing room. But the more I rub, the more smeary it gets.

I keep catching glances of myself in the glass. My hair is sticking out wildly, with a huge grotesque streak of greeny-blonde where I splashed the bleach. My face is bright red and sheeny, my hands are pink and sore from scrubbing and my eyes are bloodshot.

Why won't it get clean? Why? 'Get clean!' I cry, practically sobbing in frustration.

'Samantha.'

Abruptly I stop rubbing, to see Nathaniel standing in the doorway, looking at the smeary glass. 'Have you tried vinegar?'

'*Vinegar?*' I stare at him in suspicion.

'It cuts through the grease,' he adds. 'It's good on glass.'

'Oh. Right. Yes, I knew that.'

Nathaniel shakes his head. 'No, you didn't.'

I look at his adamant face. There's no point pretending any more. He knows I've never cleaned a house in my life.

'You're right,' I admit at last. 'I didn't.'

As I get down off the chair I feel wobbly with fatigue.

'You should have a break,' says Nathaniel firmly. 'You've been at it all day, I've seen you. Did you have any lunch?'

'No time.'

I sink down onto a chair, feeling suddenly too drained to move.

'It's . . . harder than I thought,' I say at last. 'A lot harder.'

'Uh huh.' He nods. 'What happened to your hair?'

'Bleach,' I say shortly. 'Cleaning the loo.'

He gives a muffled snort of laughter but I don't look up. To be honest, I'm beyond caring.

'I can't do it.' The words come out before I can stop them. 'I can't do this job. I'm . . . hopeless.'

'Sure you can.' He rifles in his rucksack and produces a can of Coke. 'Have this. You can't work on no fuel.'

'Thanks,' I say, taking it gratefully.

'The offer still stands,' he adds after a pause. 'My mother will give you lessons if you like.'

'Really?' I wipe my mouth, push back my sweaty hair and look up at him. 'She'd . . . do that?'

'She likes a challenge, my mum.' Nathaniel gives a little smile. 'She'll teach you your way around a kitchen. And anything else you need to know.' He glances quizzically towards the smeary mirror.

'That would be great,' I say humbly. 'I really appreciate it. Thanks.'

Five

I WAKE UP ON SATURDAY, heart pounding, and leap to my feet, my mind racing with everything I have to do . . .

And then it stops, like a car screeching to a halt. For a moment I can't move. Then, hesitantly, I sink back into bed, overcome by the weirdest, most extraordinary feeling I've ever experienced.

I have nothing to do. It's my day off. No one has any hold over me. This is my own time. *My own time.*

I check the time—and it's only 7.15 a.m. The whole day stretches before me like a clean sheet of paper. What shall I do?

I'm already sketching out a timetable for the day in my head. An hour wallowing in the bath and getting dressed. An hour lingering over breakfast. An hour reading the paper. I'm going to have the laziest, most indolent, most enjoyable morning I've ever had in my adult life.

As I head into the bathroom, I can feel muscles twinging with pain all over my body. They really should market house-cleaning as a workout. I run a deep warm bath and slosh in some of Trish's bath oil, then step into the scented water and lie back happily.

I close my eyes, letting the water lap my shoulders, and let time waft past in great swathes. I think I even fall asleep for a while. I have never spent so long in a bath in my entire life.

At last I open my eyes, reach for a towel and get out again. As I'm starting to dry myself off I reach for my watch, just out of curiosity.

It's 7.30 a.m. *What?* I was only fifteen minutes?

I feel a flash of astonishment. How on earth can I have only taken fifteen minutes? I stand, dripping, in indecision for a moment, wondering if I should get back in again and do it all again, more slowly.

But no. That would be too weird. It doesn't matter. I'll just make sure I take my time properly over breakfast. Really *enjoy* it.

At least I have some clothes to put on. Trish took me out last night to a shopping centre a few miles away, so I could stock up on underwear and shorts and summer dresses. She told me she'd leave me to it—then ended up bossing me about and picking everything out for me . . . and somehow I ended up with not a single item in black.

I cautiously put on a pink slip dress and pair of sandals, and look at myself. I've never worn pink before in my life. But to my amazement I don't look too bad! Apart from the huge streak of bleach in my hair. I'm going to have to do something about that.

As I make my way along the corridor, there's no sound from the Geigers' bedroom. I move silently past the door, feeling suddenly awkward. It'll be a bit strange, being in their house all weekend, with nothing to do. I'd better go out later. Get out of their way.

The kitchen is as silent and gleamy as ever, but it's starting to feel slightly less intimidating. I know my way around the kettle and the toaster, if nothing else. I'll have toast for breakfast, with orange and ginger marmalade, and a nice cup of coffee. And I'll read the paper from cover to cover. That'll take me to about eleven o'clock and then I can think about what else to do.

I find a copy of *The Times* on the doormat, and bring it back to the kitchen just as my toast is popping up.

This is the life.

I sit by the window, crunching toast, sipping coffee and leafing through the paper in a leisurely way. At last, after devouring three slices, two cups of coffee and all the Saturday sections, I stretch my arms in a big yawn and glance at the clock.

I don't believe it. It's only 7.56.

What is wrong with me? I was supposed to take *hours* over breakfast. I was supposed to be sitting there all morning. Not get everything finished in twenty minutes flat.

OK . . . never mind. Let's not stress about it. What do people do on days off? My mind scrolls through a series of images from TV. I could make another cup of coffee? But I've already had two. I could read the paper again? But I have an almost photographic memory. So re-reading things is a bit pointless.

My gaze drifts outside to the garden, where a squirrel is perched on a stone pillar. Maybe I'll go outside. Enjoy the garden and the wildlife and the early-morning dew. Good idea.

Except the trouble with early-morning dew is it gets all over your feet. As I pick my way over the damp grass, I'm already wishing I hadn't put on open-toed sandals. Or that I'd waited till later for my little stroll.

The garden is a lot bigger than I'd appreciated. I walk down the lawn towards an ornamental hedge where everything seems to finish, only to realise there's a whole further section beyond it, with an orchard at the end and some sort of walled garden to my left.

It's a stunning garden. Even I can see that. The flowers are vivid without being garish, every wall is covered with some beautiful creeper or vine, and as I walk towards the orchard I can see little golden pears hanging from the branches of trees.

I stroll through the fruit trees towards a huge, square, brown patch of earth with plants growing in serried rows. These must be the vegetables. I prod one of them cautiously with my foot. It could be a cabbage or a lettuce. To be honest, it could be an alien. I have no idea.

I wander round a bit longer, then sit down on a wooden bench.

Now what? I look at my watch. Still only 8.16. I can't do this. I can't do nothing all day. I'll have to go and buy another paper from the village shop. If they've got *War and Peace*, I'll buy that too. I get up and am starting to head briskly back across the lawn when a bleep from my pocket makes me stop still.

It's my mobile. It's received a text. I pull it out and look at it, feeling edgy. I haven't had any contact with the outside world for over a day.

I know there are other texts in my phone—but I haven't read any of them. I know there are messages in my voicemail—but I haven't listened to a single one. I don't want to know. I'm blocking it all out.

But now my curiosity has been sparked. As I stand there on the early-morning lawn, I can feel my mental self being dragged out of this garden, back to London, back to the office. A lot can happen in twenty-four hours. Things can change. Everything could have turned out positive in some way. Or . . . become even worse. They're prosecuting me.

The tension is rising inside me. I'm gripping my phone more and more tightly. I have to know. Good or bad. I flip open the phone and find the text. It's from a number I don't even recognise.

Feeling a little sick, I press OK to read.

hi samantha, nathaniel here.

Nathaniel? *Nathaniel?* My relief is so huge, I laugh out loud. Of course! I gave him my mobile number yesterday for his mother. I scroll down to read the rest of the message.

if you're interested, mum could start cooking lessons today. nat

Cooking lessons. I feel a spark of delight. That's it. The perfect way to fill the day. I press Reply and quickly text:

would love to. thanks. sam.

I send it with a little smile. This is fun. A minute or two later, the phone bleeps again.

what time? is 11 too early? nat

I look at my watch. Eleven o'clock is still two and a half hours away.

shall we make it 10? sam

At five to ten I'm ready in the hall. Nathaniel's mother's house is apparently tricky to find, so the plan is to meet here and he'll walk me over. As I check my reflection in the hall mirror, I wince. The streak of bleach is as obvious as ever. Maybe I could walk along with my hand carelessly positioned at my head, as if I'm thinking hard. I attempt a few casual, pensive poses in the mirror.

'Is your head all right?'

I swivel round in shock to see Nathaniel at the open door, wearing a plaid shirt and jeans.

'Er . . . fine,' I say, my hand still glued to my head. 'I was just . . .'

Oh, there's no point. I bring my hand down from my hair and Nathaniel regards the streak for a moment.

'It looks nice,' he says. 'Like a badger.'

'A *badger?*' I say, affronted. 'I don't look like a badger.'

'Badgers are beautiful creatures,' says Nathaniel with a shrug. 'I'd rather look like a badger than a stoat.'

Hang on. Since when was my choice between badger or stoat?

'Perhaps we should go,' I say with dignity. I pick up my bag and give one last glance in the mirror as I reach for the door.

OK. Maybe I look a little bit like a badger.

The summer air is already warming up outside, and as we turn out of the drive I realise this is the first time I've been out of the Geigers' grounds since I arrived here—apart from the shopping trip with Trish, when I was too busy scrabbling for her Celine Dion CD to notice my surroundings. Nathaniel has turned left and is striding easily along the road—but I can't move. I'm gazing at the sight in front of me, my jaw wide open. This village is absolutely *stunning*.

I look around, taking in the old, honey-coloured stone walls. The rows of ancient cottages with steeply pitched roofs. The river lined with willow trees. Up ahead is the pub I noticed on the first day, decorated with hanging baskets. Everything is soft and mellow and feels like it's been here for hundreds of years.

'Samantha?'

Nathaniel has finally noticed I'm pinned to the spot.

'I'm sorry.' I hurry to join him. 'It's just such a beautiful place!'

'Didn't you see any of this as you arrived?' Nathaniel regards me with amusement. 'Did you just appear in a bubble?'

I think back to that panicked, dazed, desperate journey. Getting off the train, my head throbbing, my vision a blur.

'Kind of.' I try to match his relaxed pace. 'So, did you grow up here?'

'Yup. I came back when my dad got ill. Then he died, and I had to sort things out. Take care of Mum. Everything was in a mess.'

'I'm sorry,' I say awkwardly. 'Do you have any other family?'

'My brother Jake. He came back for a week.' Nathaniel hesitates. 'He runs his own business. Very successful.'

His voice is as easy as ever, but I can detect a thread of . . . something. Maybe I won't ask any more about his family.

'Well, *I'd* live here,' I say with enthusiasm.

Nathaniel gives me an odd look. 'You do live here,' he reminds me.

I feel a tweak of surprise. I suppose he's right. Technically, I do.

I walk on a few paces, trying to process this new thought. I've never lived anywhere except London before, apart from my three years at Cambridge. I've always had an NW postcode. An 0207 number. That's who I am. That's who I . . . was.

But already the old me is feeling more distant. I'm still feeling sore and bruised. But at the same time . . . I feel more alive with possibility than I have ever done. My ribcage expands widely as I breathe in the country air and I suddenly feel a wave of optimism.

'Here we are.' Nathaniel pushes open an old iron gate and gestures me to go up a stone path towards a little cottage with blue flowered curtains at the windows. 'Come and meet your cooking teacher.'

Nathaniel's mother is nothing like I expected. I was picturing some cosy Mrs Tiggywinkle character with grey hair in a bun and half-moon spectacles. Instead, I'm looking at a wiry woman with a vivid, pretty face. Her greying hair is in plaits either side of her face, she's wearing an apron over jeans, T-shirt and espadrilles.

'Mum.' Nathaniel grins and pushes me forward into the kitchen. 'Here she is. This is Samantha. Samantha . . . my mum. Iris.'

'Samantha. Welcome.' I can see her taking me in, head to foot. 'So, you want to learn how to cook.' Her tone is friendly but businesslike.

'Yes.' I smile. 'Please.'

'And how much cooking have you done before?' Iris smiles at me. 'What can you make? What are your basics?'

'Well . . . I can . . . I can make . . . um . . . toast,' I say.

'*Toast?*' She looks taken aback. 'Just toast?'

'And crumpets,' I add quickly. 'Tea cakes . . . anything that goes in a toaster, really . . .'

'But what about *cooking*?' She looks at me more carefully. 'What about, say . . . an omelette? Surely you can cook an omelette?'

I swallow. 'Not really.'

Iris's expression is so incredulous I feel my cheeks flame. 'I never did home economics at school,' I explain.

'But your mother, surely . . . or your grandmother . . .' She breaks off as I shake my head. '*Anyone?*'

I bite my lip. Iris exhales sharply as though taking in the situation for the first time. 'So you can't cook anything at all. And what have you promised to make for the Geigers?'

Oh God.

'Trish wanted a week's worth of menus. So I . . . um . . . gave her one based on this.' Sheepishly I get the crumpled Maxim's menu out of my bag and hand it to her.

'Braised lamb and baby onion assemblé with a fondant potato and goat's cheese crust, accompanied by cardamom spinach purée,' she reads out, in tones of disbelief.

I hear a snort and look up to see Nathaniel in fits of laughter.

'It was all I had!' I exclaim defensively. 'What was I going to say, fish fingers and chips?'

'"Assemblé" is just flannel.' Iris is still perusing the sheet. 'That's souped-up shepherd's pie. We can teach you that. And the braised trout with almonds is straightforward enough . . .' She runs her finger further down the page then at last looks up, a frown creasing her brow. 'I can teach you these dishes, Samantha. But it isn't going to be easy.'

'I'm a quick learner.' I lean forward. 'And I'll work hard.'

'All right,' says Iris at last. 'Let's get you cooking.'

She reaches into a cupboard for a set of weighing scales and I take the opportunity to delve into my bag for a pad of file paper and a pen. As Iris turns round and sees me, she looks bemused.

'What's that for?' She jerks her head at the file paper.

'So I can take notes,' I explain.

'Samantha, you're not going to be taking notes,' she says. 'Cooking isn't about writing down. It's about tasting. Feeling. Touching. Smelling.'

'Right.' I nod intelligently.

I must remember that. I quickly uncap my pen and scribble down *Cooking = all about tasting, smelling, feeling etc.* I cap my pen again and look up. Iris is regarding me with incredulity.

'Tasting,' she says, removing my pen and paper from my hands. 'Not writing. You need to use your senses. Your instincts.'

She lifts the lid off a pot gently steaming on the cooker and dips a spoon into it. 'Taste this.'

Gingerly I take the spoon in my mouth. 'Gravy,' I say at once.

Iris shakes her head. 'Don't tell me what you think it is. Tell me what you can taste.'

I stare at her, puzzled. 'I can taste . . . gravy.'

Her expression doesn't change. She's waiting for something else.

'Er . . . meat?' I hazard.

'Samantha, don't think about identifying the taste. Just tell me what the sensation is.' Iris holds the spoon out a second time. 'Taste it again— and this time close your eyes.'

'OK.' I take a mouthful and close my eyes obediently.

'Concentrate on the flavours. Nothing else.' Iris's voice is in my ear.

Eyes tight shut, I focus all my attention on my mouth.

'It's salty and meaty . . .' I say slowly, without opening my eyes. 'And sweet . . . and . . . and almost fruity? Like cherries?'

I open my eyes. Iris is scrutinising me intently. Behind her I suddenly notice Nathaniel, also watching. At the sight of him, I feel a tad flustered. Tasting gravy with your eyes closed is a fairly intimate thing to do, it turns out. I'm not sure I want anyone watching me.

Iris seems to understand. 'Nathaniel,' she says briskly, 'we're going to need ingredients for all these dishes.' She scribbles a long list and hands it to him. 'Run down and get these for us, love.'

As he leaves the room, she looks at me, a faint smile on her lips. 'That was much better. Here, get a pinny on.' She hands me a red-and-white striped apron and I tie it around myself.

'It's so kind of you to help me,' I say hesitantly as she gets out onions and some orange vegetable I don't recognise. 'I'm really grateful.'

'I like a challenge.' Her eyes sparkle at me. 'And I liked the sound of you.' Iris draws down a heavy wooden chopping board. 'Nathaniel told me how you got yourself out of your mess the other night. That took some spirit.'

'I had to do something.' I give her a rueful smile.

'And they offered you a pay rise as a result. Wonderful.' As she smiles, fine lines appear round her eyes. 'Trish Geiger is a very foolish woman.'

'I like Trish,' I say, feeling a stab of loyalty.

'So do I.' Iris nods. 'She's been very supportive to Nathaniel. But you must have noticed she has little or no brain.' She sounds so matter-of-fact I want to giggle. I watch as she puts a huge, gleaming pot on the stove, then turns and looks at me. 'So you've taken them in completely.'

'Yes.' I smile. 'They have no idea who I am.'

'And who are you?'

Her question takes me completely by surprise. I open my mouth but no words come out.

'Is your name really Samantha?'

'Yes!' I say in shock.

'That was a little blunt.' Iris lifts a hand in acknowledgment. 'But a girl arrives in the middle of the countryside out of nowhere and takes a job she can't do . . .' She pauses as though choosing her words. 'Nathaniel tells me you've got out of a bad relationship?'

'Yes,' I mumble. I can feel Iris's shrewd gaze, appraising me.

'You don't want to talk about it, do you?'

'Not really. No. I don't.'

As I look up there's a thread of understanding in her eyes.

'That's fine by me.' She picks up a knife. 'Now, let's start. Roll up your sleeves, tie back your hair and wash your hands. I'm going to teach you to chop an onion.'

We spend all weekend cooking.

I learn to slice an onion finely, turn it the other way and produce tiny dice. I learn to chop herbs with a rounded blade. I learn how to rub flour and ground ginger into chunks of meat, then drop the pieces into a spitting-hot, cast-iron pan. I learn the trick of blanching French beans in boiling water before sautéing them in butter.

A week ago I didn't know what 'sauté' even meant.

On Sunday afternoon, under Iris's calm guidance, I make roast chicken with sage and onion stuffing, steamed broccoli, cumin-scented carrots and roast potatoes. As I watch Nathaniel carrying the serving dish bearing the roast chicken, all crispy golden, to the table, I feel a glow of pride. My first roast chicken.

'Wine for the cooks,' says Iris, producing a bottle from the fridge and uncorking it. She pours me a glass, then gestures to the table. 'Sit down, Samantha. You've done enough for one weekend.'

As I sink down into the nearest chair, I realise for the first time how exhausted I am.

Nathaniel carves the chicken with expert ease, and Iris dishes out the vegetables. When we're all served she sits down and raises her glass.

'To you, Samantha. You've done splendidly.'

'Thanks.' I smile and am about to sip my wine when I realise the other two aren't moving.

'And to Ben,' Iris adds softly.

'On Sundays we always remember Dad,' Nathaniel explains.

'Oh.' I hesitate, then raise my glass.

'Now.' Iris's eyes glint and she puts her glass down. 'The moment of truth.' She takes a bite of chicken and I try to hide my nerves.

'Very good.' She nods at last. 'Very good indeed.'

I can't help a beam spreading across my face.

I sit in the glow of the evening light, not talking much but eating and listening to the other two chat. The atmosphere is so relaxed and easy, so different from any meal I've ever had at home. No one's on the phone. No one's rushing to get anywhere else. I could sit here all night.

As the meal is finally drawing to a close, I clear my throat.

'Iris, I just want to say thank you again.'

'I enjoyed it. Next weekend, we'll make lasagne. And gnocchi!' Iris takes a sip of wine. 'We'll have an Italian weekend.'

'*Next* weekend?' I stare at her. 'But—'

'You don't think you've finished, do you?' She hoots with laughter. 'I've only just started on you! Now, what else do you need help with? Cleaning? Washing?'

I feel a twinge of embarrassment. Iris clearly knows exactly how much of a mess I got myself into yesterday.

'I'm not really sure how to use the washing machine,' I admit at last.

'We'll cover that.' She nods. 'I'll pop up to the house when they're out and have a look at it.'

'And I can't sew on buttons . . .'

'Buttons.' She reaches for a piece of paper and a pencil, and writes it down, still munching. 'What about ironing?' She looks up, suddenly alert. 'You must have had to iron. How did you wriggle out of that one?'

'I'm sending it out to Stacey Nicholson,' I confess. 'In the village. She charges three pounds a shirt.'

'Stacey Nicholson?' Iris puts her pencil down. 'Samantha, you are *not* paying Stacey Nicholson to do your ironing. She's fifteen years old!' She pushes back her chair, looking galvanised. 'You're going to learn how to do it yourself. I'll teach you. Anyone can iron.' She reaches into a little side room, pulls out an old ironing board covered in flowery material and sets it up, then beckons me over. 'What do you have to iron?'

'Mr Geiger's shirts, mainly,' I say, nervously.

She plugs in an iron and turns the dial. 'Hot, for cotton. Wait for the iron to heat up. Now, I'll show you the right way to tackle a shirt . . .'

She rootles, frowning, in a pile of clean laundry in the little room. 'Shirts . . . shirts . . . Nathaniel, take off your shirt a moment.'

I stiffen. As I glance at Nathaniel I see he has stiffened too.

'Mum!' He gives an awkward laugh.

'Oh, don't be ridiculous, love,' says Iris impatiently. 'You can take off your shirt for a moment. No one's embarrassed. You're not embarrassed, are you, Samantha?'

'Um . . .' My voice is a little grainy. 'Um . . . no, of course not . . .'

'Now, this is your steam.' She presses a button on the iron and a jet of steam shoots into the air. 'Always check your steam compartment has water . . . Nathaniel! I'm waiting!'

Through the steam I can see Nathaniel slowly unbuttoning his shirt. I catch a flash of smooth tanned skin and hastily lower my gaze.

Let's not be adolescent about this. So he's taking off his shirt. It's no big deal.

He tosses the shirt to his mother, who catches it deftly. My eyes are studiously fixed downwards. I'm not going to look at him.

'Start with the collar . . .' Iris is smoothing the shirt out on the ironing board. 'Now, you don't have to press hard.' She guides my hand as the iron glides over the fabric. 'Keep a smooth touch . . .'

This is ridiculous. I'm an adult, mature woman. I can look at a man with no shirt on without falling to bits. What I'll do is . . . just take a casual peek. Yes. And get this out of my mind.

'Now the yoke.' Iris turns the shirt round on the board and I start pressing again. 'Very good . . . on to the cuffs now . . .'

I lift the shirt-tail to flip it over—and as I do so, accidentally-on-purpose raise my eyes. Sweet Jesus. I'm not sure the whole getting-it-out-of-my-mind plan is going to work after all.

'Samantha?' Iris grabs the iron from me. 'You're scorching the shirt!'

'Oh!' I come to. 'Sorry. I . . . I lost concentration.'

'Your cheeks seem very flushed.' Iris puts a curious hand to my cheek. 'Are you all right, sweetie?'

'Must be the . . . steam.' I start ironing again, my face like a furnace.

Iris continues to instruct me, but I don't hear a word. As I move the iron blindly back and forth, I'm pondering obsessively on a) Nathaniel, b) Nathaniel without his shirt on, c) whether Nathaniel has a girlfriend.

At last I shake out his ironed shirt, perfectly done with all the creases in the right places.

'Very good!' says Iris, applauding. 'After some practice you'll be able to do that in four minutes flat.'

'Looks great,' Nathaniel smiles, holding out a hand. 'Thanks.'

'That's OK!' I manage in a strangled squawk, and hastily look away again, my heart thumping.

Great. One glimpse of his body and I have a full-blown crush.

Six

HE DOESN'T HAVE a girlfriend. I managed to get that information out of Trish last night, under the guise of asking about all the neighbours. The way is clear. I just need a strategy.

As I shower and get dressed the next morning, I'm totally fixated by thoughts of Nathaniel. I'm aware I've reverted to the behaviour of a fourteen-year-old adolescent; that next I'll be doodling *Samantha loves Nathaniel* with a love heart dotting the 'i'. But I don't care. It's not as though being a mature professional was working out so great for me.

I brush my hair, looking out at the misty green fields, and feel an inexplicable light-heartedness. I have no reason to feel so happy. On paper, everything is still catastrophic. My high-flying career is over. I'm earning a fraction of what I used to, for a job which involves picking other people's dirty underwear off the floor. And yet I can't help humming as I straighten my bed.

My life has changed and I'm changing with it. I've never gone after a man before. But then, until yesterday I'd never basted a chicken before. If I can do that, I can ask a man out, surely? The old Samantha would have sat back and waited to be approached. Well, not the new Samantha. I've seen the dating shows on TV, it's all about looks and body language and flirty conversation.

I reach for my make-up bag, and spend about ten minutes alternately applying and removing make-up, until I've got something which looks natural and subtle, yet defined.

Now to the body language. I wrinkle up my forehead, trying to remember the rules from TV. If a woman is attracted to a man, her pupils will dilate. Also, she will unconsciously lean forward, laugh at his jokes and expose her wrists and palms. Experimentally I lean towards my reflection, holding out my hands as I do so. I try adding a flirty laugh. 'Ha ha ha!' I'm really not sure this is adding to my chances.

I head downstairs, draw back the curtains. Nathaniel is striding across the lawn. Oh no. Full, one hundred per cent crush alert.

I cannot take my eyes off him. The sunlight is catching the ends of his tawny hair and he's wearing ancient, faded jeans. As I watch, he picks up some huge sack of something, swings it round easily and throws it onto something that might be a compost heap.

My mind is suddenly filled with a fantasy of him picking me up in exactly the same way. Swinging me round easily in his big strong arms. I mean, I can't be *that* much heavier than a sack of potatoes—

'So, how was your weekend off, Samantha?' Trish breaks my thoughts. 'We barely saw you! Did you go into town?'

'I went to Nathaniel's house,' I reply without thinking.

'Nathaniel?' Trish sounds astonished. 'The *gardener*? Why?'

Immediately I realise my huge mistake. I can't exactly say 'To have cooking lessons'. I stare back at her foolishly for a few moments, trying to fabricate an instant, convincing reason.

'Just . . . to say hello, really . . .' I say at last, aware that I sound tongue-tied. And also that my cheeks are turning pink.

Trish's face suddenly snaps in comprehension and her eyes open very wide, like dinner plates. 'Oh, I *see*,' she says. 'How *adorable!*'

'No!' I say quickly. 'It's not . . . Honestly . . .'

'Don't worry!' Trish cuts me off emphatically. 'I won't say a *word*. I am discretion itself.' She puts a finger to her lips. 'You can rely on me.'

Before I can say anything else she picks up her coffee and heads out of the kitchen. That was awkward. But I suppose it doesn't really matter. As long as she doesn't say anything inappropriate to Nathaniel.

Then I realise I'm being stupid. Of *course* she'll say something inappropriate to Nathaniel. And then who knows what he'll think.

I must go and make the situation quite clear to him. That Trish misunderstood me, and I don't have a crush on him or anything like that.

Whilst, obviously, making it clear that I do.

I force myself to wait until I've done breakfast for Trish and Eddie, mixed up some olive oil and lemon zest, and put tonight's sea bream fillets into it, just as Iris taught me.

Then I head out into the garden, holding a basket I found in the larder. If Trish wants to know what I'm doing, I'm gathering herbs for cooking.

I find Nathaniel in the orchard, standing on a ladder, tying some rope round a tree. As I make my way towards him I suddenly start feeling ridiculously nervous. My mouth feels dry—and did my legs just *wobble*?

Ignoring my jitters as best I can, I walk up to the ladder, toss back my hair and smile up at him, trying not to squint in the sun. 'Hi!'

'Hi.' Nathaniel smiles down. 'How's it going?'

'Fine, thanks! Much better. No disasters yet . . . I was after some . . . rosemary.' I gesture to my basket. 'If you have any?'

'Sure. I'll cut you some.' He jumps down off the ladder and we start walking along the path towards the herb garden.

It's totally silent, down here away from the house, apart from the odd buzzing insect and the crunch of gravel on the path. I try to think of something light and easy to say, but my brain is blank.

'Um . . . lovely herbs!' I manage at last, gesturing around the garden in genuine admiration. It's laid out in a hexagonal shape, with little paths between the sections. 'Did you do all this? It's amazing.'

'Thanks. I'm pleased with it.' Nathaniel smiles.

He pulls out a pair of secateurs from an old leather holster-type thing and starts clipping at a dark green, spiky bush.

My heart starts to thump. I have to say what I've come to say.

'So . . . um . . . it's really weird,' I begin as lightly as I can, fingering the scented leaves of some bushy plant. 'But Trish seems to have got the wrong idea about us! She seems to think we're . . . You know.'

'Ah.' He nods, his face averted.

'Which is obviously . . . ridiculous!' I add with another laugh.

'Well, of course.' At last Nathaniel looks at me properly, his tanned forehead creased in a frown. 'You won't be wanting to get into anything for a while. Not so soon after a bad relationship.'

I look at him blankly. What on earth—oh yes. My bad relationship.

'Right,' I say after a pause. 'Yes, that.'

Dammit. Why did I invent a bad relationship? What was I *thinking*?

'Actually'—I force myself to sound careless—'the relationship wasn't *that* bad. In fact, I think I've pretty much got over it.'

'You've got over a seven-year relationship in a week?' Nathaniel puts a fragrant bundle of rosemary into my arms. He looks as though he's trying to fathom me out.

'Mum said . . .' He stops, looking awkward.

'What?' I say, a little breathless.

'Mum wondered if you'd been . . . badly treated.' He shifts his gaze away. 'You're so tense and twitchy.'

'I'm not tense and twitchy!' I retort at once.

Maybe that was a little tense and twitchy.

'I'm naturally twitchy,' I explain. 'But I wasn't badly treated or anything like that. I was just . . . I always felt . . . trapped.'

The word comes out to my own surprise.

I have a flash of my life at Carter Spink. Practically living at the office. Taking work home with me. Answering emails at every hour. Maybe I did feel a little bit trapped.

'But I'm fine now.' I shake back my hair. 'Ready to move on . . . and start a new relationship . . . or something more casual . . . whatever . . . '

A one-night stand would do . . .

I gaze up at him, trying to dilate my pupils.

'You probably shouldn't rush into anything new,' Nathaniel says. He moves away without meeting my eye and starts examining a shrub.

There's an awkwardness in his back. I feel a rush of blood to my face as it hits me. He doesn't want to go out with me.

Aargh. This is hideous. Here I am, basically *offering* myself to him . . . And he's trying to let me know he's not interested. I'm mortified.

'You're right,' I say, flustered. 'It's . . . far too soon to think about anything like that. In fact, it would be a terrible idea. I'm just going to focus on my new job. Cooking and . . . and . . . so forth. I must get on. Thanks for the rosemary.'

'Any time,' says Nathaniel.

Clasping the bundle more tightly, I turn on my heel, and stride back along the gravel path up to the house.

I am *beyond* embarrassed. So much for a whole new Samantha.

Anyway, I don't care. It's for the best, really. Because I *do* have to concentrate on my work. As soon as I get back to the house I set up the ironing board, plug in the iron, turn on the radio and make a nice strong cup of coffee. This is going to be my focus from now on. Getting my tasks for the day done. Not some stupid ridiculous crush on the gardener. I'm being paid to do a job here and I'm going to do it.

By midmorning I've ironed ten shirts, put a load of laundry on and hoovered the conservatory. By lunchtime, I've dusted and hoovered all the downstairs rooms and polished all the mirrors with vinegar. By tea time, I've put on another load of laundry, shredded my vegetables in the food processor, measured out the wild rice to be steamed, and carefully prepared four filo pastry cases for my tartes de fruits, as Iris taught me.

By seven o'clock I've thrown away one lot of burnt filo cases, baked another four, topped them with strawberries and finished them with heated-up apricot jam. I've pan-fried the vegetable shreds in olive oil and garlic till they're soft. I've blanched my French beans. I've put the sea bream in the oven.

My face is bright red and my heart is beating fast and I'm moving round the kitchen in a kind of speeded-up reality . . . but I kind of feel OK. In fact, I feel almost exhilarated. Here I am, actually cooking a meal all on my own . . . and I'm just about on top of it!

I've laid the dining table with the best china I could find and put candles in the silver candlesticks. I've got a bottle of Prosecco waiting in the fridge and heated plates waiting in the oven, and I've even put Trish's CD of Enrique Iglesias love songs in the player. I feel like I'm throwing my first-ever dinner party.

With a pleasant flutter in my stomach, I smooth down my apron, push open the kitchen door and call 'Mrs Geiger? Mr Geiger?'

There's absolutely no reply. I would have thought they'd be hovering around the kitchen by now. Where *are* they?

I investigate the rooms on the ground floor, but they're all empty. Cautiously, I start to advance up the stairs.

'Er . . . Mrs Geiger?' I call hesitantly. 'Dinner's served.'

Suddenly a door is flung open violently. 'What about *Portugal*?' Trish shrieks. 'Do you remember *that*?' She strides out of the room in a whirlwind of pink and stops as she sees me.

'Um, dinner's ready,' I mumble, my eyes fixed on the carpet. 'Madam.'

'If you mention *bloody* Portugal one more *bloody* time—' Eddie comes marching out of the room.

'Eddie!' Trish cuts him off savagely, then gives a tiny nod towards me. '*Pas devant.*'

'What?' says Eddie, scowling.

'*Pas devant les . . . les . . .*' She wheels her hands, as though trying to conjure the missing word.

'*Domestiques?*' I offer awkwardly.

Trish shoots me a flinty look, then draws herself up with dignity. 'I shall be in my room.'

'It's my bloody room too!' says Eddie furiously, but the door has already banged shut.

'Um . . . I've made dinner . . .' I venture, but Eddie stalks to the stairs, ignoring me.

I feel a swell of dismay. If the sea bream isn't eaten soon it'll get all shrivelled.

'Mrs Geiger?' I knock on her door. 'I'm just worried the dinner will spoil—'

'So what?' comes back her muffled voice. 'I'm not in the mood for eating.'

I stare at the door in disbelief. I've spent all bloody day cooking dinner for them. It's all ready. The candles are lit, the plates are in the oven. They can't just not eat it.

'You *have* to eat!' I cry out, and Eddie stops, halfway down the stairs. The bedroom door opens and Trish looks out in astonishment.

'What?' she says.

OK. Play this one carefully.

'Everyone has to eat,' I improvise. 'It's a human need. So why not discuss your differences over a meal? Or put them on hold! Have a glass of wine and relax and agree not to mention . . . er . . . Portugal.'

As I say the word, I can feel hackles rising.

'I'm not the one who mentioned it,' growls Eddie.

'I only mentioned it because you were so *insensitive* . . .' Trish's voice is rising and she brushes a sudden tear from her eye. 'How do you think *I* feel, being your . . . trophy wife?'

Trophy? I must not laugh.

'Trish.' To my astonishment, Eddie is hurrying up the stairs as fast as his paunch will allow. 'Don't you *ever* say that.' He grips her shoulders and looks her fiercely in the eye. 'We've always been a partnership. You know that.'

'I know,' whispers Trish.

She's gazing up at Eddie as though no one else exists, and I suddenly feel a little pang. They really are in love.

'Let's go and eat,' says Eddie finally. 'Samantha was right. We should have a nice meal together. Sit down and talk it over.'

Thank God for that. The sea bream will still be just about OK . . . I just need to put the sauce in a jug . . .

'All right, let's.' Trish sniffs. 'Samantha, we'll be out to dinner tonight.'

My smile freezes. 'But . . . I've cooked!' I say quickly. 'It's done.'

'Oh well, never mind.' Trish makes a flapping gesture. 'Eat it yourself.'

'But it's all ready for you! Roasted fish, julienned vegetables . . .'

'Where shall we go?' says Trish to Eddie, not listening to a word. 'Shall we try to get in at the Mill House?'

As I stand there in stupefaction, she disappears into the bedroom, followed by Eddie. The door closes and I'm left on the landing.

My dinner party's ruined.

When they've roared out of the drive in Eddie's Porsche, I go into the dining room and slowly clear everything up. I put away the crystal glasses and fold up the napkins and blow out the candles. Then I head back into the kitchen and look for a moment at all my dishes, set out ready for action. My sauce, still bubbling away on the hob. My carved-lemon-slice garnishes. I was so proud of everything.

Anyway, there's nothing I can do about it.

My sea bream are looking pretty sorry for themselves, but I put one onto a plate and pour myself a glass of wine. I sit at the table, cut myself a piece of bream and raise it to my mouth. Then I put my knife and fork down without even tasting it. I'm not hungry.

A whole wasted day. And tomorrow I've got to do it all over again.

What am I doing here? I mean, really. What am I doing? Why am I not walking out right now and getting on a train back to London?

As I'm slumped there I become aware of a tapping at the open door. I look up to see Nathaniel leaning on the door frame, holding his rucksack. I feel a flash of embarrassment, as I remember this morning's encounter.

'I thought I'd come and see if you needed any help.' His eyes travel around the kitchen, at the dishes of untouched food. 'What happened?'

'They didn't eat it. They went out to dinner.'

'After you spent all day cooking for them?'

'It's their food. Their house. They can do what they like.'

I'm trying to sound careless and matter-of-fact. But I can still feel the disappointment, heavy inside me. Nathaniel puts down his rucksack, strides over to the cooker and inspects the sea bream. 'Looks good.'

'It looks like congealed, overcooked fish,' I correct him.

'My favourite.' He grins, but I'm not in the mood to smile back.

'Have some, then.' I gesture at the dish. 'No one else is going to eat it.'

'Well, then, shame to waste it.' He helps himself to everything, piling his plate ludicrously high, then pours himself a glass of wine and sits down opposite me at the table.

For a moment neither of us speaks. I'm not even looking at him.

'To you.' Nathaniel raises his glass. 'Congratulations.'

'Yeah, right.'

'Seriously, Samantha.' He waits patiently until I drag my eyes up from the floor. 'Whether they ate it or not, this is a real achievement. I mean, bloody hell.' His mouth twists humorously. 'Remember the last dinner you cooked in this kitchen?'

I give a reluctant smile. 'The lamb of doom, you mean.'

'The *chick peas*. I'll never forget those.' He takes a bite of fish, shaking his head incredulously. 'This is good, by the way.'

An image comes to me of those tiny blackened bullets; myself running around in frenzied chaos . . . and in spite of everything I want to giggle. I've already learned so much since then.

'Well, of course, I'd have been OK that night,' I say nonchalantly, 'if you hadn't insisted on *helping* me. I had it all under control till you got in my way.'

Nathaniel puts his fork down, still munching. For a few moments he looks at me, his blue eyes crinkled up with something—amusement, maybe. I can feel the heat rising in my cheeks, and as I glance downwards I notice that my hands are resting on the table, palms up.

And I'm leaning forward, I realise in sudden horror. My pupils are probably half a mile wide, too. I could not be any clearer if I wrote 'I fancy you' in felt-tip on my forehead.

I hastily move my hands to my lap, sit up straight and adopt a stony expression. I haven't got over this morning's mortification. In fact, I might take the opportunity to say something.

'So—' I begin, just as Nathaniel starts speaking too.

'Go on.' He gestures towards me and takes another bite of fish.

'Well.' I clear my throat. 'After our . . . conversation this morning, I was just going to say that you're right about relationships. Obviously I'm not ready for anything new yet. Or even interested. At all.'

There. That told him.

'What were you going to say?' I ask, pouring more wine into his glass.

'I was going to ask you out,' says Nathaniel, and I nearly flood the table with wine.

He what? The hands thing *worked*?

'But not to worry.' He takes a gulp of wine. 'I understand.'

Backtrack. I need to backtrack, very, very quickly. Yet subtly, so he doesn't actually *notice* I'm backtracking . . . oh, bugger it, I'll just be inconsistent. I'm a woman, I'm allowed to be.

'Nathaniel,' I force myself to say calmly, 'I'd love to go out with you.'

'Good.' He looks unperturbed. 'How's Friday night?'

'Perfect. I'll ask Trish and Eddie for the evening off.'

As I grin back I suddenly realise I feel hungry. I pull my plate of sea bream towards me, pick up my knife and fork and begin to eat.

Seven

I GET TO FRIDAY morning without any major calamities. At least, none that the Geigers know about.

There was the vegetable risotto disaster on Tuesday—but thank God I managed to get a last-minute substitute from the caterers. There was a peach camisole which, in hindsight, should have been ironed on a lower setting. There was the Dartington vase which I broke while trying to dust with the vacuum-cleaner attachment. But no one seems to have noticed it's gone yet. And the new one should arrive tomorrow.

So far, this week has only cost me £200, which is a vast improvement on last week.

I'm hanging out Eddie's damp underwear in the utility room, averting my eyes as best I can, when I hear Trish calling me.

'Samantha! Where *are* you?' She doesn't sound pleased, and I feel a quailing inside. What's she discovered? 'I *can't* have you walking around like that any more.' Trish arrives at the door of the utility room, shaking her head vigorously.

'I'm sorry?' I peer at her.

'Your *hair*.' She makes a face.

'Oh, right.' I touch the bleached patch with a grimace. 'I meant to get it done at the weekend—'

'You're having it done now,' she cuts across me. 'My hairdresser's here.'

'Now?' I stare at her. 'But . . . I've got hoovering to do.'

'You can make up the hours later. And I'll take the money out of your wages. Come on. Annabel's waiting!'

I guess I have no choice. I dump the rest of Eddie's underpants on the rack and follow her up the stairs.

'Now, I've been meaning to mention my cashmere cardigan,' Trish adds sternly as we reach the top. 'The cream one?'

Shit. Shit. She's found out I replaced it.

'I don't know what you've done to it.' Trish pushes open her bedroom door. 'But it looks *marvellous*. That little ink stain on the hem has completely disappeared! It's like new!'

'Right.' I give a smile of relief. 'Well . . . all part of the service!'

I follow Trish into the bedroom, where a thin woman with big blonde hair, white jeans and a gold chain belt is setting up a chair in the middle of the floor.

'Hello!' She looks up, cigarette in hand, and I realise that she's about sixty years old. She comes forward, surveys my hair and winces.

'What's all this? Thought you'd try the streaky look?' She gives a raucous laugh at her own joke.

'It was a . . . bleach accident.'

'Accident!' She runs her fingers through my hair, clicking. 'Well, it can't stay this colour. We'd better go a nice blonde.'

'I've never been blonde,' I say in alarm. 'I'm not really sure—'

'You've got the colouring for it.' She's brushing my hair out.

'Well, as long as it's not *too* blonde,' I say hurriedly. 'Not . . . you know, that fake, tarty, platinum blonde . . .'

I trail off as I realise both the other women in the room have fake, tarty, platinum-blonde hair.

I sit down on the chair, wrap a towel round my shoulders and try not to flinch as Annabel briskly pastes some chemical-smelling mixture on my head and layers in what feels like a thousand bits of silver foil.

Blonde. Oh God. What am I *doing*?

Annabel puts a magazine in my hand. Behind, Trish is opening a bottle of champagne. 'You'll look lovely. Pretty girl like you should *do* something with her hair. Now, read us our signs.'

'Signs?' I say in bewilderment.

'Horoscopes!' Annabel clicks her tongue. 'Not the brightest penny, is she?' she adds in an undertone to Trish.

'She is a little dim,' Trish murmurs back. 'But *marvellous* at laundry.'

So this is what being a lady of leisure is like. Sitting with foil in your hair, drinking Buck's Fizz and reading glossy magazines. I haven't read any magazines except *The Lawyer* since I was about thirteen. Normally I spend hairdressers' appointments typing emails or reading contracts.

But I can't relax and enjoy myself. I'm feeling more and more apprehensive as I read 'Ten Ways To Know Your Bikini Is Too Small'. By the time I've got to 'Real-Life Holiday Romances' and Annabel is blow-drying my hair, my entire body is seized up in fear.

'There we are!' Annabel gives a final blast and switches the hair dryer off. There's silence. I can't open my eyes.

'*Much* better!' Trish says approvingly.

I slowly open one eye. Then the other.

My hair isn't blonde. It's caramel. It's warm caramel with streaks of honey and the tiniest threads of gold. As I move my head it shimmers.

I swallow a few times, trying to keep control of myself. I think I might cry. 'It's wonderful,' I say, finding my voice. 'Thank you so much.'

I'm entranced by my reflection. I can't take my eyes off my new, glowing, caramel, honey self. I look alive. I look *colourful*.

I'm never going back to the way I looked before. Never.

At seven o'clock that evening, I arrive downstairs to see Trish wandering out of the living room with a cocktail glass, bloodshot eyes and a high colour.

'So!' she says benevolently. 'You're going out with Nathaniel tonight.'

'That's right.' I glance at myself in the mirror. I've gone for a fairly informal outfit. Jeans, nice simple top, sandals. New shiny hair. *Flick*.

She eyes me inquisitively over the top of her glass. 'Is that what you're wearing?' She runs her eyes over my outfit. 'It's not very *jazzy*, is it? Let me lend you a little something.'

'I don't mind not being jazzy,' I begin, feeling a few qualms, but Trish has already disappeared up the stairs. A few moments later she appears, holding a jewel box.

'Here we are. You need a bit of *glitz*.' She produces a diamanté clip in the shape of a large jewelled beetle and clips it to my hair. 'Now. You see how the emerald brings out your eyes?'

I gaze at myself. I cannot go out with a sparkly beetle on my head.

'And this is very glam!' Now she's garlanding a gilt chain round my waist. 'Let me just hang the charms on . . .'

Charms?

'Mrs Geiger . . .' I begin, flustered, as Eddie appears out of the study.

'Just got the quote in for the bathroom,' he says to Trish. 'Seven thousand, plus VAT.'

'Well, how much is it with VAT?' says Trish, rifling in her box.

I feel like a Christmas tree. She's hanging more and more glittery baubles off the belt, not to mention the beetle.

'I don't know!' retorts Eddie impatiently. 'What's seventeen and a half per cent of seven thousand?'

'One thousand, two hundred and twenty-five,' I respond absently.

There's a stunned silence.

Shit. That was a mistake. Trish and Eddie are goggling at me.

'Or . . . something.' I give a distracting laugh. 'Just a guess. So . . . have you got any more charms?'

Neither of them takes the slightest notice of me. Eddie's eyes are fixed on the paper he's holding. Very slowly he looks up.

'She's right,' he says in a strangled voice. 'She's bloody right. That's the correct answer.' He jabs the paper. 'It's here!'

'She's *right*?' Trish breathes in sharply. 'But how . . .'

'You saw her.' Eddie's voice rises to an incredulous squeak. 'She did it in her head!'

They both swivel round to gaze at me again.

'Is she *autistic*?' Trish seems beside herself.

Oh, for God's sake. *Rain Man* has a lot to answer for, if you ask me.

'I'm not autistic!' I say. 'I'm just . . . I'm just quite good with numbers.'

To my huge relief the doorbell rings, and I go to answer it. Nathaniel is standing on the doorstep, looking a little smarter than usual, in tan jeans and a green shirt.

'Hi,' I say hurriedly. 'Let's go.'

'Wait!' Eddie blocks my way. 'Young lady, you may be a lot brighter than you realise.'

Oh, no.

'What's going on?' asks Nathaniel.

'She's a mathematical genius!' says Trish. 'And we discovered it!'

I shoot Nathaniel an agonised 'she's talking nonsense' look.

'What formal education have you had, Samantha?' Eddie demands. 'Other than cooking.'

'I . . . um . . . here and there.' I spread my hands vaguely.

'It's the schools today.' Trish inhales sharply on her cigarette. 'Tony Blair should be *shot*.'

'Samantha,' Eddie says, looking self-righteous, 'I will take on your education. And if you're prepared to work hard—hard, mind—I'm sure we can get you some qualifications.'

'I don't really want any qualifications, sir,' I mumble, surreptitiously divesting myself of all the jewelled creatures and slipping them back into the jewellery box. Then I look at Nathaniel, who has been waiting on the doorstep. 'Shall we go?'

'So, what was all that about?' asks Nathaniel as we start walking along the village road. The air is soft and warm and my new hair is bouncing lightly. 'You're a mathematical genius?'

'No.' I can't help laughing. 'Of course not!'

'What *is* your background then?'

'Oh, you don't want to know.' I give him a brush-off smile. 'Very boring.'

'I don't believe that for a minute.' His tone is light but persistent. 'Did you have a career? Before you came here?'

I walk for a few paces without saying anything, my eyes on the ground, trying to think what to say. I can feel Nathaniel's eyes on me, but I twist my head away from his scrutiny.

'You don't want to talk about it,' he says at last.

'No! It's not that.' I push my hands through my hair. 'It's just . . . a long story.'

Nathaniel shrugs. 'We've got all evening.'

As I meet his steady gaze I feel a sudden pull, like a fishhook inside my chest. I want to unburden everything. Who I am, what happened, how hard it's been. He'd understand. He'd keep it secret.

'So.' He stops still in the street, his thumbs in his pockets. 'Are you going to tell me who you are?'

'Maybe,' I say at last, and find myself smiling. Nathaniel smiles back, his eyes crinkling with a slow, delicious ease.

'But not right now.' I look around the golden village street. 'It's too nice an evening to spoil. I'll tell you later.'

We walk on, passing an old stone wall covered with a profusion of climbing roses. And as I breathe in the delicious scent, I feel a sudden lightness; almost euphoria. The street is dappled with soft evening light and the last rays of sun are warm on my shoulders.

'Nice hair, by the way,' he says.

'Oh, thanks.' I give a nonchalant smile. 'It's nothing really.' *Flick.* 'So where are we going?'

'The pub,' he says. 'If that's OK?'

'Perfect!'

As we approach the Bell I see a small crowd of people outside: some standing by the door; others sitting at the wooden tables.

'What are they doing?' I say, puzzled.

'Waiting,' he says. 'Landlord's late.'

'Oh,' I say. I look around but all the tables are already taken. 'Well, never mind. We can sit here.'

I perch on an old barrel—but Nathaniel has already headed for the door of the pub.

And . . . that's weird. Everyone is standing back to let him through. I watch in astonishment as he reaches in his pocket and produces a big bunch of keys, then looks round to find me.

'Come on,' he beckons with a grin. 'Opening time.'

You own a *pub*?' I say, as the initial melee of the evening dies down.

I've watched in wonderment for fifteen minutes as Nathaniel has pulled pints, bantered with customers, given instructions to the bar staff and made sure everyone is happy. Now the initial rush is over, he's come round to where I'm perched on a bar stool with a glass of wine.

'Three pubs,' he corrects me. 'It's our family business. The Bell, the Swan over in Bingley and the Two Foxes.'

'So you're not really a gardener!'

'I am really a gardener.' He looks down briefly. 'This is . . . business.'

There's a tone in his voice as though I've trodden on something sensitive. I look away—and my attention is caught by a picture on the wall of a middle-aged man. He has Nathaniel's strong jaw and blue eyes, and the same crinkles round his eyes as he smiles.

'That's your dad?' I say cautiously. 'He looks wonderful.'

'He was the life and soul.' Nathaniel's eyes soften. 'Everyone here, they all loved him.' He takes a deep slug of beer, then puts his glass down. 'But listen. We don't have to stay here. If you'd rather go somewhere else, somewhere smarter . . .'

I look around the bustling pub. Music is playing above the noise of talk and laughter. A group of regulars are greeting each other by the bar with cheerful insults. A pair of elderly American tourists in Stratford T-shirts are being advised on local beers by a barman with red hair and twinkling eyes. I can't remember the last time I was somewhere with such an easy, friendly atmosphere.

'Let's stay. And I'll help!' I slip off my stool and head behind the bar.

'Have you ever pulled a pint before?'

'No,' I say, picking up a glass and putting it under one of the beer taps. 'But I can learn.'

'OK.' Nathaniel comes round the bar. 'You tilt the glass like this . . . now pull.'

I pull the tap, and a burst of foam splutters out. 'Damn!'

'Slowly . . .' He puts his arms round me, guiding my hands.

Mmm, this is nice. He's saying something to me, but I'm not listening to a word. I'm in a blissful happy haze, enveloped in his strong arms.

'You know,' I begin, turning my head towards him. And then I stop as my eyes focus on something. There's an old wooden notice on the wall, stating *No Muddy Boots Please* and *No Working Clothes*. Underneath, another notice has been pinned. It's printed on yellowing paper in faded marker pen—and it reads: NO LAWYERS.

I stare at it, dumbfounded. No lawyers? Am I reading that correctly?

'There we are.' Nathaniel holds up the glass, full of a gleaming amber liquid. 'Your first-ever pint.'

'Er . . . great!' I say, then gesture casually at the sign. 'What's this?'

'I don't serve lawyers,' he says without a flicker.

'Nathaniel! Get over here!' someone calls from the other end of the bar and he clicks in annoyance.

'I'll only be a moment.' He touches my hand, then moves away.

OK . . . just calm down, obviously it's a joke. Everyone hates lawyers, just like everyone hates estate agents and tax collectors. It's an accepted fact of life. But they don't all put signs up in their pubs, do they?

As I'm standing there, the barman with red hair comes up to scoop some ice out of the tank.

'Hi,' he says, holding out his hand. 'I'm Eamonn.'

'Samantha.' I shake it with a smile. 'I'm here with Nathaniel.'

'He said.' His eyes twinkle. 'Welcome to Lower Ebury.'

As I watch him serving, it suddenly strikes me that this guy might know something about the sign.

'So,' I say carelessly when he comes back over, 'that sign about lawyers. It's a joke, right?'

'Not really,' Eamonn replies cheerfully. 'Nathaniel can't stand lawyers.'

'Right!' Somehow I manage to keep on smiling. 'Um . . . why's that?'

'There was some law suit between his dad and the council. Nathaniel says Ben got talked into doing it by the lawyers. He wasn't well anyway, and he got more and more stressed by it. Then he had a heart attack.'

'God, how awful,' I say in horror. 'And Nathaniel blamed the lawyers?'

'He reckons the case should never have been brought.' Eamonn hefts a crate of orange mixers onto the bar. 'The last lawyer came in this pub . . .' He leans conspiratorially across the bar, 'Nathaniel punched him.'

'He *punched* him?' My voice comes out a petrified squeak.

'It was on the day of his dad's funeral.' Eamonn lowers his voice. 'One of his dad's lawyers came in here and Nathaniel socked him one. We tease him about it now.'

He turns away to serve someone and I take a gulp of wine. Let's not freak out here. So he doesn't like lawyers. That doesn't mean *me*. Of course it doesn't. I can still be honest with him. I can still tell him about my past. He won't take it against me. Surely.

But what if he does?

'Sorry about that.' All of a sudden Nathaniel is in front of me, his face warm and friendly. 'Are you OK?'

'I'm fine!' I say over-brightly. 'Having a lovely time!'

By the end of the evening I've pulled about forty pints. I've had a plate of cod and chips and half a dish of sticky toffee pudding—and beaten Nathaniel at darts, to loud cheers from everyone watching.

At last Nathaniel rings last orders with a resounding clang of the bell, and a good hour later the final stragglers make it to the door, each pausing to say goodbye to Nathaniel as they leave.

'We'll clear up,' says Eamonn firmly. 'You'll want to be enjoying the rest of the evening.'

'Well . . . OK.' Nathaniel claps him on the back. 'Thanks, Eamonn.' He looks at me. 'Ready to go?'

Almost reluctantly I slide down off my bar stool. 'It's been an amazing evening,' I say to Eamonn. 'Brilliant to meet you.'

'Likewise.' He grins. 'Send us your invoice.'

I beam back. I've never had an evening out like this in my life.

No one in London ever took me to a pub for a date—let alone to the other side of the bar. On my first evening out with Jacob he took me to *Les Sylphides* at Covent Garden, then left after twenty minutes to take a call from the States and never returned. He said the next day he was so bound up in a point of commercial contract law, he forgot I was there.

And the worst thing is, instead of saying 'You bastard!' and punching him, I asked what point of commercial contract law.

After the beery warmth of the pub, the summer night is fresh and cool. There are no streetlamps; the only light comes from a big full moon and curtained cottage windows.

'Did you enjoy yourself?' Nathaniel sounds a bit anxious.

'I really, really loved it,' I say with enthusiasm. 'It's a great pub. And I can't get over how friendly it is. The way everyone knows you! And the village spirit. Everyone cares about each other. You can tell.'

'How can you tell that?' Nathaniel sounds amused.

'From the way everyone claps each other on the back,' I explain. 'Like, if someone were in trouble, everyone would rally round in a heart-warming way. You can just see it.'

I hear Nathaniel stifle a laugh. 'We did get the Most Heart-warming Village award last year,' he says.

'You can laugh,' I retort. 'But in London, no one's heart-warming. If you fell over dead in the street they'd just push you into the gutter. After emptying your wallet and stealing your identity.'

'I know about Londoners.' Nathaniel looks wry. 'I lived in London for a time.'

I gape at him in the moonlight. Nathaniel lived in London? I try, and fail, to picture him strap-hanging on the tube, reading *Metro*.

'Seriously?' I say at last, and he nods.

'And I hated it. Seriously.'

'But what—why . . .'

'I was a waiter on my year off before uni. My flat was opposite a twenty-four-hour supermarket. It was lit up all night with these bright fluorescent strips. And the noise . . .' He winces. 'In ten months of living there, I never had a single moment of total darkness or total quiet. I never heard a bird. I never saw the stars.'

Instinctively, I tilt my head back to look up at the clear night sky.

'How about you?' His voice brings me back to earth.

'What do you mean?'

'You were going to tell me your story,' he says.

'Oh.' I feel a spasm of nerves. 'Yes, right. So I was.'

I have to say something. Maybe I can keep it to a minimum. Tell the truth without mentioning the lawyer bit.

'Well,' I say at last. 'I was in London. In this . . . this . . . '

'Relationship,' he prompts.

'Er . . . yes.' I swallow. 'Well. Things went wrong. I got on a train . . . and I ended up here. That's it.'

'That's *it?*' Nathaniel sounds incredulous. 'That's the long story?'

'Look.' I turn to face him in the moonlight, my heart pumping. 'I know I was going to tell you more. But are the details really important? Does it matter, what I used to do . . . or be? The point is, I'm here. And I've just had the best evening of my life. Ever.'

I can see he wants to challenge me; he even opens his mouth to speak. Then he turns away without saying whatever it was.

I feel a plunge of despair. Maybe I've ruined everything.

We walk on again into the night without speaking. Nathaniel's shoulder brushes against mine. Then I feel his hand. His fingers graze against my own casually at first, as though by accident—then, slowly, entwine themselves round mine.

I feel an arching inside as my entire body responds, but somehow force myself not to catch my breath. Neither of us says a word. There's no sound except our footsteps on the road and a distant owl hooting. Nathaniel's hand is sure and firm round my own. I can feel the roughened callouses on his skin; his thumb rubbing over mine.

We come to a stop at the entrance to the Geigers' drive. He looks down at me silently, his expression almost grave. I can feel my breath thickening. I don't care if it's obvious I want him.

He releases my hand and puts both hands round my waist. Now he's slowly pulling me towards him. I close my eyes, prepared to lose myself.

'For goodness' sake!' comes an unmistakable voice. 'Aren't you going to *kiss* her?'

I jump and open my eyes. Nathaniel looks equally shocked, and takes an automatic step away. I swivel round—and to my utter horror, Trish is leaning out of an upstairs window.

'I'm not a *prude*, you know,' she says. 'You are allowed to kiss!'

I shoot daggers at her. Has she never heard the word 'privacy'?

'Carry on!' Her cigarette end glows as she waves it. 'Don't mind me!'

Don't mind her? I'm sorry, but I am not doing this with Trish as a spectator. I glance at Nathaniel, who looks as nonplussed as I feel.

I meet his eye and suddenly feel uncontrollable laughter rising. This is disastrous. The mood is totally broken.

'Um . . . thanks for a great evening,' I say, trying to keep a straight face. 'I had a lovely time.'

'Me too.' His eyes are almost indigo in the shadows; his mouth twisted in amusement. 'So. Are we going to give Mrs Geiger her kicks? Or leave her in an unbearable frenzy of frustration?'

We both glance up at Trish, still leaning avidly out of her window.

'Oh . . . I think she probably deserves the unbearable frenzy of frustration,' I say with a tiny smile.

'So I'll see you tomorrow?'

'I'll be at your mum's at ten o'clock.'

'See you then.'

He holds out his hand and we barely brush fingertips before he turns and walks away. I watch him disappear into the darkness, then head down the drive to the house; my whole body still pulsating.

It's all very well, getting one over on Trish. But what about *my* unbearable frenzy of frustration?

Eight

I'M WOKEN THE NEXT DAY by Trish banging sharply on my door. 'Samantha! I need to speak to you! Now!'

It's not even eight o'clock on a Saturday morning. Where's the fire?

'OK!' I call blearily. 'Hang on a sec!'

I stumble out of bed, my head filled with delicious memories of last night. Nathaniel's hand in mine . . . Nathaniel's arms round me . . .

'Yes, Mrs Geiger?' I open my door to see Trish standing there in a silk dressing gown, her face flushed and her eyes bloodshot. She puts her hand over the cordless phone she's holding.

'Samantha.' There's a strange note of triumph in her voice. 'You've fibbed to me, haven't you?'

My mind frantically runs over all the fibs I've ever told Trish, up to and including 'I'm a housekeeper'. It could be something small and insignificant. Or she could have found out the whole lot.

'I don't know what you're referring to,' I say in a throaty voice. 'Madam.'

'Well.' Trish walks towards me, swishing her dressing gown crossly. 'As you can imagine, I'm *rather* upset that you never told me you'd cooked paella for the Spanish ambassador.'

My mouth hangs open. The Spanish what? Has she lost it?

'Mrs Geiger,' I say, a little nervously, 'would you like to sit down?'

'No, thank you!' she says crisply. 'I'm still on the phone with Lady Edgerly.'

The floor seems to wobble beneath me. *Freya's on the phone?*

'Lady Edgerly . . .' Trish lifts the phone to her ear. 'You're quite right, *far* too unassuming . . .' She looks up. 'Lady Edgerly would like to have a word with you.'

She hands me the phone and in a blur of disbelief I lift it to my ear. 'Hello?'

'Samantha?' Freya's familiar, raspy voice erupts into my ear through a sea of crackle. 'Are you OK? What the *fuck* is going on?'

'I'm . . . fine!' I glance at Trish, who is standing approximately two metres away. 'I'll just . . . go somewhere a bit more . . .'

Ignoring Trish's laser-like eyes, I retreat into my bedroom and close the door tight. Then I lift the phone to my ear again.

'I'm fine!' I feel a rush of joy to be talking to Freya again.

'What on earth's going on?' she demands again. 'I got this message but it made no sense! You're a *housekeeper*? Is this some huge wind-up?'

'No.' I glance at the door, then move into the bathroom and switch on the fan. 'I'm a full-time housekeeper,' I say in a lower voice. 'I've left my job at Carter Spink.'

'You've *quit*?' says Freya incredulously. 'Just like that?'

'I didn't quit. I was . . . thrown out. I made a mistake and they fired me.' It's still hard to say it. Or even to think about it.

'You were thrown out for a simple *mistake*?' Freya sounds outraged.

'It wasn't a simple mistake. It was a really big, important mistake. Anyway, that's what happened. And I decided to do something different. Become a housekeeper for a bit.'

'You decided to become a housekeeper,' echoes Freya slowly. 'Samantha, did you totally lose your mind?'

'Why not?' I say defensively. 'You were the one who said I should have a break.'

'But a *housekeeper*? You can't cook!' She's giggling now. 'I've seen your cooking. And your non-existent cleaning.'

'I know!' A wave of hysteria is coming over me. 'It was a bit of a nightmare to begin with. But I'm learning. You'd be surprised.'

'Do you have to wear an apron?'

'I've got this hideous nylon uniform . . .' I'm snuffling with laughter now. 'And I call them madam . . . and sir . . . and I curtsy . . .'

'Samantha, this is insane,' says Freya between gurgles. 'You cannot stay there. I'm going to rescue you. I'll fly back tomorrow . . .'

'No!' I say with more vehemence than I intended. 'No! I'm . . . having a good time. It's fine.'

There's a suspicious silence down the phone. Dammit. Freya knows me far too well.

'With a man?' her teasing voice comes at last.

'Maybe.' I feel an unwilling grin come to my face. 'Yes.'

'Details?'

'It's early days. But he's . . . you know. Nice.' I beam foolishly at my own reflection in the bathroom mirror.

'Well, even so. You know I'm only a phone call away. You can stay at our place . . .'

'Thanks, Freya.' I feel a tug of affection for her.

'No problem. Samantha?'

'Yes?' There's a long silence, until I think the line must have cut out.

'What about the partnership?' says Freya at last. 'It was your dream. Are you just going to abandon it?'

I feel a twinge of deep, buried grief. 'That dream's over,' I say shortly. 'Partners don't make fifty-million-quid mistakes.'

'*Fifty million quid?* Jesus,' she breathes, sounding shocked. 'I can't imagine how you've coped with all this—'

'It's fine,' I cut her off. 'I've got over it. Really.'

'You know, I had a feeling something was up. I tried to send you an email via the Carter Spink website. But your page was gone.'

'Really?' I feel an odd little tweak inside.

'And then I thought—' She breaks off, and I can hear mayhem in the background. 'Our transport's here. Listen, I'll call you soon—'

'Wait!' I say urgently. 'Before you go, Freya, what on *earth* did you say to Trish about the Spanish ambassador?'

'Oh, that.' She giggles. 'Well, she kept asking questions, so I thought I'd better make some stuff up. I said you could fold napkins into a scene from *Swan Lake* . . . and make ice sculptures . . .'

'Freya . . .' I close my eyes.

'She lapped it up! I have to go, babe. Love you.'

'Love you too.'

The phone goes dead and I stand motionless for a moment, the bathroom suddenly very silent without Freya's husky voice amid the background clamour of India.

I look at my watch. I just have time to have a look.

Three minutes later I'm sitting at Eddie's desk, tapping my fingers as I wait for the Internet connection to work. I asked Trish if I could possibly send an email to Lady Edgerly, and she was only too eager to open up the study for me.

Eddie's home page opens and I type in www.carterspink.com.

As the familiar purple logo appears, I can feel all the old tensions rising. Taking a deep breath, I click swiftly past the Introduction, straight to Associates. The list comes up—and Freya's right. The names segue straight from Snell to Taylor. No Sweeting.

I exhale, telling myself to be rational. Of course they've taken me off. I've been fired, what else did I expect? I should just close down, go to Iris's house and forget about it. That's what I should do.

Instead, I find myself reaching for the mouse and tapping 'Samantha Sweeting' into the search box. 'No result' pings up a few moments later and I stare at it, taken aback.

No result? Nowhere on the whole *website*? But . . . what about in the Media section? Or News Archives?

I quickly click on to the Done Deals box, and search for 'Euro-Sal, merger, DanCo'. That was a big European deal last year and I handled the financing. The report appears on the screen, with the headline 'Carter Spink advises on £20bn merger'. My eyes run down the familiar text. 'The Carter Spink team was led from London by Arnold Saville, with associates Guy Ashby and Jane Smilington.'

I stop in disbelief, then go back and read the text more carefully, searching for the missing words—'and Samantha Sweeting', it should read. But the words aren't there. I'm not there.

My heart is thudding as I click from deal to deal, tracking back a year. Two years. Five years. They've wiped me out. Someone has gone painstakingly through the entire website and removed my name.

I take a breath, trying to stay calm. But anger is bubbling up, hot and strong. How dare they change history? I gave them seven years of my *life*. They can't just pretend I was never even on the payroll . . .

Then a new thought hits me. Why am I such an embarrassment? I slowly type in www.google.com and enter 'Samantha Sweeting' in the box, then press the return key.

A moment later the screen fills with text. As I scan the entries I feel as though I've been hit over the head.

> . . . the **Samantha Sweeting** debacle . . .
> . . . **Samantha Sweeting** went AWOL, leaving colleagues to . . .
> . . . **Samantha Sweeting** jokes. What do you call a lawyer who . . .
> . . . **Samantha Sweeting** fired from Carter Spink . . .

I can never go back. I knew that. But I don't think I really *knew* it. Not deep down in the pit of my stomach. Not where it counts.

I feel a wetness on my cheek and jump to my feet, shutting all the web pages down; I clear History in case Eddie gets curious. I shut down the computer and look round the silent room. This is where I am. Not there. That part of my life is over.

Iris's cottage is looking as idyllic as ever as I dash up to the front door, out of breath.

'Hello.' She looks up with a smile from where she's sitting with a mug of tea. 'You seem in a hurry.'

'I just wanted to get here on time.' I look round the garden, but I can't see any sign of Nathaniel.

'Nathaniel had to go and sort out a leaking pipe at one of the pubs,' says Iris, as though reading my mind. 'But he'll be back later. Meanwhile, we're going to make bread.'

'Great!' I say. I follow her into the kitchen and put on the same stripy apron as last time.

'I've started us off already,' says Iris, going to a large, old-fashioned mixing bowl on the table. 'Yeast, warm water, melted butter and flour. Mix together and you have your dough. Now, you're going to knead it.'

'Right,' I say again, looking blankly at the dough.

She shoots me a curious look. 'Are you all right, Samantha?'

'I'm fine.' I try to smile. 'Sorry.'

She hefts the dough onto the table and kneads it briskly. 'You see? Fold it over, make a quarter turn. You need to use a bit of energy.'

Cautiously I plunge my hands into the soft dough and try to imitate what she was doing.

'That's it,' says Iris, watching carefully. 'Get into a rhythm and really *work* it. Kneading's very good for releasing stress,' she adds wryly. 'Pretend you're bashing all your worst enemies.'

'I'll do that!' I manage a cheerful tone.

But there's a knot of tension in my chest, which doesn't dwindle away as I knead. I can't stop my mind flicking back to that website.

'The more you work the dough, the better the bread will be,' says Iris, with a smile. 'Can you feel it becoming warm and elastic in your hands?'

I look at the dough in my fingers, but I can't connect with it. My mind is skittering about like a bird on ice. My upper arms are aching; my face is sweating. How dare they wipe me out? I did things for that firm. I was a *good lawyer.*

'Would you like a rest?' Iris comes over and touches my shoulder. 'It's hard work when you're not used to it.'

'What's the point of all this?' My words shoot out before I can stop them. 'I mean, making bread. You make it and you eat it. Then it's gone.'

'You could say the same of all food,' Iris points out. 'Or of life itself.'

'Exactly.' I rub my forehead with my apron. 'Exactly.'

'I think that's enough kneading,' she says, taking the dough from me and patting it into a round shape.

'Shall I put it in the oven?' I say, trying to speak more normally.

'Not yet.' Iris places the dough back in the bowl and puts it on top of the stove. 'Now we wait.' She pops a tea towel over the bowl. 'Half an hour should do it. I'll make a cup of tea.'

'But . . . what are we waiting *for*?'

'For the yeast to rise and work its magic on the dough.' She smiles. 'Underneath that towel, a small miracle is happening.'

I look at the bowl, trying to think miracles. But it isn't working. I can't feel calm or serene. My body is wound up too far.

'I'm sorry,' I hear myself say. 'I can't do it.' I head for the kitchen door and out into the garden.

'Sweetie, what's wrong?' Iris comes after me.

'I can't do this!' I wheel round. 'I can't just . . . just sit around patiently, waiting for *yeast* to get its act together.'

'Why not?'

'Because it's such a waste of time!' I clutch my head in frustration.

'What do you think we should be doing instead?' she asks.

'Something . . . *important*. OK? Something constructive.'

Iris appears amused. 'What's more constructive than making bread?'

Oh *God*. I feel an urge to scream. It's OK for her, with her apron and no wrecked career on the Internet.

'You don't understand anything,' I say, close to tears.

'Samantha, you've had a trauma,' she says in kind, even tones. 'And it's affected you very deeply—'

'I *haven't* had a trauma! I just . . . I can't do this, Iris. I can't pretend to be this. I'm not a bread-maker, OK? I'm *not* a domestic goddess.' I look around the garden desperately, as though searching for clues. 'I don't know who I am any more. Or where I'm headed in life. Or anything.'

My energy's gone and I sink down on the dry grass. A few moments later Iris comes and squats down beside me.

'Don't beat yourself up for not knowing all the answers,' she says softly. 'Sometimes it's enough just to know what you're going to do next.'

'And what *am* I going to do next?' I say, with a hopeless shrug.

'You're going to help me shell the beans for lunch.' She sounds so matter-of-fact that I can't help half smiling.

When I've finished the beans we knead the dough again. We shape it into loaves, put them into loaf tins and then have to wait another half-hour for them to rise again. But somehow this time I don't mind. I sit at the table with Iris, hulling strawberries and listening to the radio until it's time to put the tins into the oven. Then Iris loads a tray with cheese, bean salad, biscuits and strawberries, and we take it outside to a table set under the shade of a tree.

'There,' she says, pouring some iced tea into a tumbler. 'Better?'

'Yes. Thanks,' I say awkwardly. 'I'm sorry about earlier. I just . . .'

'Samantha, it's all right.' She gives me a brief look, between slicing the cheese. 'You don't have to apologise.'

'But I do.' I take a deep breath. 'I'm really grateful, Iris. You've been so kind . . . and Nathaniel . . .'

'He took you to the pub, I heard.'

'It was amazing!' I say with enthusiasm. 'You must be so proud, to have that in your family.'

Iris nods. 'Those pubs have been run by Blewetts for generations.' She sits down and helps us both to bean salad, dressed with oil and speckled with herbs. I take a mouthful, and it's absolutely delicious.

'It must have been hard when your husband died,' I venture.

'Everything was in a mess.' Iris pauses. 'There were financial difficulties. I wasn't well. If it hadn't been for Nathaniel we might have lost the pubs. He made sure they got back on track. For his father's memory.' Her eyes cloud a little and she hesitates. 'You never know how things are going to turn out, however much you plan. But you already know that.'

'I always thought my life would be a certain way,' I say, gazing down at my plate. 'I had it all mapped out.'

'But it didn't happen like that?'

For a few seconds I can't answer. I'm remembering the moment I heard I was going to be partner. That instant of undiluted, dazzling joy, when I thought my life had finally fallen into place.

'No,' I say, trying to keep my voice level. 'It didn't happen like that.'

'Don't be too hard on yourself, chicken,' she says. 'We all flounder.'

I can't imagine Iris ever floundering. She seems so calm.

'Oh, I floundered,' she says, reading my expression. 'After Ben went. It was so sudden. Everything I thought I had, gone overnight.'

'So . . . what did you . . .' I spread my hands helplessly.

'I found another way,' she says. 'But it took time.' For a moment she holds my gaze, then looks at her watch. 'Speaking of which, I'll make some coffee. And see how that bread's getting on.'

I get up to follow her, but she bats me down again. 'Sit. Stay. Relax.'

I sit there in the dappled sunlight, sipping my iced tea, trying to relax. But emotions are still darting around me like unsettled fish. I clench my eyes shut, trying to clear my mind. I should never have looked at that website. I should never have read those comments.

'Hold out your arms, Samantha.' Iris's voice is suddenly behind me. 'Don't open your eyes. Go on.'

I have no idea what she's up to, but I hold out my arms. The next moment I feel something warm being put into them. A yeasty smell is rising up. I open my eyes to see a loaf of bread.

I stare at it in utter disbelief. It looks like the kind of bread you'd see in a baker's window. Fat and plump and golden brown, with a crusty, almost flaky top. It smells so delicious I can feel my mouth watering.

'Tell me that's nothing,' says Iris, squeezing my arm. 'You made that, sweetie. And you should be proud of yourself.'

I can't reply. Something hot is wadding my throat as I clutch the warm loaf. I made this bread. I made it. I, Samantha Sweeting, who gave up seven years of her life to be wiped out of existence. Who has no idea who she even is any more. I made a loaf of bread. Right now I feel like this is the only thing I have to hold on to.

To my horror a tear suddenly rolls down my cheek, followed by another. This is ridiculous. I have to get a grip on myself.

'Looks good,' comes Nathaniel's easy voice behind me, and I wheel round in shock. He's standing next to Iris, his hair glowing in the sun.

'Hi,' I say, flustered. 'I thought you were . . . fixing a pipe.'

'Still am.' He nods. 'I just popped home.'

'I'll go and get the other loaves out,' says Iris, patting me on the shoulder, and disappears over the grass towards the house.

I stand up and look at Nathaniel over the bread. Just the sight of him is adding all sorts of emotions into the mix.

'Are you all right?' he says, glancing at my tears.

'I'm fine. It's just been a weird day,' I say, brushing the tears away in embarrassment. 'I don't usually get so emotional about . . . bread.'

'Mum said you got a bit frustrated.' He raises his eyebrows. 'All that kneading?'

'It was the rising.' I raise a rueful smile. 'Having to wait. I've never been good at waiting.'

'Uh-huh.' Nathaniel's steady blue eyes meet mine.

'For anything.' Somehow I seem to be edging closer and closer to him, I'm not entirely sure how. 'I have to have things *now*.'

'Uh-huh.'

We're inches apart now. And as I gaze up at him, breathing hard, all the frustrations and shocks of the last couple of weeks seem to be distilling inside me. A huge block of pressure is growing, until I can't bear it. I need release. Unable to stop myself, I reach up and pull his face down towards mine.

I haven't kissed like this since I was a teenager. Arms wrapped round one another; oblivious of anything else in the world. Completely lost. Trish could be standing there with a video camera, issuing directions, and I wouldn't notice.

It seems hours later that I open my eyes and we draw apart. My lips feel swollen; my legs are staggery. Nathaniel looks equally shell-shocked. His eyes are opaque and he's breathing more swiftly.

The bread is totally squashed, I suddenly notice. I try to reshape it as best I can, putting it on the table like a deformed pottery exhibit while I gather my breath.

'I don't have long,' Nathaniel says. 'I have to get back to the pub.' His hand runs lightly down my back and I feel my body curving towards his.

'I don't take long,' I say, my voice husky with desire.

When did I become so brazen, exactly?

'I *really* don't have long.' He glances at his watch. 'About six minutes.'

'I only take six minutes,' I murmur with an enticing glance.

There's silence for a few moments. An incredulous expression is coming over Nathaniel's face. 'Well . . . round here we take things a bit slower,' he says at last.

'Right,' I say, trying not to look at all disappointed. 'So . . . I'll see you,' I say, trying to sound casual. 'What are you doing tomorrow?'

'I'm not sure yet.' He gives a noncommittal shrug. 'Are you around?'

'I guess so. Maybe.'

'Well . . . I may see you.'

And with that he's striding away again over the grass, and I'm left with nothing but a misshapen loaf of bread and total confusion.

By the next morning I've thought long and hard and have got nowhere. Either a) Nathaniel was offended by my references to sex, and isn't interested any more, or b) he's fine, it's all still on, he was just being a man and not saying much, and I should stop obsessing.

Or somewhere in between.

Or some other option I haven't even considered. Or . . .

Actually, I think that might cover it. But still. I'm totally confused just thinking about it.

I stumble downstairs in my dressing gown at around nine, to find Trish in the hall, dressed in a white silk suit, with the biggest corsage of fake red roses I've ever seen.

'Morning, Samantha,' she says. 'We'll be out all day at my sister's party. Nathaniel will be coming over to work in the garden, but I expect you know that—'

'Nathaniel?' I feel an electric jolt. 'He's coming here?'

'He called this morning. The sweet peas need . . . stringing or looping or something?' She gets out a lip pencil and begins outlining her already lined lips. 'I heard he took you to his little pub?'

'Er . . . yes. He did.'

'I was *so* glad about that, really.' She takes out a mascara wand and starts adding more layers to her already spiky lashes. 'We nearly had to look for another gardener, can you *imagine*. Although of course it was a great shame for him. After all his plans.'

I look at her, nonplussed. What's she talking about?

'What was a shame?' I say.

'Nathaniel. His nursery. Plant thing.' She frowns at her reflection and flicks at a speck of mascara beneath her eye. 'Organic something or other. He showed us the business proposition. In fact, we were even considering backing him. We are very *supportive* employers, Samantha.' She fixes me with a blue gaze as though daring me to disagree.

'Of course!'

'Ready?' Eddie comes out of the study dressed very smartly in a blazer with shiny gold buttons and wearing a Panama hat. 'It's going to be bloody sweltering, you know.'

'Eddie, don't start,' snaps Trish, shoving her mascara wand back in the tube. 'We are going to this party and that's final.'

'And what happened?' I ask, trying to haul the conversation back on track. 'With Nathaniel's plans?'

Trish makes a small, regretful moue at herself in the mirror.

'Well, his father passed away very suddenly, and there was all that dreadful business with the pubs. And he changed his mind. Never bought the land.' She gives herself another, dissatisfied look. 'Should I wear my *pink* suit?'

'*No*,' Eddie and I say in unison. I glance at Eddie's exasperated face and stifle a giggle.

'You look lovely, Mrs Geiger,' I say. 'Really.'

Somehow, between us, Eddie and I manage to chivvy her away from the mirror, out of the front door and into Eddie's Porsche.

'What time will you be back?' I ask.

'Not until late this evening,' says Trish. 'Ah, Nathaniel, here you are.'

I look over the top of the car in slight apprehension. There he is, coming down the drive, in jeans and espadrilles and an old grey T-shirt, his rucksack over his shoulder. And here I am, in my dressing gown with my hair all over the place.

And still not sure how things have been left between us.

'Hi,' I say as he gets near.

'Hi.' Nathaniel's eyes crinkle in a friendly way, but he doesn't make any attempt to kiss me or even smile.

'So.' I wrench my eyes away and look at the gravel for a few moments. 'You're . . . working today.'

'I could do with some help,' he says casually. 'If you're at a loose end.'

I feel a dazzling leap of delight, which I attempt to hide with a cough.

'Right.' I shrug slightly, almost frowning. 'Well . . . maybe.'

'Great.' He nods to the Geigers and saunters off towards the garden.

Trish has been watching this exchange in increasing dissatisfaction.

'You're not very *affectionate* with each other, are you?' she says. 'You know, in *my* experience—'

'Leave them alone, for God's sake!' retorts Eddie, starting the engine. 'Let's get this bloody thing over with.'

'Eddie Geiger!' Trish shrills, swivelling round in her seat. 'This is my sister's party you're talking about! Do you realise—'

Eddie revs the engine, drowning out her voice, and with a spattering of gravel the Porsche disappears out of the drive.

Right. So . . . it's just Nathaniel and me. Alone together. Until eight o'clock this evening. That's the basic scenario.

Deliberately nonchalant, I turn on the gravel and make my way back towards the house. I force myself not to rush. I take a shower and get dressed and have breakfast, consisting of a cup of tea and an apple.

I've dressed low key. A T-shirt, a cotton skirt and flip flops. As I look in the mirror, I feel almost shivery with anticipation.

After the cool house, the garden feels scorching; the air still and almost shimmery. I stay in the shade, heading down the side path, not knowing where he's working; where I'm heading. And then I see him, in the midst of a row of lavender and lilac-coloured flowers, his brow furrowed against the sun as he knots a length of twine.

'Hi,' I say.

'Hi.' He looks up and wipes his brow. I'm half expecting him to drop what he's doing, come forward and kiss me. But he doesn't. He just carries on knotting, then cuts the twine off with a knife.

'I came to help,' I say after a pause. 'What are we doing?'

'Tying up the sweet peas.' He gestures at the plants, which are growing up what look like cane wigwams. 'They need support otherwise they just flop.' He throws a ball of twine over to me. 'Just tie them gently.'

He's not joking. I really *am* helping with the gardening. Cautiously I unwind a length of twine and follow what he's doing. The soft petals tickle me as I work, and fill the air with an amazing sweet scent.

'How's that?'

'Let's see.' Nathaniel comes over to take a look. 'Yup. You could tie a little tighter.' His hand brushes briefly against mine as he turns away. 'Let's see you do the next one.'

My hand tingles at his touch. Did he mean to do that? Uncertain, I tie up the next plant, knotting harder than before.

'Yeah, that's good.' Suddenly Nathaniel's voice is behind me and I feel his fingers on the back of my neck, tracing around my earlobe. 'You need to do the whole row.'

He definitely meant to do that. No question. He has a game plan, I suddenly realise. OK, now I really am turned on.

The pulsating is growing stronger inside me as I move from plant to plant. There's silence except the rustling of leaves as I tie up three more plants and get to the end of the row.

'Done,' I say without turning round.

'Great, let's see.' He comes over to inspect my knotted twine. I can feel his other hand edging up my thigh, pushing up my skirt, his fingers feeling for my flesh. I can't move. I'm transfixed. Then suddenly he moves away, businesslike again, picking up a pair of trugs.

'What . . .' I can't even frame a sentence properly.

He kisses me briefly, hard on the mouth. 'Let's move on. Raspberries need picking.'

THE UNDOMESTIC GODDESS

The raspberry cages are further down the garden, like rooms of green netting, with dry, earthy floors and rows of raspberry plants. As we enter there's no sound except that of buzzing insects. We work the first row wordlessly, intently, picking the fruit off the plants. By the end of the row my mouth is tangy with the taste of them; my hands are scratched and aching from the constant plucking and I'm sweating all over.

We meet at the end of the row and Nathaniel looks at me a still second, sweat running down the side of his face.

'Hot work,' he says. He puts his trug down and strips off his T-shirt.

'Yes.' There's a still beat between us. Then, defiantly, I do the same. I'm standing there in my bra, inches from him, my skin pale and milky compared to his. I meet his eyes and it's like we're playing truth or dare.

'I couldn't reach those.' I point at a cluster of fruit just out of reach.

'I'll help.' He leans over me, skin against skin, and I feel his mouth on my earlobe as he picks the fruit. My entire body responds. I can't bear this; I need it to stop. And I need it not to stop.

But it goes on. We move up and down the rows like two performers in a courtly dance. Outwardly concentrating on our moves yet aware only of each other. At the end of every row, he brushes some part of me with his mouth or fingers. I want to get at him, I want my hands all over him, but every time he turns away before anything can progress.

I'm starting to shiver all over with desire. He unhooked my bra two rows ago. I've discarded my knickers. He's unbuckled his belt. And still, *still* we're picking raspberries.

As I reach the end of the last row I put the heavy trug down and face him, unable to hide how desperate I am.

'Are we done?'

'We've done pretty well.' His gaze drifts towards the other fruit cages. 'There's still more to do . . .'

'No,' I hear myself saying. 'No more.'

I stand there in the heat and the dusty earth, panting and aching. And just as I think I might explode, he comes forward and bends his mouth down to my nipple, and I nearly swoon. And this time he doesn't move away. This time is for real. His hands are moving over my body, my skirt is falling to the ground, his jeans are sliding off. Then I'm shuddering, and clutching him, and crying out. And the raspberries are forgotten, scattered on the ground, squashed, crushed beneath us.

We seem to lie still for hours afterwards. I feel numb with euphoria. There's dust and stones embedded in my back and knees and hands and raspberry stains all over my skin.

My head is on Nathaniel's chest, his heartbeat like a deep, comforting clock tick. The sun is hot on my skin. I have no idea what time it is. I don't care what time it is. I've lost all sense of minutes and hours.

At last Nathaniel shifts his head slightly. He kisses my shoulder, then smiles. 'You taste of raspberry.'

'That was . . .' I break off, almost too stupefied to frame any sensible words. 'You know . . . normally I . . .' A huge yawn suddenly overcomes me and I clap my hand over my mouth.

Nathaniel lifts a hand and traces lazy circles round my back.

'Six minutes isn't sex,' I hear him saying as my eyes crash shut. 'Six minutes is a boiled egg.'

By the time I wake up, the raspberry cages are in partial shade. Nathaniel has removed himself from underneath me, given me a pillow constructed from my crumpled, raspberry-stained skirt, put on his jeans and brought down some beer from the Geigers' fridge. I sit up, to see him leaning against a tree on the grass, swigging from the bottle.

'How long was I asleep?' I put my hand to my face and remove a small stone. I feel totally disorientated.

'Couple of hours. You want some of this?' He gestures to the bottle.

I get to my feet, brush myself down, put on my skirt and bra as a good compromise outfit and join him on the grass. He gives me the bottle and I take a swig. I sink back against the tree trunk, my bare feet in the cool grass.

'You're not as twitchy as you were,' says Nathaniel. 'You used to jump a mile whenever I spoke to you.'

'No, I didn't!'

'Uh huh, you did.' He nods. 'Like a rabbit.'

'I thought I was a badger.'

'You're a rabbit-badger cross. Very rare breed.' He grins at me and takes a swig of beer. For a while neither of us speaks.

'Mum says you've changed, too.' Nathaniel says at last, shooting me a swift, querying look. 'She says she reckons whoever you've run away from . . . whatever happened . . . they're losing their grip on you.'

The question is there in his voice, but I don't respond. I'm thinking of Iris, yesterday. Letting me take all my frustrations out on her. It's not like she's had it easy herself.

I roll onto the grass, staring up at the blue sky. I have changed. I can feel it in myself. I feel . . . stiller.

'Who would you be?' I say, twisting a grass stem round my finger. 'If you could just run away. Become a different person.'

Nathaniel's silent for a moment, looking over his bottle at the garden.

'I'd be me,' he says at last with a shrug. 'I'm happy as I am. I like living where I live. I like doing what I do.'

I roll over onto my front and look up at him. 'There must be something else you'd like to do. Some dream you've got.'

He shakes his head, smiling. 'I'm doing what I want to do.'

'But what about the nursery you were going to set up?'

Nathaniel's face jolts in surprise. 'How did you—'

'Trish told me about it this morning. She said you had business plans and everything. What happened?'

For a moment he's silent, his eyes averted from mine. 'It was just an idea,' he says at last.

'You gave it up for your mum. To run the pubs.'

'Maybe.' He reaches for a low-growing branch and starts stripping it of leaves. 'Everything changed.'

'But do you really want to run the pubs?' I edge forward on the grass, trying to intercept his gaze. 'You said it yourself, you're not a landlord. You're a gardener.'

'It's not a question of *want*.' Nathaniel's voice has a sudden edge of frustration. 'It's a family business. Someone has to run it.'

'Why you?' I persist. 'Why not your brother?'

'He's . . . different. He does his own thing.'

'*You* could do your own thing!'

'I have responsibilities.' His frown grows heavier. 'My mum—'

'She'd want you to be happy in your life, not give it up for her.'

'I am happy. It's ridiculous to say—'

'But couldn't you be *happier*?'

There's silence in the garden. Nathaniel is looking away, his shoulders bent round as if he wants to shut out what I'm saying.

'Don't you ever want to ditch your responsibilities?' I throw my arms out wide in sudden abandon. 'Just . . . walk out into the world and see what happens?'

'Is that what you did?' he demands, wheeling round, a sudden aggression in his voice.

I stare at him uncertainly. 'I . . . we're not talking about me,' I say at last. 'We're talking about you.'

'Samantha.' He exhales and rubs his brow. 'I know you don't want to talk about the past. But I want you to tell me one thing. And be truthful. Do you have kids?'

I'm so dumbfounded, I can't speak for a moment. He thinks I have *kids*? A gurgle of relieved laughter rises through me before I can stop it.

'No, I don't have kids! I mean . . . do I *look* like I've had five kids?' I can't help a note of indignation, and he starts to laugh too.

'Maybe not *five* . . .'

'What's that supposed to mean?'

I'm about to hit him with his shirt when a voice pierces the air. 'Samanth*a*?' It's Trish. Coming from the house. They're *home*?

My eyes swivel madly over the two of us. I'm naked except for a skirt and a bra, and covered in raspberry stains. Nathaniel is much the same, except in jeans.

'Quick! My clothes!' I hiss, scrabbling to my feet.

'Where are they?' says Nathaniel, looking around.

'I don't *know*!' I look at him helplessly.

'Samanth*a*?' I can hear the conservatory doors being opened.

'Shit!' I squeak. 'She's coming!'

'It's fine,' says Nathaniel, retrieving his T-shirt from the raspberry cage. He pops it over his head and at once looks pretty normal. 'I'll create a diversion. You sneak up the side, behind the shrubs, go in the kitchen door, run upstairs and get changed. OK?'

'OK,' I say breathlessly. 'And what's our story?'

'Our story is . . .' He pauses as though thinking. 'We didn't shag in the garden or help ourselves to beer from the fridge.'

'Right.' I can't help giggling. 'Good plan.'

He kisses me, and I dart across the lawn and sneak up the side of the garden, keeping behind the shrubs. I feel about ten years old, playing hide-and-seek, the same mixture of terror and delight pounding in my heart. When I'm only ten yards or so from the house I crouch behind a shrub and wait. After a minute or two I see Nathaniel firmly leading the Geigers down the lawn towards the lily pond.

'I think we could have a case of powdery mildew,' he's saying.

I wait until they're well past, then sprint on light feet to the conservatory, in through the house and up the stairs. I hurry into the bathroom, turn on the shower full blast and stand under it for thirty seconds. Afterwards, I pull on clean underwear, a pair of fresh jeans and a demure long-sleeved top. I even add fresh lipstick. Then, slipping on a pair of espadrilles, I head downstairs and out into the garden.

Nathaniel and the Geigers are by now making their way back up to the house. Trish's heels are sinking into the lawn and both she and Eddie look hot and bothered.

'Hi,' I say casually as they approach. 'Did you enjoy the party?'

Too late I see Nathaniel making deathlike, finger-across-the-throat gestures behind their backs.

'Thank you for asking, Samantha.' Trish inhales sharply. 'But I'd rather not talk about the party, thank you.'

Eddie makes an incensed spluttering sound. 'You won't bloody give up, will you? All I said was—'

'It was the *way* you said it!' shrieks Trish. 'Sometimes I think your *sole* purpose in life is to embarrass me!'

Eddie huffs furiously and stalks off towards the house.

Uh-oh. I raise my eyebrows at Nathaniel, who grins back over Trish's quivering hairdo.

'Would you like a nice cup of tea, Mrs Geiger?' I say soothingly. 'Or . . . a Bloody Mary?'

'Thank you, Samantha,' she replies, lifting her chin in a dignified manner. 'A Bloody Mary would be very nice.'

As we walk up to the conservatory, Trish seems to calm down a little. Once inside, she even mixes her own Bloody Mary instead of bossing me around as I do it, and makes one each for me and Nathaniel, too.

'*Now*,' she says, after we've each taken a gulp and sat down among the frondy plants, 'there was something I needed to tell you, Samantha. My husband's niece is coming to stay tomorrow for a few weeks. She has some work to do, and it's *very* important she isn't disturbed. I'd like you to get the spare room ready for her.'

'Very good.' I nod dutifully.

'She's a very bright girl, Melissa.' Trish lights a cigarette with her Tiffany lighter. 'She's a lawyer.'

A lawyer? This could be bad. In fact, this could be a disaster.

What if I *know* this lawyer?

'So . . . is she called Geiger too?' I ask casually.

'No, she's called Hurst.'

Melissa Hurst. It doesn't ring any bells.

'And where does she work?' *Please let it be abroad . . .*

'Oh, she's at some high-powered place in London.' Trish gestures vaguely with her glass.

OK, so I don't know her. But this is not looking good. If she's at any of the big London law firms she's bound to have heard about me. She's bound to know about the Carter Spink lawyer who lost £50 million and ran away. All it takes is for her to recognise my name, to put two and two together . . . and the whole story will come out. Everyone will know my lies. I glance at Nathaniel. I *can't* let things be spoilt. Not now.

He winks at me and I take a deep gulp of Bloody Mary. The answer is simple. I'll just have to do whatever it takes to keep my secret hidden.

Nine

THERE'S NO REASON why this lawyer should recognise my face. But just to be on the safe side, I opt for a simple disguise. After I've prepared the spare room the following afternoon, I hurry to my own room and pin my hair up on top of my head with artistic strands falling down and concealing my face. Then I add a pair of old sunglasses I found in the dressing-table drawer. They date from the 1980s and have big green frames that make me look like Elton John, but I'll live with that. The point is, I look nothing like my old self.

As I come downstairs, Nathaniel is heading out of the kitchen, looking pissed off. He looks up at me and stops dead in surprise.

'Are those *your* sunglasses?' He peers at me incredulously.

'I've got a headache. So . . . what's up?' I hastily change the subject.

'Trish.' He scowls. 'She's been lecturing me on noise. I can't mow the lawn between ten and two. Could I tiptoe on the gravel. *Tiptoe.*'

'Why?'

'Because of this blasted visitor. A bloody *lawyer*.' He shakes his head in disbelief. '*Her* work's important. *My* work's important!'

'She's coming!' Trish's voice suddenly shrills from the kitchen and she comes hurrying out. 'Are we all ready?' She flings open the front door and I hear the sound of a car door opening in the drive.

My heart starts to bang in my chest. This is it. If I recognise this woman I'll just keep my eyes down, mumble my words and play my part. I'm a housekeeper. I have never been anything but a housekeeper.

'You should get *lots* of peace here, Melissa,' I can hear Trish saying. 'I've instructed the staff to look after you with *extra* special care . . .'

I exchange looks with Nathaniel, who rolls his eyes.

I hold my breath. A moment later Trish enters the house, followed by a girl in jeans and a tight white top, dragging a suitcase.

This is the top, high-powered lawyer?

I stare at her in bewilderment. She has long dark hair and a pert, pretty face, and can't be much out of her teens.

'Melissa, this is our *wonderful* housekeeper—' Trish breaks off in surprise. 'Samantha, what are you wearing? You look like Elton John!'

'Hello,' I say awkwardly, taking the sunglasses off, but keeping my head down. 'It's very nice to meet you.'

'It's *fab* to be here.' Melissa has a boarding-school drawl and matching toss of the hair. 'London was, like *sooo* getting me down.'

'Mrs Geiger said you're a lawyer at some . . . big place in London?'

'Yah.' She gives me a smug smile. 'I'm at Chelsea Law School.'

What? She's not even a qualified lawyer. She's a law student. She's a *baby*. I cautiously raise my head and meet her eyes—but there's not a blink of recognition. Oh, for God's sake. I have nothing to worry about from this girl. I almost want to laugh.

'And who's this?' Melissa bats her mascaraed eyelashes alluringly at Nathaniel, whose scowl deepens.

'This is Nathaniel, our gardener,' says Trish. 'And he's under *strict* instructions not to disturb you.'

'Well, I've got *loads* of revision to do.' Melissa gives a world-weary sigh and pushes a hand through her hair. 'I've been *soooo* stressed.'

'I don't know how you do it!' Trish puts an arm around her shoulders. 'Now, what would you like to do first? We're *all* at your disposal.'

'Could you unpack my things?' Melissa turns to me. 'They'll be creased, so they'll all need ironing.'

I feel a slight jolt. I've turned into this girl's personal *maid*?

'Why don't you make us all some coffee first?' Trish says. 'We'll take it on the terrace. Bring some biscuits out, too.'

'Of course, Mrs Geiger,' I say, bobbing an automatic curtsy.

'Could you make mine half caffeinated, half decaf?' Melissa adds over her shoulder. 'I, like, don't want to get too wired.'

No, I bloody couldn't, you pretentious little cow.

'Of course.' I smile through gritted teeth. 'My pleasure.'

Something tells me this girl and I are not going to get along.

I dump the coffeepot on the counter with a bang.

'Don't let her wind you up.' Nathaniel comes over, puts his arms round me and kisses me. 'She's not worth it.'

'I know.' I nestle into his hold with a little smile, feeling myself relax. 'Mmm. I've missed you.'

He runs his hands down my back and I feel a tingle of delight. Last night I stayed over with Nathaniel at the pub and crept back to the Geigers at six o'clock in the morning. Something tells me this could become a regular pattern.

I take the coffee out to Trish, Melissa and Eddie on the terrace. They are sitting at the garden table, which is covered in papers and brochures.

'It's just *sooo* difficult,' Melissa is saying, as I pour. 'I mean, this is a decision which will affect my whole life. And you wouldn't believe my workload, Uncle Eddie.'

'It'll be worth it, love.' Eddie pats her hand reassuringly. 'When you're at . . .' He picks up a brochure from the table and peers at it through his reading glasses. 'Carter Spink.'

For a few moments I can't move. Melissa is going for a job at Carter Spink?

'Looks very swanky!' says Eddie, flipping over the glossy pages, each illustrated with a photograph. 'Look at these offices!'

As he flips through, I'm transfixed. There's a picture of the foyer. There's one of the floor I used to work on. I can't tear my eyes away— but at the same time I don't want to look. That's my old life. It doesn't belong here. And then suddenly, as Eddie flips another page over, I feel a jolt of disbelief. It's a picture of me. Me.

I'm in my black suit, my hair pinned up, sitting at a meeting-room table along with Ketterman, David Elldridge and a guy who was over from the States. I look so *pale*. I look so *serious*.

'And it's like . . . do I *want* to give up all my time?' Melissa is jabbing the page. 'These people work every night! What about a social life?'

My face is right there in full view. I'm just waiting for someone to frown in recognition. But no one does. Melissa is still rabbiting on: 'Although, you know, the money *is* really good . . .' She sighs, and flips the page. The picture's gone. I'm gone. I head back to the kitchen.

I don't see the Carter Spink brochure again for two weeks, when I'm drifting into the kitchen to make lunch.

I don't know what happened to time. I don't even wear a watch any more. The minutes and hours just ebb and flow and swirl around. Yesterday I lay in a field all afternoon with Nathaniel, watching dandelion seeds floating by, and the only ticking sound came from the crickets.

I barely recognise myself any more, either. I'm tanned from lying in the sun at lunchtimes. My arms are gaining muscles from all the polishing and kneading and carting heavy saucepans around.

Every morning, before breakfast, Nathaniel walks me back through the village to the Geigers' house—and even at that hour the air is already warming up. Everything seems slow and lazy, these days. Nothing seems to matter. Everyone's in holiday mood—except Trish, who is in full frenzy mood. She is holding a big charity lunch next week.

I'm tidying up the papers that Melissa has left on the table when I spot the Carter Spink brochure. I can't resist picking it up and leafing through the familiar pictures. There are the steps I went up every day for seven years. There's Guy, looking as dazzlingly handsome as ever.

'What are you doing?' Melissa has come into the kitchen without me hearing. She eyes me suspiciously. 'That's mine.'

'Just tidying your things,' I say pointedly, putting the brochure down. 'I've got to use this table.'

'Oh. Thanks.' Melissa rubs her face. She looks haggard, these days. There are shadows under her eyes and the sheen to her hair has gone.

'So are you applying to this law firm?' I ask casually. I look down at the Carter Spink brochure again. It's open at a picture of Arnold Saville. He's wearing a bright blue spotted tie and matching handkerchief and is beaming out at the world.

'Yup. They're the best.' Melissa is getting a Diet Coke from the fridge. 'That's the guy who was supposed to be interviewing me.' She jerks her head at the picture of Arnold. 'But he's leaving.'

I feel a jerk of astonishment. Arnold's leaving Carter Spink?

'Are you sure?' I say before I can stop myself.

'Yes.' Melissa gives me an odd look. 'What's it to you?'

'Oh, nothing,' I say hastily. 'I just meant . . . he doesn't look old enough to retire.'

'Well, he's going.' She shrugs and wanders out of the kitchen, leaving me staring down in puzzlement.

Arnold is leaving Carter Spink? But he's always boasted about lasting another twenty years. Why would he be leaving now? And what else has happened that I don't know about?

So that afternoon, when I've cleared up lunch, I slip into Eddie's study, switch on the computer and click on Google. I search for 'Arnold Saville'—and sure enough on the second page I come across a little diary item about his early retirement. I read the fifty-word piece, trying to glean clues. Why would Arnold retire early? Is he ill?

I search for further items, but that's the only one I can find. After a moment's hesitation, I go to the search box and—telling myself I shouldn't—type in 'Samantha Sweeting'. Immediately a zillion stories about me pop up again on the screen. I don't feel so freaked out this time, though. It almost doesn't feel like me any more.

I scan entry after entry, seeing the same details replayed. After clicking through about five pages I add 'Third Union Bank' to my search, and scan the resulting entries. Then I type in 'Third Union Bank, BLLC Holdings', then 'Third Union Bank, Glazerbrooks'.

God, Google is addictive. I sit there, totally absorbed, clicking and typing and reading, gorging on endless web pages. After an hour I'm slumped in Eddie's chair, like a zombie. My back is aching and my neck is stiff, and the words are all running into each other.

I rub my tired eyes and glance at the web page open in front of me, wondering what I'm even doing on it. It's some obscure list of guests at a lunch held earlier this year at the Painters Hall. About halfway down is the name BLLC Holdings, which must have been the link. On autopilot I move the cursor along the page—and into view comes the name **Nicholas Hanford Jones, director**.

Something chimes inside my addled brain. *Nicholas Hanford Jones.* Why do I know that name?

I screw my eyes up tight and concentrate as hard as I can. *Nicholas Hanford Jones.* I can almost see it in my mind's eye; I'm grasping at an association . . . an image . . . Come on, think . . . This is the trouble with having a nearly photographic memory. People think it must be useful, when in fact all it does is drive you insane.

And then suddenly it comes to me. The swirly writing of a wedding invitation. It was stuck up on the pinboard in Ketterman's office, about three years ago. I used to see it every time I went in.

> *Mr and Mrs Arnold Saville*
> *request the pleasure of your company*
> *at the wedding of their daughter Fiona*
> *to Mr Nicholas Hanford Jones.*

Nicholas Hanford Jones is Arnold Saville's son-in-law? Arnold has a family connection with BLLC Holdings? I sink back in my chair, totally disconcerted. How come he never mentioned that?

And then another thought strikes me. I was on the BLLC Holdings Companies House page a minute ago. Why wasn't Nicholas Hanford Jones listed as a director? That's illegal, for a start.

I rub my brow, then out of curiosity type in 'Nicholas Hanford Jones'. A moment later the screen is full of entries, and I start picking my way down, skimming each chunk of text, clicking onto the next page and the next. And then, just as I'm about to give up, my eye falls on an entry tucked away at the bottom of the page. *William **Hanford Jones**, Finance Director of Glazerbrooks, thanked **Nicholas** Jenkins for his speech . . .*

I stare at it for a few seconds in total disbelief. The finance director at Glazerbrooks is called Hanford Jones too? Are they from the same *family*? Feeling like some kind of private detective, I log onto Friends Reunited, and two minutes later I have my answer. They're brothers.

I feel a bit dazed. This is a pretty huge connection. The finance director of Glazerbrooks, which went bust owing Third Union Bank £50 million. A director of BLLC Holdings, which lent it £50 million three days
before. And Arnold, representing Third Union Bank. All related; all in
the same extended family.

Isn't it a potential conflict of interest? Shouldn't Arnold have disclosed the information straight away? Why on earth would he keep
such an important thing secret? Unless—

No. It couldn't—he couldn't possibly . . .

I get up and thrust my hands through my hair. OK, let's just . . . stop
all this, right now. This is Arnold I'm talking about. *Arnold*. I'm turning
into some nutty conspiracy theorist.

With sudden resolution I get out my phone. I'll call Arnold. I'll wish
him well in his retirement. Then maybe I can get rid of all these ridiculous ideas floating round my head.

After three rings the phone is picked up by Lara. 'Arnold Saville's
office.'

'Hi, Lara,' I say. 'It's . . . Samantha. Samantha Sweeting.'

'*Samantha?*' Lara sounds poleaxed. 'Bloody hell! How are you?'

'I'm fine, thanks. Really good.' I quell a spasm of nerves. 'I just rang
because I've heard that Arnold's leaving. Is it true?'

'It's true!' says Lara with relish. 'He's moving to the Bahamas.'

'The *Bahamas?*' I say in astonishment.

'He's bought a house there! Looks lovely. He leaves on Friday,' Lara
continues. 'I'll be transferring to Derek Green's office, you remember
him? Taxation partner? Very nice guy, though apparently he can have a
bit of a temper—'

'Er . . . great!' I cut her off, suddenly remembering her ability to
gossip for hours without taking a breath. 'Lara, I just wanted to give
Arnold my best wishes. If you could possibly put me through?'

'Really?' Lara sounds surprised. 'That's incredibly generous of you,
Samantha. After what happened.'

'Well, you know,' I say awkwardly, 'it wasn't Arnold's fault. He did
what he could.'

There's a strange silence.

'Yes,' says Lara after a pause. 'Well. I'll put you through.'

After a few moments Arnold's familiar voice is booming down the
line. 'Samantha, dear girl! Is it really you?'

'It's really me.' I manage a smile. 'I haven't *quite* disappeared off the
face of the earth.'

'I should hope not! Now, you're all right, are you?'

'I'm . . . fine,' I say awkwardly. 'Thanks. I was just surprised to hear you're retiring.'

'I was never a glutton for punishment!' He gives an easy laugh. 'Thirty-three years at the coalface of law. That's enough for any human. Let alone any lawyer!'

Just his jovial voice is reassuring me. I must be crazy. Arnold couldn't be involved in anything untoward. He couldn't be hiding anything. He's *Arnold*. I'll mention it to him, I decide. Just to prove it to myself.

'Well . . . I hope it all goes well,' I say. 'And I . . . I guess you'll be seeing more of your family?'

'I'll be lumbered with the blighters, yes!' He laughs again.

'I never knew your son-in-law was a director of BLLC Holdings!' I attempt a casual tone. 'Quite a coincidence!'

There's a moment of silence.

'I'm sorry?' says Arnold. His voice is still as charming as ever, but the warmth has disappeared.

'BLLC Holdings.' I swallow. 'You know, the other company involved with the Third Union Bank loan? The one that registered a charge? I just happened to notice . . .'

'I have to go now, Samantha!' Arnold cuts me off smoothly. 'Delightful to chat, but I'm leaving the country on Friday and there's a lot to do. It's exceedingly busy here, so I wouldn't ring again if I were you.'

The line goes dead before I can say any more. I slowly put down the phone and stare at a butterfly fluttering outside the window.

That wasn't right. That wasn't a natural reaction. He got rid of me as soon as I mentioned his son-in-law.

Something is going on. Something is definitely going on.

What could it be? I have totally abandoned the housework for the afternoon and am sitting on my bed with a pad of paper and pencil, trying to work out the possibilities.

Who stands to gain? I stare at my scribbled facts and arrows yet again. Two brothers. Millions of pounds being transferred between banks and companies. Think. *Think* . . .

Let's get everything in logical order. Glazerbrooks went into receivership. Third Union Bank lost their money. BLLC Holdings jumped ahead in the queue . . .

I tap my pencil impatiently on the paper. But so what? They only get back the money they loaned. They don't get any advantage. Unless— what if they never paid over anything in the first place?

The thought hits my brain out of nowhere. I sit bolt upright, unable to breathe. What if that's it? *What if that's the scam?*

My mind starts to race. Suppose there are two brothers. They know that Glazerbrooks is in serious financial trouble. They know that the bank has just paid in £50 million but the bank's charge wasn't registered. That means there's a £50-million unsecured loan swilling around in the company, up for grabs by anyone else who registers a charge . . .

I can't sit down any more. I'm pacing back and forth, my brain sparking like an electrical circuit. It works. It works. They fiddle the figures. BLLC Holdings get the money that Third Union Bank paid over, Carter Spink's insurers foot the bill—

I pause in my striding. No. It doesn't work. I'm being stupid. The insurers are only covering the £50 million because I was negligent. That's the crucial element. The whole plan would have depended on me, Samantha Sweeting, making that particular mistake.

I mean . . . you can't plan a mistake in advance. You can't *make* someone forget to do something—

And then I stop dead. My skin suddenly feels clammy. The memo.

I never saw that memo on my desk until it was too late.

What if—Oh my God. What if someone planted that memo on my desk? Slipped it into a pile of papers after the deadline had passed?

What if I didn't make a mistake?

I assumed the memo was there all the time. I assumed it was my error. But what if it wasn't? Everyone at Carter Spink knew I had the messiest desk in the firm. It would be easy to slip the memo into a pile of papers. Make it look as if it had been there for weeks.

I'm breathing harder and harder, till I'm almost hyperventilating. I have lived with that mistake for two months. It's there every morning when I wake up and every day when I go to bed. Like a constant chorus in my head: Samantha Sweeting ruined her life.

But . . . what if I was used? *What if I didn't make a mistake after all?*

I have to know. I have to know the truth. Right now. With a shaking hand I reach for my mobile phone and punch in the number again.

'Lara, I need to speak to Arnold again,' I say, as soon as I'm connected.

'Samantha . . .' Lara sounds awkward. 'I'm afraid Arnold won't take any more calls from you. And he asked me to tell you that you're not to pester him about your job any more.'

I feel a flash of shock. 'Lara, I'm not pestering him about my job.' I try to keep my voice steady. 'I just need to talk to him about a . . . matter. If he won't talk to me, I'll come to the office. Can you make me an appointment, please?'

'Samantha . . .' She sounds even more embarrassed than before. 'Arnold told me to inform you . . . if you try to come here to the offices, Security will eject you.'

'*Eject* me?' I stare at the phone in disbelief.

'I'm sorry. I really am. And I don't blame you!' she adds fervently. 'I thought what Arnold did to you was really shocking! A lot of us do.'

I feel a fresh confusion. What he *did* to me? Does Lara know about the memo?

'What—what do you mean?' I stammer.

'The way he got you fired!' says Lara.

'What?' I feel like all the breath has been squeezed from my chest.

'I *did* wonder if you knew.' She lowers her voice. 'He's leaving now, so I can say it. I took the minutes at that meeting, after you ran off. And Arnold talked round all the other partners. He said you were a liability and they couldn't risk taking you back and all sorts. A lot of them wanted to give you another chance, you know.'

'Thanks for telling me, Lara. I . . . had no idea.'

I feel dizzy. Everything is turning out distorted. Arnold didn't fight my corner at all. He got me fired. With a sickening thud I suddenly recall him the day after it happened, insisting I should stay where I was, not come back. That's why. He wanted me out of the way so I couldn't fight for myself. So he could stitch me up.

And I trusted him. Totally and utterly. Like a stupid, gullible fool.

My chest is heaving painfully. All my doubts have disappeared. Arnold is in on something crooked. I know it. He set me up. He planted that memo, knowing it would destroy my career.

A bleeping from my mobile phone makes me jump, and I look up blearily. I'd almost forgotten where I was. I pick it up and see that I've got a text.

I'm downstairs. have a surprise to show you. nat

As I head downstairs, I'm really not with it. Flashes of anger keep overwhelming me as I think of Arnold's jocular smile, the way he told me he'd do his best for me, the way he listened as I blamed myself, as I apologised and grovelled . . .

'Hi.' Nathaniel waves a hand in front of my face. 'Earth to Samantha.'

'Oh . . . Sorry. Hi!' Somehow I muster a smile. 'What's the surprise?'

'Come this way.' He grins and ushers me out to his car, which is an ancient Beetle convertible. As usual, rows of seed pots are crowding the back seat and an old wooden spade is sticking out of the back.

'Madam.' He opens the door gallantly.

'So what are you showing me?' I ask as I get in.

'Magical mystery tour.' He gives an enigmatic smile, and starts up the engine.

We drive out of Lower Ebury and take a route through a tiny neighbouring village and up into the hills. Nathaniel seems in a cheerful mood and tells me stories about each farm and pub that we pass. But I barely hear a word. My mind is still churning.

I don't know what I can do. I can't even get into the building. I have no credibility. I'm powerless. And I only have three days. Once Arnold disappears off to the Bahamas that'll be it.

'Here we are!' Nathaniel turns off the road on to a gravel drive. He stops the engine. 'What do you think?'

With an effort I wrench my mind back to the present. 'Um . . .' I peer around blankly. 'Yes. Lovely.'

'Samantha, are you OK?' Nathaniel shoots me a curious glance.

'I'm fine.' I try to smile. 'Just a bit tired.'

I open the car door to get out, away from his gaze. I shut the door behind me, take a few steps forward and look around.

We're in some kind of courtyard, baking in the evening sun. There's a ramshackle house to the right, with a 'For Sale' post. Ahead are banks of greenhouses, glinting in the low sunlight. There are plots, filled with rows of vegetables, there's a Portacabin marked GARDEN CENTRE . . .

Hang on.

I swivel round in bewilderment to see that Nathaniel has got out of the car too. He's grinning at me and holding a sheaf of papers.

'A horticultural business opportunity,' he reads aloud. 'Four acres of land, with ten more available, subject to negotiation. Ten thousand square feet of glasshouses. Four-bedroom farmhouse, needs work . . .'

'You're *buying* this?' I say, my attention fully grabbed.

'I'm thinking about it. I wanted to show you first.' He spreads an arm out. 'It's a pretty good concern. Needs building up, but the land's there. We can get some polytunnels going, extend the offices . . .'

'But what about the pubs? How come you're suddenly—'

'It was you. What you said in the garden that day.' He pauses, the breeze ruffling his hair. 'I'm not a landlord, I'm a gardener. I'd be happier doing what I really want to do. So . . . I had a long talk with Mum and she understood. We both reckon Eamonn can take over. Not that he knows yet.'

'Wow.' I look around again, taking in a pile of wooden crates; stacks of seed trays; a tattered poster advertising Christmas trees. 'So you're really going to do it?'

Nathaniel shrugs, but I can see the excitement in his face. 'You only get one chance at life.'

'Well, I think it's fantastic.' I beam with genuine enthusiasm.

'And there's a house.' He nods towards it. 'Or at least, there will be a house. It's a bit run down.'

'Right.' I regard the ramshackle building with a grin. 'It does look a bit of a mess.'

'I wanted you to see it first,' says Nathaniel. 'Get your approval. I mean, one day you might . . .' He stops.

There's silence in the courtyard. All of a sudden my relationship sensors are swivelling round madly. What was he going to say?

'I might . . . stay over?' I supply at last, a little awkward.

'Exactly.' Nathaniel rubs his nose. 'Shall we have a look?'

The house is bigger than it looks from the outside, with bare boards and old fireplaces. One room has practically no plaster, and the kitchen is totally old-fashioned, with 1930s cupboards.

'Great kitchen.' I shoot him a teasing look.

'I'm sure I could refit it to your cordon bleu standards,' he returns.

We make our way upstairs and into a huge bedroom overlooking the rear of the house. From above, the vegetable plots look like an orderly patchwork quilt, stretching away into the green meadow.

'It's a beautiful place,' I say, leaning on the window sill. 'I love it.'

Standing here, looking out at the view, Carter Spink and Arnold suddenly seem part of another life. I'm not just out of the loop, I'm off the string altogether. But even as I'm gazing out at the restful country scene, I can feel myself grasping for the end of it. I can't let it go. All it would take is one phone call to the right person . . . If I had some proof . . .

'What I was wondering is . . .'

Suddenly I become aware that Nathaniel is speaking. In fact I think he could have been speaking for a while—and I haven't heard a word. I hastily turn round, to see him facing me. His cheeks are flushed and he has an unfamiliar awkwardness about him. It looks like whatever he's been saying has required some effort.

'. . . do you feel the same way, Samantha?'

I stare back at him dumbly. Do I feel the same way about what?

Oh shit. Was he saying something really heartfelt and meaningful? Was he making some sort of speech of love? And I *missed* it?

This just teaches me to obsess. The man I'm secretly falling in love with just made a romantic speech to me—probably the only one I'll get in my whole life—and *I wasn't listening*?

And now he's waiting for me to reply. What am I going to do? He's just spilled his heart to me. I can't say, 'Sorry, I didn't quite catch that.'

'Um . . .' I push my hair back, playing for time. 'Well . . . you've given me quite a lot to think about.'

'But do you agree?'

Do I agree with what? Capital punishment for burglars? Threesomes? OK, this is Nathaniel. I'm sure I agree with it, whatever it is.

'Yes.' I give him the most sincere look I can muster. 'Yes, I agree. Wholeheartedly. In fact . . . I've often thought so myself.'

A strange flicker passes over Nathaniel's face as he surveys me. 'You agree,' he says, as though to make sure. 'With everything?'

'Er . . . yes!'

'Even about the chimpanzees?'

'The *chimpanzees*?' I see Nathaniel's mouth twitching. He's twigged.

'You didn't listen to a word I was saying, did you?' he says.

'I didn't realise you were saying something important!' I wail, hanging my head. 'You should have warned me!'

Nathaniel looks at me incredulously. 'That took some nerve, you know, saying all that.'

'Say it again,' I beg. 'Say it all again! I'll listen!'

'Uh-huh.' He laughs, shaking his head. 'Maybe one day.'

'I'm sorry, Nathaniel. Really I am.' I turn away to stare out of the window again. 'I was just . . . distracted.'

'I know.' He comes over and puts his arms round me, over my own. I can feel his steady heartbeat against me, calming me down. 'Samantha, what's up? It's your old relationship, isn't it?'

'Yup,' I mutter after a pause.

'Why won't you tell me about it? I could help.'

I swivel round to face him. The sun is glowing in his eyes and on his burnished face. He's never looked more handsome. I have a sudden vision of him punching Arnold right in the face.

But I can't dump all this on him. It's too big. It's too . . . sordid.

'I don't want to bring that world into this one,' I say at last.

Nathaniel opens his mouth again but I turn away before he can speak. I stare out at the idyllic view again, blinking against the rays of the sun, my mind in turmoil.

Maybe I should just give up on the whole nightmare. Forget about it. Let it go. Close the door on my old life and leave it behind for ever. I have a job. I have Nathaniel. I have a possible future here.

But even as I'm thinking it—I know that's not what I'm going to do. I can't forget about it. I can't let go. There's one more chance and I have nothing left to lose.

Ten

OK. BEING BACK IN LONDON has thrown me a little bit. The city isn't the way I remember it. I can't believe how dirty it is. How *rushed* it is. Things I never noticed before. On automatic pilot I head down to the underground and onto a train. I can see my face in the window opposite, pale and expressionless.

As I walk back to my apartment building, my mind is buzzing. *Will he listen to me?*

I come out of the lift, two floors higher than usual. It's almost identical to my floor—same carpet, same wallpaper, same lamps. Just different numbers on the apartment doors: 31 and 32. I can't remember which one I want so in the end I plump for 31. It has a softer doormat. I sink down on the floor, put my bag down, lean against the door and wait.

My phone bleeps, but I ignore it. It'll be yet another message from Trish. She was livid when I told her I had to go away for a couple of days; in fact she tried to stop me. So I told her I had a foot complaint which needed urgent attention from my specialist in London.

In hindsight this was a huge mistake, as she wanted to know every single gory detail. She even demanded I take off my shoe and show her. I had to spend ten minutes improvising about 'bone misalignment' while she peered at my foot and said 'it looks perfectly normal to me' in tones of great suspicion.

She looked at me mistrustfully for the rest of the day. Then she left a copy of *Marie Claire* casually open at the 'Pregnant? Need Confidential Advice?' advertisement. Honestly. I have to knock that one on the head or it'll be all over the village and Iris will be knitting bootees.

I look at my watch and feel a swoop of nerves. But all I can do is wait.

By the time Ketterman emerges from the lift I've been sitting here for three hours, without anything to eat or drink. But at the sight of him I scramble to my feet.

For a moment Ketterman looks shocked. Then he resumes his usual stony expression. 'Samantha. What are you doing here?'

I take a step forward. 'I know I'm the last person you want to see.' I rub my aching brow. 'Believe me, I don't want to be here either. Out of all the people in the world I could turn to for help . . . you would be the last. So the fact that I'm here, coming to you . . . should prove it to you.' I look at him desperately. 'I'm serious. I have something to tell you, and you have to listen. You have to.'

There's a long silence between us. Ketterman's face is rigid. I can't tell what he's thinking. Then, at last, he reaches into his pocket for a key. He walks past me, unlocks the door to flat 32—and turns.

'Come in.'

I wake up to the view of a cracked, grubby ceiling. My eyes run along to a huge cobweb in the corner of the room, then down the wall to a rickety bookshelf stuffed with books, tapes, letters, old Christmas decorations and the odd bit of discarded underwear.

How did I live in this mess for seven years? How did I not *notice* it?

I push back the cover, get out of bed and look around blearily. The carpet feels gritty under my feet and I wince. It needs a good hoover. I guess the cleaner stopped coming after the money stopped appearing.

I find a dressing gown, pull it on and head out to the kitchen. I'd forgotten how bare and cold and spartan it was in here. There's nothing in the fridge, of course. But I find a camomile teabag and fill the kettle, and perch on a bar stool, looking out at the brick wall opposite.

It's already nine fifteen. Ketterman will be at the office. He'll be taking whatever action he's going to take. I wait to feel the nerves rise . . . but they don't. I feel weirdly calm. Everything's out of my hands now; there's nothing I can do.

He listened to me. He actually listened, and asked questions, and even made me a cup of tea. I was there for over an hour. He didn't tell me what he thought or what he was going to do. He didn't even say whether he believed me or not. But something tells me he did.

The kettle's coming to the boil when the phone rings. I pick up the receiver, suddenly wondering how many people must have rung this number over the last few weeks. The machine is crammed with messages, but after listening to the first three, all from Mum and each more furious than the last, I gave up.

'Hello?'

'Samantha,' comes a businesslike voice. 'John Ketterman here.'

'Oh.' In spite of myself I feel a nervous swoop. 'Hi.'

'I'd like you to come to the Carter Spink offices,' he says. 'It may be necessary for you to speak to some people.'

'People?'

There's a slight pause, then Ketterman says, 'Investigators.'

Oh my God. Oh my *God*. I feel like punching the air or bursting into tears or something. But somehow I keep my composure.

'So have you found something out? Was my theory right?'

There's a crackling silence down the phone. I can't breathe.

'Not in every detail,' says Ketterman at last, and I feel a painful thrill of triumph. That means I was right in some details.

The phone goes dead. I put the receiver down and look at my reflection in the hall mirror. My cheeks are flushed and my eyes are bright.

I was right. And they know it.

They'll offer me my job back, it suddenly hits me. They'll offer me partnership. At the thought I'm seized with excitement—and at the same time, a kind of weird fear.

I'll cross that bridge when I come to it.

I spend three hours at the Carter Spink offices, talking in turn to a man from the Law Society, two of the senior partners and some guy from Third Union Bank.

I still haven't worked out exactly what's going on. Lawyers are so bloody discreet. I know someone's been to see Arnold at his home and that's about it. But even if no one's going to admit it, I know I was right. I've been vindicated.

After the last interview, a plate of sandwiches is brought to the room I'm in, together with a bottle of mineral water and a muffin. I get to my feet, stretch, and wander over to the window. I feel like a prisoner in here. There's a tapping at the door and Ketterman comes into the room.

'Haven't I finished yet?' I say. 'I've been here hours.'

'We may need to speak to you again.' He gestures to the sandwiches. 'Have some lunch.'

I cannot stay in this room a moment longer. I have to stretch my legs, at least.'I'll just go and freshen up first,' I say, and hurry out of the room before he can object.

As I enter the Ladies, all the women in there stop talking immediately. I disappear into a cubicle and hear the sound of excited whisperings and murmurings outside. As I come out again, not one person has left the room. I can feel all the eyes on me, like sun lamps.

'So are you back now, Samantha?' says an associate called Lucy.

'Not exactly.' I turn away to the sink, feeling self-conscious.

'You look so *different*,' says another girl.

'Your arms!' says Lucy as I wash my hands. 'They're so brown. And *toned*. Have you been to a spa?'

'Er . . . no.' I give a mysterious smile. 'How's life been here?'

'Good.' Lucy nods a few times. 'Extremely busy. Clocked up sixty-six billable hours last week. Two all-nighters.'

'I had three,' puts in another girl. She speaks casually, but I can see the pride in her face. And the dark grey shadows under her eyes. Is that what I used to look like? All pale and strained and tense?

'Great!' I say politely, drying my hands. 'Well, I'd better get back now. See you.'

I exit the Ladies and am walking back to the interview room, lost in my own thoughts, when I hear a voice.

'Oh my God, *Samantha?*'

'*Guy?*' I look up in shock to see him hurrying down the corridor towards me, his smile even more dazzling than ever.

'Look at you!' He grips my shoulders tightly and scans my face. 'You look fantastic.' He lowers his voice. 'I've just been briefed on the situation. Bloody hell, Samantha, it's incredible. Only you could work all that out. *Arnold*, of all people. I was *shell-shocked*. Everyone is. Those who know,' he adds, lowering his voice still further. 'Obviously it's not out yet.'

'I don't even know what the "situation" is,' I reply, with a touch of resentment. 'No one's telling me anything.'

'Well, they will.' Guy reaches into his pocket, gets out his BlackBerry and squints at it. 'You are flavour of the month right now. I knew it all along.' He looks up. 'I knew you never made a mistake.'

I gape at him. How can he say that?

'No, you didn't,' I reply at last, finding my words. 'You said I was "unreliable".'

'I said *other* people had said you made errors.' Guy pauses in tapping at his BlackBerry and looks up, frowning. 'Shit, Samantha. I did stand up for you. I was on your side. Ask anyone!'

Yup. Sure. That's why you wouldn't have me to stay.

But I don't say anything out loud. I really don't want to get into it. It's history. 'Fine,' I say at last. 'Whatever.'

We start walking along the corridor together, Guy still engrossed in the BlackBerry. God, he's addicted to that thing, I think, with irritation.

'So where the hell did you disappear to?' At last he stops tapping. 'What have you been doing all this time?'

'I've got a job.'

'I knew you'd get snapped up.' He nods with satisfaction. 'Who's employed you?'

'Oh . . . no one you'd know,' I say after a pause.

'You're in the same area, though?' He puts his BlackBerry away. 'Doing the same kind of work?'

I have a sudden vision of me mopping Trish's bathroom floor.

'Er . . . as it happens, not really.' Somehow I keep a straight face.

Guy seems surprised. 'But you're still in banking law, right? Don't tell me you've made a complete change?' He suddenly looks galvanised. 'You haven't gone into commercial law, have you?'

'Um, no . . . not commercial law. I'd better go.' I cut him off and open the door to the interview room. 'See you later.'

I eat my sandwiches, I drink my mineral water. For half an hour no one disturbs me. I feel a bit like I'm in quarantine for some deadly illness. They could have given me some magazines, at least. I've developed quite a habit for gossip, after being surrounded by Trish's endless supply of *Heat* and *Hello!*.

At last I hear a knock at the door and Ketterman comes in.

'Samantha, we would like to see you in the boardroom.'

The *boardroom*? Blimey.

I follow Ketterman down the corridors, aware of the nudges and whisperings from everyone we pass. He opens the huge double doors to the boardroom and I walk in, to see about half the partners standing there, waiting for me. There's silence as Ketterman closes the doors.

Am I supposed to speak? Did I miss the instructions? Ketterman has joined the group of partners. Now he turns to face me.

'Samantha, as you know, an investigation of . . . recent events is under way. The results have not yet been fully determined.' He breaks off, looking tense, and I can see some of the others exchanging sober looks. 'However, we have come to one conclusion. You were wronged.'

I gape at him in stupefaction. He's *admitting* it? Getting a lawyer to admit they've made a mistake is like getting a movie star to admit they've had liposuction.

'Thank you.' I smile politely. 'I appreciate that.'

'And therefore.' Ketterman pauses. 'We would like to offer you full equity partnership in the firm. Effective immediately.'

I'm so shocked I nearly sit down on the floor. *Full equity partnership?*

I open my mouth—but I can't speak. I feel winded. Full equity partnership is the highest pinnacle. It's the most prestigious job in law. I never, ever, *ever* expected that.

'Welcome back, Samantha,' says one of the senior partners, Greg Parker.

'Welcome back,' chime in a few others. David Elldridge gives me a warm smile. Guy gives me the thumbs up.

'We have some champagne.' Ketterman nods to Guy, who opens the double doors. The next moment two waitresses from the partners' dining room are coming in with trays of champagne glasses. Someone puts one in my hand.

This is all going too fast. I have to say something.

'Er . . . excuse me?' I call out. 'I haven't said if I'll accept it yet.'

The whole room seems to freeze, like a videotape on pause.

'I'm sorry?' Ketterman's face contorts with incredulity.

Oh God. I'm not sure they're going to take this very well.

'The thing is . . .' I break off and take a sip of champagne for Dutch courage, trying to work out how to put this tactfully. I've been thinking about it all day. Being a partner at Carter Spink is the dream I've had all my adult life. The glittering prize. It's everything I ever wanted.

Except . . . all the things I never knew I wanted. Like fresh air. Like evenings off. Unburdened weekends. Making plans with friends.

I clear my throat and look round the room.

'It's a tremendous honour to be offered such an amazing opportunity,' I say earnestly. 'And I'm very grateful. Truly. However . . . the reason I came back wasn't to get my job back. It was to clear my name. To prove that I didn't make a mistake.' I can't help shooting a look at Guy. 'The truth is, since leaving Carter Spink I've . . . well . . . moved on. I have a job. Which I very much enjoy. So I won't be taking up your offer.'

There's a stunned silence.

'Is she *serious*?' says someone at the back.

'Samantha,' says Ketterman, coming forward, 'you may have found opportunities elsewhere. But you are a Carter Spink lawyer. This is where you trained, this is where you belong.'

'If it's a question of salary,' adds Elldridge, 'I'm sure we can match whatever you're currently . . .' he glances at Guy. 'Which law firm has she gone to?'

'Wherever you are, I'll speak to the senior partner,' says Ketterman in a businesslike way. 'The personnel director . . . whoever would be appropriate. If you give me a number.' He's taking out his BlackBerry.

My mouth twists. I desperately want to giggle.

'I never said I was working as a lawyer.'

It's as if I've said I think the world is flat. I have never seen so many flummoxed faces in my life.

'You're . . . not working as a lawyer?' says Elldridge at last. 'What are you working as, then?'

I was hoping it wouldn't come to this. But on the other hand, why shouldn't they know?

'I'm working as a housekeeper.' I smile.

'"Housekeeper"?' Elldridge peers at me. 'Is that the new jargon for troubleshooter? Is that what you mean?'

'No, it's not what I mean,' I say patiently. 'I'm a housekeeper. I make beds. I cook meals. I'm a domestic.'

For about sixty seconds nobody moves. God, I wish I had a camera. Their *faces*.

'You're literally . . . a *housekeeper*?' stutters Elldridge at last.

'Uh-huh.' I look at my watch. 'And I'm fulfilled and I'm relaxed and I'm happy. In fact, I should be getting back. Thank you,' I add to Ketterman, 'for listening to me.'

'You're turning down our offer?' says Greg Parker incredulously.

'I'm turning down your offer.' I give an apologetic shrug. 'Sorry.'

As I head out of the room I feel slightly wobbly about the legs. And slightly manic inside. *I turned it down.* I turned down senior partnership of Carter Spink.

What the hell is my mother going to say?

The thought makes me want to burst into hysterical laughter.

I feel too keyed up to wait for the lift so I head down the stairwell, clattering on the cold stone steps.

'Samantha!' Guy's voice suddenly echoes above me.

Oh, honestly. What does he want?

'I'm going!' I yell back. 'Leave me alone!' I can hear him accelerating down the steps, so I pick up speed myself.

'Samantha, this is crazy! I can't let you ruin your career out of . . . out of pique!' he calls.

I wheel round indignantly. 'I'm not doing this out of pique!'

'I know you're angry with us all!' Guy joins me on the staircase, breathing hard. 'I'm sure it makes you feel really good to turn us down, to say you're working as a housekeeper . . .'

'I *am* working as a housekeeper!' I retort. 'And I'm not turning you down because I'm angry, but because I don't want the job.'

'Samantha, you wanted partnership more than anything else in the world!' Guy grabs my arm. 'You can't throw it away! It's too valuable.'

'What if I don't value it any more?'

'It's only been a few weeks! Everything can't have changed!'

'It has. *I* have.' I swivel on my heel and start down the stairs again. I reach the bottom of the stairwell and burst into the foyer with Guy in hot pursuit. Hilary Grant, head of PR, is sitting on a leather sofa with some red-suited woman, and they both look up in surprise.

'Samantha, you cannot do this!' Guy is shouting after me as he emerges into the foyer. 'I cannot let you turn down senior partnership to be a . . . *housekeeper*.'

'Why not, if it's what I want to do?' I come to a halt on the marble and turn to face him. 'Guy, I've found out what it's like to have a life! I've found out what it's like, *not* feeling pressure all the time. And I like it!'

'You're going to stand there and tell me you prefer cleaning loos to being a partner of Carter Spink?' His face is flushed with outrage.

'Yes!' I say defiantly. 'Yes, I do!'

'Who's that?' says the woman in the red suit with interest.

'Samantha, you're making the biggest mistake of your entire existence!' Guy's voice follows me as I reach the doors. 'If you walk out now—'

I don't hear any more. I'm out of the door. Down the steps. Gone.

I *might have just made the biggest mistake of my entire existence.* As I sit on the train back to Gloucestershire, Guy's words keep ringing in my ears.

Once upon a time, just that thought would have sent me into a tailspin. But not any more. I almost want to laugh. He has no idea.

If I've learned one thing from everything that's happened to me, it's that there is no such thing as the biggest mistake of your existence. There's no such thing as ruining your life. Life's a pretty resilient thing, it turns out.

When I arrive at Lower Ebury I head straight to the pub. Nathaniel is behind the bar, talking to Eamonn. For a few moments I just watch him: his strong hands; the slant of his neck; the way his brow furrows as he nods. I can tell at once he disagrees with whatever Eamonn is saying. But he's waiting, wanting to be tactful about making his point.

Maybe I'm better at telepathy than I thought.

As if he's telepathic too, he looks up and smiles a welcome—but I can see the tension underneath. These last couple of days can't have been easy for him. Maybe he thought I wasn't coming back.

A roar goes up from the dartboard, and one of the guys turns and spots me walking towards the bar.

'Samantha!' he shouts. 'At last! We need you on our team!'

'In a sec!' I call over my shoulder. 'Hi,' I say as I reach Nathaniel.

'Hi,' he says casually. 'Good trip?'

'Not bad.' I nod. Nathaniel lifts up the bar for me to come through, his eyes searching my face as though for clues.

'So . . . is it over?'

'Yup.' I put my arms around him and hug him tight. 'It's over.'

And at that moment, I truly believe it is.

Eleven

NOTHING HAPPENS until lunchtime.

I make the breakfast for Trish and Eddie as usual. I hoover and dust as usual. Then I get out the chopping board and start squeezing oranges. I'm going to make bitter chocolate and orange mousse for the charity lunch tomorrow. We're going to serve it on a bed of crystallised orange slices, and each plate is going to be garnished with a real silver-leaf angel from a Christmas decoration catalogue.

This was Trish's idea. As are the angels hanging from the ceiling.

'How are we doing?' Trish comes tapping into the kitchen, looking flustered. 'Have you made the mousses yet?'

'Not yet,' I say, briskly squeezing an orange. 'Mrs Geiger, don't worry. It's all under control.'

'Do you know what I've *been* through, the last few days?' She clutches her head. 'More and more people keep accepting . . . I've had to change the seating plan . . .'

'It'll be fine,' I say soothingly. 'Try to relax.'

'Yes.' She breathes out, holding her head between two lacquered finger-nails. 'You're right. I'll just go and check the goody bags . . .'

I cannot believe how much Trish is spending on this lunch. Every time I question whether we really need to canopy the dining room in white silk, or give every guest an orchid buttonhole, she shrills 'It's all in a good cause!'

Which reminds me of something I've been meaning to ask her for quite a while now.

'Er . . . Mrs Geiger,' I say casually, 'are you charging your guests for entrance to the lunch?'

'Oh, no!' she says. 'I think that's rather *tacky*, don't you?'

'Are you holding a raffle?'

'I don't think so.' She wrinkles her nose. 'People *loathe* raffles.'

I hardly dare ask this next question. 'So . . . um . . . how exactly are you planning on making money for the charity?'

There's silence in the kitchen. Trish has frozen, her eyes wide.

'*Bugger*,' she says at last.

I knew it. She hadn't given it a thought. 'Perhaps we could ask for voluntary donations?' I suggest. 'We could hand round a little bag with the coffee and the mints?'

'Yes. Yes.' Trish peers at me as though I'm a genius. '*That's* the answer.' She exhales sharply. 'This is really very stressful, Samantha. I don't know how you stay so calm.'

I smile, feeling a sudden wave of fondness for her. When I arrived back at the house last night it was like coming home. Even though Trish had left a mountain of crockery on the counter for my return, and a note saying *Samantha, please polish all silver tomorrow.*

Trish heads out of the kitchen and I start whisking up egg whites for the mousse. Then I notice a man sidling down the drive. He's wearing jeans and an old polo shirt and has a camera slung round his neck. He disappears from view and I frown in puzzlement. Maybe he's a delivery man. I measure out the caster sugar, with half an ear out for the door-bell, and start folding it into the egg whites, just the way Iris taught me. Then, suddenly, the man is standing at the kitchen door, peering in through the window.

I'm not ruining my mixture for some door-to-door salesman. He can wait a few moments. I finish folding in the sugar—then head to the door and open it. 'Can I help?' I say politely.

The man gazes silently at me for a few seconds, glancing down every so often at a folded-up tabloid newspaper in his hand. 'Are you Samantha Sweeting?' he says at last.

I look back at him warily. 'Why?'

'I'm from the *Cheltenham Gazette*.' He flashes an ID card at me. 'I'm after an exclusive interview with you. "Why I chose the Cotswolds as my secret hideaway"—that kind of thing.'

I look at him blankly. 'Er . . . what are you talking about?'

'You haven't seen it?' He looks surprised. 'I take it this is you?'

He turns the newspaper round and as I see it, my stomach seizes up in shock.

It's a picture of me. In the newspaper. Me.

It's my official Carter Spink portrait. Above the picture, in bold black letters, is the headline: I'D RATHER CLEAN LOOS THAN BE A PARTNER AT CARTER SPINK.

With trembling hands I grab the paper and scan the text.

Top law firm Carter Spink is the most prestigious in the country. But yesterday one young woman turned down a high-ranking post as partner in order to work as a humble housekeeper.

GET A LIFE

Partners were left with egg on their faces as star £500-an-hour lawyer Samantha Sweeting rejected their offer, which carried a substantial six-figure salary. Having previously been fired, the high-flier apparently uncovered a financial scandal at the firm. However, when offered full equity partnership, Sweeting cited the pressure and lack of free time as reason for her decision.

'I've got used to having a life,' she said, as partners begged her to stay.

A former Carter Spink employee who declined to be named confirmed the brutal working conditions of the legal firm. 'They expect you to sell your soul,' he said.

A spokeswoman for Carter Spink defended the firm's practices. 'We are a flexible, modern firm with a sympathetic working ethos. We would like to talk to Samantha about her views and would certainly not expect employees to "sell their soul".'

VANISHED

She confirmed that Ms Sweeting's job offer is still open and Carter Spink partners are anxious to talk to her. However, in a further extraordinary twist, this modern-day Cinderella has not been seen since running away from the offices.

I stare at the page, numb with disbelief. How did— What did—?

A flash interrupts me and I look up in shock to see the guy pointing his camera at me.

'Stop!' I say in horror, putting my hands up in front of my face.

'Can I have a picture of you holding a toilet brush, love?' he says, zooming his lens in. 'They tipped me off at the pub it was you. Quite a scoop.' The camera flashes again and I flinch.

'No! You . . . you have made mistake.' I shove the paper back at him. 'This . . . Zees ees not me. My name is Martine. I no lawyer.'

The journalist looks at me suspiciously, and down at the photo again. I can see a flicker of doubt cross his face. I do look fairly different now from the way I did then, with my blonde hair and everything.

'That's not a French accent,' he says.

He has a point. Accents aren't exactly my strong point.

'Am . . . half Belgian.' I keep my eyes fixed on the floor. 'Please leave 'ouse now. Or I call police.'

I shove him off the doorstep, slam the door shut and turn the key. Then I pull the curtain across the window and lean back against the door, my heart thudding. Fuck. What am I going to do?

OK. The important thing is not to panic. The important thing is to stay rational and take a balanced view of the situation.

On the one hand, my entire past has been exposed in a national tabloid. On the other hand, Trish and Eddie don't read that particular tabloid. Or the *Cheltenham Gazette*. It's one silly story in one silly paper and it will die away by tomorrow. There's no reason to tell them anything. I'll just carry on making my chocolate orange mousses as though nothing has happened. Yes. Total denial is the way forward.

Feeling slightly better I reach for the chocolate and start breaking chunks into a glass bowl.

OK. Denial's not going to work, because twenty minutes later there are three more journalists in the drive.

'Do you know what's going on, Samantha?' says Trish, coming into the kitchen carrying a book called *Your Elegant Luncheon Party*. 'There seems to be a bit of a *commotion* outside in the road.'

'Is there?' I say. 'I . . . I hadn't noticed.'

'It looks like a protest.' She wrinkles her brow. 'I do hope they're not still there tomorrow. Protesters are so *selfish* . . .'

I feel like I'm in some kind of parallel reality. Everything's going to come out. It's just a matter of time. What do I do?

'Have *you* seen this protest?' Trish demands as Eddie saunters into the kitchen. 'Outside our gates! I think we should tell them to move on.'

'It's not a protest,' he says, opening the fridge. 'It's journalists.'

'*Journalists?*' Trish peers at him. 'What on earth would journalists be doing here?'

'Maybe we have a new celebrity neighbour?' suggests Eddie, pouring a beer into a glass.

At once Trish claps her hand over her mouth. 'Joanna Lumley! I *heard* a rumour she was buying in the village! Samantha, have you heard anything about this?'

'I . . . er . . . no,' I mumble, my face burning.

I have to say something. Come on. Say something. But what? Where do I start?

'Samantha, I need this shirt ironed by tonight.' Melissa comes wandering into the kitchen, holding out a sleeveless print shirt. 'And be really careful with the collar, OK?' she adds with a bad-tempered frown.

'I'm not sure I'll have time—' I begin.

'*Make* time,' she snaps. 'What's going on outside?'

'We think it's Joanna Lumley!' says Trish excitedly.

Suddenly the doorbell rings.

My stomach seems to double over. For a moment I consider bolting out of the back door.

'I wonder if that's them!' exclaims Trish. 'Eddie, go and answer it. Samantha, put on some coffee.'

I'm totally paralysed. I need to speak. I need to explain. But my mouth won't move. Nothing will move.

'Samantha?' She peers at me. 'Are you all right?'

With an almighty effort I look up. 'Um . . . Mrs Geiger . . .' My voice comes out a nervous husk. 'There's something . . . I ought to . . .'

'Melissa!' Eddie's voice interrupts me. He's hurrying into the kitchen, a huge beam spread across his face. 'Melissa, love! They want you!'

'*Me?*' Melissa looks up in surprise. 'What do you mean, Uncle Eddie?'

'It's the *Daily Mail*. They want to interview you!' Eddie turns to Trish, glowing with pride. 'Did you know that our Melissa has one of the finest legal brains in the country?'

Oh no. Oh no.

'What?' Trish nearly drops her copy of *Your Elegant Luncheon Party*.

'That's what they said!' Eddie nods. 'They said it might come as quite a surprise to me to learn we had such a high-flying lawyer in the house. I said Nonsense!' He puts an arm round Melissa. 'We've always known you were a star!'

'Mrs Geiger,' I say urgently. No one takes any notice of me.

'It must be that prize I won at law school! They must have heard about it somehow!' Melissa is gasping. 'Oh my God! The *Daily Mail*!'

'They want to take photos!' puts in Eddie. 'They want an exclusive!'

'I need to put on some make-up!' Melissa looks totally flustered.

'Here!' Trish wrenches open her handbag. 'Here's some mascara . . . and lipstick . . .'

I have to stop this. I have to break it to them.

'Mr Geiger . . .' I clear my throat. 'Are you sure . . . I mean, did they ask for Melissa by . . . by name?'

'They didn't need to!' He twinkles at me. 'Only one lawyer in this house!'

'Make some coffee, Samantha,' instructs Trish sharply. 'And use the pink cups. Quickly! Wash them up.'

'The thing is . . . I don't think they've come to see Melissa,' I say desperately. 'There's something I . . . I should have told you . . .'

No one pays any attention. They're all focused on Melissa.

'How do I look?' Melissa smooths her hair back self-consciously.

'Lovely, darling!' Trish leans forward.

'Is she ready for the interview?' An unfamiliar woman's voice comes from the kitchen door and everyone freezes in excitement.

'In here!' Eddie pulls open the door to reveal a dark-haired woman in a trouser suit, whose eyes run appraisingly over the kitchen.

'Here's our legal star!' Eddie gestures to Melissa with a beam of pride.

'Hello.' Melissa tosses back her hair, then steps forward with an out-stretched hand. 'I'm Melissa Hurst.'

The woman looks at Melissa blankly for a few moments. 'Not her,' she says. '*Her.*' And she points at me.

In puzzled silence, everyone swivels to stare at me.

'That's Samantha,' says Trish, looking perplexed. 'The housekeeper.'

'You're Samantha Sweeting, I take it?' The woman brings out her reporter's pad. 'Can I ask you a few questions?'

'You want to interview the *housekeeper*?' says Melissa, sarcastically.

The journalist ignores her. 'You *are* Samantha Sweeting, aren't you?' she persists.

'I . . . yes,' I admit at last, my face burning. 'But I don't want to do an interview. I don't have any comment.'

'*Comment*?' Trish's eyes dart around uncertainly. 'Comment on what?'

'What's going on, Samantha, love?' Eddie looks anxious. 'Are you in some kind of trouble?'

'You haven't *told* them?' The *Daily Mail* journalist looks up from her notepad. 'They have no idea?'

'Told us what?' says Trish, agitated. 'What?'

'Your "housekeeper" is a top City lawyer.' The woman throws down a copy of the tabloid on to the kitchen table. 'And she's just turned down a six-figure partnership to work for you.'

It's as though someone's thrown a grenade into the kitchen. Eddie visibly reels. Trish totters on her high-heeled clogs and grabs a chair for balance. Melissa's face looks like a popped balloon.

'I meant to tell you . . .' I bite my lip awkwardly as I look at their faces. 'I was . . . getting round to it . . .'

Trish's eyes are bulging as she reads the headline. Her mouth is opening and closing, but no sound is coming out.

'You're a . . . a *lawyer*?' she stutters at last.

'There's been a mistake!' Melissa's cheeks are bright pink. '*I'm* the lawyer. *I'm* the one who got a prize at law school! She's the *cleaner.*'

'She's the one who got three prizes at law school.' The journalist jerks her head towards me. 'And the highest law degree of her year.'

'But . . .' Melissa's face is deepening to an ugly purple. 'It's impossible.'

'Youngest ever partner of Carter Spink . . .' The journalist consults her notes. 'Is that right, Ms Sweeting?'

'No!' I say. 'I mean . . . well . . . kind of. Can I make anyone a cup of tea?' I add desperately.

No one seems interested in tea.

'I don't understand.' Eddie turns to me. 'How did you combine being a lawyer with the housekeeping?'

'Yes!' exclaims Trish, coming to life. 'How on earth could you be a City lawyer and have time to train with Michel de la Roux de la Blanc?'

Oh God. They *still* don't get it?

'I'm not really a housekeeper,' I say desperately. 'I'm not really a cordon bleu cook. Michel de la Roux de la Blanc doesn't exist. I'm a . . . a fake.'

I can't look at either of them. Suddenly I feel terrible. 'I'll understand if you want me to leave,' I mumble.

'Leave?' Trish looks horrified. 'We don't want you to leave, do we, Eddie?'

'Absolutely not.' His face becomes even more ruddy. 'You've done a fine job, Samantha. You can't help it if you're a lawyer.'

'"I'm a fake",' says the journalist, writing it carefully down on her notepad. 'Do you feel guilty about that, Ms Sweeting?'

'Stop it!' I say. 'I'm not doing an interview!'

'Ms Sweeting says she'd rather clean loos than be a partner of Carter Spink,' says the journalist, turning to Trish. 'Could I see the loos in question?'

'*Our* loos?' Spots of pink appear on Trish's cheeks. 'Well, we did have the bathrooms refitted recently, they're all Royal Doulton . . .'

'Stop this!' I clutch my hair. 'Look, I'll . . . I'll make a statement to the press. And then I want you all to leave me and my employers alone.'

I hurry out of the kitchen, the *Daily Mail* woman following behind, and fling open the front door. The crowd of journalists is still there, behind the gate. Is it my imagination or are there more than before?

'It's Martine,' says the *Cheltenham Gazette* guy sardonically.

I ignore him. 'Ladies and gentlemen of the press,' I begin. 'I would be grateful if you would leave me alone. There isn't any story here.'

'Are you going to stay a housekeeper?' calls a fat guy in jeans.

'Yes, I am.' I lift my chin. 'I've made a personal choice, for personal reasons, and I'm very happy here.'

'What about feminism?' demands a young girl, as cameras flash. 'Women have fought for years to gain an equal foothold. Now you're telling them they should go back to the kitchen?'

'I'm not telling women anything!' I say, taken aback.

'Was Carter Spink a sexist hellhole?'

'Is this a bargaining ploy?'

'Could you pose for us in your pinny?' calls out the fat guy with a lascivious wink.

'No!' I say in horror. 'I have nothing else to say! Go away!'

Ignoring the cries and shouts of 'Samantha!' I turn and run with trembling legs back up the drive to the house.

I burst into the kitchen, to find Trish, Eddie and Melissa transfixed in front of the newspaper. All three of them raise their heads and regard me as though I'm some kind of alien.

'You charge five hundred pounds an hour?' Trish doesn't seem in control of her voice.

'They offered you full equity partnership?' Melissa looks green. 'And you said *no*? Are you *crazy*?'

'Don't read this stuff!' I try to grab the paper. 'Mrs Geiger, I just want to carry on as usual. I'm still your housekeeper—'

'You're one of the country's top legal talents!' Trish jabs the paper hysterically. 'It says so here!'

'Samantha?' There's a rapping at the door and Nathaniel comes into the kitchen, holding an armful of newly picked potatoes. 'Will this be enough for the lunch?'

I stare at him, feeling a clutch at my heart. He has no idea. Oh God. I should have told him. Why didn't I tell him? *Why didn't I tell him?*

'What are *you*?' says Trish, turning to him wildly. 'A top rocket scientist? A secret government agent?'

'I'm sorry?' Nathaniel shoots me a quizzical look but I can't raise a smile.

'Nathaniel . . .' I trail off, unable to continue.

Nathaniel looks from face to face, a crease of uncertainty deepening in his brow. 'What's going on?' he says at last.

I have never made such a hash of anything as I make of telling Nathaniel. I stammer, I stutter, I repeat myself and go round in circles.

Nathaniel listens in silence. He's leaning against an old stone pillar in front of the secluded bench where I'm sitting. His face is in profile, shadowed in the afternoon sun, and I can't tell what he's thinking.

At last I come to a finish and he slowly lifts his head. If I was hoping for a smile, I don't get it. 'You're a lawyer,' he says at last.

'Yes.' I nod shamefacedly.

'I thought you were in an abusive relationship.' He thrusts his hands through his hair. 'I thought that's why you didn't want to talk about your past. And you let me believe it.'

'I'm sorry.' I wince with guilt. 'I just didn't want you to know the truth.'

'Why not?' he retorts, and I can hear the hurt in his voice. 'What, you didn't trust me?'

'No!' I say in dismay. 'Of course I trust you! If it had been anything else . . .' I break off. 'Nathaniel, you have to understand. When we first met, how could I tell you? Everyone knows you hate lawyers. You even have a sign in your pub—No Lawyers!'

'That sign's a *joke*.' He makes an impatient gesture.

'It's not. Not completely.' I meet his gaze. 'Come on, Nathaniel. If I'd told you I was a City lawyer when we first met, would you have treated me in the same way?'

Nathaniel doesn't reply. I know he's too honest to give me the easy response. He knows as well as I do, the true answer is no.

'I'm the same person.' I lean forward and take his hand. 'Even if I used to be a lawyer . . . I'm still me!'

For a while Nathaniel says nothing, just stares down at the dirt. I'm holding my breath, desperate with hope. Then he looks up with a reluctant half-smile.

'So, how much are you charging me for this conversation, then?'

I exhale in a gust of relief. He's OK. He's OK about it.

'Oh, about a thousand pounds,' I say carelessly. 'I'll send you a bill.'

'Samantha Sweeting, corporate lawyer.' He surveys me for a few moments. 'Nope. I can't see it.'

'Me neither! That part of my life is over.' I squeeze his hand tightly. 'Nathaniel, I'm really sorry. I never meant any of this to happen.'

'I know.' He squeezes my hand back and I feel myself relax.

'So what happens now?' says Nathaniel.

'Nothing. The media interest will die down. They'll get bored.' I lean forward and rest my head on his shoulder, and feel his arms close round me. 'I'm happy in my job. I'm happy in this village. I'm happy with you. I just want everything to stay the same.'

I'm wrong. The media interest doesn't die down. I wake up the next morning to find twice as many journalists as yesterday camped outside, plus two TV vans. As I come into the kitchen. Eddie is sitting at the table, which is covered in newspapers.

'You're in every single paper,' he informs me. 'Look.' He shows me a double-page spread in the *Sun*. There's a picture of me superimposed on the background of a loo, and someone's drawn a toilet brush in one of my hands. 'I'd rather clean loos!' is in huge letters next to my face.

'Oh my God.' I sink into a chair and stare at the picture. '*Why?*'

'It's August,' says Eddie, flicking through the *Telegraph*. 'Nothing else in the news. Is it true you single-handedly uncovered Mafia connections at your law firm?'

'No!' I look up in horror. 'Who said that?'

'Can't remember where I saw it now,' he says, riffling through the pages. 'This one has a poll, look.' Eddie has opened another paper. '"Samantha Sweeting: Heroine or Fool? Phone or text your vote." Then they give a number to call.'

'Samantha! You're up!'

I raise my head to see Trish coming into the kitchen, holding a bundle of newspapers under her arm. As she looks at me she has the same shell-shocked expression of awe that she had yesterday.

'Good morning, Mrs Geiger.' I hastily get to my feet. 'What can I get you for breakfast? Some coffee to begin with?'

'Don't *you* make the coffee, Samantha!' she replies, looking flustered. 'You're our guest. Eddie, *you* can make the coffee!'

'I'm not making the coffee!' objects Eddie.

'I'm not your guest!' I protest. 'I'm your housekeeper!'

I can see Eddie and Trish exchanging doubtful looks.

'Nothing's different!' I insist. 'I'm still your housekeeper! Yes, I could make a lot more money being a lawyer in London. But it's not what I want.' I spread my arms around the kitchen. 'This is what I want to do. This is where I want to be.'

I'm half expecting Trish and Eddie to look moved by my little speech. Instead, they both peer at me in total incomprehension.

'I think you should consider the offer,' says Eddie. 'It says in the paper they're desperate to woo you back.'

'We won't be at *all* offended if you leave,' adds Trish, nodding emphatically. 'We'll *completely* understand.'

'I don't want to leave!' I say crossly. 'I want to stay here and enjoy a fulfilling life at a different pace.'

The telephone rings and Trish picks it up. 'Hello?' She listens for a moment. 'Yes, of *course*, Mavis. *And* Trudy. See you later!' She puts the receiver down. 'Two more guests for the charity lunch!'

'Right.' I glance at my watch. 'I'd better get going on the starters.'

As I'm getting out my pastry the phone rings again and Trish sighs. 'If this is more late guests . . . Hello?' As she listens, her expression changes and she puts her hand over the receiver.

'Samantha,' she hisses. 'It's an ad company. Are you willing to appear in a TV commercial for Toilet Duck? You'd wear a barrister's wig and gown, and you'd have to say—'

'No!' I say, recoiling. 'Of course not!'

'You should never turn down television,' says Eddie reprovingly. 'Could be a big opportunity.'

'No, it couldn't! I don't want to be in any commercials!' I can see Eddie opening his mouth to argue. 'I don't want to do any interviews,' I add quickly. 'I just want everything to go back to normal.'

By lunchtime everything is not back to normal. In fact everything is even more surreal than before.

I've had three more requests to appear on TV and Trish has given an exclusive interview to the *Mail*. Callers to a radio phone-in which Melissa insisted on listening to have described me as an 'antifeminist moron' and a 'parasite on the taxpayers who paid for my education'. I was so furious I almost phoned up myself.

But instead I switched the radio off and took three deep breaths. I'm not going to let myself get hassled. I have other things to think about. Fourteen guests have arrived for the charity lunch and are milling around on the lawn. I have wild-mushroom tartlets to bake, asparagus sauce to finish, and salmon fillets to roast.

I desperately wish Nathaniel was here to keep me calm. But he's gone off to Buckingham to pick up some koi carp for the pond, which Trish has suddenly decided she must have. Apparently they cost hundreds of pounds and all the celebrities have them. It's ridiculous. No one ever even *looks* in the pond.

The doorbell rings just as I'm opening the oven, and I sigh. Not another guest. We've had four late acceptances this morning, which has totally thrown my schedule.

I put the tray of tarts in the oven, gather up the remaining scraps of pastry, and start to wipe down my rolling pin.

'Samantha?' Trish taps at the door. 'We have another guest!'

'*Another* one?' I turn round, wiping flour off my cheek. 'But I've just put the starters in the oven . . .'

'It's a friend of yours. He says he needs to speak to you urgently. About business?' Trish raises her eyebrow at me significantly—then steps aside. And I freeze in astonishment.

It's Guy. Standing in Trish's kitchen. In his immaculate Jermyn Street suit. I stare at him, unable to speak, utterly flabbergasted.

Judging by his expression, he's pretty gobsmacked, too.

'Oh my God,' he says slowly, his eyes running over my uniform, my rolling pin, my floury hands. 'You really are a housekeeper.'

'Yes.' I lift my chin. 'I really am.'

'Samantha . . .' says Trish from the door. '*Not* that I want to interrupt, but . . . Starters in ten minutes?'

'Of course, Mrs Geiger.' I automatically bob a curtsy as Trish leaves and Guy's eyes nearly fall out of his head.

'You *curtsy?*'

'The curtsying was a bit of a mistake,' I admit. I catch his appalled eye and feel a giggle rising. 'Guy, what are you *doing* here?'

'I'm here to persuade you to come back.'

'I'm not coming back. Excuse me.' I get my asparagus sauce out of the fridge, pour it into a pan and and set it on a gentle heat.

Guy is watching in bemusement. 'Samantha,' he says. 'We need to talk.'

'I'm busy.' The kitchen timer goes off and I open the bottom oven to take out my rosemary garlic rolls. I feel a surge of pride as I see them, all golden brown and wafting a delicious, herby scent. I can't resist taking a nibble out of one, then offering it to Guy.

'You *made* these?' He looks astounded. 'I didn't know you could cook.'

'I couldn't. I learned.' I reach into the fridge again for some unsalted butter and break a knob into the foaming asparagus sauce.

'I have a job offer for you,' says Guy. He reaches into his inside pocket and produces a white letter. 'Here. Take a look.'

'I'm not interested!' I reply. 'Don't you understand?' I turn the hob down to a simmer and lean against the counter. 'I've learned a different way to live. I do my day's work, and I finish . . . and that's it. I'm *free*. I don't need to take paperwork home. I don't need to have my BlackBerry switched on twenty-four hours a day, seven days a week. I don't have that constant pressure any more. I'm not stressed out. And it suits me.'

I open the bottom oven, take out my trays of tartlets and start decanting them onto small warmed plates.

'I'll help,' says Guy, coming over.

'You can't *help*.' I roll my eyes.

'Of course I can.' To my astonishment he takes off his jacket, rolls up his sleeves and puts on a cherry-sprigged apron. 'What do I do?'

I can't help a tiny giggle. He looks so incongruous.

'Fine.' I hand him a tray. 'You can take in the starters with me.'

We head to the dining room, carrying the mushroom tartlets and the bread rolls. As we enter the white-canopied room, the chatter breaks off and fourteen dyed, lacquered heads turn. Trish's guests are seated round the table, sipping champagne, each wearing a suit of a different pastel colour. It's like walking into a Dulux paint chart.

'And this is Samantha!' says Trish, whose cheeks are a bright shade of pink. 'Our housekeeper . . . and also top lawyer!'

To my embarrassment a spattering of applause breaks out.

'We saw you in the papers!' says a woman in cream.

'This is Guy, who's helping me out today,' I say, beginning to serve the mushroom tarts.

'He's *also* a partner at Carter Spink,' adds Trish proudly.

I can see impressed glances being exchanged across the table. An elderly woman at the end turns to Trish, looking bewildered.

'Is *all* your help lawyers?'

'Not all,' says Trish airily. 'But having *had* a Cambridge-educated housekeeper, I could never go back.'

'Where do you get them from?' a red-haired woman asks avidly. 'Is there a special agency?'

'It's called Oxbridge Housekeepers,' says Guy, placing a mushroom tart in front of her. 'Only those with first-class honours can apply.'

'Shut *up*,' I mutter. 'Just serve the food.'

At last all the ladies are served and we retreat to the empty kitchen.

'Very funny,' I say, plonking the tray down with a crash.

'Well, for God's sake, Samantha. Do you expect me to take all this *seriously*?' He takes off the apron and throws it down on the table. 'Serving food to a bunch of airheads. You have more brains than anyone in that room, and you're serving them? You're *curtsying* to them? You're cleaning their *bathrooms*?'

He sounds so passionate, I turn round, shocked. His face is flushed and all traces of teasing have gone.

'Samantha, you're living in fantasyland!' he shouts. 'This is all fun because you've never done it before! But it'll wear off! Can't you *see*?'

I feel a pricking of uncertainty inside, which I ignore. 'No, it won't.' I give my asparagus sauce a determined stir. 'I love this life.'

'Will you still love it when you've been cleaning bathrooms for ten years? Get real.' He comes over to the cooker and I turn away. 'So you needed a break. Fine. But now you need to come back to real life.'

'This *is* real life for me,' I shoot back. 'It's more real than my life used to be. I'm not going back to that pressure. I worked seven days a week, for seven bloody years—'

'Exactly. Exactly! And just as you get the reward, you *bail out*?' He clutches his head. 'Samantha, do you realise how bad this all looks for Carter Spink? You have them over a barrel! They want the world to see you walking back into that office. They'll pay you whatever you want. You can earn enough to retire after ten years. You'll be set up for life! *Then* you can go and pick strawberries or sweep floors or whatever it is you want to do.'

I open my mouth automatically to respond . . . but all of a sudden my words have dried up. I can't quite track my thoughts. They're jumping about all over the place in confusion.

'You earned your partnership,' says Guy, his tone quieter. 'You earned it, Samantha. Use it.'

Guy doesn't say any more on the subject. He's always known exactly when to close an argument. He helps me serve the salmon, then gives me a hug and tells me to call him as soon as I've had time to think. And then he's gone, and I'm left alone in the kitchen, my thoughts churning.

I was so certain. I was so sure of myself. But now . . .

His arguments keep playing out in my mind. Maybe this is all a novelty. Maybe after a few years of a simpler life I won't be content.

I have a brain. I worked for my partnership. I earned it.

I bury my head in my hands, resting my elbows on the table, listening to my own heartbeat in my chest, thumping away like a question. *What am I going to do? What am I going to do?*

And yet all the time I'm being pushed towards one answer. The rational answer. The answer which makes most sense.

I know what it is. I'm just not sure I'm ready to face up to it yet.

It takes me until six o'clock. The lunch is over and I've cleared it away. Trish's guests have wandered round the garden and had cups of tea and melted away. As I walk out into the soft, balmy evening, Nathaniel and Trish are standing by the pond, with a plastic tank by Nathaniel's feet.

'This is a kumonryu,' Nathaniel is saying as he scoops something out of the tank with a big green net. 'Want to have a look?' As I get nearer I see an enormous patterned fish flapping noisily in the net. He offers it to Trish and she reels back with a little shriek.

'Get it away! Put it in the pond!'

'It cost you two hundred quid,' says Nathaniel with a shrug. 'I thought you might want to say hello.'

'Put them all in.' Trish shudders. 'I'll come and see them when they're swimming about.' She turns and heads back towards the house.

'All right?' Nathaniel looks up at me. 'How was the charity lunch?'

'It was fine.'

'Did you hear the news?' He scoops another fish into the pond. 'Eamonn's got engaged! He's having a party next weekend at the pub.'

'That's . . . that's great.' My mouth is dry. Come on. Just tell him.

'Nathaniel, I'm going back.' I close my eyes, trying to ignore the stab of pain inside. 'I'm going back to London.'

For a moment he doesn't move. Then very slowly he turns round, the net still in his hand, his face expressionless. 'Right,' he says.

'I'm going back to my old job as a lawyer.' My voice shakes a little. 'Guy from my old firm came down today, and he made me realise . . .' I break off and gesture helplessly.

'Realise what?' Nathaniel says, his brow furrowing a little.

'I can't be a housekeeper all my life!' I sound more defensive than I'd like. 'I'm a trained lawyer! I have a brain!'

'I know you have a brain.' Now *he* sounds defensive. Oh God. I'm not managing this well.

'I've earned partnership. Full equity partnership at Carter Spink.' I gaze up at him, trying to convey the significance of this. 'It's the most prestigious . . . lucrative . . . amazing . . . I can make enough money in a few years to retire!'

Nathaniel doesn't seem too impressed. 'At what cost?'

'What do you mean?'

'I mean that when you turned up here, you were a nervous wreck. You were like some freaked-out rabbit. White as a sheet. Stiff as a board. You looked like you hadn't ever seen the sun, you looked like you hadn't ever *enjoyed* yourself—'

'You're exaggerating.'

'I'm not. Can't you *see* how much you've changed? You're not edgy any more. You're not a bundle of nerves.'

'OK, so I've relaxed a bit!' I throw up my hands. 'I know I've calmed down and I've learned to cook and iron and pull pints . . . and I've had a wonderful time. But it's like a holiday. It can't last for ever.'

Nathaniel shakes his head in despair. 'So after all this you're just going to go back, and carry on as though nothing happened?'

'It'll be different this time! I'll make it different. I'll keep a balance.'

'Who are you kidding?' Nathaniel grips my shoulders. 'Samantha, it'll be the same stress, the same lifestyle—'

I feel a sudden surge of anger towards him for not understanding; for not supporting me.

'Well, at least I *tried* something new!' My words pour out in a torrent. 'At least I went out and tried a different life for a bit!'

'What's that supposed to mean?' His grasp loosens in shock.

'It means, what have *you* ever tried, Nathaniel?' I know I sound shrill and aggressive but I can't help myself. 'You live in the same village you grew up in, you run the family business, you're buying a nursery down the road . . . you're practically still in the *womb*. So before you lecture me on the way to live my life, try living one of your own, OK?'

I break off, panting, to see Nathaniel looking as though I've slapped him. 'I . . . didn't mean it,' I mumble.

I take a few steps away, feeling near to tears. This isn't the way things were supposed to go. Nathaniel was supposed to support me and give me a hug and tell me I was making the right decision. Instead here we are, standing yards apart, not even looking at each other.

'I thought about spreading my wings.' Nathaniel's voice sounds stiff. 'There's a nursery in Cornwall I'd die to own. Fantastic piece of land, fantastic business . . . but I didn't look at it. I preferred not to be six hours' drive away from you.' He shrugs.

I don't know how to reply. For a while there's silence, except for the cooing of pigeons down at the end of the garden.

'Nathaniel . . . I have to go back.' My voice isn't quite steady. 'I don't have any choice. But we can still be together. The two of us. We can still make it work. We'll have holidays . . . weekends . . . I'll come back for Eamonn's party . . . You won't know I've gone!'

He's silent for a moment, fiddling with the handle of the bucket. When at last he looks up, his expression makes my heart constrict.

'Yeah,' he says in a quiet voice. 'I will.'

Twelve

THE NEWS MAKES the front page of the *Daily Mail*. I am a genuine celebrity: SAMANTHA CHOOSES LAW OVER LOOS. As I come into the kitchen the next morning, Trish is poring over it, with Eddie reading another copy.

'Trish's interview has been printed!' he announces. 'Look!'

'"I always knew Samantha was a cut above the average housekeeper," says Trish Geiger, thirty-seven,"' reads out Trish proudly. '"We often discussed philosophy and ethics together over the Hoover.""'

She looks up and her face changes. 'Samantha, are you all right? You look absolutely washed out.'

'I didn't sleep that well,' I admit, and flick on the kettle.

I spent the night at Nathaniel's. We didn't talk any more about my going. But at three o'clock, when I looked over at him, he was awake too, staring up at the ceiling.

'You need energy!' says Trish, perturbed. 'It's your big day! You need to look your best!'

'I will.' I try to smile. 'I just need a cup of coffee.'

It's going to be a huge day. The Carter Spink PR department swung into action as soon as I made my decision, and have turned my return into a full media event. There's going to be a big press conference at lunchtime in front of the Geigers' house, where I'll say how delighted I am to be going back to Carter Spink. Several of the partners are going to shake my hand for the photographers and I'll give a few short interviews. And then we're all going back to London on the train.

'So,' says Eddie as I spoon coffee into the pot. 'All packed up?'

'Pretty much. And Mrs Geiger . . . here.' I hand Trish the folded blue uniform which I've been carrying under my arm. 'It's clean and pressed. Ready for your next housekeeper.'

As Trish takes the uniform she looks suddenly stricken. 'Of course,' she says, her voice jumpy. 'Thank you, Samantha.' She clasps a napkin to her eyes.

'There, there,' says Eddie, patting her on the back. He looks rather moist around the eyes himself. Oh God, now I feel like crying myself.

'I'm really grateful for everything,' I gulp. 'And I'm sorry for leaving you in the lurch.'

'We know you've made the right decision.' Trish dabs her eyes.

'We're very proud of you,' chips in Eddie gruffly.

'Anyway!' Trish pulls herself together and takes a sip of coffee. 'I've decided to make a *speech* at the press conference. I'm sure the press will be expecting me to speak.'

'Absolutely,' I say, a little nonplussed. 'Good idea.'

'After all, now we're becoming media personalities—'

'Media personalities?' interrupts Eddie incredulously. 'We're not media personalities!'

'Of course we are! I'm in the *Daily Mail*!' A faint flush comes to Trish's face. 'This could be just the beginning for us, Eddie. If we hired the right publicist we could be on reality TV! Or . . . advertise Campari!'

'Campari?' expostulates Eddie. 'Trish, you don't *drink* Campari!'

'I could!' Trish is saying defensively as the doorbell rings. 'Or they could use coloured water . . .'

Smiling, I head into the hall, pulling my dressing gown around myself. Maybe it's Nathaniel, come to wish me luck.

But as I open the door, I see the entire PR team from Carter Spink standing on the doorstep, all in identical trouser suits.

'Samantha.' Hilary Grant, head of PR, runs her eyes over me. 'Ready?'

By twelve o'clock I'm wearing a black suit, black tights, black high heels, and the crispest white shirt I've ever seen. I've been professionally made up and my hair has been scraped back into a bun.

Hilary brought the clothes and the hairdresser and make-up artist. Now we're in the drawing room while she preps me on what to say to the press. For the thousand millionth time.

'What's the most important thing to remember?' she's demanding.

'Not to mention loos,' I say wearily.

'And if they ask about recipes?'

'I answer, "I'm a lawyer. My only recipe is the recipe for success."' Somehow I manage to utter the words straight-faced.

'The *News Today* team will follow you back to London.' Hilary consults her BlackBerry. 'We've given them access for the rest of the day.'

I cannot believe how big this has become. A news programme actually wants to do a fly-on-the-wall TV documentary section about my return to Carter Spink. Is there nothing else happening in the world?

The door opens and I hear Melissa's voice coming from the hall.

'So I can call you at the office to talk about my career plan?'

'Absolutely. Er . . . good idea.' Guy appears in the room and quickly shuts the door before Melissa can follow him in. 'Who the hell's *that*?'

'Melissa.' I roll my eyes heavenwards. 'Don't ask.'

'She says you taught her everything she knows.' Guy gives an amused grin. 'Would that be in corporate law—or scone-baking?'

'Ha ha,' I say politely.

'So,' Guy raises his eyebrows. 'How are you? Excited?'

'Yes!' I smile.

'You made the right decision, you know,' says Guy.

'I know.' I brush a fleck of cotton off my skirt.

Hilary taps her watch. 'It's nearly time!'

The entire world seems to have descended on the Geigers' house. As I venture out of the front door with Hilary and two PR managers, there are what looks like hundreds of people in the drive. A row of TV cameras is trained on me, photographers and journalists are in a crowd behind, and Carter Spink PR assistants are milling around and handing out coffee from a refreshments stand that has sprung up from nowhere.

I can see David Elldridge and Greg Parker standing by the cappuccino machine, both typing on their BlackBerries. The PR department wanted as many partners as possible for the photocall, but none of the others could make it.

'Samantha.' I look up to see Nathaniel coming across the gravel. His face is shadowed and his blue eyes are tense. 'How are you doing?'

'I'm . . . fine.' I look at him for a couple of seconds. 'It's all a bit crazy.'

I feel his hand clasping mine and intertwine my fingers between his as tightly as I can. I can feel his thumb rubbing mine, just like he did that first evening we had together. Like some private language.

'Are you going to introduce me, Samantha?' Guy saunters over.

'This is Guy,' I say reluctantly. 'I work with him at Carter Spink. Guy . . . Nathaniel.'

'Delighted to meet you!' Guy holds out his hand and Nathaniel is forced to let go of mine to shake it.

'So you look after the garden.' Guy looks around the drive. 'Very nice.'

I can see Nathaniel's fist forming at his side.

Please don't punch him, I pray urgently. *Don't* punch him—

To my relief I notice Iris coming through the gate, peering at all the journalists with interest.

'Look!' I say quickly to Nathaniel. 'Your mum.'

I greet Iris with a wave. As she reaches me she just looks at me for a few moments: at my bun, my black suit, my high-heeled shoes. 'Goodness,' she says at last.

'I know.' I give an awkward laugh 'A bit different.'

'So, Samantha.' Her eyes rest softly on mine. 'You found your way.'

'Yes.' I swallow. 'Yes, I did. This is the right way for me, Iris. I'm a lawyer. I always was. It's a great opportunity.'

Iris nods, her expression guarded. 'Nathaniel told me all about it. I'm sure you've made the right decision.' She pauses. 'Well . . . goodbye, chicken. And good luck. We'll miss you.'

As I lean forward to hug her, I feel tears pricking my eyes. 'Iris . . . I don't know how to thank you,' I whisper. 'For everything you did.'

'You did it all yourself.' She squeezes me tight. 'I'm proud of you.'

'And it's not really goodbye.' I wipe my eyes with a tissue, praying my make-up hasn't run. 'I'll be back before you know it. I'm going to visit as many weekends as I can . . .'

'Samantha?' Hilary calls me from the refreshments stand, where she's talking to David Elldridge and Greg Parker. 'Can you come over here?'

'I'll be right there!' I call back.

'Samantha, before you go . . .' Iris takes hold of both my hands, her face twisted a little in anxiety. 'Sweetie, I'm sure you're doing what's best for you. But just remember, you only get your youth once.' She looks at my hand, smooth against hers. 'You only get these precious years once.'

'I'll remember.' I bite my lip. 'I promise.'

'Good.' She pats my hand. 'Off you go.'

As I walk over to the refreshments stand, Nathaniel's hand is tightly in mine. We're going to have to say goodbye in a couple of hours.

No. I can't think about that.

Hilary is looking a little stressed as I approach. 'Got your statement?'

'All set.' I take out the folded sheet of paper. 'Hilary, this is Nathaniel.'

Hilary's eyes run over him without interest. 'Hello,' she says. 'Now, Samantha, we'll start in about three minutes. The team are just distributing press packs . . .'

Three more minutes. Three minutes before my old life begins again.

'So . . . I'll be back for Eamonn's party,' I say, still clutching Nathaniel's hand. 'It's only a few days away. I'll catch the train down on Friday night, spend the weekend . . .'

'Not next weekend,' chips in Guy, shaking chocolate on to a cappuccino. He looks up. 'You'll be in Hong Kong.'

'What?' I say stupidly.

'Samatron are delighted you're back and they've asked for you on this merger. We're flying to Hong Kong tomorrow. Has no one told you?'

'No,' I say, staring at him in shock. 'No one's even mentioned it. So when will we be back?'

Guy shrugs. 'Couple of weeks?'

'Samantha!' says Elldridge, coming up. 'Has Guy mentioned, we want you on a corporate shooting weekend at the end of September? Up in Scotland, should be fun.'

'Right. Um, yes, that sounds great. The only thing is, I'm trying to keep some weekends free . . . keep a bit of balance in my life . . .'

Elldridge looks puzzled. 'You've *had* your break, Samantha,' he says jovially. 'Now it's back to work.'

'Realistically, I'd say you're not going to have a free weekend till Christmas,' puts in Guy.

Everything's moving too fast. I thought it would be different this time. I thought I'd have more control.

'Christmas,' echoes Nathaniel at last, looking thunderstruck.

'No,' I say at once. 'He's exaggerating. It won't be that bad.' I rub my brow. 'I'll be back before Christmas. I promise. Whatever it takes.'

A strange flicker passes over his face. 'Don't turn it into a duty.'

'*Duty?*' I stare at him. 'That's not what I meant.'

'Samantha!' snaps Hilary. 'You *really* don't have time for this!'

'You should go.' Nathaniel gestures with his head. 'You're busy.'

This is awful. It feels like everything is disintegrating between us. I have to do something. Reach out to him.

'Nathaniel, just tell me.' My voice trembles. 'Tell me before I go. That day in the farmhouse . . . what did you say to me?'

Nathaniel looks at me for a long moment, then something in his eyes seems to close up. 'It was long and boring and badly put.' He shrugs.

'Right! I'm going to announce you,' says Hilary.

She marches on to the lawn. 'Ladies and gentlemen of the press!' Hilary's voice is blaring through the microphone. 'I'm delighted to welcome you all here this morning. And to introduce our newest partner at Carter Spink, Samantha Sweeting!'

Applause breaks out as I cross the lawn but it barely touches my consciousness. All of a sudden I'm stranded in front of the nation's press and I don't know what I want. I don't know what I should do.

Slowly I unfold my statement and smooth it down.

'Good morning,' I say into the microphone, my voice stilted. 'I am delighted to be able to share my exciting news with you. After being made a wonderful offer by Carter Spink, I will be returning to the firm today as a partner. Needless to say . . . I'm thrilled.'

Somehow I can't make my voice sound thrilled. I glance across to where Nathaniel and Guy are standing together. Guy's talking and Nathaniel is listening, his face taut. What's Guy saying?

'I have been overwhelmed by the warmth and generosity of the Carter Spink welcome,' I continue hesitantly, 'and am honoured to be joining such a prestigious partnership of . . .'

My eyes return to Guy and Nathaniel but Nathaniel's vanished. Where's he gone? I can't concentrate on what I'm saying.

'Talent and excellence!' snaps Hilary from the sidelines.

'Um . . . yes.' I find my place on the sheet. 'Talent. And excellence.'

A titter goes through the journalists. I'm not doing a good job here.

'Carter Spink's quality of service is . . . um . . . second to none,' I continue, trying to sound convincing.

'Better quality than the toilets you used to clean?' calls out a journalist with ruddy cheeks.

'We are not taking questions at this stage!' says Hilary crossly. 'And we are taking no questions on the subject of toilets, bathrooms, or any other form of sanitary ware. Samantha, carry on.'

'Unspeakable, were they?' laughs the ruddy-cheeked guy.

'Samantha, carry *on*,' spits Hilary, looking livid.

'They certainly were not unspeakable!' Trish comes striding on to the lawn, her fuchsia heels sinking into the grass. 'I will not have my toilets maligned! They're all Royal Doulton. They're Royal Doulton,' she repeats into the microphone. 'Highest quality. You're doing very well, Samantha!' She pats me on the shoulder.

All the journalists are laughing by now. Hilary's face is puce.

'Excuse me,' she says to Trish with suppressed fury. 'We are in the middle of a press conference here. Could you please leave?'

'This is my lawn!' says Trish, lifting her chin. 'The press want to hear from me, too! Eddie, where's my speech?'

'You're not making a *speech*!' says Hilary in horror, as Eddie darts on to the lawn with a printed scroll sheet.

'I would like to thank my husband Eddie for all his support,' begins Trish, ignoring Hilary. 'I would like to thank the *Daily Mail* . . .'

'This isn't the bloody Oscars!' Hilary looks apoplectic.

'Don't swear at me!' retorts Trish sharply. 'I am the owner of this residence, I'd like to remind you.'

'Mrs Geiger, have you seen Nathaniel?' I look desperately around the crowd for the millionth time. 'He's disappeared.'

'Who's Nathaniel?' asks one of the journalists.

'He's the gardener,' puts in the ruddy-faced guy. 'Lover boy.'

'Samantha,' says Hilary furiously. 'Please get back to the official statement!' She pushes Trish away from the microphone.

'Don't you touch me!' shrills Trish. 'I'll sue. Samantha Sweeting is my lawyer, you know.'

'Oy, Samantha! What does Nathaniel think about you going back to London?' shouts someone.

'Have you put your career over love?' chimes in a bright-faced girl.

'No!' I say desperately. 'I just . . . I need to talk to him. Where *is* he? Guy!' I hurry towards him over the grass. 'What did you say to Nathaniel? You have to tell me.'

'I advised him to keep his dignity.' Guy gives an arrogant shrug. 'To be honest, I told the him the truth. You won't be back.'

'How *dare* you?' I gasp in fury. 'How *dare* you say that? I will be back! And he can come to London—'

'Oh, please.' Guy raises his eyes. 'He doesn't want to hang around like some sad bastard, getting in your way, embarrassing you . . .'

'Embarrassing me?' I stare at Guy, aghast. 'Is that what you *said* to him? Is that why he left?'

'For God's sake, Samantha,' snaps Guy impatiently. 'He's a *gardener*.'

My fist acts before I can think. It hits Guy right on the jaw.

I can hear gasps and shouts and cameras snapping all around, but I don't care. That is the best thing I have ever done.

'Ow! Fuck!' He clasps his face. 'What the fuck was that for?'

The journalists are all crowding round now, hurling questions at us, but I ignore them.

'It's you who embarrass me,' I spit at Guy. 'You're worth nothing compared to him. *Nothing.*' To my horror I can feel tears coming to my eyes. I have to find Nathaniel. Right now.

'Everything's fine! Everything's fine!' Hilary comes thundering across the grass, a blur of pinstripe trouser suit. 'Samantha's a little overwrought today!' She grabs my arm in a vice-like grip, her teeth bared in a rictus smile. 'Just a friendly disagreement between partners! Samantha is looking forward to the challenges of leading a world-renowned legal team. Aren't you, Samantha?' Her grip tightens.

'I . . . don't know,' I say in despair. 'I'm sorry, Hilary.' I wrench my arm out of hers and start running over the grass, towards the gates.

'Stop her!' Hilary is yelling to all the PR staff. 'Block her way!'

Girls in trouser suits start coming at me from all directions like some kind of SWAT team. Somehow I dodge them. One makes a grab for my jacket and I wriggle out of it. I throw off my high heels too, and pick up my pace, barely wincing at the gravel under my soles as I push open the gate and run down the street, not looking back.

By the time I arrive at the pub my tights have been torn to shreds on the road, my hair has come out of its bun and half fallen down my back, my make-up is swimming in sweat, and my chest is burning with pain.

But I don't care. I have to find Nathaniel. I have to tell him he's the most important thing in my life, more important than any job.

I have to tell him I love him.

I don't know why I didn't realise it before, why I never said it before. It's so obvious. It's so blinding.

'Eamonn!' I call as I approach, and he looks up in surprise from where he's collecting glasses. 'I have to talk to Nathaniel. Is he here?'

'Here?' Eamonn appears lost for words. 'Samantha, you've missed him. He's already gone.'

'Gone?' I come to a halt, panting. 'Gone where?'

'To look at this business he wants to buy.'

'The one in Bingley?' I gulp in relief, still out of breath.

'That's not where . . .' Eamonn looks awkward. I stare at him, feeling a sudden foreboding. 'Samantha . . . he's gone to Cornwall. He said he might be down there a couple of weeks. I thought he'd have told you.'

'Um, no,' I say, my voice barely working. 'He didn't.'

Suddenly my legs feel like jelly. I sink down onto one of the barrels, my head pounding. He's gone to Cornwall, just like that. Without even saying goodbye. Without even talking about it.

'He left a note in case you dropped by.' Eamonn feels in his pocket and produces an envelope.

'Thanks, Eamonn.' I take the envelope and pull out the paper.

S, I think we both know this is the end of the line. Let's quit while we're ahead. Just know that this summer was perfect. N

Tears are flooding down my cheeks as I read it, over and over. I can't believe he's gone. How can he have given up on us? Whatever Guy said to him, whatever he thought. How can he have just *left*?

I hear a sound and look up to see Guy and a crowd of journalists gathered around me. I hadn't even noticed.

'Samantha,' says Guy, his voice low and conciliatory. 'Things may seem bad at the moment.' He glances at the note. 'But you have a fantastic career to get on with.'

I don't answer. My shoulders are hunched over, my nose is running and my hair is falling around my face in lacquered strands.

'There's nothing to keep you here now.' Guy takes a step forward and puts my glossy high-heeled shoes on the table beside me. 'Come on, partner. Everyone's waiting.'

Thirteen

I FEEL NUMB. It really is all over. I'm sitting in a first-class compartment on the train to London, with the other partners. It's an express train. In a couple of hours we'll be back. I have a new pair of tights on. My make-up has been repaired. I've even given a fresh statement to the press, hastily constructed by Hilary: 'Although I will always feel affection for my friends in Lower Ebury, nothing is more exciting and important in my life right now than my career with Carter Spink.'

I said it pretty convincingly. I even found a smile from somewhere as I shook David Elldridge's hand. It's just possible they might print a picture of that, rather than the one of me punching Guy. You never know.

Wedged in the corner opposite me is the TV cameraman for the news documentary, together with the producer, Dominic, a guy with trendy glasses and a denim jacket. I can feel the camera lens on me, following every move, zooming in and out, catching every expression.

'And so lawyer Samantha Sweeting leaves the village where she was known only as a domestic help,' Dominic is saying into his microphone in a low, TV-commentary voice. 'The question is . . . does she have any regrets?' He gives me a questioning glance.

'I thought you were supposed to be fly-on-the-wall,' I snap with a baleful look.

'Here you go!' Guy dumps a heavy set of contracts on my lap. 'Here's the Samatron deal. Get your teeth into that.'

I look at the pile of paper, inches thick. Once upon a time, seeing a brand-new, fresh contract gave me a rush of adrenaline. Now I feel blank.

I leaf through the contract, trying to summon up some enthusiasm.

'From cookery books to contracts,' murmurs Dominic into his microphone. 'From wooden spoons to writs.'

This guy is really starting to piss me off.

I turn back to my contract, but the words are jumbling in front of my eyes. All I can think about is Nathaniel. I've tried calling him but he isn't answering. Or replying to texts. It's like he doesn't want to know any more. My eyes are starting to blur with tears again and I blink them away furiously. I can't cry. I'm a partner. Partners do not cry. Trying to get a grip on myself, I look out of the window instead. We seem to be slowing down, which is a bit weird.

'An announcement for all passengers . . .' A voice comes crackling out of the loudspeakers. 'This train has been rescheduled as a slow train. It will be stopping at Hitherton, Marston Bridge, Bridbury . . .'

'What?' Guy looks up. 'A *slow* train?'

'. . . and will arrive at Paddington half an hour after the scheduled time,' the voice is saying. 'Apologies for any . . .'

'*Half an hour?*' David Elldridge whips out his mobile phone, looking livid. 'I'm going to have to reschedule my meeting.'

'I'll have to put off the Pattinson Lobb people.' Guy looks equally pissed off, and is already jabbing at the speed-dial on his phone.

'Davina,' Greg Parker is saying into his phone. 'Tell the team I'll be half an hour late, I'm sending an email—' He puts down his phone and immediately starts typing into his BlackBerry.

I'm watching all this frenzied action incredulously. They all look so stressed. So the train's going to be late. It's *half an hour*. It's thirty minutes. How can anyone get so het up over thirty minutes?

The train pulls into Hitherton station and comes slowly to a halt. I glance out of the window—then gasp aloud. A huge hot-air balloon is hovering in the air, just a few feet above the station building. It's bright red and yellow, with people waving from a basket.

'Hey, look!' I exclaim. 'Look at that! It's amazing!'

No one lifts their head. They're all frantically tapping their keyboards.

No one is interested in anything except the contents of their BlackBerry. Is this what I'm supposed to be like? Because I've forgotten how. I look at them all, the cream of the legal world, dressed in their handmade suits, holding state-of-the-art computers. Missing out. Not even *caring* that they're missing out. Living in their own world.

I don't belong here. That's not my world any more. *I'm not one of them.*

I suddenly know it, with the deepest certainty I've ever felt. I don't fit. Maybe I did once, but not any more. I shouldn't be here. This isn't what I want from my life. This isn't who I want to be.

I have to get out. Now.

Up and down the train people are stepping in and out, banging doors, hefting bags. As calmly as I can I reach for my suitcase, pick up my bag and stand up.

'I'm sorry,' I say. 'I made a mistake. I've only just realised.'

'*What?*' Guy looks up.

'I'm sorry I've wasted your time.' My voice wavers slightly. 'But . . . I can't stay. I can't do this.'

'Is this to do with the gardener?' Guy sounds exasperated. 'Because quite frankly—'

'No! It's to do with *me*! I just . . .' I hesitate, searching for the words. 'I don't want to be someone who doesn't look out of the window.'

Guy's face doesn't register an iota of understanding.

'Goodbye.' I open the train door and step out, but Guy grabs me roughly.

'Samantha, stop this crap! I *know* you. And you're a *lawyer.*'

'You *don't* know me, Guy!' My words burst out in a surge of sudden anger. 'Don't define me! I'm not a lawyer! I'm a *person.*'

I pull my arm out of his and slam the door shut, shaking all over. The next moment it opens again and Dominic and the cameraman pile out after me.

'And so!' Dominic is murmuring excitedly into his microphone. 'In a shock turn of events, Samantha Sweeting has rejected her glittering legal career!'

I am really going to thump him in a minute.

'This morning she was devastated to lose the man she loved. Now she has no career either.' He pauses, then adds in sepulchral tones, 'Who knows what dark thoughts are going through her mind?'

What's he trying to imply? That I'm going to throw myself under the next train? He'd love that, wouldn't he? He'd probably win an Emmy.

'Do you have a plan, Samantha?' asks Dominic, thrusting his microphone at me. 'A goal?'

'Sometimes you don't need a goal in life,' I say defensively. 'You don't need to know the big picture. You just need to know what you're going to do next.'

'And what are you going to do next?'

'I'm . . . working on it.' I turn and march away from the camera, towards the waiting room. As I near it, I see a guard coming out.

'Um, hello,' I say. 'I'd like to know how to get to . . .' I trail off, uncertainly. Where am I going? 'To . . . um . . . Cornwall,' I hear myself saying.

'*Cornwall?*' He looks taken aback. 'Whereabouts in Cornwall?'

'I don't know.' I swallow. 'Not exactly. But I need to get there, as quickly as possible.'

There can't be that many nurseries for sale in Cornwall. I'll track down the right one. I'll find him. Somehow.

'Well.' The guard's brow creases. 'I'll have to consult the book.' He disappears into his room. I can hear Dominic whispering feverishly into his microphone, but I don't care.

'Here we are.' The guard emerges, holding a piece of paper covered in pencil. 'Six changes, I'm afraid, to Penzance. And it'll be one hundred and twenty pounds. Train'll be a while,' he adds. 'Platform Two.'

'Thanks.' I pick up my suitcase and head over the footbridge. I can hear Dominic hurrying after me with the cameraman.

'Samantha appears to have taken leave of her senses,' he's panting into his microphone. 'Who knows what rash move she will make next?'

He *so* wants me to jump, doesn't he? I'm just going to ignore him.

'With no address,' I hear him continuing, 'Samantha is setting off on a long and uncertain journey to find the man who rejected her this morning. Is this a wise plan?'

OK, I've had enough.

'Maybe it isn't a wise plan!' I turn to face him. 'Maybe I won't find him. Maybe he won't even want to know. But I have to try.'

Dominic opens his mouth again to speak.

'Shut up,' I say. 'Just shut up.'

It seems like hours before I hear the sound of the train in the distance. But it's the wrong side. It's another train for London. As it pulls in I can hear the doors opening and people piling on and off.

'London train!' the guard is shouting. 'Platform One.'

My eyes move idly over the windows, at people in their seats, talking, sleeping, reading, listening to iPods—

And then everything seems to freeze. Am I *dreaming?*

It's Nathaniel. On the London train. He's three yards away, sitting in a window seat, staring ahead rigidly.

What—Why is he—

'Nathaniel!' I try to shout, but my voice has turned into a husk. 'Nathaniel!' I wave my arms frantically, trying to get his attention.

'It's him!' exclaims Dominic. 'Nathaniel!' he yells, his voice like a foghorn. 'Over here, mate!'

'Nathaniel!' At last my voice is working. 'Na-than-iel!'

At my desperate scream he finally looks up and jolts with shock as he sees me. For a moment his expression is sheer disbelief. Then his whole face seems to expand in a slow explosion of delight.

I can hear the train doors slamming. It's about to leave.

I can see him getting up inside the train, grabbing his rucksack, squeezing past the woman in the next seat. Then he disappears from view, just as the train starts pulling out of the station.

'Too late,' says the cameraman lugubriously. 'He'll never make it.'

My chest is too tight for me to answer. All I can do is stare at the departing train, moving past carriage by carriage, speeding up, faster and faster . . . until finally it's gone.

And Nathaniel is standing on the platform. He's there.

Without moving my eyes from his I begin to walk along the platform, speeding up as I reach the footbridge. On the opposite side he does the same. We reach the top of the steps, walk forward a way and both come to a halt, a few feet apart.

'I thought you were going down to Cornwall,' I say at last. 'To buy your nursery.'

'I changed my mind. Thought I might . . . visit a friend in London instead.' He glances at my suitcase. 'Where were you going?'

I clear my throat. 'I was thinking . . . Cornwall.'

'Cornwall?' He stares at me.

'Uh huh.'

Nathaniel leans against the barricade, his thumbs in his pockets, and surveys the wooden slats of the bridge. 'So . . . where are your friends?'

'Gone. And they're not my friends. I punched Guy,' I add proudly.

Nathaniel throws back his head and laughs. 'So they fired you.'

'I fired them,' I correct him.

'You did?' says Nathaniel in amazement. He reaches out for my hand but I don't take it. Underneath my joy I'm still feeling unsettled. The hurt of this morning hasn't gone. I can't pretend everything's OK.

'I got your note.' I lift my eyes to his and Nathaniel flinches.

'Samantha . . . I wrote you a different one on the train. In case you wouldn't see me in London.'

He fishes awkwardly in his pocket and pulls out a letter, several sheets long; both sides of the paper covered in writing. I hold it for a few moments without reading it.

'What does it say?' I raise my eyes.

'It's long and boring.' His gaze burns into mine. 'And badly put.'

I turn the pages slowly over in my fingers. Here and there I glimpse words that make my eyes fill instantly.

'So,' I manage.

'So.' Nathaniel's arms come round my waist; his warm mouth lands on mine. As he holds me tight I can feel the tears spilling onto my cheeks. This is where I belong. This is where I fit. I finally draw away and look up at him, wiping my eyes.

'Where now?' He looks down over the bridge and I follow his gaze. The railway track extends in both directions, way into the distance. 'Which way?'

I look along the endless line, squinting in the sunshine. I'm twenty-nine years old. I can go anywhere. Do anything. Be anyone I like.

'There's no rush,' I say at last and reach up to kiss him again.

SOPHIE KINSELLA

When Sophie Kinsella breezed into the Wimbledon restaurant where we had arranged to meet for lunch, she looked fresh and stunning, even though it was a baking hot June day and she was six months' pregnant with her third child. 'It's another boy,' she told me with a grin. 'Hugo and Freddy are absolutely delighted.' So is her husband, Henry.

As we ordered lunch, we talked about *The Undomestic Goddess*. 'The novel came from two ideas that were in my head,' Sophie began. 'I am completely useless domestically and I've always thought it would be a good source of comedy. And then I've always loved the concept of making a horrendous mistake and running away. I thought that was really interesting because you hear about someone being dishonest, embezzling and trying to cover it up, but you don't hear about someone basically making an honest mistake.'

I asked Sophie to explain what she meant when she described herself as 'useless domestically'? She pulled a face. 'Well, let's say I can't iron, find tidying up soul-destroying and I have to psyche myself up to cook. I can make easy family meals but I'm not brave enough to host a proper grown-up dinner party!' So would she get caterers in, as Samantha does in the novel, and try to pass the food off as her own? 'I'd love to try but I know I couldn't carry it off—my friends know me too well, sadly. No, I'm not a good cook—although I did learn to bake bread for this novel. I have a good friend who is

a domestic goddess and we spent the day baking bread and it was fantastic fun and very therapeutic. We made four gorgeous loaves, ate one for tea—hoovering it all up in minutes with her homemade jam—and I could see that the other three would be gone equally quickly and I kept thinking, God, now we need to do it all over again! For that day it was lovely, but never again.'

I asked Sophie if she had any memorable domestic disasters that she was willing to share? 'Well, the meringue scene in the book is lifted straight from my life. But my favourite is when I took one of Nigella Lawson's recipes and make cupcakes with my children. It was all going really well and we had filled all the little cases and put them in the oven. After they had been cooking for about ten minutes, I suddenly noticed the flour that I had measured out still sitting on the side. And it was awful because the boys were so excited. So I didn't tell them. I just baked the cupcakes and they were like these eggy, horrendous things!'

Bearing in mind that her new baby is expected in the next few months, I asked Sophie if she was planning to take some time away from writing? 'Yes, a little. But I am not someone who can just switch off and not think about books for six months, especially as I want to write another *Shopaholic* novel. So I'll be thinking, if not actually writing—and shopping, of course, lots and lots of shopping! Well, a girl has to do her research, doesn't she?'

Jane Eastgate

No Place
Like Home

Mary Higgins Clark

When Alex Nolan sets eyes upon the
eighteenth-century mansion in Old Mill
Lane, he knows that it is the perfect
birthday gift for his wife, Celia. The
agent tries to tell him the history of the
house—known locally as Little Lizzie's
Place—where a ten-year-old girl killed
her mother and tried to kill her stepfather,
but Alex is not interested. All he wants
is to surprise Celia.

PROLOGUE

TEN-YEAR-OLD LIZA was dreaming her favourite dream, the one about the day when she was six, and she and Daddy were at the beach, in New Jersey, at Spring Lake. They'd been in the water, holding hands and jumping together whenever a wave broke near them. Then a much bigger wave rushed in and began to break right over them. Daddy grabbed her. 'Hang on, Liza,' he yelled, and the next minute they were tumbling underwater and being thrown around by the wave. Liza had been so scared.

She could still feel her forehead slamming into the sand when the wave crashed them onto the shore. She had swallowed water and was coughing and her eyes were stinging and she was crying but then Daddy pulled her onto his lap. 'Now *that* was a wave!' he said, as he brushed the sand from her face, 'but we rode it out together, didn't we, Liza?'

That was the best part of the dream—having Daddy's arms round her and feeling so safe.

Before the next summer came around, Daddy had died. After that she'd never really felt safe again. Now she was always afraid, because Mom had made Ted, her stepfather, move out of the house, but Ted didn't want a divorce and kept pestering her to let him come back. Liza knew she wasn't the only one afraid; Mom was afraid, too.

Liza wanted to go back into the dream of being in Daddy's arms, but the voices kept waking her up. Someone was crying and yelling. Did she hear Mom calling Daddy's name? What was she saying?

Liza sat up and slid out of bed. She could see the light in the hall. It was Ted's voice she heard now. He was yelling at Mom, and Mom was screaming. 'Let go of me!'

Liza knew that Mom was so afraid of Ted, and that she even kept Daddy's gun in her night table. Liza rushed down the hall, her feet moving noiselessly on the carpet. The door of Mom's sitting room was open and inside she could see that Ted had Mom pinned against the wall and was shaking her. Liza ran past the sitting room and into her mother's bedroom. She hurried round the bed and yanked open the night table drawer. Trembling, she grabbed the gun and ran back to the sitting room.

Standing in the doorway, she pointed the gun at Ted and screamed, 'Let go of my mother!'

Ted spun round, holding on to Mom, his eyes wide and angry. The veins in his forehead were sticking out. Liza could see the tears streaming down her mother's cheeks.

'Sure,' he yelled. With a violent thrust, he shoved Liza's mother at her. When she crashed into Liza, the gun went off. Then Liza heard a funny little gurgle and Mom crumpled to the floor. Liza looked down at her mother, then up at Ted. He began to lunge towards her, and Liza pointed the gun at him and pulled the trigger. She pulled it again and again, until he fell down and then began crawling across the room and tried to grab the gun from her. When it wouldn't fire any more, she dropped it and got down on the floor and put her arms round her mother. There was no sound, and she knew her mother was dead.

After that Liza had only a hazy memory of what happened. She remembered Ted's voice on the phone, the police coming, someone pulling her arms from her mother.

She was taken away, and she never saw her mother again.

1

Twenty-four years later

I CANNOT BELIEVE I am standing in the exact spot where I was standing when I killed my mother. I ask myself if this is a nightmare, or if it is really happening. In the beginning, after that terrible night, I had nightmares all the time. I spent a good part of my childhood drawing pictures of them for Dr Moran, a psychologist in California, where I went to live after the trial. This room figured in many of those drawings.

The mirror over the fireplace is the one my father chose when he restored the house. In it, I see my reflection. My face is deadly pale. My eyes no longer seem dark blue, but black, reflecting all the terrible visions that are leaping through my mind. The colour of my eyes is a heritage from my father. My mother's eyes were lighter, a sapphire blue, picture perfect with her golden hair. My hair would be dark blonde if I left it natural. I have darkened it, though, ever since I came back east sixteen years ago to attend the Fashion Institute of Technology in Manhattan. I am also taller than my mother was by five inches. Yet, as I grow older, I believe I am beginning to resemble her, and I have always lived in dread of someone saying, 'You look familiar . . .' My mother's image still turns up periodically in stories that rehash the circumstances of her death. So if anyone says I look familiar, I know it's her they have in mind. I, Celia Foster Nolan, formerly Liza Barton, the child the tabloids dubbed 'Little Lizzie Borden', am far less likely to be recognised as that chubby-faced girl with golden curls who was acquitted—not exonerated—of killing her mother and trying to kill her stepfather.

My second husband, Alex Nolan, and I have been married for six months. Today I thought we were going to take my four-year-old son, Jack, to see a horse show in Peapack, a town in northern New Jersey, when suddenly Alex detoured to Mendham, a neighbouring town. It was only then that he told me he had a wonderful surprise for my birthday and drove to this house. Alex parked the car, and we went inside.

Jack is tugging at my hand, but I remain frozen to the spot. Energetic, as most four-year-olds are, he wants to explore. I let him go, and in a flash he is running down the hall.

Alex is standing a little behind me. I can feel his anxiety. He believes he has found a beautiful home for us to live in, and his generosity is such that the deed is solely in my name, his birthday gift to me. 'I'll catch up with Jack, honey,' he reassures me. 'You look around and start figuring how you'll decorate.'

'Your husband tells me you're an interior designer,' Henry Paley, the real-estate agent, says as Alex leaves the room. 'This house has been well kept up, but every woman, especially one in your profession, wants to put her own signature on her home.'

Not yet trusting myself to speak, I look at him. Paley is a small man of about sixty, with thinning grey hair, and neatly dressed in a dark pin-striped suit. I realise he is waiting for me to show enthusiasm for my wonderful birthday gift.

'As your husband may have told you, I was not the selling agent,' Paley explains. 'My boss, Georgette Grove, was showing your husband properties nearby when he spotted the FOR SALE sign on the lawn. The house is quite simply an architectural treasure, situated on ten acres in the premier location in a premier town.'

I know it is a treasure. My father was the architect who restored a crumbling eighteenth-century mansion into this charming and spacious home. I look past Paley at the fireplace. Mother and Daddy found the mantel in France, in a chateau about to be demolished. Daddy told me the meanings of its sculptured work, the cherubs and pineapples . . .

Ted pinning Mother against the wall . . .

Mother sobbing . . .

I am pointing the gun at him. Daddy's gun . . .

Ted spinning Mother round and shoving her at me . . .

The gun going off . . .

Lizzie Borden took an axe . . .

'Are you all right, Mrs Nolan?' Henry Paley is asking me.

'Yes, of course,' I manage, with some effort. My mind is racing with the thought that I should not have let Larry, my first husband, make me swear that I wouldn't tell the truth about myself to anyone, not even to someone I married. In this moment I am fiercely angry at Larry for wringing that promise from me. He was ashamed of my past, afraid of its impact on our son's future. That fear has brought us here, now.

Already the lie is a wedge driven between Alex and me. He talks about wanting to have children soon, and I wonder how he would feel if he knew that Little Lizzie Borden would be their mother.

It's been twenty-four years, but such memories die hard. Will anyone in town recognise me? Probably not. But though I agreed to live in this area, I did not agree to live in this town, or in this house. I can't live here. I simply can't.

To avoid the curiosity in Paley's eyes, I walk over to the mantel and pretend to study it.

'Beautiful, isn't it?' Paley says enthusiastically. 'The master bedroom is very large, and has two separate, wonderfully appointed baths.' He opens the door to the bedroom and, reluctantly, I follow him.

Memories flood my mind. Weekend mornings in this room. I used to get in bed with Mother and Daddy. Daddy would bring up coffee for Mother and hot chocolate for me. Looking out of the back windows I see the Japanese maple he planted so long ago, now mature and beautiful.

Tears are pressing against my eyelids. I want to run out of here. If necessary I will have to break my promise to Larry and tell Alex the truth. I am not Celia Foster, nee Kellogg, the daughter of Kathleen and Martin Kellogg of Santa Barbara, California. I am Liza Barton, reluctantly acquitted by a judge of murder and attempted murder.

'Mom, Mom!' My son's footsteps clatter on the floorboards. He hurries into the room, energy encapsulated, small and sturdy, a bright quickness about him, a handsome little boy, the centre of my heart. At night I steal into his room to listen to his even breathing. He is not interested in what happened years ago. He is satisfied if I am there to answer when he calls.

I bend down and catch him in my arms. Jack has Larry's light brown hair and high forehead. His beautiful blue eyes are my mother's, but then Larry had blue eyes, too. In those last moments of fading consciousness, Larry had whispered that he didn't want Jack to ever have to deal with the tabloids digging up those old stories about me. I taste again the bitterness of knowing that his father was ashamed of me.

Ted Cartwright swears estranged wife begged for reconciliation . . .

State psychiatrist testifies ten-year-old Liza mentally competent to form the intent to commit murder. . . .

Was Larry right to swear me to silence? At this moment, I can't be sure of anything. I kiss the top of Jack's head.

'I really, really, really like it here,' he tells me excitedly.

Alex is coming into the bedroom. He planned this surprise for me with so much care. When we came up the driveway, it had been festooned with birthday balloons, swaying on this breezy August day—all painted with my name. But the exuberant joy with which he handed me the key and the deed is gone. He can read me too well.

'When I told the women at the office what I'd done, they said no matter how beautiful the house, they'd want the chance to decide about it,' he says, his voice forlorn.

They were right, I think as I look at him, at his reddish-brown hair and brown eyes. Tall and wide-shouldered, Alex has a strength about him that makes him enormously attractive. Jack adores him. Now Jack slides from my arms and puts his arm round Alex's leg.

My husband and my son.

And my house.

The Grove Real Estate Agency was on East Main Street in the New Jersey town of Mendham. Georgette Grove parked in front of it and got out of the car. The August day was unusually cool, and her short-sleeved linen suit was not warm enough for the weather. She moved with a quick step up the path to the door of her office.

Sixty-two years old, Georgette was a handsome, whippet-thin woman with hazel eyes and short wavy hair the colour of steel. She was pleased at how smoothly the closing had just gone on one of the smaller houses in town. Even though she had split the commission with another broker, it would give her a few months' reserve until she landed another sale.

So far it had been a disastrous year, saved only by her sale of the house on Old Mill Lane to Alex Nolan. She had very much wanted to be present this morning when Nolan presented it to his wife. I hope she likes surprises, Georgette thought for the hundredth time. She had tried to warn him about its history, but Nolan didn't seem to care. She was also worried that, since he put it in his wife's name only, if his wife didn't like it, she—Georgette—might be open to a nondisclosure suit.

It was part of New Jersey's real-estate code that a prospective buyer had to be notified if a house was a stigmatised property—one impacted by a factor that could cause apprehension or fears. Since some people would not want to live in a house in which a crime or a suicide had occurred, the real-estate agent was obliged to reveal any such history.

I tried to tell Alex Nolan that there had been a tragedy in the house, Georgette thought defensively as she opened the office door and stepped into the reception room. But he cut me off, saying that his family used to rent a 200-year-old house on Cape Cod, and its history would curl your hair. But this is different, Georgette thought. I should have told him that around here the house he bought is known as 'Little Lizzie's Place'.

She wondered if Nolan had become nervous about his surprise. At his request, the driveway had been decorated with birthday balloons and the porch had been draped with festive papier-mâché. He had asked that champagne and a birthday cake be waiting at the expensive glass patio table and chairs he had ordered from a nearby furniture store. He had also asked Georgette to be sure there were a dozen roses in every room. 'Roses are Ceil's favourite flowers,' he explained. 'When we got married, I promised her that she'd never be without them.'

He's rich. He's handsome. He's charming. And he's clearly devoted to his wife, Georgette thought. From half the marriages I've seen, she's a damn lucky woman.

But how will she react when she starts hearing the stories?

Georgette tried to push the thought away. She glanced around her reception room, which was a matter of special pride to her. Robin Carpenter, her secretary-receptionist, was at an antique mahogany desk to the right. On the left, a brightly upholstered sectional couch and chairs were grouped round a coffee table where clients sipped coffee or wine while she or Henry ran tapes showing available properties.

'How did the closing go?' Robin asked Georgette.

'Smoothly, thank God. Is Henry back?'

'No, I guess he's still drinking champagne with the Nolans. I still can't believe it. A gorgeous guy buys a gorgeous house for his wife for her thirty-fourth birthday. That's exactly my age. She's so lucky. Did you ever find out if Alex Nolan has a brother?' Robin sighed.

'Let's all hope that after she hears the story of that house, Celia Nolan still considers herself lucky,' Georgette snapped nervously. 'Otherwise, we might have a real problem on our hands.'

Robin knew exactly what she meant. Small, slender and very pretty, with a heart-shaped face and a penchant for frilly clothes, Robin gave the initial impression of an air-headed blonde. Or so Georgette had believed when she applied for the job a year ago. Five minutes of conversation, however, had led her to reversing that opinion and hiring Robin on the spot. Now Robin was about to get her own real-estate licence, and Georgette welcomed the prospect. Henry simply wasn't pulling his weight any more.

'You *did* try to warn the husband about the history of the house. I can back you up on that, Georgette.'

'That's something,' Georgette said, as she headed down the hall to her private office at the rear of the building. But then she turned abruptly and faced the younger woman. 'I tried to speak to Alex Nolan about the background of the house one time only, Robin,' she said emphatically. 'And that was when I was alone in the car with him. You couldn't have heard me discussing it.'

'I'm sure I heard you bring it up one of the times Alex Nolan was in here,' Robin insisted.

'I mentioned it to him once in the car. I never said anything about it to him here. Robin, you're not doing me or yourself any favours by lying to a client,' Georgette snapped. 'Keep that in mind, please.'

The outside door opened. They both turned as Henry Paley came into the reception room. 'How did it go?' Georgette asked.

'I would say that Mrs Nolan put up a very good act of seeming delighted by her husband's birthday surprise,' Paley answered. 'I believe she convinced him. However, she did not convince me.'

'Why not?' Robin asked.

'I wish I could tell you,' Henry said. He looked at Georgette, obviously afraid that he had somehow let her down. 'Georgette,' he said apologetically, 'I swear, when I was showing her the master suite, all I could visualise was that kid shooting her mother and stepfather in the sitting room years ago. Maybe it's all those flowers the husband ordered. It's the same scent that hits you in funeral homes. I got it full force in the master suite of Little Lizzie's Place today. And I have a feeling that Celia Nolan had a reaction like that, too.'

Henry realised that unwittingly he had used the forbidden words in describing the house on Old Mill Lane. 'Sorry, Georgette,' he mumbled as he brushed past her.

'You should be,' Georgette said bitterly. 'I can just imagine the kind of vibes you were sending out to Mrs Nolan.'

'Maybe you'll take me up on my offer to back you up on what you told Alex Nolan, Georgette,' Robin suggested, a touch of sarcasm in her voice.

But Ceil, it's what we were *planning* to do. We're just doing it a little faster. It makes sense for Jack to start pre-K in Mendham. We've been cramped for these six months in your apartment, and you didn't want to move downtown to mine.'

It was the day after my birthday, the day following the big surprise. We were having breakfast in my apartment, the one that six years ago I had been hired to decorate for Larry, who became my first husband. Jack had rushed through a glass of juice and a bowl of cornflakes, and was now getting dressed for day camp.

I don't think I had closed my eyes all night. Instead I lay in bed, my shoulder brushing against Alex, staring into the dark, remembering, always remembering. Now wrapped in a blue and white linen robe, I was trying to appear calm as I sipped my coffee. Across the table, impeccably dressed as always in a dark blue suit, white shirt and figured blue and red tie, Alex was rushing through the slice of toast and mug of coffee that was his everyday breakfast.

My suggestion that, while the house was beautiful, I would want to redecorate it completely before we moved in had met with resistance from Alex. 'Ceil, I know it was probably insanity to buy the house without consulting you, but it was exactly the kind of place we had in mind. You'd agreed to the area, now that the firm is moving me to New Jersey. We talked about Peapack or Basking Ridge, and Mendham is only minutes from both of them. The added plus is that I can get in some early morning rides. Central Park just doesn't do it for me. And I want to teach you how to ride. You said you'd enjoy taking lessons.'

I studied my husband. His expression was both contrite and pleading. He was right. This apartment really was too small for the three of us. Alex had given up so much when we married. His apartment in SoHo had included a large study, with room for his splendid sound system and even a grand piano, which was now in storage. Alex has a natural gift for music, and I know he misses the pleasure of playing. He's worked hard to accomplish all he has. Though a distant cousin of my late husband, who himself had come from wealth, Alex is decidedly a 'poor relation'. I knew how proud he was to be able to buy this new house.

'You've been saying you want to get back to decorating,' Alex reminded me. 'Once you're settled, there'll be plenty of opportunity for that. There's a lot of money in Mendham, and big houses being built. Please give it a try, Ceil.' He came round the table to put his arms round me. 'Please.'

I hadn't heard Jack come into the room. 'I like the house, too, Mom,' he piped up. 'Alex is going to buy me my own pony when we move there.'

I looked at my husband and son. 'It looks as though we have a new home,' I said, trying to smile. Eventually I'll find a house in one of the other towns, I thought. It won't be hard to persuade Alex to move. He *did* admit that it was a mistake to buy without consulting me, after all.

One month later the moving vans were pulling away from 895 Fifth Avenue and heading for the Lincoln Tunnel. Their destination was 1 Old Mill Lane, Mendham, New Jersey.

Her eyes ablaze with curiosity, fifty-four-year-old Marcella Williams stood to one side of her living-room window, watching the long moving van chug slowly past her home. Twenty minutes ago she had seen Georgette Grove's silver BMW go up the hill. Marcella was sure the Mercedes sedan that arrived shortly after that belonged to her new neighbours. She had heard that they were rushing to move in because the four-year-old was starting pre-kindergarten. She wondered what they'd be like.

People didn't tend to stay in that house long, she reflected, and it wasn't surprising. Nobody likes to have their home known as 'Little Lizzie's Place'. Jane Salzman was the first buyer after Liza Barton went on her shooting spree. She claimed the house had a creepy feeling, but then Jane was into parapsychology, which Marcella thought was a lot of nonsense. Last year's Halloween prank was the finish for Mark and Louise Harriman, the last owners. Louise flipped out when she saw the sign on her lawn and the life-sized doll with a pistol on her porch. She and Mark had been planning to relocate to Florida anyhow, so they simply moved out in February, and the house had been empty since then.

Marcella had been living there when the tragedy occurred, and she could still picture little Liza at age ten, with her blonde, curly hair and quiet, mature manner. She had a way of looking at people, as if she were sizing them up. I like a child to act like a child, Marcella thought. I went out of my way to be nice to her after Will Barton died. Then when Audrey married Ted Cartwright I said to Liza that she must be thrilled to have a new father. I'll never forget the way that little snip looked at me when she said, 'My mother has a new husband. I don't have a new father.'

I told them that at the trial, Marcella reminded herself with some satisfaction. And I told them that I was in the house when Ted collected all

Will Barton's personal stuff in boxes to store in the garage. Liza was screaming at him, and kept dragging the boxes into her room. She wouldn't give Ted an inch. She made it so hard for her mother. And it was clear that Audrey was crazy about Ted.

At least, in the *beginning* she was crazy about him, Marcella thought, mentally correcting herself as she watched a second van follow the first up the hill. Who knows what happened there? Audrey certainly didn't give the marriage much time to work out and that restraining order she got against Ted was absolutely unnecessary. I believed Ted when he swore that Audrey had phoned and asked him to come over that night.

Ted was always so grateful for my support, Marcella remembered. My testimony helped him in the civil case he filed against Liza. Well, the poor fellow *should* have been compensated. It's nasty to go through life with a shattered knee. He still has a limp. It's a miracle he wasn't killed.

When Ted got out of the hospital, he had moved a few towns away, to Bernardsville. He was now a major New Jersey developer, and his latest venture had been building town houses in Madison. Over the years, Marcella had bumped into him at various functions. He'd had a string of girlfriends, but he always claimed that Audrey was the love of his life. Marcella admitted to herself that she'd been casting around for a reason to call him. Maybe I'll let him know that the house has changed hands again, she thought, and headed for the phone.

As she crossed the spacious living room, Marcella gave a brief smile of approval to her reflection in the mirror. Her shapely body showed the benefits of daily exercise. Her frosted blonde hair framed a smooth face tightened by Botox treatments. She was confident that the new liner and mascara she was using enhanced her hazel eyes.

Marcella called information and got the number for Ted Cartwright's office, and finally reached his voicemail. Her voice distinctly coquettish, she said, 'Ted, this is Marcella Williams. I thought you'd be interested to hear that your former home has changed hands again, and the new owners are in the process of moving in.'

The sound of a police siren interrupted her message. An instant later a police car hurtled past her window. She gave a shiver of delight. 'Ted, I'll call you back,' she said breathlessly. 'The cops are on the way to your old house. I'll let you know what develops.'

'I am so sorry, Mrs Nolan,' Georgette stammered. 'I just got here myself. I've called the police.'

I looked at her. She was dragging a hose across the bluestone walk, hoping, I suppose, to wash away some of the destruction.

The house was set back one hundred feet from the road. On the lawn, painted in red, in thick, billboard-sized letters, were the words:

LITTLE LIZZIE'S PLACE. BEWARE!

Splashes of red paint stained the shingles and limestone on the front of the house. A skull and crossbones was carved in the mahogany door. A straw doll with a toy gun in its hand was propped against the door. I assumed it was meant to represent me.

'What's this supposed to be about?' Alex snapped.

'Some kids, I guess,' Georgette Grove explained nervously. 'I'm so sorry. I'll get a cleanup crew here right away, and I'll call my landscaper. He'll returf the lawn today. I can't believe . . .'

Her voice trailed off as she looked at us. Thank God I was wearing dark glasses. I was standing beside the Mercedes, my hand on the door. Next to me, Alex was clearly angry and upset.

Hang on, I told myself desperately. I knew that if I let go of the car door, I would fall. It was a hot and muggy August day, and the sun was streaming down, making the red paint glisten.

Mother's blood. I could feel my arms and neck and face becoming sticky with her blood.

'Celia, are you OK?' Alex had his hand on my arm. 'Honey, I'm so sorry. I can't imagine what would make anyone do this.'

Jack had scrambled out of the car. 'Mommy, are you OK? You're not sick, are you?'

Jack, who had only a dim memory of his own father, was instinctively frightened that he would lose me, too. I forced myself to focus on him, on his need for reassurance. Then I looked at the concern on Alex's face. A terrible possibility rushed through my mind. Does he *know*? Is this some terrible, cruel joke? As quickly as the thought came, I dismissed it. Alex had no idea that I had ever lived here. He had been on his way to see another house when he spotted the FOR SALE sign. It was one of those horrible coincidences that just happen. But my God, what shall I do?

'I'll be all right,' I told Jack, managing to force the words out through lips that felt numb and spongy.

Jack ran onto the lawn. 'I can read that,' he said proudly. 'L-i-t-t-l-e L-i-z-z-i—'

'That's enough, Jack,' Alex said firmly. He looked at Georgette. 'Is there any explanation for this?'

'I tried to explain to you when we first viewed the house,' Georgette said, 'but you weren't interested. A tragedy took place here nearly twenty-five years ago. A ten-year-old child, Liza Barton, accidentally killed her mother and shot her stepfather. Because of the similarity of her name to the infamous Lizzie Borden, the tabloids called her 'Little Lizzie Borden'. There have been incidents here since then, but never anything like this.' Georgette was on the verge of tears. 'I should have made you listen.'

The first moving van was pulling into the driveway. Two men jumped out and ran behind it to open the door.

'Alex, tell them to stop,' I demanded, my voice rising to a near shriek. 'Tell them to turn around right now. I can't live under this roof.'

Alex and the real-estate agent were staring at me, their expressions shocked. 'Mrs Nolan, don't think like that,' Georgette Grove protested. 'I am so sorry this has happened. I can't apologise enough. I assure you that some kids did this as a joke.'

'Honey, you're overreacting,' Alex said. 'This is a beautiful home. I'm sorry I didn't listen to Georgette about what happened here, but I'd have bought it for you anyway. Don't let some stupid kids spoil it.' He put his hands on my face. 'Look at me. I promise, before the day is over this mess will be gone. Come on round the back. I have a surprise for Jack.'

One of the moving men was heading for the house, Jack scampering behind him.

'No, Jack, we're going round to the barn,' Alex called. 'Come on, Ceil,' he urged. 'Please.'

I wanted to protest, but then I saw the blinking lights of a patrol car rushing up the road.

When they pulled my arms away from my mother's body they made me sit in the patrol car. I was wearing my nightgown and someone got a blanket and tucked it round me. And then the ambulance came.

'Come on, honey,' Alex coaxed. 'Let's show Jack his surprise.'

'Mrs Nolan, I'll talk to the police,' Georgette Grove volunteered.

I walked quickly along the path with Alex to the spacious grounds behind the house. I was startled to see that in the month since I had been here a riding enclosure had been built. Alex had promised Jack a pony. Was it here already? The same thought must have occurred to Jack because he began running towards the barn. He pulled open the door, and then I heard a whoop of joy.

'It's a pony, Mom,' he shouted. 'Alex bought me a pony!'

Five minutes later, his eyes shining with delight, his feet secure in the stirrups of his new saddle and Alex at his side, Jack was walking the pony round the enclosure. I stood at the split-rail fence, taking in the expression of pure bliss on his face.

'Now Jack can ride every single day,' Alex said as he passed me. 'Right, Jack?'

There was somebody clearing his throat behind me. Startled, I turned round to face a police officer, standing next to Georgette Grove. I hadn't heard them approaching.

'Mrs Nolan, I'm Sergeant Earley. I very much regret this incident. This is no way to welcome you to Mendham.' He was a man who appeared to be in his late fifties, with an outdoorsman's complexion and thinning sandy hair. 'I know just which kids to question,' he said grimly. 'Trust me. Their parents will pay for whatever has to be done.'

Earley, I thought. I know that name. When I packed my files last week I read the hidden one again, the file that began with the night I killed my mother. There had been a cop named Earley mentioned somewhere.

Alex had left Jack on the pony to join us. Georgette Grove introduced him to Sergeant Earley.

'Sergeant, I know I speak for my wife when I say that we don't want to start our life in this town by signing complaints against neighbourhood kids,' Alex said. 'But I hope that when you find those vandals you make them understand they're lucky we're being this generous.'

Earley, I thought. In my mind I was seeing the tabloid articles about me, the ones that had made me heartsick when I reread them only a week ago. There had been a picture of a cop tucking a blanket round me in the back of the police car. Earley had been his name. Afterwards he had commented to the press that he'd never seen a kid so composed. 'She was covered in her mother's blood, but when I put the blanket round her she said, "Thank you very much, officer." You'd think I'd given her an ice-cream.' And now I was facing this same man again.

'Mom, I love my pony,' Jack called. 'I want to name her Lizzie, after the name on the grass. Isn't that a good idea?'

Lizzie!

Before I could respond, I heard Georgette Grove murmur in dismay, 'Oh, Lord, here comes the busybody.'

A moment later I was being introduced to Marcella Williams, who, as she grabbed and shook my hand, told me, 'I've been living next door for twenty-eight years, and I'm delighted to welcome my new neighbour.'

Marcella Williams. She still lives here! She testified against me. She verified everything Ted told the court, helping him to get the financial settlement that had left me with almost nothing.

'Mom, is it all right if I name her Lizzie?' Jack called.

I *have* to protect him, I thought. I have to get rid of the memories. I have to act the part of a newcomer annoyed by vandalism, nothing more.

I forced a smile, turned, and leaned on the fence. 'You call your pony any name you want, Jack,' I called.

I've got to get inside, I thought. Sergeant Earley, Marcella Williams—how soon will they see something familiar about me?

One of the moving men was hurrying across the lawn. 'Mr Nolan,' he said, 'the media is out front taking pictures of the vandalism. A television reporter wants you and Mrs Nolan to make a statement on camera.'

'No!' I looked at Alex imploringly. 'Absolutely not.'

'I have a key to the back door,' Georgette Grove said quickly.

But it was too late. As I tried to escape, reporters came hurrying round the corner of the house. Light bulbs flashed, and, as I raised my hands to my face, my knees crumbled and a rush of darkness enveloped me.

Dru Perry had been on Route 24 on her way to the courthouse in Morris County when she got the call on her carphone from her newspaper, the *Star-Ledger*. Sixty-three years old, a veteran reporter, Dru was a big-boned woman with iron-grey, shoulder-length hair that always looked somewhat unkempt. Wide glasses exaggerated her penetrating brown eyes.

'Dru, forget the courthouse. Keep going to Mendham,' her editor ordered. 'There's been more vandalism at that house they call "Little Lizzie's Place", on Old Mill Lane.'

Little Lizzie's Place, Dru thought as she drove through Morristown. When she had covered the story last Halloween, the cops had been tough on the kids; they had ended up in juvenile court. What would make kids try it again, and in August?

The answer became obvious when she drove up Old Mill Lane and saw the moving vans. Whoever did this wanted to rattle the new owners, she thought. Then she caught her breath as the full impact of the vandalism registered. This was serious damage.

She parked on the road, behind the truck from the local television station. As she opened the door of her car, she saw two reporters and a cameraman start to run round the side of the house. Running herself, Dru caught up with them. She got her digital camera out just in time to snap Celia toppling over in a faint.

Then, with the gathering media, she waited until an ambulance pulled up and Marcella Williams came out of the house. The reporters pounced on her, peppering her with questions.

She's in her glory, Dru thought, as Mrs Williams explained that Mrs Nolan had revived and seemed shaken but otherwise fine. Then, as she posed for pictures, she went into the history of the house.

'I knew the Bartons,' she explained. 'It was all such a tragedy.'

It was a tragedy she was happy to recall for the media, going into great detail, including her belief that Liza Barton at age ten knew exactly what she was doing when she took her father's gun out of the drawer.

Dru stepped forward. 'Not everyone believes that version,' she said.

'Not everyone knew Liza Barton as well as I did,' Marcella retorted.

When Mrs Williams went back inside, Dru walked up to the front door to study the skull and crossbones. There was an initial carved in each eye socket—an *L* in the left and a *B* in the right.

Whoever did this is really creepy, Dru thought. This wasn't slapped together. She stepped away from the door and waited around to see if anyone representing the new owners came out to make a statement.

Ten minutes later, Alex Nolan appeared before the cameras. 'As you can understand, this is a most regrettable incident. My wife will be fine. She's exhausted from the packing, and the shock of the vandalism simply overwhelmed her. She is resting now.'

'Is it true that you bought the house as a birthday present for her?' Dru asked.

'Yes, that's true, and Celia is delighted about it. Now if you'll excuse me.' Alex turned, went into the house and closed the door.

Dru took a long sip from the bottle of water she kept in her shoulder bag. Marcella Williams had explained that she lived just down the road. I'll go wait for her there, Dru decided. Then, after I talk to her, I'll look up every detail I can find about the Little Lizzie case. I'd like to do a feature article about it, see if I can find out where Liza Barton is now. If she did deliberately kill her mother and try to kill her stepfather, chances are she's got into trouble again somewhere along the way.

2

WHEN I OPENED my eyes, I was lying on a couch the moving men had hastily placed in the living room. The first thing I saw was the terrified look in Jack's eyes. He was bending over me.

Instinctively, I reached up my arm and pulled him down beside me. 'I'm OK, pal,' I whispered.

'You scared me,' he whispered back. 'You really scared me.'

Alex was on the cellphone, demanding to know why the ambulance was taking so long to arrive.

Still holding Jack, I pushed myself up on one elbow. 'I don't need an ambulance,' I said. 'I'm all right, really I am.'

Georgette Grove was standing at the foot of the couch. 'Mrs Nolan—Celia—I really think it would be better if—'

'You really must be checked,' Marcella Williams said.

'Jack, Mommy's fine. We're getting up.' I swung my legs round and, ignoring the wave of dizziness, pulled myself to my feet. I could see the look of protest on Alex's face. 'Alex, you know how busy this week has been,' I said. 'I simply need to get the movers to put your big chair and a hassock in one of the bedrooms and let me take it easy for a couple of hours.' I looked directly at Georgette Grove and Marcella Williams. 'I know you'll understand if I just want to rest quietly.'

'Of course,' Georgette agreed. 'I'll take care of things outside.'

'Maybe you'd like a cup of tea,' Marcella Williams offered, clearly unwilling to leave.

Alex put his hand under my arm. 'We don't want to keep you, Mrs Williams. If you'll excuse us, please.'

The wail of a siren told us that the ambulance had arrived.

The emergency medical technician examined me in the first-floor room that had once been my playroom. 'You got kind of a nasty shock, I'd say,' he observed. 'Take it easy for the rest of the day, if that's possible.'

The sounds of furniture being hauled around seemed to be coming from every direction. I remembered how, after my trial, the Kelloggs, my distant cousins from California, came to take me back with them. I asked them to drive past the house. An auction was going on, and they were carrying out furniture and rugs and paintings. Remembering how awful that moment had been, I felt tears streaming from my eyes.

'Mrs Nolan, maybe you should come to the hospital.' The EMT was in his fifties, fatherly-looking.

'No, absolutely not.'

Alex was leaning over me, brushing the tears from my cheeks. 'Celia, I have to go outside to those reporters. I'll be right back.'

'Where did Jack go?' I whispered.

'The moving guy in the kitchen asked Jack to help him unpack the groceries. He's fine.'

Not trusting myself to speak, I nodded and felt Alex slip a handkerchief into my hand. As desperately as I tried, I could not stem the river of tears that poured from my eyes.

I can't hide any more, I thought. I can't live in fear that someone will find out about me. I have to tell Alex. I have to be honest. Better Jack learns about me when he's young than have the story hit him in twenty years.

When Alex came back, he slid down beside me on the chair and lifted me onto his lap. 'Ceil, what is it? It can't be just the condition of the house. What else is upsetting you?'

I felt the tears finally stop, and an icy calm come over me. Maybe this was the moment to tell him.

'That story Georgette Grove told about the child who accidentally killed her mother—'

'Georgette's spin isn't the one I heard from Marcella Williams,' Alex interrupted. 'According to her, that kid should have been convicted. She must have been a little monster. After she killed her mother she kept on shooting the stepfather until the pistol was empty. Marcella says it came out in court that it took a lot of strength to pull that trigger.'

I struggled from his embrace. With his preconceived notion, how could I possibly tell Alex the truth now? 'Are all those people gone?' I asked.

'Everyone's gone except the movers.'

'Then I'd better tell them where I want the furniture placed.'

'Ceil, tell me what's wrong.'

I will tell you, I thought, but only after I can somehow prove that Ted Cartwright lied about that night, and that when I held that gun I was trying to defend my mother, not kill her. I am going to tell the whole world who I am, but I'm going to do it when I am able to learn everything I can about that night, and why Mother was so afraid of Ted. She did not let him in willingly. I know that. There must be a trial transcript, an autopsy report. Things I have to find and read.

'Ceil, what is wrong?'

I put my arms round him. 'Nothing and everything, Alex,' I said. 'But that doesn't mean that things can't change.'

He stepped back and put his hands on my shoulders. 'Ceil, there's something not working between us. I know that. Frankly, living in the apartment that was yours and Larry's made me feel like a visitor. That's why when I saw this house, and thought it was the perfect place for us, I couldn't resist. I know I shouldn't have bought it without you. I should have let Georgette Grove tell me the background, although, from what I know now, she would have glossed over the facts even if I *had* listened.'

There were tears in Alex's eyes. I brushed them dry. 'It's going to be all right,' I said. 'I promise.'

Jeffrey MacKingsley, prosecutor of Morris County, had a particular interest in seeing that the mischief that had once again flared up at the Barton home be squelched once and for all. He had been fourteen and in his first year in high school when the shooting happened. Even then he'd been avidly interested in crime and criminal law, so he'd read everything he could about the case.

Over the years, he had remained intrigued with the question of whether ten-year-old Liza Barton had accidentally killed her mother and shot her stepfather in defence of her mother, or was one of those kids who are born without a conscience. And they exist, Jeff thought with a sigh. They sure do exist.

Sandy-haired, with dark brown eyes, a lean-athletic body, six feet tall and quick to smile, Jeff was the kind of person law-abiding people instinctively liked and trusted. He'd been prosecutor of Morris County for four years now. As a young assistant prosecutor, he'd understood that if he'd been defending instead of prosecuting a case, he often could have found a loophole that would allow even a dangerous felon to walk. That was why, when offered lucrative positions in private firms, he elected to stay in the prosecutor's office, where he'd quickly become a star.

On both sides of the courthouse he was known as a straight arrow, tough on crime, but able to understand that many offenders, with the right combination of supervision and punishment, could be rehabilitated.

Jeff had his next goal in mind—to run for governor after the incumbent's second term ended. In the meantime, he intended to exercise his authority as prosecutor to make sure that Morris County was a safe place to live. That was why the repeated vandalisms of property at the Barton home infuriated and challenged him.

'Those kids, privileged as they are, have nothing better to do than to rake up that old tragedy and turn that beautiful home into the local haunted house,' Jeff fumed to Anna Malloy, his secretary, when the incident was reported to him.

Anna put him through to police headquarters in Mendham, and Sergeant Earley brought him up to date.

'I answered the phone call from the real-estate agent. A couple named Nolan bought the house. She was really upset, actually fainted.'

'I understand that this time whoever did it wasn't satisfied with wrecking the lawn.'

'This goes beyond anything that's been pulled before. I went straight over to the school to talk to the kids who pulled the Halloween trick last year. Michael Buckley was the ringleader. He's twelve and a smart aleck. He swears he had nothing to do with it.'

'Do you believe him?'

'His father backs him up, says they were both home last night.' Earley hesitated. 'Jeff, I believe Mike, not because he isn't capable of pulling the wool over his father's eyes, but because this just wasn't a kid's trick.'

'How do you know?'

'This time they used real paint, not that stuff that washes off. This time they did a job on the front of the house, and from the height of the carving it's clear that someone a lot taller than Michael did it. Something else—the skull and crossbones was done by someone artistic. And the doll wasn't a beat-up rag doll like the other one was. This one cost money.'

'That should make it easier to trace.'

'I hope so. We're working on it.'

The next morning when I awoke, I looked at the clock and was startled to realise that it was already quarter past eight. In a reflex gesture, I turned my head. The pillow beside me was still indented where Alex's head had rested. Then I saw a note propped against his bedside lamp.

'Darling Ceil,

Woke at 6 a.m. So glad to see that you were sleeping after all you went through yesterday. Took off for an hour's ride at the club. Will make it a short day and be home by three. Hope Jack takes well to his first day at school. Love you both, A.'

I got up, pulled on a robe and walked down the hall to Jack's room. His bed was empty. I walked back into the hall and called his name, but he did not answer. Suddenly frightened, I began to call louder, 'Jack . . . Jack . . . Jack'—and realised there was a note of panic in my voice. I forced my lips shut, scolding myself for being ridiculous. He probably just went to the kitchen and fixed himself some cereal. He's an independent little boy, and often did that in the apartment. But the house had a disconcerting silence about it as I raced down the stairs and from one room to the other. I couldn't find a trace of him. In the kitchen there was no empty cereal bowl or juice glass on the counter or in the sink.

Jack was adventurous. Suppose he had become tired of waiting for me to wake up and had wandered outside and become lost? He didn't know this neighbourhood. I would have to call the police.

And then, in a moment of breathtaking release, I knew where he was. Of course. He would have hurried out to visit his new pony. I yanked open the door leading to the patio, then sighed with relief. The barn door was open, and I could see Jack's small pyjama-clad figure inside.

The relief was quickly followed by anger. Last night we had set the security alarm, but Alex had not reset it when he left this morning. If he had, I would have known that Jack was on the loose.

Alex was trying so hard, but he still was not used to being a parent, I reminded myself as I walked across the back yard. Trying to calm down,

I forced myself to concentrate on the fact that it was a perfectly beautiful early September morning, with just a touch of coolness that hinted of an early fall. Autumn has always been my favourite time of the year. Even after my father died and it was just Mother and me, I remember evenings with her in the little library off the living room, the fire crackling and both of us deep in our books. I'd be propped up with my head on the arm of the couch, close enough to her to touch her side with my toes.

I walked into the barn and tousled Jack's head. 'Hey, you scared me,' I told him. 'Don't ever go out before I'm up. OK?'

Jack nodded sheepishly. 'I just wanted to talk to Lizzie,' he said earnestly, then added, 'Who are those people, Mom?'

I turned and looked at a newspaper photo that had been taped to the post of the stall. It was a copy of a snapshot of my mother and father and me on the beach in Spring Lake. My father was holding me in one arm. His other arm was round my mother. I had a copy of the picture and the article that accompanied it in my secret file.

'Do you know that man and woman and that little girl?' Jack asked.

Of course, I had to lie: 'No, Jack, I don't.'

'Then why did someone leave their picture here?'

Why indeed? Was this another bit of malicious mischief, or had somebody recognised me? I tried to keep calm. 'Jack, we won't tell Alex about the picture. He'd be mad if he thinks anyone came here and put it up.'

Jack looked at me with the penetrating wisdom of a child who senses something is very wrong. 'Did whoever put the picture near Lizzie come while we were asleep?' he asked.

'I don't know.' My mouth went dry. Suppose whoever taped it on the post had been in the barn when Jack walked in here alone. What might he have done to my son?

Jack was standing on tiptoe, stroking the pony's muzzle. 'Lizzie's pretty, isn't she, Mom?' he asked, his attention completely diverted from the picture, which was now in the pocket of my robe.

The pony was rust-coloured with a small white marking on the bridge of her nose. 'Yes, she is, Jack,' I said, trying not to show the fear that was making me want to snatch him in my arms and run away. 'But I think she's too pretty to be called Lizzie. Let's think up another name for her.'

Jack looked at me. 'I like to call her Lizzie,' he said. 'Yesterday you said I could call her any name I wanted.'

He was right, but maybe there was a way I could change his mind. I pointed to the white marking. 'I think any pony with a star on its face should be called "Star",' I said. 'That will be my name for Lizzie. Now we'd better get you ready for school.'

By pleading, cajoling and offering a handsome bonus, Georgette Grove managed to find a landscaper who would cut out the damaged grass and lay turf that same afternoon. She also secured a painter to cover the red paint on the shingles. She had not yet been able to hire a mason to repair the stone, nor a woodwork expert to remove the skull and crossbones carved in the front door.

The events of the day had resulted in an almost sleepless night. At six o'clock, when Georgette heard the sound of the newspaper delivery service in her driveway, she leapt out of bed and hurried to the side door to retrieve the papers from the drive. The dreadful worry that was sitting like a slab of concrete on her head was that Celia Nolan would demand that the sale of the house be voided.

Georgette sat at the breakfast bar and opened the newspapers. The *Daily Record* gave the picture of the house its entire front page. On the third page of the *Star-Ledger* there was a picture of Celia Nolan, caught at the exact moment she began to faint. The *New York Post* had a close-up of the skull and crossbones on the front door. Both the *Post* and the *Star-Ledger* rehashed the sensational case. 'Unhappily, "Little Lizzie's Place" has acquired a sinister mythology in our community over the years,' the reporter for the *Daily Record* wrote.

That reporter had interviewed Ted Cartwright about the vandalism. He had posed for the picture in his home in nearby Bernardsville, his walking stick in his hand. 'I have never recovered from the death of my wife, physically or emotionally. I don't need a reminder,' he was quoted as saying. 'I still have nightmares about the expression on that child's face when she went on her shooting spree. She looked like the devil incarnate.'

It's the same story he's been telling for nearly a quarter of a century, Georgette thought. He doesn't want anyone to forget it. It's a damn shame Liza was too traumatised to defend herself. I'd give anything to hear her version of what happened that night. I've seen Ted Cartwright conduct business. If he had his way, we'd have strip malls instead of riding trails in Mendham and Peapack. He may fool a lot of people, but I've been on the zoning board and I've seen him in action. Behind that bereaved-husband façade, he's ruthless.

Georgette continued reading. Dru Perry of the *Star-Ledger* had obviously done research on the Nolans. 'Alex Nolan, a partner in Ackerman and Nolan, a New York law firm, is a member of the Peapack Riding Club. His wife, Celia Foster Nolan, is the widow of Laurence Foster, former president of Bradford and Foster investment firm.'

Even though I did try to tell Alex Nolan about the stigma on the house, Georgette thought for the hundredth time, it's in his wife's name, and she could find out about the stigma law and demand that the sale be voided. Tears of frustration in her eyes, Georgette studied the picture of Celia Nolan caught in the process of fainting. I could probably let her take me to court, but that picture would have a big impact on a judge.

Georgette went into her bedroom and began to untie the knot of her robe. Is it time to close the agency? she wondered. I can't keep on losing money. The frame house on East Main Street would sell in a minute. But this is my livelihood. What would I do? I can't afford to retire, and I don't want to work for anyone else.

Then a faint hope occurred to her. Alex Nolan is a member of the riding club, and he told me his law firm asked him to head up their new Summit office, so there are reasons he wants to be in this area. There are a few other listings that might interest him and his wife. If I offer to forgo my sales commission, maybe Celia Nolan will go along with me.

She showered and dressed. One Old Mill Lane started out as a happy home, she thought, when Audrey and Will Barton bought it. He saw the possibilities in that broken-down mansion. I remember driving by to watch the progress of the renovation, and seeing Will and Audrey planting flowers together, with Liza standing in her playpen on the lawn.

I never believed for a minute that Liza intended to kill her mother or tried to kill Ted Cartwright that night. She was a child, for heaven's sake. If that ex-girlfriend of Ted's hadn't testified that he roughed her up after they split, Liza probably would have been raised in a juvenile detention home. I never could understand what Audrey saw in Ted in the first place. He wasn't fit to carry Will Barton's hat. If only I hadn't encouraged Will to take riding lessons . . .

Half an hour later, reinforced with juice, toast and coffee, Georgette got into her car. As she backed out of the driveway, she gave an appreciative glance at the pale yellow clapboard house that had been her home for thirty years. Despite her business worries, she never failed to feel cheered by the cosy appeal of the former carriage house.

I want to spend the rest of my life here, she thought, then tried to brush off the sudden chill that washed over her.

St Joseph's Church was built on West Main Street in 1860. A school wing was added in 1962. Behind the church there is a cemetery where some of the early settlers of Mendham are buried. Among them are my ancestors.

My mother's maiden name was Sutton, a name that goes back to the late eighteenth century, when gristmills and sawmills and forges dotted the rolling farmland. My mother grew up on Mountainside Road, the child of older parents who did not live to suffer her death at the age of thirty-six. Their home, like so many others, has been restored and expanded. I have the vaguest of childhood memories of being in that house. One firm memory I *do* have is of my grandmother's friends telling my mother that my grandmother never approved of Ted Cartwright.

When I was enrolled at St Joseph's School, there were still mostly nuns on the staff. But this morning, as I walked down the hall to the pre-K class, Jack's hand in mine, I could see that the teachers were almost all members of the laity.

Jack had already been to nursery school in New York, and he loves to be with other children. Even so, he clung to my hand as the teacher, Miss Durkin, came over to greet him. 'You will come back for me, won't you, Mom?' he asked.

His father has been dead two years. Surely whatever memory he has of Larry has faded, replaced probably by a vague anxiety about losing me. I know, because after the day a priest from St Joseph's, accompanied by the owner of the Washington Valley stables, came to our home to tell us that my father's horse had bolted, and that he had died instantly in a fall, I was always afraid that something would happen to my mother.

And it did. By my hand.

My mother blamed herself for my father's accident. A born rider, she had often said she wished he could ride with her. Looking back, I believe he had a secret fear of horses, and, of course, horses sense that. For my mother, it was as necessary to ride as it was to breathe.

I felt a tug on my hand. Jack was waiting for me to reassure him. 'What time is class over?' I asked Miss Durkin.

She knew what I was doing. 'Twelve o'clock,' she said.

Jack can tell time. I knelt down so that our faces would be even. Jack has a sprinkle of freckles across his nose. His mouth is quick to smile, but his eyes sometimes hold a hint of worry, even of fear. I held up my watch. 'What time is it?' I demanded with mock seriousness.

'Ten o'clock, Mom.'

'What time do you think I'm going to be back?'

He smiled. 'Twelve o'clock on the dot.'

I kissed his forehead. 'Agreed.'

I got up quickly, as Miss Durkin took his hand. 'Jack, I want you to meet Billy. You can help me cheer him up.'

Tears were streaming down Billy's face. It was clear he'd rather be anywhere than in this pre-K class. When Jack turned towards him, I slipped out of the classroom and made my way back down the hall.

In the month since my birthday, I had avoided coming to Mendham. But now I got in the car and drove a few minutes down Main Street.

Reaching a shopping centre, I bought the newspapers and went into a coffee shop, where I ordered black coffee. I forced myself to read every word of the stories about the house, and cringed at the picture of me, my knees buckling. If there was any morsel of comfort, it was that the only personal information was the brief mention that I was the widow of the philanthropist Laurence Foster, and that Alex was a member of the riding club and about to open a branch of his law firm in Summit.

Alex. What was I doing to him? Yesterday, typical of his thoughtfulness, he had hired enough help so that by six o'clock the house was in as good shape as it could possibly be on move-in day. How hurt he had been by my refusal to allow the movers to unpack the good china and silver and crystal. Instead I had them placed in one of the guest bedrooms. I could see his disappointment as I sent more and more boxes to be stacked. He knew that it meant our stay in the house would probably be measured in weeks, not months or years.

I knew when I married Alex that he wanted to live in this area. I sipped my coffee and reflected on that fact. Summit is only half an hour from here, and he was already a member of the Peapack Club when I met him. Is it possible that subconsciously I have always wanted to come back here to the familiar scenes that are embedded in my memory? Certainly I could not in my wildest dreams have imagined that Alex would happen to buy my childhood home, but the events of yesterday and the newspaper pictures have proved to me that I'm tired of running.

I sipped the coffee slowly. I want to learn the reason that my mother became deathly afraid of Ted Cartwright, I decided. After what happened yesterday, it would not seem inappropriate for me to go to the courthouse and make enquiries, saying that I would like to learn the truth of that tragedy. I might even find a way to clear my own name.

'Excuse me, but aren't you Celia Nolan?'

I judged the woman who was standing at the table to be in her early forties. I nodded.

'I'm Cynthia Granger. I just wanted to tell you how terrible the townspeople feel about the vandalism to your house. We want to welcome you here. Do you ride?'

I skirted the answer. 'I'm thinking of starting.'

'Wonderful. I'll give you a chance to get settled, and then I'll drop a note. I hope you and your husband will join us for dinner sometime.'

I thanked her and she left. I paid for my coffee, and for the next hour drove around town, up Mountainside Road to get a look at my grandparents' home, around Horseshoe Bend, along Hilltop Road. I drove past Pleasant Valley Mill, better known as 'the pig farm'. Sure enough, there was a sow grazing in the enclosure. My parents had taken me to observe the litter of piglets in the spring. I wanted to show Jack as well.

I did some quick food shopping and got back to St Joe's well before twelve to be sure that Jack would spot me the minute his pre-K session ended. Then we went home. After Jack had gulped down a peanut butter and jelly sandwich, he begged for a ride on Lizzie. Even though I refused to ride after my father died, the knowledge of how to saddle the pony seemed second nature as my hands moved to tighten the girth.

'Where did you ever learn that?'

I whirled round. Alex was smiling at me.

'Oh,' I stammered, 'I told you. My friend Gina loved to ride when we were kids. I used to watch her take lessons.'

Lies. Lie following lie.

'I don't remember you mentioning that,' Alex said. 'But who cares?' He picked up Jack and hugged me. 'My afternoon client cancelled. She wanted to change her will again, but she wrenched her back. When I knew she wasn't coming, I beat it out fast.'

Alex had opened the top button of his shirt and pulled down his tie. I kissed the nape of his neck and his arm tightened round me. 'Tell me about your first day at school,' he demanded of Jack.

'First, can I have a ride on Lizzie?'

'Sure. And then tell me about your day.'

'I'll tell you about how they asked us about our most exciting day this summer, and I talked about moving here and the cops coming, and how today I went out to see Lizzie and there was a picture—'

'Why don't you tell Alex after your ride, Jack?' I interrupted.

'Good idea,' Alex said.

'Jack had a sandwich, but I'll start lunch for us,' I said.

'How about having it on the patio?'

'That would be fun,' I said and headed into the house. I rushed upstairs.

My father had redesigned the second floor to have two large corner rooms that could be used for any purpose. When I was little, one of them was his office, the other a playroom for me. I had directed the movers to place my desk in Daddy's office. The desk is a nondescript antique I purchased for one primary reason. One of the file drawers has a concealed panel that is secured by a combination lock that looks like a decoration. The panel can only be opened if you know the combination.

I yanked the files out of the drawer and tapped out the code, and the panel opened. I pulled out a thick file, opened it and grabbed the newspaper photo that had been taped to the post in the barn.

If Jack ended up telling Alex about it, Alex, of course, would ask to see it. If Jack then realised he had promised me not to talk about it to Alex, he'd probably blurt that out, too.

And I would have to cover with yet more lies.

Putting the picture in the pocket of my slacks, I went downstairs. Knowing Alex loved it, I had bought smoked salmon at the supermarket. I fixed it on salad plates with capers, onions and slices of hard-boiled eggs. I set out place mats and silver on the wrought-iron patio set Alex had bought, then the salads and iced tea, along with heated French bread.

When I called out that everything was ready, Alex and Jack came to sit on the patio. There had been a change in the emotional atmosphere. Alex looked serious, and Jack was on the verge of tears. After a moment of silence, Alex asked in a level tone, 'Was there any reason you weren't planning to tell me about the picture you found in the barn, Ceil?'

'I didn't want to upset you,' I said.

'You don't think the police should know that someone was trespassing here during the night?'

There was only one answer that might be plausible: 'Have you seen today's papers?' I asked quietly. 'Do you think I want any follow-up? For God's sake, give me a break.'

'Ceil, Jack tells me he went out before you woke up. Suppose he had come across someone in the barn? I'm beginning to wonder if there isn't some kind of nut around here.'

Exactly the worry I had but could not share. 'Jack wouldn't have been able to get out if you had reset the alarm,' I said sharply.

'Mommy, why are you mad at Alex?' Jack asked.

'Why indeed, Jack?' Alex pushed back his chair and went inside.

The morning after her new neighbours moved in, Marcella Williams was enjoying a second cup of coffee and devouring the newspapers when her phone rang. She picked it up and murmured, 'Hello.'

'By any chance, would a beautiful lady be free for lunch?'

Ted Cartwright! Marcella felt her pulse begin to race.

'No beautiful ladies around here,' she said coyly, 'but I do know someone who'd very much enjoy lunching with Mr Cartwright.'

Three hours later, having carefully dressed in tan slacks and a vivid silk shirt, Marcella was sitting opposite Ted Cartwright in the Black Horse Tavern on West Main Street, telling him all about her new neighbours. 'When she saw the vandalism, Celia Nolan was *really* upset. She *fainted*, for heaven's sake. Probably she was worn out from the move. No matter how much help you have, there's so much you have to do yourself.'

'It still seems a strong reaction,' Cartwright observed sceptically.

'I agree, but it was a shocking sight. Ted, I tell you, that skull and cross-bones was plain chilling, and you'd swear that red paint was real blood.'

Cartwright reached for his glass and took a long sip of pinot noir. 'Tell me more about your new neighbours.'

'Very attractive,' Marcella said emphatically. 'She could be anywhere from twenty-eight to early thirties. I'd guess he's in his late thirties. The little boy, Jack, is really cute.' She took a bite of her Cobb salad. 'I dropped over to Georgette Grove's office yesterday afternoon. She was so upset about the vandalism, and I was a little concerned about her.'

Seeing Ted's raised eyebrows, she decided to acknowledge that she knew what he was thinking. 'You know me too well,' she laughed. 'I wanted to see what was going on. Georgette wasn't there so I chatted with Robin, her receptionist or whatever she is.'

'What did you find out?'

'That the Nolans have been married six months and that Alex bought the house as a surprise for Celia's birthday.'

Cartwright again raised his eyebrows. 'The only surprise a man gives a woman should be measured in carats.'

Marcella smiled across the table at Ted. He was studying her. I know I look darn good, Marcella thought, and if I can judge a man's expression, he thinks so, too. 'Want to know what I'm thinking?' she challenged him.

'Of course.'

'I'm thinking a lot of men pushing sixty are losing their looks. They put on weight. They just go all-around blah. But you're even more attractive now than when we were neighbours. I love it that your hair has turned white. With those blue eyes of yours, it makes a great combination.'

'You flatter me and I don't mind a bit. Now how about a cup of coffee? After I drop you off, I've got to get to the office.'

Ted had suggested that she meet him at the Black Horse, but she had asked him to pick her up. 'I know I'll have a glass of wine, and I don't want to drive afterwards,' she had explained. The fact was that she wanted the intimacy of being in a car with him.

Half an hour later, Ted pulled into her driveway. He got out of the car and walked round to open the door. As she stood up, a car passed along the road. They both recognised the driver—Jeff MacKingsley.

'What's that all about?' Cartwright asked sharply. 'The Morris County prosecutor doesn't usually get involved with simple vandalism.'

'I can't imagine. Yesterday, Sergeant Earley acted as if he was running the show. I wonder if anything else happened. I was planning to make some cinnamon rolls tomorrow morning and take them up to the Nolans,' Marcella told him. 'I'll give you a call if I hear anything.'

3

I TRIED TO CALM myself down after Alex left and to calm Jack as well. I could see that the events of the past few days were overwhelming him, and suggested that he should curl up on the couch in the den and I would read to him. He willingly selected one of his favourite books. Within minutes he was in the deep sleep that tired four-year-olds achieve so easily. He did not stir when the telephone rang in the kitchen. I ran to answer it. Let it be Alex, I prayed.

But it was Georgette Grove. Her voice hesitant, she said that if I decided I did not want to live in this house, she had others in the area to show me. 'If you saw one you liked, I'd forego my sales commission,' she said. 'And make every effort to sell your house without commission.'

It was a generous offer. Of course it did assume that we could afford to buy a second house without first having the money that Alex had put into this one, but then I am sure Georgette realised that, as Laurence Foster's widow, I had my own resources. I told her that I'd be very interested and was surprised at the relief I could hear in her voice.

When I hung up the phone, I felt more hopeful. When Alex came back, I would tell him that if Georgette found a house I would lay out the money to purchase it myself.

Feeling restless, I wandered through the ground-floor rooms. Yesterday the movers had arranged the furniture marked for the living room and the placement was all wrong. I am not into feng shui, but I am, after all, an interior designer. Before I was even aware of what I was doing, I was shoving the couch across the room and rearranging chairs and tables and carpets so that the room no longer looked like a furniture store.

The doorbell rang. Suppose it was a reporter? But then I remembered that before she hung up, Georgette Grove had told me that a mason was on his way to repair the limestone, so I opened the door.

Standing in front of me was a man in his late thirties with an air of authority about him. He introduced himself as Jeffrey MacKingsley, the prosecutor of Morris County, and I invited him in.

'I was in the vicinity and decided to express my regrets at the unfortunate incident yesterday,' he said, following me into the living room.

374

As I mumbled, 'Thank you, Mr MacKingsley,' his eyes were darting around the room and I was glad that I had rearranged the furniture. The slipper chairs were facing each other on either side of the couch. The love seat was in front of the fireplace. The rugs are mellow with age, and their muted but rich colours were caught in the rays of the afternoon sun. Although there were no curtains or paintings, the room suggested that I was a normal owner with good taste settling into a new home.

That realisation calmed me, and I was able to smile when Jeffrey MacKingsley said, 'This is a lovely room, and I only hope that you will be able to get past what happened and enjoy this home. I assure you my office and the local police will work together to find the culprits. There won't be any more incidents, Mrs Nolan, if we can help it.'

'I hope not.' I hesitated. Suppose Alex walked in now and brought up the photo in the barn. 'Actually . . .'

The prosecutor's expression changed. 'Has there been another incident, Mrs Nolan?'

I reached into the pocket of my slacks and pulled out the newspaper photo. 'This was taped to a post in the barn. My little boy found it.' Choking at the deception, I asked, 'Do you know who these people are?'

MacKingsley took the picture, carefully holding it by its edge. He looked at me. 'Yes, I do. This is the family who restored this house.'

'The Barton family?' I knew my voice was nervous and strained.

'Yes,' he said. 'Mrs Nolan, we might be able to lift some fingerprints from this picture. Who else has handled it?'

'No one else. My husband had already left this morning. It was taped to the post too high up for Jack to reach it.'

'I see. Do you by any chance have a plastic bag that I could drop it in?'

'Of course.'

He followed me into the kitchen and I took a sandwich bag out of the drawer and handed it to him. He dropped the picture into it.

'I won't take any more of your time,' he said. 'Were you planning to let the police know that you'd had another trespasser on your property?'

'This seemed so trivial,' I hedged.

'I agree that it doesn't compare with what happened yesterday. But the fact remains that someone was trespassing on your property again. Fingerprints we get off this picture may help us find who is responsible. We'll need your fingerprints for comparison. I'll arrange for a police officer to come over in a few minutes. He can take them right here.'

A frightening possibility occurred to me. Would they just use my fingerprints to distinguish them from any others on the picture, or would they also run them through the system? Suppose the police decided to check the juvenile files. Mine might be on record there.

'Mrs Nolan, if you find any evidence of someone being on this property, *please* give us a call. I'm also going to ask the police to ride past the house regularly.'

'I think that's a very good idea,' Alex said from the doorway.

I had not heard him come in, and I guess MacKingsley hadn't either, because we both turned abruptly. I introduced them, and MacKingsley repeated to Alex that he would check the picture for fingerprints.

To my relief, Alex did not ask to see it. MacKingsley left after that, then Alex and I looked at each other. He put his arms round me.

'Peace, Ceil,' he said. 'I'm sorry I blew up. It's just that you've got to let me in on things. I am your husband, remember?'

He took up my offer to get out the salmon he had left on the lunch table. We ate together on the patio and I told him about the proposal Georgette Grove had made. 'Certainly, start looking,' he agreed. 'And if we end up with two houses for a while, so be it.'

The doorbell rang. I opened the door, and the Mendham police officer with the fingerprint kit stepped inside. As I rolled my fingertips in the ink, I thought of having done this before—the night I killed my mother.

When she arrived at the office, Georgette Grove sensed the tension in the air between Henry and Robin. Henry's habitual timid Casper Milquetoast expression was now one of petulance, and Robin's eyes were sending angry darts at him.

'What's up?' Georgette asked brusquely. She was not in the mood for petty coworker hissy fits.

'It's very simple,' Robin snapped. 'Henry is in one of his doom-and-gloom moods, and I told him you had enough on your plate without him hanging out the crepe and wringing his hands.'

'If you call the potential of a lawsuit that would finish this agency "doom and gloom", you ought not to come into the real-estate business,' Henry snapped back. 'Georgette, I assume you've read the newspapers? I ask you to remember I have a stake in this agency, too.'

'A twenty per cent stake,' Georgette said levelly, 'which, if my arithmetic hasn't failed me, means I own eighty per cent.'

'I also own twenty per cent of the property on Route 24, and I want my money from it. We have an offer. Either sell it or buy me out.'

'Henry, you know perfectly well that the people who want to buy that property are fronting for Ted Cartwright. If he gets his hands on it, he'll have enough land to press for commercial zoning. Long ago, we agreed we'd eventually deed that property to the state.'

'Or that you would buy me out,' Henry insisted stubbornly. 'Georgette, let me tell you something. That house on Old Mill Lane is cursed. You're the only real-estate agent in town who would accept the exclusive listing on it. You've wasted this firm's money advertising it. When Alex Nolan asked to see it, you should have told him the truth about it right then. I saw the picture in the newspaper of that poor girl collapsing, and *you* are responsible for it.'

'All right, Henry, you've had your say,' Robin said, her tone even and firm. 'Why don't you calm down?' She looked at Georgette. 'I was hoping to spare you from getting hit with this the minute you walked in.'

Georgette looked gratefully at Robin. I was her age when I opened this agency, she thought. She's got what it takes to make people want the houses she shows them. Henry doesn't give a damn any more whether he makes a sale or not. He wants to retire so much he can taste it. 'Look, Henry,' she said, 'there is a potential solution. I'm going to line up some houses to show Celia Nolan. If I find something she likes, I'll waive the commission. I have a feeling she'll be amenable to settling this quietly.'

Henry Paley shrugged and, without answering, turned and walked down the hall to his office.

It was an unexpectedly busy morning. A young couple dropped in who seemed seriously interested in buying a home in the Mendham area. Georgette spent several hours driving them to view places in their price range. Then she had a quick sandwich and coffee at her desk, and for the next two hours went through the multiple-broker listing of residences for sale, studying it carefully in the hope that one of them would jump out as an attractive prospect for Celia Nolan. She finally culled the list down to four possibilities. Her fingers crossed, she called the Nolans' number, and was delighted that Celia was amenable. Next, she made phone calls to the owners and asked to see the houses immediately.

At four o'clock she was on her way. 'I'll be back,' she told Robin. 'Wish me luck.'

Three of the houses she eliminated from consideration. All were charming in their own way, but not, she was sure, what Celia Nolan would be interested in. The one she had saved for last seemed, from the description, to be a real possibility. It was a farmhouse that had been restored, and was vacant now because the owner had been transferred on short notice. It was near the town line of Peapack, in the same area in which Jackie Kennedy had once had a home.

A beautiful piece of property, she thought as she drove up the long driveway. It has twelve acres, so there's room for the pony. She parked at the house's front door, opened the lockbox and took out the key. Then she let herself in and walked through the rooms. The house was immaculate. Every room had been repainted recently. The kitchen was state-of-the-art, while retaining the look of an old-fashioned country kitchen.

With growing hope, she inspected the finished basement. A storage closet near the stairs was locked and the key for it was missing. I know Henry showed this house the other day, Georgette thought with irritation. I wonder if he absentmindedly pocketed the key.

There was a splotch of red on the floor outside the closet. Georgette knelt down to examine it. It was paint—she was sure of that. The dining room was a rich, deep shade of red. This was probably the storage closet for leftover cans of paint.

She went back upstairs, locked the door and returned the house key to the lockbox. As soon as she reached the office, she called Celia Nolan and raved about the farmhouse.

'It does sound worth taking a look at.'

'If ten tomorrow morning is all right, I'll pick you up.'

'No, that's all right. I'd rather drive myself. I like to have my own car. That way I can be sure I'll be on time to pick up Jack at school.'

'I understand. Well, let me give you the address.' Georgette listened as Celia repeated it after her. She was about to give directions, but Celia interrupted.

'There's another call coming in. I'll meet you there at ten sharp.'

Georgette snapped shut her cellphone and shrugged. That house isn't the easiest place to find, she thought, but perhaps Celia has a navigation system in her car.

'Georgette, I want to apologise.'

She looked up. Henry Paley was standing at the door to her office.

Before she could answer, he continued, 'That is not to say I didn't mean every word, but I apologise for the way I said it.'

'Accepted,' Georgette told him, then added, 'Henry, I'm taking Celia Nolan to see the farmhouse on Holland Road. Do you remember if the key to the storage closet in the basement was there last week?'

'I believe it was.'

'Did you look in the closet?'

'No. The couple I took out were obviously not interested in the house. It was too pricey for them. We stayed only a few minutes. Well, I'll be on my way. Good night, Georgette.'

Georgette sat for long minutes after he left. I always said I could smell a liar, she thought, but what in the name of God has Henry got to lie about? And why, after he viewed it, didn't he tip me off to the fact the house is sure to move fast?

After she wrote up the vandalism on Old Mill Lane, Dru Perry went straight to Ken Sharkey, her editor, and told him she wanted to do a feature story on the Barton case. 'It's absolutely perfect for my "Story Behind the Story" series,' she said.

'Any idea where Liza Barton is now?' Sharkey asked.

'No, not a clue.'

'What will make it a real story is if you can track her down and get her version of what happened that night.'

'I intend to try.'

'Go ahead. Knowing you, you'll find something juicy.' Ken Sharkey's quick smile was a dismissal.

'By the way, Ken, I'm going to work at home tomorrow.'

'OK with me.'

Early the next morning, Dru settled at her desk in the office she had created in the second bedroom of her house. The wall in front of her was covered with a corkboard. When she was writing a feature story, she tacked onto it all the information she downloaded from the Internet. By the time she completed the story, the wall would be a jumble of pictures, clippings and scrawled notes that made sense only to her.

She had downloaded everything available about the Liza Barton case. Twenty-four years ago, it had stayed in the news for weeks. When the verdict was released, psychiatrists, psychologists and pseudo-mental-health experts had been invited to comment on Liza's acquittal.

'Rent-a-Psychiatrist,' Dru mumbled aloud as she read the quotes attributed to several medical professionals who believed that Liza Barton was one of those children capable of cold-blooded murder. One psychiatrist had said, 'I wouldn't be surprised if she was able to fake that so-called trauma when she didn't say a word for months.'

Dru always listed on the board any name she came across connected in any way with the story. Benjamin Fletcher, the lawyer appointed to defend Liza, was someone who set Dru's antenna quivering. When she looked him up, she found that he had got a law degree when he was forty-six, had worked as a public defender for only two years, then quit to open a one-man office handling divorces, wills and house closings. He was still in practice in Chester, a town not far from Mendham. Dru calculated his age now to be seventy-five. He'd be a good starting point, she decided. It's obvious that Fletcher never specialised in juvenile defence. So why, she wondered, was someone who was relatively inexperienced appointed to defend a child on a murder charge?

She leaned back in her swivel chair and began twirling her glasses—a gesture her friends compared to a fox picking up a scent.

Marcella hasn't changed a bit, Ted Cartwright thought bitterly as he sipped a Scotch in his office in Morristown. Still the same nosy gossip and still potentially dangerous. He picked up the glass paperweight from his desk and hurled it across the room, watching with satisfaction as it slammed into the centre of the leather chair in the corner of his office. I never miss, he thought, as he visualised the faces of the people he wished were sitting in that chair.

What was Jeff MacKingsley doing on Old Mill Lane today? The question had been repeating in his mind ever since he saw MacKingsley drive past Marcella's house. Prosecutors don't personally investigate vandalism.

The phone rang—his direct line. His sharp bark of 'Ted Cartwright' was greeted by a familiar voice.

'Ted, I saw the newspapers. You take a good picture and tell a good story. I can vouch for how brokenhearted a husband you were. I can prove it, too. And, as you've probably guessed, I'm calling because I'm a little short of cash.'

When Georgette phoned to suggest seeing other houses, I was quick to respond. Once we are out of this house and living in a different one, we will simply be the new people in town. We will have regained our anonymity. That thought kept me going all through the afternoon.

Alex had asked the movers to put his desk, computer and boxes of books in the library. On my birthday, when he led me from room to room, Alex had enthusiastically announced that he would take the library as his home office, pointing out that it was also large enough to accommodate his grand piano. I was nervous about asking him if he had cancelled delivery of the piano, which was scheduled for next week.

After our late lunch, Alex escaped to the library and began unpacking his books. When Jack woke up, I brought him upstairs. Luckily, he's a child who can amuse himself. Jack loves to build with blocks, creating houses, bridges and the occasional skyscraper. While he played, I busied myself going through files I had meant to clean out before we moved.

By five o'clock, Jack had tired of the blocks, so we went downstairs. Tentatively I looked into the library. Alex had papers scattered over his desk, but I could also see newspapers on the floor beside him. He looked up and smiled. 'Hey, you two, I was getting lonesome down here. Jack, we never did get very far with your pony ride. How about we try it now?'

That was all Jack needed. He rushed for the back door. Alex got up, came to me, and cradled my face in his hands.

'Ceil, I read those newspapers. I think I'm beginning to understand how you feel about living here. Maybe this house is cursed. At least, a lot

380

of people apparently think it is. Personally, I don't believe in that stuff, but my first goal is your happiness. Do you believe that?'

'Yes, I do,' I said over the lump in my throat.

The phone in the kitchen rang, and I hurried to answer it. It was Georgette Grove telling me about a wonderful farmhouse she wanted me to see. I agreed to meet her, then heard the 'call waiting' click. I switched to the other call as Alex started out through the back door. He must have heard me gasp, because he turned quickly, but then I shook my head and hung up the phone. 'The beginning of a sales pitch,' I lied.

What I had heard was a husky voice, obviously disguised, whispering, 'May I speak to Little Lizzie, please?'

The three of us went out for dinner that evening, but all I could think of was the call. Had someone recognised me, I wondered anxiously, or was it the kind of prank that kids play. I did my best to act festive with Alex and Jack, but I knew I wasn't fooling Alex. When we got home, I pleaded a headache and went to bed early.

The next morning, after I dropped Jack off at pre-K, I headed out to keep my appointment with Georgette Grove. I knew exactly how to get to Holland Road. My grandmother lived near that road. It's in a beautiful section. On one side of the road, you look down into the valley; on the other, the properties are built along the hill. The moment I saw the house where I was meeting Georgette, I thought it could be the answer.

Georgette's silver BMW sedan was in front of the house. I glanced at my watch. It was only a quarter to ten. I parked behind the BMW and went up onto the porch and rang the bell. I waited, then rang it again. Not sure what to do, I turned the doorknob and found it unlocked. I went in, and called Georgette's name as I walked from room to room.

The house was bigger than the one on Old Mill Lane. In addition to the family room and library, it had a second dining room and a study. I checked them all. Georgette was nowhere on the ground floor. I stood at the bottom of the staircase and called her name. There was only silence.

In the kitchen I had noticed a door that was open a few inches. I guessed that it led to the basement, so I walked back to the kitchen, pulled the door wide open and switched on the light. I called Georgette's name and started down the stairs, wondering if she had had an accident.

When I turned on the switch at the foot of the stairs, the oak-panelled recreation room blazed with lights. There was a faint but pungent odour in the room, a smell I recognised as turpentine.

It became stronger as I crossed the room and went down a hallway, past a bathroom. As I turned a corner, I stumbled over a foot.

Georgette was lying on the floor, her eyes open, drying blood caked on her forehead. A can of turpentine was at her side. She was still holding a rag in her hand. The gun that had killed her was lying on the floor, precisely in the centre of a splotch of red paint.

I remember screaming.

I remember running out of the house and into my car.

I remember driving home.

I remember dialling 911, but I could not get a word out when the operator answered.

The next thing I remember is waking up in the hospital.

Jarrett Alberti, a locksmith, was the second person to find Georgette Grove. He had an appointment to meet her at the farmhouse on Holland Road at eleven thirty. When he got there, he saw that the front door was open and went inside looking for her. He duplicated Celia's grim search, found Georgette's body, then dialled 911.

An hour later, the place was swarming. Yellow tape kept the media away, the coroner was with the body and the forensic team was searching the house and grounds. Prosecutor Jeff MacKingsley and Lola Spaulding, a police detective, were questioning him on the porch.

'What time did Georgette call you?' MacKingsley asked.

'About nine o'clock. She said the key was missing for a storage closet in this house. She wanted me to get over here by nine in the morning to replace the lock. I told her I couldn't get here until ten, and she said in that case to make it eleven thirty.'

'Why was that?' Jeff asked.

'She said that she didn't want me working on the lock while her client was here, and that she surely would be gone by eleven thirty.'

'Georgette referred to the client as "she".'

'Yes,' Jarrett confirmed.

'Do you know where she was when she called you?'

'Yes. She told me she was still in her office.'

'OK, when the body is removed, you can work on the closet.'

Forty minutes later, Jarrett removed the lock and opened the door. A light went on automatically over shelves with neatly labelled paint cans.

MacKingsley looked at the cans on the bottom shelf, the only ones that were not sealed. Three were empty. The fourth was half full. The lid was missing. The splotch on the floor that Georgette had been trying to clean up probably came from this one, Jeff thought. All were labelled 'dining room'. All had contained red paint. It doesn't take a genius to figure out where the vandals got the paint they used on the Nolans' house, he thought. Is *that* why Georgette was murdered? To keep her quiet?

'Is it OK if I take off now?' Jarrett asked.

'Of course. We will need a formal statement from you, but that can be done later. Thanks for all your help, Jarrett.'

As the locksmith walked down the hallway, Clyde Earley crossed the room, his expression grim.

'I just came from the hospital,' Earley said. 'We took Celia Nolan there in an ambulance. At ten after ten she dialled 911, then just gasped into the phone. They alerted us, so we went to her house. She was in shock. No response. In the emergency room, she started to come out of it. She says she was here this morning, found the body and drove home.'

'She found the body and drove home! How is she now?'

'Sedated, but OK. The husband is on his way and she insists she's going home with him. There was a scene at the school when she didn't pick up her son. The kid got hysterical. He saw her faint the other day, and apparently is scared she's going to die. One of the teachers brought him to the hospital. He's with her now.'

'We have to talk to her,' Jeff said. 'She must have been the client Georgette Grove was expecting to meet.'

'Well, I don't think she'll buy this place. Looks like she has her hands full living in one crime scene.'

'Jeff, we found something in the victim's shoulder bag.' Detective Spaulding was holding a newspaper clipping in her gloved hands. She brought it over for him to see. It was the picture of Celia Nolan fainting. 'It looks as if it was put in Georgette's bag after she was killed,' Spaulding said. 'We've checked it for fingerprints, and there aren't any.'

4

I THINK WHAT REALLY calmed me down was the absolute panic I saw in Jack's face. When he came into the emergency room cubicle, he was still sobbing. He usually goes willingly into Alex's arms, but after I wasn't there to pick him up at school, he would only cling to me.

We rode home in the back seat of the car, Jack's hand in mine. Alex was heartsick for both of us. 'God, Ceil,' he said. 'I can't even imagine what a horrible experience that was for you. What's going on in this town?'

What indeed? I thought.

It was nearly a quarter to two, and we were all hungry. Alex opened a can of soup for us and made Jack his favourite, a peanut butter and jelly sandwich. We had barely finished eating when reporters started ringing the doorbell. Alex went outside. For the second time in forty-eight hours, he made a statement to the press.

When he came back inside, I said, 'What did they ask you?'

'I guess what you'd expect: Why didn't you call the police immediately? Weren't you carrying a cellphone? I pointed out that the killer might still have been in the house, and you did the smartest thing possible—you got out of there.'

A few minutes later, Jeffrey MacKingsley called. Alex wanted to put him off, but I immediately agreed to see him. Every instinct told me that it was important I give the appearance of being a cooperative witness.

MacKingsley arrived with a man I'd guess to be in his early fifties. Chubby-faced, with thinning hair and a serious demeanour, he was introduced as Paul Walsh, the detective in charge of the investigation into Georgette Grove's death.

With Alex sitting on the couch beside me, I responded to their questions. I explained that the history of this house and the vandalism was too upsetting, and that Georgette had offered to forego her commission if she found a house for us.

'You were not aware of the background of this house before you saw it last month?' Detective Walsh asked.

I felt my palms begin to sweat. I chose my answer carefully. 'I was not aware of the reputation of this house before I saw it last month.'

'Mrs Nolan, do you know about the law in New Jersey that mandates that a real-estate broker must inform a prospective buyer if a house has a stigma—meaning, for example, if a crime has been committed in it?'

'I did *not* know that,' I said, my astonishment unfeigned. 'So Georgette wasn't being all that generous when she offered to forego her commission.'

'She did try to tell me that the house had a history, but I cut her off,' Alex explained. 'As I told her, when I was a kid my family used to rent a run-down house in Cape Cod that the natives swore was haunted.'

'Nevertheless, from what I read in yesterday's papers, you bought this house as a gift for your wife,' MacKingsley said. 'It's in her name only, so Ms Grove had a responsibility to disclose the history to her.'

'No wonder she was so upset about the vandalism,' I said. I felt a flash of anger. But then I thought of Georgette as I had seen her in that split second before I ran, the blood crusting her forehead, the rag in her hand. She had been trying to get rid of that red paint on the floor.

'Mrs Nolan, had you met Ms Grove before you moved to this house?'

'No,' I said. My mother might have known Georgette, but I had no memory of her.

'Then you only saw her the day you moved in, for a brief time?'

'That's right,' Alex said, and I caught the edge in his voice. 'Georgette didn't stay long on Tuesday. She wanted to get back to her office and arrange for the house and the lawn to be restored.'

Walsh was taking notes. 'Mrs Nolan, if I may, let's go through this step by step. You had an appointment to meet Ms Grove this morning.'

'I dropped Jack off at school at about a quarter to nine, went to the coffee shop in the shopping centre, then drove to meet Georgette.'

'She gave you directions to Holland Road?'

'No. I mean YES, of course she did!'

I caught a flicker of surprise on both their faces.

'Did you have any trouble finding the house?' Walsh asked. 'Holland Road isn't that clearly marked.'

'I drove slowly,' I said. Then I described finding the gate open, seeing Georgette's car, walking through the ground-floor rooms, going down into the basement, smelling the turpentine, finding the body.

'Did you touch anything, Mrs Nolan?' MacKingsley asked.

In my mind I retraced my steps. Was it only a few hours ago that I had been in that house? 'I turned the front door handle,' I said. 'I don't think I touched anything else until I pushed open the basement door.'

'Do you own a pistol, Mrs Nolan?' Walsh asked.

The question came out of the blue. 'No, of course not.'

'Have you ever fired a pistol?'

I looked at my inquisitor. Behind his round glasses, his eyes were a muddy brown. What kind of question was that to ask of an innocent person who had been unfortunate enough to discover a murder victim?

Of course, once again I lied. 'No, I have not.'

Walsh pulled out a newspaper clipping that was in a plastic bag. It was the photograph of me in the process of fainting. 'Have you any idea why this would be in Ms Grove's shoulder bag?'

'Why in God's name would my wife know what Georgette Grove was carrying in her shoulder bag?' Alex said. He stood up. 'I am sure you can understand that this has been another stressful day for our family.'

Both men got up immediately. 'We may need to talk to you again, Mrs Nolan,' the prosecutor said. 'You're not planning any trips, are you?'

Only to the ends of the earth, I wanted to say. 'No, Mr MacKingsley,' I answered instead, 'I'll be right here, at home.'

Zach Willet's leathery face, hard-muscled body and calloused hands gave testimony to the fact that he was a lifelong outdoorsman. Now sixty-two, Zach had worked at the Washington Valley Riding Club from the time he was twelve years old. He started by mucking out the stables on weekends. At sixteen, he quit school to work at the club full time.

Lack of ambition had kept him from progressing beyond the role of all-round handyman. He liked grooming and exercising horses. He could skilfully repair tack. On the side he ran a tidy business reselling expensive equipment for members of the horsy set. And when the regular instructors were booked, Zach would sometimes give riding lessons.

Thirty years ago, Ted Cartwright had kept his horses at Washington Valley. A couple of years later, he had moved them to the nearby but more prestigious Peapack stables.

By early Thursday afternoon, the word of Georgette Grove's death had spread through the club. Zach had known and liked Georgette. From time to time she had recommended him to people looking to board a horse.

'Why would anybody want to kill a nice lady like Georgette Grove?' was the question everyone was asking.

Zach did his best thinking when he was out riding. Frowning thoughtfully, he saddled up one of the horses he was paid to exercise and took off on the trail up the hills behind the club. Near the top, he veered off onto a trail on which very few riders ventured. The descent was too steep for anyone but an experienced rider, but that was not the reason Zach usually avoided it. What passed for his conscience did not need reminding of what had happened there so many years ago.

If you can do that to one human being who's in your way, you can do it to another, he reasoned, as he kept the horse to a walk. No question, I heard enough around town to know that Georgette was in his way. He needs that land on Route 24 for the commercial buildings he wants to put up. Bet the cops get onto his tail fast. If he did it, wonder if he'd be stupid enough to use the same gun?

Zach thought of the bent cartridge he had hidden in his apartment on the upstairs floor of a two-family house in Chester. Last night, when Ted slipped him the envelope in Sammy's Bar, there was no mistaking the threat Ted had whispered: 'Be careful, Zach. Don't push your luck.'

Ted's the one pushing his luck, Zach thought, as he stared down into the valley. At the spot where the trail turned sharply, he tightened his fingers on the reins and the horse stopped. Zach pulled his cellphone out of his vest pocket, pointed it and clicked. A picture is worth a thousand words, he thought as he pressed his knees against the horse's body, and it began to pick its way obediently along the treacherous path.

Because she had been covering a trial in the Morris County courthouse, Dru Perry did not learn immediately about Georgette Grove's death. When the judge declared a lunch break, she checked messages on her cellphone and called Ken Sharkey, her editor. Five minutes later, she was on her way to the crime scene on Holland Road in Peapack.

She was there when Jeff MacKingsley held a brief press conference. The bombshell was that Celia Nolan had been the one to find the body and it raised a barrage of questions. Dru next headed to the Nolan home. She arrived only a few minutes before Alex Nolan made his statement.

Her next stop was the Grove Real Estate Agency on East Main Street. She half expected to find it closed, but to her astonishment Marcella Williams opened the door, invited her in and introduced her to Georgette Grove's associates, Robin Carpenter and Henry Paley. They both looked annoyed, and were obviously about to refuse her request for an interview.

Marcella intervened on her behalf. 'You really should talk to Dru,' she told Carpenter and Paley. 'In the *Star-Ledger* yesterday, she wrote very sympathetically about how distressed Georgette was at the vandalism.'

'Georgette Grove was important to Mendham,' Dru said. 'I think she deserves to be remembered for all her community activities.'

As she spoke she was studying Carpenter. Despite the fact that her blue eyes were swollen and her face blotched from recent tears, there was no mistaking the fact that Robin Carpenter was beautiful. She's a natural blonde, Dru decided, but those highlights came from the hairdresser. Lovely face. Big, wide-set eyes. Come-hither lips. She also knows how to dress, Dru thought, noting Robin's well-tailored, cream-coloured gabardine trouser suit and frilly, low-cut pink and cream print blouse.

If she's trying to be sexy, though, she's wasting her efforts here, Dru decided as she concentrated on Henry Paley. The thin, nervous-looking, sixtyish real-estate agent appeared to be more worried than grieved, a thought she tucked away for later consideration.

They told her they were just about to have coffee and invited her to join them. Cup in hand, Dru followed Robin across the room to the couch and chairs.

'What do you think happened to Georgette?' Dru asked.

'I think somebody found a way to get into that house on Holland Road and was surprised when she showed up, or else somebody followed her in with the idea of robbing her, then panicked.'

'Did she come into the office this morning?'

'No, and we didn't expect her,' Robin said. 'When Henry and I were leaving yesterday, she told us she planned to go directly to the farmhouse.'

'Why did Georgette stay here after you left? Was she meeting someone?'

'This was Georgette's second home. She often stayed late.'

Dru could tell that Henry Paley was about to object to her questions. 'Let's talk about the kind of person Georgette was. I know she's been a leader in community affairs.'

'She kept a scrapbook,' Robin said. 'Why don't I get it for you?'

Fifteen minutes later, her notebook filled with jottings, Dru was ready to leave. Marcella Williams got up to go with her. Outside the office, when Dru started to say goodbye, Marcella said, 'I'll walk you to your car.'

'It's terrible isn't it?' she began. 'I still can't believe Georgette is dead. The prosecutor and a detective were just leaving when I got to the office. I guess they'd been questioning Robin and Henry. I came over because I wanted to see if there was anything I could do.'

'That was nice of you,' Dru said drily.

'Robin told me that Henry cried like a baby when he heard about Georgette, and I believe it,' Marcella continued. 'From what I understand, ever since his wife died a few years back, he's had a thing for Georgette, but she apparently wasn't interested. I also heard that since he's been getting ready to retire, his attitude has changed. He's told people he'd like to close the agency and sell the office. In addition to that, Henry bought property on Route 24 with Georgette as an investment years ago. He's been wanting to sell it, but she wanted to deed it to the state.'

'What will happen to it now?' Dru asked.

'Your guess is as good as mine. Georgette has a couple of cousins in Pennsylvania she was close to, so I bet she remembered them in her will.' Marcella's laugh was sardonic. 'One thing I'm sure of. If she left that land to her cousins, the state can whistle for that property. They'll sell it in a heartbeat.'

When they reached her car, Dru said goodbye to Marcella and agreed to keep in touch. As she drove away, she reflected on the fact that Marcella Williams had gone out of her way to tell her that Henry Paley would profit by Georgette Grove's death. Does she have a personal grudge against Henry, Dru wondered—or is she trying to protect someone else?

Charley Hatch lived in one of the smallest houses in Mendham, a four-room nineteenth-century cottage. He had bought it after his divorce. The attraction of the property was that it had a barn, which housed his land-scaping and snowploughing equipment. Forty-four years old and mildly attractive, with dark blonde hair and an olive complexion, Charley made a good living out of the residents of Mendham, but he had a deep-seated resentment towards his wealthy clients. He cut their lawns from spring until fall, then ploughed their driveways in the winter, and always he wondered why he hadn't been the one to be born into money and privilege.

A handful of his oldest customers trusted him with a key, and paid him to check their homes when they were away. If he was in the mood, he sometimes spent the night watching television in their family rooms and helping himself to whatever he liked from their liquor cabinets. This gave him a satisfying feeling of one-upmanship—the same feeling he had when he agreed to vandalise the house on Old Mill Lane.

On Thursday evening, after the news of Georgette Grove's death had broken, Charley was settled in his imitation leather recliner when his cellphone rang. He took his phone from his pocket, recognised the number of his caller and mumbled a greeting.

The familiar voice snapped, 'Charley, you were a fool to leave those empty paint cans in the closet. Why didn't you get rid of them?'

'Are you crazy?' he answered heatedly. 'With all that publicity, don't you think cans of red paint might be noticed in the trash? You got what you wanted. I did a great job.'

'Nobody asked you to carve the skull and crossbones on the front door. I warned you to hide those carvings of yours. Have you done it yet?'

'I don't think—' he began.

'That's right. You *don't* think! You're bound to be questioned. They'll find out you do the landscaping there.'

Without answering, Charley snapped shut his cellphone, breaking the connection, and stood up. With growing anxiety, he looked around the cluttered room and counted six carved figures. Cursing quietly, he picked them up, went into the kitchen, wrapped them in a roll of plastic and carefully stacked them in a garbage bag. He carried the bag out to the barn, hiding it behind some fifty-pound bags of rock salt.

Sullenly, he went back into the house, opened his cellphone and dialled. 'What did you get me into anyhow?' he asked, his voice rising. 'Why would the police talk to me? I hardly knew that real-estate woman.'

This time, it was the other person who broke the connection.

After the prosecutor and detective had left, Alex went into his office to make phone calls, because he'd had to cancel appointments when he rushed home. I took Jack outside and let him have a long ride on the pony. I didn't go through the farce of asking Alex to help me with the saddle. He had seen that I was perfectly capable of tacking up the pony myself.

After a few times of walking around the enclosure next to him, I gave in to Jack's pleadings and let him hold the reins. 'Just sit on the fence and watch, Mom,' he begged. 'I'm big.'

Hadn't I asked my mother something like that when I was Jack's age? She started me on a pony when I was only three. It's funny how a flash of memory like that will come over me. I always tried not to think about my early life, even the happy times, because it hurt too much to remember it. But now it feels as if the memories are crashing around me.

Dr Moran, my psychologist for years in California after the trial, told me that suppressed memories never stay suppressed. But there's still something I've tried to remember about that night, and it always seems I can't dig deep enough in my mind to find it. When I woke up, it was my mother's voice I heard first, and I am sure she called my father's name or spoke of him. *What did she say to Ted?*

Then, as though I'd pushed a remote and changed channels, Georgette Grove's face loomed in my mind. Did that appointment cost Georgette her life? Did someone follow her in, or was someone already hiding in the house? She couldn't have suspected anything. She must have been on her knees working away on the stain when she was shot.

That moment, as Jack rode by, I made the connection. Was that red paint on the floor the same paint someone had used on this house?

It was. I was sure of it. I was sure also that the police would be able to prove it. Then they would be questioning me not only because I found Georgette's body but because her death may have been tied to the vandalism. Whoever killed Georgette had carefully placed the pistol on that splotch of paint. The paint was supposed to be tied to her death.

And tied to me, I thought. But I can't drop the mask. I can't enquire about a trial transcript. I can't get a copy of Mother's autopsy report. How can I possibly be seen walking around the Morris County courthouse looking for that information? If they find out who I am, will they think that when I got to that house and saw Georgette cleaning up the paint that I connected her with the vandalism and shot her?

Beware! Little Lizzie's Place . . .

Lizzie Borden took an axe . . .

'Mom, isn't Lizzie a great pony?' Jack called.

'Don't call her Lizzie,' I screamed. 'You can't! I won't have it!'

Jack began to cry. I rushed over to him, encircled his waist with my arms and tried to comfort him. Then Jack pulled away. I helped him down from the pony. 'You scared me, Mom,' he said, and ran into the house.

On Friday morning, the day after Georgette Grove was murdered, Jeff MacKingsley called a meeting in his office for the team of detectives assigned to solve her homicide. Joining Paul Walsh were two veteran investigators, Mort Shelley and Angelo Ortiz.

After the barest of greetings, Jeff went straight to the point. 'The red paint used to vandalise the Nolan home came from Tannon Hardware in Mendham and was custom-mixed for the Holland Road house. It shouldn't have taken a call from me to the owners in San Diego to find *that* out.'

Ortiz responded, his tone defensive: 'I looked into that. Rick Kling, with the Mendham police, was assigned to check out the paint stores. The kid on duty at Tannon Hardware was new and didn't know anything about checking records on paint sales. Sam Tannon was on a business trip until yesterday. Rick was planning to see him.'

'We knew on Tuesday the brand of paint used by whoever vandalised the Nolan house,' Jeff replied firmly. 'Since Tannon Hardware is the only store in the area that sells that brand, Detective Kling might have decided it was worth a phone call to Sam Tannon, wherever he was.'

'Kling realises he dropped the ball,' Ortiz said. 'If we'd known that the red paint was part of what was left over from that redecoration, we'd have been on Holland Road on Wednesday, confiscating the remaining paint.'

The weight of what he was saying hung in the air. 'That doesn't mean we could have saved Georgette's life,' Jeff acknowledged. 'She may have been the victim of a random robbery attempt.'

'Jeff, in my opinion the importance of the paint is that it was used on Little Lizzie's Place. The murder weapon was centred on the splash of paint to emphasise that fact, which brings us to Celia Nolan, a lady I think needs a lot of investigating.' Paul Walsh's dry tone bordered on insolence.

'That gun was deliberately placed, that was obvious,' Jeff said. 'I do not agree with your theory that Mrs Nolan is concealing something. I think the woman has had one shock after another in the past three days, and naturally she is nervous and distressed. Clyde Earley said that she couldn't have faked the state of shock she was in. She couldn't even speak until she got to the hospital.'

'We have her fingerprints on that picture she found in the barn. I want to run them through the data-base file,' Walsh said stubbornly. 'I wouldn't be surprised if that lady has a past she might not want us to find out about.'

'Go ahead,' Jeff snapped. 'But I want you concentrating on finding a killer, not wasting your time on Celia Nolan.'

'Jeff, do you remember when I asked her if Georgette Grove gave her directions to Holland Road? She contradicted herself. First she said "No," then in a heartbeat she said, "Yes, of course." She knew she'd blundered. Incidentally, I checked the time she called 911. It was ten past ten.'

'Your point is?'

'My point is that, according to her testimony, she went into the house

391

on Holland Road at a quarter to ten, and walked around the ground floor calling Georgette's name. That's a big house, Jeff. I went back last night and clocked the trip between Holland and Old Mill Road. Normal driving, by which I mean about ten over the speed limit, it took me nineteen minutes. So let's do the arithmetic. If Nolan left that house by nine minutes of ten, she was in it only four to six minutes.'

'Which is possible,' Jeff said. 'Fast, but possible.'

'That would also assume she drove straight as an arrow, and knew exactly when to turn on unfamiliar and confusing roads while she was in a state of severe shock.'

'I would suggest you make your point,' Jeff said grimly.

'My point is that she either got there much earlier and was waiting for Georgette, or that she has been at that house before and was sure of the roads back and forth.'

'Again, your point?'

'Nolan's generous husband bought the house for her, and she wanted no part of it, but didn't dare tell him. She somehow learned about the vandalism last Halloween, got someone to mess up the house for her, arrives and pulls the fainting act, and now she has her way out. Then somehow Georgette caught on to her act. She was carrying a picture of Celia Nolan doing her swan dive in her purse. I say she was going to show it to Nolan and tell her she wasn't going to get away with it.'

'Then why weren't there any fingerprints on the picture, including Georgette's?' Ortiz asked.

'Nolan wiped it clean. She may have handled it but been afraid to take it in case people had seen Georgette with it.'

'You've missed your calling, Paul,' Jeff snapped. 'You should have been a trial attorney. You sound persuasive on the surface, but it's full of holes. Celia Nolan is a wealthy woman. She could have bought another house with a snap of her fingers, *and* sweet-talked her husband into going along with it. It's obvious he's crazy about her. Go ahead and check her prints in the data base and then let's move on. What's happening, Mort?'

Mort Shelley pulled a notebook from his pocket. 'We're putting together a list of the people who had access to that house, then we're interviewing them. People like other real-estate agents who have keys to the lockbox, and people who do any kind of service, like house-cleaning or land-scaping. We're investigating to see if Georgette Grove had any enemies, if she owed any money, if there's a boyfriend in the picture.'

'All right. Keep me posted.' Jeff stood up, signifying the meeting was over. As they were leaving he called out to Anna, his secretary, to hold any calls for an hour.

Ten minutes later she buzzed him on the intercom. 'Jeff, there's a woman on the phone who claims she was in the Black Horse Tavern last night and heard Ted Cartwright threatening Georgette Grove. I knew you'd want to talk to her.'

'Put her on,' Jeff said.

After she left Marcella Williams, Dru Perry went directly to the *Star-Ledger* offices to write her story about the homicide on Holland Road. She then cleared it with her editor, Ken Sharkey, that she would work at home in the morning to put together a weekend feature on Georgette.

That was why, with a mug of coffee in her hand and still in her pyjamas and robe, she was watching local Channel 12 on Friday morning. The news anchor was interviewing Grove's cousin, Thomas Madison, who had come from Pennsylvania when he received the news of her death. Madison, a soft-spoken man in his early fifties, expressed his family's grief and outrage at her cold-blooded murder. He announced that a memorial service would be held on Monday at Hilltop Presbyterian, the church Georgette had attended all her life. As Dru pressed the remote button and snapped off the television, she decided to go to the service.

Dru turned on her computer and began to search the Internet for references to Georgette Grove. 'Pay dirt,' she said aloud an hour later, as she came across a school picture of Georgette Grove and Henry Paley when they were seniors in Mendham High. Henry's skinny arm was round Georgette, and while she smiled directly into the camera, his fatuous smile was only for her.

Boy, he looks lovesick, Dru thought—he must have been sweet on Georgette even then. I don't see Henry as a murderer, but love and money are the two main reasons people kill or get killed.

She leaned back in her chair and looked up at the ceiling. When they talked yesterday, did Henry Paley talk about his whereabouts when Georgette was killed? Dru pulled out her notebook and jotted down the questions and facts that were jumping into her mind.

Where was Henry Paley the morning of the murder? Did he go to the office at the usual time? Lockboxes have a computerised record. It should show how often Henry visited Holland Road. Was he aware of the paint cans in that storage closet? He wanted the agency to close. Would he deliberately sabotage the Old Mill property to kill the sale?

Dru closed her notebook and went back to the Internet. In the next two hours she was able to form a clear picture of Georgette Grove, an independent woman who, judging from her many awards, was a dynamic force in preserving the quality of life, as she saw it, in Mendham.

Lots of people must have wanted to strangle her, Dru thought, as she came upon reference after reference to Georgette Grove successfully arguing against bending the existing zoning guidelines.

Or maybe one of them wanted to shoot her, she amended. She picked up the phone and dialled the agency. Henry Paley answered her call.

'Henry, I'm so glad to reach you. I'm working on the article about Georgette, and I was thinking how nice it would be to include some of those wonderful pictures from her scrapbook. I'd like to borrow it, or at least copy some of the pictures.'

After some encouragement, Paley reluctantly agreed to allow her to photograph the pages. 'I don't want the book to leave the office,' he said, 'and I don't want anything taken out of it.'

'Henry, I want you to stand beside me when I'm doing it. Thanks very much. I'll see you around noon. I won't take too much of your time.'

5

MARTIN AND KATHLEEN KELLOGG of Santa Barbara, California, were the distant cousins who adopted me. At the time of Mother's death, they had been living in Saudi Arabia. They did not learn anything about what had happened until Martin's engineering firm relocated them back to Santa Barbara. By then the trial was over and I was living in the juvenile shelter here in New Jersey while the Division of Youth and Family Services decided where to place me.

In a way, it was good that the Kelloggs hadn't had any contact with me until that time. Childless themselves, they came to Morris County and, quietly and without publicity, petitioned to adopt me. The court readily approved them as my guardians and adoptive parents.

At that time, the Kelloggs were in their early fifties, not too old to parent an eleven-year-old. More important, though, they were genuinely compassionate. The first time I met Kathleen, she said that she hoped I would like her and, in time, come to love her. 'I always wanted a little girl,' she said. 'Now I want to give you back the rest of your childhood, Liza.'

I went with them willingly. Of course, no one can give you back something that has been destroyed. I was no longer a child—I was an acquitted killer. They desperately wanted me to get beyond the 'Little Lizzie' horror, and so the story we told to anyone who had known them before we came to Santa Barbara was that I was the daughter of a widowed friend who, terminally ill with cancer, asked them to adopt me. They helped me choose my new name, Celia, because my grandmother's name had been Cecilia. They were wise enough to understand that I needed some link to the past, even though it would be secret.

I lived with them for seven years. During all that time, I saw Dr Moran once a week. When I could not speak, he had me draw pictures. Over and over, I drew the same ones. I drew a ferocious apelike figure holding a woman against the wall. I drew a gun poised in midair with bullets flying from it. I drew a picture that was the reverse of the *pietà*. Mine depicted the child holding the dead figure of the mother.

I had lost a year of grammar school but made it up quickly and went to a local high school. In both places I was known as 'quiet but nice'. I had friends, but never let anyone get close to me. I was constantly having to guard my tongue and conceal my emotions.

The same year I moved to New York to attend the Fashion Institute, Martin reached compulsory retirement and they moved to Naples, Florida. Now past eighty, he has become what Kathleen calls 'forgetful', but I fear it is the beginning stages of Alzheimer's.

When we married, Alex and I had a quiet wedding in the Lady Chapel of St Patrick's Cathedral, just the two of us and Jack, Richard Ackerman, the senior partner of Alex's law firm, and Joan Donlan, who was my right hand when I had the interior design business. Shortly after that, Alex and Jack and I flew down to visit Martin and Kathleen. One day when we were lingering over lunch on the patio, Martin called me 'Liza'. Fortunately, Alex and Jack had headed to the beach for a swim.

After my outburst over the pony's name, I followed Jack into the house. He had run to Alex and was sitting on his lap, tearfully telling him that Mommy scared him. 'She scares me too, sometimes, Jack,' Alex said. I know he meant it to be a joke, but the underlying truth was undeniable: he obviously thought I was having some sort of breakdown.

He tried to explain to Jack about the pony: 'You know, a long time ago a little girl named Lizzie lived in this house and she did some very bad things. Nobody liked her and they made her go away. We think about that bad girl when we hear her name. What's something you hate more than anything else?'

'When the doctor gives me a booster shot.'

'Well, would you want to call your pony Booster Shot?'

'Noooooooo.'

'So now you know how Mommy feels when she hears the name Lizzie. Let's think about another name for that pretty pony.'

'Mommy said we should call her "Star" because she has a star on her forehead.'

'That's a great name, and we should make it official. Mommy, don't we have some birthday wrapping paper?'

'Yes, I think so.' I was so grateful to Alex for calming Jack down, but oh, dear God, the explanation he gave!

'Why don't you make a big star and we'll put it on the barn door so everyone will know that a pony named "Star" lives there?'

Jack loved the idea. I drew the outline of a star on a section of glittery wrapping paper and he cut it out. We made a ceremony of pasting it on the door of the barn. I recited the poem I remembered from childhood:

'Star light, star bright,
First star I see tonight,
I wish I may, I wish I might,
Have the wish I wish tonight.'

By then the evening shadows were beginning to settle in. 'What is your wish, Mommy?' Jack asked.

'I wish that the three of us will be together for ever.'

'What do you wish, Alex?' Jack asked.

'I wish that you'll start to call me "Daddy" soon, and that by this time next year you'll have a little brother or sister.'

That night, when Alex tried to draw me close to him, he sensed my resistance and immediately released me. 'Ceil, why don't you take a sleeping pill?' he suggested. 'You need to relax. I'm not sleepy. I'll go downstairs and read for a while.'

When I take a sleeping pill, I usually break it in half, but that night I swallowed a whole one and for the next eight hours slept soundly. When I awoke it was almost eight o'clock, and I pulled on a robe and rushed downstairs. Jack was up and dressed, having breakfast with Alex.

Alex came over and kissed me. 'I've got to be off. You OK?'

'I'm good.' And I was. I knew what I was going to do. After I dropped Jack at school, I would go to one of the other real-estate agents and try to find a house we could rent or buy immediately.

Later that morning, I went to the Mark W. Grannon Agency, and Mark Grannon himself took me around.

'Georgette was the one who got the exclusive listing on your house,' he told me. 'None of the rest of us wanted to touch it. But Georgette always had a guilty feeling about the place. She and Audrey Barton had been good friends at one time. They went to Mendham High at the same time.'

I listened, hoping Grannon could not sense the tension gripping me.

'Audrey was a great horsewoman, you know. Her husband, Will, was deathly afraid of horses and embarrassed about it. He wanted to be able to ride with her. Georgette suggested that he ask Zach at Washington Valley Riding Club to give him lessons, something they agreed to keep secret from Audrey. She knew nothing about it until the police came to tell her that Will was dead. She and Georgette never spoke again.'

Zach!

The name hit me like a thunderbolt. It was one of the words my mother had screamed at Ted the night I killed her.

Zach. It was part of the puzzle!

On Friday afternoon, Ted Cartwright's secretary informed him that a Detective Paul Walsh from the prosecutor's office was in the waiting room and needed to ask a few questions.

In a way, Ted had been expecting the visit, but now that it had actually happened he felt perspiration form on the palms of his hands. 'I wasn't aware Mr Walsh had an appointment to see me,' he spat into the intercom. 'However, send him in.'

Walsh's rumpled, off-the-rack look triggered Cartwright's contempt, which put him somewhat at ease. 'I don't like unexpected drop-ins,' he said. 'I'm going to be on a conference call in ten minutes, so we'd better get to the point, Mr Walsh. It is Mr Walsh, isn't it?'

'That's right,' Walsh replied. He handed Cartwright his card and, uninvited, sat down in the chair facing Cartwright's desk.

Cartwright sat down again himself. 'What can I do for you?'

'I am investigating the murder yesterday morning of Georgette Grove. You knew Ms Grove, presumably. Were you friends?'

'We'd been friendly enough,' He paused, choosing his words carefully. 'In recent years, Georgette became very confrontational. On the zoning board, she was an obstructionist. For that reason, I, along with a number of other people, ended any semblance of friendship with her.'

'When was the last time you saw her?'

'On Wednesday night, at the Black Horse Tavern.'

'What time was that, Mr Cartwright?'

'Between nine fifteen and nine thirty. She was alone, having dinner.'

'Did you approach her?'

'She beckoned to me and I went to greet her and was astonished when she all but accused me of being responsible for the vandalism of the house on Old Mill Lane. I told her she was turning into a crackpot and demanded to know why she would think that. She said that I was working with Henry Paley to put her out of business so that she'd have to sell the property on Route 24.'

'What was your response?'

'I told her I was not working with Paley. I told her that while I would certainly *like* to develop that property, I had plenty of other projects I was working on. And that was the end of it.'

'I see. Where were you yesterday morning between eight and ten o'clock, Mr Cartwright?'

'At eight o'clock I was riding my horse on a trail at the Peapack Riding Club. I rode until nine o'clock, showered at the club and drove here, arriving at about nine thirty.'

'The house on Holland Road in which Ms Grove was shot has wooded property behind it. Isn't there a riding path on that property that connects to a Peapack trail?'

Cartwright stood up. 'Get out of here,' he ordered angrily. 'And don't come back. If I have to talk further with anyone from your office, I'll do it in the presence of my lawyer.'

Paul Walsh stood and walked to the door. As he turned the handle, he said quietly, 'You will be seeing me again, Mr Cartwright. And if you speak to your friend Mr Paley, tell him he'll be seeing me as well.'

At four o'clock on Friday afternoon, Charley Hatch pulled his van into the dirt driveway behind his barn, then unhitched the trailer he'd used to haul his riding mower. Some nights he didn't bother to do that but tonight he was going out again, meeting some pals at a bar to watch the Yankee game. He was looking forward to it.

It had been a long day. The sprinkler system at one of the places he serviced had broken down and the owner was due home from vacation soon. It was one of Charley's easier jobs, and he didn't want to lose it, so he had spent time getting the sprinkler guy to fix the system, then hung around until the grass was properly soaked.

Still upset by his phone conversation the previous night, he'd used the time while he was waiting to carefully examine his clothes. He was wearing the same jeans he had worn on Monday night, and he found three drops of red paint on the right knee. The jeans were old but very comfortable, and he didn't want to dump them. He'd have to see if he could get the paint off with turpentine.

Charley put away the trailer and went into the house, heading straight to the refrigerator. He pulled out a beer, flipped off the top and began to drink. A glance out of the front window made him withdraw the bottle from his lips. A squad car was turning into his driveway.

Charley glanced down. The three drops of paint suddenly looked as if they were billboard size. He rushed into his bedroom, pulled off his sneakers and was dismayed to see that the sole of his left one was smeared with paint. He pulled on a pair of corduroy pants, shoved his feet into loafers and managed to answer the door after the second ring.

Sergeant Clyde Earley was standing there. 'Mind if I come in, Charley?' he asked. 'Just want to ask you a few questions.'

'Sure, sure, come on in, Sergeant.' Charley stood aside and watched as Earley's eyes swept the room. 'Sit down. I just got home, opened a beer for myself. It's hot out there. Funny how all of a sudden, bang, it's back to summer. How about a beer?'

'Thanks, but I'm on duty, Charley.' Earley selected a straight chair, one of two at the butcher-block table where Charley ate his meals. Charley sat on the edge of a worn club chair.

'Terrible thing what happened on Holland Road yesterday,' Earley began.

'I should say so. It gives you the creeps, doesn't it?'

Earley's face was flushed. He had removed his uniform hat and his sandy hair was damp. 'You just get home from work, Charley?'

'That's right.'

'Any reason you changed into corduroy pants and leather shoes? You didn't work in them, did you?'

'Trouble with a sprinkler system. My jeans and sneakers were soaked. I was heading for the shower when I saw your car, so I pulled these on.'

'I see. Well, I'm sorry to keep you from your shower, but I just need a few facts. You do the landscaping for 10 Holland Road, right?'

'Yeah. When Mr Carroll got transferred, they asked me to keep up the place until it's sold. Mow the lawn, trim the bushes, sweep the walk.'

'Have you got a key to the house?'

'Yes. I go in every couple of days to dry mop. Sometimes the realtors bring people in when it's raining and they track in mud.'

'When was the last time you were in the house?'

'Monday. I always go in after the weekend.'

'Did you know there was red paint in the storage room?'

'Sure. There are a lot of paint cans there, all different colours. I guess the decorator ordered more than they needed.'

'You didn't know that red paint was stolen and used to vandalise the house on Old Mill Lane?'

'I read about Little Lizzie's Place being messed up, but I didn't know that the paint came from the Holland Road house.'

'The key to the storage room is missing. Did you know that, Charley?'

'It was there last week. I didn't notice it wasn't there on Monday.'

Earley smiled. 'I didn't say it was missing then. I don't know it was.'

'Well that was the last time I was there,' Charley said defensively. 'That's what I meant.'

Clyde Earley got up to go. 'Let me know if you think of anything that will help, Charley. The way I look at it, maybe the person who did that job on Little Lizzie's Place got scared because Ms Grove was on to him, so he killed her. That's the real shame. The most time somebody would get for vandalism would be a year or so, but if that person killed Grove to keep her quiet, he could get the death penalty. Well, I'll see you, Charley.' Earley let himself out.

Charley held his breath until the squad car drove away, then pulled out his cellphone and dialled. A computerised voice announced that the number he was calling was out of service.

At five o'clock, when Thomas Madison entered the Grove Real Estate office, Henry and Robin were just about to lock up. Like his late cousin, Madison was very clear about what he wanted.

'I'm glad I caught you,' he said. 'I thought I'd stay for the weekend, but there really isn't any point, so I'll come back Sunday night. We'll all be here for the service—I mean my wife, my sisters and their husbands.'

'We'll be open tomorrow,' Henry told him. 'As fate would have it, we seem to be about to close several sales. Have you been to Georgette's house yet?'

'No. The police haven't finished going through it. I don't know what they're looking for.'

'I would imagine any personal correspondence that might give them a lead to her killer,' Robin said. 'They went through her desk here as well.'

'It's a lousy business,' Madison said. 'It's just . . .' His shrug conveyed his dismay at the circumstances. 'I've really got to get home,' he said. 'I'm the coach of my kid's soccer team, and we have a game tomorrow.'

Henry smiled politely. He had absolutely no interest in Georgette's cousin's soccer team. What he *did* care about was immediately nailing down business details with Georgette's heir. 'Tom,' he said, 'from what I understand, you and your two sisters will share in Georgette's estate.'

'That's right. Orin Haskell, her lawyer, has a copy of the will. He's submitting it for probate, but that's the way it reads.' Madison shrugged again. 'Henry, I know that you own twenty per cent of both this place and some property on Route 24. I'll tell you this—we have absolutely *no* interest in continuing the business. My suggestion is that we get three appraisals, then you buy us out, or if you're not interested in keeping the business going, we close the office and sell everything.'

'You do know that Georgette intended to deed the property on Route 24 to the state,' Robin said, ignoring Henry's angry glance.

'I know about that. Frankly we'd all like to kiss Henry's feet for not letting her play Lady Bountiful to the state of New Jersey. I've got three kids, my sisters each have two, and whatever we get from the sale of Georgette's real estate will go towards paying to educate them.'

'I'll start getting appraisals immediately,' Henry promised.

'The sooner the better.' Madison turned to leave, then stopped. 'The family will be having lunch after the church service. We'd like to have you join us. I mean, you two were Georgette's other family.'

Henry waited until the door closed behind Madison. '*Are* we her other family?' he asked dryly.

'I was very fond of Georgette,' Robin said quietly.

'Were you so fond of her that you don't mind the fact that Wednesday night she went through your desk?' Henry asked.

'I wasn't going to say anything about it. You mean she went through your desk as well?'

'She not only went through my desk, she removed a file that belonged to me. Did she take anything from yours?'

'Not that I've noticed. There's nothing of any interest to her.'

'You're *sure* of that, Robin?'

They were still standing in the reception room. Henry was not a tall man, and Robin's three-inch heels put her at eye level with him. For a long moment they looked directly at each other.

'Want to play *I've Got a Secret?*' he asked.

The weekend went unexpectedly well. Both days were very warm. Alex went for an early morning ride on Saturday, and, when he returned, I suggested we go to Spring Lake. A client of mine had been married there in July. We had attended her wedding and stayed at the Breakers Hotel. Because we'd been there together, it was one place that I didn't have to worry too much about letting slip the fact that I was familiar with it.

'Now that Labor Day's over, we can get a reservation,' I said.

Alex liked the idea. Jack loved it. Alex called over to the club and was able to hire one of the kids who worked weekends at the stable to come over Saturday evening and Sunday morning to take care of Star.

It worked out just as I had hoped. We got two connecting ocean-front rooms at the Breakers. We stayed on the beach all afternoon. After dinner, we took a stroll on the boardwalk, and the breeze carried the salty scent of the ocean. Oh, how the ocean calms my soul. I was even able to think about being here before, when I was a child, like Jack, my hand in my mother's, as his was now in mine.

In the morning, we went to early Mass at St Catherine's, a church that never fails to comfort me. We spent the rest of the day on the beach, went to Rod's Olde Irish Tavern in Sea Girt for an early dinner, then, happily tired, started back to Mendham. On the way, I told Alex that I was signing up for lessons at the Washington Valley Riding Club.

'Why not at Peapack?' he asked.

'Because there's a guy at Washington Valley who's supposed to be a wonderful teacher. I called Friday afternoon and he agreed to take me on. I told him that I didn't want to start out at a place where my husband's friends could see how inexperienced I was.'

My throat choked on the lie. The truth was, of course, that I was afraid it would be my experience, not my inexperience, that would trip me up.

And of course, taking lessons from Zach would be the most natural way for me to be around a man whose name had been on my mother's lips seconds before she died.

Detective Paul Walsh was one of the first to arrive at Hilltop Presbyterian Church for Georgette Grove's memorial service on Monday morning. He chose a seat in the last pew.

The weekend search of Georgette's house had proved fruitful. One of the Mendham cops had found a file hidden in her bedroom closet containing an exchange of emails between Henry Paley and Ted Cartwright. Cartwright had promised Paley a bonus if he could force Georgette to sell the property on Route 24. Paley had written that the agency was in a shaky financial situation and that he was doing everything possible to keep it that way. Nice guy, Walsh thought.

MacKingsley's mind set was that Paley was the killer, having panicked because Georgette got her hands on his Cartwright file, but Walsh wasn't convinced. It was common knowledge that Jeff MacKingsley intended to run for the governor's office in two years, and this kind of high-profile case was just what he wanted. Well, Paul Walsh thought, solving this case would be a nice feather in *my* cap, too.

At ten minutes to ten, the organ began to play and the church filled with people. Walsh recognised some members of the local media who, like him, stayed in the back pews. Dru Perry was easy to pick out with her mane of grey hair. Marcella Williams, the neighbour on Old Mill Lane, sat in the fourth pew. Then Thomas Madison and his two sisters went down the aisle and took seats in the front. Henry Paley, looking suitably mournful, and Robin Carpenter also took front seats.

Just as the minister stepped before the altar, Celia and Alex Nolan took seats a few rows ahead of him. Dark glasses shielded Celia's eyes. Her long dark hair was twisted into a knot at the back of her head. When she turned to whisper something to her husband, Walsh had a full view of her profile. Classy-looking, he admitted to himself.

A soloist began to sing 'The Lord Is My Shepherd', and the congregation rose. The pastor, in his eulogy, spoke of a woman who gave selflessly for the good of others: 'Time after time, people have told me of Georgette's efforts to preserve the tranquil beauty of our community . . .'

At the end of the ceremony, Walsh stayed in his pew, observing the expressions of the people as they filed out of the church. When Celia Nolan passed him, Walsh could see that she was very pale, and was holding on tightly to her husband's hand. For a split second, their eyes locked. Be afraid of me, lady, Walsh thought. I can't wait to cuff you.

As he left the church, he found Robin Carpenter waiting outside.

'Detective Walsh,' she said hesitantly, 'when we were sitting inside at the service, I kept thinking about Georgette, of course, and then of something she happened to say to me on Wednesday evening. It was about six o'clock, and I went in to say good night to her. She had her scrapbook on her desk and she was looking at it so intently. She never even heard me push open the door. It wasn't fully closed, you see, and I heard her say something that maybe I should share with you.'

Walsh waited.

'Georgette was talking to herself, but she said something like, "Dear God, I'll never tell anyone I recognised her."'

'Where is that scrapbook?' Walsh demanded.

'Dru Perry persuaded Henry to lend it to her for the story about Georgette that ran in the *Star-Ledger*. She's returning it this afternoon.'

'I'll be over to get it. Thank you, Ms Carpenter.'

Deep in thought, Paul Walsh walked to his car. This information has to do with Celia Nolan, he thought. I *know* it does.

Sue Wortman was the young woman who had taken care of the pony while we were in Spring Lake. She was in the barn with Star when we got home Sunday evening, having stopped by to check on her.

Sue is a striking girl with golden-red hair and blue-green eyes. She has a way with children, and Jack took to her immediately. He explained to her that his pony used to be called Lizzie, but now she was Star. Sue told Jack that she would bet he was going to become a champion rider on a pony named Star.

On the way home from Spring Lake, Alex had suggested that we ought to attend Georgette's service. I had to agree with him. That was why, when Sue told me she was available for baby-sitting, I hired her on the spot. I had planned to go to the Washington Valley Riding Club while Jack was in school, but with Sue to take care of Jack, I was able to change my riding lesson with Zach from 10 a.m. to 2 p.m. on Monday.

Four hours wasn't much, but in a way I was glad to have that extra time before meeting Zach. All Sunday night I had disturbing dreams. In one, I was drowning and too weak to fight. In another, Jack was missing. Then he was near me in the water, and I couldn't reach him. I awoke Monday morning feeling as if I had been in a battle. I took a long, hot shower, as though I could wash the bad dreams away.

I had assumed that we would drive to the memorial service in separate cars because Alex was going to work afterwards, but he said he'd drop me back home when it was over. Sitting there in that church, all I could think of was Georgette as I saw her for the first time, the distress on her face, her frantic apologies. Then my mind jumped to that moment on Holland Road when I almost tripped over her body.

Of course, Alex sensed my distress. 'This was a lousy idea, Ceil,' he whispered. 'I'm sorry.'

On the way out of church, we passed Detective Walsh, and he and I looked at each other. I swear the hatred in his face was palpable, and I knew he wanted me to see it.

Alex and I walked back to the car. I knew by now that Alex was concerned about the time. I said I was sorry I hadn't driven my car, that I knew he was running late. Unfortunately, Marcella Williams had walked up behind us in the parking lot and overheard our conversation.

'Why waste time dropping off Celia?' she insisted. 'I'm going straight home, and it will give us a chance to visit.'

Alex and I exchanged glances. Mine reflected dismay, I know, but I climbed into Marcella's car. She was wearing a Chanel suit, in a cream and light-green fabric edged with a deeper shade of green. It occurred to me that she had come to the service dressed to be seen and admired.

'I'm so glad to have the chance to be with you, Celia,' she said warmly, as she steered her BMW convertible along Main Street. 'That was a nice turnout, wasn't it? It was so good of you to come. Georgette sold that house to your husband without telling him the background, then you had the horror of being the one to find her body. Even with all that, you came to pay your respects.'

'Georgette gave Alex a great deal of time when he was house-hunting. He felt we should be there.'

'I understand that you were already looking for a different house, and that was why you went to Holland Road. I'd love to keep you for a neighbour, but I can certainly understand. I'm very good friends with Ted Cartwright. He's the stepfather Liza Barton shot after she killed her mother. I guess you know the full story of that tragedy?'

'Yes, I do.'

'You wonder where that kid is now. Of course she isn't really a kid any more. She'd be in her early thirties. Ted said he doesn't give a damn. He hopes she fell off the earth.'

Was she toying with me? 'I can understand that he wants to put everything behind him,' I said.

'In all these years, he never remarried. Oh, he's had girlfriends, of course, but he sure was crazy about Audrey. When she dropped him for Will Barton, it just about broke his heart.'

My mother dropped Ted for my father! I'd never known that. I tried to sound casual when I asked, 'You mean Audrey was serious about Cartwright before she married Barton?'

'Oh, my dear, was she ever. Big engagement ring, plans for a wedding. But then she was maid of honour at a friend's wedding in Connecticut. Will Barton was the best man, and as they say, the rest is history.'

Why didn't I ever know that? I wondered.

We were turning down Old Mill Lane. 'How about stopping at my house for a cup of coffee?' Marcella asked.

I managed to get out of that by saying I had phone calls to make before I picked up Jack. Uttering the vaguest of promises to get together soon, I got out of her car and let myself in the kitchen door.

The message light was blinking on the phone. I picked up the receiver, pushed the play button and listened.

It was that same shadowy voice I had heard the other day. This time it whispered, 'More about Little Lizzie . . .

'And when she saw what she had done,

'She gave her father forty-one.

'Thursday got another gun,

'Shot Georgette and began to run.'

Jeff MacKingsley called a two o'clock meeting of the detectives assigned to the Georgette Grove investigation. Paul Walsh, Mort Shelley and Angelo Ortiz were present and ready to give their reports.

Shelley went first: 'The personal codes of eight local brokers were programmed into the lockbox on Holland Road. Two of those eight were Georgette Grove and Henry Paley. There's a computer record of which broker's code was punched in and the time it was punched. Paley told us he'd been out there once. The fact is, he was there three times. The last time was Sunday afternoon, a week ago. The paint in that storage room was used on the Nolan house sometime Monday night.'

He glanced down at his notes. 'The other brokers who showed the house last week all swear they did not leave the kitchen or patio doors unlocked. But they did agree that it's been known to happen. The alarm system is programmed for fire and carbon monoxide, not for entry or exit, since the house is empty and Charley Hatch keeps an eye on things.'

'Do any of the brokers you spoke to remember seeing the key in the door of the storage closet?' Jeff asked.

'One of them, from the Mark Grannon Agency, showed the house on Sunday morning. He said the key was there. He remembers because he opened the door. The cans of paint were all unopened.'

'Let's go step-by-step,' Jeff suggested. 'We know the key was there on Sunday morning. Paley showed the house on Sunday afternoon and claims he didn't notice if the key was there. Wednesday, in the Black Horse Tavern, Georgette publicly accused Ted Cartwright of conniving with Henry to force her to sell her property on Route 24. Now that we found Henry's file in her closet, we know she had proof. I don't see Paley painting that lawn or carving that skull and crossbones, but I *can* see that either he or Cartwright might pay someone to do it. I can also understand why Henry might panic if Georgette had proof that he was connected to the vandalism.'

Jeff linked his fingers together and leaned back in his chair. 'Henry knew the paint was there. He wanted to get his money out of the office property, and out of the Route 24 parcel. Cartwright had promised him a hefty bonus if he forced the sale. If Georgette Grove knew all that, from what I hear of her, she would have hung on to that property even if she was starving. I say that Paley and Cartwright are our primary suspects, so let's keep the heat on them. Cartwright will never crack, but I bet we can put the squeeze on Paley.'

'Jeff, you're barking up the wrong tree,' Paul Walsh said. 'Georgette's death has everything to do with the pretty lady on Old Mill Lane.'

'You were going to run Celia Nolan's fingerprints through the data base,' Jeff said quietly, suppressing his anger. 'What did you find?'

'Oh, she's clean,' Walsh admitted. 'She never committed a crime for which she's been caught. But there's something fishy there. Celia Nolan is scared and defensive; she's hiding something. This morning, Robin Carpenter told me that on Wednesday evening, when she went to say good night to Georgette, her door was ajar and Robin pushed it open.

406

Georgette was looking at her scrapbook, and, not realising she was being overheard, said, "Dear God, I'll never tell anyone I recognised her."'

'Who was she talking about?' Jeff asked.

'My guess is that a picture of Celia Nolan may be in that book.'

'Have you got the scrapbook?'

'No. Henry lent it to Dru Perry from the *Star-Ledger*, who promises to return it this afternoon. I'm going to pick it up later.'

'Once again, Paul, I think it's necessary to keep an open mind, or else you're going to miss the obvious,' Jeff snapped. 'We had this conversation on Friday. Let's move on. What about fingerprints?'

'They're all in the usual spots in the Holland Road house,' Mort Shelley reported. 'Doorknobs, light switches, kitchen drawers—we've run them all through the data base and we came up with zip.'

'How about the gun?'

'Saturday night special, impossible to trace.'

Angelo Ortiz was next: 'Clyde Earley talked to the landscaper, Charley Hatch, Friday afternoon. He felt that Hatch was nervous, defensive, like he's got something to hide.'

'Is Earley checking Hatch out?' Jeff asked.

'Yes. I talked to him this morning. He hadn't uncovered any reason for Hatch to have a grudge against Georgette Grove. But Earley's got one of his hunches. He's still sniffing around Hatch.'

'Well, tell him not to pull any of his tricks,' Jeff said. 'The trouble with Clyde is that ever since he got publicity on the Barton case, twenty-four years ago, he's been trying to find a way back into the spotlight again.' He stood up. 'OK, that's it.'

Ten miles away, Sergeant Clyde Earley was standing outside Charley Hatch's barn. He'd already established that Charley wasn't home, having seen his landscaping van at one of the houses on Kahdena Road. I'm just paying a little visit to go over Charley's Holland Road schedule, Earley told himself. Sorry that he's not here.

The trash barrels by the barn were full. Wouldn't hurt to take a look, would it? Clyde thought. I know I can't get a search warrant at this point, because I don't have probable cause, so I'll have to make do without one.

The first barrel was stuffed with two black trash bags, securely tied and knotted. With a yank of his strong hands, Clyde opened the top one. It contained the unappetising remains of Charley Hatch's most recent meals. With a muttered expletive, Clyde threw it back in the barrel, then he opened the other bag. This one was stuffed with shabby clothes, which suggested that Charley had cleaned out his closet.

Clyde shook the contents onto the ground. The last items to fall out were sneakers, jeans and a bag of carved figurines. With a satisfied smile, he examined the items closely and found what he was looking for: drops of red paint on the jeans, a smear of red paint on the sole of the left-foot sneaker. Charley must have jumped into those corduroy pants when he saw me coming, Clyde thought.

The figurines were a half-dozen statuettes of animals and birds, all intricately carved, all about six inches tall. These are good, Clyde thought. Why would he get rid of these? Doesn't take a genius to figure that one out, he decided. He doesn't want them around because he got creative at Lizzie's place and carved the skull and crossbones on the door. Somebody has to know about his little hobby.

Thoroughly satisfied with his detective work, Sergeant Clyde Earley carefully placed the figurines, the sneakers and the jeans in the squad car. He stuffed the rest of the clothing Hatch had discarded back in the trash bag, retied it, but deliberately left it on the ground. Let him sweat blood when he sees someone's been here, he thought.

Earley got back in the squad car. I don't think I have to worry about Charley Hatch reporting a theft, he told himself. That ludicrous possibility made him snicker out loud as he drove away.

6

My FIRST INSTINCT was to erase that horrible message, but I didn't do it. Instead I took the tape out of the answering machine and brought it up to my office. I pulled out the file drawer of my desk and tapped in the combination that opened the hidden panel. As if my fingers were burning from touching it, I dropped the tape in the file. When the panel was safely secured again, I sat at my desk, holding my hands down on my knees to keep them from trembling. I simply could not believe what I had heard. Someone who knew I was Liza Barton was accusing me of murdering Georgette Grove. I've spent twenty-four years wondering when someone would point at me and shout my real name, but how could anyone think I would kill a woman I've met once in my life, and for less than an hour?

Detective Walsh. His name sprang into my mind. *'Have you ever fired a gun?*' It was the kind of question you ask a person you view as a sus-pect. Was it possible that Walsh had left that phone message, and was playing a cat-and-mouse game with me?

But even if he knows I'm Liza Barton—and *how* would he know?—why would he think I would kill Georgette Grove? Did Walsh imagine that I was angry enough at Georgette to kill her? Could he possibly believe my mind is so twisted? That possibility made me sick with fear.

Even if Walsh is not the one who knows I am Liza Barton, he's suspi-cious of me. I've already lied to him. I can't answer any more questions. I've got to hire a criminal lawyer.

But how would I explain that to my lawyer husband?

It was time to pick up Jack. I got up, went into the bathroom and washed my face with cold water, trying to shock myself into reality. I changed into jeans and a cotton sweater. As I got in the car, I reminded myself that I had to buy a new tape for the answering machine.

I collected Jack at St Joe's and suggested we have lunch at the coffee shop. I managed to persuade him to eat a grilled cheese sandwich instead of peanut butter and jelly. He was filled with stories about pre-K, including the fact that a girl had tried to kiss him.

'Did you let her kiss you?' I asked.

'No, it's stupid.'

'You let *me* kiss you,' I teased.

'That's different.'

It's funny how my love for Jack was the root cause of my marrying Alex. I had met Alex for the first time at Larry's funeral two years ago. Even standing at my husband's casket, I couldn't help being aware that Alex Nolan was a very attractive man. I didn't see him again until he came up to me at a charity dinner a year later. We had lunch the next week, and went to dinner and the theatre a few nights later. It was obvi-ous that he was interested in me, but I had no intention of getting involved with anyone. I had genuinely loved Larry, but the realisation of how disturbed he had been about my past had unsettled me terribly.

Larry was the man who had told me that the happiest part of his life began the day he met me. Larry was the man who put his arms round me and said, 'My God, you poor kid,' when I showed him the sensational stories of Little Lizzie. Larry was the man who shouted with joy the day I told him I was pregnant, and who did not leave me for a single minute of my long and difficult delivery. Larry was the man who, in his will, left me a third of his wealth, and made me residual heir of Jack's estate.

Larry was also the man who on his deathbed, his hand clutching mine, begged me not to disgrace his son by revealing my past.

MARY HIGGINS CLARK

Alex and I began to date with the understanding that this was going nowhere, that it was all platonic. 'I'll be platonic for as long as you want, Ceil,' he would joke. 'But don't for a minute believe I *think* platonic.' Then he'd turn to Jack. 'Hey, guy, how can I make your mother like me?'

We'd been in that mode for four months when one night everything changed. Jack's baby sitter was late. By the time she got to the apartment it was ten to eight, and I was expected at an eight o'clock dinner party on the West Side. The doorman was getting a cab for someone else. I rushed out to hail another cab. I didn't see the limo pulling out from the kerb.

I woke up in the hospital two hours later, battered and bruised, and with a concussion. Alex was sitting by my bedside. He answered my question before I asked: 'Jack's fine. Your baby sitter called me. The police couldn't reach your parents in Florida.'

He ran his hand across my cheek. 'Ceil, you could have been killed!' Then he answered my next unasked question. 'I'll stay at your place with Jack tonight. You know he'll be comfortable with me.'

Alex and I were married two months later. While we were seeing each other without commitment, I owed him nothing. Now that I am his wife, I owe him the truth.

All these thoughts were leaping through my mind as I watched Jack finish the last crumb of his sandwich. I paid the bill and we left the coffee house and started to drive home, but then I remembered that I hadn't bought the answering-machine tape. We backtracked, and as a result, it was twenty to two by the time we got to the house. Sue was there, ready to baby-sit, and I rushed upstairs to trade my sneakers for boots that would work well enough for my first riding lesson.

It didn't occur to me to cancel the lesson. I was distraught at the dual threat that somebody knew I was Liza Barton and that Detective Walsh was suspicious of me. But my instincts told me that by getting to know Zach I might learn why my mother had screamed his name that night.

I left the car in the parking lot of the Washington Valley Riding Club, went inside and told the receptionist that I had an appointment with Zach Willet.

Zach came to fetch me. I judged him to be about sixty. His lined face suggested long exposure to the elements, and the broken capillaries in his cheeks made me suspect he liked his liquor. His eyes were an odd shade of hazel, almost faded. As he looked me over, I detected a hint of insolence in his manner. I was sure I knew what he was thinking: I was one of those people who thought it would be glamorous to learn how to ride a horse, and I would probably end up quitting after a couple of lessons.

Introductions over, he said, 'I tacked up a horse that's used to beginners.'

410

As we walked back to the stables, he asked, 'Ever ridden before?'

'My friend had a pony. She'd let me have rides on it.'

'Uh-huh.' Clearly he was unimpressed.

There were two horses saddled and tied to the hitching post. The large mare was obviously his. A docile-looking gelding was there for me. I listened attentively to Zach's first instructions about mounting a horse. Then he said, 'His name is Biscuit. Here, I'll boost you up.'

It had been a long time since I had sat on a horse, but I immediately felt at home. We walked the horses side by side around the ring. I was with Zach for an hour, and while he was far from gregarious I did get him to talk. He told me how being around horses was a lot more satisfying than being around most of the people he knew. He told me that horses were herd animals and liked each other's company. I remembered to make the mistakes new riders do, like letting the reins slide, giving a squeal when Biscuit picked up the pace.

Of course, when Zach realised I lived on Old Mill Lane, he connected me with Little Lizzie's Place. 'You're the one who found Georgette's body!'

'Yes, I am.'

'Lousy experience for you. Georgette was a nice lady. I read that your husband bought that house as a birthday present. Some present! Ted Cartwright, the stepfather the kid shot that night, used to keep his horses here. We're old friends.'

I tried to sound casual. 'Didn't I hear that Liza's father died as a result of a riding accident somewhere around here?'

'That's right. Next time you come, I'll show you the spot. Well, not the exact spot. That's on a trail only the real experts take. Nobody can understand why Will Barton went on it. He knew better. I was supposed to be with him that day.'

'Were you? What happened?'

'He'd had about ten lessons and could tack up his own horse. My horse had picked up a stone in its hoof and I was trying to get it out. Will said he'd start ahead. I was about five minutes behind him, and I started to get worried that I wasn't catching up. Never occurred to me to look for him on that trail. But I couldn't find him anywhere, and by the time I got back to the stable, the word was all over the place. He and the horse had gone over the cliff.'

'Why do you think he went on the trail?'

'Got confused.'

'Weren't there signs to warn him?'

'Sure there were, but I bet the horse got frisky and Will didn't notice them. Then when he saw what he was up against, my bet is that he yanked on the reins and the horse reared. In a way I've blamed myself all these years. I should have made Will Barton wait for me.'

So that was how it happened, I thought. Knowing that, Mother might have blamed Zach. But why would she have screamed his name at Ted?

'We'll turn back to the stable,' Willet told me. 'You're OK. Stick to it and you'll make a good rider.'

Dru Perry wrote a brief story about Georgette Grove's memorial service, turned it in to her boss at the *Star-Ledger*, and then went back to work on the 'Story Behind the Story' feature. She was thoroughly intrigued with the prospect of taking a fresh look at the Liza Barton case.

She had left a message on the answering machine of Benjamin Fletcher, the lawyer who had defended Liza at her trial. He finally called her back on her cellphone, and they had arranged that she would come to his office in Chester at four o'clock. Now Dru sat in his cubbyhole office, staring at him across a jumble of files and family pictures. She didn't know what she had expected, but it wasn't that he'd be a giant of a man, six feet three or four and at least a hundred pounds overweight. His few remaining strands of hair were damp with perspiration.

'Do you have any idea how many times over the years some reporter has called me about the Barton case?' he asked. 'Don't know what you think you're going to find to write about that hasn't been written before.'

'I guess we all know the basic facts of the case,' Dru agreed. 'But I'd like to talk about Liza. You were appointed by the court to defend her. Is it true that she never spoke to anyone?'

'From the time she thanked that cop for putting a blanket round her in the squad car, she didn't say a single word for two months. Even after that, the psychiatrists couldn't get much out of her. They asked her about her stepfather, and she said, "I hate him."'

'Isn't that understandable, as she blamed him for her mother's death?'

Fletcher pulled a handkerchief out of his pocket and rubbed his face with it. 'Ms Perry, that little girl never intended to kill her mother, that's a given. But Ted Cartwright, the stepfather, is something else. I was always surprised that the press didn't dig a little more into Audrey Barton's relationship with him. Oh, sure they knew she'd been engaged to Ted, then broke it off when she married Will Barton, and that the old flame got rekindled after she was widowed. What they all missed was what went on during that marriage. Barton was an intellectual, a fine architect, but not a particularly successful one. What money there was came from Audrey. From the time she was a child, Audrey rode every day. She still was riding every day after she married Barton, and guess who was in that Peapack club riding with her? Ted Cartwright. And her husband never went with her because he was terrified of horses."

'Are you saying that Audrey was having an affair with Ted while she was married?' Dru asked quickly.

'I don't know if that's true. But she saw him at the club practically every day, and they'd often go on the trails together. At the time, Ted was expanding his construction business and starting to make lots of money.'

'You're suggesting that Audrey regretted her marriage to Will Barton?'

'I heard that from a half-dozen people at the club when I was preparing for the trial. If it was such an open secret, wouldn't a smart kid like Liza have caught on to it too? From the time Audrey buried her husband, she was seeing Ted Cartwright. She waited a couple of years to marry him because the kid resented him from the get-go."

'Then why did Audrey file for divorce. Why was she so afraid of him?'

'My guess is that life with the three of them under the same roof was unbearable, and obviously Audrey couldn't dump her child. But don't forget one more point that kept coming up: the alarm system. One of the things we did get out of Liza was that her mother set the alarm that night before the two of them went upstairs. But when the cops came, the alarm was off. Cartwright didn't break in. If he'd disconnected the alarm from the outside, there'd be a record of a malfunction. I believed him when he said Audrey had called him and invited him over to discuss a reconciliation.'

'I read an interview with Ted's former girlfriend Julie Brett in one of those trashy tabloids, about two years after the trial. She testified at the trial that Cartwright physically abused her.'

Fletcher chuckled. 'She sure did, but the abuse she got from Cartwright was that he dropped her for another woman.'

'You mean she was lying?'

'Now I didn't say that, did I? I think the truth is they'd had an argument. In sympathy for Liza, Julie dressed up her story a little. She's got a good heart. That's off the record, of course.' The lawyer's face became stern. 'Ms Perry, trust me, if it wasn't for Julie, Liza Barton would have been confined in a juvenile detention centre until she was twenty-one.'

'Have you any idea where Liza is now?'

'No. I wonder about her from time to time. I just hope she got the psychiatric help she needed. If she didn't, I wouldn't put it past her to sneak back around here someday and blow Ted's brains out.'

Late Monday afternoon, Charley Hatch sat in his living room, drinking beer and waiting nervously for the call he'd been told to expect. He was going over in his mind how he would explain that there was a problem.

It's not my fault, he thought. After that cop Earley left on Friday, I tried to call the usual number. Then my phone rings. I'm told to go out and buy one of those cellphones with minutes on it so nobody can trace it.

Then, just to show I was being careful, I mentioned that I'd noticed some spots of paint on my jeans and sneakers, and managed to change them before I let the cop in. I thought that would show I'm on the ball, but instead I'm told to get rid of the jeans and sneakers, and to make sure there's no paint spots on the van. Then I have to listen to more bull about how dumb I was to do the carving in that door.

So over the weekend I left the jeans and sneakers bundled with my carvings in the garage, and then I decided I'd better get rid of them for good. My garbage is picked up every Tuesday and Friday. I thought putting it in the bin Sunday night would be OK. I'll bet it was that nosy .cop who rummaged through it and found my jeans and sneakers and carvings. Anyway, they're gone. I admit I was a dope to put on those corduroy pants on a hot day. Earley even said something about it.

Charley's regular cellphone rang. His throat suddenly tight, he took a deep breath, then answered. 'Hello.'

'Give me the number of the other phone. I'll call you on it.'

When his new phone rang, he picked it up. Instead of giving his carefully rehearsed explanation, he blurted nervously out, 'I threw my sneakers, jeans and my carved figures in the garbage. Someone fished them out. I think it was that cop who came to see me Friday.'

The long silence that followed was worse than the angry tirade he'd been subjected to because of the skull and crossbones.

When his caller spoke, the voice was calm and even. 'Why did you put that stuff in the garbage?'

'It was supposed to be picked up tomorrow.'

'I didn't ask for the garbage schedule. You should have just thrown it in a Dumpster behind some store. Listen, I don't know who shot Georgette Grove, but if the cops have evidence that you did the job on the Nolan house, they'll blame you for it.'

'Blame *us* for it,' Charley corrected.

'Don't threaten me, Charley. I'm pretty sure that cop had no right to go through your garbage without a search warrant, so even if they found something incriminating they can't use it. They can, however, wear you down. So get a lawyer, and refuse to answer questions.'

'A lawyer! Who's going to pay for a lawyer?'

'You know damn well I'll pay for it.' There was a pause. 'Charley, you'll never have to worry about money again if you can get through this without messing it up.'

NO PLACE LIKE HOME

On Monday night, Zach had a hamburger and a couple of drinks at Marty's Bar and debated in his mind about calling Ted Cartwright. The picture he had mailed him must have arrived at his office by now.

The cops had to be questioning Ted about Georgette Grove, he figured. Everyone in town knew how furious he was that she was always blocking his building plans. The case against him would be a lot stronger if a certain Zach Willet decided to share a certain memory with the police.

I'm the minnow who can lead them to the shark, Zach thought.

He decided against having a third Scotch and got into his car to drive home. *Home!* He used to really like his place. Three rooms and a back porch, where on nice days when he wasn't working he could settle down with the papers and his portable TV. But last year Old Lady Potters died, and her daughter moved into the downstairs apartment. She had four kids, and one of them had a drum kit. The racket was driving Zach nuts.

Ted is building town houses in Madison, Zach thought. They're about finished and they look real nice. I wouldn't mind having a little more room. And a place to park, he added to himself, as he drove down his street and found every spot taken. It was clear the landlady's kids were having a gang of friends over.

Zach finally parked a block and a half away, and sullenly walked back to the house. It was a warm evening, and when he went up the steps to the porch, kids were everywhere. He unlocked the door that led to the first-floor apartment and climbed the stairs with a deliberately heavy foot. He had looked forward to settling down on his back porch with a cigar, but there were more kids in the back yard, all shouting at each other.

He got out his cellphone and put it on the table, trying to decide whether or not to make the call. He'd hit Ted up only a week or so ago. But that was before Georgette took a bullet in the head. Ted must be real nervous now, Zach told himself.

The sudden beat of the drums from downstairs made him jump. Muttering a curse, he dialled Ted's cellphone.

'The customer you are trying to reach is unavailable . . .'

Zach waited impatiently until the computerised voice had finished, then he said, 'Sorry to miss you Ted. Know how upset you must be about Georgette's death. I bet you're taking it real hard. Hope you can hear me. The racket downstairs is driving me nuts. I really need another place to live, like one of those town houses you're building. I hope you got that nice picture I sent you.'

All Monday evening, I struggled to tell Alex that I wanted to hire a criminal defence lawyer, but the words kept dying in my throat. The pleasant weekend at Spring Lake had eased the tension between us, and I was coward enough to want that good feeling to last a little while longer.

Then, after dinner, when Alex said he had to go to Chicago tomorrow afternoon to take a deposition, and would be there for one night, possibly two, I was almost relieved. If any more of those terrible calls came in, he wouldn't be around to hear them. And I wanted to call Dr Moran. He's retired now, but I have his number. I needed his advice. Now, if I didn't reach him, I wouldn't have to worry about leaving a message for him to call me back.

All this I was thinking while I was getting Jack ready for bed. I read him a story, then left him to read one himself before it was time to turn off the light. I went down the stairs and into the kitchen. Alex had volunteered to clear the table and to put the dishes in the dishwasher.

'Espresso's ready,' he said with a smile. 'Let's have it in the living room.'

We sat opposite each other in the fireside chairs. By then, I had a feeling he was picking the right moment to bring up something.

'What time did you tell Jack he has to turn out the light?' he asked.

'Eight thirty. But you know the routine. He'll be asleep before that.'

'I'm still getting used to the way a kid begs for more time, then falls asleep the minute his head hits the pillow.' Alex looked at me. 'Ceil, my piano is being delivered on Saturday.'

He raised a hand before I could protest. 'I miss having the piano. It's been six months since I put it in storage. You may find a different house tomorrow, or it could be a year from tomorrow.'

'You want to stay here in this house, don't you?' I asked.

'Yes, I do, Ceil. I know that with your talent, if you decorated it, this would be a showplace. We can put up a security fence to be sure we never have a vandalism episode again.'

'But it will still be "Little Lizzie's Place" in people's minds,' I protested.

'Ceil, I know a way to put a stop to that. This house was originally called Knollcrest. Let's call it that again, and have a sign made to put at the gate. Then we could have a cocktail party, have a picture of the house on the invitation, and welcome people to Knollcrest. I believe the name would begin to stick. How about it?'

The look on my face must have conveyed my answer.

'Well, never mind,' Alex said. 'It was a lousy idea.' Then as he stood up, he added, 'But I *am* going to have the piano delivered on Saturday.'

The next morning Alex gave me a hurried kiss on his way out. 'I'm going for a ride. I'll shower at the club. I'll call you tonight from Chicago.'

I don't know if he suspected that I had been awake most of the night.

He came to bed about an hour after me, moving very quietly, assuming that I was asleep, and settling on his side of the bed without even the perfunctory kiss that was becoming our nightly routine.

After I dropped Jack at school, I went to the coffee shop again. Cynthia Granger, the woman who had chatted with me last week, was seated at a nearby table with another lady. When she saw me come in, she got up and asked me to join them. After expressing concern for the shock I had experienced on Holland Road, she told me the general feeling in the community was that Ted Cartwright was involved in Georgette's death.

'Ted's always been considered a Mafia-type,' Cynthia explained to me. 'Not that I mean he's *in* the Mafia, but you sense that underneath his surface charm you're dealing with one very tough cookie. I understand that somebody from the prosecutor's office was in his office Friday afternoon.'

For what turned out to be a very short interval, I felt as if everything might be all right. If the prosecutor thought Ted Cartwright was connected to Georgette's death, I might have been wrong about Detective Walsh zeroing in on me. Maybe, after all, in their eyes, I was only the lady from New York who had the incredibly bad luck to buy a stigmatised house, and then to find a murder victim.

Lee Woods, the woman seated with Cynthia, had moved to Mendham last year from Manhattan. It turned out that she had a friend whose apartment I had decorated before I married Larry, and she was effusive in her praise of it. 'Then you're Celia Kellogg,' she said. 'Talk about coincidence. I was redoing our apartment so I called your number, but your assistant said you had a baby and wouldn't be taking on clients. Is that still true?'

'It won't be much longer,' I said. 'Sooner or later, I do plan to hang out my shingle around here.'

It felt so good to be Celia Kellogg, interior designer, again. Cynthia and Lee even had a suggestion for a housekeeper. Gratefully, I took her name. But as we got up to leave, I had a sudden sense of being watched. I turned around and saw the man who was sitting at a nearby table.

It was Detective Paul Walsh.

At three o'clock on Tuesday afternoon, feeling irritable and unsettled, Jeff MacKingsley told his secretary, Anna, to hold his calls.

Paul Walsh had come back to the office at noon and reported that he had followed Celia Nolan around all morning. 'I really jolted her when she saw me in the coffee shop,' he said. 'Then I followed her over to Bedminster, where she went into that place where they sell riding clothes. When she came out with a bunch of boxes and saw me parked behind her, I thought she'd have a heart attack. I knew she was picking up the kid, so I let it go for today.'

He looked at me as if he was defying me to take him off the case, Jeff thought, and I won't do that, at least not yet. As far as I'm concerned, the investigations into Georgette Grove's death and the vandalism on Old Mill Lane are going nowhere fast.

Who had a motive in killing Georgette? Two people. Ted Cartwright and Henry Paley. Cartwright had been riding Wednesday morning and conceivably could have turned onto the trail that went behind the house on Holland Road. He could have been waiting for Georgette and followed her into the house.

The problem with that scenario, as Jeff saw it, was that Cartwright would have to have known that Georgette was showing the house that morning. Of course, Henry Paley could have tipped him off, but how could Cartwright be sure that Celia Nolan wouldn't have driven over with Georgette? If Nolan and Grove had shown up together, would Ted Cartwright have killed both of them?

Henry Paley is the one who makes the most sense for both crimes, Jeff decided. He knew that Georgette was scheduled to meet Nolan at the Holland Road house. He could have been waiting for Georgette to show up, then followed her in, killed her and made his escape before Celia Nolan arrived. Money was his motive, and fear of disclosure. If she was able to tie him to the vandalism, he knew he was facing a jail term.

Henry Paley admits to being in the vicinity of Holland Road on Thursday morning, he reflected. He was at a nine o'clock open house. The other realtors Angelo talked to remember seeing him there at about nine fifteen. Celia Nolan arrived at the Holland Road house at a quarter to ten. So Henry had around twenty minutes to leave the open house, cut through those woods, shoot Georgette, go back to his car and take off.

But if Henry is the killer, then whom did he hire to vandalise the Nolan house? I don't think he did it all by himself, Jeff thought. Those paint cans were heavy. Also, there was nothing amateurish about the carving in the door.

The telephone rang. He had told Anna to hold calls unless they were urgent. He picked up the phone. 'Yes, Anna.'

'Sergeant Earley is on the line. He says it's very important.'

'Put him through.' Jeff heard a click and said, 'Hello, Clyde, what's up?'

'Jeff, I got to thinking about who would be likely to do that job on Little Lizzie's Place, and I started to think about that landscaper, Charley Hatch. He had round-the-clock access to the Holland Road house, and would have known about the paint cans in the storage closet. Anyhow, I had a little talk with him Friday afternoon.'

'Go on,' Jeff said.

'I got the feeling that Charley was real nervous. Remember how hot it was Friday afternoon? First thing I noticed was that he was wearing real heavy corduroy pants and loafers. Frankly, I got curious about where his regular work pants and shoes might be. So this morning I waited by Charley's place until the guy who picks up the garbage showed up, and I followed him till he was off Charley's property. I think, as of then, we can consider the bags to be legally abandoned. I asked the waste engineer, as he calls himself, to open Charley's trash, and lo and behold, we found a pair of jeans with red spots, sneakers with red paint, and nice little carved figures with the initials CH on the bottom. Apparently, Charley Hatch loves to do wood carvings. I've got all these items in my office.'

At the other end of the call, at his desk in the Mendham police station, Clyde Earley smiled to himself. He did not think it necessary to inform the prosecutor that at 4 a.m. today, while it was still pitch-dark outside, he had returned to Charley's property and had put these items back into their original bag, with all the old clothes that still sat in the bin awaiting today's pick-up. The plan had worked perfectly when he had retrieved the evidence in full view of a reliable witness—Mr Waste Engineer.

'The garbage man witnessed you opening the bag, and he knew it came from Charley's?' Jeff asked.

'Absolutely. He had carried the bags to the truck on the street, right in front of Charley's place.'

'Clyde, this is a real breakthrough,' Jeff said. 'That's great police work. Where is Charley now?'

'Out landscaping somewhere.'

'We'll send the clothes to the state lab, and I'm sure they'll match the paint, but that could take a day or two. I think that we have enough probable cause to file a complaint for criminal mischief and pick him up. Clyde, I can't thank you enough.'

Jeff hung up the phone and went on the intercom. 'Come in please, Anna. I've got a complaint to dictate.'

She had barely settled in the chair across from his desk when the phone rang again.

The call was from Earley. 'We just heard from the 911 dispatcher. A hysterical woman on Sheep Hill Drive reported that she found her landscaper lying on the ground at the north end of her property. Charley Hatch was shot in the face, and she thinks he's dead.'

At twelve thirty on Tuesday afternoon, Henry Paley walked from his office to the Black Horse Tavern to meet Ted Cartwright, who had called and insisted they have lunch together. When he arrived, he glanced around the dining room, half expecting to see either Detective Shelley or Detective Ortiz at a table. Over the weekend, both of them had separately stopped by the office to ask again what Georgette had said to him that last evening—and what Georgette meant when Robin overheard her say, 'I'll never tell anyone that I recognised her.'

I told them both I have no idea who she recognised, Henry thought, and both acted as if they didn't believe me.

As usual, most of the tables were occupied. Ted Cartwright was already at a corner one. He's probably halfway through his first Scotch, Henry thought, as he made his way across the room.

'Do you think this meeting is a good idea, Ted?' he asked as he pulled out a chair and sat down.

'Hello, Henry. Yes, I think it's an excellent idea. As the owner of twenty per cent of the Route 24 property, you had every right to be in contact with someone interested in buying it. I could wish that you hadn't put our bonus arrangement on paper, but nothing can be done about that now.'

'You sound a lot less upset about those notes than you did the other day,' Henry commented, then realised the waiter was at his side. 'A glass of Merlot, please,' he said.

'Bring another one of these while you're at it,' Cartwright told the waiter. Then, as the man reached for his glass, he added irritably, 'I'm not finished this one. Leave it alone.'

He's drinking fast even for him, Henry thought. He's not as calm as he wants me to think he is.

Cartwright looked across the table at Henry. 'I do feel better, and I'll tell you why. I've hired a lawyer, and the reason for this lunch is not only to let people see we have nothing to hide, but to tell you you'd better hire a lawyer, too. The prosecutor wants to solve this case, and one approach he's going to take is to try to prove that we agreed to get rid of Georgette, and that one of us actually shot her, or hired someone else to do it.'

Henry stared at Cartwright, but said nothing until the waiter returned with the drinks. Then he took a sip of the Merlot and said reflectively, 'I had not even considered that the prosecutor would see me as a possible suspect. Not, to be perfectly honest, that I am burdened with grief about it. At one time I was quite fond of her, but the older Georgette got, the more set in her ways she became, as you well know. However, it simply isn't in my nature to hurt anyone. I have never even held a gun.'

'If you're practising for your defence,' Cartwright said, 'you're wasting it on me. I know your type, Henry. You're a sneak. Were you behind what happened on Old Mill Lane? It's just the sort of trick I'd expect of you.'

'Shall we order?' Henry suggested. 'I have an appointment to take some people house-hunting this afternoon. It's interesting that Georgette's death gave our agency a shot in the arm. We've had quite a few drop-ins.'

The two men did not speak again until the steak sandwiches they both ordered were served. Then, in a conversational tone, Henry said, 'Ted, now that I've persuaded Georgette's cousin to sell the Route 24 property, I'd appreciate the bonus cheque you offered me. I believe the sum we agreed was one hundred thousand dollars.'

Cartwright stopped the fork he was holding in midair. 'You have *got* to be kidding,' he said.

'No, I am not kidding. We made a deal.'

'The deal was that you would persuade Georgette to sell that property instead of deeding it to the state.'

'The deal was, and is, that the property is for sale. Somehow, I anticipated that you might not wish to pay the bonus you owe me. Over the weekend I got in touch with Thomas Madison. I pointed out that, while your offer was reasonable, other offers for that property have also been made. I suggested that I contact the people who made them and see if they would like to begin negotiations.'

'You're bluffing,' Cartwright said, anger rising in his face.

'I really am *not* bluffing, Ted. But you are. You're scared to death that you'll be arrested for Georgette's murder. You were horseback riding near the house on Holland Road. You had a quarrel with Georgette in this very room the night before her death. Now, shall I pursue those other interested parties, or shall I expect your cheque within forty-eight hours?'

Without waiting for an answer, Henry stood up. 'Ted, thanks for lunch. Oh, by the way, why not satisfy my curiosity. Are you still seeing Robin? Or was she only last year's diversion for you?'

Lorraine Smith was the woman whose hysterical 911 call about Charley Hatch had brought not only the police but also an ambulance, the medical examiner, the media and the team from the Morris County prosecutor's office, including the prosecutor himself.

Fifty years old and mother of eighteen-year-old twins, Lorraine eventually regained her composure sufficiently to join the investigative team in the breakfast room of her home on Sheep Hill Road. 'Charley got here about one o'clock,' she told Jeff, Paul Walsh, Angelo Ortiz and Mort Shelley. 'He comes every Tuesday.'

'Did you talk to him at all?' Jeff asked.

'Today I did. Normally I don't talk to him when he's just doing the lawn, but today I was annoyed at him for being late.' Lorraine took a sip of coffee. 'Charley's supposed to come at nine o'clock, and I had friends over for lunch. We were on the patio and had to listen to the roar of his power mower. I finally went and told him to finish tomorrow.'

'What did he say?'

'He kind of laughed and said something like, "You know, Mrs Smith, it's OK for me to be tired and sleep in once in a while. You better take advantage of my services while you still have the chance."'

'Then what happened?'

'His cellphone rang.' Lorraine Smith paused. 'Or I should say, one of his cellphones rang. He took one out of his breast pocket, then, when the ringing kept going, he rushed to get the other one out of his back pocket.'

'Did you happen to hear the name of the person who called him?'

'No. He obviously didn't want to talk in front of me. He told the person to wait a minute, then said, "I'll load my stuff and get out of here now, Mrs Smith." I went back inside, my friends and I finished lunch, and they left at about two fifteen. I didn't realise that Charlie's van was still in the back. When I saw it, I went looking to see where he was.'

'How long was that after your friends left?' Angelo Ortiz asked.

'Only a few minutes. I could see he wasn't in the back yard, so I walked round the pool and tennis court. Just past them is that row of boxwoods where our property ends at Valley Road. Charley was lying on his back in the little space between two of them. His eyes were open and staring, and there was a lot of blood on his face.' Lorraine Smith rubbed her hand over her forehead as if to erase the memory.

Jeff stood up. 'Mrs Smith, we'll ask you to sign a statement later, but thank you for being so helpful. It makes our job easier.'

The four men walked through the foyer to the front door. Detective Lola Spaulding from the forensic unit met them as they came out of the house.

'Jeff, his wallet is in the van. Doesn't look touched. No sign of a cellphone. But we did find something in his vest pocket.' She offered him a plastic bag containing a photograph.

The photograph, like the one that had been in Georgette Grove's shoulder bag, had been cut out of a newspaper. It showed a stunningly attractive blonde woman in her early thirties. She was wearing riding breeches and a hunt coat and holding a silver trophy.

'This hasn't been tested for fingerprints,' Lola said. 'Any idea who it is?'

'Yes,' Jeff said. 'It's Liza Barton's mother, Audrey, and this is one of the pictures the newspapers used last week for the story of the vandalism.'

He gave the picture back to Spaulding and walked to the yellow crime-scene tape that had been strung up to hold back the media. Audrey Barton lived on Old Mill Lane, he thought. The psycho who killed two people is leaving those pictures, and is either playing a game with us, or is begging to be stopped.

What are you telling us? Jeff mentally asked the killer as light bulbs began to flash. How can we stop you before you kill again?

7

ON THE WAY HOME from shopping in Bedminster, I kept looking in the rearview mirror to see if Detective Walsh was still following me. I decided he wasn't, because I couldn't see any trace of that black Chevrolet sedan. I picked up Jack at school, brought him home, washed his face and hands, and drove him around the corner for a play date. After promising to be back at four o'clock, I went home.

Jack's friend's mother had invited me to have a cup of coffee with her while she gave the boys lunch, but I begged off, saying that I had phone calls to make. Unlike yesterday, when I'd given Marcella Williams that excuse, this time I was being honest. I had to talk to Dr Moran. It was about ten o'clock in California, a good time to reach him. And I also wanted to call Kathleen. Now that Martin was failing mentally, she was the only one other than Dr Moran in whom I could confide.

As soon as I got home, I ran to the answering machine. When Jack and I stopped at the house, I'd noticed the light was blinking, but I was afraid to play the message for fear it was one of the Lizzie Borden calls.

The message was from Detective Walsh. He thought that possibly I had been wrong about the time I found Georgette's body, saying it was impossible that someone who didn't know the route from Holland Road to my house could have made the trip so quickly. 'I understand that you were traumatised, Mrs Nolan,' he said, his voice smooth but sarcastic, 'but by now I imagine you could sort out the time a little better.'

I pushed the delete button, but erasing Walsh's voice from my answering machine could not erase the implication of what he was saying. Now I was even more anxious to talk to Dr Moran.

He answered on the second ring. 'Celia,' he said, his voice as warm and reassuring as always, 'you've been on my mind a lot lately. How is everything going?'

'Not that great, Doctor.' I told him about Alex buying this house, about the vandalism, about Georgette's death, the bizarre phone calls, and the threatening way Detective Walsh was treating me.

His voice became increasingly grave as he asked questions. 'Celia, you should tell Alex the truth,' he said.

'I can't, not now, not yet, not until I can show him that what they say about me isn't true.'

'Celia, there's a chance that detective will dig into your past and find out who you are. I think you should protect yourself. Is the lawyer still practising who defended you when you were a child?'

'Benjamin Fletcher? I don't know. I didn't like him.'

'But he got you acquitted. Get a directory and look him up.'

The telephone books were in the cabinet under the phone. I pulled out the yellow pages. 'He's listed here,' I told Dr Moran. 'He practises in Chester. That's only twenty minutes away.'

'I think you should consult him. Anything you tell him will be protected by attorney–client privilege. At the very least, he could recommend a suitable lawyer. Call him, and keep in touch with me.'

'Yes, I will.'

I called Kathleen next. We talk every few weeks. When she answered, I could hear Martin in the background. 'It's Celia,' she called to him. I heard his response, and it chilled my blood.

'Her name is Liza,' he called back. 'She made up the other name.'

'Kathleen, does he *tell* that to people?'

'He's got so much worse,' she whispered. 'I never know *what* he's going to say. I'm at the end of my rope. I took him to a wonderful nursing home only a mile away, but he cried like a baby. For a little while he was perfectly lucid, and begged me to keep him home.'

I could hear the despair in her voice. 'Oh, Kathleen,' I said. Then I insisted that she find a live-in aide and that I would gladly take care of the expense. By the time the conversation ended, I think I had cheered her a little. Of course, I didn't talk to her about what was going on in my life. It was clear she had enough on her plate.

I took the only action open to me. I dialled Benjamin Fletcher's office and made an appointment. Then I called the Washington Valley Riding Club, reached Zach and asked if he was free for another lesson at two o'clock. He agreed, and I rushed upstairs to change into the breeches and boots and riding jacket that I'd just bought.

I drove to the club, arriving there at ten to two. We went out on the trail, and I remembered how my mother enjoyed riding on an afternoon like this. As I thought of her, the riding expertise I had gained as a child started to return. Zach was much quieter today, but seemed in a good mood. On the way back to the stable he said I was doing just fine. As we hit the open field, he said, 'Let's go,' and began to canter. Biscuit immediately followed him, and we raced across the grass to the barn.

We pulled up, and slid off the horses. Zach faced me, his eyes wary. 'You've done a lot of riding,' he said flatly. 'Why didn't you tell me?'

'I told you my friend had a pony.'

'Uh-huh. Well, unless you want to waste your money, why don't we figure out exactly how good you are, and start your lessons from there.'

'That would be fine, Zach,' I said quickly.

Ted, you admitted that Zach . . .

Suddenly I was hearing my mother's voice—those were a few of the words I had heard her screaming when I woke up that night.

What had Ted admitted to her? Trying not to let my face give me away, I mumbled to Zach that I would call him, then I went straight to the car.

As I drove down Sheep Hill Road, I could see that something must have happened at the corner house. There were squad cars and media trucks parked in the driveway. It was a sight that I wanted to avoid, and I tried to take a right turn onto Valley Road. It was closed to traffic and I could see a mortuary van at a break in the hedge. I kept going straight, not caring where the road took me, because all I wanted to do was to get away from the sight of police cars and all the trappings of death.

It was a quarter to four when I got home. Still dressed in my riding outfit, I walked over to pick up Jack from his play date, then strolled home with him hand in hand.

We were barely inside and having a soda together in the kitchen when the bell rang. My heart in my throat, I went to the door, knowing that when I opened it I would be looking at Detective Paul Walsh.

I was right. But this time he was accompanied not only by the prosecutor but also by two other men, who were introduced to me as Detectives Ortiz and Shelley.

There was something about the way they all stared at me as I stood there in my riding clothes that made me know that my appearance had startled them. As I would later learn, all four of them were mentally comparing me with the newspaper picture of my mother that they had found in Charley Hatch's breast pocket.

Dru Perry went to the courthouse late Tuesday morning to search through old records. At first she thought she was wasting her time. Liza Barton's adoption records were sealed. The record of Liza's trial was sealed. She'd expected that, but wanted to see if there was any point in the *Star-Ledger* testing the public's 'right to know' law.

'Forget it,' she was told matter-of-factly by a clerk. 'Juvenile and adoption cases don't come under that law.'

Then, as she was leaving the courthouse, a grandmotherly woman who introduced herself as Ellen O'Brien caught her at the door. 'You're Dru Perry. I have to tell you I love your "Story Behind the Story" series in the *Star-Ledger*. Are you going to do one of them again soon?'

'I'd like to do one on the Liza Barton case,' Dru admitted. 'I thought I'd do some research here, but I'm hitting a stone wall.'

'That would make a great story,' Ellen enthused. 'I've been at this courthouse thirty years, and I've seen a lot of cases, but nothing like that one.'

Thirty years, Dru thought. That means she worked here when that case was going on. She noticed it was twelve o'clock. 'By any chance, are you on your way to lunch?'

'Yes, I am. I'm just popping into the cafeteria.'

'Then is it all right if I join you?'

Fifteen minutes later, over a Cobb salad, Ellen O'Brien was willingly sharing her recollections about what happened from the time Liza Barton was taken into custody. 'They photographed and fingerprinted her at the Mendham police station. She was cool as a cucumber. Never once asked about her mother or stepfather. Then she was taken to the juvenile detention centre and examined by a state psychiatrist.'

Dru broke off a piece of roll. 'I understand that Liza didn't say a word for the first several months she was in custody.'

'That's right, except my friend who was an aide in the detention centre said that Liza used to say the name "Zach" sometimes, then start shaking her head and moving her body.'

Important, Dru thought. She made a notation in her book: *Zach*.

'It leaked out that she was profoundly depressed and on a suicide watch for months,' Ellen continued. 'When she was acquitted, the Division of Youth and Family Services tried to find her a home. Then some relatives showed up and adopted her. It was very hush-hush. I gather they felt Liza's chance for a normal life meant burying the past.'

'Has anybody any idea who they were?'

'From what I understand, there weren't any close relatives. Audrey and Will Barton were both only children. It's almost ironic. Audrey's ancestors settled here before the Revolutionary War. Liza's mother's maiden name was Sutton. But the family has died out around here. So God knows how far distant the cousin might have been who took her in.'

Ellen took a final sip of iced tea. 'The State of New Jersey calls,' she announced. 'I can't tell you what a pleasure it has been talking to you,

Dru. But maybe it's better if you don't mention my name in your story.'

'Of course,' Dru agreed. 'I can't thank you enough. You've been a great help, Ellen. Now if you'll point me to where the marriage records are kept, I'll get back to work.'

I'll trace Liza's ancestry back at least three generations, Dru thought as she paid the bill. My hunch is that it's more likely that Liza was adopted by a member of her mother's family than her father's. I'll collect the names of the people the Sutton women married and trace their descendants to see if one of them has a thirty-four-year-old daughter. It's worth a shot.

I knew I had to take a stand. I could not have these four men come into my house and question me about the death of a woman I had met only once. These people from the prosecutor's office did not know I was Liza Barton. They were trying to tie me to Georgette's death only because I had not dialled 911 from Holland Road and had driven home so quickly.

Jack had followed me to the door, and now he slipped his hand in mine. I'm not sure if he was seeking reassurance or trying to give it.

My anger at what this might be doing to him gave me the backbone to go on the attack. 'Mr MacKingsley,' I began, 'will you please explain to me why Detective Walsh was following me around this morning?'

'Mrs Nolan, I apologise for any inconvenience,' MacKingsley said. 'Would you mind if we stepped in to speak with you for a few minutes? Let me explain what it's about. The other day, you showed me a photograph of the Barton family that was taped to the post in the barn. There were no fingerprints on it except yours, which, as you can understand, is unusual. You took it off the post, but someone had to have handled it first. We have not released this information publicly, but in Georgette Grove's shoulder bag we found a newspaper picture of you taken just as you fainted. That also had no fingerprints on it. Today we found a picture of Audrey Barton at another crime scene.'

I almost blurted out, 'A picture of my mother!' My nerves were just that raw. Instead I asked, 'What has that got to do with me?' trying to sound as calm as possible.

I was still standing in the doorway, and MacKingsley saw that I had no intention of inviting them in. 'Mrs Nolan, the landscaper for the house on Holland Road was shot to death a few hours ago. We have proof that he vandalised this property. He had a picture of Audrey Barton in his pocket, and I doubt that he put it there himself. What I am trying to say is that Georgette Grove's murder, and this homicide, are somehow connected to this house.'

'Did you know Charley Hatch, Mrs Nolan?' Walsh asked.

'No, I did not. Why were you in the coffee shop this morning, and why did you follow me to Bedminster?'

'Mrs Nolan,' Walsh said, 'I believe you either left the Holland Road house, where you discovered the body of Georgette Grove, much earlier than you have admitted, or that you are so familiar with these roads you could make a number of rather confusing turns and still make that phone call to 911 at the time it was received.'

Before I could respond, MacKingsley said, 'Mrs Nolan, Georgette Grove sold this house to your husband. Charley Hatch vandalised it. You live in it. There's an obvious connection and we are trying to solve two homicides. That is why we are here.'

'Are you *sure* you never met Charley Hatch?' Walsh asked.

Anger put steel in my voice. 'I have never even *heard* of the man.'

'Mom.' Jack tugged at my hand.

'It's all right, Jack.' I looked straight at Jeff MacKingsley. 'I arrived here last week to find this house vandalised. I had an appointment to meet Georgette Grove, and found her dead. I do not know what is going on, but I suggest that you concentrate on trying to find whoever is guilty of these crimes, and have the decency to leave me and my family alone.'

I began to close the door. Walsh put his foot forward to block it. 'One more question, Mrs Nolan. Where were you between one thirty and two o'clock this afternoon?'

That one seemed easy to answer: 'I had a two o'clock riding lesson at the Washington Valley Riding Club. I arrived there at five to two. Why don't you clock the distance from here to there, Mr Walsh? That way you can figure out all by yourself what time I left this house.'

I slammed the door against his shoe and he withdrew it, but as I turned the lock, a horrible possibility occurred to me. The police activity on Sheep Hill—could that have anything to do with the death of the land-scaper? If so, I had placed myself directly in the area where he died.

On Tuesday afternoon at four o'clock, Henry Paley returned to the realty office. 'How did it go?' Robin asked.

'I think we have a sale. This is the third time the Muellers have looked at the house, and this time his parents came with them. His father is obviously the one with the chequebook.' Henry smiled, walked over and stood at her desk. 'Robin, you're looking quite provocative today. I don't think Georgette would have approved of that revealing sweater, but then she wouldn't have approved of your boyfriend, would she?'

'Henry, I'm not very comfortable with this subject,' Robin said matter-of-factly.

'I'm sure you're not. I wonder if Georgette wasn't on to you. But maybe not. She certainly never got wind of the fact that you and Cartwright were seeing each other last year. If she had, you'd have been out on your ear.'

'I knew Ted Cartwright before I started work here. I do not have a personal relationship with him. The fact that I knew him never undermined my loyalty to Georgette.'

'Robin, you're the one who fielded phone enquiries about available properties. You're the one who handled the drop-ins. I admit that I haven't worked hard for a while, but you're something else. Was Ted paying you to turn away potential business?"

'You mean like the bonus he was paying you to get Georgette to sell the Route 24 property?' Robin asked sarcastically. 'Of course not.'

The door that fronted East Main Street opened. Startled, they looked up to see a grim-faced Sergeant Earley come into the office.

'I'm glad to catch you together,' he said. 'You know Charley Hatch, the landscaper who took care of the Holland Road property?'

'I've seen him around,' Paley answered.

'This afternoon, sometime between one thirty and two o'clock, he was shot to death while he was working at Sheep Hill Road.'

Robin jumped up, her face pale. 'Charley! That can't be!'

Both men stared at her.

'Charley was my half-brother,' she wailed. 'He *can't* be dead.'

At five o'clock on Tuesday afternoon, Zach Willet drove to the neighbouring town of Madison and parked in front of the sales office of the Cartwright Town Houses Corporation. Inside, he found a sales clerk, a woman in her thirties, tidying up for the day.

'Hi, Amy,' Zach said, noting the nameplate on her desk. 'I can see you're ready to skedaddle, so I won't take two minutes of your time.'

On the walls were sketches of different models of the town houses. Zach walked from one to the other. Brochures on the table listed prices, sizes and particular features. He picked up one and read aloud. 'Four-storey town house, four bedrooms, master bedroom suite, state-of-the-art kitchen, three fireplaces, four baths, double garage, private patio and yard, all services.' Zach smiled appreciatively. 'Looks as though you just can't go wrong with that one.' He pointed to the biggest picture. 'Now, Amy, I know you're probably rushing to meet your boyfriend, but how about showing me that fancy homestead.'

'I'll be glad to take you over, Mr . . .' Amy hesitated. 'I don't think you introduced yourself.'

'That's right. I didn't. I'm Zach Willet.'

Amy opened her desk drawer and fished for her key ring. 'That's 8 Pawnee Avenue. I have to warn you that is our top-of-the-line town house. It's fully loaded with every conceivable extra, and naturally that is reflected in the cost. It's also the furnished model.'

'Sounds better and better. Let's take a look at it.'

On the way through the development, Amy pointed out that the land-scaping was scheduled to be featured in a national gardening magazine, and that the driveways were heated to prevent ice forming in the winter. 'Mr Cartwright has thought of everything,' she said.

'Ted's a good friend of mine,' Zach said expansively. 'Has been since we were kids riding bareback at the stable.'

Amy walked a few steps more. 'Here we are at number 8. As you can see, it's a corner unit, and it really is the crown jewel of the development.'

Zach's smile broadened as Amy opened the door and led him into the family room on the entry level. 'Raised-hearth fireplace, wet bar—what's not to like?' he asked rhetorically.

'Some people use the room on the other side for a gym, and, of course, there's a bathroom with a hot tub right beside it. It's such a convenient arrangement.' Amy's voice crackled with professional enthusiasm.

Zach insisted on riding the elevator to each of the floors. Like a child opening presents, he took pleasure in every detail. 'Plate-warmer drawer! I remember my momma putting the plates on top of the burners on the stove to keep them warm. She always ended up with blistered fingers.'

'Two guest bedrooms! I don't have close family, but I'd better look up those cousins of mine in Ohio and have them out for a weekend.'

They rode back down in the elevator, went outside, and Zach said, 'I'll take it. As is. Furnished.'

'That's wonderful.' Amy locked the front door. 'Are you prepared to make a deposit now?'

'Didn't Ted Cartwright tell you he's giving me this unit?' Zach asked, his tone astonished. 'I saved his life once, and Ted never forgets a favour. You must be proud to be in his employ.'

Alex called shortly after the prosecutor and his entourage left. He was at the airport in Chicago. 'I'm going to have to go back tomorrow for a couple of days more,' he said. 'But I miss you guys and just want to get back for the night. Why don't you see if Sue is available to baby-sit, so you and I can go out for a late dinner in Morristown at the Grand Cafe?'

'Sounds great,' I told him. 'Jack had a play date, so he'll be ready for bed early, and I'll call Sue right away.'

I phoned Sue. She was free to come over. I gave Jack a ride on Star, then settled him in front of the television with a Muppet tape and went upstairs. In the bathroom that my father had designed for my mother, I luxuriated in her deep English tub, trying to wash away the bewildering events of the day.

How much should I tell Alex? Or should I just say nothing, and try to have a stress-free evening with him? He has to go back to Chicago tomorrow morning. Maybe in the next few days they would solve these two crimes and the prosecutor's office would lose interest in me. I tried hard to believe that; it was the only thing I *could* believe and stay sane.

When I got out of the tub, I put on a robe, fed Jack, bathed him and put him to bed. Then I went to get changed.

I have a dark green silk shantung trouser suit that's dressy without being fussy. I decided to wear it tonight. While living in New York, Alex and I had got in the habit of going out a couple of times a week for a late dinner. We would go to Neary's, our favourite Irish pub, or, if we were in the mood for pasta, to Il Tennille. Sometimes we'd go with friends, but more often it would be just the two of us.

That newlywed feeling certainly has been erased since we moved in here last week, I thought as I touched my eyelashes with mascara and applied blush to my lips. I clipped on my emerald and gold earrings, and decided to let my hair hang loose, knowing Alex likes it that way.

I hadn't heard Alex come in, and didn't know he was there until I felt his arms round me. He laughed at my startled gasp, then turned me to him. His lips found mine and I responded, eager for his embrace.

'I've missed you,' he said. 'Those stupid depositions are turning out to be endless. I simply had to get home overnight.'

I smoothed his hair back. 'I'm so glad you did.'

Jack came running in. 'You didn't say hello to me.'

'I thought you were asleep,' Alex said, as he scooped him up, so that now his strong arms were hugging both of us. It felt so good. It felt so right, and for a few hours, I was able to pretend that it was.

Several people stopped by our table at the Grand Cafe. They turned out to be friends of Alex's from the Peapack Riding Club. All of them offered their regrets about the vandalism and my experience of having found Georgette's body. Alex's response was that we were thinking of giving the house its old name again, 'Knollcrest', and he promised each visitor, 'When Ceil does her magic, we'll have the mother of all cocktail parties.'

When we were alone at our table, he smiled and said, 'You can't blame me for hoping.'

That was when I told him about the prosecutor coming to the house, and about Detective Walsh following me and telling me there was something suspicious about my getting home so quickly from Holland Road. I watched as the muscles in Alex's face tightened. 'Do you mean those people have nothing better to do than worry about the fact that you managed to get home quickly in a catatonic state?'

'It gets worse,' I said, and told him about the murder of the landscaper. 'Alex, I don't know what to do. They say it all has to do with our house, but I swear to you, they're looking at me as though I was responsible for Georgette's death.'

'Oh, Ceil, that's ridiculous,' Alex protested, but then he saw that I was again on the verge of breaking down. 'Honey,' he said, 'I'm going to talk to that prosecutor tomorrow. He has one hell of a nerve to let his detectives follow you around. I'll straighten the bunch of them out fast.'

On the one hand, I felt gratitude. My husband wants to fight my battles, I thought. On the other hand, what will Alex think when, the next time Walsh or Jeff MacKingsley shows up, I refuse to answer their questions on the grounds that I might incriminate myself?

'Ceil, you have nothing to be concerned about. This is ridiculous.' Alex reached across the table, but I pulled my hand away, fishing in my purse for my handkerchief.

'Maybe this isn't the best time for me to stop by, Celia. You seem upset.'

I looked up at Marcella Williams. Her voice was kindly and soothing, but her eyes were alive with curiosity.

The man standing at her side was Ted Cartwright.

At four thirty on Tuesday afternoon, Jeff MacKingsley had just returned to his office when Sergeant Earley phoned to tell him that Robin Carpenter was Charley Hatch's half-sister. 'I've called a press conference for five o'clock,' Jeff told him. 'Ask her to come to my office at six. Or better yet, drive her over.'

As he had expected, the press conference was confrontational. 'There have been two homicides in Morris County in one week, both at million-dollar-plus homes. Were the deaths connected?' the *Record* reporter asked.

'The man who collected Charley Hatch's garbage claims that Sergeant Earley confiscated a bag from Hatch's trash and took out jeans and sneakers and figurines. Was Hatch a suspect in Georgette Grove's death?' That was from the *New York Post* reporter.

Jeff cleared his throat. 'Charley Hatch was shot sometime between one forty and two ten this afternoon. We believe his assailant was known to him and possibly had arranged to meet him. We believe the deaths of Charley Hatch and Georgette Grove were connected, and may also be linked to the Old Mill Lane vandalism. We are pursuing several leads, and will keep you all informed.'

He made his way back to his office, aware that his frustration and irritation were landing on Clyde Earley. I'll bet anything that he didn't wait to go through Charley Hatch's garbage until it was off the premises, he fumed. I'll bet Charley knew it had been disturbed and panicked.

And where does that sexy receptionist who claims to be Charley Hatch's half-sister fit in the picture?

At six o'clock, Robin Carpenter arrived at Jeff's office. Walsh, Ortiz, and Shelley sat in on the meeting.

'Ms Carpenter, I'd like to extend my sympathy,' Jeff said. 'I'm sure your brother's death has been quite a shock for you.'

'Thank you, Mr MacKingsley, but I don't want to give the wrong impression. I am very sorry about Charley, but I must explain that I never even knew he existed until a year ago.'

Robin told them that at the age of seventeen her mother had given birth to a baby. In a private adoption, she had signed him over to a childless couple. 'My mother's been dead for ten years. Then one day last year, Charley showed up on my father's doorstep. He had his birth certificate and pictures of himself in my mother's arms.

'In all honesty, Charley may be my half-brother, but I didn't much care for him. I mean he was always whining. He complained that he had to pay too much to his wife when they were divorced. He said he hated landscaping, and couldn't stand most of the people he worked for.'

'Did you have much contact with him?' Jeff asked.

'He'd call occasionally and ask me to have a cup of coffee with him. The divorce was fairly recent, and he was at loose ends.'

'Ms Carpenter, we have reason to believe that Charley Hatch was the person who vandalised the house on Old Mill Lane.'

'That's impossible,' Robin protested. 'Why would Charley do that?'

'That's exactly what we want to know,' Jeff replied. 'Did he ever come into your office to see you?'

'No, never.'

'Would Georgette or Henry have had contact with him?'

'Possibly. I mean if Georgette had an exclusive listing on a property, she'd be the one making sure that it was kept up, so it's possible that she knew Charley if he was working on one of those properties. But his name never came up.'

'Then Henry Paley also might have known Charley.'

'Of course.'

'When was the last time you spoke to your half-brother?'

'It was at least three months ago.'

'Where were you today between one forty and two ten?'

'In the office. You see, Henry was having lunch with Ted Cartwright. When he came back a little after one, I ran across the street to get a sandwich and bring it back in. Henry had an appointment at one thirty to take a client out.'

'Did he keep that appointment?'

Robin hesitated, then said, 'Yes he did, but Mr Mueller, the potential buyer, phoned to say he was delayed until two thirty.'

'Then Henry was in the office with you until that time?'

Robin Carpenter's eyes moistened, and she bit her lip. 'I can't believe that Charley is dead. Is that why . . .?'

Jeff waited, then said, 'Ms Carpenter, if you have any information that would assist this investigation, it is your obligation to reveal it. What did you just start to say?'

Robin's composure broke. 'Henry has been trying to blackmail me,' she burst out. 'Before I went to work for Georgette, I dated Ted Cartwright a few times. When I realised how much she despised him, I didn't mention it. Henry's been trying to twist everything to make it sound as if I was undermining Georgette. That wasn't true, but what is true is that Henry was not in the office from one fifteen today until nearly four o'clock.'

At a quarter to three, Dru Perry received a call from Ken Sharkey telling her that Charley Hatch, the landscaper at the house where Georgette Grove had been murdered, had been shot to death. Ken wanted Dru to attend the press conference that MacKingsley was sure to call.

Dru assured Ken that she would wait around for the press conference, but she did not share the stunning information she had just uncovered. She had traced back three generations of Liza Barton's maternal ancestors. Liza's mother and grandmother had been only children. Her great-grandmother had three sisters. One never married. Another married and died without issue. The third married a man named William Kellogg.

Celia Foster Nolan's maiden name is Kellogg, Dru remembered. I think it was the guy from the *Post* who gave the background about her—that she had her own design business, Celia Kellogg Interiors.

Maybe that's merely the wildest of coincidences, Dru thought. But no, I don't believe in that kind of coincidence. Celia Nolan is *exactly* the right age to be the grown-up Liza Barton. Is it really a coincidence that Alex Nolan happened to buy that house as a surprise? If he did, it has to mean that Celia never told him about her true background. How shocked she must have been. And she moved in to be greeted by that vandalism. No wonder she fainted when she saw all the media charging at her.

Did it unbalance her? Dru wondered. Was she in such a frenzy about being in the house and all that publicity that she killed Georgette?

At the press conference, Dru was uncharacteristically silent. Later she went back to the office. On the Internet she found a seven-year-old article in *Architectural Digest* calling Celia Kellogg one of the most innovative new designers. It gave her background as the daughter of Martin and Kathleen Kellogg of Naples, Florida.

It was an easy matter to get their telephone number from the directory. Dru copied it in her notebook. It's not time to call them yet, she decided. They're sure to deny that their adopted daughter is Liza Barton. But, if I'm right, Little Lizzie Borden is not only back, she's very possibly unhinged and on a killing spree. Her own lawyer said he wouldn't be surprised if someday she blew Ted Cartwright's brains out.

And I've got to find out who Zach is. If his name sent her into spasms of grief, maybe she has a grudge against him, too.

8

EVEN AS TED CARTWRIGHT was being introduced to me I was sure that seeing me was triggering something inside him. He could not take his eyes off my face, and I am certain that he was seeing my mother in it.

'It's very nice to meet you, Mrs Nolan,' he said.

His voice was jarring—hearty, resonant, commanding, confident, the same voice that had risen to an ugly jeer as he shoved my mother at me.

I looked up at him. I did not touch his extended hand, but neither did I want to raise questions by being overtly rude. I murmured, 'How are you?' and turned back to Alex. Unaware of what was going on, Alex covered the awkward silence with polite conversation, telling me that Ted was a member of the Peapack Club, and that they'd run into each other occasionally.

Of course, Marcella Williams could not leave without trying to find out why I had been dabbing at my eyes. 'Celia, is there anything at all I can do to help you?' she asked.

'Perhaps minding your own business would be a start,' I said.

Marcella's sympathetic smile froze on her face. Before she could say anything, Ted took her arm and pulled her away.

I saw distress in Alex's face. 'Ceil, what was *that* all about? There was no reason to be so rude.'

'I think there was,' I said. 'We were having a private conversation. That woman couldn't wait to find out what is upsetting me. As for Mr Cartwright, he gave the newspapers that long interview, raking up that lurid story about the house you want us to live in.'

'He answered a few questions a reporter asked him, that's all. Ceil, I barely know Cartwright, but he's very well thought of at the club. I think Marcella was genuinely trying to be helpful. My God, she drove you home yesterday when I had a time problem.'

You told me Zach saw you!

My mother's voice was shouting in my mind. Hearing Ted's voice again had verified the flash of memory I had this past week. Mother had spoken Zach's name, and now I had a few words more: '*You told me Zach saw you!*'

What did Zach see Ted do?

The day my father died, he had ridden ahead of Zach, then taken the wrong trail. At least, that was the story Zach told me. But Zach also bragged that he was Ted Cartwright's longtime friend. Had Ted also been riding that day? Did he have anything to do with my father's accident?

'Ceil, what is it?' Alex said. 'You look as pale as a ghost.'

I had literally felt the blood drain from my face, and quickly searched my mind for a plausible explanation. At least I could tell a half-truth. 'Before Marcella barged over, I was about to tell you that I had been talking to my mother. She tells me my dad's Alzheimer's is worse.'

'Oh, Ceil, I'm so sorry. Is there anything we can do?'

The 'we' was so comforting to hear. 'I've told Kathleen to hire a full-time aide. I told her I'd take care of it.'

'Let me do that.'

I shook my head as I thanked him. 'That's not necessary, but I love you for wanting to help.'

'Ceil, you know I'd give you the world on a platter if you'd take it.'

'I just want a tiny piece of the world,' I said, 'a nice, normal piece of it, with you and Jack.'

'And Jill and Junior,' Alex said, smiling.

Our bill came. As we got up, Alex suggested we stop by Marcella and Ted's table. 'It wouldn't hurt to smooth things over,' he urged.

I was on the verge of an angry reply, but then something occurred to me. 'I think that's a good idea,' I said.

I was sure Marcella and Ted had been looking over at us, but when we turned in their direction they looked at each other and acted as if they were deep in conversation. We walked over to their table.

'I'm so sorry, Marcella,' I said. 'I got very bad news about my father today. He's quite ill.' I looked at Ted. 'I've been taking riding lessons from a man who claims he's a great friend of yours. His name is Zach. He's a wonderful teacher. I'm so glad to have lucked on to him.'

Later, when we were home and getting ready for bed, Alex said, 'Ceil, you looked beautiful tonight, but you went so pale I thought you were going to faint. I know you haven't been sleeping well lately. Is it this Detective Walsh guy who's upsetting you, as well as your Dad being sick?'

'Detective Walsh hasn't helped,' I said.

'I'll be on the prosecutor's doorstep at nine o'clock. I'll go straight to the airport from there, but I'll call and tell you how it went.'

'OK.'

'As you know, I'm not much for sleeping pills, but I think you should take one. A decent night's sleep makes the whole world look different.'

'I think that's a good idea,' I agreed. Then I added, 'I'm not being much of a wife to you these days.'

Alex kissed me. 'There are thousands of days ahead of us.' He kissed me again. 'And nights.'

The sleeping pill worked. It was nearly eight o'clock when I woke up. My first awareness was that sometime during my dreams I had heard the first part of what my mother had screamed at Ted.

You admitted it when you were drunk.

Jeff MacKingsley was at his desk promptly at eight thirty on Wednesday morning. He had a sense that it was going to be a long day and not a good one. When Anna came in to tell him a Mr Alex Nolan was at her desk, Jeff's immediate instinct was to welcome the opportunity to have a talk with Celia Nolan's husband. On the other hand, he did not want to have a meeting after which he might be misquoted.

'Is Mort Shelley in his office?' he asked.

'He just went by with a container of coffee.'

'Tell him to put it down and come in here at once, then send Mr Nolan in. And I don't want Paul Walsh to know that Nolan is here.'

Barely a minute later, Mort Shelley came in.

'Celia Nolan's husband is here, and I need a witness to the conversation,' Jeff told him. 'Don't take notes in front of him. I get the feeling that this is not going to be a friendly chat.'

It was clear from the moment Alex Nolan entered the room that he was spoiling for a fight. He barely acknowledged the introduction to Shelley, then demanded, 'Why is one of your detectives following my wife?'

Jeff admitted to himself that if he had been Celia Nolan's husband he would have reacted exactly the same way.

'Mr Nolan, please sit down and let me explain something,' he said. 'Your new home was vandalised. The agent who sold it to you was murdered. We have evidence that a man who was shot yesterday committed the vandalism. I'm going to lay my cards on the table. You know, of course, that Liza Barton fatally shot her mother and wounded her stepfather in your house. There was a picture of the Barton family in your barn the day after you moved in.'

'The one of them on the beach?' Alex asked.

'Yes. There were no fingerprints on it except those of your wife, who took it down and gave it to me. The picture had been wiped clean of fingerprints. Georgette Grove had a picture in her shoulder bag of your wife fainting. It had been cut out of the *Star-Ledger*. It also had no fingerprints on it. Finally, Charley Hatch, the landscaper who was shot yesterday, had a picture of Audrey Barton in the pocket of his vest. Like the others, it had no fingerprints on it.'

'I still fail to see what that has to do with my wife.'

'It may not have anything to do with your wife, but it has everything to do with your house, and we have to find the connection. We know Mrs Nolan had to have driven past the house on Sheep Hill Road where Charley Hatch was shot, within the time frame of his death. We have checked at the Washington Valley Riding Club, where she arrived for a riding lesson at approximately eight minutes to two. She may have seen another car when she came down that road. She may have seen someone walking on it. Don't you think it's reasonable that we question her?'

'I am sure Celia would want to cooperate with your investigation,' Alex Nolan said. 'But I insist that you call off this Detective Walsh. I will *not* have her harassed and distressed. Celia has gone through a lot in the last several years.' He got up and extended his hand. 'Mr MacKingsley, do I have your word that Celia will not be bullied by your staff?'

Jeff got up. 'Yes, you do,' he said. 'I need to ask her about driving past the house where Charley Hatch died, but I'll do it myself.'

'Do you consider my wife a suspect in these homicides?'

'Based upon the evidence we have now, I do not.'

'In that case, I will advise my wife to talk with you.'

'Thank you. That will be very helpful. I'll try to arrange a meeting for later today. Will you be around, Mr Nolan?'

'Not for the next few days. I've been taking depositions in Chicago and I'm going straight back there now.'

After the door had closed behind Nolan, Jeff looked at Mort Shelley.

'What do you think?' he asked.

'I agree with you. I don't consider Celia Nolan a suspect, but I think there's something she hasn't told us yet. I swear, when she opened the door yesterday in those riding clothes, I thought for a minute she had posed for the picture we found in Charley Hatch's pocket.'

'I had the same reaction, but, of course, the difference is obvious. Nolan is much taller, her hair is darker, the shape of her face is different. She just happened to be wearing the same kind of outfit.'

The difference was obvious, Jeff told himself, but there was still something about Celia Nolan that reminded him of Audrey Barton. And it was more than the fact that they were both beautiful women in riding clothes.

On Wednesday morning, Ted Cartwright made a stop at the Cartwright Town Houses Corporation in Madison. A smiling Amy greeted him by chirping, 'How are things at the North Pole, Santa Claus?'

'Amy,' Cartwright said irritably, 'I don't know what that's supposed to mean and I'm not interested in finding out. I've got a busy day lined up.'

'I'm sorry, Mr Cartwright,' Amy said. 'But I can't help thinking how few people would be so generous, even to someone who saved their life.'

Cartwright had been about to pass her desk to go into his office, but stopped suddenly. 'What are you talking about?'

Amy swallowed nervously. 'I'm so sorry,' she said. 'Mr Willet didn't tell me that it was a secret you were giving him the model town house because he saved your life years ago.'

'*Are you telling me that is what Zach Willet told you?*'

'Yes, and if it isn't true, we may have lost a sale. The couple from Basking Ridge called and I told them it was sold.'

Cartwright stared at Amy, his normally ruddy complexion draining of colour, his eyes boring into her face.

'Mr Willet phoned a little while ago,' she went on. 'He intends to move in over the weekend. I told him that since that unit is our furnished model, maybe he could wait until we're sold out, but he said that wouldn't be possible.'

'I'll talk to Mr Willet,' Ted Cartwright said quietly. Then, unexpectedly, he smiled. 'Amy, I have to tell you that for a minute, I was just as taken in as you were. All this is Zach's idea of a joke. A lousy joke, I admit. We've been friends for many years. Last week we made a bet on the Yankees–Red Sox game. He's a passionate Red Sox fan. Our bet was a hundred bucks, but Zach threw in that if the difference in the score was over ten runs, I owed him a town house.' Cartwright chuckled. 'I guess Zach decided to test the waters. I'm sorry he wasted your time.'

I dropped Jack off at school at eight fifteen. There was no way I was going to go into the coffee shop this morning, what with the possibility that Detective Walsh would be waiting there for me. Instead, I drove directly to Chester. My appointment with Benjamin Fletcher was for nine o'clock. I managed to find a delicatessen round the corner from his office where I could get hot coffee and nibble at a piece of bagel.

There was the tang of fall in the clear, crisp air. At one minute to nine I climbed the steps to Fletcher's second-floor office. I walked into a small anteroom that held a shabby desk, two small armchairs covered in vinyl and a table with a pile of dogeared magazines on it.

'That's got to be Celia Nolan,' a voice from the inner room yelled.

Just hearing that voice made my palms sweat. I wanted to turn and run down the stairs. But I was too late. That giant of a man was filling the doorway, his hand extended, his smile as mirthless as I remembered it. He was walking towards me, taking my hand. 'Always glad to help a pretty lady in trouble. Come on in.'

There was nothing I could do but follow him into his cluttered office. He settled himself behind his desk, beads of perspiration on his face even though the window was open. With his shirtsleeves rolled up and the top two buttons opened, he looked like what I suspected he was: a retired lawyer who kept his shingle out because it gave him a place to go.

But he was not stupid. I could tell that the minute I reluctantly took the seat he offered me and he began to talk. 'Celia Nolan of 1 Old Mill Lane in Mendham,' he said. 'That's a very exciting address.'

'Yes, it is,' I agreed. 'That's why I'm here.'

'I read all about you. There's a lot going on in your life. Now how did you hear about me and why are you here?'

Before I could even attempt to answer, he raised his hand. 'I charge three fifty an hour plus expenses and a ten thousand dollar retainer before you get to say, "Help me, counsellor, for I have sinned."'

I pulled out my chequebook and wrote the cheque. 'I'm glad you looked me up,' I said. 'Then you'll understand how it feels to have the prosecutor's office practically accuse me of murdering Georgette Grove.'

'Why would they even begin to think that?'

I told him about the three pictures without fingerprints, about how I had managed to drive home quickly after I found Georgette, and that logistically it was evident I had driven past the house on Sheep Hill Road around the time the landscaper was killed. 'I know they think I'm involved in some way, and it's all because of that house.'

'Surely you must know the history of it by now.'

'Of course. My point is that because of those three pictures, the

440

prosecutor's office feels all this has to do with the Barton family.' I don't know how I managed to say my surname so matter-of-factly, all the while looking right at him.

And then he said something that chilled me to the bone. 'I always thought that kid Liza would come back here someday and shoot her stepfather. But it's crazy that those birds in the prosecutor's office are bothering a stranger who had the hard luck to get that house as a birthday present. Celia, I promise you, we'll take care of them, because you know what will happen? You start answering their questions, and they'll trip you up and confuse you so much that in a day or so *you'll* believe you killed those people simply because you didn't like the house.'

'Do you mean I shouldn't answer questions?' I asked.

'That's exactly what I mean. I know that Paul Walsh. He's out to make a name for himself. Now if he or Jeff MacKingsley or anyone else in that crowd tries to question you, send them to me. I'll take good care of you.'

Lena Santini, the divorced wife of the late Charley Hatch, agreed to speak to Angelo Ortiz at eleven o'clock in Charley's home in Mendham. A small, thin woman of about forty-five, with flaming red hair that had not been granted to her naturally, she seemed genuinely sorry about his death.

'I'm sad for Charley, not for myself,' she explained. 'I can't pretend that there was ever much between us. We got married ten years ago. I'd been married before, but it hadn't worked. That guy was a drinker. It could have been good between Charley and me.'

They were sitting in the living room. Lena took a puff of her cigarette. 'Look at this place,' she said. 'It's so messy it makes my skin crawl. That's the way it was when I was living with Charley. He always dropped his underwear and socks on the floor. Guess who picked them up? I'd say, "Charley, when you have a snack, rinse off the plate and glass and knife or whatever and put them in the dishwasher." It never happened. He left stuff on the table or on the rug near where he'd been sitting. And he'd complain. Let me tell you, he was a prize-winner in the complaint department. I finally couldn't take it any more, and we split a year ago.'

Lena's face softened. 'But those figures he carved were beautiful. I used to tell him he should start selling them, but of course he wouldn't listen. He only felt like carving them once in a while. Oh well, God rest him.' A smile appeared on her lips briefly, then disappeared.

Ortiz, perched on the edge of Charley's lounge chair, had been listening sympathetically. Now he moved into the questioning. 'Did you see much of Charley since you've been divorced?'

'Not much. Once in a while he'd give me a call and we'd have coffee.'

'Was he close to his half-sister, Robin Carpenter?'

'That one!' Lena raised her eyes to the ceiling. 'That was another thing. The people who adopted Charley were real nice folks. When the mother was dying, she told Charley his real name. I guess he hoped his birth family would turn out to be worth a lot of money. Boy, was he disappointed. But he met his half-sister Robin, and ever since then she's been playing him like a fiddle.'

Ortiz tensed. 'Then they saw each other regularly?'

'Did they ever! "Charley, can you drive me into the city? Charley, would you mind taking my car to be serviced?"'

'Did she pay him?'

'No, but she made him feel important. You've met her, I guess. She's the kind that guys look at. Anyhow, she used to take Charley out for dinner in New York sometimes. She didn't want to be seen with him around here because she's got a rich boyfriend. Oh, and get this. Charley told her he had the keys to the houses of people who were away, and knew the security codes, so Robin had the nerve to ask him to let her use those houses when she was with her boyfriend. Can you *imagine*?'

'Ms Santini, we have reason to believe that Charley committed the vandalism on Old Mill Lane.'

'You've got to be kidding. Charley would never do that.'

'Would he do it if he was paid to do it?'

'Who'd ask him to do a crazy thing like that?' Lena Santini crushed the butt of her cigarette in the ashtray. 'Come to think of it, the only person I know who could get Charley to do a stupid trick like that is Robin.'

'Robin Carpenter told us that she has not been in touch with Charley for three months.'

'Then why did she have dinner with him in New York recently at Patsy's Restaurant on West Fifty-sixth Street?'

'Do you happen to remember the exact date?'

'It was Saturday of Labor Day weekend. I remember because it was Charley's birthday, and I called and offered to buy him dinner. He told me Robin was taking him out to Patsy's.'

Lena's eyes suddenly glistened. 'If that's all you want to ask me, I have to go. I asked you to meet me here because I wanted to get a couple of Charley's carvings to put in the casket, but they're all gone.'

'We have them,' Ortiz told her. 'Unfortunately, since these items are evidence, we have to keep them.'

Detective Mort Shelley walked into the Grove Real Estate Agency with the late Georgette Grove's scrapbook under his arm. Everyone on the team, including Jeff, had gone through every page of the book and found not one newspaper clipping that might be tied to Georgette having suddenly recognised someone. The pictures were of Georgette at civic affairs, or smiling with minor celebrities to whom she had sold property.

But it's serving its purpose, Shelley thought. Returning it gives me good reason to have another chat with Robin and Henry.

Robin was at her desk, and looked up on hearing the door open. Her professional smile vanished when she saw who her visitor was.

'Thanks for lending the scrapbook,' Mort said mildly.

'I hope it was useful,' Robin said. She dropped her eyes to the papers on her desk.

With the air of a man who has nothing to do, Mort sat down on the sectional sofa that faced Robin's desk.

Clearly annoyed, she looked up. 'If you have a question, I'll be glad to answer it, Mr . . . I'm sorry, but I've forgotten your name.'

'Shelley. Like the poet. Mort Shelley.'

'Mr Shelley, I went to the prosecutor's office yesterday. I can't add a single word to what I said, and while this agency is still functioning I have a job to do.'

'And so do I, Ms Carpenter, and so do I. It's half past twelve. Have you had lunch yet?'

'No. I'll wait till Henry returns. He's out with a client.'

'Now suppose he didn't come back till, let's say, four o'clock? Would you have something sent in?'

'No. I'd put the sign with the clock on the door and run across the street and grab something.'

'Isn't that what you did yesterday, Ms Carpenter?'

'I already told you that I brought my lunch in yesterday.'

'Yes, but you *didn't* tell us that you put that clock on the door sometime before two o'clock, did you? The elderly lady in the curtain shop down the street noticed that sign at two oh-five.'

'Oh, I see what you're getting at. With all that's been going on, I had a dreadful headache. I ran to the drugstore to get aspirin. I was in and out in a few minutes.'

'Uh-huh. On another subject, my partner was talking to your ex-half-sister-in-law, if that's the proper way to put it, a little while ago.'

'Lena?'

'That's right. Now you told us you hadn't talked to Charley in three months. Lena says you had dinner with him in New York less than two weeks ago. Who's right?'

'I am. About three months ago he happened to phone when my car wouldn't start. I was meeting a friend in New York at Patsy's, and he drove me in. That night he said he wanted me to take him there for his birthday, and I jokingly said, "It's a date." Then I left a message on his phone saying it wouldn't work out. The poor guy thought I was serious about going.'

'Are you involved with any particular man at this time?'

'No, I am not. As I told all of you yesterday, Ted Cartwright is just a friend. We dated a few times. Period.'

'One last question, Ms Carpenter. Your half-brother's former wife tells us that you asked Charley to allow you and your rich boyfriend to stay overnight in houses he was looking after. Is that true?'

Robin Carpenter stood up. 'That does it, Mr Shelley. Tell Mr MacKingsley that if he or any of his lackeys want to ask more questions, they can contact my lawyer.'

On Wednesday morning, Dru Perry phoned into the office and spoke to Ken Sharkey. 'I'm on to something big,' she told him. 'Get someone else to cover the courthouse.'

'Sure. Want to talk about it?'

'Not on the phone.'

'OK. Keep me posted.'

Dru had a problem. She mulled it over as she spread marmalade on wholewheat toast and sipped coffee. None of the news photographs reprinted after the vandalism had been particularly clear. She considered how to go about getting access to other photos, then got an idea.

At nine o'clock she phoned Marcella Williams. 'Mrs Williams, this is Dru Perry of the *Star-Ledger*. I write a feature called "The Story Behind the Story" for the Sunday edition—'

'I always look forward to reading that feature,' Marcella interrupted.

'I'm preparing one on Liza Barton. You knew the family intimately, and I wonder if I could come and interview you.'

'I'd be delighted to be interviewed by a fine writer like you.'

'Do you happen to have any pictures of the Bartons?'

'Yes, of course I do. When Audrey married Ted, I took a slew of pictures, but I have to warn you, there isn't a single one of Liza smiling.'

This is my lucky day, Dru thought. 'Would eleven o'clock be convenient for you?'

'Perfect. I do have a lunch date at twelve thirty.'

'An hour will be more than enough. And Mrs Williams . . .'

'Oh, please, call me Marcella, Dru.'

'How nice. Marcella, will you just think and try to remember if Audrey or Will Barton had a friend named Zach?'

NO PLACE LIKE HOME

'Oh, I know who Zach is. He's the riding instructor Will had at Washington Valley stables. The day he died, Will rode out ahead of Zach and got on the wrong trail. That's why he had that fatal accident.'

That fatal accident, Dru thought. Was it Zach's fault that Will Barton died? Had he been careless to let Barton ride off without him? And if Barton's death was *not* an accident, when did Liza learn the truth about it?

At one o'clock, Ted Cartwright rounded the corner of the Washington Valley clubhouse and headed to the stable. 'Is Zach around?' he asked Manny Pagan, one of the grooms.

Manny was brushing a skittish mare. 'Easy, girl,' he muttered soothingly.

'Is Zach around?' Cartwright shouted. 'Are you deaf?'

An annoyed Manny was about to snap, 'Find him yourself,' but when he looked up he realised that Cartwright, whom he knew by sight, was trembling with fury. 'I'm pretty sure he's eating his lunch at the picnic table,' he said, pointing to a grove of trees about a hundred yards away.

Ted covered the ground with rapid strides. Zach was eating the second half of a baloney sandwich. Ted sat down opposite him. 'Who the hell do you think you are?' he asked, his voice now a menacing whisper.

Zach took another bite of the sandwich and a swig of soda. 'Now that's no way for a friend to talk to a friend,' he said mildly.

'What makes you think you can go over to my town houses and tell my sales rep I am giving you the model unit?'

'Did she tell you that I'm planning to move in over the weekend?' Zach asked. 'I tell you, Ted, that place where I'm living has turned out to be sheer hell. The landlady's kids are having parties every night, playing the drums till I think my ears are gonna bust, and here you have that nice place, and I just know you want me to have it.'

'I'll call the police if you try to set one *foot* inside it.'

'Now why do I think that won't happen?' Zach asked.

'Zach, you've been bleeding me for twenty-seven years. You've got to stop or you won't be around to bleed me any more.'

'Ted, that constitutes a threat, and I'm sure you don't mean it. Maybe *I* should be going to the police. The way I look at it, I've been keeping you out of prison all these years.'

'There is also a penalty for blackmail,' Cartwright spat out.

'Ted, that town house is a drop in the bucket to you, but it would be a comfort to me. And then there's the matter of my conscience. Suppose I were to wander down to the Mendham police station and say that I knew about an accident that wasn't an accident at all, and that I have proof? I'd have guaranteed immunity. I think I mentioned this before.'

Ted stood up. The veins in his temples were bulging. His hands gripped the edge of the picnic table. 'Be careful, Zach. Be very careful.' His words were clipped, and sharp as a dagger.

'I am being careful,' Zach assured him cheerfully. 'That's why, if anything happens to me, the proof of what I'm saying will be found immediately. Well, gotta get back. I have a nice lady coming in for a riding lesson. She lives in your old house—you know, the one where you were shot? She's real interested in that accident you and I know about.'

'Have you been talking to her about it?'

'Oh, sure. Everything but the good stuff. Think it over, Ted. Maybe you'll want Amy to have the refrigerator stocked when I move in on Saturday. That would be a nice welcoming gesture, don't you think?'

At two o'clock on Wednesday afternoon, Paul Walsh, Angelo Ortiz and Mort Shelley gathered in Jeff MacKingsley's office to review their findings in what the media was now calling the 'Little Lizzie Homicides'. They had all brought paper bags with sandwiches and coffee or a soft drink.

Ortiz started with his report. He gave them a quick run-down of his interview with Lena Santini.

'You mean Carpenter's story yesterday was a bold-faced lie?' Jeff asked.

'I saw Carpenter this morning,' Shelley said. 'She explained away the so-called birthday date by saying it was his idea and she left a message for him that it wouldn't happen. She denies being in Patsy's that night.'

'Let's get pictures of Carpenter and Hatch, and show them to the maitre d', the bartenders and all the waiters at Patsy's,' Jeff said. 'We'll subpoena her credit-card and E-ZPass statements as well. Either Carpenter or the ex-wife is lying. Let's find out which it is.'

'Jeff, you're planning to see Celia Nolan today?' Paul Walsh asked.

'I'm not seeing her today,' Jeff said shortly. 'When I called she referred me to her lawyer, Benjamin Fletcher.'

'Benjamin Fletcher!' Shelley exclaimed. 'He was Little Lizzie's lawyer! Why on earth would Celia Nolan go to him?'

'He got her off before, didn't he?' Walsh asked quietly.

'Got who off?'

'Liza Barton, who else?' Walsh said.

Jeff, Mort and Angelo stared at him. Enjoying the astonishment on their faces, Walsh smiled. 'I lay odds with you that the deranged ten-year-old who shot her mother and stepfather has now resurfaced as Celia Nolan, a woman who flipped when she found herself back in home sweet home.'

'You're crazy,' Jeff snapped. 'And *you're* the reason she ran to get a lawyer. She'd have cooperated with us if you hadn't been in her face.'

'I have taken the time to look up Celia Nolan's background. She is adopted. She is thirty-four years old, exactly Liza Barton's present age. We all felt the impact of seeing her in those riding clothes yesterday, and I'll tell you why: Audrey Barton was her mother.'

Jeff sat silently for a moment, not wanting to believe what he was beginning to believe—that perhaps Walsh was on to something.

'After I saw Celia Nolan in riding clothes, I made a few enquiries. She's taking lessons at the Washington Valley Riding Club. Her teacher, Zach Willet, was giving Will Barton riding lessons at the time of his death from a fall with his horse,' Walsh continued, barely able to conceal his satisfaction at the impact he was making.

'If Celia Nolan *is* Liza Barton, do you think she holds Zach Willet responsible?' Mort asked quietly.

'Let me put it this way: if I were Zach Willet, I wouldn't want to be alone with that lady for long,' Walsh answered.

'Your theory, Paul, overlooks the fact that Charley Hatch vandalised the house,' Jeff told him. 'Are you suggesting that Celia Nolan knew Hatch?'

'No, I'm not, and I accept that she'd never met Georgette before she moved into the house. I *do* say that she became unbalanced when she saw the writing on the lawn and the splattered paint. She wanted revenge on the people who put her in that position. If she *is* Liza Barton, there's an explanation for why she knew her way home from Holland Road. Her grandmother lived only a few streets away. She admits that she was driving past in the exact time frame when Hatch was killed. Those pictures we found are a way of begging us to recognise her.'

'That still doesn't fly so far as her killing Hatch. How would she have found out he vandalised the house?' Ortiz asked.

'The garbage man was talking about Clyde Earley taking Hatch's sneakers and jeans and carvings out of the trash.'

'Are you suggesting,' Jeff said, 'that Celia Nolan, even if she is Liza Barton, happened to hear the gossip of a garbage man, figured out where Charley Hatch, whom she'd never met, was working, got him standing at the hedge, shot him, and then went off to have a riding lesson?'

'She put herself on that road at the right time,' Walsh insisted.

'Paul, you want to pin everything on Celia Nolan, and I agree that it will make a great story: LITTLE LIZZIE STRIKES AGAIN. But someone else hired Charley Hatch. I don't for a minute believe Earley's story. I bet Clyde went through that garbage when it was on Hatch's property. I wouldn't be surprised if he took it and Hatch knew it was gone. Then Earley could put it back in the trash barrel and wait to have a witness see him open it after it's been abandoned. If Hatch panicked, whoever hired him may have panicked. And my guess is that Georgette Grove learned who ordered the vandalism and paid for it with her life.'

'Jeff, you'd have made a great defence lawyer. Celia Nolan is very attractive, isn't she? I've noticed the way you look at her.' When he saw the prosecutor's icy stare, Walsh realised he had gone too far. 'Sorry,' he mumbled. 'But I stand by my theory.'

'When this case is over, I'm sure you'll be happier reassigned to another division in the office,' Jeff said. 'You're a smart man, Paul, and you could be a good detective, except for one thing—you don't keep an open mind, and frankly, I'm sick and tired of it.

'Here is what we're going to do now. We should be getting Charley Hatch's phone records later today. Mort, you prepare an affidavit for the judge to get the phone records of Carpenter, Paley and Cartwright—I think we have sufficient grounds. I also want Carpenter's and Hatch's credit-card bills and E-ZPass statements. And I am going to petition the Family Court to allow us to unseal Liza Barton's adoption records.'

Jeff looked at Paul Walsh. 'I'll lay you odds that even if Celia Nolan is Liza Barton, she is a victim of what is going on. For whatever reason, someone is trying to trap her into being accused of committing these murders.'

9

WHEN I LEFT Benjamin Fletcher's office I drove around aimlessly for a while, trying to decide if I should have told him I was Liza Barton, or even if I should have gone to him at all. I told myself that hiring Fletcher would ease my explanation to Alex of my refusal to cooperate with the prosecutor's office. I now could reasonably say that since everything that had happened seemed connected to the Liza Barton case, I went to Liza Barton's lawyer for help. It seemed like a natural thing to do.

I knew that eventually I would have to tell Alex the truth about myself—and risk losing him—but I didn't want to do it yet. If only I could remember exactly what my mother shouted at Ted that night. I would have the key to why he threw her at me, and perhaps the answer to whether I shot him deliberately. In all the pictures I drew for Dr

Moran when I was a child, the gun is in midair. I know the impact of my mother's body caused it to go off in my hand the first time. I only wish I could somehow prove that when I shot Ted I was in a catatonic state.

Zach was the key. All those years, I had never considered my father's death anything but an accident. But now, as I tried to piece together my mother's final words, I couldn't find the missing ones.

You admitted it when you were drunk . . . Zach saw you . . .

What did Ted tell my mother? And what did Zach see?

It was only ten o'clock. I called the *Daily Record* and was told that all back issues were on microfilm in the county library on Randolph Street. At ten thirty I was in the reference room, requesting the microfilm that included May 9, the day my father died, twenty-seven years ago.

Of course, the minute I read the May 9 edition, I realised that any account of my father's death would be printed the next day. I glanced through it anyway, and noticed that an antique-gun marksmanship contest was scheduled that day at Jockey Hollow at noon. Twenty antique-gun collectors were competing in it, including Ted Cartwright.

I looked at the picture of Ted. He was in his late thirties then, his hair still dark, a swaggering, devil-may-care look about him. He was holding in his hand the gun he planned to use in the contest.

I moved the microfilm to the next day. On the front page I found the story about my father. His picture was exactly as I remember him—the thoughtful eyes that always held a hint of a smile, the aristocratic nose and mouth, the dark blond hair. The account of his accident was the same as the one Zach Willet had told me. The consensus of opinion was that something may have frightened the horse, and that 'Barton, an inexperienced rider, was unable to control him.'

Then one sentence seemed to explode before my eyes: 'A groom, Herbert West, who was exercising a horse on a nearby trail, reported hearing a loud noise that sounded like a gunshot at the time. Mr Barton would have been near the fork that led to the treacherous slope.'

I moved the microfilm to the sports pages of that day's edition. Ted Cartwright was holding a trophy in one hand and an old Colt .22 target pistol in the other. He had won the marksmanship contest, and the article said he was going to celebrate by having lunch at the Peapack Club with friends, and then going for a long horseback ride.

My father died at three o'clock—plenty of time for Ted to have had lunch and gone out for a ride, travelling along the trail that leads to the Washington Valley trails. Was it possible he came upon my father, the man who had taken my mother from him?

The only way I could learn the truth was from Zach Willet.

I printed out the articles. It was time to pick up Jack. I left the library, got in my car and drove to St Joe's.

I could tell by Jack's woebegone face that the morning hadn't gone well. He didn't want to talk about it, but by the time we got home and were having lunch, he opened up.

'One of the kids in my class said that I live in a house where a kid shot her mother. Is that right, Mom?' he asked.

I took a deep breath. 'From what I understand, Jack, that little girl lived in this house with her mother and father, and she was very, very happy. Then her father died, and one night someone tried to hurt her mother, and so she tried to save her.'

'If someone tried to hurt you, I'd save you,' Jack promised.

'I know you would, sweetheart. So if your friend talks about that little girl again, say she was very brave. She couldn't save her mother, but that's what she was trying so hard to do.'

'Mommy, don't cry.'

'I don't want to, Jack. I just feel sorry for that little girl.'

'I'm sorry for her, too,' Jack decided.

I told him that if it was OK with him, Sue was going to come over, and I'd go for another riding lesson. I saw a shadow of doubt cross his face. 'Sue is teaching *you* to ride, and I'm taking lessons so I can keep up.'

That helped, but then Jack pushed back his chair, came around and lifted his arms to me. 'Can I sit on your lap for a little while?' he asked.

'You bet.' I picked him up and hugged him. 'Who thinks you're a perfect little boy?' I asked him.

This was a game we played. I saw a hint of a smile. 'You do.'

'Who loves you to pieces?'

'You do, Mommy.'

'You're so smart. I can't believe how smart you are.'

Now he was laughing. 'I love you, Mommy.'

My little boy fell asleep in my arms, just for about twenty minutes. I wondered if I gave him the same sense of security my father had given me that day the wave crashed us to shore. I prayed to learn the truth about my father's death. Then I thought of my mother at my father's funeral, wailing, 'I want my husband! I want my husband!'

You admitted it when you were drunk. You killed my husband. You told me Zach saw you do it.

That was what my mother had screamed that night! I was as certain of it as I was that my little boy was in my arms. The pieces had fallen into place. For a long time I sat quietly, absorbing the import of those words.

When Sue arrived, I left for my riding lesson with Zach Willet.

Marcella Williams had a stack of pictures that she thought might interest Dru Perry. 'After Liza went on her shooting spree,' she explained, 'I got them all together and gave some of them to the media.'

I'll just bet you did, Dru thought. But as she went through them, and studied the close-ups of Will and Audrey Barton, she could barely hide her emotions from Marcella's inquisitive eyes.

Celia Nolan *is* Liza Barton, she thought. She's a combination of both her parents. She looks like both of them.

'Marcella, did you ever meet this Zach guy, the one who gave Will Barton riding lessons?'

'No. Why would I? Audrey was furious when she heard that Will had been taking lessons from him without her knowledge, but Will wanted to learn to ride so that he could keep his wife company.'

'Do you know if Audrey blamed Zach for the accident?'

'She really couldn't. Everyone at the stable told her that Will insisted on starting out alone, despite Zach's asking him to wait.'

Marcella's phone rang just as Dru got up to go. Marcella rushed to answer it, and it was clear that it was disappointing news.

'That's the way it goes,' she told Dru. 'My lunch date was with Ted Cartwright, but he has to see someone on an urgent matter. Maybe it's just as well. Sounds to me as though Ted is in one of his ugly moods.'

After Dru left, she drove to the county library. She submitted her request for the microfilm of the *Daily Record*, including the day after Will Barton's death. The reference librarian smiled. 'That day is mighty popular this morning. I released that same segment an hour ago.'

Celia Nolan, Dru thought. If she's been talking to Zach Willet, she may suspect something about the accident. 'Could that have been my friend Celia Nolan?' she asked. 'We're both working on the same project.'

'Why, yes it is. She did several print-outs.'

Several, Dru thought. I wonder why several.

Five minutes later, she was printing out the account of Will Barton's death. Then she kept going through the paper until she found the sports section, and, like Celia Nolan, reasoned that Ted Cartwright might very well have been in the vicinity at the time of Will Barton's accident.

Desperately troubled by what Celia's state of mind might be, Dru made one more stop, this one at the police station in Mendham. As she had hoped, Sergeant Clyde Earley was on duty, and was delighted to be interviewed by her about the Little Lizzie case.

'I bet that night is still clear in your mind,' she mused.

'You bet it is, Dru. I can still see that kid sitting cool as a cucumber in my squad car, thanking me for the blanket I wrapped round her.'

'You drove off with her, didn't you? Where did you take her?'

'Right here. I fingerprinted her and took her picture.'

'Do you still have her fingerprints?'

'Once a juvenile is cleared of any wrongdoing, we're supposed to destroy them.'

'Did you destroy Liza's fingerprints, Clyde?'

He winked. 'Off the record, no. I kept them in the file, like souvenirs.'

Dru thought of the way Celia Nolan had tried to run from the photographers that first day she'd met her. She felt sorry for her, but knew she had to finish her investigation.

'Clyde, there's something you have to do,' she said. 'Get Liza's fingerprints to Jeff MacKingsley right away. I think Liza has come back, and may be taking revenge on the people who hurt her.'

I sensed there was something different about Zach when I met him at the stable. He seemed somewhat tense, guarded. I knew he was trying to figure me out, but I didn't want him to become wary. I had to get him to talk.

He helped me tack the horse up, then we walked the horses to the spot where the trails begin to snake through the woods. 'Let's take the trail to the fork where Will Barton had his accident,' I said.

'You sure are interested in that accident,' he commented.

'I've been reading up on it. It was interesting that a groom heard a shot. His name was Herbert West. Is he still around?'

'He's a starter at Monmouth Park Racetrack now.'

'Zach, how far were you behind Will Barton that day? Three minutes? Five minutes?'

Zach and I were travelling side by side. A strong breeze had blown the clouds away, and now it was sunny and cool, a perfect afternoon for a ride. The trees were showing the first sign of fall. The smell of damp soil under the horses' hooves reminded me of the times I rode on my pony with my mother at the Peapack club. Sometimes my father would drive over with us and read a book while we were on the trail.

'I'd say I was about five minutes behind him,' Zach answered. 'And, young lady, I think we better have a showdown. Why all the questions about that accident?'

'Let's discuss it at the fork,' I suggested. Making no further effort to conceal my ease on horseback, I pressed my legs against my horse's sides and he broke into a canter. Six minutes later we drew rein at the fork.

'You see, Zach,' I said, 'we left the stable at ten past two. It's two nineteen now, and part of the time we've been going at a pretty good pace. So you couldn't have been only five minutes behind Will Barton, could you?'

I saw the way his mouth tightened.

'Zach, I'm going to level with you,' I began. Of course, I was only going to level with him up to a point. 'My grandmother's sister was Will Barton's mother. She went to her grave sure that there was more to his death than was reported. That gunshot that Herbert West heard would have scared a horse, wouldn't it? I mean, I wonder if when you were looking for Will Barton, you might have seen him galloping down that danger-ous trail on a horse you knew you couldn't stop. And maybe you saw the man who fired the gun. And maybe that man was Ted Cartwright.'

'I don't know what you're talking about,' Zach said.

'Zach, you're a good friend of Cartwright. I can understand you'd be reluctant to get him in trouble. But Will Barton should not have died. Our family is pretty comfortable. I've been authorised to pay you one million dollars if you will go to the police. The only thing that you did wrong was to lie to them about what happened, and I really doubt they could charge you for that after so many years. You'd be a hero, a man with a conscience trying to right a wrong.'

'Did you say one million dollars?'

'Cash. Wired to your bank.'

Zach's thin lips narrowed. 'Is there a bonus if I tell the cops that I saw Cartwright charge his horse at Barton's, forcing it up that trail, and then fire the shot?'

I felt my heart begin to pound. 'There'll be a ten per cent bonus, an extra hundred thousand dollars. Is that the way it happened?'

'That's the way it happened, all right. Cartwright had his old Colt pistol. That takes a special bullet. The second he fired it, he turned and went back on the trail that connects to Peapack.'

'What did you do?'

'I heard Barton yell when he went over the edge. I knew he didn't have a chance. I guess I was pretty shocked. I just rode around on the different trails as if I was looking for him. Eventually, somebody spotted the body down in the ravine. In the meantime, I'd gotten a camera and gone back to the fork in the trail. I wanted to protect myself. I'd grabbed a copy of the morning newspaper that contained a picture of Ted hold-ing the Colt .22 he was planning to use in a marksmanship contest. I put that picture next to the bullet he'd fired—which was sticking out of a tree trunk—and photographed it. I prised the bullet out carefully with my hoof pick. I found the casing, too. Then I walked onto the steep trail and took a picture of the scene below.'

'Will you show me those pictures? Do you still have the casing and the bullet?'

'I'll show you the photos. But I keep them until I get the money. And yes, I also have the bullet and the casing.'

I don't know why I asked this next question, but I did: 'Zach, is money the only reason you're telling me this?'

'Mostly,' he said, 'but there is another reason. I'm kind of sick of Ted getting away with murder, then coming here and threatening me.'

'When can I get this proof you're talking about?'

'Tonight, when I go home.'

'If my baby sitter is free, can I drive over and get it about nine o'clock?'

'That's OK with me. I'll give you my address.'

We rode back to the stable in silence. Zach's cellphone rang as we were dismounting. He answered, then winked at me. 'Hello,' he said. 'What's up? . . . Oh, the town house is worth seven hundred thousand, so you'll give me the money? You're too late. I've had a better offer. Goodbye.

'That felt real good,' Zach told me as he scrawled his address on the back of an envelope. 'See you around nine. The house number is kind of hard to read from the street, but you can tell it by the kids swarming around and the drums banging.'

'I'll find it,' I said.

I left, knowing that if Ted Cartwright ever went to trial, his lawyer would argue that Zach's testimony had been paid for. But how could they refute physical evidence that Zach had kept all these years? And how different was this from what the police do all the time—post rewards for people to come forward with evidence?

I was just offering a lot more than they do.

At four o'clock, Sergeant Clyde Earley and Dru Perry were waiting outside Jeff MacKingsley's office. 'I don't know if he's going to like the fact that you're with me,' Clyde groused.

'Listen, Clyde, I'm a newspaperwoman. This is my story. I'm going to protect my exclusive.'

Anna was at her desk. 'Hope you're bringing good news to the prosecutor,' she told Clyde in a friendly tone. 'He's in one horrible mood.'

As she watched Clyde's shoulders slump, her intercom went on. 'Send them in,' Jeff said.

'Let me talk first,' Dru murmured to Clyde as he held the door to Jeff's office open for her.

'Dru, Clyde,' Jeff acknowledged them. 'What can I do for you?'

'Jeff,' Dru said, 'what I have to tell you is very important, and I need to have your word that there'll be no leak to the press. I *am* the press in this story, and I'm bringing it to you because I think I have an obligation to do that. I'm worried that another life may be in danger.'

Jeff leaned forward, his arms crossed on his desk. 'Go on.'

'I think Celia Nolan is Liza Barton, and thanks to Clyde, you may be able to prove it.'

Seeing the grave look on Jeff's face, Dru realised two things right away: Jeff MacKingsley had been aware of the possibility, and he would not be happy to have it verified. She took out the pictures of Liza that she had taken from Marcella Williams. 'Look at them, Jeff, and then think of Celia Nolan. She's a combination of her mother and father.'

Jeff laid the pictures out on his desk and turned to Clyde. 'Why are you here?'

'Well, you see—'

'Clyde is here,' Dru interrupted, 'because Celia Nolan may already have killed two people, and she may be gunning for the man who was at least partly responsible for her father's accident. Clyde booked Liza the night she killed her mother.'

'I kept her fingerprints,' Clyde Earley said bluntly. 'I have them with me now. You can find out fast if Celia Nolan is Liza Barton.'

'If Celia is Liza, she may be out for revenge,' Dru said. 'The lawyer who defended her twenty-four years ago told me he wouldn't be surprised if someday she came back and blew Ted Cartwright's head off. And a court clerk told me that she had heard that when Liza was in the juvenile detention centre, still in shock, she would say the name "Zach", and then go into spasms of grief. Take a look at these articles from the library. Maybe they show why that happened. I phoned Washington Valley this afternoon to speak to Zach. They told me he was giving Celia a riding lesson.'

'All right. Thank you,' Jeff said. 'Clyde, we have a law that says, when a juvenile is acquitted of a crime, the record is expunged, including fingerprints. You know what I think of your habit of ignoring the law to suit your purposes, but I'm glad you had the guts to give me these. Dru, it's your story. You have my word.'

When they were gone, Jeff sat for long minutes at his desk, studying the pictures of Liza Barton. She's Celia, he thought. We can make sure by checking her fingerprints against the ones on the picture in the barn. I can't use the old ones in court, but at least I'll know who I'm dealing with.

The picture in the barn.

Deep in thought, Jeff was now gazing blankly at the photos that were on his desk. Was this what he had been missing?

In Criminology 101 they tell us that the motive for most homicides is either love or money, he thought.

He turned on the intercom. 'Send Mort Shelley in.'

When Shelley came in, Jeff said, 'Drop whatever you're doing. There's someone I want checked out from top to bottom.' He showed Mort a name he had written on his notepad.

Shelley's eyes widened. 'You think?'

'I don't know what I think yet, but put as many of our people on it as you need. I want to know when this guy cut his first tooth and which one it was.'

As Mort Shelley got up, Jeff handed him the copies of the newspaper stories. 'Give these to Anna, please.' He turned on the intercom. 'Anna, there was a death at the Washington Valley Riding Club twenty-seven years ago. I want the complete file on the investigation. You'll get the details from the papers Mort is giving you. Also, call that club and see if you can get Zach Willet on the phone.'

When I got home from the stable, the barn was empty, and Jack and Sue were gone. She was evidently taking him for a walk around the neighbourhood on Star, and that was fine with me. I called my accountant to be sure that I had at least $1.1 million at the ready in my cash account at the brokerage house.

'It's your money, Celia,' Larry's investment counsellor said. 'But I must warn you, wealthy as you are, that's a substantial sum.'

'I would pay ten times that to accomplish what I am hoping to with that money,' I said.

And it was true. If Zach Willet had the proof he claimed to have, and if Ted went on trial, I would happily take the witness stand and testify to those final words my mother screamed at Ted. And for the first time the world would hear *my* version of what happened.

Alex phoned at dinner time. He was staying at the Ritz-Carlton in Chicago, his favourite hotel there. 'Ceil, I'm definitely going to be stuck here till Friday afternoon but I was thinking, do you want to go into New York this weekend? We could see a couple of plays? Maybe your old baby sitter would mind Jack on Saturday night, and then Sunday we could go to a matinee that he'd enjoy. How about it?'

It sounded wonderful. 'I'll make a reservation at the Carlyle,' I told him. Then I took a deep breath. 'Alex, there's something I have to tell you that may change the way you feel about me, and if it does I will respect your decision.'

'Ceil, nothing would ever change the way I feel about you.'

'We'll see, but I have to take the chance. I love you.'

When I replaced the receiver, my hand was trembling. I knew, though, I had made the right decision.

'Mommy, are you happy?' Jack asked as I was drying him after his bath.

'I'm always happy when I'm with you, Jack,' I said. 'But I'm getting happy in a lot of other ways, too.' Then I told him Sue was coming again because I had errands to run.

Sue arrived at eight thirty.

Zach lived in Chester. I had looked up his street on the map. He lived in a neighbourhood of small two-family homes. I found his house—the number was 358—but I had to drive to the next block before I could find a parking space. There were streetlights, but they were hidden by the heavy trees that lined the sidewalk.

Zach had been right—you could identify his house by the sound of drums being played somewhere inside. I went up the stairs onto the porch. There were two doors, a centre one and one to the side with a name over the doorbell, and I was able to make out the letter Z. I rang the bell and waited, but there was no answer. I tried again and listened, but with the drums beating I could not be sure if the bell was working.

I was uncertain what to do. It was just nine o'clock. I decided that maybe he had gone out for dinner and wasn't home yet. I went down the porch steps and stood on the sidewalk looking up. The windows on the first floor were dark. I didn't want to stand there any longer, but I didn't want to give up hope that Zach would be along any minute. I decided to get my car and double-park in front of his house.

I don't know what made me turn and look at the car parked directly in front of the house. I could see Zach sitting in it. The driver's window was open and he seemed to be asleep. 'Hi, Zach,' I said as I walked over. 'I was afraid you were standing me up.'

When he didn't respond, I touched his shoulder, and he fell forward against the steering wheel. My hand felt sticky. I looked down. It was covered with blood. I grabbed the door of his car to steady myself, then I frantically wiped it with my handkerchief. Then I rushed back to my own car and drove home, trying to wipe the blood away on my slacks. I don't know what I was thinking. I just knew I had to escape.

When I walked in the house, Sue was watching television in the family room. Her back was to me. 'Sue,' I called. 'I'm late phoning my mother. I'll be down in a minute.'

Upstairs, I rushed into the bathroom, stripped, and turned on the shower. I felt as though my whole body had been washed with Zach's blood. I threw my slacks in the shower tray and watched the water turn red at my feet. I dressed hurriedly and went back downstairs.

'The person I was supposed to see wasn't home,' I said.

After Sue left, I poured a stiff Scotch and sat in the kitchen sipping it, wondering what I was going to do. Zach was dead, and I had no way of knowing if the evidence he had for me was gone.

I finished the Scotch, went upstairs, undressed, got into bed, and realised I was facing a sleepless night of worry, even of despair. Knowing it was the wrong thing to do, I took a sleeping pill. Somewhere around eleven, I was aware that the phone was ringing.

It was Alex. 'Ceil, you must be in a dead sleep. I'm sorry I woke you up. I had to let you know that no matter what you say you have to tell me, it won't change one iota of the way I feel about you.'

I was glad to hear his voice. 'I believe that's true,' I whispered sleepily.

Then with a smile in his tone, Alex said, 'I wouldn't even care if you told me you were Little Lizzie Borden. Good night, sweetheart.'

The body of Zachary Eugene Willet was found by a sixteen-year-old drummer, Tony 'Rap' Corrigan, at 6 a.m., as he was leaving on his bicycle to do his morning paper route.

'I thought old Zach had tied one on,' he explained to Jeff MacKingsley and Angelo Ortiz, who had rushed to the scene after the Chester police notified them of the 911 call. 'But when I saw all that dried blood, I thought I'd throw up.'

No one in the Corrigan family remembered seeing Zach park the car. 'It had to be after dark,' said Rap's mother, Sandy. 'I know because there was an SUV parked there when I got home from work. Zach was planning to move over the weekend,' she volunteered.

'Did he tell you where he was moving?'

'He was taking the model unit at Cartwright Town Houses in Madison.'

'Cartwright?' Jeff said casually. 'I would think that one of those town houses would be quite expensive.'

'Especially if it comes furnished,' Sandy Corrigan agreed. 'Zach claimed Mr Cartwright was going to give it to him because he saved his life once.'

'Two moving men came by to pack for Zach yesterday,' Rap said. 'I told them one of them could have done the whole job in an hour. Zach didn't have much stuff. They only took out a couple of boxes.'

'Did they give you their cards?' Jeff asked.

'Well, no. I mean they had uniforms on and a truck.'

Jeff and Angelo looked at each other. 'Can you describe these men?' Jeff asked.

'One of them was a big guy. He had dark glasses and funny-looking blond hair. I think it was dyed. He was kind of old—more than fifty. The other guy was short, and maybe about thirty or so.'

'I see.' Jeff turned to Sandy. 'Have you got a key to Zach's apartment?'

'Of course.'

The forensic unit was dusting the doorbell to Zach's apartment. 'We've got a nice clean one here,' Dennis from the lab commented. 'We got a partial off the door of the car, too. That one someone tried to wipe off.'

'I haven't had a chance to tell you,' Jeff told Angelo as he turned the key and pushed the door open. 'I spoke to Zach Willet by phone at five o'clock last night.'

They started upstairs. 'What kind of guy did he seem?' Ortiz asked.

'Cocky. Very sure of himself. When I asked if I could come talk with him, he told me that he was thinking of arranging a meeting with me. He said he might have some interesting things to tell me, that between the three of us he was sure we could come to an understanding.'

'The three of us?' Angelo asked.

'Yes, the three of us—Celia Nolan, Zach and me.'

There was a narrow hallway at the top of the stairs. They walked a few steps and looked into what was meant to be a living room.

'What a mess,' Angelo said.

The couch and chairs had been slit in every direction. Stuffing oozed out from the faded upholstery. The rug had been rolled up. Silently, they walked into the kitchen and the bedroom. Everywhere it was the same—contents of drawers had been tossed onto towels or blankets; the mattress on the bed had been sliced open.

'The self-proclaimed moving men,' Jeff said quietly. 'Looks more like a wrecking crew. I wonder if they found what they were looking for.'

'Time to talk to Mrs Nolan?' Angelo asked.

'Maybe she'll answer some questions with her lawyer present.'

They stopped again in the living room. 'The kid said the moving men took out some boxes,' Ortiz said. 'What do you think was in them?'

'Papers,' Jeff said briefly. 'Do you see a single bill or letter or scrap of paper in this place? Whoever was here didn't find what they wanted. Maybe they were looking for safe-deposit-box or storage-room receipts.'

'How's this for artwork?' Ortiz asked dryly, lifting a broken picture frame. 'Looks as though this was the mirror over the couch, and Zach took the mirror out and made this monstrosity.' In the centre of the frame there was a large caricature of Zach Willet, and dozens of pictures and notes had been taped around it. Ortiz read the inscription under the caricature. "To Zach, on the occasion of your twenty-fifth anniversary at Washington Valley."'

'Let's take that with us,' Jeff said. 'We might find something interesting. And now, it's past eight o'clock, not too early to pay a visit to Mrs Nolan.'

Or a visit to Liza Barton, he corrected himself silently.

10

'MOMMY, CAN I STAY home with you today?' Jack asked.

The request was so unexpected that I was taken aback. But I soon had an explanation.

'You were crying. I can tell,' he said matter-of-factly.

'No, Jack,' I protested. 'I just didn't sleep very well last night, and my eyes are tired.'

'You were crying,' he said simply.

'Want to bet?'

'What kind of bet?' Jack asked.

'I'll tell you what. After I drop you off at school, I'll take a nap, and if my eyes are nice and bright when I pick you up, you owe me a hundred trillion dollars.'

'And if they're not nice and bright, you owe me a hundred trillion dollars.' Jack began to laugh. We usually settled those bets with an ice cream cone or a trip to the movies.

The wager decided upon, Jack willingly let me drop him off at school. I managed to get home before I started to break down again. I felt so trapped and helpless. For all I knew, Zach had told other people I was meeting him. How could I explain he had proof Ted Cartwright killed my father? And where was that proof now? I had touched Zach. Maybe my fingerprints were on his car.

I was dead tired, and decided that maybe I should do what I had told Jack I would do, and try to take a nap. I was halfway up the stairs when the bell rang. My hand froze on the banister. I was sure it was going to be someone from the prosecutor's office. All I have to say, I reminded myself, is that I will not answer questions unless my attorney is present.

When I opened the door, Jeff MacKingsley was standing on the porch with the younger detective with black hair.

I could only imagine what they thought when they saw me with my red-rimmed, swollen eyes. For a moment, I don't think I cared. I was tired of running, tired of fighting. I wondered if they had come to arrest me.

'Mrs Nolan, I know you're represented by an attorney,' Jeff MacKingsley said. 'But I believe you may have some information that could help us regarding a crime that was just committed. Zach Willet was found shot to death early this morning.'

I did not say anything. Let them think my silence indicated shock.

'You took a riding lesson from Zach yesterday afternoon,' MacKingsley said. 'Did he indicate to you that he had plans to meet anyone?'

'Was he planning to meet anyone?' I repeated, and heard my voice rising into near hysteria. I clasped my hand against my mouth. 'I have an attorney.' I managed to lower my pitch. 'I won't speak to you without him being present.'

'I understand. Mrs Nolan, this is a simple question. The picture of the Barton family that you found taped to your barn. Did you ever show it to your husband?'

At least the question was one I could answer without fear. 'My husband had already gone to work when I found it. He came home as I was giving it to you. No, Mr MacKingsley, he did not see it.'

The prosecutor nodded and thanked me, then said in a tone that sounded strangely sympathetic, 'Celia, I really think everything is falling into place. I think that you are going to be all right.'

Jeff MacKingsley was quiet on the drive back to the office, and Angelo Ortiz knew better than to intrude. It was clear his boss was troubled, and he was sure he knew why. Celia Nolan seemed to be on the verge of a total breakdown.

The forensic group was waiting for them when they arrived. 'We've got nice prints for you, Jeff,' Dennis, the fingerprint expert from the lab, announced with great satisfaction. 'A nice index finger from the doorbell, and a thumbprint from the car.'

'Were there any in Zach's apartment?' Jeff asked.

'Lots and lots and lots of Zach's. Nobody else.'

'Dennis, I have two sets of fingerprints I want you to check for me,' Jeff said, then added, 'And check them against the ones you just got.'

Dennis was back in half an hour. 'You've got yourself a match, Prosecutor. The three sets belong to the same person.'

'Thanks, Dennis.' Jeff sat quietly for almost twenty minutes, then he reached for his phone, and dialled information to get the number of Benjamin Fletcher, attorney-at-law.

Jimmy Franklin was a newly appointed detective, unofficially under the guidance of his good friend Angelo Ortiz. On Thursday morning, with his cellphone camera and following Angelo's instructions, he stopped at the Grove Real Estate office, ostensibly to enquire about the availability of a small starter house in Mendham.

Jimmy was twenty-six, but like Angelo he had a boyish look that was very appealing. Robin explained pleasantly that there were very few starter houses available in Mendham, but that she did have some in neighbouring towns.

While she marked listings for him to study, Jimmy pretended to be on the phone. What he was doing was taking close-up pictures of Robin. The night before he had managed to get a picture of Charley Hatch from Lena Santini, a picture she assured him did not do poor Charley justice.

Jimmy took the pictures of Robin and Charley with him when he drove into Manhattan, parking on West 56th Street near Patsy's Restaurant.

It was a quarter to twelve when he arrived. There was an enticing aroma of tomato sauce and garlic, but the restaurant had not yet begun to fill with the luncheon crowd. Jimmy brought out his pictures and laid them on the bar. 'Cranberry juice,' he ordered as he flashed his badge. 'Recognise either of these people?' he asked the bartender.

The bartender studied the pictures. 'They look familiar, especially the woman, but I can't be sure.'

Jimmy had better luck with the maître d'. 'She comes in sometimes, but that's not who she's usually with. Let me ask the waiters.'

When he returned, the maitre d' had a waiter in tow and the satisfied look of a man who had completed his mission.

'Dominick will fill you in. He never forgets a face.'

Dominick was holding the pictures. 'She comes in once in a while. Good-looking. You know, sexy. That guy was with her once a couple of weeks ago. Reason I remember, it was the guy's birthday. She had us put a candle on a slice of cheesecake, then gave him an envelope. I could see she'd laid some nice change on him. Twenty hundred dollar bills.'

'That's a nice birthday present,' Jimmy agreed. 'You say she comes in here with some other guy. Can you describe him?'

'Sure.'

Jimmy got out his notebook and jotted down the description. Then, feeling pleased with the success of his morning, he decided it would be in the line of duty to have some of Patsy's linguini.

Sobered by his boss's threat of reassignment, Paul Walsh accepted the job of checking out Zach's landlady's claim that he had been planning to move into a town house that Ted Cartwright was giving him. At nine thirty on Thursday morning, Paul was talking to Amy Stack, who told him how Zach Willet had played a practical joke on her and Mr Cartwright.

'He sounded so convincing when he said that Mr Cartwright was giving him the model unit. I feel like such a dope for believing him.'

'What did Mr Cartwright say when you told him?'

'I thought he'd go into orbit. But then he laughed, and explained it was just a silly bet they had made, and Zach was acting as if he'd really won.'

'But bet or no bet, it was not your impression that Mr Cartwright had any intention of giving Zach Willet that town house?' Walsh asked.

'Even if he did save Mr Cartwright's life years ago, Zach Willet had no chance in the world of ever setting foot in that condo,' Amy said.

'Did Mr Cartwright spend the day here yesterday?'

'No, he was in for a short while between nine and ten. He said he was coming back at four o'clock, but I guess he changed his mind.'

'Thank you, Ms Stack,' Walsh said. 'You've been very helpful.'

The news of Zach's death had spread through the Washington Valley Riding Club. The idea that someone had shot him seemed unthinkable to the people who worked in the stables. 'He wouldn't harm a fly,' a scrawny old-timer named Alonzo said when Paul Walsh asked if Zach Willet had any enemies. 'Zach kept to himself. Never got in an argument in the fifty years I've known him.'

'Do you know if anybody had it in for him for any reason?'

No one could think of anything until Alonzo remembered that Manny Pagan had made some comment about Ted Cartwright getting into an argument with Zach yesterday. 'Manny's exercising a horse in the ring. I'll get him,' Alonzo offered.

Manny Pagan came over to the stable, leading his horse. 'Mr Cartwright shouted at me. I never saw a guy so mad in my life. I pointed out where Zach was eating lunch at the picnic table and saw Cartwright go charging over to him. I swear there was steam coming out of his ears.'

'That was yesterday at lunchtime?'

'That's right.'

Paul Walsh had learned what he had come to find out.

'Mr Fletcher, returning your call,' Anna announced on the intercom.

Jeff MacKingsley drew a deep breath and picked up the receiver. 'Hello, Ben,' he said warmly. 'How are you?'

'Hello, Jeff,' Benjamin Fletcher replied. 'Nice to hear from you, but I'm sure you're not interested in the state of my health.'

'Of course I'm interested, but you're right, that's not the reason I called. I need your help.'

'I'm not so sure I'm feeling very helpful, Jeff. That viper you call a detective, Walsh, has been intimidating my new client.'

'Yes, I realise that and I'm sorry. But listen to me. Do you know that your new client, Celia Nolan, is actually Liza Barton?'

Jeff heard a sharp intake of breath at the other end of the phone.

'I have absolute proof,' he said. 'Fingerprints.'

'You better not have fingerprints from the juvenile case.'

'Ben, for now, never mind where I got them. I need to talk to Celia. I won't ask her one word about the homicides last week, but there's something else I have to ask her. Do you remember the name Zach Willet?'

'Sure. What about him?'

'Zach was shot in his car sometime last evening. Celia must have had an appointment to meet him. Her fingerprints are on Zach's car door and on his doorbell. I don't for one minute think she had anything to do with Zach's death, but I need to know why she was meeting him. Will you let her talk to me? I'm worried there may be lives at risk—including hers.'

'I'll talk to her. If she agrees, I must be present, of course, and at any point, if I say stop, you stop. I'll get back to you later, Jeff. And I'll tell you another thing. With all those people you've got working for you, have someone protect her. Make sure nothing happens to that pretty lady.'

Jack had won the bet. I agreed that my eyes still looked tired, but insisted that it was because I had a headache. Instead of paying him one hundred trillion dollars, I took him to lunch at the coffee shop and bought him an ice cream cone for dessert. I kept on my dark glasses and told Jack the light hurt my eyes because of the headache. Did he believe me? I doubt it. He's a smart and perceptive kid.

We arrived home to find two messages on the phone. As always, I was afraid it was one of the Lizzie Borden messages, but both were from Benjamin Fletcher, with instructions to call him immediately.

They are going to arrest me, I thought. They have my fingerprints. I misdialled twice before I finally reached him.

'It's Celia Nolan, Mr Fletcher,' I said.

'First thing, a client has to trust her attorney, Liza.'

Liza. With the exception of Dr Moran in my early days of treatment, and the time Martin's mind was wandering, I have not been called Liza since I was ten years old. The matter-of-fact way in which Fletcher said my name helped to reduce the shock that he knew who I was.

'I wasn't sure whether to tell you yesterday,' I said. 'I'm still not sure if I can trust you. How did you know it was me? Did you recognise me?'

'Can't say that I did. Jeff MacKingsley told me about an hour ago.'

'Jeff MacKingsley told you!'

'He wants to talk to you, Liza. But first, I must be certain it's in your best interest. Don't worry, I'll be there with you, but I am *very* concerned. He tells me you left your fingerprints where a dead body was found.'

'Am I going to be arrested?' I could barely make my lips form the words.

'Not if I can help it. This is all very unusual, but the prosecutor tells me he believes you had nothing to do with it.'

I closed my eyes as relief flooded every inch of my body. Then I told Benjamin Fletcher about Zach Willet. I told him about my suspicion that my father's death had not been an accident, that yesterday I had promised Zach $1.1 million if he would tell the police what really happened, and that Zach kept the evidence of Ted Cartwright's guilt.

'You're going to be giving MacKingsley some powerful stuff, Liza. But how did your fingerprints get on that car and doorbell?'

I told him all about my appointment to see Zach. About seeing him in the car, and panicking and rushing home.

'Does anyone else know you were there?'

'No, but I did call my investment adviser yesterday and ask him to be ready to wire the money I promised Zach. He can verify that.'

'All right, Liza,' Benjamin Fletcher said. 'What time is good for you to go to the prosecutor's office?'

'I'll need to get my baby sitter. Four o'clock would be all right.'

'Four o'clock it is,' Fletcher said.

I hung up the phone, and from somewhere behind me, Jack asked, 'Mommy, are you going to be arrested?'

Most of the investigators in the prosecutor's office had been pulled off their own units to concentrate on the Mendham homicides. At three o'clock, the group analysing the phone records of Hatch, Cartwright, Carpenter and Paley were ready to report their findings to Jeff.

'In the last two months, Ted Cartwright has been in touch with Zach Willet six times,' Liz Reilly, a new investigator, announced. 'The last time was yesterday afternoon at three oh-six.'

'Cartwright and Henry Paley have been talking to each other a lot,' Nan Newman, one of the veteran investigators, reported, 'but there was no contact on Henry's phone with Charley Hatch.'

'Paley's a low life,' Jeff said, 'and he hasn't accounted for his where-abouts when Hatch was shot. I've asked him to come in with his lawyer at five o'clock, and Ted Cartwright is coming at six.

'We know Robin Carpenter is a liar,' he continued. 'She lied about the date in Patsy's Restaurant with her brother. His E-ZPass shows that he drove into New York at six forty that night. In Patsy's, Robin was seen giving Hatch what appeared to be two thousand dollars.'

'There are no calls from Carpenter to Hatch since last Friday. I believe that she was using a prepaid phone with no subscriber name to contact him. She must have told him to get one, too, because the woman whose lawn he was cutting saw him holding two phones. I also think that when he answered that call, he made an appointment to meet someone at the break in the hedge. Of course, we can't be sure that it was Robin who made that last call.'

The investigators were listening quietly, following Jeff's reasoning, hoping for an opportunity to make a significant contribution.

Then Mort Shelley opened the door to Jeff's office. They exchanged glances, and Shelley answered Jeff's unspoken question:

'He's where he said he'd be. We've got a tag on him.'

'Make sure you don't lose him,' Jeff said quietly.

11

THIS WAS THE COURTHOUSE in which the trial had taken place. As I walked through the corridors, I remembered those terrible days. I remembered the inscrutable gaze of the judge. I remembered being afraid of my lawyer. I remember listening to the witnesses who testified that I meant to kill my mother. I remember how I tried to sit up straight because my mother was always after me not to slouch.

Benjamin Fletcher was waiting for me inside the main door of the prosecutor's office. His white shirt looked crisp; his dark blue suit was pressed. He took my hand and held it. 'It would seem I owe a little ten-year-old girl an apology,' he said. 'I got that child off, but I admit that I bought Cartwright's version of what happened.'

'I know you did,' I said. 'But you did get me off.'

'The verdict was not guilty,' he continued, 'but it was based on reasonable doubt. Most people felt that you were guilty. When we get this behind us, I'm going to see that everyone understands what you have been through, so they know that you were an innocent victim.'

I could feel my eyes brighten with the ever-ready tears.

'No charge,' he added, 'and it rattles my soul to utter those words.'

I laughed, which was what he wanted. I suddenly felt confident that this hulking septuagenarian would take care of me.

Jeff MacKingsley's corner office was large and pleasant. I had always instinctively liked this man, even when I resented him showing up on my doorstep. Now he got up from his desk and came round it to greet us. I had done the best job I could, trying to disguise my swollen eyes, but I don't think I fooled him.

With Benjamin Fletcher sitting beside me, I told Jeff everything I knew about Zach. I told him that it was only in these last two weeks that I had remembered clearly my mother's last words: 'You admitted it when you were drunk. You killed my husband. You told me Zach saw you.'

Detective Ortiz and a stenographer were in the room, but I ignored them. Jeff let me talk almost without interruption. I guess in my own way, I was answering all the questions he had planned to ask me. When I described going to Zach's house, he did prod me for additional details.

When I was finished, I said, 'Mr MacKingsley, I want you to ask me any questions you have about Georgette Grove and Charley Hatch—'

'Wait a minute,' Benjamin Fletcher interrupted. 'We agreed we were not going to discuss those cases.'

'We have to. It's going to get out that I'm Liza Barton.' I looked at Jeff. 'Does anyone in the media know yet?'

'It was a person in the media, Dru Perry, who disclosed it to us,' he admitted. 'You may want to talk with her. I think she'd be sympathetic.' Then he added, 'Is your husband aware that you are Liza Barton?'

'No he is not,' I said. 'It was a terrible mistake, but I promised Jack's father, my first husband, that I would not reveal my past to anyone. Of course, I will tell Alex now.'

For the next forty minutes I answered every question the prosecutor asked me about Georgette Grove and Charley Hatch. I even told him about the Little Lizzie phone calls. At ten to five, Fletcher and I said goodbye and left the private office.

There was a woman with wild grey hair at Jeff's secretary's desk. She was obviously very angry. Her back was to me, and I heard her say, 'I told Jeff about Celia Nolan because I thought it was my duty. My thanks is that I lose my exclusive. The New York Post is giving all of page three to the "Return of Little Lizzie" story, and they're practically going to accuse her of committing all three murders.'

Somehow I made it to my car. Somehow I said goodbye to Benjamin Fletcher. Somehow I got home, paid Sue, and thanked her.

Jack was listless. I think he was starting to get a cold. I sent out for a pizza, and before it came I got him into pyjamas and changed into my own pyjamas and robe.

I decided I would go to bed after I tucked Jack in. All I wanted to do was to sleep and sleep and sleep. There were calls from Mr Fletcher and Jeff MacKingsley. I did not answer them, and both left messages expressing concern at how upset I must be.

Of course I'm upset, I thought. Tomorrow I'll be starring in 'The Return of Little Lizzie'. From this day forward, I will never travel far enough or hide deep enough to escape being called Little Lizzie.

When the pizza came, Jack and I had a couple of slices. Jack definitely was catching some kind of bug. I took him upstairs. 'Mom, I want to sleep with you,' he said fretfully.

That was fine with me. I locked up and set the alarm, then I called Alex's cellphone. He didn't answer, but he had said something about a dinner meeting. I left a message saying that I was going to bed early, and to please call me at 6 a.m., Chicago time. I said there was something important I had to tell him.

I took a sleeping pill, got into bed and, with Jack cuddled in my arms, fell fast asleep.

I don't know how long I slept, but it was pitch-dark when I felt my head being raised and heard a voice whispering, 'Liza, drink this.'

I tried to close my lips, but a strong hand was forcing them open, and I was gulping a bitter liquid that I knew contained crushed sleeping pills.

From a distance, I heard Jack's wail as someone carried him away.

'**D**ru, that leak did not come from this office,' Jeff snapped, finally out of patience. 'You seem to forget that Clyde Earley, among others, knows that Celia Nolan is Liza Barton. Frankly, I think that whoever planned that vandalism was well aware of her identity. The *Post* is barking up the wrong tree. Hang around, and I may have some real news for you.'

Dru's anger began to subside. 'You're playing straight with me?'

'Have I ever been known not to play it straight with you?' Jeff replied.

Henry Paley and his lawyer arrived at five o'clock. Henry read a statement into the record that had obviously been prepared by his attorney. In a wooden voice he admitted that he had been at the Holland Road house several times more than he had indicated, but he insisted that it was only carelessness in keeping his daily reminder. He went on to acknowledge that about a year ago he had been offered $100,000 by Ted Cartwright if he could to persuade Georgette to sell the land on Route 24.

'There has been a question as to my whereabouts on or around the time of the demise of Charley Hatch, the landscaper,' Henry read. 'I left my office at one fifteen and went directly to the Mark Grannon Real Estate Agency. There I met Thomas Madison, Georgette Grove's cousin.

Mr Grannon had made an offer to buy our agency.

'As for the late Charley Hatch—I may have seen Mr Hatch when I was showing properties. I do not remember ever exchanging a word with him. I never met the most recent homicide victim, Zach Willet.'

Looking pleased with himself, Henry folded his statement neatly and looked at Jeff. 'I trust that covers the situation.'

'Maybe,' Jeff said pleasantly. 'But I do have one question: don't you think that Georgette Grove, knowing of your cosy relationship with Ted Cartwright, would have lived out her life holding on to the Route 24 property rather than sell it commercially?'

'I object to that question,' Paley's lawyer said heatedly.

'You were in the vicinity of Holland Road when Georgette was shot, Mr Paley, and her death made it possible for you to get a better deal than Cartwright was offering. That will be all for today. Thank you for coming in to make your statement, Mr Paley.'

The heavy frame surrounding Zach Willet's twenty-fifth anniversary memorabilia had been placed on a desk in a vacant office down the hall from Jeff MacKingsley. Investigator Liz Reilly had been instructed to review every card and picture and note taped within the frame.

Liz had a feeling that this collage would be a perfect place to secrete a picture or any small object that might be easily discovered in a file.

The tape on the pictures and cards was cracked and dry, and easily separated from the corkboard that Zach had inserted for backing. Liz got a kick out of reading the first several notes of congratulation: 'Here's to another 25, Zach'; 'Ride 'em, cowboy'; 'Happy trails to you.'

She removed them, one by one, until only the caricature itself remained in the frame. It had been drawn in crayon on heavy cardboard, and was tacked to the corkboard. When she removed it, she turned the caricature over. Taped to the back was a sealed envelope. Liz decided to have a witness when she opened it.

She went down the hall to the prosecutor's office. Jeff MacKingsley was standing at the window.

'Mr MacKingsley, can I show you something?'

'Sure, Liz, what is it?'

'This was taped behind that caricature of Zach Willet.'

Jeff looked from the envelope to Liz and back to the envelope. He went to his desk and got a letter opener from the drawer. He opened the enveloped and shook it. Two metal objects clanked onto his desk.

Jeff pulled some photographs out of the envelope. One was a close-up showing a bony hand pointing to a tree in which a bullet was clearly

469

embedded. A newspaper was positioned below the hole to display the date—May 9—and the year, which was the year Will Barton had died.

A two-page letter, neatly handwritten but filled with misspellings and addressed to 'Whoever it could concern', contained Zach's graphic yet oddly dignified description of how he had watched Will Barton die.

Jeff turned to Liz. 'Good work. This is enormously important, and just might be the break we need.'

Liz left Jeff's office, delighted with the prosecutor's reaction.

As Jeff stood thinking, he was interrupted again as investigator Nan Newman rushed into his office. 'Boss, you're not going to believe this. Rap Corrigan, the kid who found Zach Willet's body, came in to give me a statement. While he was there, Ted Cartwright came into the outer office with his attorney. Rap did a double-take and practically pulled me down the hall to talk to me.

'Jeff, Rap swears that Ted Cartwright, minus a dopey looking blond wig, is one of the two so-called moving men he let into Zach Willet's apartment yesterday.'

Ted Cartwright was dressed in an impeccably tailored dark blue suit, a light blue shirt and a red and blue tie. With his crown of white hair and imposing carriage, he was every inch the powerful executive as he strode ahead of his lawyer into Jeff's office.

Seated behind his desk, Jeff calmly observed the arrival and waited until Cartwright and his lawyer were in front of him before he got up. He did not offer to shake the hand of either man, but indicated the chairs that were pulled close to the desk. Detectives Angelo Ortiz and Paul Walsh were already seated to the side of the prosecutor.

Cartwright's attorney introduced himself. 'Prosecutor MacKingsley, I am Louis Buch, counsel to Mr Theodore Cartwright. I wish to state for the record that my client has appeared here today with the desire to assist in your investigation into the death of Zach Willet.'

His face impassive, Jeff MacKingsley looked at Ted. 'How long have you known Zach Willet, Mr Cartwright?'

'Oh, I think about twenty years,' Ted answered.

'Think again, Mr Cartwright. Isn't it over thirty years?'

'Twenty, thirty.' Cartwright shrugged. 'A long time, whichever it is.'

'Would you say you were friends?'

Ted hesitated. 'It depends on how you define friendship. I knew Zach. I liked him. I love horses and I admired his skill at handling them. On the other hand, it wouldn't occur to me to invite him to my home for dinner, or really socialise with him in any way.'

'Then you don't count having a drink with him at the bar at Sammy's as socialising with him?'

'Of course, if I bumped into him at a bar, I would have a drink with him, Mr MacKingsley.'

'I see. When was the last time you spoke with him?'

'I called him yesterday afternoon, around three o'clock.'

'And what was the reason for the call?'

'We had a good laugh over the joke he pulled on me.'

'What was that joke, Mr Cartwright?'

'A few days ago, Zach went over to my development in Madison and told my sales rep that I was giving him a town house. We had a bet on the Yankees–Red Sox game, and he had kidded me that if the Red Sox won by more than ten runs, I would have to give him a town house.'

'When was the last time you saw Zach?'

'Yesterday, around noon.'

'Where did you see him?'

'At the Washington Valley stables.'

'I understand you had a quarrel with him.'

'I blew off a little steam. Because my rep took him seriously, we almost lost a sale. I simply wanted to tell Zach that his joke went too far. But I called and apologised at three o'clock.'

'That's very odd, Mr Cartwright,' Jeff said, 'because a witness heard Zach tell you that he didn't need the money the town house was worth because he had a better offer. Do you remember him saying that?'

'That wasn't the conversation we had,' Ted said mildly. 'You're mistaken, Mr MacKingsley, as is your witness.'

'I don't think so. Mr Cartwright, did you ever promise Henry Paley one hundred thousand dollars if he could persuade Georgette Grove to sell the property they jointly owned on Route 24?'

'I had a business arrangement with Henry Paley.'

'Georgette was pretty much in your way, wasn't she?'

'Georgette had her way of doing things. I have mine.'

'Where were you on September fourth at about ten a.m.?'

'I was out for an early morning ride on my horse.'

'Weren't you on a trail that connects directly to the private trail behind the Holland Road house where Georgette died?'

'I do not ride on private trails.'

'Mr Cartwright, did you know Will Barton?'

'Yes, I did. He was the first husband of my late wife, Audrey.'

'You were separated from your wife at her time of death?'

'The evening of her death she had called me to discuss a reconciliation.

We were very much in love. Her daughter, Liza, hated me because she didn't want anyone to replace her father, and she hated her mother for loving me.'

'Why did you and your wife separate, Mr Cartwright?'

'The strain of Liza's antagonism became too much for Audrey. We only planned the separation to be temporary, until she could get psychological help for her troubled daughter.'

'You didn't separate because, when you were drunk one night, you confessed you had killed her first husband?'

'Don't answer that, Ted,' Louis Buch ordered. He looked angrily at Jeff. 'We're here to talk about Zach Willet. I was not informed of other matters.'

'It's all right, Lou. I'll answer their questions.'

'Mr Cartwright,' Jeff said, 'Audrey Barton was terrified of you. Her mistake was that she didn't go to the police. But you were afraid that she would go one day. There was always some question about the gunshot heard at the time Will Barton's horse went over the cliff.'

'This is ridiculous,' Cartwright snapped.

'No, it's not. Zach Willet witnessed what you did to Will Barton. We found interesting evidence in Zach's apartment—a statement he had written, plus a picture he took. He retrieved a bullet, and its casing, and kept them all these years. Let me read his statement to you.'

Jeff picked up Zach Willet's letter and read it.

'That is fiction and inadmissible in court,' Louis Buch snapped.

'Zach's murder isn't fiction,' Jeff said. 'He was bleeding you for twenty-seven years and finally got so cocksure when he realised you killed Georgette Grove that he decided to be taken care of on a higher scale.'

'I did *not* kill Georgette or Zach Willet,' Cartwright said.

'Were you in Zach Willet's apartment yesterday?'

'No, I was not.'

Jeff looked past him. 'Angelo, will you ask Rap to come in?'

As they waited, Jeff said, 'Mr Cartwright, as you can see, I have the evidence you were searching for in Zach's apartment—the bullet and casing from the gun that you fired to terrify Will Barton's horse, and the pictures that show where and when it happened. Later you donated that gun to the collection of firearms at a Washington museum, didn't you? I am subpoenaing it so that we can determine if the bullet and casing were fired from that gun.' Jeff looked up. 'Oh, here's Zach's landlady's son.'

At Angelo's prodding, Rap came forward to the desk.

'Do you recognise anyone in this room, Rap?' Jeff asked.

'I recognise you, Mr MacKingsley, and Detective Ortiz. And I recognise this guy.' He pointed at Ted. 'Yesterday he came to our house dressed like a moving man. He had another guy with him. I gave him Zach's key.'

'Are you positive this man came to your home yesterday and went up to Zach Willet's apartment?'

'I'm positive. He had a wig on, but I'd know that face anywhere.'

'Thank you, Rap.'

Jeff waited to speak until Rap had left the room. 'Robin Carpenter is your girlfriend,' he told Cartwright. 'You gave her the money to bribe her half-brother, Charley Hatch, to vandalise the house known, thanks to you, as "Little Lizzie's Place". You shot Georgette Grove. Hatch became a threat and you, or Robin, took him out.'

'That's not true,' Cartwright shouted, jumping to his feet.

Louis Buch stood up, stunned and totally furious.

Jeff glared at Cartwright. 'We know that you went to Audrey Barton's home to kill her that night. We know that you caused Will Barton's death. We know that you killed Zach Willet.' He stood up. 'Mr Cartwright, you are under arrest for the burglary of Zach Willet's apartment. Mr Buch, we anticipate that Mr Cartwright will be formally charged with these murders in the next several days.'

Jeff paused, then turned to Detective Ortiz and said, 'Please read Mr Cartwright his rights.'

I am being carried downstairs. I can't open my eyes. 'Jack.' I try to call his name, but can only whisper it. My lips feel rubbery. I have to wake up. *Jack needs me.*

'It's all right, Liza. I'm taking you to Jack.'

Alex is talking to me. Alex, my husband. He is home, not in Chicago. I have to tell him tomorrow I'm really Liza Barton.

But he called me Liza.

There were sleeping pills in that glass. Maybe I'm dreaming.

Jack. He's crying. 'Mommy. Mommy. Mommy.'

'Jack. Jack.' I try to scream, but can only mouth his name.

There is cold air on my face. My eyes won't open. Alex is carrying me. Where is he taking me? Where is Jack?

I hear a door opening—the garage door. Alex is laying me down. I know where I am. My car, the back seat of my car. 'Jack . . .'

'You want him? You can have him.' It's a woman's voice, harsh.

'Mommmmmmy!' Jack's arms are round my neck. His head is buried against my heart.

'Get outside, Robin, I'm starting the engine.'

I hear the garage door close. Jack and I are alone.

I'm so tired. I can't help it. I am falling asleep.

At 10.30 p.m., still in his office, Jeff MacKingsley waited for Mort Shelley. He had already been notified that a search of Ted Cartwright's house had uncovered the blond wig, the movers' uniforms and the boxes of Zach's papers. More important, a 9 mm pistol had been found in his safe.

We'll have Cartwright cold on this one, Jeff thought. The satisfaction he would normally feel from the possibility of closing such a case was outweighed by his concern for Celia Nolan. Or Liza Barton, he corrected himself. I'm going to have to tell her that her husband was setting her up to be accused of murdering Georgette Grove, he thought, and it's all about the money she inherited from his cousin, Laurence Foster.

There was a light tap at the door and Shelley came in. 'Beats me how this guy has managed to stay out of prison.'

'What have you got, Mort?'

'Alex Nolan is a phoney,' Mort said. 'He *is* a lawyer and *he* is affiliated with a law firm that used to be prestigious, but it's now just a two-man operation. Nolan claims to specialise in wills and trusts, but has only a handful of clients. He's had several ethics violations filed against him, and has been suspended twice.' Shelley consulted the thick file he was carrying. 'He never made an honest dollar in his life. His money came from a bequest he received four years ago from a seventy-seven-year-old widow he was romancing. Nolan got three million dollars out of that scam.'

'That's pretty good,' Jeff said. 'Most people would settle for it.'

'Alex Nolan wants real money, the kind that means private planes and yachts and mansions.'

'Celia—I mean Liza—doesn't have that kind of money.'

'Her son does. Laurence Foster took good care of her, but the two-thirds of his estate that he left to Jack contain Foster's share of patents for research he financed. There are three different companies that are about to go public, and that will mean tens of millions of dollars one day.'

'And Nolan knew this?'

'It was public knowledge that Foster was an investor in start-up companies. Wills are on file where they were probated. Nolan didn't need to be a genius.'

Shelley picked another page out of the file. 'We tracked down Foster's private nurses from the last time he was in the hospital. One of them admitted she took big tips from Nolan to let him in when Foster was dying and visitors were limited to immediate family. Nolan was probably hoping to get himself written into the will, but Foster's mind was beginning to wander, so maybe it was he, himself, who told Nolan about Celia's past.'

Jeff's mouth tightened as he listened.

'Nolan is all smoke and mirrors,' Mort continued. 'He didn't own that

474

apartment in SoHo. The furniture wasn't his. He was using that three million bucks to convince Liza that he was a prominent attorney. And I spoke to Celia's investment advisor. He told me that Foster left one-third of his estate to Celia and two-thirds to Jack. If Jack dies before he reaches twenty-one, everything goes to Celia. After her marriage to Nolan, Celia split her estate between Nolan and Jack. She also made him Jack's guardian, as well as the trustee of his estate.'

Jeff nodded. 'When Nolan sat in this office yesterday and referred to the picture Liza found in the barn as the one of the Barton family on the beach, I knew he must be the one who put it there. Last week when Liza gave it to me, Nolan came in as I was putting it in a plastic bag. He didn't ask to look at it then, but yesterday, despite all the Barton pictures that have been in the newspapers, he knew exactly which one it was.'

'Robin has been his girlfriend for at least three years,' Shelley said. 'I took a picture of Nolan I got in the bar association directory to Patsy's. One of the waiters remembers seeing them when he was new on the job.'

'I wonder if the plan to get Liza back into her old home was hatched after Robin went to work at the Grove Agency,' Jeff mused. 'Buy the house as a gift. Move her into it. Vandalise it to rattle her. Expose her as Little Lizzie. Count on a psychological breakdown so he could get control of the estate. But then something went wrong. That last evening in the office, Georgette must have found something that linked Robin to Alex. Henry told us that Georgette had gone through both their desks. She made a call to Robin at ten o'clock. Unless Robin comes clean, we'll probably never know the reason for it.'

'My guess is that Robin was the one waiting for Georgette in the house on Holland Road,' Mort volunteered, 'then she and Alex decided to point the finger at Celia by leaving her picture in Georgette's bag. And Robin might have taken something out of the bag, something Georgette had found in her desk. Then, when Charley Hatch's jeans and sneakers and carvings were confiscated, he became too much of a danger.'

'This may not be the first time Nolan has been involved in a homicide,' Jeff told Shelley. 'He was a suspect in the death of a wealthy young woman he'd dated in college. She had dropped him for someone else and he apparently went crazy and stalked her for over a year. I only learned that this afternoon.'

His expression became grave. 'First thing tomorrow, I'm going to tell Liza what we know. After that, I'll order protection for her and Jack. If Nolan weren't in Chicago, I'd have a guard on them now. He and his girlfriend have to be getting very nervous.'

The phone rang. Anna turned on the intercom. 'Jeff, there's a Detective

Ryan on the phone from Chicago. He says Alex Nolan slipped out of a dinner meeting three hours ago and hasn't showed up at the Ritz-Carlton.'

Jeff and Mort jumped up. '*Three hours!*' Jeff exclaimed. 'He could have flown back here by now!'

The car's engine was running. The fumes were making me drowsier, but I knew I had to fight it. Now that he was with me, Jack was falling asleep again. I tried to move him. I *had* to turn off the engine. If we stayed here, we were going to die. I had to move. But my limbs wouldn't function. What was it that Alex had forced me to drink?

I was slumped against the cushion, half lying, half sitting. The sound of the engine was deafening. Something must be wedged against the gas pedal. Soon we would be unconscious. Soon my little boy would die.

No. No. Please, no.

'Jack, Jack.' My voice was a broken whisper, but it went directly into his ear. 'Jack, Mommy is sick. Help me.'

He turned his head restlessly, then settled again under my neck.

'Jack, Jack, wake up, wake up.'

I was starting to fall asleep again. I bit my lip so hard that I could taste blood. 'Jack, help Mommy,' I pleaded. He lifted his head. I sensed he was looking at me. 'Jack, climb . . . into front seat. Take car key . . . out.'

He was moving. He sat up and slid off my lap. 'It's dark, Mommy.'

'Climb in . . . front seat,' I whispered. 'Climb . . .' I could feel myself sinking slowly, words disappearing from my mind.

Jack's foot grazed my face. He was climbing over the seat.

'The key, Jack . . .'

From far off, I heard him say, 'I can't get it out.'

'Turn it, Jack. Turn it . . . then . . . pull . . . it . . . out.'

Suddenly there was silence, total silence in the garage. Followed by Jack's sleepy but proud cry, 'Mommy, I *did* it.'

I knew the fumes could still kill us. We had to get out.

'Mommy, are you sick?'

The garage door opener, I thought—it's clipped onto the visor. I often let Jack press it. 'Jack, open . . . garage door,' I begged. 'You know how.'

I think I slipped away for a minute. The rumbling sound of the rising door woke me up for a moment, and it was with a vast sense of deliverance and relief that I finally stopped fighting and lost consciousness.

I woke up in an ambulance. The first face I saw was Jeffrey MacKingsley's. The first words he said were the ones I wanted to hear: 'Don't worry, Jack is fine.' The second words seemed filled with promise. 'Liza, I told you everything was going to be all right.'

EPILOGUE

WE HAVE LIVED in the house for two years now. After much thought, I decided to stay there. For me it was no longer the house in which I had killed my mother, but the home in which I had tried to save her life. I have used my skills as an interior designer to complete my father's vision for it. It is truly beautiful, and each day we build happy memories.

Ted Cartwright accepted a plea bargain. He got thirty years for murdering Zach Willet, fifteen years for killing my father and twelve years for causing the death of my mother, the sentences to be served concurrently. Part of his agreement was that he would confess that he came to the house that night intending to kill my mother.

He had lived in the house, and he knew that there was one basement window that for some inexplicable reason had never been wired into the security system. That was the way he got in.

He admitted that he had planned to strangle my mother as she slept, and if I had awakened while he was there, he would have killed me, too.

Knowing that the impending divorce would make him a suspect in her death, he had placed a call from our basement phone to his home and waited an hour before starting upstairs on his murderous journey. He had planned to tell the police that my mother had asked him to come to our house the next day to discuss a reconciliation.

But that planned explanation had to be changed when the shooting occurred. Instead, at my trial, he testified that my mother had called and pleaded with him to come to the house while I was asleep.

Once in the house, Ted got the new code out of my mother's address book and disarmed the security system. He unlocked the kitchen door to make it seem that my mother's carelessness had allowed an intruder to sneak in. At my trial, his story was that my mother had disarmed it and unlocked the door because she was expecting him.

Ted also indicated that the other 'moving man' was Sonny Ingers, a construction worker on his town-house project. His identification of Ingers was corroborated by Rap Corrigan.

Henry Paley emerged without any criminal charges. The prosecutor's office concluded that his conspiracy with Ted Cartwright was limited to trying to convince Georgette Grove to sell the Route 24 property.

Robin Carpenter and Alex Nolan are both serving life sentences for the murders of Georgette Grove and Charley Hatch, and for the attempted murders of Jack and me. Robin admitted that she had shot both Georgette and her half-brother Charley. She had taken from Georgette's shoulder bag a picture of her and Alex that Georgette had found in her desk.

So many people stopped by our house during the weeks after Jack and I were nearly killed, bringing food, flowers and friendship. Some told me how their grandmothers and mine were schoolmates. I love it here. My roots are here. I've opened an interior design shop in Mendham. Life is busy. Jack is in the first grade and plays on every team he can find.

In the weeks and months following Alex's arrest, my relief over Ted's confession was overshadowed by my sadness at Alex's betrayal. It was Jeff who helped me to understand that the Alex I thought I knew had never existed.

I'm not exactly sure of the moment when I realised I was falling in love with Jeff. I think he knew before I did that we were meant to be together.

That's another reason why I am so busy. My husband, Jeffrey MacKingsley, is getting ready to run for governor.

MARY HIGGINS CLARK

Ever since she was a child, Mary Higgins Clark has enjoyed writing and 'I loved to tell scary stories from the time I was about five,' she says. 'I also loved reading Nancy Drew, Agatha Christie and Josephine Tey and I was always trying to keep up with the author and find the real clues. I thought, "I understand these books. Let's see if I can write one."' Her career, first in advertising and then as a Pan Am air hostess, distracted her from her writing ambitions for a while, but in 1964 things changed. Tragically, she was left a widow at only thirty-five years of age and, with five children to support, was forced to put her writing talent to profitable use. She started writing radio scripts on all sorts of subjects ranging from babies to food and travel. 'I was an instant expert on everything,' she says. 'It was a wonderful discipline and very useful when it came to writing suspense.' She used to fit the work in around her children's lives. 'I got up at five and wrote at the kitchen table until seven, when I had to get the children ready for school.' In response to the suggestion that this must have been difficult, Mary states, 'For me, writing is a need. It's the degree of yearning that separates the real writer from the "would-be's". Those who say "I'll write when I have time" will probably never do it. I always knew I'd make it as a writer. It may

sound crazy, but I always knew. There was no question in my mind.'

And how right she was. For nearly thirty years, Mary Higgins Clark's page-turning mysteries have been hugely successful in her native America and abroad, and many have been based on real-life crimes or interesting points of law. 'I got the idea for *No Place Like Home* because a realtor in New Jersey, where I live, told me about this law in New Jersey where a realtor must tell a prospective buyer if the house has a history—if there's been a crime committed, a suicide, even if it's reputed to be haunted. A murder, certainly. You must disclose that or else the buyer can come back and say, "give me my money back".' Mary's heroine in *No Place Like Home*, Liza Barton, is taunted by comparisons to the case of Lizzie Borden, the infamous Massachusetts spinster who was accused, but later acquitted, of murdering both her parents on August 4, 1892.

So does the author ever scare herself while she is writing? 'I hope to. It's wonderful if I do. When I get nervous or jump when the phone rings, I think, "Gee, that's great. I'm doing a good job." I still love telling scary stories!'

Since all her novels become instant best sellers, does Mary Higgins Clark still feel the same sense of excitement each time one is published? 'Oh, sure, because any writer who takes a reader for granted is very foolish.'

Jane Eastgate

601-032-1